Hilarious, exuberant, subtle, tender, brutal, spectacular, and above all unexpected: these two extraordinary volumes contain the limitless possibilities of the British short story.

This is the first anthology capacious enough to celebrate the full diversity and energy of its writers, subjects and tones. The most famous authors are here, and many others, including some magnificent stories never republished since their first appearance in magazines and periodicals. *The Penguin Book of the British Short Story* has a permanent authority, and will be reached for year in and year out.

This volume takes the story from its origins with Defoe, Swift and Fielding to the 'golden age' of the *fin de siècle* and Edwardian period.

Philip Hensher is a novelist, critic, librettist and short story writer. *The Northern Clemency* was shortlisted for the Booker Prize. His most recent novel is *The Emperor Waltz*.

The Penguin Book of

THE
PENGUIN BOOK
of the
BRITISH
SHORT
STORY

VOLUME 1

From DANIEL DEFOE
to JOHN BUCHAN

———

Selected with a General Introduction by
PHILIP HENSHER

PENGUIN BOOKS

PENGUIN CLASSICS

UK | USA | Canada | Ireland | Australia
India | New Zealand | South Africa

Penguin Books is part of the Penguin Random House group of companies
whose addresses can be found at global.penguinrandomhouse.com.

This collection first published in Penguin Classics 2015
002

Introduction and editorial matter copyright © Philip Hensher, 2015
The acknowledgements on pp. 715–18 constitute an extension of this copyright page
All rights reserved

The moral rights of the editor and authors of the stories have been asserted

Set in 11.25/14.75 pt Adobe Caslon Pro
Typeset by Jouve (UK), Milton Keynes
Printed in Great Britain by Clays Ltd, St Ives plc

ISBN: 978–0–141–39599–9

To A. S. Byatt

Contents

Contents

Contents

General Introduction

The British short story is probably the richest, most varied and most historically extensive national tradition anywhere in the world. But before introducing a *Penguin Book of the British Short Story*, it's as well to admit that every single substantive word in the title, apart from 'Penguin', is under fierce debate. Certainly I felt unclear about what 'British' might mean, and was completely unable to lay down rules for who might qualify as British. It might make sense to include everyone who wrote as an inhabitant of the British Isles and as a subject of the government in London. That would include all Irish writers until 1922, but it is most unlikely that anyone would expect to find a story from James Joyce's *Dubliners* in this anthology. Foreign-born writers resident in the UK I ruled out where there was a strong movement to regard them, as in the case of Katherine Mansfield, as conferring merit on their place of birth rather than their residence. On the other hand, I have chosen to include Elizabeth Bowen, whose subject seems indubitably British. There are undoubtedly writers here who, to some readers, will seem to contribute to the British short story, rather than belong to it; there might, indeed, be a strong argument for including Henry James in an anthology of this sort. But Britishness is slippery and debatable, as indeed the British short story often is.

'Short story' is still more problematic. What is a short story? Eager pundits queue up to explain that a short story must consist of a single situation, a short space of time, a small number of characters, be less than a certain number of words, and so on. These restrictive demands have been around for a long time, often ultimately deriving from Poe's grandiose suggestion, applying Aristotle to a new literary form, that 'unity of effect or impression is a point of the greatest importance'.[1] Although this insistence comes from the same writer, who insists that 'the death then of a beautiful woman is unquestionably the most poetical topic in the world'[2], the point about unity has been taken very seriously ever since. Certainly, in this country, reviewers for an 1880s London journal, *The Athenaeum*, which took an interest in the American short story, were already regularly insisting on 'economy and unity of effect'.

The market for such restrictive explanations seems to have expanded with the rise of creative writing as an academic discipline, but they remain uncertain and unconvincing. All of these pundits would quickly find themselves having to explain away the existence of great short stories that seem hardly to have the slightest notion of any of the single situation, a limitation of time, a consistent tone, or anything else. D. H. Lawrence's 'Daughters of the Vicar' covers thirty years in its marriage of the sublime and the minute, and takes a detailed comparison of four marriages as its grand subject. Restrictions of length, too, seem unsustainable, and there are short stories by Conrad that press on to 30,000 words and beyond. Why 'Typhoon', at 30,000 words, is universally regarded as a short story and *Nightmare Abbey*, at 26,000 words and possessing a more uniform setting, is described as a novel is a question only answerable by the accidents of publication history. Practical concerns prevented this anthology from acknowledging the occasional expansion of the short story, which in general flourishes at between 4,000 and 15,000 words, into much longer forms.

If it is difficult to reach a conclusion about what the formal literary limits of the short story are, the debate about the historical phenomenon of the short story also shows no sign of resolution. There are two general views about the short story, one inclusive in tendency, the other more rigid. In the inclusive account, a story told in brief is as old as mankind, and there are short stories to be found in ancient Greek literature, and in the Bible, before turning up in the English language (one friend firmly told me) in a short story in the *Anglo-Saxon Chronicle*. A generous and open account might include a Canterbury Tale before moving on to Mandeville's fantasy travel writing, and starting in earnest with Elizabethan prose romances.

On the other hand, the exclusive and rigid account of the short story sees it as a very particular historical phenomenon. The term 'short story' only occurs towards the end of the nineteenth century, although it is difficult to be quite sure when: the *OED*'s first citations, which are from 1877 and (Trollope's autobiography) 1882, seem to use the phrase as an established usage. To a surprising degree, authors of the time do seem to regard it as a much newer form than the novel. In 1894, the short-story writer Lanoe Falconer talked about 'the literary capabilities of the short story, still in its infancy'. [2] In Britain, writers were relatively slow to perceive the possibilities of short fiction, both artistically and commercially. American writers were obliged to develop a practice in short fiction as early as the 1790s, and certainly by the 1820s, because the American public generally preferred cheap, copyright-evading editions of English novels. One authority explains: 'The American short story . . . emerged in the 1830s when the flood of British imports drowned the American novel and left magazines and gift-books as the only paying outlets for native fiction.'[3] Those English novelists, by contrast, found their principal markets in the long form. The restrictive history of the short story maintains that, despite foreign practitioners such as Pushkin, Kleist and Washington Irving, the British short story only seriously begins with the establishment of major, well-paying short-story magazines such as *The Strand* in 1891.

Both historical accounts have something to be said for them, and both are, in the end, wrong. There doesn't seem to be anything to be gained from regarding any piece of made-up narrative as a short story, even if it is in verse. Even such pieces of imaginative prose as the Elizabethan prose romances seem to me so different from the short story when it emerged under that name, and to contribute so little to its development, that nothing was to be gained by starting so very early. (I admit, too, to finding almost all of them agonizingly dull.) On the other hand, indisputable short stories were being written and published in Britain long before *The Strand* and even the mid-Victorian journals such as *All the Year Round* started taking an interest in short fiction. In this anthology, the Scottish writers Hogg and Galt will be seen to be writing perfectly shaped and conceived short stories by the 1820s.

It made sense, however, not to start at that point, but to go back somewhat, and examine the different and often intriguing ways in which prose pieces of short imaginative fiction were trying to make sense of themselves in relation to the novel. The first pieces in this anthology are not, in the modern sense, short stories. But they bear in a vital, animating way on the short story's historical development. They are trying to distinguish themselves from the long form, and are drawing on a number of literary counter-examples. The Fielding is a compacted, sequential romance; the Defoe a mock-documentary account of confected reality; a morality tale starts to get out of hand in Hannah More. In other stories, possibilities are set out which will bear fruit long afterwards in the history of the form: Mary Lamb's entrancingly static idyll is a story about a life with no story. I include Swift's extraordinary 'Directions to the Footman' in part because it shows how narrative was always lurking, ready to rip up the most morally directive of stories, and partly because it foreshadows in an unmistakable way a tendency of recent years, to cast short stories in the form of non-fictional lists, instruction booklets and other secretly story-telling sequences of prose (Lorrie Moore's 'How to Talk to Your Mother (Notes)' from *Self-Help* is a good recent example). All these are working towards a definition of the short story in distinction to the emerging form of the novel. By the time Galt (and Scott) start to publish their short stories, the definition is clear, and confident; and it did not emerge from nothing.

2

Nowadays, when we read short stories, we read them in an unusual way, and one that may not resemble the way they were originally intended to be read. We read short stories in anthologies like this one, but mostly in substantial collected or selected editions, intermediate or summary accounts of a short-story writer's career. We are used to reading the short fiction of a single author one piece after another. Of course, the single-author collection can be a marvellous thing, introducing the reader to an author's world with intensity and power. Some of the most powerful encounters I had in the course of compiling this book, indeed, were with beautifully conceived and executed collections from which it was hard to choose a single example, such as Douglas Dunn's superb *Secret Villages* or E. M. Delafield's *The Entertainment*. But it's important to recognize that short stories were not first written to be read in this way, for the most part, but to be read singly and in very varied company. Short-story collections, and especially volumes entitled *Collected Stories*, I found, may be misleading, heavily revising short stories written much earlier, organizing an author's short stories in ways designed to obscure their publishing history, or even omitting most of an author's work under a title implying completeness. Some of the worst offenders in this regard are 'collected' editions compiled by the authors themselves. Sometimes, collected editions are calculated to make a particular effect by including works never regarded as within the author's body of short fiction. Readers were very surprised to see the huge bulk of Alasdair Gray's collected short fiction, *Every Short Story*, when it was published by Canongate. On investigation, Mr Gray had chosen to include an entire novel, previously published as *Something Leather*, under a new title. To gain an accurate sense of a writer's short fiction, it is often necessary to return to their first publication – usually in journals.

For the greater part of the short story's history in Britain, the main publishers of short fiction were the editors of magazines and journals. Even very distinguished and famous writers did not write their short stories to be first read in a collection between hard covers; their stories were submitted to the editors of magazines like – in roughly chronological order - *Blackwood's, Chambers's Edinburgh Journal, Household Words, All the Year Round, Cassell's, The Fortnightly Review, The Strand, Black and White, The Yellow Book, Adelphi, Life and Letters, Lilliput, Encounter, Horizon, The London Magazine, Granta* and very many others. There were journals to publish stories in very many different genres and styles, and each had its particular flavour. Some journals dabbled in short fiction and serial novels – *Country Life* published a short story from time to time, occasionally hitting gold or digging deep into its coffers to bring out something by a star author (it published John Masefield's 'Davy Jones's Gift', for example). Others were overtaken by fashion and broadened their scope to include fiction: *The Gentleman's Magazine*, published from 1731, gave in and brought out fiction between 1868 and 1890 before withdrawing from the fiction market in its remaining seventeen years. Fiction was a core part of the endeavour of many popular journals, even of daily newspapers – at first, usually novels or serial works, but as time went on, increasingly relying on the short story. The quantity of short fiction published by the *Daily Mail* in its early history beggars belief, none of it collected, all of it now effectively lost. Much of it must have given a lot of pleasure in its day.

The breadth of publications taking and paying for short fiction in this country, and the equally wide spread of possibilities in America and elsewhere, made it perfectly possible for a successful writer of short fiction to earn a good living, and even (like Conan Doyle) to become rich. In the 1890s, after the appearance of *The Strand* and *Black and White* as magazines that would publish only short fiction rather than serialized novels, at least twenty-three magazines were founded that published short fiction significantly or exclusively. In the decade and a half before the First World War, there were 'at least thirty-four high circulation magazines publishing substantial quantities of short stories'.[4] The primary market, and the primary source of income for these writers, was publication in the journals.

Some instances might reveal how, even without the consistently higher payments available from American magazines, British authors could attain real professional competence through selling short stories to magazines, and it was clearly worth investing a good deal in time, money and skilful craft. Some payments: Hardy's payments for a single short story went from £20 in 1878 to £100 in 1894. Twenty pounds was a fairly standard payment for decades. It is what Stevenson was paid for *Dr Jekyll and Mr Hyde* in 1886, and by the 1930s E. M. Delafield's customary price for a story had only risen to £30. There were still less well-paying journals – the *Yellow Book* paid Arnold Bennett £3 for a short story – but often hard-nosed and flush journals took a view about what an author could do for them, and paid accordingly. An interesting study by Reginald Pound has revealed the range of payments made by *The Strand* to authors in 1914 for single short stories, and it shows what they thought they could gain by star names. Britten Austin was paid £31/10s, P. G. Wodehouse £40, A. E. W. Mason £166/13/4, rising to £350 for W. W. Jacobs. It is complicated to translate these sums into modern-day equivalents, but it is worth noting that studies of the middle classes at the time cite a family doctor's average annual salary before the First World War as around £400. These, of course, are just the payments for first serial rights in Britain. Many, perhaps most, authors of short stories could also sell the story in the United States, and subsequently second serial rights in both Britain and the US, so that a story for which a British magazine paid £50 could easily end up earning three times as much merely from serial publication. These individual magazine payments, impressive as they are, fall short of Conan Doyle's extraordinary income. He was paid £50 each by *The Strand* for the first four Sherlock Holmes stories, and then engineered a colossal increase. After 1895, the magazine never paid less than £100 per thousand words for anything he wrote. After Sherlock Holmes had been killed off and – through public demand – resurrected, Doyle was offered £3,000 for twelve stories by an English publisher and £6,000 by an American. Later still, Doyle received an offer of 75,000 dollars, or approximately £12,500 at the conversion rate of the time, for twelve short stories.[5] There was no question that magazine publishing of short stories could be among the most financially lucrative form of writing long into the twentieth century. This investment encouraged the most able and ingenious writers of the day to place it at the centre of their practice.

After the turn of the twentieth century, many and perhaps most of the best authors who published in journals found it possible to put together a volume for sale by a publisher. It is, inevitably, largely from these authors that the compiler of an anthology of this sort will find himself drawing. These collections would carry on supplying some kind of income to the author, and no doubt satisfy some authors in their sense of preserving their short fiction, as well as their novels, for the benefit of posterity. This was a possibility available to a good number of authors; according to the lists compiled at the time by Edward J. O'Brien, the editor of an annual 'Best Short Stories' volume between the wars, over a hundred collections by UK authors were published in the UK almost every year between 1925 and 1936. Publishers, however, were much more cautious than magazine editors, and often offered very small advances and limited royalty terms. H. E. Bates received £20 for a 1931 collection, and even a very successful writer like E. M. Delafield or Walter de la Mare might only receive £150 or £200 – about the same that could be raised by a single well-syndicated short story in the magazines. There was a strong belief among publishers that 'we reckon', as Victor Gollancz put it, 'that short stories [in collections] sell between a quarter and a sixth of an established author's novels – but with a very rigid maximum of about 4,000'.[6] The collection of stories, which is the way in which we read an author's work, was for most authors for most of this period a useful and prestigious, but not very profitable, addition to initial publication. The primary income, and the most exciting appearance of each work, came with the first publication, in magazines and journals.

Posterity has on the whole acted as it was supposed to, and kept an interest only in the short-story writers who stretched to published collections. Although only quite rare and aesthetically minded authors published their short fiction primarily in volume form in preference to journal publication of individual stories – George Egerton in the 1890s, Dorothy Edwards in the 1920s – this is the form in which the short story is invariably considered, and the way in which its history has come down to us. But to read the short story not in much later collections but as it first appeared is to gain a much more detailed sense of how it developed, and what it actually meant. Of course, it is beyond human capacity to read more than a few of the principal journals that published short fiction in the last quarter-millennium – *Chambers's Edinburgh Journal* was brought out between 1832 and 1956, and to read all the fiction it published is a major undertaking with doubtful reward. Moreover, the publisher taking a punt on an author who has made a splash in periodical form turns out to be quite an efficient filter of talent. In putting together this anthology, I have nevertheless tried to go beyond the *oeuvres* of celebrated and once-celebrated authors brought out in collected and selected form by mainstream publishers. In reading through a dozen or so journals, I have tried to gain a sense of how short stories initially appeared to the people they were written for, as well as looking for the occasional excellent story by an author who never quite attained the body of work or the popularity a publisher would need in order to bring out a *Collected Stories*. In this anthology, examples of fine stories that had, as far as I can tell, no life beyond first publication are those by T. Baron Russell and Jack Common – it may not be a coincidence that many such stories I read were by working-class writers. Occasionally, a story might be taken up by a well-meaning anthologist, such as Edward J. O'Brien's excellent *Best Short Stories* annual volumes during the 1920s and 1930s, giving a second wind, for instance, to the terrifying and heartrending short story by Leslie Halward I include here – Halward, in fact, did not include, or did not have was a sense that a writer of fiction, and perhaps especially a writer of short stories, would not normally be expected to address a subject as controversial and lively as Mrs Thatcher's reputation, even thirty years on. Even though the story and its author had carefully waited until Thatcher had died before engaging with the reading public, it still seemed brave, shocking and above all, surprising to see a short story about (more or less) contemporary politics.

It is fair to say that this attitude would have greatly surprised previous generations. One of the very striking aspects of the British short story, as revealed by the experience of reading through weekly news-oriented journals, was its capacity to react immediately to events of the most public order. Novels seem to take a few years to ruminate over the news, to develop the impact of social changes or dramatic public events on lives – the great novels of Napoleonic upheaval are written between thirty and fifty years after his defeat at Waterloo. Short stories, on the other hand, may in some circumstances be written quickly, in the heat of the moment, responding with utter immediacy to a mere facet of a huge situation as it unfolds.

A large number of the best short stories are written as a sort of commentary on a changing social situation, as a writer thinks him- or herself into a new situation. Many of the stories in the *Yellow Book*, for instance, explore the new situation of women as independent-minded and perhaps even gainfully employed. From very early on, short-story writers saw the possibility for writers of fiction of the railway, and by the middle of the nineteenth century, railways are being exploited for all sorts of non-modern reasons, such as a hallucinatory ghost story – there is a good, standard example, 'Going Through the Tunnel' in *Chambers's Journal*.[7] Many of William Trevor's most interesting stories from the 1960s and 1970s are specifically about the human impact of social changes – wife-swapping parties in 'Angels at the Ritz' – just as Elizabeth Taylor and Samuel Selvon found the short story the best and swiftest medium to write about the impact of immigration in Britain in 'Tall Boy' and 'Knock on Wood'. In this anthology, one fine example of immediate response to events is a story by Adam Mars-Jones on an aspect of the AIDS crisis, written less than half a decade after the diagnosis of the first patient. To show how very swift this response could be, it's necessary to look at the impact of a huge public event on the pages of a fiction journal.

The Second World War quickly inspired a large body of first-rate short fiction, including Alun Lewis's marvellous accounts of the lives of ordinary soldiers, and there was no hesitation or delay between event and fictional rendering. In the first instance, full-scale novels of the conflict were either prophetic, written before anything had taken place, like Nevil Shute's *What Happened to the Corbetts*, written in the 1930s about a speculative air raid on Southampton, or out of date before they were published, like Evelyn Waugh's *Put Out More Flags*, whose subject was the phoney war but which had to be published as thousands were being killed in the London Blitz. The short story was much quicker and could more reliably speak to participants in a current situation. Mollie Panter-Downes, one of a number of British women writers whom the *New Yorker* has always supported, published the first of many short stories on wartime themes a mere fortnight after the outbreak of war in 1939 – its subject the outbreak of war itself.

This swiftness of response in the form of fiction now strikes us as surprising, and perhaps even indecorous. In a recent biography, the writer Adam Begley expressed some surprise that the American short-story writer John Updike regularly took real-life events from the very recent past and transformed them, as if transcribing, into saleable short fiction. There is no way of knowing how swiftly other short-story writers translated private, real-life experiences into imaginary prose, but we can see that when a public event occurred, its fictional representations in short fiction were never far behind. The First World War broke out in August 1914. At the earliest possible opportunity, in its September 1914 issue, *Blackwood's Magazine* published a story about a battle in the Great War, realistically written and edited almost before anyone had experienced one ('Five-Four-Eight', by Jeffery E. Jeffery). These responses to events were not automatically populist: another very early response in *Blackwood's* to the war, 'The Old Junker' by Charles Oliver, published in February 1915, goes to some length to expound the figure of the idealistic, kindly German, before 'he had taken the Moloch form that he wears today'. Such immediate responses have not gone away entirely. One of Graham Greene's last stories was a horrified warning against the imminent opening of a Channel Tunnel, first published in the *Independent* newspaper. But the effective separation of paying journal and practising short-story writer in recent years has diminished this important aspect of the British short story, and when it turns up, we are often rather shocked.

4

The possibilities for the writer of short stories have narrowed significantly in recent years. Where once there was any number of paying journals and magazines offering handsome sums for first serial rights, now the principal outlet for many writers of short stories is not publication but competitions. With no intention of mockery, I quote the acknowledgements page of a recent collection of short stories, published by a small press, the work of a writer who says she has been publishing short stories for twenty years.

> Placed 2nd in round 6 of The Whitaker Prize 2012; placed 1st in the live Write-Invite Competition 28th January 2012; placed 3rd in The Meridian Summer Competition 2012; 4th place in A Very Short Story Competition September 2011; shortlisted in Five Stop Story Competition 2012; one of twelve shortlisted in The Knock On Effect Competition 2012; shortlisted in the Erewash Writers' Short Story Competition; shortlisted in the Writers' Forum Competition July 2012; won second prize in the Green-acre Writers' Short Story Competition; placed 1st in the Word Hut Number 3 Short Story Competition; shortlisted in the Wells Short Story Competition 2000; longlisted in The Fish Short Story Prize 2011; specially commended in the Infanca Helene James Short Story Competition 2012 . . .

And so on. These competitions sometimes offer reasonable prizes – the Fish short story competition, for instance, offers a first prize of 2,000 Euros plus 1,000 Euros travelling expenses. Sometimes there are rather thinner rewards on offer. The Word Hut Prize offers only £70 for first prize. These prizes are funded by the eager contestants paying to enter – the Fish competition demands 22 Euros from entrants, and the Word Hut only £4. The possibility that anyone might pay in order to read these short stories seems hardly to be envisaged. But what alternative is there?
One Sunday newspaper offers an annual lavishly funded prize for the

short story, culminating in a dinner for 150 or so and a first prize of £30,000. The winner is subsequently printed in the newspaper. The year that I went, the chair of the judges, a retired don, congratulated himself and his fellow judges for having produced a shortlist which contained no short story set in Britain, before handing over the cheque to an utterly routine piece of work by an American author about a tragically dead rock star and a terminal illness. It was, of course, in the approved present tense. There seemed no point in suggesting that with the same money, the newspaper could develop any number of short-story talents by, for instance, commissioning and running a short story every week for £1,000. Similarly, the BBC's annual short-story competition much prefers handing over £20,000 in prize money to paying writers properly to write stories for broadcast. I inquired about the fees payable by BBC Radio 4's short-story slot, *Afternoon Reading*. Enough to say that it would not pay for my weekly laundry bill. The sort of relationship, too, between magazine and author that existed in the past, permitting *Adelphi* to help to contribute towards the development of Jack Common as a writer and editor, or *Horizon* towards that wayward, fascinating experimentalist Anna Kavan, has completely disappeared.

There are very few outlets still able to pay a writer for a short story in a way that could encourage a writer to persist, and with the sort of editorial investment that will enable a writer to develop. Most of them are in the United States. The *New Yorker* has, happily, been able to develop the short-story writing careers of two of the best short-story writers now at work, Tessa Hadley and Zadie Smith. There is no British journal that would have published Hadley's stories, as the *New Yorker* has, twenty-one times, and paid properly for them. *Granta* very occasionally publishes a British short story; some newspapers, notably the *Guardian*, sometimes publish a short story by a very firmly established and celebrated 'name'; some popular magazines, such as *Good Housekeeping*, do still take short stories; others develop short, fervent periods of enthusiasm for short fiction before abandoning it again. The *New Statesman* is currently in such a fit of enthusiasm, publishing a short story every two months by, admittedly, very well-established authors. The stories now published by British outlets are, it must be pointed out, very rarely more than 2,000 words, which is at the very lower limit of the form's usual scale. If there is a paying British outlet for the classical short story of 7,000 words or so, I have not been able to discover it. The writer of short stories is largely reduced to persuading publishers to publish whole volumes in exchange for minuscule advances, making stories available for nothing or very little in niche journals whose editorial expertise may be uncertain and whose circulation is certainly tiny, or entering competitions. The result is a definite shift in the quality of short stories over the last fifteen years or so.

The problem with relying on competitions as a means of developing talent, rather than the response of a paying public, is that they reward what they think ought to be good, and not what contains any real energy. Repeatedly, reading short stories rewarded by competitions, I was struck by present-tense solitary reflections, often with characters lying on their beds affectlessly pondering; major historical events were considered gravely; social media were dutifully brought in to indicate an eye on the contemporary without disturbing the safely solitary nature of the character. Pondering preceded, by a very long way, the social interaction which is the proper subject of fiction. There was nothing there at all, apart from a fervent desire to win £30,000.

The insistence that short stories should be serious in theme, with an underlying contempt for anything not about major issues of public policy, and yet not permitting the short story of contemporary public events either, is nothing new. Lena Milman in the 1890s wrote that 'The contempt for the short story prevalent in England, but unknown elsewhere, is surely as traceable to Puritan influence as the destruction of the Mary Altar at Ely, and the shrine of St Thomas; for, insisting, as it has become our English bent to do, upon some serious side-purpose in art, we are not content with a beautiful suggestion, with a sketch be it never so masterly; the narrative must illustrate a principle, the picture, a fact.'[8] Not until the rise of literary competitions in the second half of the twentieth century, however, did the British hit upon a method ingeniously devised to suppress everything that had previously been good about a literary form.

The system of competitions replacing a system of commissions, payments, circulation and readers looks tempting as a guarantee of literary quality; no one, however, ever invited, or required Conan Doyle or V. S. Pritchett or Kipling or P. G. Wodehouse to put on a dinner jacket and shake the hand of a retired academic before they could receive a cheque for a short story. They might even have considered the idea somewhat humiliating. Moreover, no competition will ever produce or reward a 'Silver Blaze', a 'When My Girl Comes Home', a 'Wireless', or a 'Fiery Wooing of Mordred'. It is perhaps no accident that the dullest short stories I read from the last fifteen years were winners of competitions: a lot of the most exciting and interesting short stories, on the other hand, were science fiction, fantasy and horror. Clive Barker's *Books of Blood*, from the early 1980s, spawned a very engaged and argumentative readership which in turn created some brilliantly inventive writers – China Miéville, Neil Gaiman and Adam Marek are possible through a readership, a system of circulation, and not through the rewards offered by the conventional tastes of prize committees. If an ordinary newspaper took to publishing, once a week, a short story and paying the same that it currently pays for the celebrity interview that fills the same space, then the short story in all its forms would soon return to the energy and inventiveness that it possessed until recently. In the meantime, we can only be grateful for the British writers who are still nurtured by generous American magazines, the ones who can persist in writing collections of short stories for publishers for the same small advances that publishers always offered for collections, and the ones who are lucky enough to work in a field with an engaged and passionate readership.

5

With some embarrassment and some self-consciousness, I set out to suggest some of the qualities that distinguish the British short story in the last three hundred years, and make it worth reading.

In the 1990s, A. S. Byatt edited a groundbreaking and inspiring *Oxford Book of the English Short Story*. It was based on a principle which, curiously, had never been put into practice before: limiting its grounds to authors of English nationality. Byatt confessed to some doubt about setting out on such an endeavour, on the grounds that 'I feared that the great short-story writers were indeed from elsewhere ... I feared being marooned amongst buffers and buffoons, bucolics, butties and Blimps.' In the event, her anthology was a revelation of quality and a particular range of expertise. It came as such a revelation because the English, and perhaps the British too, *qua* British, are not accustomed to think of their own literary qualities. There is always a risk, in case some claim of supremacy starts rearing its head from the dark ages. It is as if the particular quality of writing from these islands cannot be considered because, inevitably, it will lead to distasteful claims of superiority that we signed away in 1947 with the end of Empire. Anthologies of English short stories, apart from Byatt's, tend to conflate 'writing in the English language' with 'writing by the English', as Byatt herself pointed out. Even Malcolm Bradbury's interesting *Penguin Book of the Modern British Short Story* mysteriously included a story by Samuel Beckett.

Not everyone shrinks away from national pride in this area, I wincingly discover. In fact, the practice of the short story appears to be, for much of the world, an opportunity for such jingoistic sentiments that one wonders that it hasn't been declared an Olympic sport. While I was preparing this book, the American short-story writer Lorrie Moore was reported as telling a presumably not incredulous Brooklyn audience that 'American short story writing is the best in the world really . . . partly because it has been nourished by universities.'[9] I was interested to read the unqualified opinion of the veteran Indian writer Khushwant Singh in an anthology of Indian short stories that 'Western short stories tend to be prolix, leaving the reader to guess what they are all about. That is why many critics believe that the West has lost the art of writing short stories. In India, on the other hand, the short story is as vibrant as ever.'[10]

No doubt very similar statements of national pride could be gathered from many nations, but it is simply impossible to imagine any British writer now asserting anything of the kind. That is not because of any serious doubt about the quality and the energy of the tradition, but because we just don't say that sort of thing. I don't want to enter into nationalist competitions: there is no point in trying to elevate one nation's writers in the form over another. Chekhov, Alice Munro, Kleist, John Cheever and Kipling are, in the best sense, freaks, and their genius is at once local and irrelevant to a local tradition. The consequences of this national modesty, or at any rate the refusal to bang the national drum, are that the British short story has been consistently underestimated and even dismissed. It is much easier, for instance, to find reviews of American collections in British newspapers than British collections. Reading some ill-informed accounts of British short fiction, I was reminded of the foreword to the first edition of the *London Magazine* in 1954, where the editor expressed a recurrent attitude through allegory.

> Two small boys came across a walnut tree one day at the bottom of a large, neglected garden. One of them said 'I can't see any walnuts on that tree.' The other replied: 'I bet you there are some, all the same.' And he swung up into the tree with his stick. The first boy was staring into the leaves where his companion had disappeared, when suddenly a walnut hit him on the nose and then a shower of them crashed into the grass all round him. A voice from the top of the tree shouted out in triumph: 'Who said there weren't any walnuts?' To which a voice from the ground replied: 'How do you know they aren't rotten? Rotten ones don't count.' But when the boy who had climbed the tree slithered down, he found that the other boy had walked away without bothering to look.

I found, preparing this book, that there were people who, like that boy, were prepared to dismiss the local tradition immediately; on investigation, sometimes this attitude came shortly before the revelation that they had never read, and sometimes never heard of, V. S. Pritchett, A. E. Coppard or Kipling's short stories.

But what is that local tradition? What do Britain's short-story writers do most characteristically? In some ways, I came to think of the exemplary British short story as Arthur Conan Doyle's masterpiece, 'Silver Blaze'. It is extraordinarily playful with the conventions of its own genre, beginning with an indication of the murderer that could hardly be more explicit or blatant. It is concerned with a huge range of significant and interesting physical objects, including the elaborate dress that is never seen and its owner never identified. It is about the actions of the overlooked and misunderstood. It is about social class, of course. Like many great short stories from Britain, it revolves around a general social gathering with its own rituals – William Sansom's wonderful 'A Contest of Ladies' is a good comparison. It appears to be telling a thrilling story while in fact being entirely contemplative and thoughtful about events in the past – the action of the story is mostly confined to two train journeys and a long walk.

It is macabre, and draws some ingenious amusement from its most grotesque elements – the cleverest and most enchanting surely the detail of the lame sheep that Sherlock so brilliantly intuits. (He tells us how brilliant he is, too.) It gives the appearance of being richly exact, while in fact being an utter fantastic fabrication – as Doyle himself noted, if the events had happened in real life, half the characters would have been in jail and the others banned from racing for life. And it shows no terror of literary genre, while doing with the conventions of that genre whatever it feels like.

Playfulness is never far from the British short story. This playfulness encourages the form in unexpected directions at different times; the brilliant outbreak of experimental short fiction in the 1960s, including Christine Brooke-Rose and J. G. Ballard – I should also like to have included Anna Kavan – started to influence quite unexpected people including Kingsley Amis. But long before that, the quality of playfulness never prevents the British short story from attaining real seriousness and emotional depth. Arnold Bennett's simply magnificent 'The Matador of the Five Towns' finds space for engaged amusement in its fabulous social panorama, closing down on meanness and tragedy in a little room. Kipling's 'The Village that Voted the Earth was Flat', surely the howling artificial pinnacle of Kipling's genius, was written and published a couple of months before the outbreak of the Great War; as a consideration of hysteria and wildness in the public mind, it has never been matched. Unexpectedly, it is both painfully cruel and fascinated by comedy in the most detailed way. More recently, the brilliant flippancy of tone of Georgina Hammick's masterly 'Grist' shading by degrees into real, wailing grief sustains a long-established tone in British writing. That interest in the overlooked, the apparently insignificant, finds a parallel not just in Dickens's great 'Mrs Lirriper's Lodgings' but in a flurry of superb and often richly orchestrated writing on proletarian subjects from the 1890s onwards – the *Yellow Book* stories and, here, Jack Common's beautiful story, are followed by the magical G. F. Green and Alan Sillitoe, one of the greatest of the writers here. In recent years, I very much admired David Rose, and would have liked to include a story by him about roadmenders. Above all, the great British short story is outward-facing, analysing the world. *Chambers's Journal* promised, on its foundation in

1832, 'lots of nice little stories about travellers in Asia and Africa'.[11] As it moved into its heyday, the fascination with the outwardly exotic was supplemented by a much richer vein, finding considerable exotic interest in territories closer to hand.

There are sumptuous riches in the British short story, and the raucously exuberant piece of playfulness is only part of it. There is, too, an exquisitely withdrawn and precise vein, often claimed by women writers: these were among my most precious discoveries while reading, and I came to see the tradition that runs through Malachi Whitaker, Dorothy Edwards, Viola Meynell and Elizabeth Taylor to Shena Mackay – Jackie Kay and Jane Gardam should also be mentioned here – as a sublime, vulnerable one. Withdrawn exactitudes are an important part of the tradition, but only part. It often needs to be stressed that the British short story can be most itself when rumbustious, violent, extravagant, fantastical; above all, when it yields to a national taste for the theatrical.

So often, the great British short story seems to be fascinated by performance. A recurrent form is the narrator after dinner, who shares the best story he ever heard: as time goes on, and leisurely dinners become less universal in the real world, the story starts to turn towards the tale told in a railway carriage, like Graham Greene's thrillingly preposterous 'The Hint of an Explanation', or – surprisingly common – the tale told by a barber to his client, of which the greatest must surely be V. S. Pritchett's 'You Make Your Own Life' with its final brutal slash of the razorblade. Pritchett was the greatest of British short-story writers, and embedded in the art of performance, whether in the sardonic explanation of a stage trick in 'The Fall' that opens up a man's relationship with his absent brother, or the performance that has no idea that it's going on until its last line, as in 'When My Girl Comes Home', or the stage monologue which 'The Camberwell Beauty' initially seems to be. The monologue, as of a stage character, is a very common form in the British short story; I regretted not being able to include more after Dickens's 'Mrs Lirriper' set an unmatchable standard that only Pritchett began to reach. Too many others were ultimately rather limp interwar matinée offerings, but the indirect relationship with the stage, and with performance generally, animated many of the best short stories here.

The quality of performance drives two recurrent qualities of the British short story: its dependence on comedy in any and all circumstances, and its love of Grand Guignol. Wild and impossible violence often emerges from physical specificity, as in the Aickman or the great T. H. White story. The physically specific can be the source of comedy, too, and often these two very British modes combine. Adam Marek's eye-popping story 'The 40-Litre Monkey' has plenty of prec-edents. Even a writer as unfailingly sympathetic as Tessa Hadley can give a story of considerable suffering the detached and borderline flippant title 'Buckets of Blood'. Readers may be surprised at the things they are asked to laugh at by Somerset Maugham, Wilkie Collins or Max Beerbohm. The violence in the splendid Wodehouse story is always, it seems, waiting to break out. Sometimes the territory that seems to interest the writer is the exact moment when the laughter freezes on the lips, not just in the sublime and terrifying Kipling story but, in a minor key, in the A. E. Coppard and Rhys Davies. Both Coppard and Davies were masters of what A. S. Byatt very accurately calls 'mixed tones', and in their very best stories, as represented here, the reader is often moved to laughter before wondering whether laughter is quite the thing. The uncertainty, exactly pinpointed, is at the heart of their achievement.

It's common, in compilations of this sort, for the anthologizer to make a case for his general subject by playing down the comic element. Comedy is so much at the centre of the British short story that, by contrast, I've sometimes included a short story by a writer not primarily known for his or her humour. Elizabeth Taylor's virtuoso late 'In and Out the Houses' has all her social precision of detail (the ravioli!) but is cast as a broad farce where only one character ever goes anywhere – the technical command is stunning, like a Mozart rondo. I wanted, too, to highlight Elizabeth Bowen's gift for comedy with a savage edge with a relatively unfamiliar early piece rather than the acknowledged greatness of 'Mysterious Kôr'. That gift for comedy in surprising places continues: it beautifully lightens Zadie Smith's wonderful 'The Embassy of Cambodia' with some unexpectedly broad, Dickensian characters. I don't think it will ever go away, however superficially serious the subject of the short story.

From that valuing of comedy comes, I think, a characteristic of the British short story to entwine, reverse, overturn itself and take directions that nobody could foresee; this emerges most consistently in tone and flavour. The great British short story is often a ferocious ride with hidden traps and unpredictable bogs, explosions and patches of tranquillity or exhaustion. Surprise is a quality often prized; even the surprise offered by a story that never changes its tone, like Dorothy Edwards's or Mary Lamb's stories. In an extraordinary story by Penelope Gilliatt I came close to including, a well-planted fictional robot called FRANK does exactly nothing, but deserves the story's title. The surprise may be in the point of view, as in the wild shifts of direction in the Jean Rhys short story, or realizing that the person who places himself at the centre of the story has no significance whatsoever, as in Pritchett's 'The Camberwell Beauty'. Comedy, the tripping up of expectations, the overturning of an established world: these things have a tendency to shape the form even when laughter is not contemplated.

Some of these distinctive qualities are more or less permanently present in the British short story. Some, however, ebb and flow with fashion, and I have tried to suggest in my selection how the short story has a predominant flavour and urgent themes at different moments in its history. The feeling of growing hysteria with a diabolic edge before the Great War is striking – the feeling, perhaps, as Richard Strauss's Salomé puts it, that '*es sind noch nicht genug Tote*', there aren't enough dead yet. There is speculation about what women are to do with their lives in the 1920s that emerges in a spate of brilliant feminine two-handers. New subjects emerge; new themes interest the best talent at work.

A confident relationship with genre has never limited the British short story, though some genres have proved more fruitful to the form than others. The love story and the detective story were evidently very popular forms in magazine fiction: they did not seem to me to be natural candidates for short fiction, often requiring as they do a slow expansion on the significance of details and a warm growth of feeling over time. Perhaps for the same reason, there was no shortage of historical short stories, but, apart from Jean Rhys and the unique genius of Penelope Fitzgerald, very few I could much admire. Other forms, however, that could rest on suggestion and airy implication were natural. I sometimes felt, reading through the collected stories of classic authors, that an anthology of this sort could be made up of nothing other than the occasional ghost story that almost every British writer produced; there is at least one first-rate example from the works of many writers, including Saki, Elizabeth Bowen and Penelope Fitzgerald, as well as specialists like E. F. Benson and M. R. James. Ghost stories are British in the most conventional way; the great practitioners, like M. R. James and Robert Aickman, rely on a background of propriety and high respectability. When those moments of propriety are broken, sometimes with screaming terror, sometimes merely with the narrator being physically touched for the first time in the story, or by gatecrashing a party, a different, less orderly side of the British is revealed. Science fiction, too, which can rest on the suggestion of vast unknowable changes, was as natural to short fiction from the start as horror. Fine as G. K. Chesterton's 'The Honour of Israel Gow' is, it would be perfect if it ended before the solution started being put together, at the point of maximum bafflement, with all the horror and grotesquery in full untethered flight. Another point of genre possibility comes with the curious, dreamlike fantasy that sometimes overtakes the short story: the burst of allegorical mysticism in late-1940s short stories, including T. F. Powys and Sylvia Townsend Warner, is a very striking one – one should perhaps add Tolkien's long and beautiful 'Leaf by Niggle', a story it proved impractical to include.

Was there a regional aspect? Perhaps. The Scottish short story has aspects of folklore and a consistent interest in experiments with voice that is their own – I was sorry not to find space for Eric Linklater, and to have included some more early compilers of folklore would have taken the anthology in a direction too rich to be merely sampled. The Welsh short story produces profound mastery, and its fascination with the unexpected direction and the superficially relaxed, conversational purpose emerges in Rhys Davies and the breathtaking Alun Lewis story – a hearty, skirling, raucous quality, too.

It may be that the British short story offers the longest and richest national tradition in the world, and with its own particular qualities of genre, extroversion, confidence and improvisation escapes any kind of predictability. This anthology could very easily have been twice as long as it is. I was determined that I would not include famous writers on the basis of achievement that, in reality, lay elsewhere – neither Firbank nor

Virginia Woolf would command our interest on the basis of their stories if they had never written novels. E. M. Forster was a difficult case. The stories I most admired were published posthumously, ruling them out of consideration, and the ones he published in his lifetime suffered from the whimsy that his novels, at greater length, command and subdue. Nor was it right to include stories that were merely historically interesting; Scott's short stories are important, but I couldn't admire any of them as much as the best of Galt. I also thought that Walter de la Mare was in the unusual position of requiring lengthy submersion in his peculiar tone. It was impossible to imagine any of his stories making sense in an anthology of this sort, and I could not make up my mind whether he was a writer of genius or a writer of essentially entranced badness.

I thought it was my duty to shut my ears against the noise of fashionable approbation. Particularly in the case of contemporary writers, it would have been easy to have gone along with some lazily acclaimed writers. Of course, there are some writers at work now whom I omitted at the last with immense regret, such as Jane Gardam, David Rose, Gerard Woodward or Helen Dunmore. There were other highly acclaimed practitioners, however, who never came near a final selection. Reading through an author's successive collections of stories was a salutary lesson in discovering that a large reputation really had no idea how to put a story together, or had only one idea, much repeated over the course of decades. Other restrictions made themselves felt. It was agony to confine myself to a single story by a very varied and fecund writer. Worst of all, it sometimes had to be accepted that an author who had done something rather brilliant with a short story couldn't quite justify his or her space at the expense of a greater master. While not feeling much guilt about the omission of a fashionable name or a Woolf – they will survive my neglect – I do feel guilty about these unfamiliar names who had made something strong and beautiful and striking, and yet, at the last, I found that a J. E. Buckrose, a Margery Sharp, an Elizabeth Goudge, an H. A. Manhood or an R. Murray Gilchrist (much admired by Arnold Bennett) had to drop back into oblivion. With all that, the task of systematically reading thousands of short stories by hundreds of writers in journals, collections and magazines must count as the most rewarding and surprising of my professional life.

6

Many conversations, much correspondence and casual discussion over the years contributed to this anthology. I would like to thank John Mullan, John Sutherland, Tessa Hadley, Alan Hollinghurst, Nicola Barr, Harriet Harvie-Wood, Georgia Garrett, Georgie Hammick, Peter Parker, D. J. Taylor, Jane Feaver, Ginny Baily, Maggie Fergusson and Candia McWilliam for very helpful suggestions. The idea of the anthology was Simon Winder's at Penguin. Simon both confidently went along with the notion of an anthology on a very generous scale, and, just as importantly, kept the project within bounds. I should also say that he coped manfully with the loss of a splendid Ian Fleming story at the very last stage. The detailed investigation of both journals and collections of stories was only possible thanks to the London Library and the British Library. I would also like to thank Bath Spa University, which gave me time off from teaching at a crucial stage to allow me to get through a very large quantity of reading. Above all, the work of selection owes most to A. S. Byatt, who carved a pioneering path with her 1997 *Oxford Book of the English Short Story* and whose selfless interest and engagement in conversation and correspondence gave me a lot to think about. I am very happy to dedicate this anthology to Antonia, and to correct at least one glaring omission from her anthology; she modestly left herself out, and it is a pleasure to be able to include a superb story by my predecessor.

Philip Hensher, 2015

Notes

1. Review of N. Hawthorne, 'Twice-Told Tales', in Poe, Edgar Allen, *Essays and Reviews*, ed. G. R. Thompson (New York, 1984), p. 571.
2. 'The Philosophy of Composition', *ibid*, p. 19.
3. *The Collected Stories of Lanoe Falconer* (Palo Alto, 2010), p. 13.

4. Baldwin, Dean, *Art and Commerce in the British Short Story, 1880–1950* (London, 2013), p. 8.

5. Baldwin, p. 44.

6. Lycett, Andrew, *Conan Doyle: The Man Who Created Sherlock Holmes* (London, 2007), pp. 294, 299.

7. Baldwin, p. 101.

8. *Chambers's Journal*, 3 June 1871.

9. 'A Few Notes upon Mr James', *The Yellow Book*, vol. 7, p. 71.

10. Reported on Twitter by an audience member called Koa Beck, 1 February 2014, after a talk at Beth Elohim, Park Slope, Brooklyn.

11. *Khushwant Singh Selects: Best Indian Short Stories*, vol. 2 (Harper Collins, India), p. 9.

12. Quoted by W. Forbes Gray, 'A Hundred Years Old: *Chambers's Journal, 1832–1932*', *Chambers's Journal* (1932), p. 83.

THE
PENGUIN BOOK
of the

BRITISH
SHORT
STORY

VOLUME 1

DANIEL DEFOE

A True Relation of the Apparition of Mrs Veal

This thing is so rare in all its circumstances, and on so good authority, that my reading and conversation has not given me anything like it: it is fit to gratify the most ingenious and serious inquirer. Mrs Bargrave is the person to whom Mrs Veal appeared after her death; she is my intimate friend, and I can avouch for her reputation, for these last fifteen or sixteen years, on my own knowledge; and I can confirm the good character she had from her youth, to the time of my acquaintance. Though, since this relation, she is calumniated by some people, that are friends to the brother of this Mrs Veal, who appeared; who think the relation of this appearance to be a reflection, and endeavour what they can to blast Mrs Bargrave's reputation, and to laugh the story out of countenance. But by the circumstances thereof, and the cheerful disposition of Mrs Bargrave, notwithstanding the ill-usage of a very wicked husband, there is not yet the least sign of dejection in her face; nor did I ever hear her let fall a desponding or murmuring expression; nay, not when actually under her husband's barbarity; which I have been witness to, and several other persons of undoubted reputation.

Now you must know, Mrs Veal was a maiden gentlewoman of about thirty years of age, and for some years last past had been troubled with fits; which were perceived coming on her, by her going off from her discourse very abruptly to some impertinence. She was maintained by an only brother, and kept his house in Dover. She was a very pious woman, and her brother a very sober man to all appearance; but now he does all he can to null or quash the story. Mrs Veal was intimately acquainted with Mrs Bargrave from her childhood. Mrs Veal's circumstances were then mean; her father did not take care of his children as he ought, so that they were exposed to hardships; and Mrs Bargrave, in those days, had as unkind a father, though she wanted neither for food nor clothing, whilst Mrs Veal wanted for both; insomuch that she would often say, Mrs Bargrave, you are not only the best, but the only friend I have in the world, and no circumstance of life shall ever dissolve my friendship. They would often condole each other's adverse fortunes, and read together Drelincourt upon Death, and other good books; and so, like two Christian friends, they comforted each other under their sorrow.

Some time after, Mr Veal's friends got him a place in the custom-house at Dover, which occasioned Mrs Veal, by little and little, to fall off from her intimacy with Mrs Bargrave, though there was never any such thing as a quarrel; but an indifferency came on by degrees, till at last Mrs Bargrave had not seen her in two years and a half; though above a twelvemonth of the time Mrs Bargrave hath been absent from Dover, and this last half year has been in Canterbury about two months of the time, dwelling in a house of her own.

In this house, on the 8th of September, 1705, she was sitting alone in the forenoon, thinking over her unfortunate life, and arguing herself into a due resignation to providence, though her condition seemed hard. And, said she, I have been provided for hitherto, and doubt not but I shall be still; and am well satisfied that my afflictions shall end when it is most fit for me: and then took up her sewing-work, which she had no sooner done, but she hears a knocking at the door. She went to see who was there, and this proved to be Mrs Veal, her old friend, who was in a riding-habit. At that moment of time the clock struck twelve at noon.

Madam, says Mrs Bargrave, I am surprised to see you, you have been so long a stranger; but told her, she was glad to see her, and offered to salute her; which Mrs Veal complied with, till their lips almost touched; and then Mrs Veal drew her hand across her own eyes, and said, I am not very well; and so waived it. She told Mrs Bargrave, she was going a journey, and had a great mind to see her first. But, says Mrs Bargrave, how came you to take a journey alone? I am amazed at it, because I know you have a fond brother. Oh! says Mrs Veal, I gave my brother the slip, and came away because I had so great a desire to see you before I took my journey. So Mrs Bargrave went in with her, into another room within the first, and Mrs Veal sat her down in an elbow-chair, in which Mrs Bargrave was sitting when she heard Mrs Veal knock. Then says Mrs Veal, My dear friend, I am come to renew our old friendship again, and beg your pardon for my breach of it; and if you can forgive me, you are the best of women. O, says Mrs Bargrave, do not mention such a thing; I have not had an uneasy thought about it; I can easily forgive it. What did you think of me? said Mrs Veal. Says Mrs Bargrave, I thought you were like the rest of the world, and that prosperity had made you forget yourself and me. Then Mrs Veal reminded Mrs Bargrave of the many friendly offices she did her in former days, and much of the conversation they had with each other in the times of their adversity; what books they read, and what comfort, in particular, they received from Drelincourt's Book of Death, which was the best, she said, on that subject ever written. She also mentioned Dr Sherlock, the two Dutch books which were translated, written upon death, and several others. But Drelincourt, she said, had the clearest notions of death, and of the future state, of any who had handled that subject. Then she asked Mrs Bargrave, whether she had Drelincourt. She said, Yes. Says Mrs Veal, Fetch it. And so Mrs Bargrave goes up stairs and brings it down. Says Mrs Veal, Dear Mrs Bargrave, if the eyes of our faith were as open as the eyes of our body, we should see numbers of angels about us for our guard. The notions we have of heaven now, are nothing like what it is, as Drelincourt says; therefore be comforted under your afflictions, and believe that the Almighty has a particular regard to you; and that your afflictions are marks of God's favour; and when they have done the business they are sent for, they shall be removed from you. And, believe me, my dear friend, believe what I say to you, one minute of future happiness will infinitely reward you for all your sufferings. For, I can never believe, (and claps her hand upon her knee with great earnestness, which indeed ran through most of her discourse,) that ever God will suffer you to spend all your days in this afflicted state; but be assured, that your afflictions shall leave you, or you them, in a short time. She spake in that pathetical and heavenly manner, that Mrs Bargrave wept several times, she was so deeply affected with it.

Then Mrs Veal mentioned Dr Kenrick's Ascetick, at the end of which he gives an account of the lives of the primitive Christians. Their pattern she recommended to our imitation, and said, their conversation was not like this of our age: For now, says she, there is nothing but frothy, vain discourse, which is far different from theirs. Theirs was to edification, and to build one another up in faith; so that they were not as we are, nor are we as they were: but, says she, we ought to do as they did. There was an hearty friendship among them; but where is it now to be found? Says Mrs Bargrave, It is hard indeed to find a true friend in these days. Says Mrs Veal, Mr Norris has a fine copy of verses, called Friendship in Perfection, which I wonderfully admire. Have you seen the book? says Mrs Veal. No, says Mrs Bargrave, but I have the verses of my own writing out. Have you? says Mrs Veal, then fetch them. Which she did from above stairs, and offered them to Mrs Veal to read, who refused, and waived the thing, saying, holding down her head would make it ache; and then desired Mrs Bargrave to read them to her, which she did. As they were admiring friendship, Mrs Veal said, Dear Mrs Bargrave, I shall love you for ever. In these verses there is twice used the word Elysian, Ah! says Mrs Veal, these poets have such names for heaven. She would often draw her hand across her own eyes, and say, Mrs Bargrave, do not you think I am mightily impaired by my fits? No, says Mrs Bargrave, I think you look as well as ever I knew you. After all this discourse, which the apparition put in much finer words than Mrs Bargrave said she could pretend to, and as much more than she can remember, (for it cannot be thought, that an hour and three quarters' conversation could all be retained, though the main of it she thinks she does,) she said to Mrs Bargrave, she would have her write a letter to her brother, and tell him, she would have him give rings to such and such; and that there was a purse of gold in her cabinet, and that she would have two broad pieces given to her cousin Watson.

Talking at this rate, Mrs Bargrave thought that a fit was coming upon her, and so placed herself in a chair just before her knees, to keep her from falling to the ground, if her fits should occasion it: for the elbow-chair, she thought, would keep her from falling on either side. And to divert Mrs Veal, as she thought, took hold of her gown-sleeve several times, and commended it. Mrs Veal told her, it was a scowered silk, and newly made up. But for all this, Mrs Veal persisted in her request, and told Mrs Bargrave, she must not deny her: and she would have her tell her brother all their conversation, when she had opportunity. Dear Mrs Veal, says Mrs Bargrave, this seems so impertinent, that I cannot tell how to comply with it; and what a mortifying story will our conversation be to a young gentleman? Why, says Mrs Bargrave, it is much better, methinks to do it yourself. No, says Mrs Veal, though it seems impertinent to you now, you will see more reason for it hereafter. Mrs Bargrave then, to satisfy her importunity, was going to fetch a pen and ink; but Mrs Veal said, Let it alone now, but do it when I am gone; but you must be sure to do it: which was one of the last things she enjoined her at parting; and so she promised her.

Then Mrs Veal asked for Mrs Bargrave's daughter; she said, she was not at home: But if you have a mind to see her, says Mrs Bargrave, I'll send for her. Do, says Mrs Veal. On which she left her, and went to a neighbour's to see for her; and by the time Mrs Bargrave was returning, Mrs Veal was got without the door in the street, in the face of the beast-market, on a Saturday, which is market-day, and stood ready to part, as soon as Mrs Bargrave came to her. She asked her, why she was in such haste. She said she must be going, though perhaps she might not go her journey till Monday; and told Mrs Bargrave, she hoped she should see her again at her cousin Watson's, before she went whither she was going. Then she said, she would take her leave of her, and walked from Mrs Bargrave in her view, till a turning interrupted the sight of her, which was three quarters after one in the afternoon.

Mrs Veal died the 7th of September, at twelve o'clock at noon, of her fits, and had not above four hours' senses before her death, in which time she received the sacrament. The next day after Mrs Veal's appearing, being Sunday, Mrs Bargrave was mightily indisposed with a cold, and a sore throat, that she could not go out that day; but on Monday morning she sent a person to captain Watson's, to know if Mrs Veal was there. They wondered at Mrs Bargrave's inquiry; and sent her word, that she was not there, nor was expected. At this answer Mrs Bargrave told the maid she had certainly mistook the name, or made some blunder. And though she was ill, she put on her hood, and went herself to captain Watson's though she knew none of the family, to see if Mrs Veal was there or not. They said, they wondered at her asking, for that she had not been in town; they were sure, if she had, she would have been there. Says Mrs Bargrave, I am sure she was with me on Saturday almost two hours. They said, it was impossible; for they must have seen her if she had. In comes Capt. Watson, while they were in dispute, and said, that Mrs Veal was certainly dead, and her escutcheons were making. This strangely surprised Mrs Bargrave, when she sent to the person immediately who had the care of them, and found it true. Then she related the whole story to captain Watson's family, and what gown she had on, and how striped; and that Mrs Veal told her, it was scowered. Then Mrs Watson cried out, You have seen her indeed, for none knew, but Mrs Veal and myself, that the gown was scowered. And Mrs Watson owned, that she described the gown exactly: For, said she, I helped her to make it up. This Mrs Watson blazed all about the town, and avouched the demonstration of the truth of Mrs Bargrave's seeing Mrs Veal's apparition. And captain Watson carried two gentlemen immediately to Mrs Bargrave's house, to hear the relation of her own mouth. And when it spread so fast, that gentlemen and persons of quality, the judicious and sceptical part of the world, flocked in upon her, it at last became such a task, that she was forced to go out of the way. For they were, in general, extremely satisfied of the truth of the thing, and plainly saw that Mrs Bargrave was no hypocondriac; for she always appears with such a cheerful air, and pleasing mien, that she has gained the favour and esteem of all the gentry; and it is thought a great favour, if they can but get the relation from her own mouth. I should have told you before, that Mrs Veal told Mrs Bargrave, that her sister and brother-in-law were just come down from London to see her. Says Mrs Bargrave, How came you to order matters so strangely? It could not be helped, says Mrs Veal. And her brother and sister did come to see her, and entered the town of Dover just as Mrs Veal was expiring. Mrs Bargrave asked her, whether she would drink some tea. Says Mrs Veal, I do not care if I do; but I'll warrant you, this mad fellow, (meaning Mrs Bargrave's husband,) has broke all your trinkets. But, says Mrs Bargrave, I'll get something to drink in for all that; but Mrs Veal waived it, and said, It is no matter, let it alone; and so it passed.

All the time I sat with Mrs Bargrave, which was some hours, she recollected fresh sayings of Mrs Veal. And one material thing more she told Mrs Bargrave, that old Mr Breton allowed Mrs Veal ten pounds a year; which was a secret, and unknown to Mrs Bargrave, till Mrs Veal told it her.

Mrs Bargrave never varies in her story; which puzzles those who doubt of the truth, or are unwilling to believe it. A servant in the neighbour's yard, adjoining to Mrs Bargrave's house, heard her talking to somebody an hour of the time Mrs Veal was with her. Mrs Bargrave went out to her next neighbour's the very moment she parted with Mrs Veal, and told her what ravishing conversation she had with an old friend, and told the whole of it. Drelincourt's Book of Death is, since this happened, bought up strangely. And it is to be observed, that notwithstanding all the trouble and fatigue Mrs Bargrave has undergone upon this account, she never took the value of a farthing, nor suffered her daughter to take anything of anybody, and therefore can have no interest in telling the story.

But Mr Veal does what he can to stifle the matter, and said, he would see Mrs Bargrave; but yet it is certain matter of fact that he has been at captain Watson's since the death of his sister, and yet never went near Mrs Bargrave; and some of his friends report her to be a liar, and that she knew of Mr Breton's ten pounds a year. But the person who pretends to say so, has the reputation of a notorious liar, among persons whom I know to be of undoubted credit. Now Mr Veal is more of a gentleman than to say she lies; but says, a bad husband has crazed her. But she needs only present herself, and it will effectually confute that pretence. Mr Veal says he asked his sister on her death-bed, whether she had a mind to dispose of anything? And she said, No. Now, the things which Mrs Veal's apparition would have disposed of, were so trifling, and nothing of justice aimed at in their disposal, that the design of it appears to me to be only in order to make Mrs Bargrave so to demonstrate the truth of her appearance, as to satisfy the world of the reality thereof, as to what she had seen and heard; and to secure her reputation among the reasonable and understanding part of mankind. And then again, Mr Veal owns, that there was a purse of gold; but it was not found in her cabinet, but in a comb-box. This looks improbable; for that Mrs Watson owned, that Mrs Veal was so very careful of the key of the cabinet, that she would trust nobody with it. And if so, no doubt she would not trust her gold out of it. And Mrs Veal's often drawing her hand over her eyes, and asking Mrs Bargrave whether her fits had not impaired her, looks to me as if she did it on purpose to remind Mrs Bargrave of her fits, to prepare her not to think it strange that she should put her upon writing to her brother to dispose of rings and gold, which looked so much like a dying person's request; and it took accordingly with Mrs Bargrave, as the effects of her fits coming upon her;

and was one of the many instances of her wonderful love to her, and care
of her, that she should not be affrighted; which indeed appears in her
whole management, particularly in her coming to her in the day-time,
waiving the salutation, and when she was alone; and then the manner of
her parting, to prevent a second attempt to salute her.

Now, why Mr Veal should think this relation a reflection, as it is plain
he does, by his endeavouring to stifle it, I cannot imagine; because the
generality believe her to be a good spirit, her discourse was so heavenly.
Her two great errands were to comfort Mrs Bargrave in her affliction, and
to ask her forgiveness for the breach of friendship, and with a pious discourse to encourage her. So that, after all, to suppose that Mrs Bargrave
could hatch such an invention as this from Friday noon till Saturday noon,
supposing that she knew of Mrs Veal's death the very first moment, without jumbling circumstances, and without any interest too; she must be
more witty, fortunate, and wicked too, than any indifferent person, I dare
say, will allow. I asked Mrs Bargrave several times, if she was sure she felt
the gown? She answered modestly, If my senses be to be relied on, I am
sure of it. I asked her, if she heard a sound when she clapped her hand
upon her knee? She said, she did not remember she did; but said she
appeared to be as much a substance as I did, who talked with her. And I
may, said she, be as soon persuaded, that your apparition is talking to me
now, as that I did not really see her: for I was under no manner of fear,
and received her as a friend, and parted with her as such. I would not, says
she, give one farthing to make any one believe it: I have no interest in it;
nothing but trouble is entailed upon me for a long time, for aught I know;
and had it not come to light by accident, it would never have been made
public. But now, she says, she will make her own private use of it, and keep
herself out of the way as much as she can; and so she has done since. She
says, she had a gentleman who came thirty miles to her to hear the relation; and that she had told it to a room full of people at a time. Several
particular gentlemen have had the story from Mrs Bargrave's own mouth.

This thing has very much affected me, and I am as well satisfied, as I
am of the best-grounded matter of fact. And why we should dispute matter of fact, because we cannot solve things of which we can have no certain
or demonstrative notions, seems strange to me. Mrs Bargrave's authority
and sincerity alone, would have been undoubted in any other case.

JONATHAN SWIFT

Directions to the Footman

Your employment being of a mixt nature, extends to a great variety of business, and you stand in a fair way of being the favourite of your master or mistress, or of the young masters and misses; you are the fine gentleman of the family, with whom all the maids are in love. You are sometimes a pattern of dress to your master, and sometimes he is so to you. You wait at table in all companies, and consequently have the opportunity to see and know the world, and to understand men and manners; I confess your vails are but few, unless you are sent with a present, or attend the tea in the country; but you are called Mr in the neighbourhood, and sometimes pick up a fortune, perhaps your master's daughter; and I have known many of your tribe to have good commands in the army. In town you have a seat reserved for you in the play-house, where you have an opportunity of becoming wits and cricks: you have no profest enemy except the rabble, and my lady's waiting-woman, who are sometimes apt to call you skip-kennel. I have a true veneration for your office, because I had once the honour to be one of your order, which I foolishly left by demeaning my self with accepting an employment in the custom-house. But that you, my brethren, may come to better fortune, I shall here deliver my instructions, which have been the fruits of much thought and observation, as well as of seven years experience.

In order to learn the secrets of other families, tell your brethren those of your master's; thus you will grow a favourite both at home and abroad, and be regarded as a person of importance.

Never be seen in the streets with a basket or bundle in your hands, and carry nothing but what you can hide in your pocket, otherwise you will disgrace your calling: to prevent which, always retain a blackguard boy to carry your loads; and if you want farthings, pay him with a good slice of bread or scrap of meat.

Let a shoe-boy clean your own shoes first, for fear of fouling the chamber, then let him clean your master's; keep him on purpose for that use and to run of errands, and pay him with scraps.

When you are sent on an errand, be sure to hedge in some business of your own, either to see your sweet-heart, or drink a pot of ale with some brother-servants, which is so much time clear gained.

There is a great controversy about the most convenient and genteel way of holding your plate at meals; some stick it between the frame and the back of the chair, which is an excellent expedient, where the make of the chair will allow it: others, for fear the plate should fall, grasp it so firmly, that their thumb reacheth to the middle of the hollow; which however, if your thumb be dry, is no secure method; and therefore in that case, I advise your wetting the bowl of it with your tongue: as to that absurd practice of letting the back of the plate lye leaning on the hollow of your hand, which some ladies recommend, it is universally exploded, being liable to so many accidents. Others again, are so refined, that they hold their plate directly the left arm-pit, which is the best situation for keeping it warm; but this may be dangerous in the article of taking away a dish, where your plate may happen to fall upon some of the company's heads. I confess my self to have objected against all these ways, which I have frequently tryed; and therefore I recommend a fourth, which is to stick your plate up to the rim inclusive, in the left side between your waistcoat and your shirt: this will keep it at least as warm as under your arm-pit, or ockster (as the Scots call it). This will hide it so, as strangers may take you for a better servant, too good to hold a plate; this will secure it from falling, and thus disposed, it lies ready for you to whip it out in a moment, ready warmed, to any guest within your reach, who may want it. And lastly, there is another convenience in this method, that if at any time during your waiting, you find yourself going to cough or sneese, you can immediately snatch out your plate, and hold the hollow part close to your nose or mouth, and, thus prevent spirting any moisture from either, upon the dishes or a lady's head-dress: you see gentlemen and ladies observe a like practice on such an occasion, with a hat or a handkerchief; yet a plate is less fouled and sooner cleaned than either of these; for, when your cough or sneese is over, it is but returning your plate to the same position, and your shirt will clean it in the passage.

Take off the largest dishes, and set them on with one hand, to shew the ladies your vigour and strength of back; but always do it between two ladies, that if the dish happens to slip, the soup or sauce may fall on their cloaths, and not daub the floor: by this practice, two of our brethren, my worthy friends, got considerable fortunes.

Learn all the new-fashion words, and oaths, and songs, and scraps of plays that your memory can hold. Thus, you will become the delight of nine ladies in ten, and the envy of ninety-nine beaux in a hundred.

Take care, that at certain periods, during dinner especially, when persons of quality are there, you and your brethren be all out of the room together, by which you will give yourselves some ease from the fatigue of waiting, and at the same time leave the company to converse more freely, without being constrained by your presence.

When you are sent on a message, deliver it in your own words, altho' it be to a duke or a dutchess, and not in the words of your master or lady; for how can they understand what belongs to a message as well as you, who have been bred to the employment? But never deliver the answer till it is called for, and then adorn it with your own style.

When dinner is done, carry down a great heap of plates to the kitchen, and when you come to the head of the stairs, trundle them all before you: there is not a more agreeable sight or sound, especially if they be silver, besides the trouble they save you, and there they will lie ready near the kitchen door, for the scullion to wash them.

If you are bringing up a joint of meat in a dish, and it falls out of your hand, before you get into the dining room, with the meat on the ground, and the sauce spilled, take up the meat gently, wipe it with the lap of your coat, then put it again into the dish, and serve it up; and when your lady misses the sauce, tell her, it is to be sent up in a plate by itself.

When you carry up a dish of meat, dip your fingers in the sauce, or lick it with your tongue, to try whether it be good, and fit for your master's table.

You are the best judge of what acquaintance your lady ought to have, and therefore, if she sends you on a message of compliment or business to a family you do not like, deliver the answer in such a manner, as may breed a quarrel between them, not to be reconciled: or, if a footman comes from the same family on the like errand, turn the answer she orders you to deliver, in such a manner, as the other family may take it for an affront.

When you are in lodgings, and no shoe-boy to be got, clean your master's shoes with the bottom of the curtains, a clean napkin, or your landlady's apron.

Ever wear your hat in the house, but when your master calls; and as soon as you come into his presence, pull it off to shew your manners.

Never clean your shoes on the scraper, but in the entry, or at the foot of the stairs, by which you will have the credit of being at home, almost a minute sooner, and the scraper will last the longer.

Never ask leave to go abroad, for then it will be always known that you are absent, and you will be thought an idle rambling fellow; whereas, if you go out, and no body observes, you have a chance of coming home without being missed, and you need not tell your fellow-servants where you are gone, for they will be sure to say, you were in the house but two minutes ago, which is the duty of all servants.

Snuff the candles with your fingers, and throw the snuff on the floor, then tread it out to prevent stinking: this method will very much save the snuffers from wearing out. You ought also to snuff them close to the tallow, which will make them run, and so encrease the perquisite of the cook's kitchen-stuff; for she is the person you ought in prudence to be well with.

While grace is saying after meat, do you and your brethren take the chairs from behind the company, so that when they go to sit down again, they may fall backwards, which will make them all merry; but be you so discreet as to hold your laughter till you get to the kitchen, and then divert your fellow-servants.

When you know your master is most busy in company, come in and pretend to settle about the room, and if he chides, say, you thought he rung the bell. This will divert him from plodding on business too much, or spending himself in talk, or racking his thoughts, all which are hurtful to his constitution.

If you are ordered to break the claw of a crab or a lobster, clap it between the sides of the dining room door between the hinges: thus you can do it gradually without mashing the meat, which is often the fate of the street-door-key, or the pestle.

When you take a foul plate from any of the guests, and observe the foul knife and fork lying on the plate, shew your dexterity, take up the plate, and throw off the knife and fork on the table without shaking off the bones or broken meat that are left: then the guest, who hath more time than you, will wipe the fork and knife already used.

When you carry a glass of liquor to any person who hath called for it, do not bob him on the shoulder, or cry sir, or madam, here's the glass, that would be unmannerly, as if you had a mind to force it down one's throat; but stand at the person's right shoulder and wait his time; and if he strikes it down with his elbow by forgetfulness, that was his fault and not yours.

When your mistress sends you for a hackney coach in a wet day, come back in the coach to save your cloaths and the trouble of walking; it is better the bottom of her pettycoats should be daggled with your dirty shoes, than your livery be spoiled, and yourself get a cold.

There is no indignity so great to one of your station, as that of lighting your master in the streets with a lanthorn; and therefore, it is very honest policy to try all arts how to evade it: besides, it shews your master to be either poor or covetous, which are the two worst qualities you can meet with in any service. When I was under these circumstances, I made use of several wise expedients, which I here recommend to you: sometimes I took a candle so long, that it reached to the very top of the lanthorn and burned it: but, my master after a good beating, ordered me to paste the top with paper. I then used a middling candle, but stuck it so loose in the socket that it leaned towards one side, and burned a whole quarter of the horn. Then I used a bit of candle of half an inch, which sunk in the socket, and melted the solder, and forced my master to walk half the way in the dark. Then he made me stick two inches of candle in the place where the socket was; after which, I pretended to stumble, put out the candle, and broke all the tin part to pieces: at last, he was forced to make use of a lanthorn-boy out of perfect good husbandry.

It is much to be lamented, that gentlemen of our employment have but two hands to carry plates, dishes, bottles, and the like out of the room at meals; and the misfortune is still the greater, because one of those hands is required to open the door, while you are encumbered with your load: therefore, I advise, that the door may be always left at jarr, so as to open it with your foot, and then you may carry out plates and dishes from your belly up to your chin, besides a good quantity of things under your arms, which will save you many a weary step; but take care that none of the burthen falls till you are out of the room, and if possible, out of hearing.

If you are sent to the post-office with a letter in a cold rainy night, step to the ale-house, and take a pot, until it is supposed you have done your errand, but take the next fair opportunity to put the letter in carefully, as becomes an honest servant.

If you are ordered to make coffee for the ladies after dinner, and the pot happens to boil over, while you are running up for a spoon to stir it, or are thinking of something else, or struggling with the chamber-maid for a kiss, wipe the sides of the pot clean with a dishclout, carry up your coffee boldly, and when your lady finds it too weak, and examines you whether it has not run over, deny the fact absolutely, swear you put in more coffee than ordinary, that you never stirred an inch from it, that you strove to make it better than usual, because your mistress had ladies with her, that the servants in the kitchen will justify what you say: upon this, you will find that the other ladies will pronounce your coffee to be very good, and your mistress will confess that her mouth is out of taste, and she will for the future suspect herself, and be more cautious in finding fault. This I would have you do from a principle of conscience, for coffee is very unwholsome; and out of affection to your lady, you ought to give it her as weak as possible: and upon this argument, when you have a mind to treat any of the maids with a dish of fresh coffee, you may, and ought to substract a third part of the powder, on account of your lady's health, and getting her maids good-will.

If your master sends you with a small trifling present to one of his friends, be as careful of it as you would be of a diamond ring: therefore, if the present be only half a dozen pippins, send up the servant who received the message to say, that you were ordered to deliver them with your own hands. This will shew your exactness and care to prevent accidents or mistakes; and the gentleman or lady cannot do less than give you a shilling: so when your master receives the like present, teach the messenger who brings it to do the same, and give your master hints that may stir up his generosity; for brother servants should assist one another, since it is for all their master's honour, which is the chief point to be consulted by every good servant, and of which he is the best Judge.

When you step but a few doors off to tattle with a wench, or take a running pot of ale, or to see a brother footman going to be hanged, leave the street door open, that you may not be forced to knock, and your, master discover you are gone out; for a quarter of an hour's time can do his service no injury.

When you take away the remaining pieces of bread after dinner, put them on foul plates, and press them down with other plates over them, so as no body can touch them; and thus, they will be a good perquisite to the blackguard boy in ordinary.

When you are forced to clean your master's shoes with your own hands, use the edge of the sharpest case knife, and dry them with the toes an inch from the fire, because wet shoes are dangerous; and besides, by these arts you will get them the sooner for yourself.

In some families the master often sends to the tavern for a bottle of wine, and you are the messenger: I advise you, therefore, to take the smallest bottle you can find; but however, make the drawer give you a full quart, then you will get a good sup for yourself, and your bottle will be filled. As for a cork to stop it, you need be at no trouble, for your thumb will do as well, or a bit of dirty chewed paper.

In all disputes with chairmen and coachmen, for demanding too much, when your master sends you down to chaffer with them, take pity of the poor fellows, and tell your master that they will not take a farthing less: it is more for your interest to get share of a pot of ale, than to save a shilling for your master, to whom it is a trifle.

When you attend your lady in a dark night, if she useth her coach, do not walk by the coach side, so as to tire and dirt yourself, but get up into your proper place, behind it, and so hold the flambeau sloping forward over the coach roof; and when it wants snuffing, dash it against the corners.

When you leave your lady at church on Sundays, you have two hours safe to spend with your companions at the ale-house, or over a beef stake and a pot of beer at home with the cook, and the maids; and indeed poor servants have so few opportunities to be happy, that they ought not to lose any.

Never wear socks when you wait at meals, on the account of your own health, as well as of theirs who sit at table; because as most ladies like the smell of young mens toes, so it is a sovereign remedy against the vapours.

Chuse a service, if you can, where your livery colours are least tawdry and distinguishing: green and yellow, immediately betray your office, and so do all kinds of lace, except silver, which will hardly fall to your share, unless with a duke, or some prodigal just come to his estate. The colours you ought to wish for, are blue, or filemot, turned up with red; which with a borrowed sword, a borrowed air, your master's linnen, and an improved confidence added to a natural, will give you what title you please, where you are not known.

When you carry dishes or other things out of the room at meals, fill both your hands as full as possible; for, although you may sometimes spill, and sometimes let fall, yet you will find at the year's end, you have made great dispatch, and saved abundance of time.

If your master or mistress happens to walk the streets, keep you on one side, and as much on the level with them as you can, which people observing, will either think you do not belong to them, or that you are one of their companions; but, if either of them happen to turn back and speak to you, so that you are under the necessity to take off your hat, use but your thumb and one finger, and scratch your head with the rest.

In winter time light the dining-room fire but two minutes before dinner is served up, that your master may see, how saving you are of his coals.

When you are ordered to stir up the fire, clean away the ashes from between the bars with the fire-brush.

When you are ordered to call a coach, although it be midnight, go no further than the door, for fear of being out of the way when you are wanted; and there stand bawling, coach, coach, for half an hour.

Although you gentlemen in livery have the misfortune to be treated scurvily by all mankind, yet you make a shift to keep up your spirits, and sometimes arrive at considerable fortunes. I was an intimate friend to one of our brethren, who was footman to a court lady: she had an honourable employment, was sister to an earl, and the widow of a man of quality. She observed something so polite in my friend, the gracefulness with which he tript before her chair, and put his hair under his hat, that she made him many advances; and one day taking the air in her coach with Tom behind it, the coachman mistook the way, and stopt at a priviledged chaple, where the couple were marryed, and Tom came home in the chariot by his lady's side: but he unfortunately taught her to drink brandy, of which she dyed, after having pawned all her plate to purchase it, and Tom is now a journeyman malster.

Boucher, the famous gamester, was another of our fraternity, and when he was worth 50,000l. he dunned the Duke of B—m for an arrear of wages in his service; and I could instance many more, particularly another, whose son had one of the chief employments at court; and is sufficient to give you the following advice, which is to be pert and sawcy to all mankind, especially to the chaplain, the waiting-woman, and the better sort of servants in a person of quality's family, and value not now and then a kicking, or a caning; for your insolence will at last turn to good account; and from wearing a livery, you may probably soon carry a pair of colours.

When you wait behind a chair at meals, keep constantly wriggling the back of the chair, that the person behind whom you stand, may know you are ready to attend him.

When you carry a parcel of china plates, if they chance to fall, as it is a frequent misfortune, your excuse must be, that a dog ran across you in the hall; that the chamber-maid accidentally pushed the door against you; that a mop stood across the wntry, and tript you up; that your sleeve stuck against the key, or button of the lock.

When your master and lady are talking together in their bed-chamber, and you have some suspicion that you or your fellow-servants are con-cerned in what they say, listen at the door for the publick good of the servants, and join all to take proper measures for preventing any innova-tions that may hurt the community.

Be not proud in prosperity: you have heard that fortune turns on a wheel; if you have a good place, you are at the top of the wheel. Remember how often you have been stripped, and kicked out of doors, your wages all taken up beforehand, and spent in translated red-heel'd shoes, second-hand toupees, and repair'd lace ruffles, besides a swinging debt to the ale-wife and the brandy-shop. The neighbouring tapster, who before would beckon you over to a savoury bit of ox-cheek in the morning, give it you gratis, and only score you up for the liquor, immediately after you were packt off in disgrace, carried a petition to your master, to be paid out of your wages, whereof not a farthing was due, and then pursued you with bailiffs into every blind cellar. Remember how soon you grew shabby, thread-bare, and out-at-heels; was forced to borrow an old livery coat, to make your appearance while you were looking for a place; and sneak to every house where you have an old acquaintance to steal you a scrap, to keep life and soul together; and upon the whole, were in the lowest station of human life, which, as the old ballad says, is that of a skipkennel turned out of place: I say, remember all this now in your flourishing condition. Pay your contributions duly to your late brothers the cadets, who are left to the wide world: take one of them as your dependant, to send on your lady's messages when you have a mind to go to the ale-house; slip him out privately now and then a slice of bread, and a bit of cold meat, your master can afford it; and if he be not yet put upon the establishment for a lodging, let him lye in the stable, or the coach-house, or under the back-stairs, and recommend him to all the gentlemen who frequent your house, as an excellent servant.

To grow old in the office of a footman, is the highest of all indignities: therefore when you find years coming on, without hopes of a place at court, a command in the army, a succession to the stewardship, an employ-ment in the revenue (which two last you cannot obtain without reading and writing) or running away with your master's niece or daughter; I directly advise you to go upon the road, which is the only post of honour left you: there you will meet many of your old comrades, and live a short life and a merry one, and make a figure at your exit, wherein I will give you some instructions.

The last advice I shall give you, relates to your behaviour when you are going to be hanged; which, either for robbing your master, for house-breaking, or going upon the high-way, or in a drunken quarrel, by killing the first man you meet, may very probably be your lot, and is owing to one of these three qualities; either a love of good fellowship, a generosity of mind, or too much vivacity of spirits. Your good behaviour on this article, will concern your whole community: at your tryal deny the fact with all solemnity of imprecations: a hundred of your brethren, if they can be admitted, will attend about the bar, and be ready upon demand to give you a good character before the court: let nothing prevail on you to confess, but the promise of a pardon for discovering your comrades: but, I suppose all this to be in vain, for if you escape now, your fate will be the same another day. Get a speech to be written by the best author of Newgate: some of your kind wenches will provide you with a Holland shirt, and white cap crowned with a crimson or black ribbon: take leave chearfully of all your friends in Newgate: mount the cart with courage: fall on your knees: lift up your eyes: hold a book in your hands although you cannot read a word: deny the fact at the gallows: kiss and forgive the hangman, and so farewell: you shall be buried in pomp, at the charge of the fraternity: the surgeon shall not touch a limb of you; and your fame shall continue until a successor of equal renown succeeds in your place.

HENRY FIELDING

The Female Husband

That propense inclination which is for very wise purposes implanted in the one sex for the other, is not only necessary for the continuance of the human species; but is, at the same time, when govern'd and directed by virtue and religion, productive not only of corporeal delight, but of the most rational felicity.

But if once our carnal appetites are let loose, without those prudent and secure guides, there is no excess and disorder which they are not liable to commit, even while they pursue their natural satisfaction; and, which may seem still more strange, there is nothing monstrous and unnatural, which they are not capable of inventing, nothing so brutal and shocking which they have not actually committed.

Of these unnatural lusts, all ages and countries have afforded us too many instances; but none I think more surprising than what will be found in the history of Mrs Mary, otherwise Mr George Hamilton.

This heroine in iniquity was born in the Isle of Man, on the 16th Day of August, 1721. Her father was formerly a serjeant of grenadiers in the Foot-Guards, who having the good fortune to marry a widow of some estate in that island, purchased his discharge from the army, and retired thither with his wife.

He had not been long arrived there before he died, and left his wife with child of this Mary; but her mother, tho' she had not two months to reckon, could not stay till she was delivered, before she took a third husband.

As her mother, tho' she had three husbands, never had any other child, she always express'd an extraordinary affection for this daughter, to whom she gave as good an education as the island afforded; and tho' she used her with much tenderness, yet was the girl brought up in the strictest principles of virtue and religion; nor did she in her younger years discover the least proneness to any kind of vice, much less give cause of suspicion that she would one day disgrace her sex by the most abominable and unnatural pollutions. And indeed she hath often declared from her conscience, that no irregular passion ever had any place in her mind, till she was first seduced by one Anne Johnson, a neighbour of hers, with whom she had been acquainted from her childhood; but not with such intimacy as afterwards grew between them.

This Anne Johnson going on some business to Bristol, which detained her there near half a year, became acquainted with some of the people called Methodists, and was by them persuaded to embrace their sect.

At her return to the Isle of Man, she soon made an easy convert of Molly Hamilton, the warmth of whose disposition rendered her susceptible enough of Enthusiasm, and ready to receive all those impressions which her friend the Methodist endeavoured to make on her mind.

These two young women became now inseparable companions, and at length bed-fellows: for Molly Hamilton was prevail'd on to leave her mother's house, and to reside entirely with Mrs Johnson, whose fortune was not thought inconsiderable in that cheap country.

Young Mrs Hamilton began to conceive a very great affection for her friend, which perhaps was not returned with equal faith by the other. However, Mrs Hamilton declares her love, or rather friendship, was totally innocent, till the temptations of Johnson first led her astray. This latter was, it seems, no novice in impurity, which, as she confess'd, she had learnt and often practiced at Bristol with her methodistical sisters.

As Molly Hamilton was extremely warm in her inclinations, and as those inclinations were so violently attached to Mrs Johnson, it would not have been difficult for a less artful woman, in the most private hours, to turn the ardour of enthusiastic devotion into a different kind of flame.

Their conversation, therefore, soon became in the highest manner criminal, and transactions not fit to be mention'd past between them.

They had not long carried on this wicked crime before Mrs Johnson was again called by her affairs to visit Bristol, and her friend was prevail'd on to accompany her thither.

Here when they arrived, they took up their lodgings together, and lived in the same detestable manner as before; till an end was put to their vile amours, by the means of one Rogers, a young fellow, who by his extraordinary devotion (for he was a very zealous Methodist) or by some other charms, (for he was very jolly and handsome) gained the heart of Mrs Johnson, and married her.

This amour, which was not of any long continuance before it was brought to a conclusion, was kept an entire secret from Mrs Hamilton; but she was no sooner informed of it, than she became almost frantic, she tore her hair, beat her breasts, and behaved in as outrageous a manner as the fondest husband could, who had unexpectedly discovered the infidelity of a beloved wife.

In the midst of these agonies she received a letter from Mrs Johnson, in the following words, or as near them as she can possibly remember.

Dear Molly,

I know you will condemn what I have now done; but I condemn myself much more for what I have done formerly: For I take the whole shame and guilt of what hath passed between us on myself. I was indeed the first seducer of your innocence, for which I ask GOD's pardon and yours. All the amends I can make you, is earnestly to beseech you, in the name of the Lord, to forsake all such evil courses, and to follow my example now, as you before did my temptation, and enter as soon as you can into that holy state into which I was yesterday called. In which, tho' I am yet but a novice, believe me, there are delights infinitely surpassing the faint endearments we have experienc'd together. I shall always pray for you, and continue your friend.

This letter rather increased than abated her rage, and she resolved to go immediately and upbraid her false friend; but while she was taking this resolution, she was informed that Mr Rogers and his bride were departed from Bristol by a messenger, who brought her a second short note, and a bill for some money from Mrs Rogers.

As soon as the first violence of her passion subsided, she began to consult what course to take, when the strangest thought imaginable suggested itself to her fancy. This was to dress herself in mens cloaths, to embarque for Ireland, and commence Methodist teacher.

Nothing remarkable happened to her during the rest of her stay at Bristol, which adverse winds occasioned to be a whole week, after she had provided herself with her dress; but at last having procured a passage, and the wind becoming favourable, she set sail for Dublin.

As she was a very pretty woman, she now appeared a most beautiful youth. A circumstance which had its consequences aboard the ship, and had like to have discovered her, in the very beginning of her adventures.

There happened to be in the same vessel with this adventurer, a Methodist, who was bound to the same place, on the same design with herself.

These two being alone in the cabin together, and both at their devotions, the man in the extasy of his enthusiasm, thrust one of his hands into the other's bosom. Upon which, in her surprize, she gave so effeminate a squawl, that it reached the Captain's ears, as he was smoking his pipe upon deck. Hey day, says he, what have we a woman in the ship! and immediately descended into the cabbin, where he found the two Methodists on their knees.

Pox on't, says the Captain, I thought you had had a woman with you here; I could have sworn I had heard one cry out as if she had been ravishing, and yet the Devil must have been in you, if you could convey her in here without my knowledge.

I defy the Devil and all his works, answered the He Methodist. He has no power but over the wicked; and if he be in the ship, thy oaths must have brought him hither: for I have heard thee pronounce more than twenty since I came on board; and we should have been at the bottom before this, had not my prayers prevented it.

Don't abuse my vessel, cried the Captain, she is as safe a vessel, and as good a sailer as ever floated, and if you had been afraid of going to the bottom, you might have stay'd on shore and been damn'd.

The Methodist made no answer, but fell a groaning, and that so loud, that the Captain giving him a hearty curse or two, quitted the cabbin, and resumed his pipe.

He was no sooner gone, than the Methodist gave farther tokens of brotherly love to his companion, which soon became so importunate and troublesome to her, that after having gently rejected his hands several times, she at last recollected the sex she had assumed, and gave him so violent a blow in the nostrils, that the blood issued from them with great Impetuosity.

Whether fighting be opposite to the tenets of this sect (for I have not the honour to be deeply read in their doctrines) or from what other motive it proceeded, I will not determine; but the Methodist made no other return to this rough treatment, than by many groans, and prayed heartily to be delivered soon from the conversation of the wicked; which prayers were at length so successful, that, together with a very brisk gale, they brought the vessel into Dublin harbour.

Here our adventurer took a lodging in a back-street near St Stephen's Green, at which place she intended to preach the next day; but had got a cold in the voyage, which occasioned such a hoarseness that made it impossible to put that design in practice.

There lodged in the same house with her, a brisk widow of near forty years of age, who had buried two husbands, and seemed by her behaviour to be far from having determined against a third expedition to the land of matrimony.

To this widow our adventurer began presently to make addresses, and as he at present wanted tongue to express the ardency of his flame, he was obliged to make use of actions of endearment, such as squeezing, kissing, toying, etc.

These were received in such a manner by the fair widow, that her lover thought he had sufficient encouragement to proceed to a formal declaration of his passion. And this she chose to do by letter, as her voice still continued too hoarse for uttering the soft accents of love.

A letter therefore was penned accordingly in the usual stile, which, to prevent any miscarriages, Mrs Hamilton thought proper to deliver with her own hands; and immediately retired to give the adored lady an opportunity of digesting the contents alone, little doubting of an answer agreeable to her wishes, or at least such a one as the coyness of the sex generally dictates in the beginning of an amour, and which lovers, by long experience, know pretty well how to interpret.

But what was the gallant's surprize, when in return to an amorous epistle, she read the following sarcasms, which it was impossible for the most sanguine temper to misunderstand, or construe favourably.

Sir,

I Was greatly astonished at what you put into my hands. Indeed I thought, when I took it, it might have been an Opera song, and which for certain reasons I should think, when your cold is gone, you might sing as well as Farinelli, from the great resemblance there is between your persons. I know not what you mean by encouragement to your hopes; if I could have conceived my innocent freedoms could have been so misrepresented, I should have been more upon my guard: but you have taught me how to watch my actions for the future, and to preserve myself even from any suspicion of forfeiting the regard I owe to the memory of the best of men, by any future choice. The remembrance of that dear person makes me incapable of proceeding farther.

And so firm was this resolution, that she would never afterwards admit of the least familiarity with the despairing Mrs Hamilton; but perhaps that destiny which is remarked to interpose in all matrimonial things, had taken the widow into her protection: for in a few days afterwards, she was married to one Jack Strong, a cadet in an *Irish* regiment.

Our adventurer being thus disappointed in her love, and what is worse, her money drawing towards an end, began to have some thoughts of returning home, when fortune seemed inclined to make her amends for the tricks she had hitherto played her, and accordingly now threw another mistress in her way, whose fortune was much superior to the former widow, and who received Mrs Hamilton's addresses with all the complaisance she could wish.

This lady, whose name was Rushford, was the widow of a rich cheesemonger, who left her all he had, and only one great grand-child to take care of, whom, at her death, he recommended to be her heir; but wholly at her own power and discretion.

She was now in the sixty eighth year of her age, and had not, it seems, entirely abandoned all thoughts of the pleasures of this world: for she was no sooner acquainted with Mrs Hamilton, but, taking her for a beautiful lad of about eighteen, she cast the eyes of affection on her, and having pretty well outlived the bashfulness of her youth, made little scruple of giving hints of her passion of her own accord.

It has been observed that women know more of one another than the wisest men (if ever such have been employed in the study) have with all their art been capable of discovering. It is therefore no wonder that these hints were quickly perceived and understood by the female gallant, who animadverting on the conveniency which the old gentlewoman's fortune would produce in her present situation, very gladly embraced the opportunity, and advancing with great warmth of love to the attack, in which she was received almost with open arms, by the tottering citadel, which presently offered to throw open the gates, and surrender at discretion.

In her amour with the former widow, Mrs Hamilton had never had any other design than of gaining the lady's affection, and then discovering herself to her, hoping to have had the same success which Mrs Johnson had found with her: but with this old lady, whose fortune only she was desirous to possess, such views would have afforded very little gratification. After some reflection, therefore, a device entered into her head, as strange and surprizing, as it was wicked and vile; and this was actually to marry the old woman, and to deceive her, by means which decency forbids me even to mention.

The wedding was accordingly celebrated in the most public manner, and with all kind of gaiety, the old woman greatly triumphing in her shame, and instead of hiding her own head for fear of infamy, was actually proud of the beauty of her new husband, for whose sake she intended to disinherit her poor great-grandson, tho' she had derived her riches from her husband's family, who had always intended this boy as his heir. Nay, what may seem very remarkable, she insisted on the parson's not omitting the prayer in the matrimonial service for fruitfulness; drest herself as airy as a girl of eighteen, concealed twenty years of her age, and laughed and promoted all the jokes which are usual at weddings; but she was not so well pleased with a repartee of her great-grandson, a pretty and a smart lad, who, when somebody jested on the bridegroom because he had no beard, answered smartly: There should never be a beard on both-sides: For indeed the old lady's chin was pretty well stocked with bristles.

Nor was this bride contented with displaying her shame by a public wedding dinner, she would have the whole ceremony compleated, and the stocking was accordingly thrown with the usual sport and merriment.

During the three first days of the marriage, the bride expressed herself so well satisfied with her choice, that being in company with another old lady, she exulted so much in her happiness, that her friend began to envy her, and could not forbear inveighing against effeminacy in men; upon which a discourse arose between the two ladies, not proper to be repeated, if I knew every particular; but ended at the last, in the unmarried lady's declaring to the bride, that she thought her husband looked more like a woman than a man. To which the other replied in triumph, he was the best man in Ireland.

This and the rest which past, was faithfully recounted to Mrs Hamilton by her wife, at their next meeting, and occasioned our young bridegroom to blush, which the old lady perceiving and regarding as an effect of youth, fell upon her in a rage of love like a tygress, and almost murdered her with kisses.

One of our English Poets remarks in the case of a more able husband than Mrs Hamilton was, when his wife grew amorous in an unseasonable time.

> *The doctor understood the call,*
> *But had not always wherewithal.*

So it happened to our poor bridegroom, who having not at that time the wherewithal about her, was obliged to remain meerly passive, under all this torrent of kindness of his wife, but this did not discourage her, who was an experienced woman, and thought she had a cure for this coldness in her husband, the efficacy of which, she might perhaps have essayed formerly. Saying therefore with a tender smile to her husband, I believe you are a woman, her hands began to move in such direction, that the discovery would absolutely have been made, had not the arrival of dinner, at that very instant, prevented it.

However, as there is but one way of laying the spirit of curiosity, when once raised in a woman, *viz.* by satisfying it, so that discovery, though delayed, could not now be long prevented. And accordingly the very next night, the husband and wife had not been long in bed together, before a storm arose, as if drums, guns, wind and thunder were all roaring together. Villain, rogue, whore, beast, cheat, all resounded at the same instant, and were followed by curses, imprecations and threats, which soon waked the poor great-grandson in the garret; who immediately ran down stairs into his great-grandmother's room. He found her in the midst of it in her shift, with a handful of shirt in one hand, and handful of hair in the other, stamping and crying, I am undone, cheated, abused, ruined, robbed by a vile jade, impostor, whore . . . What is the matter, dear Madam, answered the youth; O child, replied she, undone! I am married to one who is no man. My husband? a woman, a woman, a woman. Ay, said the grandson, where is she? . . . Run away, gone, said the great-grandmother, and indeed so she was: For no sooner was the fatal discovery made than the poor female bridegroom, whipt on her breeches, in the pockets of which, she had stowed all the money she could, and slipping on her shoes, with her coat, waiste-coat and stockings in her hands, had made the best of her way into the street, leaving almost one half of her shirt behind, which the enraged wife had tore from her back.

As Mrs Hamilton well knew that an adventure of that kind would soon fill all Dublin, and that it was impossible for her to remain there undiscovered, she hastened away to the Key, where by good fortune, she met with a ship just bound to Dartmouth, on board of which she immediately went, and sailed out of the harbour, before her pursuers could find out or overtake her.

She was a full fortnight in her passage, during which time, no adventure occurred worthy remembrance. At length she landed at Dartmouth, where she soon provided herself with linnen, and thence went to Totness, where she assumed the title of a doctor of physic, and took lodgings in the house of one Mrs Baytree.

Here she soon became acquainted with a young girl, the daughter of one Mr Ivythorn, who had the green sickness; a distemper which the doctor gave out he could cure by an infallible nostrum.

The doctor had not been long intrusted with the care of this young patient before he began to make love to her: for though her complexion was somewhat faded with her distemper, she was otherwise extremely pretty.

This Girl became an easy conquest to the doctor, and the day of their marriage was appointed, without the knowledge, or even suspicion of her father, or of an old aunt who was very fond of her, and would neither of them have easily given their consent to the match, had the doctor been as good a Man as the niece thought him.

At the day appointed, the doctor and his mistress found means to escape very early in the morning from Totness, and went to a town called Ashburton in Devonshire, where they were married by a regular Licence which the doctor had previously obtained.

Here they staid two days at a public house, during which time the Doctor so well acted his part, that his bride had not the least suspicion of the legality of her marriage, or that she had not got a husband for life. The third day they returned to Totness, where they both threw themselves at Mr Ivythorn's feet, who was highly rejoic'd at finding his daughter restor'd to him, and that she was not debauched, as he had suspected of her. And being a very worthy good-natur'd man, and regarding the true interest and happiness of his daughter more than the satisfying his own pride, ambition or obstinacy, he was prevailed on to forgive her, and to receive her and her husband into his house, as his children, notwithstanding the opposition of the old aunt, who declared she would never forgive the wanton slut, and immediately quitted the house, as soon as the young couple were admitted into it.

The Doctor and his wife lived together above a fortnight, without the least doubt conceived either by the wife, or by any other person of the Doctor's being what he appeared; till one evening the Doctor having drank a little too much punch, slept somewhat longer than usual, and when he waked, he found his wife in tears, who asked her husband, amidst many sobs, how he could be so barbarous to have taken such advantage of her ignorance and innocence, and to ruin her in such a manner? The Doctor being surprized and scarce awake, asked her what he had done. Done, says she, have you not married me a poor young girl, when you know, you have not . . . you have not . . . what you ought to have. I always thought indeed your shape was something odd, and have often wondered that you had not the least bit of beard; but I thought you had been a man for all that, or I am sure I would not have been so wicked to marry you for the world. The Doctor endeavoured to pacify her, by every kind of promise, and telling her she would have all the pleasures of marriage without the inconveniences. No, no, said she, you shall not persuade me to that, nor will I be guilty of so much wickedness on any account. I will tell my Papa of you as soon as I am up; for you are no husband of mine, nor will I ever have any thing more to say to you. Which resolution the Doctor finding himself unable to alter, she put on her cloaths with all the haste she could, and taking a horse, which she had bought a few days before, hastened instantly out of the town, and made the best of her way, thro' bye-roads and across country, into Somersetshire, missing Exeter, and every other great town which lay in the road.

And well it was for her, that she used both this haste and precaution: For Mr Ivythorn having heard his daughter's story, immediately obtained a warrant from a justice of peace, with which he presently dispatch'd the proper officers; and not only so, but set forward himself to Exeter, in order to try if he could learn any news of his son-in-law, or apprehend her there; till after much search being unable to hear any tidings of her, he was obliged to set down contented with his misfortune, as was his poor daughter to submit to all the ill-natured sneers of her own sex, who were often witty at her expence, and at the expence of their own decency.

The Doctor having escaped, arrived safe at Wells in Somersetshire, where thinking herself at a safe distance from her pursuers, she again sat herself down in quest of new adventures.

She had not been long in this city, before she became acquainted with one Mary Price, a girl of about eighteen years of age, and of extraordinary beauty. With this girl, hath this wicked woman since her confinement declared, she was really much in love, as it was possible for a man ever to be with one of her own sex.

The first opportunity our Doctor obtain'd of conversing closely with this new mistress, was at a dancing among the inferior sort of people, in contriving which the Doctor had herself the principal share. At that meeting the two lovers had an occasion of dancing all night together; and the Doctor lost no opportunity of shewing his fondness, as well by his tongue as by his hands, whispering many soft things in her ears, and squeezing as many soft things into her hands, which, together with a good number of kisses, &c. so pleased and warmed this poor girl, who never before had felt any of those tender sensations which we call love, that she retired from the dancing in a flutter of spirits, which her youth and ignorance could not well account for; but which did not suffer her to close her eyes, either that morning or the next night.

The day after that the Doctor sent her the following letter.

My Dearest Molly,

Excuse the fondness of that expression; for I assure you, my angel, all I write to you proceeds only from my heart, which you have so entirely conquered, and made your own, that nothing else has any share in it; and, my angel, could you know what I feel when I am writing to you, nay even at every thought of my Molly, I know I should gain your pity if not your love; if I am so happy to have already succeeded in raising the former, do let me have once more an opportunity of seeing you, and that soon, that I may breathe forth my soul at those dear feet, where I would willingly die, if I am not suffer'd to lie there and live. My sweetest creature, give me leave to subscribe myself

Your fond, doating,
Undone SLAVE.

This letter added much to the disquietude which before began to torment poor Molly's breast. She read it over twenty times, and, at last, having carefully survey'd every part of the room, that no body was present, she kissed it eagerly. However, as she was perfectly modest, and afraid of appearing too forward, she resolved not to answer this first letter; and if she met the Doctor, to behave with great coldness towards him.

Her mother being ill, prevented her going out that day; and the next morning she received a second letter from the Doctor, in terms more warm and endearing than before, and which made so absolute a conquest over the unexperienc'd and tender heart of this poor girl, that she suffered herself to be prevailed on, by the intreaties of her lover, to write an answer, which nevertheless she determin'd should be so distant and cool, that the woman of the strictest virtue and modesty in England might have no reason to be asham'd of having writ it; of which letter the reader hath here an exact copy:

Sur,

I Haf recevd boath your too litters, and sur I ham much surprise hat the loafe you priten to have for so pur a garl as mee. I kan nut beleef you wul desgrace yourself by marring sutch a yf as mee, and Sur I wool nut be thee hore of the gratest man in the kuntry. For thof mi vartu his all I haf, yit hit is a potion I ham rissolv to kare to mi housband, soe noe moor at present, from your umble savant to cummand.

The Doctor received this letter with all the ecstasies any lover could be inspired with, and, as Mr Congreve says in his Old Batchelor, Thought there was more eloquence in the false spellings, with which it abounded, than in all Aristotle. She now resolved to be no longer contented with this distant kind of conversation, but to meet her mistress face to face. Accordingly that very afternoon she went to her mother's house, and enquired for her poor Molly, who no sooner heard her lover's voice than she fell a trembling in the most violent manner. Her sister who opened the door informed the Doctor she was at home, and let the impostor in; but Molly being then in dishabille, would not see him till she had put on clean linnen, and was arrayed from head to foot in as neat, tho' not so fine a manner, as the highest court lady in the kingdom could attire herself in, to receive her embroider'd lover.

Very tender and delicate was the interview of this pair, and if any corner of Molly's heart remain'd untaken, it was now totally subdued. She would willingly have postponed the match somewhat longer, from her strict regard to decency; but the earnestness and ardour of her lover would not suffer her, and she was at last obliged to consent to be married within two days.

Her sister, who was older than herself, and had over-heard all that had past, no sooner perceiv'd the Doctor gone, than she came to her, and wishing her joy with a sneer, said much good may it do her with such a husband; for that, for her own part, she would almost as willingly be married to one of her own sex, and made some remarks not so proper to be here inserted. This was resented by the other with much warmth. She said she had chosen for herself only, and that if she was pleased, it did not become people to trouble their heads with what was none of their business. She was indeed so extremely enamoured, that I question whether she would have exchanged the Doctor for the greatest and richest match in the world.

And had not her affections been fixed in this strong manner, it is possible that an accident which happened the very next night might have altered her mind: for being at another dancing with her lover, a quarrel arose between the Doctor and a man there present, upon which the mother seizing the former violently by the collar, tore open her wastecoat, and rent her shirt, so that all her breast was discovered, which, tho' beyond expression beautiful in a woman, were of so different a kind from the bosom of a man, that the married women there set up a great titter; and tho' it did not bring the Doctor's sex into an absolute suspicion, yet caused some whispers, which might have spoiled the match with a less innocent and less enamoured virgin.

It had however no such effect on poor Molly. As her fond heart was free from any deceit, so was it entirely free from suspicion; and accordingly, at the fixed time she met the Doctor, and their nuptials were celebrated in the usual form.

The mother was extremely pleased at this preferment (as she thought it) of her daughter. The joy of it did indeed contribute to restore her perfectly to health, and nothing but mirth and happiness appeared in the faces of the whole family.

The new married couple not only continued, but greatly increased the fondness which they had conceived for each other, and poor Molly, from some stories she told among her acquaintances, the other young married women of the town, was received as a great fibber, and was at last universally laughed at as such among them all.

Three months past in this manner, when the Doctor was sent for to Glastonbury to a patient (for the fame of our adventurer's knowledge in physic began now to spread) when a person of Totness being accidentally present, happened to see and know her, and having heard upon enquiry, that the Doctor was married at Wells, as we have above mentioned, related the whole story of Mr Ivythorn's daughter, and the whole adventure at Totness.

News of this kind seldom wants wings; it reached Wells, and the ears of the Doctor's mother before her return from Glastonbury. Upon this the old woman immediately sent for her daughter, and very strictly examined her, telling her the great sin she would be guilty of, if she concealed a fact of this kind, and the great disgrace she would bring on her own family, and even on her whole sex, by living quietly and contentedly with a husband who was in any degree less a man than the rest of his neighbours.

Molly assured her mother of the falsehood of this report; and as it is usual for persons who are too eager in any cause, to prove too much, she asserted some things which staggered her mother's belief, and made her cry out, O child, there is no such thing in human nature.

Such was the progress this story had made in Wells, that before the Doctor arrived there, it was in every body's mouth; and as the Doctor rode through the streets, the mob, especially the women, all paid their compliments of congratulation. Some laughed at her, others threw dirt at her, and others made use of terms of reproach not fit to be commemorated. When she came to her own house, she found her wife in tears, and having asked her the cause, was informed of the dialogue which had past between her and her mother. Upon which the Doctor, tho' he knew not yet by what means the discovery had been made, yet too well knowing the truth, began to think of using the same method, which she had heard before put in practice, of delivering herself from any impertinence; for as to danger, she was not sufficiently versed in the laws to apprehend any.

In the mean time the mother, at the solicitation of some of her relations, who, notwithstanding the stout denial of the wife, had given credit to the story, had applied herself to a magistrate, before whom the Totness man appeared, and gave evidence as is before mentioned. Upon this a warrant was granted to apprehend the Doctor, with which the constable arrived at her house, just as she was meditating her escape.

The husband was no sooner seized, but the wife threw herself into the greatest agonies of rage and grief, vowing that he was injured, and that the information was false and malicious, and that she was resolved to attend her husband wherever they conveyed him.

And now they all proceeded before the Justice, where a strict examination being made into the affair, the whole happened to be true, to the great shock and astonishment of every body; but more especially of the poor wife, who fell into fits, out of which she was with great difficulty recovered.

The whole truth having been disclosed before the Justice, and something of too vile, wicked and scandalous a nature, which was found in the Doctor's trunk, having been produced in evidence against her, she was committed to Bridewell, and Mr Gold, an eminent and learned counsellor at law, who lives in those parts, was consulted with upon the occasion, who gave his advice that she should be prosecuted at the next sessions, on a clause in the vagrant act, *for having by false and deceitful practices endeavoured to impose on some of his Majesty's subjects.*

As the Doctor was conveyed to Bridewell, she was attended by many insults from the mob; but what was more unjustifiable, was the cruel treatment which the poor innocent wife received from her own sex, upon the extraordinary accounts which she had formerly given of her husband.

Accordingly at the ensuing sessions of the peace for the county of Somerset, the Doctor was indicted for the abovementioned diabolical fact, and after a fair trial convicted, to the entire satisfaction of the whole court.

At the trial the said Mary Price the wife, was produced as a witness, and being asked by the council, whether she had ever any suspicion of the Doctor's sex during the whole time of the courtship, she answered positively in the negative. She was then asked how long they had been married, to which she answered three months; and whether they had cohabited the whole time together? to which her reply was in the affirmative. Then the council asked her, whether during the time of this cohabitation, she imagined the Doctor had behaved to her as a husband ought to his wife? Her modesty confounded her a little at this question; but she at last answered she did imagine so. Lastly, she was asked when it was that she first harboured any suspicion of her being imposed upon? To which she answered, she had not the least suspicion till her husband was carried before a magistrate, and there discovered, as hath been said above.

The prisoner having been convicted of this base and scandalous crime, was by the court sentenced to be publickly and severely whipt four several times, in four market towns within the county of Somerset, to wit, once in each market town, and to be imprisoned, &c.

These whippings she has accordingly undergone, and very severely have they been inflicted, insomuch, that those persons who have more regard to beauty than to justice, could not refrain from exerting some pity toward her, when they saw so lovely a skin scarified with rods, in such a manner that her back was almost flead; yet so little effect had the smart or shame of this punishment on the person who underwent it, that the very evening she had suffered the first whipping, she offered the goaler money, to procure her a young girl to satisfy her most monstrous and unnatural desires.

But it is to be hoped that this example will be sufficient to deter all others from the commission of any such foul and unnatural crimes: for which, if they should escape the shame and ruin which they so well deserve in this world, they will be most certain of meeting with their full punishment in the next: for unnatural affections are equally vicious and equally detestable in both sexes, nay, if modesty be the peculiar characteristick of the fair sex, it is in them most shocking and odious to prostitute and debase it.

In order to caution therefore that lovely sex, which, while they preserve their natural innocence and purity, will still look most lovely in the eyes of men, the above pages have been written, which, that they might be worthy of their perusal, such strict regard hath been had to the utmost decency, that notwithstanding the subject of this narrative be of a nature so difficult to be handled inoffensively, not a single word occurs through the whole, which might shock the most delicate ear, or give offence to the purest chastity.

HANNAH MORE

Betty Brown, the St Giles's Orange Girl: with Some Account of Mrs Sponge, the Money Lender

Betty Brown, the Orange Girl, was born nobody knows where, and bred nobody knows how. No girl in all the streets of London could drive a barrow more nimbly, avoid pushing against passengers more dextrously, or cry her 'Fine China Oranges' in a shriller voice. But then she could neither sew, nor spin, nor knit, nor wash, nor iron, nor read, nor spell. Betty had not been always in so good a situation as that in which we now describe her. She came into the world before so many good gentlemen and ladies began to concern themselves so kindly that the poor might have a little learning. There was no charitable Society then, as there is now, to pick up poor friendless children in the streets and put them into a good house, and give them meat, and drink, and lodging, and learning, and teach them to get their bread in an honest way, into the bargain. Whereas, this now is often the case in London; blessed be God for all his mercies.

The longest thing that Betty can remember is, that she used to crawl up out of a night cellar, stroll about the streets, and pick cinders from the scavengers' carts. Among the ashes she sometimes found some ragged gauze and dirty ribbons; with these she used to dizen herself out, and join the merry bands on the first of May. This was not however quite fair, as she did not lawfully belong either to the female dancers who foot it gaily round the garland, or to the sooty tribe, who, on this happy holiday, forget their whole year's toil; she often, however, got a few scraps, by appearing to belong to both parties.

Betty was not an idle girl; she always put herself in the way of doing something. She would run of errands for the footmen, or sweep the door for the maid of any house where she was known: she would run and fetch some porter, and never was once known either to sip a drop or steal the pot. Her quickness and fidelity in doing little jobs got her into favour with a lazy cook-maid, who was too apt to give away her master's cold meat and beer, not to those who were most in want, but to those who waited upon her, and did the little things for her which she ought to have done herself.

The cook, who found Betty a dextrous girl, soon employed her to sell ends of candles, pieces of meat and cheese, and lumps of butter, or any thing else she could crib from the house. These were all carried to her friend Mrs Sponge, who kept a little shop and a kind of eating-house for poor working people, not far from the Seven Dials. She also bought as well as sold many kinds of second hand things, and was not scrupulous to know whether what she bought was honestly come by, provided she could get it for a sixth part of what it was worth. But if the owner presumed to ask for its real value, she had sudden qualms of conscience, suspected the things were stolen, and gave herself airs of honesty, which often took in poor silly people, and gave her a sort of half reputation among the needy and the ignorant, whose friend she pretended to be.

To this artful woman Betty carried the cook's pilferings, and as Mrs Sponge would give no great price for these in money, the cook was willing to receive payment for her eatables in Mrs Sponge's drinkables; for she dealt in all kinds of spirits. I shall only just remark here, that one receiver, like Mrs Sponge, makes many pilferers, who are tempted to these petty thieveries, by knowing how easy it is to dispose of them at such iniquitous houses.

Betty was faithful to both her employers, which is extraordinary, considering the greatness of the temptation, and her utter ignorance of good and evil. One day, she ventured to ask Mrs Sponge if she could not assist her to get into a more settled way of life. She told her, that when she rose in the morning she never knew where she should lie at night, nor was she ever sure of a meal before hand. Mrs Sponge asked her what she thought herself fit for. Betty, with fear and trembling, said, there was one trade for which she thought herself qualified, but she had not the ambition to look so high. It was far above her humble views. This was, to have a barrow, and sell fruit, as several other of Mrs Sponge's customers did, whom she had often looked at with envy.

Mrs Sponge was an artful woman. Bad as she was, she was always aiming at something of a character; this was a great help to her trade.

While she watched keenly to make every thing turn to her own profit, she had a false fawning way of seeming to do all she did out of pity and kindness to the distressed; and she seldom committed an extortion, but she tried to make the person she cheated believe themselves highly obliged to her kindness. By thus pretending to be their friend she gained their confidence, and she grew rich herself while they thought she was only shewing favour to them. Various were the arts she had of getting rich. The money she got by grinding the poor, she spent in the most luxurious living; and, while she would haggle with her hungry customers for a farthing, she would spend pounds on the most costly delicacies for herself.

Mrs Sponge, laying aside that haughty look and voice, well known to such as had the misfortune to be in her debt, put on the hypocritical smile and soft tone which she always assumed, when she meant to *take in* her dependants. 'Betty,' said she, 'I am resolved to stand your friend. These are sad times to be sure. Money is money now. Yet I am resolved to put you into a handsome way of living. You shall have a barrow, and well furnished, too.' Betty could not have felt more joy or gratitude, if she had been told that she should have a coach. 'O, madam,' said Betty, 'it is impossible. I have not a penny in the world towards helping me to set up.' 'I will take care of that,' said Mrs Sponge; 'only you must do as I bid you. You must pay me interest for my money. And you will of course be glad also to pay so much every night for a nice hot supper which I get ready, quite out of kindness, for a number of poor working people. This will be a great comfort for such a friendless girl as you, for my victuals and drink are the best; and my company the merriest of any house in all St Giles's.' Betty thought all this only so many more favours, and, courtesying to the ground, said, 'to be sure, Ma'am, and thank you a thousand times into the bargain.'

Mrs Sponge knew what she was about. Betty was a lively girl, who had a knack at learning any thing; and so well looking through all her dirt and rags, that there was little doubt she would get custom. A barrow was soon provided, and five shillings put into Betty's hands. Mrs Sponge kindly condescended to go to shew her how to buy the fruit, for it was a rule with this prudent gentlewoman, and one from which she never departed, that no one should cheat but herself.

Betty had never possessed such a sum before. She grudged to lay it out all at once, and was ready to fancy she could live upon the capital. The crown, however, was laid out to the best advantage. Betty was carefully taught in what manner to cry her oranges; and received many useful lessons how to get off the bad with the good, and the stale with the fresh. Mrs Sponge also lent her a few bad sixpences, for which she ordered her to bring home good ones at night. – Betty stared. Mrs Sponge said, 'Betty, those who would get money, must not be too nice about trifles. Keep one of these sixpences in your hand, and if an ignorant young customer gives you a good sixpence do you immediately slip it into your other hand, and give him the bad one, declaring, that it is the very one you have just received, and that you have not another sixpence in the world. You must also learn how to treat different sorts of customers. To some you may put off with safety goods which would be quite unsaleable to others. Never offer bad fruit, Betty, to those who know better; never waste the good on those who may be put off with worse; put good oranges at top, and the mouldy ones under.'

Poor Betty had not a nice conscience, for she had never learnt that grand, but simple rule of all moral obligation, 'Never do that to another which you would not have another do to you.' She set off with her barrow as proud and as happy as if she had been set up in the finest shop in Covent Garden. Betty had a sort of natural good-nature, which made her unwilling to impose, but she had no principle which told her it was a sin. She had such good success, that, when night came she had not an orange left. With a light heart, she drove her empty barrow to Mrs Sponge's door. She went in with a merry face, and threw down on the counter every farthing she had taken. 'Betty,' said Mrs Sponge, 'I have a right to it all, as it was got by my money. But I am too generous to take it. I will therefore only take sixpence for this day's use of my five shillings. This is a most reasonable interest, and I will lend you the same sum to trade with to-morrow, and so on; you only paying me sixpence for the use of it every night, which will be a great bargain to you. You must also pay me my price every night for your supper, and you shall have an excellent lodging above stairs; so you see every thing will now be provided for you in a genteel manner, through my generosity.'

Poor Betty's gratitude blinded her so completely that she forgot to calculate the vast proportion which this generous benefactress was to receive out of her little gains. She thought herself a happy creature, and went in to supper with a number of others of her own class. For this supper, and for more porter and gin than she ought to have drank, Betty was forced to pay so high, that it eat up all the profits of the day, which, added to the daily interest, made Mrs Sponge a rich return for her five shillings.

Betty was reminded again of the gentility of her new situation, as she crept up to bed in one of Mrs Sponge's garrets five stories high. This loft, to be sure, was small, and had no window, but what it wanted in light was made up in company, as it had three beds, and thrice as many lodgers. Those gentry had one night, in a drunken frolic, broke down the door, which happily had never been replaced; for, since that time, the lodgers had died much seldomer of infectious distempers. For this lodging Betty paid twice as much to her good friend as she would have done to a stranger. Thus she continued, with great industry and a thriving trade, as poor as on the first day, and not a bit nearer to saving money enough to buy her even a pair of shoes, though her feet were nearly on the ground.

One day, as Betty was driving her barrow through a street near Holborn, a lady from a window called out to her that she wanted some oranges. While the servants went to fetch a plate, the lady entered into some talk with Betty, having been struck with her honest countenance and civil manner. She questioned her as to her way of life, and the profits of her trade – and Betty, who had never been so kindly treated before by so genteel a person, was very communicative. She told her little history as far as she knew it, and dwelt much on the generosity of Mrs Sponge, in keeping her in her house, and trusting her with so large a capital as five shillings. At first it sounded like a very good-natured thing but the lady, whose husband was one of the Justices of the new Police, happened to know more of Mrs Sponge than was good, which led her to inquire still further. Betty owned, that to be sure it was not all clear profit, for that besides that the high price of the supper and bed ran away with all she got, she paid sixpence a day for the use of the five shillings. 'And how long have you done this?' said the lady. 'About a year, Madam.'

The lady's eyes were at once opened. 'My poor girl,' said she, 'do you know that you have already paid for that single five shillings the enormous sum of 7*l*. 10*s*.? I believe it is the most profitable five shillings Mrs Sponge ever laid out.' 'O, no, Madam,' said the girl, 'that good gentlewoman does the same kindness to ten or twelve other poor friendless creatures like me.' 'Does she so?' said the lady; 'then I never heard of a better trade than this woman carries on, under the mask of charity, at the expence of her poor deluded fellow-creatures.'

'But, Madam,' said Betty, who did not comprehend this lady's arithmetic, 'what can I do? I now contrive to pick up a morsel of bread without begging or stealing. Mrs Sponge has been very good to me; and I don't see how I can help myself.'

'I will tell you,' said the lady. 'If you will follow my advice, you may not only maintain yourself honestly, but independently. Only oblige yourself to live hard for a little time, till you have saved five shillings out of your own earnings. Give up that expensive supper at night, drink only one pint of porter, and no gin at all. As soon as you have scraped together the five shillings, carry it back to your false friend; and if you are industrious, you will, at the end of the year, have saved 7*l.* 10*s.* If you can make a shift to live now, when you have this heavy interest to pay, judge how things will mend when your capital becomes your own. You will put some cloaths on your back, and by leaving the use of spirits, and the company in which you drink them, your health, your morals, and your condition will mend.'

The lady did not talk thus to save her money. She would gladly have given the girl the five shillings; but she thought it was beginning at the wrong end. She wanted to try her. Besides, she knew there was more pleasure as well as honour in possessing five shillings of one's own saving than of another's giving. Betty promised to obey. She owned she had got no good by the company or the liquor at Mrs Sponge's. She promised that very night to begin saving the expence of the supper, and that she would not taste a drop of gin till she had the five shillings beforehand. The lady, who knew the power of good habits, was contented with this, thinking, that if the girl could abstain for a certain time, it would become easy to her. In a very few weeks Betty had saved up the five shillings. She went to carry back this money with great gratitude to Mrs Sponge. This kind friend began to abuse her most unmercifully. She called her many hard names not fit to repeat, for having forsaken the supper, by which she swore she got nothing at all; but as she had the charity to dress it for such beggarly wretches, she insisted they should pay for it, whether they eat it or not. She also brought in a heavy score for lodging, though Betty had paid for it every night, and had given notice of her intending to quit her. By all these false pretences, she got from her not only her own five shillings, but all the little capital with which Betty was going to set up for herself. As all was not sufficient to answer her demands, she declared she would send her to prison; but while she went to call a Constable, Betty contrived to make off.

With a light pocket and a heavy heart, she went back to the lady; and with many tears told her sad story. The lady's husband, the Justice, condescended to listen to Betty's tale. He said Mrs Sponge had long been upon his books as a receiver of stolen goods. Betty's evidence strengthened his bad opinion of her. 'This petty system of usury,' said the gentleman, 'may be thought trifling, but it will no longer appear so, when you reflect, that if one of these female sharpers possesses a capital of seventy shillings, or 3*l*. 10*s*. with fourteen steady regular customers, she can realize a fixed income of 100 guineas a year. Add to this the influence such a loan gives her over these friendless creatures, by compelling them to eat at her house, or lodge, or buy liquors, or by taking their pawns, and you will see the extent of the evil. I pity these poor victims: you, Betty, shall point out some of them to me. I will endeavour to open their eyes on their own bad management. It is one of the greatest acts of kindness to the poor to mend their economy, and to give them right views of laying out their little money to advantage. These poor blinded creatures look no farther than to be able to pay this heavy interest every night, and to obtain the same loan on the same hard terms the next day. Thus are they kept in poverty and bondage all their lives; but I hope as many as hear of this will get on a better plan, and I shall be ready to help any who are willing to help themselves.' This worthy Magistrate went directly to Mrs Sponge's with proper officers; and he soon got to the bottom of many iniquities. He not only made her refund poor Betty's money, but committed her to prison for receiving stolen goods, and various other offences, which may perhaps make the subject of another history.

Betty was now set up in trade to her heart's content. She had found the benefit of leaving off spirits, and she resolved to drink them no more. The first fruits of this resolution was, that in a fortnight she bought herself a new pair of shoes, and as there was now no deduction for interest or for gin, her earnings became considerable. The lady made her a present of a gown and a hat, on the easy condition that she should go to church. She accepted the terms, at first rather as an act of obedience to the lady than from a sense of higher duty. But she soon began to go from a better motive. This constant attendance at church, joined to the instructions of the lady, opened a new world to Betty. She now heard for the first time that she was a sinner; that God had given a law which was holy, just, and good; that she had broken this law, had been a swearer, a sabbath-breaker, and had lived without God in the world. All this was sad news to Betty; she knew, indeed, that there were sinners, but she thought they were only to be found in the prisons, or at Botany Bay, or in those mournful carts which she had sometimes followed, with her barrow, with the unthinking crowd, to Tyburn. She was deeply struck with the great truths revealed in the Scripture, which were quite new to her. She was desirous of improvement, and said, she would give up all the profits of her barrow, and go into the hardest service, rather than live in sin and ignorance.

'Betty,' said the lady, 'I am glad to see you so well disposed, and will do what I can for you. Your present way of life, to be sure, exposes you to much danger; but the trade is not unlawful in itself, and we may please God in any calling, provided it be not a dishonest one. In this great town there must be barrow women to sell fruit. Do you, then, instead of forsaking your business, set a good example to those in it, and shew them, that though a dangerous trade, it need not be a bad one. Till Providence points out some safer way of getting your bread, let your companions see, that it is possible to be good even in this. Your trade being carried on in the open street, and your fruit bought in an open shop, you are not so much obliged to keep sinful company as may be thought. Take a garret in an honest house, to which you may go home in safety at night. I will give you a bed and a few necessaries to furnish your room; and I will also give you a constant Sunday's dinner. A barrow woman, blessed be God and our good laws, is as much her own mistress on Sundays as a Duchess; and the Church and the Bible are as much open to her. You may soon learn all that such as you are expected to know. A barrow woman may pray as heartily morning and night, and serve God as acceptably all day, while she is carrying on her little trade, as if she had her whole time to spare.

To do this well, you must mind the following

RULES FOR RETAIL DEALERS:

Resist every temptation to cheat.
Never impose bad goods on false pretences.
Never put off bad money for good.
Never use profane or uncivil language.
Never swear your goods cost so much, when you know it is false.
By so doing you are guilty of two sins in one breath, a lie and an
oath.

To break these rules, will be your chief temptation. God will mark how
you behave under them, and will reward or punish you accordingly. These
temptations will be as great to you as higher trials are to higher people;
but you have the same God to look to for strength to resist them as they
have. You must pray to him to give you this strength. You shall attend a
Sunday School, where you will be taught these good things; and I will
promote you as you shall be found to deserve.'

Poor Betty here burst into tears of joy and gratitude, crying out, 'What,
shall such a poor friendless creature as I be treated so kindly and learn to
read the word of God too? Oh, Madam, what a lucky chance brought me
to your door.' 'Betty,' said the lady, 'what you have just said, shews the
need you have of being better taught: there is no such thing as chance;
and we offend God when we call that luck or chance which is brought
about by his will and pleasure. None of the events of your life have happened by chance; but all have been under the direction of a good and kind
Providence. He has permitted you to experience want and distress, that
you might acknowledge his hand in your present comfort and prosperity.
Above all, you must bless his goodness in sending you to me, not only
because I have been of use to you in your worldly affairs, but because he
has enabled me to shew you the danger of your state from sin and ignorance, and to put you in a way to know his will and to keep his
commandments.'

How Betty, by industry and piety, rose in the world, till at length she
came to keep that handsome sausage-shop near the Seven Dials, and was
married to an honest hackney-coachman, may be told at some future time,
in a Second Part.

MARY LAMB

The Farm House

My name is Louisa Manners; I was seven years of age last birthday, which was on the first of May. I remember only four birthdays. The day I was four years old was the first that I recollect. On the morning of that day, as soon as I awoke, I crept into mamma's bed, and said, 'Open your eyes, mamma, for it is my birthday. Open your eyes and look at me!' Then mamma told me I should ride in a post-chaise, and see my grandmamma and my sister Sarah. Grandmamma lived at a farmhouse in the country, and I had never in all my life been out of London; no, nor had I ever seen a bit of green grass, except in the Drapers' Garden, which is near my papa's house in Broad Street; nor had I ever rode in a carriage before that happy birthday.

I ran about the house talking of where I was going, and rejoicing so that it was my birthday, that when I got into the chaise I was tired, and fell asleep.

When I awoke, I saw the green fields on both sides of the chaise, and the fields were full, quite full, of bright shining yellow flowers, and sheep and young lambs were feeding in them. I jumped, and clapped my hands together for joy, and I cried out, 'This is

"Abroad in the meadows to see the young lambs,"'

for I knew many of Watts's hymns by heart.

The trees and hedges seemed to fly swiftly by us, and one field, and the sheep, and the young lambs, passed away; and then another field came, and that was full of cows; and then another field, and all the pretty sheep returned; and there was no end of these charming sights till we came quite to grandmamma's house, which stood all alone by itself, no house to be seen at all near it.

Grandmamma was very glad to see me, and she was very sorry that I did not remember her, though I had been so fond of her when she was in town but a few months before. I was quite ashamed of my bad memory. My sister Sarah showed me all the beautiful places about grandmamma's house. She first took me into the farmyard, and I peeped into the barn; there I saw a man thrashing, and as he beat the corn with his flail, he made such a dreadful noise that I was frightened, and ran away; my sister persuaded me to return; she said Will Tasker was very good-natured; then I went back, and peeped at him again; but as I could not reconcile myself to the sound of his flail, or the sight of his black beard, we proceeded to see the rest of the farmyard.

There was no end to the curiosities that Sarah had to show me. There was the pond where the ducks were swimming, and the little wooden houses where the hens slept at night. The hens were feeding all over the yard, and the prettiest little chickens, they were feeding too, and little yellow ducklings that had a hen for their mamma. She was so frightened if they went near the water! Grandmamma says a hen is not esteemed a very wise bird.

We went out of the farmyard into the orchard. Oh, what a sweet place grandmamma's orchard is! There were pear-trees, and apple-trees, and cherry-trees, all in blossom. These blossoms were the prettiest flowers that ever were seen; and among the grass under the trees there grew buttercups, and cowslips, and daffodils, and blue-bells. Sarah told me all their names, and she said I might pick as many of them as ever I pleased.

I filled my lap with flowers, I filled my bosom with flowers, and I carried as many flowers as I could in both my hands; but as I was going into the parlour to show them to my mamma, I stumbled over a threshold which was placed across the parlour, and down I fell with all my treasure.

Nothing could have so well pacified me for the misfortune of my fallen flowers as the sight of a delicious syllabub which happened at that moment to be brought in. Grandmamma said it was a present from the red cow to me because it was my birthday; and then, because it was the first of May, she ordered the syllabub to be placed under the May-bush that grew before the parlour-door, and when we were seated on the grass round it, she helped me the very first to a large glass full of the syllabub, and wished me many happy returns of that day, and then she said I was myself the sweetest little May-blossom in the orchard.

After the syllabub, there was the garden to see, and a most beautiful garden it was; – long and narrow, a straight gravel walk down the middle of it; at the end of the gravel walk there was a green arbour with a bench under it.

There were rows of cabbages and radishes, and pease and beans. I was delighted to see them, for I never saw so much as a cabbage growing out of the ground before.

On one side of this charming garden there were a great many beehives, and the bees sung so prettily.

Mamma said, 'Have you nothing to say to these pretty bees, Louisa?' Then I said to them –

'How doth the little busy bee improve each shining hour,
And gather honey all the day from every opening flower.'

They had a most beautiful flower-bed to gather it from, quite close under the hives.

I was going to catch one bee, till Sarah told me about their stings, which made me afraid for a long time to go too near their hives; but I went a little nearer, and a little nearer every day, and before I came away from grandmamma's, I grew so bold, I let Will Tasker hold me over the glass windows at the top of the hives, to see them make honey in their own home.

After seeing the garden, I saw the cows milked, and that was the last sight I saw that day; for while I was telling mamma about the cows, I fell fast asleep, and I suppose I was then put to bed.

The next morning my papa and mamma were gone. I cried sadly, but was a little comforted at hearing they would return in a month or two, and fetch me home. I was a foolish little thing then, and did not know how long a month was. Grandmamma gave me a little basket to gather my flowers in. I went into the orchard, and before I had half-filled my basket I forgot all my troubles.

The time I passed at my grandmamma's is always in my mind. Sometimes I think of the good-natured pied cow that would let me stroke her while the dairy-maid was milking her. Then I fancy myself running after the dairy-maid into the nice clean dairy, and see the pans full of milk and cream. Then I remember the wood-house; it had once been a large barn, but being grown old, the wood was kept there. My sister and I used to peep about among the faggots, to find the eggs the hens sometimes left there. Birds' nests we might not look for. Grandmamma was very angry once, when Will Tasker brought home a bird's nest full of pretty speckled eggs for me. She sent him back to the hedge with it again. She said the little birds would not sing any more if their eggs were taken away from them.

A hen, she said, was a hospitable bird, and always laid more eggs than she wanted, on purpose to give her mistress to make puddings and custards with.

I do not know which pleased grandmamma best, when we carried her home a lapful of eggs, or a few violets; for she was particularly fond of violets.

Violets were very scarce; we used to search very carefully for them every morning round by the orchard hedge, and Sarah used to carry a stick in her hand to beat away the nettles; for very frequently the hens left their eggs among the nettles. If we could find eggs and violets too, what happy children we were!

Every day I used to fill my basket with flowers, and for a long time I liked one pretty flower as well as another pretty flower; but Sarah was much wiser than me, and she taught me which to prefer.

Grandmamma's violets were certainly best of all, but they never went in the basket, being carried home, almost flower by flower, as soon as they were found, therefore blue-bells might be said to be the best, for the cowslips were all withered and gone before I learned the true value of flowers. The best blue-bells were those tinged with red; some were so very red that we called them red blue-bells, and these Sarah prized very highly indeed. Daffodils were so very plentiful, they were not thought worth gathering unless they were double ones; and buttercups I found were very poor flowers indeed, yet I would pick one now and then, because I knew they were the very same flowers that had delighted me so in the journey; for my papa had told me they were.

I was very careful to love best the flowers which Sarah praised most, yet sometimes, I confess, I have even picked a daisy, though I knew it was the very worst flower of all, because it reminded me of London, and the Drapers' Garden; for, happy as I was at grandmamma's, I could not help sometimes thinking of my papa and mamma, and then I used to tell my sister all about London; how the houses stood all close to each other; what a pretty noise the coaches made; and what a great many people there were in the streets. After we had been talking on these subjects, we generally used to go into the old wood-house and play at being in London. We used to set up bits of wood for houses; our two dolls we called papa and mamma; in one corner we made a little garden with grass and daisies, and that was to be the Drapers' Garden. I would not have any other flowers here than daisies, because no other grew among the grass in the real Drapers' Garden. Before the time of hay-making came, it was very much talked of. Sarah told me what a merry time it would be, for she remembered everything which had happened for a year or more. She told me how nicely we should throw the hay about. I was very desirous, indeed, to see the hay made.

To be sure, nothing could be more pleasant than the day the orchard was mowed: the hay smelled so sweet, and we might toss it about as much as ever we pleased; but, dear me, we often wish for things that do not prove so happy as we expected; the hay, which was at first so green and smelled so sweet, became yellow and dry, and was carried away in a cart to feed the horses; and then, when it was all gone, and there was no more to play with, I looked upon the naked ground, and perceived what we had lost in these few merry days. Ladies, would you believe it, every flower, blue-bells, daffodils, buttercups, daisies, all were cut off by the cruel scythe of the mower. No flower was to be seen at all, except here and there a short solitary daisy, that a week before one would not have looked at.

It was a grief, indeed, to me, to lose all my pretty flowers; yet when we are in great distress, there is always, I think, something which happens to comfort us; and so it happened now that gooseberries and currants were almost ripe, which was certainly a very pleasant prospect. Some of them began to turn red, and as we never disobeyed grandmamma, we used often to consult together, if it was likely she would permit us to eat them yet; then we would pick a few that looked the ripest, and run to ask her if she thought they were ripe enough to eat, and the uncertainty what her opinion would be made them doubly sweet if she gave us leave to eat them.

When the currants and gooseberries were quite ripe, grandmamma had a sheep-shearing. All the sheep stood under the trees to be sheared. They were brought out of the field by old Spot, the shepherd. I stood at the orchard-gate and saw him drive them all in. When they had cropped off all their wool, they looked very clean, and white, and pretty, but, poor things, they ran shivering about with cold, so that it was a pity to see them. Great preparations were making all day for the sheep-shearing supper. Sarah said a sheep-shearing was not to be compared to a harvest-home, *that* was so much better, for that then the oven was quite full of plum-pudding, and the kitchen was very hot indeed with roasting beef; yet I can assure you there was no want at all of either roast-beef or plum-pudding at the sheep-shearing.

My sister and I were permitted to sit up till it was almost dark, to see the company at supper. They sat at a long oak table, which was finely carved, and as bright as a looking-glass.

I obtained a great deal of praise that day, because I replied so prettily when I was spoken to. My sister was more shy than me; never having lived in London was the reason of that. After the happiest day bedtime will come! We sat up late; but at last grandmamma sent us to bed; yet though we went to bed, we heard many charming songs sung; to be sure, we could not distinguish the words, which was a pity, but the sound of their voices was very loud, and very fine indeed.

The common supper that we had every night was very cheerful. Just before the men came out of the field, a large faggot was flung on the fire; the wood used to crackle and blaze, and smell delightfully; and then the crickets, for they loved the fire, they used to sing; and old Spot, the shepherd, who loved the fire as well as the crickets did, he used to take his place in the chimney corner; after the hottest day in summer, there old Spot used to sit. It was a seat within the fireplace, quite under the chimney, and over his head the bacon hung.

When old Spot was seated, the milk was hung in a skillet over the fire, and then the men used to come and sit down at the long white table.

JAMES HOGG

John Gray o' Middleholm

There was once a man of great note, of little wit, some cunning, and inexhaustible good nature, who lived in the wretched village of Middleholm, on the border of Tiviotdale, to whom the strangest lot befell, that ever happened to a poor man before. He was a weaver to his trade, and a feuar; about six feet four inches in height; wore a black coat with horn buttons of the same colour, each of them twice as broad and thick as a modern lady's gold watch. This coat had wide sleeves, but no collar, and was all clouted about the elbows and armpits, and moreover the tails of it met, if not actually overlapped each other, a little above his knee. He always wore a bonnet, and always the same bonnet, for ought that any one could distinguish. It was neither a broad nor a round bonnet, a Highland bonnet nor a Lowland bonnet, a large bonnet nor a small bonnet; nevertheless, it was a bonnet, and a very singular one too, for it was a *long bonnet*, shaped exactly like a miller's meal-scoop. He was altogether a singular figure, and a far more singular man. Who has not heard of John Gray, weaver and feuar in Middleholm?

John had a garden, which was a middling good one, and would have been better, had it been well sorted; he had likewise a cow that was a very little, and a very bad one; but he had a wife that was the worst of all. She was what an author would call a half-witted inconsiderate woman; but the Middleholm wives defined her better, for they called her 'a tawpie, and an even-down haverel'. Of course John's purse was very light, and it would never throw against the wind; his meals were spare and irregular, and his cheek-bones looked as if they would peep through the face. It is impossible for a man to be in this state without knowing the value of money, or at least regretting the want of it. His belly whispers to him every hour of the day, that it would be a good thing to have; and when parched with drought of an evening, and neighbours are going into the alehouse to enjoy their crack and their evening draught, how killing the reflection, that not one penny is to spare! It even increases a man's thirst, drying the very glands of his mouth to a cinder – It makes him feel more hungry, and creates a sort of void, either in idea or in the stomach, which it is next to impossible to fill up. Such power over the internal feelings has this same emptiness of the purse.

John had all these feelings most keenly in his way; for his sides were so long, and so lank, and enclosed in such a bound of space, that it was no easy matter to fill it up. Now, it being a grand position in philosophy, that no space within the earth's atmosphere can remain a void, owing to the intolerable pressure of air, amounting to the inconceivable weight of fifteen pounds on every square inch, it may well be conceived what an insufferable column pressed constantly on John's spacious tube. Nothing gave John so much uneasiness as the constant suggestions of this invidious column of air.

There was but one thing on earth that could counter-work this pressure of elemental fluid, and keep it up to its proper sphere, and that was money. This was a grand discovery made by John, which Bacon himself never thought on, or thought of only to be completely mistaken. That sage says, 'The state of all things here is, to extenuate, and turn things to be more pneumatical and rare; and not to retrograde from pneumatical to that which is dense.' How absurd! It is evident that Mr Bacon had never been a feuar in Middleholm.

John's system was exactly the reverse of this, and it was the right one. He conceived, and felt, that the tangible part of the body ought always to prevail over the pneumatical; and then, as to the means of accomplishing this, he discovered that money – money alone, was the equivalent power that could equiponderate in such a case. But as to the means of procuring this great universal anodyne, that puzzled John more than the great discovery itself.

Every man, however, has some prospects, or at least some hopes, of increasing his stock of this material. John had his hopes of doing so too; but no man, or woman either, will guess on what these hopes were founded. It could not possibly be by the profits of his weaving, at least with such a wife as he had; for John's proficiency in that useful art was far short of what was expected of a country weaver in those days. He could work a pair of blankets, or a grey plaid; but beyond that his science reached not. When any customer offered him a linen web, however coarse, or a brace of table-cloths, he modestly declined them, by assuring the good-wife, 'that his loom didna answer thae kind o' things, and when fo'k teuk in things that didna answer their looms, they whiles fashed them mair than if they had keepit them out.' It could not be by the profits of the miserable feu that he hoped to make money, for the produce of that was annually consumed before it came half to maturity. He had no rich friends; and his live stock consisted of, a small lean cow, two wretched-looking cats, a young one and an old one; six homely half-naked daughters, one son, and his wife, Tibby Stott.

But it is hard for a man to give up the idea of advancing somewhat in life, either by hook or by crook. To stand still, and stagnate as it were, or yield to a retrograde motion, are among the last things that the human mind assents to. John's never assented to any such thing. Notwithstanding all these disadvantages that marshalled against him, he had long-cherished and brilliant hopes of making rich; and that by the simplest and most natural way in the world, namely, by finding a purse, or *a pose*, as he more emphatically called it.

Was not John the true philosopher of nature? What others illustrated by theory, he exemplified in practice; namely, that the mind must grasp at something before. John longed exceedingly to have money – every other method of attaining it seemed fairly out of his reach, save this; and on this he fixed with avidity, and enjoyed the prospect as much as one does who believes he must fall heir to an estate. He knew all the folks in the kingdom that had got forward in life by finding poses; but the greatest curiosity of all was, that he never believed money to be made in any other way. John never saw money made by industry in his life; there was never any made at Middleholm, neither in his days nor those of any other man, and what he had never seen exemplified he could not calculate on: so that, whenever he heard of a man in the neighbourhood who had advanced his fortune rapidly, John uniformly attributed it to his good fortune in having found a pose.

But it was truly amazing, how many of these he believed to be lying hid all over the country, especially in the vicinity of the old abbeys. And

John reasoned in this manner: 'The monks and the abbots amassed all the money in the country; they had the superiority of all the lands, and all the wealth, and all the rents at their control. Then, on the approach of any marauding army, it was well known that they went always out and hid their enormous wealth in the fields, from whence a great part of it was never again lifted.' And then there was all the fields of battle, with which the Border counties abound, concerning which fields John argued in this way: 'Suppose now there were 20,000 English and 15,000 Scots met on a field; there might be mony mae, and there might be fewer; but, supposing there were so many, every one of these would hide his purse before he came into the battle, because he kend weel, that if he were either woundit or taen prisoner, he wad soon be strippit o' that. In ony o' thae cases, when it was hidden, he could get it again; whereas, if he was killed, it was o' nae mair use to him, an' was as weel there as in the hands o' his enemies. There was then 35,000 purses, or poses rather, a' hid in a very sma' bounds. An' then, to consider how many great battles war foughten a' o'er the country, an' often too when the tae party was laden wi' spulzie.' In short, John believed that all these Border districts were lined with poses, and that we every day walked over immense sums of old sterling coinage.

He had several times visited the fields of Philliphaugh, of Middlestead, and Ancrum Moor; and on each of these he had delved a great deal, looking for poses; but, as he simply and good-naturedly remarked, never chanced to light on the right spot. For all that he was nothing discouraged, but every year grew more and more intent on realizing some of these hidden treasures.

He had heard of a large sum of money that was hid in a castle of Liddesdale, and another at Tamleuchar Cross; and of these two he talked so long, and so intently, that he resolved at last to go and dig, first for the one treasure, and then for the other. So one evening he got some mattocks ready, and prepared for his journey, being resolved to set out the next morning.

But that night he had a singular dream, or rather a vision, that deterred him. The narrative must be given in John's own words, as it has doubtless never been so well told by any other person. No one else could be so affected by the circumstances, and when the heart is affected, the language, however diffuse, has something in it that approximates to nature.

'I was lying in my bed, close yerkit against the stock; for my wife, poor creature! had twae o' the weans in ayont her, an' they war a' sniffin an' sleepin; an' there was I, lying thinking and thinking what I wad do wi' a' my money aince I had it howkit up; when, ere ever I wist, in comes an auld grey-headit man close to my bed-side. He was clad in a grey gown, like the auld monks lang syne; but he had nae cross hingin at his breast; an' he lookit me i' the face, an' says to me, – says he, "John Gray o' Middleholm, do you ken me?" Na, honest man, quo' I; "how should I ken you?"

'"But I ken you, John Gray; an' I hae often been by your side, an' heard what ye war sayin, an' kend what ye war thinkin, an' seen what ye war doing, when ye didna see me. Ye're a very poor man, John Gray."

'"Ye needna tell me that, honest man; there needs nae apparition come frae the dead to tell me that."

'"An' ye hae a very ill wife, John Gray, an' a set o' ill-bred menseless bairns. Now, how mony o' them will ye gie me, an' I'll mak ye rich? Will ye gie me Tibby Stott hersel?"

'"Weel I wat, honest man, she wad be better wi' ony body than me; but I can never gie away auld Tibby Stott, ill as she is, against her will. She has lien sae lang by my side, an' sleepit i' my bosom, that she's turned like a second nature to me; an', I trow, we maun just tak the gude wi' the ill, an' fight thegither as lang as our heads wag aboon the ground, though mony a sair heart an' hungry wame she has gart me dree." He then named o'er a' the bairns to me, ane by ane, an' pledd an' fleeched me for this an' the tither ane; but, after a' he could say, an' a' the promises he could make, I wadna condescend to part wi' ane o' my bairns.

'"John Gray o' Middleholm," quo' he, "ye're a great fool; I kend ay ye were a fool; an' a' the country kens it as weel as me; but ye're no just sae ill as I thought you had been. How do you propose to maintain a' thae tawpies, young an' auld?

'"Aye, that's the question, friend," quo' I; "an it's easier to speer than answer it. But I hae a plan i' my head for that too; yet I dinna ken how far it may be advisable to tell you a' about it."

'"O poor daft Jock Gray o' Middleholm!" quo' he; "ye're that lazy ye winna work, an' ye're that stupid that ye hae married a wife that canna work, an' ye hae gotten a bike o' gillygawpie weans, that ye're breedin up like a wheen brute beasts; and the hale o' ye can neither work nor want; an' ye're gaun away the morn to mine the auld Castle o' Hermitage, an' carry away the mighty spoils that are hidden there. An' then ye're gaun away to Tamleuchar Cross, –

> To houk the pots o' goud, that lie
> Atween the wat grund an' the dry,
> Where grows the weirdest an' the warst o' weeds,
> Where the horse never steps, an' the lamb never feeds.

But, John Gray o' Middleholm, you'll never finger a plack o' thae twa poses, for the deil keeps the taen, an' me the tither."

'"Eh! gudesooth, friend, an that be the case, I fear I may drink to them. But wha are ye, an it may be speer'd?"

'"I am ane that kens a' the secrets o' a' the hidden poses in Scotland; an' I'm a great friend to you, John Gray o' Middleholm."

'"I'm unco glad to hear it, man; troth am I! I'm right blithe to hear it! Then, there shall be houkin an' shoolin, countin and coupin ower!"

'"Nane where ye trow; for ye're but a short-sightit carle; an' the warst faut that ye hae – ye're daft, John Gray. But, if ye'll be ruled by me, I'll tell you where ye'll find a pose that will mak you a rich man for the langest day ye hae to live. Gang ye away down to the town o' Kelso, an' tak a line frae the end o' the auld brigg to the north neuk o' the abbey, an' exactly at the middle step you will find a comically shapen stane; raise ye up that when nae body sees, an' there you will find an auld yettlin oon-pan filled fu' o' goud an' siller to the very ee."

'"But, friend, I never was at Kelso, and I never saw either the brigg or the abbey-kirk; an' how am I to find the stane? an', ower an' aboon a', gin I fa' to an' houk up the fok's streets, what will they say to me?"

'"Weel, weel, tak your ain way, John Gray; I hae tauld ye. But ye're daft, poor man; there, ye're gaun away to mine a' the vaults o' the biggest castle o' Liddesdale, an' then ye're gaun to trench a hale hillside at Tamleuchar, a' upon mere chance. An' here, I tell you where the pose is lying, an' ye'll no be at the pains to gang an' turn ower ae stane an' lift it. Ye're clean daft, John Gray o' Middleholm; but I hae tauld ye, sae tak your ain daft gate."

An' wi' that the auld body elyed away, an' left me. I was sae grieved that he had gane away in a pet, for he was the very kind o' man I wantit, that I hollo'd, an' called after him, as loud as I could, to come back. But, gude sauf us a'! at that moment, my wife, Tibby Stott, poor creature! wakened me; for I was roaring through my sleep, an' the hale had been a dream.'

John was terribly puzzled next day, and knew not which way to proceed. He did not like to go to hand-gripes with the devil, after such a warning as he had got, and therefore he judged it as safe to delay storming his Castle of Hermitage, till he considered the matter more maturely. On the other hand, it was rather ungenerous to go and seize on his friend's treasure at the Cross of Tamleuchar, after such a friendly visit; and he feared, likewise, that the finding of it was very uncertain; yet he did not know but this might be some malicious spirit, whose aim was to put him by getting the money. And as to Kelso, he had never thought of it before; and it took such a long time to train his ideas to any subject, that he never once thought of going there: so all the schemes were postponed for some time.

'A while after that,' says John, 'I was sitting at my loom, an' I was workin an' workin, an' thinkin an' thinkin, how to get ane o' thae hidden poses. "I maun either hae a pose soon," says I to mysel, "or else I maun dee o' hunger; an' Tibby Stott, poor creature! she maun dee o' hunger; an' a' my innocent bairns maun dee o' hunger, afore I get them up to do for theirsels." Thae war heavy concerns on me, an' I was sair dung down. When, or ever I wist, in comes my auld friend, the grey-headit monk. "John Gray o' Middleholm," quo' he; "do you ken me?" "Ay, that I do, honest man; an' weel too! Right blithe am I to see your face again, for I was unco vexed when ye gaed away an' left me sae cuttily afore."

'"Yere a daft man, John Gray, that's the truth o' the matter; but ye hae some good points about ye, an' I'm your friend. Ye say, ye dinna ken Kelso, nor the place where the pose is lying: now, if ye'll gang wi' me, I'll let you see the very place, an' the very stane that the money is lying aneath; an' if ye winna be at the pains to turn it ower and take the pose, I'll e'en gie it to some ither body; I hae tauld ye, John Gray o' Middleholm."

'"Dinna gie it to nae other body, an' it be your will, honest man,' quo' I; I says till him, "An' I's gang w'ye, fit for fit, when ye like." Sae up I gets, just as I was workin at the loom, wi' my leather apron on, an' a rash o' loom needles in my cuff; an' it wasna a rap till we were at Kelso, where I soon saw the situation o' the town, an' the brigg, an' the auld abbey. Then he takes me to a stane, a queer three-neukit stane, just like a cockit hat. "Now," says he, "John Gray o' Middleholm, the siller's in aneath this; but it winna be very easily raised; put ye a mark on it, till ye get mattocks an' a convenient time, for I maunna be seen here." I first thought o' leaving my apron on it, but thinking that wad bring a' the fock o' the town, I took ane o' the loom needles to stick in beside it, thinking naebody wad notice that. Bless me! friend, quo' I, this is the saftest an' the smoothest stane that ever I fand in my life; it is surely made o' chalk; an' wi' that, I rammed ane o' the loom needles down through the middle o' the stane into the very head. But I hadna' weel done that, afore there was sic yells an' cries rase out frae aneath the stane, as gin a' the devils o' hell had been broken loose on me; an' the blood sprang frae the chalk stane; an' it spoutit on my hands, an' it spoutit on my face, till I was frightit out o' my wits! Sae I bang'd up, an' ran for bare life; but sic a fa' as I got! I had almost broken my neck. Where think ye I had been a' the time, but lyin' sound sleepin' i' my bed; an' instead o' rinning the needle into the three-neukit stane, I had rammed it to the head in the haunch o' Tibby Stott, poor creature. Then there was sic a whillibalu as never was heard! An' she threepit, an' insistit on me, that I was ettling to murder her. "Dear Tibby Stott, woman," quo' I; "Tibby," says I to her, "If I had been ettling to murder you, wadna' I hae run the loom needle into some other part than where I did? It will be lang or ye murder there, Tibby Stott, especially wi' a loom needle."

'I had now gotten Kelso sae completely i' my head, that away I sets again, to see, at least, if the town was set the same way as I had seen it in my vision. I fand every thing the same; the brig, the auld abbey, an' the three-neukit stane shapit like a cockit hat, mid-way between them; but I coudna' get it houkit, for the fo'k were a' gaun asteer, an' ay this ane was spying an' looking at me, an' the tither ane was spying an' looking at me. Sae I hides my mattocks in a corner o' the auld abbey-kirk, an' down I gaes to saunter a while about the water side, to see if the Kelso fo'k wad settle within their ain doors, an' mind their ain business. I hadna' been lang at the water side, till I sees a hare sitting sleeping in her den. Now, thinks I, that wad be a good dinner for Tibby an' the bairns, an' me. Sae I slides away very cunningly, never letting wit that I saw her; but I had my ee gledgin' out at the tae side; an' as soon as I wan fornent her, I threw mysel' on aboon her a' my length. Then she waw'd, an' she scream'd, an' she sprawled, till I thought she wad win away frae me; but at length I grippit her by the throat. "Ye auld bitch, that ye are," quo' I; "I's do for ye now." But, wi' that, the hare gae me sic a drive wi' a' her four feet at ance, that she gart me flee aff frae aboon her like a drake into the hard stanes at the water side, till I was amaist fell'd. An' there I lay groaning; an' the hare she lay i' the bit screamin. Pity my case! where had I been a' the time, but sound sleepin' i' my ain bed? An' instead o' catchin' a hare, I had catch'd naething but auld Tibby Stott, poor creature; an' had amaist smothered her an' choakit her into the bargain.

'I was really excessively grieved this time; but what could I help it? I ran an' lightit a candle; an' I thought my heart should hae broken, when the poor thing got up on her bare knees, an' beggit me to spare her life. "Dear Tibby Stott!" quo' I; "Tibby, my woman," I says to her, "It will be the last thing that ever I'll think of to harm your life, poor creature!" says I.

'"Na, na, but John, I heard ye ca' me an awfu' like name for a man to ca' his wife; an' ye said that ye wad do for me now."

'"Tibby Stott, my woman," quo' I; "I'm really sorry for what has happened; but ye maun forgie me, for in faith an' troth I thought ye war a hare."

'"A hare! Na na, John, that winna gang down – Had ye said ye thought I was a mare, I might hae excused ye. I'm sure there wad hae been far less difference in size wi' the tane as the tither."

'Tibby Stott's no that far wrang there, thinks I to mysel, horn daft as she is.

'"But, John, what did ye tak me for the ither night, when ye stickit me wi' a loom needle into the bane?"

'"Indeed, Tibby, I'm amaist ashamed to say it; but I thought ye war a three-neukit stane, i' the shape of a cockit hat."'

When Tibby Stott heard this, she drew quietly to her clothes, and hastened out of the house. She was now quite alarmed, thinking that her husband had lost his reason; and, running to one of the neighbouring cottages, she awakened the family, and related to them her tale of dismay; informing them, that her husband had, in the first place, mistaken her for a three-cornered stone, and had stabbed her through the haunch with a loom needle. This relation only excited their merriment; but when she told them, that a few minutes ago he had mistaken her for a hare, and getting above her, had seized her by the throat, trying to worry her for one, it made them look aghast, and they all acquiesced in the belief, that John had been bitten by a mad dog, and was now seized with the malady; and that, when he tried to worry his wife for a hare, he had believed himself to be a dog, a never failing symptom of the distemper. Their whole concern now was, how to get the poor children out of the house; for they dreaded, that on the return of his fit, he might mistake them all for hares crouching in their dens, and worry every one of them. Two honest weavers therefore volunteered their services to go and reconnoitre, and to try if possible to get out the unfortunate children.

Now it so happened, that John was curiously engaged at the very time that these men went to the window, which was productive of another mistake, and put the villagers into the most dreadful dismay. As soon as he observed that Tibby Stott stayed so long away from her bed, he suspected that she had left the house; and, on rising to search for her, he soon found his conjecture too true. This he regretted, thinking that she would make fools both of herself and him, a thing which John accounted very common for wives to do, as the man had no better experience; and, not doubting but that his presence would be likely to make things worse, he awoke the eldest girl, whose name was *Grace*, (the most unappropriate one that could have been bestowed,) and desired her to go and bring back her mother. At first she refused to move, grumbling excessively, and bidding her father go himself; but John, at last, by dint of expostulation, getting her to comply, she requested him to bring her some clothes, and her stockings and shoes from beyond the fire. John called her a good girl, and ran, naked as he was, to bring her apparel. The clothes he found as she directed him, and hastening to the form beyond the fire to bring her stockings and shoes, he set down the lamp and lifted them. The stockings being tied together by a pair of long red garters, John found that he could not carry them all conveniently, so he took the clothes and the shoes in one hand, the lamp in the other, and the staniraw stockings and red garters, in his hurry, he took in his teeth. In this most equivocal situation was John first discovered by the two men as they peeped in at the window, on which they fled with precipitation, while their breasts were throbbing with horror.

When they returned to the house which they had lately left, they found a number of the villagers assembled, all gaping in dismay at the news, that *the lang weaver*, as they always stiled John Gray, was gone mad, and had tried to worry his wife for a hare. Scarcely had they swallowed this uncommon accident, when the two men entered; and the additional horror of the party may hardly be described, when they told what they had seen. 'Mercy on us a', sirs!' cried they, 'what will be done? John Gray has worried ane o' the lasses already; an' we saw him wi' our een, rinning up an' down the house naked, wi' her claes a' torn i' the tae hand, an' her heart, liver, and thrapple in his teeth, an' his een glancin' like candles!' The women uttered an involuntary scream; the men groaned in spirit; and the Rev. John Mathews, the Antiburgher minister of the village, who had likewise been called up, and had joined the group, proposed that they should say prayers. The motion was agreed to without a division; the minister became a mouth, as he termed it, to the party, and did not fail to remember the malady of the lang weaver, and the danger to which his children were exposed.

While they were yet in the midst of their devotions, the amiable Grace Gray entered, inquiring for her mother; but, after many interrogations, both by the minister and others, the villagers remained in uncertainty with regard to the state of John's malady until it was day. But then, on his appearance, coming in a hurried manner toward the house to seek his wife and daughter, there was such a dispersion! He ran, and she ran, and there was no one ran faster than the Antiburgher minister, who escaped praying, as he flew, that the Lord would make his feet as the feet of hinds upon the mountains. However, the whole fracas of John's hydrophobia ended without any thing very remarkable, save these: that Tibby Stott asked her daughter with great earnestness, 'Whilk o' them it was that was worried? an' hoped in God that it wasna' little Crouchy.' This was a poor decrepid, insignificant child, who was however her mother's darling, and whose loss would have been more regretted by her than all the rest of the family put together. The other remarkable circumstance was, that the story had spread so rapidly, that it never could be recalled or again assimilated to the truth, and it is frequently related as a fact over all the south country to this day, among the peasantry. Many a time have I heard it, and shuddered at the story; and I am sure many, into whose hand these tales may fall, have likewise heard the woful relation, that a weaver in Middleholm was once bit by his own terrier, and that five years afterwards, he went mad, and tried to worry his wife, who escaped; but that he succeeded in worrying his daughter, and on the neighbours assembling and breaking into the house, that he was found in the horrible guise in which the two men had described him.

John continued to be eyed with dark and lurking suspicion for some time; but he cared very little about such vulgar mistakes, for his mind was more and more taken up about finding poses. This reiterated vision of the old gray-headed monk, the town of Kelso, the bridge, the abbey, and the three-neukit stane like a cockit hat, had now taken full and ample possession of his brain, that he thought of it all day, and by night again visited it in his dreams. Often had he been there in idea, and, as he believed, in spirit, while his mortal part was lying dormant at the wrong side of Tibby Stott; but, at the long and the last, he resolved to go there in person, and, at all events, to see if the town was the same as had been represented to him in his visions.

Accordingly John set out, one morning early in the spring, on his way to the town of Kelso; but he would neither tell his wife, nor any one about Middleholm, where he was going, or what he was going about. He went as he was, with his staff in his hand, and his long bonnet on his head, without any of his mattocks for digging or heaving up broad stones, although he knew that purses were generally hid below them. Therefore John felt as disconsolate by the way, as a parish-minister does who goes from home to preach without a sermon in his pocket, or like a warrior going out to battle without his armour or weapons. He had, besides, but very little money in his pocket; only a few halfpence, and these he found could be but ill spared at home; and the only hope he had, was in the great sum of money that lay hid beneath the three-neukit stane like a cockit hat, which stane, he knew, lay exactly mid-way between the end of the bridge and the north corner of the abbey.

John arrived at the lovely town of Kelso a little before the going down of the sun, and immediately set out about surveying the premises; but, to his great disappointment, he found that nothing was the same as it had been shown to him in his dream. The town and the abbey were both on the wrong side of the river, and he scarcely felt convinced that it was the same place. Moreover, the middle space between the end of the bridge and the abbey it was impossible to fix on, owing to some houses that interrupted the line. However, he looked narrowly and patiently all the way, from the one to the other, for the three-cornered stone, often stopping to scrape away the dust with his hands or feet from the sides of every broad one, to ascertain its exact form. He found many broadish stones, and some that inclined a little to a triangular form, but none of them like the one he had dreamed of; though there were some that he felt a strong inclination to raise up, merely that he might see what was below them.

But the more he looked, the better was he convinced, that the middle space between the abbey and the bridge was occupied by an old low-roofed house, within which the three-cornered stone, and the pose of course, behoved to be. Four or five times, in the course of his investigations, did John draw near to the door of this house, and every time stood hesitating whether or not he should enter; but, as he had resolved to tell his errand to no one living, not for fear of being laughed at, but for fear any one should come between him and the pose, he declined going in.

Not having enough of money to procure himself a night's lodging at an inn, he went and bought a pennyworth of bread at a baker's shop, that he might not be chargeable to any one; and, going down to the side of the river, he made a hearty supper on his roll, drinking a little pure water to it. It was here that John, to his infinite pleasure, first discovered a similarity between his vision and the existing scene. For, be it remembered, that, in one of his dreams, he went down to the side of the River Tweed to while away the time, and there discovered a hare sitting in her form. He now remembered having seen this very scene in his dream, which he now looked on, all in the same arrangement, and thenceforward felt a conviction, that this vision would not go for nothing. He then went into a narrow street that stretched to the eastward, as he described it, and went on till he heard the well-known sound of the jangling of weavers' treadles. As the proverb goes, 'Birds of a feather, flock ay thegither'; into that house John went, and asked the privilege of a bed, telling them, he himself was a poor weaver, who had come a long journey, in hopes to recover a large sum of money in the town, but not having as yet been successful, he had not wherewith to pay his night's lodging at an inn. The honest people made him very welcome, for the people of that beautiful town, from the highest to the lowest, are noted for a spirit of benevolence. But they tried in vain to pry into his business, and to learn who the creditor was from whom he expected to recover the sum of money. John, on the other hand, was very inquisitive of his host about the old abbey – what sort of people the monks were – how they were dressed, and if they had much money – what they did with it on a sudden invasion by the English? and, in particular, *Where he supposed to be exactly the middle space between the bridge and the abbey?* The man answered all his queries civilly; and, though he sometimes suspected his guest of a little derangement in intellect, gave him what information he could on these abstruse points; manifesting all the while, however, a disposition rather to enter into a debate about some of the modern tenets of religion. This John avoided as much as possible; for, though John was an Antiburgher, he knew little more about the matter, save that his sect was right and all the rest of the world wrong, which was quite sufficient for him; but, finding that the Kelso weaver was not disposed so readily to admit this, he waved the engagement from time to time, and always introduced the more interesting and not less mysterious subject, of purses hidden in the earth.

Next morning John was early astir, and busily engaged in search of the three-cornered stone; but still with the same success; and ever and anon his investigations brought him to the door of the low-roofed ancient house before mentioned, which he still surveyed with a wistful look, as if desirous to enter. The occupier of this old mansion was a cobler, a man stricken in years, who had a stall in the one end of it, while his wife and daughter kept a small fruit-shop in the other, and by these means earned a decent livelihood. This cobler, being a very industrious man, was at his work both late and early, and had noted all John's motions the evening before, as well as that morning. Curious to know what were the stranger's motives in prying so much about his door, he went out and accosted him, just as he was in the act of stooping to clean the dust away from the sides of a broad stone to see what shape it was. As he spoke, John turned round his head and looked at him; but he was so amazed at the figure he saw, that he could not articulate a syllable. 'What's the matter w'ye, friend?' said the cobler; 'or what is it you hae lost?' John still could not speak a word; but there he stuck, with his one knee leaning on the ground, his muddy hands hanging at a distance from his body, like a man going to leap, his head turned round, and his mouth open, gaping on this apparition of a cobler. The latter, at once conceiving that he had addressed a maniac, stood and gazed at him in silence and pity. John was the first who broke silence, and certainly his address had not the effect of removing the cobler's apprehensions. 'The warld be a wastle us! friend, is this you?' said John. 'There's nae doubt o't ata', man,' returned the cobler; 'this is *me*, as sure as that is *you*; but wha either you or me is, I fancy me or you disna very weel ken.' 'Honest man, do you no ken me?' said John; 'tell me honestly, did you never see my face afore?' 'Why,' said the cobler, 'I now think I have seen it before; but where, I do not recollect.' 'Was it in the night-time or the day-time that you saw me?' said John. 'Certainly, never in the night-time,' returned the cobler. 'Then I fancy I am wrang,' said John; 'I'm forgetting mysel', an' no thinkin what I'm speakin about; but I aux your pardon.' 'O there's nae offence, honest friend,' quoth the cobler; 'no ae grain: it is only a sma' mistake; you thought it was *me*, and I thought it was *you*, an' it seems it turns out to be neither the one nor the other.' The cobler's wit was lost upon John, who again sunk into silence and gazed; for he saw that this ancient cobler was the very individual person that had appeared to him in his sleep, and told him of the treasure. And, still to approximate the vision closer to reality, the cobler wore a large three-cocked hat on his head. John was in utter consternation, and knew not what to make of it. He saw that it was not a three-neukit stane which the cobler wore on his head, and though very like one in colour, yet that it had once been felt. Still the hat had such a striking resemblance to the stone which John had so often seen in his vision, that he was satisfied the one was represented by the other. He saw there was something extraordinary in the case, and something that boded him luck; but how to solve this mystery of the three-neukit stane and the cockit hat, John was greatly at a loss. He had no doubt that he had found the cue to the treasure; for he had found this cockit hat exactly mid-way between the bridge and the north corner of the abbey, as nearly as he could judge or measure. It was not indeed a three-neukit stane, but it was very like one; and at any rate, it was the very thing, shape, and size, and all, that he had dreamed about, and under which he had been assured the gold was hid. Above all, here was the very person, in form, voice, size, and feature, whose image had appeared to him in his sleep, and had held repeated conversations with him on the subject of the hidden pose; but then, what was there below the hat save the cobler, and he could not possibly be a pan full of gold and silver? The coincidence was however too striking to be passed over without scrutiny. Even the wisest of men would have been struck with it, and have tried to find out some solution; and curious would I be to know what a wise man, in such a case, would have thought of the matter.

John, as I said, was the philosopher of nature, and always fixed on the most obvious and simple solutions, in determining on effects from their general causes. He first asked of the cobler a sight of his hat; which being granted, he looked inside of it; but perceiving that there was neither money nor lining of any sort there, he returned it, saying, it was a curious hat. He then asked the cobler, seriously, if he had never swallowed any gold. The other said, he had not to his knowledge. 'At least,' said John; 'you certainly could not swallow any very large quantity? Very weel, then, frien'; if ye'll be sae gude as to stand a wee bit back.' The cobler did so; and John, marking the precise spot where he had been standing, and on which he had first seen him in his real corporeal being, went directly to procure mattocks to dig with, thinking it would to a certainty be below that spot, and of course virtually covered by the hat at the time he first saw its ample and triangular form.

He soon got a pick and spade, and fell to digging on the side of the narrow street with all expedition, to the great amusement of the old cobler, who, for fear of incurring blame from his townsmen, went into his stall, and awaited the issue of this singular adventure.

Poor John was hungry, and the column of air was become so oppressive on him, that he felt as if his life depended on his success, and wrought with no ordinary exertion. The pit waxed in its dimensions, and deepened exceedingly. He first came to sand, and then to loam, at which time his hopes ran very high, for he found two or three small bones, which he was sure had once formed a part of the body of some immensely rich abbot; and finally, he came to a stiff, almost an impenetrable till. Nevertheless he continued to dig, until the town's people, beginning to move about as the morning advanced, gathered about him, and asked him what he meant? He desired them to mind their own business, and let him mind his; and on this the first comers went away, thinking he was a man employed in repairing the street; but it was not long ere two town officers arrived, and forced him to desist, threatening, that if he refused to comply, and to fill up the hole exactly as he found it, they would carry him to prison, and have him punished. John was forced to yield, and once more abandon his golden dream. He filled up the pit with evident marks of chagrin and disappointment, some averring that they even saw the tears dropping from his eyes, and mixing with the gravel. He had now nothing for it, but to return as he came, and apply to the wretched loom once more. He even knew not where he was to procure a breakfast, and still less how Tibby Stott, poor creature! and the children, were breakfasting at home. The officers asked him whence he came, and what he wanted; but he refused to satisfy them; and after he had made the street as it was, and to their satisfaction, they left him.

There was something so whimsical in all that the cobler had witnessed, that he determined, if possible, to find out something of the man's meaning. He dreaded that he was a little deranged in his intellects; still there was a harmless simplicity about the stranger that interested him; and he thought he discerned glimpses of shrewdness that could not possibly be inherent in an ideot. Accordingly, as soon as the crowd had dispersed, and John had lifted his plaid and staff, and blown his nose two or three times, as he took a last look of the bridge and the old abbey, the cobler went out to him, addressed him with kindness, and beseeched him to go in, and take share of his breakfast.

Thankfully did John accept of the invitation, and seldom has a man done more justice to his entertainer's hospitality, than our hero did that morning. After despatching a bowlfull of good oat meal parritch, washed down with a bottle of brisk treacle ale, the cobler's daughter presented them with a large cut of broiled salmon. This rich and solid fare answering John's complaint exceedingly well, he set to it with so much generous avidity, that the cobler restrained himself, and suffered his guest to realize the greater part of it. The delightful sensations excited by this repast raised John's heart a little above his late disappointment, and even before the salmon was finished, he had begun to converse with some spirit. But his sphere of conversation was rather of a circumscribed nature, being confined to one object, namely, that of poses hidden in the earth, with its collateral branches. He asked the cobler what sort of men the monks were, who had lived in that grand abbey – Of the abbots that governed them – The sources of their great riches, and how they disposed of these on any invasion by the English.

There was no subject on which the cobler loved more to converse, having himself come of that race, and, as he assured John, the sixth in descent from the last abbot and a lady of high quality; he, and his forebears so far back, having been the fruits of a Christmas confession; and that, had the establishment still continued, he would in all likelihood have at that day been abbot himself. He showed John an old charter on emblazoned vellum, granted by Malcolm the fourth to the abbey of Kelso, on the removal of the Cistertian Monks from Selkirk to that place; and he talked so long on the customs and usages of the monks, the manner of lives they led, their fasts, holidays, and pilgrimages, that John never thought to be so weary of monachism; no mention having ever been made of their poses, in all this lengthened discourse.

After breakfast, the cobler pledged John in a bumper of brandy, and then handed his guest another, which John took with a blushing smile, and after holding it up between him and the light to enjoy its pure dark colour, he drank to the good health of the cobler; and, as the greatest blessing on earth that he could think of, wished he might find a good pose.

The cobler, thinking he now had his guest in the proper key, asked him to explain to him, if he pleased, the motives of his procedure that morning and last night? John laughed with a sly leer, bit his lip, and looking at the women who were bustling but and ben, at length told his host, that if he was to tell him that, he must tell him by himself; on which they went into the stall, and after John had desired the cobler to shut the door, he addressed him as follows:

'Now, ye see, friend, ye're sic an honest kind man, that I canna refuse to tell you ony thing; an' for that cause, I'll tell you the plain truth; but, as I ken you will think me a great fool, I'll neither tell you my name, nor my wife's name, nor the name o' the place where I bide; but it is a wee bit out o' Kelso; no very far; I can gang hame to my dinner. Ye maun just let that satisfy you on that score. Weel, ye see, disna I dream ae night, that there's an auld oon-pan, fu' o' gold an' silver, hidden aneath a queer shapen stane, exactly mid-way atween the end o' your brig an' the north neuk o' the auld abbey there; an' I dreamed it sae aft, that I could get nae rest; for troth it was like to mislead me, an' pit me by mysel a' thegither. To sickan a height did the fleegary rin in my imagination, (hee, hee, hee! Is the door closs, think ye?) that I mistook the stane that was happin the pose, and, meaning to pit a mark in it to ken it by, (Will naebody hear us, think ye?) disna I rin a lang sharp bodkin into the head i' the wrang side o' my wife, poor creature! till I e'en gart her skirl like a gait, an' was amaist fleyed her out o' her wits. An' there was ae night after that, she ran a greater risk still. Sae, troth, just to prevent me frae fa'ing till her wi' a pick an' a spade some night, an' to see gin it wad help me to ony better blink o' rest, I was fain to come to Kelso yestreen, to see if there was sic a thing or no. An' this morning, when you and I first met, for reasons that I needna an' canna weel explain, I thought I had found the very spot. Now, that's the main truth, an' I daresay you will think me a great fool.'

The cobler, who was mightily amused by this statement of facts, answered as follows: 'A man, my good friend, may act foolishly at a time, an' yet no be a'thegither a fool. To be a fool, you see, is to – is to – In short, it's to be a fool – a born fool like. But it is a Gallic word that, an' has mony meanings. Now, dreaming disna make a man a fool; but it makes him a fool sae far, that he may play the fool in his dream. He may rise in his sleep, an' play the fool; but if he dinna play the fool after he wakens, he canna just be ca'd an absolute fool. But it is the fool, who, after he has dreamed, takes a' his dreams for reality. At least, it is acting very foolishly to do that.' 'I thought your speech wad land there,' said John. 'No, but stay till I explain mysel,' said the cobler. 'O, ye needna fash, the thing's plain enough,' said John; 'I maun think about setting awa' hame.' 'Stop a wee bit, man,' said the cobler, taking hold of John's coat as he was rising, 'I hae a queer story to tell you about a purse afore ye gang away, that will explain the matter wi' mair clearness an' precision than a' the learning an' logic that I'm master o'.

'It is ower true, what I maun tell you, honest man, that I am very ill for dreaming mysel, an' mony a wild unsonsy dream I hae had; an' the mair I strave against it, I grew aye the waur. When I was a young child, there was hardly a night that I didna' dream I was a monk, an' confessing some ane or ither o' the bonny lasses an' wives about Kelso. An' sic tales as I thought they tauld me! Then, when I saw them again sittin' i' the kirk, wi' their douse decent faces, I couldna' get their confessions out o' my mind, gude forgie me! an' I had some kind o' inklin' about my heart, that they were a' true. There was the folly o' the thing! Then I had nae sooner closed my een the neist night than I was a monk again, and hard engaged at the auld business. There was ane Bess Kelly, a fine sponkin' lass, that a' the lads were like to gang wudd about; I'm sure I confessed Bess mair nor a hunder times i' my sleep, an' mony was the sin I pardoned till her.' John chuckled, and grinned, and made every now and then a long neck by the cobler, to see if the door was close enough shut; but when he reached thus far, John rose, passed him, and felt the latch, and though the door was shut, he gave it a push with his shoulder, to make it, if possible, go a little closer. 'Friend, I can tell you,' said John; 'there may be here that ken, an' here that dinna ken; but that's a very queer story. So you always dreamed you were a monk?' 'So often,' said the cobler, 'that the idea became familiar to me; and even in the day time, I often deemed myself one.' 'So did I,' said John, 'it became familiar to me too, and I thought you a monk both by night and by day.' The cobler stared at John, and thought him mad in good earnest; but the latter, feeling that he was going to divulge more perhaps than prudence and caution with regard to hidden poses warranted, corrected himself by saying, that he thought he resembled one of that order, in his grave, decent appearance, which was all he meant to say. The cobler then went on.

'Weel, I'm no yet come to the story I was gaun to tell you. I had sic a dream last night, as I hae nae had these twenty years; and, I think, I never had sic a queer dream in my life. An' then it was sae like your ain, too; for it was about a hidden purse.' 'Aye aye, man!' said John, 'Gude sauf us! what was't? but stop a wee till I see if the door be close steekit.' John again felt the door, gave it another push, and then sat down, with open mouth and ears, to drink in the story of the cobler's dream.

'I was as usual a monk, and had gane out after vespers to take a walk by the side o' the Tweed; an' as I was gaun down by the boat-pool foot, I sees an ill-faur'd-looking carle, something like yoursel', sitting eating a roll, an' he'd a living hare lying beside him that he had catched in her den.' – 'Hout, friend!' said John, 'but did you really dream that?' 'In very deed I did,' said the cobler, 'why do you doubt it?' 'Because, friend,' said John, 'they may be here that ken, an' here that dinna ken; but that's a very queer dream indeed.' 'There's nae doubt o't,' said the cobler; 'but stay till you hear it out. Weel, I says to the carle, (he was very like you,) friend, will you sell your hare? "Hout na'," quo' he, "you palmer bodies are a' poor, ye hae nae sae muckle siller atween you an' poverty as wad buy my hare. Ye're a very poor man, monk, for a' the rich confessions ye hae made, an' ye're a daft man, that's waur; but, an' ye wad like to be rich, I can tell you where you will get plenty o' goud an' siller." I thankit the carle, an' said there were few that wadna' like to be richer than they were, an' I had nae objections at a' to the thing. "Weel, weel," quo' he; "he that hides kens best where to seek; but there was mony ane i' the days o' langsyne, wha haid weel, but never wan back to howk again. Gang ye your ways west the country the morn, an' spier for a place they ca' Middleholm; an' when ye come there, speer for a man they ca' John Gray. Gang ye into his garden, an' ye will find thirteen apple-trees in it, six at the head, an' six at the foot, an' ane in the middle."' – 'Hout friend!' said John, interrupting him, 'but are ye no joking? did you really dream that?' "As sure as yon sun is in the heaven, I did,' said the cobler; 'why should you doubt it?' 'Because ye see, friend,' said John, 'they are here that ken, an' here that dinna ken; but, let me tell you, that's a very queer dream indeed. Weel, what did the fearsome carle say mair?'

'"Gang ye into that garden," quo' he, "an' begin at the auld apple-tree in the middle, an' howk deep in the yird below that tree, an' you will find an auld pan filled fu' o' money to the ee. When ye hae disposed o' that, if ye like to gang back to that man's garden, an' howk weel, you will find a pose o' reid goud aneath every apple-tree that's in it." Now, wadnae ye hae reckoned me as a fool if I had taen a' this for truth? an' thought I was acting very foolishly, if I had gane away into the west country, asking for a place an' a man that perhaps hae nae existence? To hae gane about, as our school rhyme says, spearing for

> "The town that ne'er was framed,
>   An' the man that ne'er was named,
>   The tree that never grew,
>   An' the bird that never flew."'

'O there's nae doubt o' the thing, friend, it wad hae been great nonsense – there's nae doubt o't at a'. But yet, for a' that, its the queerest dream, ae way an' a' ways, that I ever heard i' my life; an' I hae a great mind to gang an' speer after the place an' the man mysel'. If I get as good a breakfast, an' as good a dram, as I did for the last pose I howkit, my labour winna' be lost a' thegither.'

The cobler laughed, and wished John all manner of success; and the latter parted from him with many professions of esteem; and, in higher spirits than ever he was before, he went straight home to Tibby Stott and Middleholm, and prepared next morning to begin and root up the old apple-tree in the middle of the garden. Now, there were exactly thirteen trees in it, as the cobler said; a circumstance of which the owner was not aware till that very night when he returned from Kelso.

Poor Tibby Stott was right glad to see her husband again, for the report in the village was, that he had run away mad; and, as the country people were in terrible alarm about that time for mad dogs, and pursuing and killing them every day, Tibby dreaded that poor John would be shot, or sticked with long forks, like the rest. She viewed him at first with a jealous eye; but, on seeing him so good-humoured and kind to the children and herself, she became quite reconciled to him, and wept for joy, poor creature! at getting him back again; for she found she would have been utterly helpless without him, although ten times a-day she called him *a cool-the-loom*. John told her how he had travelled to Kelso, and spent a day and a night there on some important business, and had only wared one penny; and, among other things, how he had learned to cultivate his garden so as to make it produce great riches.

Next morning, as soon as it was day, John began a digging at one side of the old apple-tree, but he was terribly impeded by roots, and came very ill speed. Some of these he cut, and digged in below others; for he found, that when they were cut, they impeded his progress nearly as much as before. By the time the villagers rose, John had made a large pit; but then the alarm began, and spread like wild-fire, that the lang weaver was come home again madder than ever, and had been working all night digging a grave in his garden, which every one suspected he meant for Tibby Stott. The pit that he had made, by chance, bore an exact resemblance to a grave, and great was the buzz in the village of Middleholm that morning. The people gathered around him, at first looking cautiously over the garden wall; but at last they came close about him, every man with his staff in his hand, and asked him how he did, and what he was engaged in. John said he had been away down the country, inquiring by what means to improve his garden, and he had been instructed to prune the roots of his apple-trees in place of the branches; for that they had run to wood below the earth, which had been the cause of their growing wild and barren. The villagers knew not what to make of this, it was so unlike any thing that the lang weaver had ever done before; so they continued to hang over him, and watch his progress, with all manner of attention. John saw this would never do, for they would discover all; and then there were so many who would be for sharing the money along with him, that a small share might only fall to him; and, moreover, if they told the lord of the manor, he would claim it altogether.

John had a good deal of low cunning; and, as he had now got very deep on one side of the tree, in order to mislead the villagers, he took a wheel-barrow, and hurled a kind of sour dung that had been accumulating around his cow-house for years, with which he crammed the pit that he had made below the tree, and, after covering it over with the mould, he tramped it down. His neighbours then went away and left him, convinced that he had got some new chimera into his head about gardening, which would turn out a piece of folly at the last. John was now left to prosecute his grand research quietly; save that Tibby Stott never ceased intreating him 'to mind his loom an' let the trees alane.' John answered with great rationality, 'sae I will, Tibby, my woman, I will mind the loom; but ye ken a man maun do ae thing afore anither.'

Towards the evening, Mr Mathews, the minister, went into the garden to *get a crack wi' John*, and see his new scheme of gardening. John had now got to a considerable depth on the south side of the tree, and not much regarding the tame moral remarks, or the threadbare puns of his pastor, (these two little amiable characteristics of the Calvinistical divine,) was plying at his task with all his might, for still as he grew more hungry his exertions increased; and just at that precious instant, his spade rattled along the surface of a broad stone. 'John,' said the minister, 'What have you got there, John?' 'I fancy I'm come to the solid rock now, sir,' said John, 'I needna' howk nae deeper here.' 'John, give me the mattock, John,' said the minister; 'I propine, that it would be nothing inconsistent with prudence and propriety to investigate this matter a little. This garden, as I understand, was planted by four friars of the order of St Benedict, who were the first founders of this village; and these people had sometimes great riches, John. Give me the mattock, John, and if I succeed in raising that stone, I shall claim all that is below it.' 'I wad maybe contest that point wi' your worship,' said John; 'for I can tell you what you will find below it.' 'And pray, what would I find below it, John?' said the Antiburgher minister. 'Just yird an' stane to the centre o' the globe,' said John; 'an' sic a pit wad spoil my bit garden.' 'Why, you are grown a wit, John,' said the divine, 'as well as a gardener. That answer is very good; nevertheless, give me the mattock, John.'

The minister might as well have asked John's heart's blood. He determined to keep hold of his spade, and likewise the possession of his pit; yet he did not wish to fight the minister. So, turning his face to him, and keeping his spade behind his back, he said to him, 'Hout na', sir, ye dinna ken how to handle spades an' shools, gin' it be nae maybe the shool o' the word to delve into our hearts an' souls wi'.' 'There's more strength than propriety in that remark, John,' said the minister. 'But I can tell you, sir,' continued John, with a readiness that was not customary with him, 'the hale secret o' the stane. Thae monk bodies were good gardeners, an' they laid aye a braid stane aneath the roots o' ilka fruit-tree that they plantit, to keep the bits o' tendrils frae gripping down to the cauld till, whilk wad soon spoil the tree.' 'Why, John, I have heard of such an experiment, indeed; and I suspect you have guessed nearer to the truth than might have been gathered from the tenor of the foregoing chapter of your life, John; it is therefore vain for a man to waste his strength for nought. A good evening to you, John.' 'Gude e'en, gude e'en to your Reverence,' said John, as he turned about in his hole, chuckling and laughing with delight; and when the Antiburgher minister was fairly out at the gate, he nodded his head, and said to himself, 'Now, if I hae nae mumpit the minister, my name's no John Gray o' Middleholm. Thae gospel bodies want to hae a finger in ilka ane's pye, but they manna hae things a' their ain gate neither. O there's nae set o' men on the face o' the yird, as keen o' siller as the ministers! Ane wad think, to hear them preach, that they held the warld quite at the staff's end; but a' the time they're nibblin

nibblin at it just like a trout at a worm, or a hare at a kailstock. He thought to hae my pose! Let him haud him wi' his steepin' – screw'd as it is off the backs an' the meltiths o' mony a poor body.'

John took hold of a stone hammer, and gave the broad stone a smash on the one side. As he struck, the stone tottered, and John heard distinctly, something that jingled below it. The very hairs of his head stood upright, he was in such agitation! the hammer dropped from his hand, and he jumped out of the pit, gazed all around him, and then ran towards the house, impelled by some inward feeling to communicate his good fortune to his partner; but by the way reflection whispered in his ear, that Tibby Stott, poor creature! was not the person calculated for keeping such an important secret. This set him back to his pose; which, in trembling anxiety, he resolved to survey; and, cleaning all the earth from above the stone, he heaved it up, and there beheld * * * * * * * *

It must not here be told what John beheld. – It would be too much for the reader's happiness to bear. He must be left to conjecture what it was that John discovered below that broad stone, and it is two to one he will guess wrong, for all that he has heard about it, and for as plain as matters have been made to him. John let the stone sink down again – took the wheel-barrow and filled the pit full of wet straw, which he judged better than dung; then, covering it over with earth, he went into his supper of thin bleared sowins, amid his confused and noisy family, all quarrelling about their portions; and finally, to his bed with Tibby Stott.

That night, John drew nearer to Tibby than usual, and put his arm around her neck. 'Wow, John, hinny!' quoth she, 'what means a' this kindness the night?' 'Tibby Stott, my woman Tibby,' said John, 'I hae a secret to tell you; but ye're to promise, an' swear to me, that ye're never to let it to the tap o' your tongue, as lang as ye hae life, afore ony body but mysel.' Tibby promised all that John desired her, and she repeated as many oaths after him as he chose, eager to learn this great secret; and John, after affecting great hesitation and scruples, addressed her as follows:

'Tibby Stott, do ye ken what was the matter wi' me, when I was last sae unweel?' 'Na, John, I didna ken then, nor ken I yet.' 'But I kend, Tibby Stott; and there's no anither in this world kens, or ever maun ken, but yoursel. I was very ill then, Tibby; an' I was in a very queer way. Ay, I was waur than ony body thought! But do you ken how I got better, Tibby?'

'Indeed, I dinna ken that nouther, John.' 'But I'll tell you, Tibby. I was brought to bed o' twa black birds; an' I hae them keepin concealed i' the house; an' they're twa ill spirits, far waur than cockatrices. Now, if this war kend, I wad be hanged, an' ye wad be burnt at the stake for a witch; therefore, keep the secret as you value both our lives. An' Tibby, ye maun never gang to look for thae twa birds, for if ever ye find them, they'll flee away wi' you to an ill place; an' mind ye an' dinna gang to be telling this to ony living flesh, Tibby Stott.'

'Na, na, John; sin' ye bid me, I sall never tak the tale o'er the tap o' my tongue. But, oh! alak! an wae's me! what's to come o' us? Ye hae gart a' my flesh girrel, John; to think that ever my gudeman sude hae been made a mither! an' then to think what he's mither to! Mither o' twa deils! The Lord have a care o' us, John! wad it no be better to let the twa imps flee away, or get Mr Mathews to lair them?'

'But tent me here, Tibby Stott, my woman, Tibby, they're sent for gude luck –'

'It can only be deil's luck, at the best, John; an' his can never be good luck.'

'The best o' a' luck, Tibby; for I can tell you, we'll never want as lang as they are in the house. They'll bring me siller when I like, an' what I like; an' a' that ye hae to do, is to haud your tongue, an' ye'll find the good o't; but if ever ye let this secret escape you, we're ruined hip and thigh for ever.'

Tibby promised again for the sake of the money; but the next morning before she swept her house, she ran in unto a neighbouring gossip, and addressed her as follows:

'Wow, Jean, I hae gotten a screed o' unco news sin' I last saw you! I trow ye didna ken that we had a crying i' this town the tither week?'

'I wat, Tibby, I never heard o' sic a thing afore.'

'Aye, but atween you an' me, there's a pair o' braw twins come to the warl, though nane o' the best-hued anes that may be. But they'll be snug-keepit anes, an' weel-tochered anes, and weel keepit out o' sight, as maiden's bairns should be. Aye, Jean, my dow; but an' ye kend wha's the mither o' them, your een wad stand i' back water wi' laughin!'

'What? Hout fie Tibby! I wat weel it isna Bess Bobagain, the Antiburgher minister's housekeeper?'

'Waur nor that yet; an' that wad hae been ill eneuch. But ye see the thing maunna be tauld; or else ye maun swear never to tell it again, as lang as ye live.'

'Me tell it again! Nah! It is weel kend I never tauld a secret i' my life. Ane may safely trust me wi' ony thing. My father, honest man, used to say to me, even when I was but a wee toddlin thing, that he had sae muckle to lippen to me, that he could hae trustit me wi' a housefu' o' untelled millstanes. The thing that's bred i' the bane, winna easily ding out o' the flesh. When I was sae trusty then, what should I be now?'

'Aye, to be sure, there's a great deal in that. It says muckle for ane, when ane's pawrent can trust ane, sae as to do as ane likes i' ane's house. My father wad never trust me wi' a boddle; but mony a time he said I wad be a good poor man's wife, for that the best thing ony body could do for a poor man, was to gie him employment, an' I was the ane that wad haud mine busy for the maist part o' the four and twenty hours. But for a' my father's far-seen good sense, I hae had eneuch ado wi' John Gray, for though he's nae bad hand when he's on the loom, it is nae easy matter to keep him at the batt. But that's a' away frae our story. Sin your father could trust you sae far, I think I may trust you too, only ye're to say *as sure as death*, you will never tell it again.'

Jane complied, as was most likely, for the sake of this mysterious and scandalous story, as she deemed it to be, and after every precaution on the part of Tibby Stott, her gossip was entrusted with the whole. It would be endless to recount all the promises that were stipulated for, made, and broken at Middleholm, in the course of that day. Suffice it, that before night, every one, both old and young in the village, knew that the lang weaver had been *brought to bed o' twa black craws.*

This was too ridiculous a story to be believed, even by the ignorant inhabitants of that ancient village; and, as John shrewdly anticipated, they only laughed at John Gray's crazy wife. It proved however to him, that it would never do to trust his helpmate with the secret of finding hidden poses, and that whatever money he drew from such funds, it behoved him to ascribe it to the generosity of the two black birds.

So John arose one moonlight night, while others slept, went into his garden, and removing the wet straw, he again lifted up the broad stone, and took from under it the valuable treasure of which he had formerly made discovery. This was neither less nor more than the very thing he had always been told of, both by the vision of the cobler in his dream, and by the cobler himself; namely, an old pan filled with coins, of a date and reign John knew nothing about. Nearly one fourth of the whole bulk was made up of broad pieces of gold, but very thin, enclosed in one side of the pan; the rest was all silver, in a considerable state of decay. There were likewise among the gold, four rude square coins, about a quarter of an inch in thickness, and nearly the weight of a dollar each. John emptied them into a bag, and marched straight to Edinburgh with his treasure; where, after a great deal of manœuvring, he sold the whole for the miserable sum of £213:12:6, being the exact value of the metal (as the man assured him) to a scruple. John got his payment in gold and silver, for he would have nothing to do with bank notes, and brought the whole home with him. He knew nothing about putting money out at interest; and, still in fear lest he should be discovered, he hid it in the corner of his chest, resolved to live well on it till it was done, and then dig up another tree, take the pose from below it, and sell, and spend that in course; and so on: for John knew perfectly well, that he had a dozen of poses more to begin to, when the first was done.

Thenceforward, John's meals became somewhat more plentiful, but improved nothing in quality. He had been so long used to a life of poverty, that parsimony was become natural to him, and it was but seldom that he applied to the two birds for assistance. He could not rest however until he digged below one other tree, that he might have some guess what the extent of his treasure was, and what he had to depend on.

He accordingly began, and digged all round the next, and in beneath it, until the pits on each side met below the stem of the tree at a great depth, so that every one of the downward roots were cut; but for all that he could do, he could find no treasure whatever, and was obliged to give up the scrutiny considerably disappointed. Having, however, discovered, in the former adventure, that the removal of a part of the immense quantity of miry sour dung, from about his cowhouse, had been attended with some conveniences, he likewise filled up this latter pit with a farther portion of that, and again betook himself to his loom and his twa black craws.

The next year, to the astonishment of all, but more particularly to John himself, who had never once calculated on such an event, these two trees, after being literally covered over with healthy blossoms, bore such a load of fruit as never had been witnessed in that country. Almost every branch required a prop to prevent it being torn from the tree, by the increasing weight. John pulled the apples always as they ripened, and sent a quantity down every week by the carrier to his friend, the Cobler of Kelso, whose wife and daughter, it will be remembered, kept a fruit shop in one end of his dwelling. At the close of the year, when John went down to settle with his old friend, and the three-cocked hat, the latter paid him gratefully £7, 10s. for the produce of these two trees, and thanked him for his credit; not forgetting to treat him at breakfast with a cut of broiled salmon and a glass of brandy.

John, perceiving that this was good interest for a few wheel-barrows full of sour mire, followed the same mode with all his apple-trees, and planted more, so that in the course of a few years, the cobler paid him annually from 30 to 45 pounds Sterling for fruit, a great sum in those days; and thus was the cobler's extraordinary dream thoroughly fulfilled, not alone with regard to the main pose in the old pan, but that below every tree of the garden.

John now lived comfortably, with his family, all the days of his life, and there were no lasses had such trim and elegant cockernonies in all the Antiburgher meeting-house of Middleholm as the daughters of the lang weaver. But Tibby Stott, poor creature! believed till her dying-day, that their wealth was supplied by the twa mysterious black craws, whose place of concealment she never found out, nor ever sought after.

JOHN GALT

The Howdie

Part I – Anent Births

When my gudeman departed this life, he left me with a heavy handful of seven childer, the youngest but a baby at the breast, and the elder a lassie scant of eight years old. With such a small family what could a lanely widow woman do? Greatly was I grieved, not only for the loss of our bread-winner, but the quenching of that cheerful light which was my solace and comfort in straitened circumstances, and in the many cold and dark hours which the needs of our necessitous condition obliged us to endure.

James Blithe was my first and only Jo; and but for that armed man, Poverty, who sat ever demanding at our hearth, there never was a brittle minute in the course of our wedded life. It was my pleasure to gladden him at home, when out-of-door vexations ruffled his temper; which seldom came to pass, for he was an honest young man, and pleasant among those with whom his lot was cast. I have often, since his death, thought, in calling him to mind, that it was by his natural sweet nature that the Lord was pleased, when He took him to Himself, to awaken the sympathy of others for me and the bairns, in our utmost distress.

He was the head gairdner to the Laird of Rigs, as his father had been before him; and the family had him in great respect. Besides many a present of useful things which they gave to us, when we were married, they came to our wedding; a compliment that James often said was like the smell of the sweet briar in a lown and dewy evening, a cherishment that seasoned happiness. It was not however till he was taken away that I experienced the extent of their kindness. The ladies of the family were most particular to me; the Laird himself, on the Sabbath after the burial, paid me a very edifying visit; and to the old Leddy Dowager, his mother, I owe the meal that has ever since been in the basin, by which I have been enabled to bring up my childer in the fear of the Lord.

The Leddy was really a managing motherly character; no grass grew beneath her feet when she had a turn to do, as was testified by my case: for when the minister's wife put it into her head that I might do well in the midwife-line, Mrs Forceps being then in her declining years, she lost no time in getting me made, in the language of the church and gospel, her helper and successor. A blessing it was at the time, and the whole parish has, with a constancy of purpose, continued to treat me far above my deserts; for I have ever been sure of a shortcoming in my best endeavours to give satisfaction. But it's not to speak of the difficulties that the hand of a considerate Providence has laid upon me with a sore weight for an earthly nature to bear, that I have sat down to indite this history book. I only intend hereby to show, how many strange things have come to pass in my douce way of life; and sure am I that in every calling, no matter however humble, peradventures will take place that ought to be recorded for the instruction, even of the wisest. Having said this, I will now proceed with my story.

All the har'st before the year of dearth, Mrs Forceps, my predecessor, had been in an ailing condition; insomuch that, on the Halloween, she was laid up, and never after was taken out of her bed a living woman. Thus it came to pass that, before the turn of the year, the midwifery business of our countryside came into my hands in the natural way.

I cannot tell how it happened that there was little to do in the way of trade all that winter; but it began to grow into a fashion that the genteeler order of ladies went into the towns to have there han'lings among the doctors. It was soon seen, however, that they had nothing to boast of by that manœuvre, for their gudemen thought the cost overcame the profit; and thus, although that was to a certainty a niggardly year, and great part of the next no better, it pleased the Lord, by the scanty upshot of the har'st before spoken of, that, whatever the ladies thought of the doctors, their husbands kept the warm side of frugality towards me and other poor women that had nothing to depend upon but the skill of their ten fingers.

Mrs Forceps being out of the way, I was called in; and my first case was with an elderly woman that was long thought by all her friends to be past bearing; but when she herself came to me, and rehearsed the state she was in, with a great sough for fear, instead of a bairn, it might turn out a tympathy, I called to her mind how Sarah the Patriarchess, the wife of Abraham, was more than fourscore before Isaac was born: which was to her great consolation; for she was a pious woman in the main, and could discern in that miracle of Scripture an admonition to her to be of good cheer.

From that night, poor Mrs Houselycat grew an altered woman; and her gudeman, Thomas Houselycat, was as caidgy a man as could be, at the prospect of having an Isaac in his old age; for neither he nor his wife had the least doubt that they were to be blest with a man-child. At last the fulness of time came; and Thomas having provided a jar of cinnamon brandy for the occasion, I was duly called in.

Well do I remember the night that worthy Thomas himself came for me, with a lantern or a bowit in his hand. It was pitch-dark; the winds rampaged among the trees, the sleet was just vicious, and every drop was as salt as pickle. He had his wife's shawl tied over his hat, by a great knot under the chin, and a pair of huggars drawn over his shoes, and above his knees; he was just a curiosity to see coming for me.

I went with him; and to be sure when I got to the house, there was a gathering; young and old were there, all speaking together; widows and grannies giving advice, and new-married wives sitting in the expectation of getting insight. Really it was a ploy; and no wonder that there was such a collection; for Mrs Houselycat was a woman well-stricken in years, and it could not be looked upon as any thing less than an inadvertency that she was ordained to be again a mother. I very well remember that her youngest daughter of the first clecking was there, a married woman, with a wean at her knee, I'se warrant a year-and-a-half old; it could both walk alone, and say many words almost as intelligible as the minister in the poopit, when it was a frosty morning; for the cold made him there shavelin-gabbit, and every word he said was just an oppression to his feckless tongue.

By and by the birth came to pass: but, och on! the long faces that were about me when it took place; for instead of a lad-bairn it proved a lassie;

and to increase the universal dismay at this come-to-pass, it turned out that the bairn's cleading had, in a way out of the common, been prepared for a man child; which was the occasion of the innocent being, all the time of its nursing in appearance a very doubtful creature.

The foregoing case is the first that I could properly say was my own; for Mrs Forceps had a regular finger in the pie in all my heretofores. It was, however, good erls; for no sooner had I got Mrs Houselycat on her feet again, than I received a call from the head inns in the town, from a Captain's lady, that was overtaken there as the regiment was going through.

In this affair there was something that did not just please me in the conduct of Mrs Facings, as the gentlewoman was called; and I jaloused, by what I saw with the tail of my eye, that she was no better than a light woman. However, in the way of trade, it does not do to stand on trifles of that sort; for ours is a religious trade, as witness what is said in the Bible of the midwives of the Hebrews; and if it pleased Providence to ordain children to be, it is no less an ordained duty of the midwife to help them into the world. But I had not long been satisfied in my own mind that the mother was no better than she should be, when my kinder feelings were sorely tried, for she had a most extraordinar severe time o't; and I had but a weak hope that she would get through. However, with my help and the grace of God, she did get through: and I never saw, before nor since, so brave a baby as was that night born.

Scarcely was the birth over, when Mrs Facings fell into a weakly dwam that was very terrifying; and if the Captain was not her gudeman, he was as concerned about her, as any true gudeman could be, and much more so than some I could name, who have the best of characters.

It so happened that this Mrs Facings had been, as I have said, overtaken on the road, and had nothing prepared for a sore foot, although she well knew that she had no time to spare. This was very calamitous, and what was to be done required a consideration. I was for wrapping the baby in a blanket till the morning, when I had no misdoubt of gathering among the ladies of the town a sufficient change of needfu' baby clouts; but among other regimental clanjamphry that were around this left-to-hersel' damsel, was a Mrs Gooseskin, the drum-major's wife, a most devising character. When I told her of our straits and jeopardy, she said to give myself no uneasiness, for she had seen a very good substitute for child-linen, and would set about making it without delay.

What she proposed to do was beyond my comprehension; but she soon returned into the room with a box in her hand, filled with soft-teazed wool, which she set down on a chair at the bed-stock, and covering it with an apron, she pressed the wool under the apron into a hollow shape, like a goldfinch's nest, wherein she laid the infant, and covering it up with the apron, she put more wool over it, and made it as snug as a silk-worm in a cocoon, as it has been described to me. The sight of this novelty was, however, an affliction, for if she had intended to smother the bairn, she could not have taken a more effectual manner; and yet the baby lived and thrived, as I shall have occasion to rehearse.

Mrs Facings had a tedious recovery, and was not able to join him that in a sense was her gudeman, and the regiment, which was to me a great cause of affliction; for I thought that it might be said that her case was owing to my being a new hand, and not skilful enough. It thus came to pass that she, when able to stand the shake, was moved to private lodgings, where, for a season, she dwined and dwindled, and at last her life went clean out; but her orphan bairn was spared among us, and was a great means of causing a tenderness of heart to arise among the lasses, chiefly on account of its most thoughtless and ne'er-do-weel father, who never inquired after he left the town, concerning the puir thing; so that if there had not been a seed of charity bred by its orphan condition, nobody can tell what would have come of it. The saving hand of Providence was, however manifested. Old Miss Peggy Needle, who had all her life been out of the body about cats and dogs, grew just extraordinar to make a pet, in the place of them all, of the laddie Willie Facings; but, as I have said, I will by and by have to tell more about him; so on that account I will make an end of the second head of my discourse, and proceed to the next, which was one of a most piteous kind.

In our parish there lived a young lad, a sticket minister, not very alluring in his looks; indeed, to say the truth, he was by many, on account of them, thought to be no far short of a haverel; for he was lank and most uncomely, being in-kneed; but, for all that, the minister said he was a young man of great parts, and had not only a streak of geni, but a vast deal of inordinate erudition. He went commonly by the name of

Dominie Quarto; and it came to pass, that he set his affections on a weel-faured lassie, the daughter of Mrs Stoups, who keepit the Thistle Inn. In this there was nothing wonderful, for she was a sweet maiden, and nobody ever saw her without wishing her well. But she could not abide the Dominie: and, indeed, it was no wonder, for he certainly was not a man to pleasure a woman's eye. Her affections were settled on a young lad called Jock Sym, a horse-couper, a blithe heartsome young man, of a genteel manner, and in great repute, therefore, among the gentlemen.

He won Mally Stoups' heart; they were married, and, in the fulness of time thereafter, her pains came on, and I was sent to ease her. She lay in a back room, that looked into their pleasant garden. Half up the lower casement of the window, there was a white muslin curtain, made out of her mother's old-fashioned tamboured aprons, drawn across from side to side, for the window had no shutters. It would be only to distress the reader to tell what she suffered. Long she struggled, and weak she grew; and a sough of her desperate case went up and down the town like the plague that walketh in darkness. Many came to enquire for her, both gentle and semple; and it was thought that the Dominie would have been in the crowd of callers: but he came not.

In the midst of her suffering, when I was going about my business in the room, with the afflicted lying-in woman, I happened to give a glint to the window, and startled I was, to see, like a ghost, looking over the white curtain, the melancholious visage of Dominie Quarto, with watery eyes glistening like two stars in the candle light.

I told one of the women who happened to be in the way, to go out to the sorrowful young man, and tell him not to look in at the window; whereupon she went out, and remonstrated with him for some time. While she was gone, sweet Mally Stoups and her unborn baby were carried away to Abraham's bosom. This was a most unfortunate thing; and I went out before the straighting-board could be gotten, with a heavy heart, on account of my poor family, that might suffer, if I was found guilty of being to blame.

I had not gone beyond the threshold of the back-door that led into the garden, when I discerned a dark figure between me and the westling scad of the setting moon. On going towards it, I was greatly surprised to find the weeping Dominie, who was keeping watch for the event there, and had just heard what had happened, by one of the women telling another.

This symptom of true love and tenderness made me forget my motherly anxieties, and I did all I could to console the poor lad; but he was not to be comforted, saying, 'It was a great trial when it was ordained that she should lie in the arms of Jock Sym, but it's far waur to think that the kirk-yard hole is to be her bed, and her bridegroom the worm.'

Poor forlorn creature! I had not a word to say. Indeed, he made my heart swell in my bosom; and I could never forget the way in which he grat over my hand, that he took between both of his, as a dear thing, that he was prone to fondle and mourn over.

But this cutting grief did not end that night; on Sabbath evening following, as the custom is in our parish, Mrs Sym was ordained to be interred; and there was a great gathering of freends and neighbours; for both she and her gudeman were well thought of. Everybody expected the Dominie would be there, for his faithfulness was spoken of by all pitiful tongues; but he stayed away for pure grief; he hid himself from the daylight and the light of every human eye. In the gloaming, however, after, as the betherel went to ring the eight o'clock bell, he saw the Dominie standing with a downcast look, near the new grave, all which made baith a long and a sad story, for many a day among us: I doubt if it's forgotten yet. As for me, I never thought of it without a pang, but all trades have their troubles and the death of a young wife and her unborn baby, in her nineteenth year, is not one of the least that I have had to endure in mine.

But, although I met like many others in my outset both mortifications and difficulties, and what was worse than all, I could not say that I was triumphant in my endeavours; yet, like the Doctors, either good luck or experience made me gradually gather a repute for skill and discernment, insomuch that I became just wonderful for the request I was in. It is therefore needless for me to make a strive for the entertainment of the reader, by rehearsing all the han'lings that I had; but, as some of them were of a notable kind, I will pass over the generality and only make a Nota Bena here of those that were particular, as well as the births of the babies that afterwards came to be something in the world.

Between the death of Mally Stoups and the Whitsunday of that year, there was not much business in my line, not above two cases; but, on the day after, I had a doing, no less than of twins in a farmer's family, that was already overstocked with weans to a degree that was just a hardship; but, in that case, there was a testimony that Providence never sends mouths into the world without at the same time giving the wherewithal to fill them.

James Mashlam was a decent, douce, hard-working, careful man, and his wife was to all wives the very patron of frugality; but, with all their ettling, they could scarcely make the two ends of the year to meet. Owing to this, when it was heard in the parish that she had brought forth a Jacob and Esau, there was a great condolence; and the birth that ought to have caused both mirth and jocundity was not thought to be a gentle dispensation. But short-sighted is the wisdom of man and even of woman likewise; for, from that day, James Mashlam began to bud and prosper, and is now the toppingest man far or near; and his prosperity sprang out of what we all thought would be a narrowing of his straitened circumstances.

All the gentry of the country-side, when they heard the tydings, sent Mrs Mashlam many presents, and stocked her press with cleeding for her and the family. It happened, also, that, at this time, there was a great concourse of Englishers at the castle with my Lord; and one of them, a rattling young gentleman, proposed that they should raise a subscription for a race-purse; promising, that, if his horse won, he would give the purse for the behoof of the twins. Thus it came to pass, that a shower of gold one morning fell on James Mashlam, as he was holding the plough; for that English ramplor's horse, lo and behold! won the race, and he came over with all the company, with the purse in his hand full of golden guineas galloping upon James; and James and his wife sat cloking on this nest-egg, till they have hatched a fortune; for the harvest following, his eldest son was able to join the shearers, and from that day plenty, like a fat carlin, visited him daily. Year after year his childer that were of the male gender grew better and better helps: so that he enlarged his farm, and has since built the sclate house by the water side; that many a one, for its decent appearance, cannot but think it is surely the minister's manse.

From that time I too got a lift in the world; for it happened, that a grand lady, in the family way, came on a visit to the castle, and by some unaccountable accident she was prematurely brought to bed there. No doctor being at hand nearer than the burgh town, I was sent for and, before one could be brought, I had helped into the world the son and heir of an ancient family; for the which, I got ten golden guineas, a new gown that is still my best honesty, and a mutch that many a one came to see for it is made of a French lace. The lady insisted on me to wear it at the christening; which the Doctor was not overly pleased to hear tell of, thinking that I might in time clip the skirts of his practice.

For a long time after the deliverance of that lady I had a good deal to do in the cottars' houses; and lucky it was for me that I had got the guineas aforesaid, for the commonalty have not much to spare on an occasion; and I could not help thinking how wonderful are the ways of Providence, for the lady's gift enabled me to do my duty among the cottars with a lighter heart than I could have afforded to do had the benison been more stinted.

All the remainder of that year, the winter and the next spring, was without a remarkable: but just on the eve of summer, a very comical accident happened.

There was an old woman that come into the parish, nobody could tell how, and was called Lucky Nanse, who made her bread by distilling peppermint. Some said that now and then her house had the smell of whiskey; but how it came, whether from her still or the breath of her nostrils, was never made out to a moral certainty. This carlin had been in her day a by-ordinair woman, and was a soldier's widow forby.

At times she would tell stories of marvels she had seen in America, where she said there was a moose so big that a man could not lift its head. Once, when old Mr Izet, the precentor, to whom she was telling anent this beast, said it was not possible, she waxed very wroth, and knocking her neives together in his face, she told him that he was no gentleman to misdoubt her honour: Mr Izet, who had not much of the sweet milk of human kindness in his nature, was so provoked at this freedom, that he snapped his fingers as he turned to go away, and said she was not better than a ne'er-do-weel camp-randy. If she was oil before she was flame now, and dancing with her arms extended, she looted down, and, grasping a gowpin of earth in each hand, she scattered it with an air to the wind, and cried with a desperate voice, that she did not value his opinion at the worth of that dirt.

By this time the uproar had disturbed the clachan, and at every door the women were looking out to see what was the hobble-show; some with bairns in their arms and others with weans at their feet. Among the rest that happened to look out was Mrs Izet, who, on seeing the jeopardy that her gudeman was in, from that rabiator woman, ran to take him under her protection. But it was a rash action, for Lucky Nanse stood with her hands on her henches and daured her to approach, threatening, with some soldier-like words, that if she came near she would close her day-lights.

Mrs Izet was terrified, and stood still.

Home with you, said Nanse, ye mud that ye are, to think yourself on a par with pipeclay, with other hetradox brags, that were just a sport to hear. In the meantime, the precentor was walking homeward, and called to his wife to come away, and leave that tempest and whirlwind with her own wrack and carry.

Lucky Nanse had, by this time, spent her ammunition, and, unable to find another word sufficiently vicious, she ran up to him and spat in his face.

Human nature could stand no more, and the precentor forgetting himself and his dignity in the parish, lifted his foot and gave her a kick, which caused her to fall on her back. There she lay sprawling and speechless, and made herself at last lie as like a corpse, as it was possible. Every body thought that she was surely grievously hurt, though Mr Izet said his foot never touched her; and a hand-barrow was got to carry her home. All present were in great dismay, for they thought Mr Izet had committed a murder and would be hanged in course of law; but I may be spared from describing the dolorosity that was in our town that night.

Lucky Nanse being carried home on the barrow like a carcase, was put to bed; where, when she had lain some time, she opened a comical eye for a short space, and then to all intents and purposes seemed in the dead throes. It was just then that I, drawn into the house by the din of the straemash, looked over a neighbour's shoulder; but no sooner did the artful woman see my face than she gave a skirle of agony, and cried that her time was come, and the pains of a mother were upon her; at which to hear, all the other women gave a shout, as if a miracle was before them, for Nanse was, to all appearance, threescore; but she for a while so enacted her stratagem that we were in a terrification lest it should be true. At last she seemed quite exhausted, and I thought she was in the natural way, when in a jiffy she bounced up with a derisive gaffaw, and drove us all pell-mell out of the house. The like of such a ploy had never been heard of in our countryside. I was, however, very angry to be made such a fool of in my profession before all the people, especially as it turned out that the old woman was only capering in her cups.

Sometime after this exploit another come-to-pass happened that had a different effect on the nerves of us all. This fell out by a sailor's wife, a young woman that came to lie in from Sandy-port with her mother, a most creditable widow, that kept a huckstry shop for the sale of parliament cakes, candles, bone-combs, and prins, and earned a bawbee by the eydency of her spinning wheel.

Mrs Spritsail, as the young woman was called, had a boding in her breast that she could not overcome, and was a pitiable object of despondency, from no cause; but women in her state are often troubled by similar vapours. Hers, however, troubled everybody that came near her, and made her poor mother almost persuaded that she would not recover.

One night when she expected to be confined, I was called in: but such a night as that was! At the usual hour, the post woman, Martha Dauner, brought a letter to the old woman from Sandy-port, sealed with a black wafer; which, when Mrs Spritsail saw, she grew as pale as a clout, and gave a deep sigh. Alas! it was a sigh of prophecy; for the letter was to tell that her husband, John Spritsail, had tumbled overboard the night before, and was drowned.

For some time the young widow sat like an image, making no moan: it was very frightful to see her. By and by, her time came on, and although it could not be said that her suffering was by common, she fell back again into that effigy state, which made her more dreadful to see than if she had been a ghost in its winding sheet; and she never moved from the posture she put herself in till all was over, and the living creature was turned into a clod of church-yard clay.

This for a quiet calamity is the most distressing in my chronicle, for it came about with little ceremony. Nobody was present with us but only her sorrowful mother, on whose lap I laid the naked new-born babe. Soon after, the young widow departed to join her gudeman in paradise; but as it is a mournful tale, it would only be to hurt the reader's tender feelings to make a more particular account.

All my peradventures were not, however, of the same doleful kind; and there is one that I should mention, for it was the cause of meikle jocosity at the time and for no short season after.

There lived in the parish a very old woman, upwards of fourscore: she was as bent in her body as a cow's horn, and she supported herself with a staff in one hand, and for balance held up her gown behind with the other; in short, she was a very antideluvian, something older than seemed the folk at that time of the earth.

This ancient crone was the grandmother to Lizzy Dadily, a light-headed winsome lassie, that went to service in Glasgow; but many months she had not been there when she came back again, all mouth and een; and on the same night her granny, old Maudelin, called on me. It was at the gloaming: I had not trimmed my crusie, but I had just mended the fire, which had not broken out so that we conversed in an obscurity.

Of the history of old Maudelin I had never before heard ony particulars; but her father, as she told me, was out in the rebellion of Mar's year, and if the true king had gotten his rights, she would not have been a needful woman. This I, however, jealouse was vanity; for although it could not be said that she was positively an ill-doer, it was well known in the town that old as she was, the conduct of her house in many points was not the best. Her daughter, the mother of Lizzy, was but a canary-headed creature. What became of her we never heard, for she went off with the soldiers one day, leaving Lizzy, a bastard bairn. How the old woman thereafter fenn't, in her warsle with age and poverty, was to many a mystery, especially as it was now and then seen that she had a bank guinea note to change, and whom it cam frae was a marvel.

Lizzy coming home, her granny came to me, as I was saying, and after awhile conversing in the twilight about this and that, she told me that she was afraid her oe had brought home her wark, and that she didna doubt they would need the sleight of my hand in a short time, for that Lizzy had only got a month's leave to try the benefit of her native air; that of Glasgow, as with most young women, not agreeing with her.

I was greatly taken aback to her hear talk in such a calm and methodical manner concerning Lizzy, whom I soon found was in that condition that would, I'm sure, have drawn tears of the heart's blood from every other grandmother in the clachan. Really I was not well pleased to hear the sinful carlin talk in such a good-e'en and good-morn way about a guilt of that nature; and I said to her, both hooly and fairly, that I was not sure if I could engage myself in the business, for it went against my righteous opinion to make myself a mean of filling the world with natural children.

The old woman was not just pleased to hear me say this, and without any honey on her lips, she replied,

'Widow Blithe, this is an unco strain! and what for will ye no do your duty to Lizzy Dadily; for I must have a reason, because the minister or the magistrates of the borough shall ken of this.'

I was to be sure a little confounded to hear the frail though bardy old woman thus speak to her peremptors, but in my mild and methodical manner I answered and said,

'That no person in a trade with full hands ought to take a new turn; and although conscience, I would allow, had its weight with me, yet there was a stronger reason in my engagements to others.'

'Very well,' said Maudelin, and hastily rising, she gave a rap with her staff, and said, 'that there soon would be news in the land that I would hear of'; and away she went, stotting out at the door, notwithstanding her age, like a birsled pea.

After she was gone, I began to reflect; and I cannot say that I had just an ease of mind, when I thought of what she had been telling anent her oe: but nothing more came to pass that night.

The following evening, however, about the same hour, who should darken my door but the minister himself, a most discreet man, who had always paid me a very sympathysing attention from the death of my gudeman, so I received him with the greatest respect, wondering what could bring him to see me at that doubtful hour. But no sooner had he taken a seat in the elbow chair than he made my hair stand on end at the wickedness and perfidy of the woman sec.

'Mrs Blithe,' said he, 'I have come to have a serious word with you, and to talk with you on a subject that is impossible for me to believe. Last night that old Maudelin, of whom the world speaks no good, came to me with her grand-daughter from Glasgow, both weeping very bitterly;

the poor young lass had her apron tail at her face, and was in great distress.'

'What is the matter with you,' said I, quoth the minister; 'and thereupon the piteous grandmother told me that her oe had been beguiled by a false manufacturing gentleman, and was thereby constrained to come back in a state of ignominy that was heartbreaking.'

'Good Maudelin, in what can I help you in your calamity?'

'In nothing, nothing,' said she; 'but we are come to make a confession in time.'

'What confession? quo' I' – that said the minister.

'Oh, sir,' said she, 'it's dreadful, but your counselling may rescue us from a great guilt. I have just been with Widow Blithe, the midwife, to bespeak her helping hand; oh, sir, speir no questions.'

'But,' said the minister, 'this is not a business to be trifled with; what did Mrs Blithe say to you?'

'That Mrs Blithe,' replied Maudelin, 'is a hidden woman; she made sport of my poor Lizzy's misfortune, and said that the best I could do was to let her nip the craig of the bairn in the hour of its birth.'

'Now, Mrs Blithe,' continued the Minister, 'is it possible that you could suggest such a crime?'

I was speechless; blue sterns danced before my sight, my knees trembled, and the steadfast earth grew as it were coggly aneath my chair; at last I replied,

'That old woman, sir, is of a nature, as she is of age enough, to be a witch – she's no canny! to even me to murder! Sir, I commit myself into your hands and judgment.'

'Indeed, I thought,' said the minister, 'that you would never speak as Maudelin said you had done; but she told me to examine you myself, for that she was sure, if I was put to the straights of a question, I would tell the truth.'

'And you have heard the truth, sir,' cried I.

'I believe it,' said he; 'but, in addition to all she rehearsed, she told me that, unless you, Mrs Blithe, would do your duty to her injured oe, and free gratis for no fee at all, she would go before a magistrate, and swear you had egged her on to bathe her hands in innocent infant blood.'

'Mr Stipend,' cried I; 'the wickedness of the human heart is beyond the computations of man: this dreadful old woman is, I'll not say what; but oh, sir, what am I to do; for if she makes a perjury to a magistrate my trade is gone, and my dear bairns driven to iniquity and beggary?'

Then the minister shook his head, and said, 'It was, to be sure, a great trial, for a worthy woman like me, to be so squeezed in the vice of malice and malignity; but a calm sough in all troubles was true wisdom, and that I ought to comply with the deceitful carlin's terms.'

Thus it came to pass, that, after the bastard brat was born, the old wife made a brag of how she had spirited the worthy minister to terrify me. Everybody laughed at her souple trick: but to me it was, for many a day, a heartburning; though, to the laive of the parish, it was a great mean, as I have said, of daffin and merriment.

No doubt, it will be seen, by the foregoing, that, although in a sense I had reason to be thankful that Providence, with the help of the laird's leddy-mother, had enabled me to make a bit of bread for my family, yet, it was not always without a trouble and an anxiety. Indeed, when I think on what I have come through in my profession, though it be one of the learned, and the world not able to do without it, I have often thought that I could not wish waur to my deadliest enemy than a kittle case of midwifery; for surely it is a very obstetrical business, and far above a woman with common talons to practise. But it would be to make a wearisome tale were I to lengthen my story; and so I mean just to tell of another accident that happened to me last year, and then to make an end, with a word or two of improvement on what shall have been said; afterwards I will give some account of what happened to those that, through my instrumentality, were brought to be a credit to themselves and an ornament to the world. Some, it is very true, were not just of that stamp; for, as the impartial sun shines alike on the wicked and the worthy, I have had to deal with those whose use I never could see, more than that of an apple that falleth from the tree, and perisheth with rottenness.

The case that I have to conclude with was in some sort mystical; and long it was before I got an interpretation thereof. It happened thus: –

One morning in the fall of the year and before break of day, when I was lying wakerife in my bed, I heard a knuckling on the pane of the window and got up to inquire the cause. This was by the porter of the

Thistle Inns, seeking my help for a leddy at the crying, that had come to their house since midnight and could go no further.

I made no more ado, but dressed myself off-hand, and went to the Inns; where, to be sure, there was a leddy, for any thing that I then knew to the contrary, in great difficulty. Who she was, and where she had come from, I heard not; nor did I speir; nor did I see her face; for over her whole head she had a muslin apron so thrown and tied, that her face was concealed; and no persuasion could get her to remove that veil. It was therefore plain to me that she wished herself, even in my hands, not to be known; but she did not seem to jalouse that the very obstinacy about the veil would be a cause to make me think that she was afraid I would know her. I was not, however, overly-curious; for, among the other good advices that I got when I was about to take up the trade, from the leddy of Rigs, my patron, I was enjoined never to be inquisitive anent family secrets; which I have, with a very scrupulous care, always adhered to; and thus it happened, that, although the leddy made herself so strange as to make me suspicious that all was not right, I said nothing but I opened both my eyes and my ears.

She had with her an elderly woman; and, before she came to the worst, I could gather from their discourse, that the lady's husband was expected every day from some foreign land. By and by, what with putting one thing together with another, and eiking out with the help of my own imagin-ation, I was fain to guess that she would not be ill pleased to be quit of her burden before the Major came home.

Nothing beyond this patch-work of hints then occurred. She had an easy time of it; and, before the sun was up, she was the mother of a bonny bairn. But what surprised me was, that, in less than an hour after the birth, she was so wonderful hale and hearty, that she spoke of travelling another stage in the course of the day, and of leaving Mrs Smith, that was with her, behind to take care of the babby; indeed, this was settled; and, before noon, at twelve o' clock, she was ready to step into the post-chaise that she had ordered to take herself forward – but mark the upshot.

When she was dressed and ready for the road – really she was a stout woman – another chaise drew up at the Inn's door, and, on looking from the window to see who was in it, she gave a shriek and staggered back to a sofa, upon which she fell like one that had been dumbfoundered.

In the chaise I saw only an elderly weather-beaten gentleman, who, as soon as the horses were changed, pursued his journey. The moment he was off, this mysterious mother called the lady-nurse with the babby, and they spoke for a time in whispers. Then her chaise was brought out and in she stepped, causing me to go with her for a stage. I did so and she very liberally gave me a five pound note of the Royal Bank and made me, without allowing me to alight, return back with the retour-chaise; for the which, on my account, she settled with the driver. But there the story did not rest, as I shall have occasion to rehearse by and by.

Part II – Anent Bairns

Although I have not in the foregoing head of my subject mentioned every extraordinary han'ling that came to me, yet I have noted the most remarkable; and made it plain to my readers by that swatch of my professional work, that it is not an easy thing to be a midwife with repute, without the inheritance from nature of good common sense and discretion, over and above skill and experience. I shall now dedicate this second head, to a make-mention of such things as I have heard and known anent the bairns, that in their entrance into this world, came by the grace of God through my hands.

And here, in the first place, and at the very outset, it behoves me to make an observe, that neither omen nor symptom occurs at a birth, by which any reasonable person or gossip present can foretell what the native, as the unchristened baby is then called, may be ordained to come through in the course of the future. No doubt this generality, like every rule, has an exception; but I am no disposed to think the exceptions often kent-speckle; for although I have heard many a well-doing sagacious carlin notice the remarkables she had seen at some births, I am yet bound to say that my experience has never taught me to discern in what way a come-to-pass in the life of the man was begotten of the uncos at the birth of the child.

But while I say this, let me no be misunderstood as throwing any doubt on the fact, that births sometimes are, and have been, in all ages, attended with signs and wonders manifest. I am only stating the truth as it has fallen out in the course of my own experience; for I never misdoubt that it's in the power of Providence to work miracles and cause marvels, when a child is ordained with a superfluity of head-rope. I only maintain, that it is not a constancy in nature to be regular in that way, and that many prodigies happen at the times of births, of which it would not be a facile thing for a very wise prophet to expound the use. Indeed, my observes would go to the clean contrary; for I have noted that, for the most part, the births which have happened in dread and strange circumstances, were not a hair's-breadth better, than those of the commonest clamjamphry. Indeed, I had a very notable instance of this kind in the very first year of my setting up for myself, and that was when James Cuiffy's wife lay in of her eldest born.

James, as all the parish well knew, was not a man to lead the children of Israel through the Red Sea, nor she a Deborah to sing of butter in a lordly dish; but they were decent folk; and when the fulness of her time was come, it behoved her to be put to bed, and my helping hand to be called for. Accordingly I went.

It was the gloaming when James came for me; and as we walked o'er the craft together, the summer lightning ayont the hills began to skimmer in a woolly cloud: but we thought little o't, for the day had been very warm, and that flabbing of the fire was but a natural outcoming of the same cause.

We had not, however, been under the shelter of the roof many minutes, when we heard a-far off, like the ruff of a drum or the hurl of a cart of stones tumbled on the causey, a clap of thunder, and then we heard another and another, just like a sea-fight of Royal Georges in the skies, till the din grew so desperate, that the crying woman could no more be heard than if she had been a stone image of agony.

I'll no say that I was not in a terrification. James Cuiffy took to his Bible, but the poor wife needed all my help. At last the bairn was born; and just as it came into the world, the thunder rampaged, as if the Prince of the Powers of the air had gaen by himself; and in the same minute, a thunder-bolt fell doun the lum, scattered the fire about the house, whiskit out of the window, clove like a wedge the apple-tree at the house-end, and slew nine sucking pigs and the mother grumphy, as if they had been no better than the host of Sennacherib; which every body must allow was most awful: but for all that, nothing afterwards came to pass; and the bairn that was born, instead of turning out a necromancer or a geni, as we had so much reason to expect, was, from the breast, as silly as a windlestraw. Was not this a plain proof that they are but of a weak credulity who have faith in freats of that kind?

I met, likewise, not in the next year, but in the year after, nearer to this time, another delusion of the same uncertainty. Mrs Gallon, the exciseman's wife, was overtaken with her pains, of all places in the world, in the kirk, on a Sabbath afternoon. They came on her suddenly, and she gave a skirle that took the breath with terror from the minister, as he was enlarging with great bir on the ninth clause of the seventh head of his discourse. Every body stood up. The whole congregation rose upon the seats, and in every face was pale consternation. At last the minister said, that on account of the visible working of Providence in the midst of us, yea in the very kirk itself, the congregation should skail: whereupon skail they did; so that in a short time I had completed my work, in which I was assisted by some decent ladies staying to lend me their Christian assistance; which they did, by standing in a circle round the table seat where the ploy was going on, with their backs to the crying mother, holding out their gowns in a minaway fashion, as the maids of honour are said to do, when the queen is bringing forth a prince in public.

The bairn being born, it was not taken out of the kirk till the minister himself was brought back, and baptized it with a scriptural name; for it was every body's opinion that surely in time it would be a brave minister, and become a great and shining light in the Lord's vineyard to us all. But it is often the will and pleasure of Providence to hamper in the fulfilment the carnal wishes of corrupt human nature. Matthew Gallon had not in after life the seed of a godly element in his whole carcase; quite the contrary, for he turned out the most rank ringing enemy that was ever in our country-side; and when he came to years of discretion, which in a sense he never did, he fled the country as a soldier, and for some splore with the Session, though he was born in the kirk; – another plain fact that shows how little reason there is in some cases to believe that births and prognostifications have no natural connexion. Not that I would condumaciously maintain that there is no meaning in signs sometimes, and may be I have had a demonstration; but it was a sober advice that the auld leddy of Rigs gave me, when she put me in a way of business, to be guarded in the use of my worldly wisdom, and never to allow my tongue to describe what my eyes saw or my ears heard at an occasion, except I was well convinced it would pleasure the family.

'No conscientious midwife,' said she, 'will ever make causey-talk of what happens at a birth, if it's of a nature to work dule by repetition on the fortunes of the bairn'; and this certainly was most orthodox, for I have never forgotten her counsel.

I have, however, an affair in my mind at this time; and as I shall mention no names, there can be no harm done in speaking of it here; for it is a thing that would perplex a philosopher or a mathematical man, and stagger the self-conceit of an unbeliever.

There was a young Miss that had occasion to come over the moor by herself one day, and in doing so she met with a hurt; what that hurt was, no body ever heard; but it could not be doubted that it was something most extraordinar; for, when she got home, she took to her bed and was very unwell for several days, and her een were blear't with greeting. At last, on the Sabbath-day following, her mother foregathert with me in coming from the kirk; and the day being showery, she proposed to rest in my house as she passed the door, till a shower that she saw coming would blow over. In doing this, and we being by ourselves, I speired in a civil manner for her daughter; and from less to more she told me something that I shall not rehearse, and, with the tear in her eye, she entreated my advice; but I could give her none, for I thought her daughter had been donsie; so no more was said anent it; but the poor lassie from that day fell as it were into a dwining, and never went out; insomuch that before six months were come and gone, she was laid up in her bed, and there was a wally-wallying on her account throughout the parish, none doubting that she was in a sore way, if not past hope.

In this state was her sad condition, when they had an occasion for a gradawa at my Lord's; and as he changed horses at the Cross Keys when he passed through our town, I said to several of the neighbours, to advise the mother that this was a fine opportunity she ought not to neglect, but should consult him anent her dochter. Accordingly, on the doctor returning from the castle, she called him in; and when he had consulted the ailing lassie as to her complaint, every body rejoiced to hear that he made light of it, and said that she would be as well as ever in a month or two; for that all she had to complain of was but a weakness common to womankind, and that a change of air was the best thing that could be done for her.

Maybe I had given an advice to the same effect quietly before, and therefore was none displeased to hear, when it came to pass, that shortly after, the mother and Miss were off one morning, for the benefit of the air of Glasgow, in a retour chaise, by break of day, before anybody was up. To be sure some of the neighbours thought it an odd thing that they should have thought of going to that town for a beneficial air; but as the report soon after came out to the town that the sick lassie was growing brawly, the wonder soon blew over, for it was known that the air of a close town is very good in some cases of the asthma.

By and by, it might be six weeks or two months after, aiblins more, when the mother and the daughter came back, the latter as slimb as a popular tree, and blooming like a rose. Such a recovery after such an illness was little short of a miracle, for the day of their return was just ten months from the day and date of her hurt.

It is needless for me to say what were my secret thoughts on this occasion, especially when I heard the skill of the gradawa extolled, and far less how content I was when, in the year following, the old lady went herself on a jaunt into the East Country to see a sick cousin, a widow woman with only a bairn, and brought the bairn away with her on the death of the parent. It was most charitable of her so to do, and nothing could exceed the love and ecstasy with which Miss received it from the arms of her mother. Had it been her ain bairn she could not have dandalized it more!

Soon after this the young lady fell in with a soldier officer, that was sent to recruit in the borough, and married him on a short acquaintance, and went away with him a regimenting to Ireland; but 'my cousin's wee fatherless and motherless orphan,' as the old pawkie carlin used to call the bairn, stayed with her, and grew in time to be a ranting birkie; and in the end, my lord hearing of his spirit, sent for him one day to the castle, and in the end bought for him a commission, in the most generous manner, such as well befitted a rich young lord to do; and afterwards, in the army, his promotion was as rapid as if he had more than merit to help him.

Now, is not this a thing to cause a marvelling; for I, that maybe had it in my power to have given an explanation, was never called on so to do; for everything came to pass about it in such an ordained-like way, that really I was sometimes at a loss what to think, and said to myself surely I have dreamt a dream; for, although it could not be said to have been a case of prognostications, it was undoubtedly one of a most kittle sort in many particulars. Remembering, however, the prudent admonition I had received from the auld leddy of Rigs, I shall say no more at present, but keep a calm sough.

It is no doubt the even-down fact that I had no hand in bringing 'my cousin's wee fatherless and motherless orphan' into the world, but maybe I might have had, if all the outs and ins of the story were told. As that, however, is not fitting, I have just said enough to let the courteous reader see, though it be as in a glass darkly, that my profession is no without the need of common sense in its handlings, and that I have not earned a long character for prudence in the line without ettle, nor been without jobs that cannot be spoken of, but, like this, in a far-off manner.

But it behoves me, before I go farther, to request the reader to turn back to where I have made mention of the poor deserted bairn, Willy Facings; how he was born in an unprepared hurry, and how his mother departed this life, while his ne'er-do-weel father went away like a knotless thread. I do not know how it happened, but come to pass it did, that I took a kindness for the forsaken creature, insomuch that, if his luck had been no better with Miss Peggy Needle, it was my intent to have brought him up with my own weans; for he was a winsome thing from the hour of his birth, and made every day a warmer nest for his image in my heart. His cordial temper was a mean devised by Providence as a compensation to him for the need that was in its own courses, that he would never enjoy a parent's love.

When Miss Peggy had skailed the byke of her cats, and taken Billy, as he came to be called, home to her house, there was a wonderment both in the borough-town and our clachan how it was possible for her, an inexperienced old maid, to manage the bairn; for by this time he was weaned, and was as rampler a creature as could well be, and she was a most prejinct and mim lady. But, notwithstanding her natural mimness and prejinkity, she was just out of the body with love and tenderness towards him, and kept him all day at her foot, playing in the inside of a stool whamled up-side down.

It was the sagacious opinion of every one, and particularly both of the doctor and Mr Stipend, the minister, that the bairn would soon tire out the patience of Miss Peggy; but we are all short-sighted mortals, for instead of tiring her, she every day grew fonder and fonder of him, and hired a lassie to look after him, as soon as he could tottle. Nay, she bought a green parrot for him from a sailor, when he was able to run about; and no mother could be so taken up with her own get as kind-hearted Miss Peggy was with him, her darling Dagon; for although the parrot was a most outstrapolous beast, and skrighed at times with louder desperation than a pea-hen in a passion, she yet so loved it on his account, that one day when it bit her lip to the bleeding, she only put it in its cage, and said, as she wiped her mouth, that it was 'a sorrow.'

By and by Miss Peggy put Billy to the school; but, by that time, the condumacious laddie had got the upper hand of her, and would not learn his lesson, unless she would give him an apple or sweeties; and yet, for all that, she was out of the body about him, in so much that the minister was obligated to remonstrate with her on such indulgence; telling her she would be the ruin of the boy, fine creature as he was, if she did not bridle him, and intended to leave him a legacy.

In short, Miss Peggy and her pet were just a world's wonder, when, at last, Captain Facings, seven years after Billy's birth, being sent by the king to Glasgow, came out, one Sunday to our town, and sent for me to learn what had become of his bairn. Though I recollected him at the first sight, yet, for a matter of policy, I thought it convenient to pretend doubtful of my memory, till, I trow, I had made him sensible of his sin in deserting his poor baby. At long and length I made him to know the blessing that had been conferred by the fancy of Miss Peggy, on the deserted child, and took him myself to her house. But, judge of my consternation, and his likewise, when, on introducing him to her as the father of Billy, whom I well recollected, she grew very huffy at me, and utterly denied that Billy was any such boy as I had described, and foundled over him, and was really in a comical distress, till, from less to more, she grew, at last, as obstinate as a graven image, and was not sparing in the words she made use of to get us out of her habitation.

But, not to summer and winter on this very unforeseen come-to-pass, the Captain and I went to the minister, and there made a confession of the whole tot of the story. Upon which he advised the Captain to leave Billy with Miss Peggy, who was a single lady, not ill-off in the world; and he would, from time to time, see that justice was done to the bairn. They then made a paction concerning Billy's education; and, after a sore struggle, Miss Peggy, by the minister's exhortation, was brought to consent that her pet should be sent to a boarding-school, on condition that she was to be allowed to pay for him.

This was not difficult to be agreed to; and, some weeks after, Bill was accordingly sent to the academy at Green Knowes, where he turned out a perfect delight; and Miss Peggy sent him every week, by the carrier, a cake, or some other dainty. At last, the year ran round, and the vacance being at hand, Bill sent word by the carrier, that he was coming home to spend the time with Mamma, as he called Miss Peggy. Great was her joy at the tidings; she set her house in order, and had, at least, twenty weans, the best sort in the neighbourhood, for a ploy to meet him. But, och hone! when Billy came, he was grown such a big creature, that he no longer seemed the same laddie; and, at the sight of him, Miss Peggy began to weep and wail, crying, that it was an imposition they were attempting to put upon her, by sending another callan. However, she became, in the course of the night, pretty well convinced that he was indeed her pet; and, from that time, though he was but eight years old, she turned over a new leaf in her treatment.

Nothing less would serve her, seeing him grown so tall, than that he should be transmogrified into a gentleman; and, accordingly, although he was not yet even a stripling – for that's a man-child in his teens – she sent for a taylor next day and had him put into long clothes, with top boots; and she bought him a watch, and just made him into a curiosity, that nowhere else could be seen.

When he was dressed in his new clothes and fine boots, he went out to show himself to all Miss Peggy's neighbours; and, it happened, that, in going along, he fell in with a number of other childer, who were sliding down a heap of mixed lime, and the thoughtless brat joined them; by which he rubbed two holes in the bottom of his breeks, spoiled his new boots, and, when the holes felt cold behind, he made his hat into a seat, and went careering up the heap and down the slope with it, as if he had been a charioteer.

Everybody who saw the result concluded that certainly now Miss Peggy's favour was gone from him for ever. But she, instead of being angry, just exclaimed and demonstrated with gladness over him; saying, that, till this disaster, she had still suspected that he might turn out an imposture. Was there ever such infatuation? But, as I shall have to speak more anent him hereafter, I need not here say how he was sent back to the academy, on the minister's advice, just dress'd like another laddie.

FREDERICK MARRYAT

South West and by West three-quarters West

Jack Littlebrain was, physically considered, as fine grown, and moreover as handsome a boy as ever was seen, but it must be acknowledged that he was not very clever. Nature is, in most instances, very impartial; she has given plumage to the peacock, but, as every one knows, not the slightest ear for music. Throughout the feathered race it is almost invariably the same; the homeliest clad are the finest songsters. Among animals the elephant is certainly the most intelligent, but, at the same time, he cannot be considered as a beauty. Acting upon this well ascertained principle, nature imagined, that she had done quite enough for Jack when she endowed him with such personal perfection; and did not consider it was at all necessary that he should be very clever; indeed, it must be admitted not only that he was not very clever, but (as the truth must be told) remarkably dull and stupid. However, the Littlebrains have been for a long while a well-known, numerous, and influential family, so that, if it were possible that Jack could have been taught any thing, the means were forthcoming: he was sent to every school in the country; but it was in vain; at every following vacation, he was handed over from the one peda-gogue to the other, of those whose names were renowned for the Busbian system of teaching by stimulating both ends: he was horsed every day and still remained an ass, and at the end of six months, if he did not run away before that period was over, he was invariably sent back to his parents as incorrigible and unteachable. What was to be done with him? The Lit-tlebrains had always got on in the world, somehow or another, by their interest and connections; but here was one who might be said to have no brains at all. After many *pros* and *cons*, and after a variety of consulting letters had passed between the various members of his family, it was decided, that as his maternal uncle, Sir Theophilus Blazers, G.C.B., was at that time the second in command in the Mediterranean, he should be sent to sea under his command; the Admiral, having in reply to a letter on the subject, answered that it was hard indeed if he did not lick him into some shape or another; and that, at all events, he'd warrant that Jack should be able to box the compass before he had been three months nibbling the ship's biscuit; further, that it was very easy to get over the examination necessary to qualify him for lieutenant, as a turkey and a dozen of brown stout sent in the boat with him on the passing day, as a present to each of the passing captains, would pass him, even if he were as incompetent as a camel (or, as they say at sea, a cable,) to pass through the eye of a needle; that having once passed, he would soon have him in command of a fine frigate, with a good nursing first lieutenant; and that if he did not behave himself properly, he would make his signal to come on board of the flag-ship, take him into the cabin, and give him a sound horsewhipping, as other admirals have been known to inflict upon their own sons under similar circumstances. The reader must be aware that, from the tenour of Sir Theophilus's letter, the circumstances which we are narrating must have occurred some fifty years ago.

When Jack was informed that he was to be a midshipman, he looked up in the most innocent way in the world, (and innocent he was, sure enough,) turned on his heels, and whistled as he went for want of thought. For the last three months he had been at home, and his chief employment was kissing and romping with the maids, who declared him to be the handsomest Littlebrain that the country had ever produced. Our hero viewed the preparations made for his departure with perfect indifference, and wished every body good-by with the utmost composure. He was a happy, good-tempered fellow who never calculated, because he could not; never decided, for he had not wit enough to choose; never foresaw, although he could look straight before him; and never remembered, because he had no memory. The line, 'If ignorance is bliss, 'tis folly to be wise,' was certainly made especially for Jack: nevertheless he was not totally deficient: he knew what was good to eat or drink, for his taste was perfect, his eyes were very sharp, and he could discover in a moment if a peach was ripe on the wall; his hearing was quick, for he was the first in the school to detect the footsteps of his pedagogue; and he could smell any thing savoury nearly a mile off, if the wind lay the right way. Moreover, he knew that if he put his fingers in the fire that he would burn himself; that knives cut severely; that birch tickled, and several other little axioms of this sort which are generally ascertained by children at an early age, but which Jack's capacity had not received until at a much later date. Such as he was, our hero went to sea; his stock in his sea-chest being very abundant, while his stock of ideas was proportionally small.

We will pass over all the trans-shipments of Jack until he was eventually shipped on board of the Mendacious, then lying at Malta with the flag of Sir Theophilus Blazers at the fore – a splendid ship, carrying 120 guns, and nearly 120 midshipmen of different calibers. (I pass over captain, lieutenant, and ship's company, having made mention of her most valuable qualifications.) Jack was received with a hearty welcome by his uncle, for he came in pudding-time, and was invited to dinner; and the Admiral made the important discovery, that if his nephew was a fool in other points, he was certainly no fool at his knife and fork. In a short time his messmates found out that he was no fool at his fists, and his knock-down arguments ended much disputation. Indeed, as the French would say, Jack was perfection in the *physique*, although so very deficient in the *morale*.

But if Pandora's box proved a plague to the whole world, Jack had his individual portion of it, when he was summoned to *box* the compass by his worthy uncle Sir Theophilus Blazers; who in the course of six months discovered that he could not make his nephew box it in the three, which he had warranted in his letter; every day our hero's ears were boxed, but the compass never. It required all the cardinal virtues to teach him the cardinal points during the forenoon, and he made a point of forgetting them before the sun went down. Whenever they attempted it (and various were the teachers employed to drive the compass into Jack's head) his head drove round the compass; and try all he could, Jack never could compass it. It appeared, as some people are said only to have one idea, as if Jack could only have one *point* in his head at a time, and to that point he would stand like a well-broken pointer. With him the wind never changed until the next day. His uncle pronounced him to be a fool, but that did not hurt his nephew's feelings; he had been told so too often already.

I have said that Jack had a great respect for good eating and drinking, and, moreover, was blessed with a good appetite: every person has his peculiar fancies, and if there was any thing which more titillated the palate and olfactory nerves of our hero, it was a roast goose with sage and onions. Now it so happened, that having been about seven months on board of the Mendacious, Jack had one day received a summons to dine with the Admiral, for the steward had ordered a roast goose for dinner, and knew not only that Jack was partial to it, but also that Jack was the Admiral's nephew, which always goes for something on board of a flag-ship. Just before they were sitting down to table, the Admiral wishing to know how the wind was, and having been not a little vexed with the slow progress of his nephew's nautical acquirements, said, 'Now, Mr Littlebrain, go up, and bring me down word how the wind is; and mark me, as, when you are sent, nine times out of ten you make a mistake, I shall now bet you five guineas against your dinner, that you make a mistake this time: so now be off and we will soon ascertain whether you lose your dinner or I lose my money. Sit down, gentlemen; we will not wait for Mr Littlebrain.'

Jack did not much admire this bet on the part of his uncle, but still less did he like the want of good manners in not waiting for him. He had just time to see the covers removed, to scent a whiff of the goose, and was off.

'The Admiral wants to know how the wind is, sir,' said Jack to the officer of the watch.

The officer of the watch went to the binnacle, and setting the wind as nearly as he could, replied, 'Tell Sir Theophilus that it is *S. W. and by W. ¾ W.*'

'That's one of those confounded long points that I never can remember,' cried Jack, in despair.

'Then you'll "*get goose,*" as the saying is,' observed one of the midshipmen.

'No; I'm afraid that I sha'n't get any,' replied Jack, despondingly. 'What did he say, S. W. and by N. ¾ E.?'

'Not exactly,' replied his messmate, who was a good-natured lad, and laughed heartily at Jack's version. 'S. W. and by W. ¾ W.'

'I never can remember it,' cried Jack. 'I'm to have five guineas if I do, and no dinner if I don't; and if I stay here much longer, I shall get no dinner at all events, for they are all terribly peckish, and there will be none left.'

'Well, if you'll give me one of the guineas, I'll show you how to manage it,' said the midshipman.

'I'll give you two, if you'll only be quick and the goose a'n't all gone,' replied Jack.

The midshipman wrote down the point from which the wind blew, at full length, upon a bit of paper, and pinned it to the rim of Jack's hat. 'Now,' said he, 'when you go into the cabin, you can hold your hat so as to read it, without their perceiving you.'

'Well, so I can; I never should have thought of that,' said Jack.

'You hav'n't wit enough,' replied the midshipman.

'Well, I see no wit in the compass,' replied Jack.

'Nevertheless, it's full of point,' replied the midshipman; 'now be quick.'

Our hero's eyes served him well, if his memory was treacherous; and as he entered the cabin door he bowed over his hat very politely, and said, as he read it off, 'S. W. and by W. ¾ W.,' and then he added, without reading at all, 'if you please, Sir Theophilus.'

'Steward,' said the Admiral, 'tell the officer of the watch to step down.' 'How's the wind, Mr Growler?'

'S. W. and by W. ¾ W.' replied the officer.

'Then, Mr Littlebrain, you have won your five guineas, and may now sit down and enjoy your dinner.'

Our hero was not slow in obeying the order, and ventured, upon the strength of his success, to send his plate twice for goose. Having eaten their dinner, drunk their wine, and taken their coffee, the officers, at the same time, took the hint which invariably accompanies the latter beverage, made their bows and retreated. As Jack was following his seniors out of the cabin, the Admiral put the sum which he had staked into his hands, observing, that 'it was an ill wind that blew nobody good.'

So thought Jack, who, having faithfully paid the midshipman the two guineas for his assistance, was now on the poop keeping his watch, as midshipmen usually do; that is, stretched out on the signal lockers, and composing himself to sleep after the most approved fashion, answering the winks of the stars by blinks of his eyes, until at last he shut them to keep them warm. But, before he had quite composed himself, he thought of the goose and the five guineas. The wind was from the same quarter, blowing soft and mild; Jack laid in a sort of reverie, as it fanned his cheek, for the weather was close and sultry.

'Well,' muttered Jack to himself, 'I do love that point of the compass, at all events, and I think that I never shall forget S. W. and by W. ¾ W. No I never – never liked one before, though—'

'Is that true?' whispered a gentle voice in his ear; 'do you love "S. W. and by W. ¾ W.," and will you, as you say, never forget her?'

'Why, what's that?' said Jack, opening his eyes, and turning half round on his side.

'It's me – "S. W. and by W. ¾ W.," that you say you love.'

Littlebrain raised himself and looked round; – there was no one on the poop except himself and two or three of the after-guard, who were lying down between the guns.

'Why, who was it that spoke?' said Jack, much astonished.

'It was the wind you love, and who has long loved you,' replied the same voice; 'do you wish to see me?'

'See you, – see the wind? – I've been already sent on that message by the midshipmen,' thought Jack.

'Do you love me as you say, and as I love you?' continued the voice.

'Well, I like you better than any other point of the compass, and I'm sure I never thought I should like one of them,' replied Jack.

'That will not do for me; will you love only me?'

'I'm not likely to love the others,' replied Jack, shutting his eyes again; 'I *hate* them all.'

'And love me?'

'Well, I do love you, that's a fact,' replied Jack, as he thought of the goose and the five guineas.

'Then look round, and you shall see me," said the soft voice.

Jack, who hardly knew whether he was asleep or awake, did at this summons once more take the trouble to open his eyes, and beheld a fairy female figure, pellucid as water, yet apparently possessing substance; her features were beautifully soft and mild, and her outline trembled and shifted as it were, waving gently to and fro. It smiled sweetly, hung over him, played with his chestnut curls, softly touched his lips with her own, passed her trembling fingers over his cheeks, and its warm breath appeared as if it melted into his. Then it grew more bold, – embraced his person, searched into his neck and collar, as if curious to examine him.

Jack felt a pleasure and gratification which he could not well compre-hend: once more the charmer's lips trembled upon his own, now remaining for a moment, now withdrawing, again returning to kiss and kiss again, and once more did the soft voice put the question, –

'Do you love me?'

'Better than goose,' replied Jack.

'I don't know who goose may be,' replied the fairy form, as she tossed about Jack's waving locks; 'you must love only me, promise me that before I am relieved.'

'What, have you got the first watch, as well as me?' replied Jack.

'I am on duty just now, but I shall not be so long. We southerly winds are never kept long in one place; some of my sisters will probably be sent here soon.'

'I don't understand what you talk about,' replied Jack. 'Suppose you tell me who you are, and what you are, and I'll do all I can to keep awake; I don't know how it is, but I've felt more inclined to go to sleep since you have been fanning me about, than I did before.'

'Then I will remain by your side while you listen to me. I am, as I told you, a wind—'

'That's puzzling,' said Jack, interrupting her.

'My name is "S. W. and by W. ¾ W."'

'Yes, and a very long name it is. If you wish me to remember you, you should have had a shorter one.'

This ruffled the wind a little, and she blew rather sharp into the corner of Jack's eye, – however, she proceeded, –

'You are a sailor, and of course you know all the winds on the compass by name.'

'I wish I did; but I don't,' replied Littlebrain, 'I can recollect you, and not one other.'

Again the wind trembled with delight on his lips, and she proceeded: – 'You know that there are thirty-two points on the compass, and these points are divided into quarters; so that there are, in fact, 128 different winds.'

'There are more than I could ever remember; I know that,' said Jack.

'Well, we are in all 128. All the winds which have northerly in them, are coarse and ugly; all the southern winds are pretty.'

'You don't say so?' replied our hero.

'We are summoned to blow, as required, but the hardest duty generally falls to the northerly winds, as it should do, for they are the strongest; although we southerly winds can blow hard enough when we choose. Our characters are somewhat different. The most unhappy in disposition, and I may say, the most malevolent, are the north and easterly winds; the N.W. winds are powerful, but not unkind; the S.E. winds vary, but, at all events, we of the S.W. are considered the mildest and most beneficent. Do you understand me?'

'Not altogether. You're going right round the compass, and I never could make it out, that's a fact. I hear what you say, but I cannot promise to recollect it; I can only recollect S. W. and by W. ¾ W.'

'I care only for your recollecting me; if you do that, you may forget all the rest. Now you see we South Wests are summer winds, and are seldom required but in this season; I have often blown over your ship these last three months, and I always have lingered near you, for I loved you.'

'Thank you – now go on, for seven bells have struck sometime, and I shall be going to turn in. Is your watch out?'

'No, I shall blow for some hours longer. Why will you leave me – why wo'n't you stay on deck with me?'

'What, stay on deck after my watch is out! No, if I do, blow me! We midshipmen never do that – but I say, why can't you come down with me, and turn in my hammock; it's close to the hatchway, and you can easily do it.'

'Well, I will, upon one promise. You say that you love me, now I'm very jealous, for we winds are always supplanting one another. Promise me that you will never mention any other wind in the compass but me, for if you do, they may come to you, and if I hear of it I'll blow the masts out of your ship, that I will.'

'You don't say so?' replied Jack, surveying her fragile, trembling form.

'Yes, I will, and on a lee shore too; so that the ship shall go to pieces on the rocks, and the Admiral and every soul on board her be drowned.'

'No, you wouldn't, would you?' said our hero, astonished.

'Not if you promise me. Then I'll come to you and pour down your windsails, and dry your washed clothes as they hang on the rigging, and just ripple the waves as you glide along, and hang upon the lips of my dear love, and press him in my arms. Promise me, then, on no account ever to recollect or mention any other wind but me.'

'Well, I think I may promise that,' replied Jack, 'for I'm very clever at forgetting; and then you'll come to my hammock, wo'n't you, and sleep with me? you'll be a nice cool bedfellow these warm nights.'

'I can't sleep on my watch as midshipmen do; but I'll watch you while you sleep, and I'll fan your cheeks, and keep you cool and comfortable, till I'm relieved.'

'And when you go, when will you come again?'

'That I cannot tell – when I'm summoned; and I shall wait with impatience, that you may be sure of.'

'There's eight bells,' said Jack, starting up; 'I must go down and call the officer of the middle watch; but I'll soon turn in, for my relief is not so big as myself, and I can thrash him.'

Littlebrain was as good as his word; he cut down his relief, and then thrashed him for venturing to expostulate. The consequence was, that in ten minutes he was in his hammock, and 'S. W. and by W. ¾ W.' came gently down the hatchway, and rested in his arms. Jack soon fell fast asleep, and when he was wakened up the next morning by the quarter-master, his bedfellow was no longer there. A mate inquiring how the wind was, was answered by the quarter-master that they had a fresh breeze from the N. N. W., by which Jack understood that his sweetheart was no longer on duty.

Our hero had passed such a happy night with his soft and kind companion, that he could think of nothing else; he longed for her to come again, and, to the surprise of every body, was now perpetually making inquiries as to the wind which blew. He thought of her continually; and in fact was as much in love with 'S. W. and by W. ¾ W.' as he possibly could be. She came again – once more did he enjoy her delightful company; again she slept with him in his hammock, and then, after a short stay, she was relieved by another.

We do not intend to accuse the wind of inconstancy, as that was not her fault; nor of treachery, for she loved dearly; nor of violence, for she was all softness and mildness; but we do say, that 'S. W. and by W. ¾ W.' was the occasion of Jack being very often in a scrape, for our hero kept his word; he forgot all other winds, and, with him, there was no other except his dear 'S. W. and by W. ¾ W.' It must be admitted of Jack, that, at all events, he showed great perseverance, for he stuck to his point.

Our hero would argue with his messmates, for it is not those who are most capable of arguing who are most fond of it; and, like all arguers not very brilliant, he would flounder and diverge away right and left, just as the flaws of ideas came into his head.

'What nonsense it is your talking that way,' would his opponent say, 'Why don't you come to the point?'

'And so I do,' cried Jack.

'Well then, what is your point?'

'S. W. and by W. ¾ W.,' replied our hero.

Who could reply to this? But in every instance, and through every difficulty, our hero kept his promise, until his uncle Sir Theophilus was very undecided, whether he should send him home to be locked up in a Lunatic Asylum, or bring him on in the service to the rank of post-captain. Upon mature consideration, however, as a man in Bedlam is a very useless member of society, and a tee-total non-productive, whereas a captain in the navy is a responsible agent, the Admiral came to the conclusion, that Littlebrain must follow up his destiny.

At last, Jack was set down as the greatest fool in the ship, and was pointed out as such. The ladies observed, that such might possibly be the case, but at all events he was the handsomest young man in the Mediterranean fleet. We believe that both parties were correct in their assertions.

Time flies – even a midshipman's time, which does not fly quite so fast as his money – and the time came for Mr Littlebrain's examination. Sir Theophilus, who now commanded the whole fleet, was almost in despair. How was it possible that a man could navigate a ship, with only one quarter point of the compass in his head?

Sir Theophilus scratched his wig; and the disposition of the Mediterranean fleet, so important to the country, was altered according to the dispositions of the captains who commanded the ships. In those days, there were martinets in the service; officers who never overlooked an offence, or permitted the least deviation from strict duty; who were generally hated, but at the same time were most valuable to the service. As for his nephew passing his examination before any of those of the first, or second, or even of the third degree, the Admiral knew that it was impossible. The consequence was, that one was sent away on a mission to Genoa, about nothing;

another to watch for vessels never expected, off Sardinia; two more to cruize after a French frigate which had never been built: and thus, by degrees, did the Admiral arrange, so as to obtain a set of officers sufficiently pliant to allow his nephew to creep under the gate which barred his promotion, and which he never could have vaulted over. So the signal was made – our hero went on board – his uncle had not forgotten the propriety of a little *douceur* on the occasion; and, as the turkeys were all gone, three couple of geese were sent in the same boat, as a present to each of the three passing captains. Littlebrain's heart failed him as he pulled to the ship; even the geese hissed at him, as much as to say, 'If you were not such a stupid ass, we might have been left alive in our coops.' There was a great deal of truth in that remark, if they did say so.

Nothing could have been made more easy for Littlebrain than his examination. The questions had all been arranged beforehand; and some kind friend had given him all the answers written down. The passing captains apparently suffered from the heat of the weather, and each had his hand on his brow, looking down on the table at the time that Littlebrain gave his answers, so that of course they did not observe that he was reading them off. As soon as Littlebrain had given his answer, and had had sufficient time to drop his paper under the table, the captains felt better and looked up again.

There were but eight questions for our hero to answer. Seven had been satisfactorily got through; then came the eighth, a very simple one: – 'What is your course and distance from Ushant to the Start?' This question having been duly put, the captains were again in deep meditation, shrouding their eyes with the palms of their hands.

Littlebrain had his answer – he looked at the paper. What could be more simple than to reply? – and then the captains would have all risen up, shaken him by the hand, complimented him upon the talent he had displayed, sent their compliments to the commander-in-chief, and their thanks for the geese. Jack was just answering, 'North—'

'Recollect your promise!' cried a soft voice, which Jack well recollected.

Jack stammered – the captains were mute – and waited patiently.

'I must say it,' muttered Jack.

'You shan't,' replied the little Wind.

'Indeed I must,' said Jack, 'or I shall be turned back.'

The captains, surprised at this delay and the muttering of Jack, looked up, and one of them gently inquired if Mr Littlebrain had not dropped his handkerchief or something under the table? and then they again fixed their eyes upon the green cloth.

'If you dare, I'll never see you again,' cried 'S. W. and by W. ¾ W.,' – 'never come to your hammock, – but I'll blow the ship on shore, every soul shall be lost, Admiral and all; recollect your promise!'

'Then I shall never pass,' replied Jack.

'Do you think that any other point in the compass shall pass you except me? – never! I'm too jealous for that; come now, dearest,' and the Wind again deliciously trembled upon the lips of our hero, who could no longer resist.

'S. W. and by W. ¾ W.,' exclaimed Jack firmly.

'You have made a slight mistake, Mr Littlebrain,' said one of the captains. '*Look* again – I meant to say, *think* again.'

'S. W. and by W. ¾ W.,' again repeated Jack.

'Dearest! how I love you!' whispered the soft Wind.

'Why, Mr Littlebrain,' said one of the captains, for Jack had actually laid the paper down on the table, 'what's in the wind now?'

'She's obstinate,' replied Jack.

'You appear to be so, at all events,' replied the captain. 'Pray try once more.'

'I have it!' thought Jack, who tore off the last answer from his paper. 'I gained five guineas by that plan once before.' He then handed the bit of paper to the passing captain: 'I believe that's right, sir,' said our hero.

'Yes, that is right; but could you not have said it instead of writing it, Mr Littlebrain?'

Jack made no reply; his little sweetheart pouted a little, but said nothing; it was an evasion which she did not like. A few seconds of consultation then took place, as a matter of form. Each captain asked of the other if he was perfectly satisfied as to Mr Littlebrain's capabilities, and the reply was in the affirmative; and they were perfectly satisfied, that he was either a fool or a madman. However, as we have had both in the service by way of precedent, Jack was added to the list, and the next day was appointed lieutenant.

Our hero did his duty as lieutenant of the forecastle; and as all the duty of that officer is, when hailed from the quarter-deck, to answer '*Ay, ay, sir,*' he got on without making many mistakes. And now he was very happy; no one dared to call him a fool except his uncle; he had his own cabin, and many was the time that his dear little 'S. W. and by W. ¾ W.' would come in by the scuttle, and nestle by his side.

'You wo'n't see so much of me soon, dearest,' said she, one morning, gravely.

'Why not, my soft one?' replied Jack.

'Don't you recollect that the winter months are coming on?'

'So they are,' replied Jack. 'Well, I shall long for you back.'

And Jack did long, and long very much, for he loved his dear wind, and the fine weather which accompanied her. Winter came on, and heavy gales and rain, and thunder and lightning; nothing but double-reefed top-sails, and wearing in succession; and our hero walked the forecastle, and thought of his favourite wind. The N.E. winds came down furiously, and the weather was bitter cold. The officers shook the rain and spray off their garments when their watch was over, and called for grog.

'Steward, a glass of grog,' cried one, 'and let it be strong.'

'The same for me,' said Jack; 'only I'll mix it myself.'

Jack poured out the rum till the tumbler was half full.

'Why, Littlebrain,' said his messmate, 'that is a dose, that's what we call a regular *Nor-wester.*'

'Is it?' replied Jack. 'Well then, Nor-westers suit me exactly, and I shall stick to them like coblers' wax.'

And during the whole of the winter months our hero showed a great predilection for Nor-westers.

It was in the latter end of February that there was a heavy gale; it had blown furiously from the northward for three days, and then it paused and panted as if out of breath – no wonder; and then the wind shifted, and shifted again, with squalls and heavy rain, until it blew from every quarter of the compass.

Our hero's watch was over, and he came down and called for a 'Nor-wester' as usual.

'How is the wind, now?' asked the first lieutenant to the master, who came down dripping wet.

'S. S. W., but drawing now fast to the Westward,' said old Spunyarn.

And so it was; and it veered round until 'S. W. and by W. ¾ W.,' with an angry gust, came down the sky-light, and blowing strongly into our hero's ear, cried, –

'Oh! you false one!!'

'False!' exclaimed Jack. 'What! you here, and so angry too? – what's the matter?'

'What's the matter! – do you think I don't know? What have you been doing ever since I was away, comforting yourself during my absence with *Nor-westers?*'

'Why, you an't jealous of a Nor-wester, are you?' replied Littlebrain. 'I confess, I'm rather partial to them.'

'What! – this to my face! – I'll never come again, – without you promise me that you will have nothing to do with them, and never call for one again. Be quick – I cannot stay more than two minutes, for it is hard work now, and we relieve quick – say the word.'

'Well, then,' replied Littlebrain, 'you've no objection to *half-and-half?*'

'None in the world; that's quite another thing, and has nothing to do with the wind.'

'It has, though,' thought Jack, 'for it gets a man in the wind; but I wo'n't tell her so; and,' continued he, 'you don't mind a raw nip do you?'

'No – I care for nothing except a Nor-wester.'

'I'll never call for one again,' replied Jack; 'it is but making my grog a little stronger; in future it shall be *half-and-half.*'

'That's a dear! – now I'm off, don't forget me;' and away went the wind in a great hurry.

It was about three months after this short visit, the fleet being off Corsica, that our hero was walking the deck, thinking that he soon should see the object of his affections, when a privateer brig was discovered at anchor a few miles from Bastia. The signal was made for the boats of the fleet to cut her out, and the Admiral, wishing that his nephew should distinguish himself somehow, gave him the command of one of the finest boats. Now Jack was as brave as brave could be; he did not know what danger was; he hadn't wit enough to perceive it, and there was no doubt but he would distinguish himself. The boats went on the service. Jack was the very first on board, cheering his men as he darted into the closed ranks of his opponents. Whether it was that he did not think that his head was worth defending, or that he was too busy in breaking the heads of others to look after his own; this is certain, that a tomahawk descended upon it with such force as to bury itself in his skull (and his was a thick skull, too). The privateer's men were overpowered by numbers, and then our hero was discovered, under a pile of bodies, still breathing heavily. He was hoisted on board, and taken into his uncle's cabin: the surgeon shook his head when he had examined that of our hero.

'It must have been a most tremendous blow,' said he to the Admiral, 'to have penetrated—'

'It must have been, indeed,' replied the Admiral, as the tears rolled down his cheeks; for he loved his nephew.

The surgeon having done all that his art would enable him, left the cabin to attend to the others who were hurt; the Admiral also went on the quarter-deck, walking to and fro for an hour in a melancholy mood. He returned to the cabin, and bent over his nephew; Jack opened his eyes.

'My dear fellow,' said the Admiral, 'how's your head now?'

'S. W. and by W. ¾ W.,' faintly exclaimed our hero, constant in death, as he turned a little on one side and expired.

It was three days afterwards, as the fleet were on a wind, making for Malta, that the bell of the ship tolled, and a body, sewed up in a hammock and covered with the Union Jack, was carried to the gangway by the Admiral's bargemen. It had been a dull cloudy day, with little wind; the hands were turned up, the officers and men stood uncovered; the Admiral in advance with his arms folded, as the chaplain read the funeral service over the body of our hero, – and as the service proceeded, the sails flapped, for the wind had shifted a little; a motion was made, by the hand of the officer of the watch, to the man at the helm to let the ship go off the wind, that the service might not be disturbed, and a mizzling soft rain descended. The wind had shifted to our hero's much loved *point*, his fond mistress had come to mourn over the loss of her dearest, and the rain that descended were the tears which she shed at the death of her handsome but not over-gifted lover.

WILLIAM THACKERAY

A Little Dinner at Timmins's

I

Mr and Mrs Fitzroy Timmins live in Lilliput Street, that neat little street which runs at right angles with the Park and Brobdingnag Gardens. It is a very genteel neighbourhood, and I need not say they are of a good family.

Especially Mrs Timmins, as her mamma is always telling Mr T. They are Suffolk people, and distantly related to the Right Honourable the Earl of Bungay.

Besides his house in Lilliput Street, Mr Timmins has Chambers in Fig-tree Court, Temple, and goes the Northern Circuit.

The other day, when there was a slight difference about the payment of fees between the great Parliamentary Counsel and the Solicitors, Stoke and Pogers, of Great George Street, sent the papers of the Lough Foyle and Lough Corrib Junction Railway to Mr Fitzroy Timmins, who was so elated that he instantly purchased a couple of looking-glasses for his drawing-rooms (the front room is 16 by 12, and the back, a tight but elegant apartment, 10 ft 6 by 8 ft 4), a coral for the baby, two new dresses for Mrs Timmins, and a little rosewood desk, at the Pantechnicon, for which Rosa had long been sighing, with crumpled legs, emerald-green and gold morocco top, and drawers all over.

Mrs Timmins is a very pretty poetess (her 'Lines to a Faded Tulip', and her 'Plaint of Plinlimmon', appeared in one of last year's Keepsakes), and Fitzroy, as he impressed a kiss on the snowy forehead of his bride, pointed out to her, in one of the innumerable pockets of the desk, an elegant ruby-tipped pen, and six charming little gilt blank books, marked

'My Books', which Mrs Fitzroy might fill, he said, (he is an Oxford man, and very polite) 'with the delightful productions of her Muse'. Besides these books, there was pink paper, paper with crimson edges, lace paper, all stamped with R. F. T. (Rosa Fitzroy Timmins), and the hand and battle-axe, the crest of the Timminses (and borne at Ascalon by Roaldus de Timmins, a crusader, who is now buried in the Temple Church, next to Serjeant Snooks), and yellow, pink, light-blue, and other scented sealing-waxes, at the service of Rosa when she chose to correspond with her friends.

Rosa, you may be sure, jumped with joy at the sight of this sweet present; called her Charles (his first name is Samuel, but they have sunk that) the best of men! embraced him a great number of times, to the edification of her buttony little page, who stood at the landing; and as soon as he was gone to Chambers, took the new pen and a sweet sheet of paper, and began to compose a poem.

'What shall it be about?' was naturally her first thought. 'What should be a young mother's first inspiration?' Her child lay on the sofa asleep, before her; and she began in her neatest hand –

LINES

ON MY SON, BUNGAY DE BRACY GASHLEIGH TYMMYNS,

AGED TEN MONTHS.

Tuesday.

'How beautiful! how beautiful thou seemest,
  My boy, my precious one, my rosy babe!
Kind angels hover round thee, as thou dreamest:
Soft lashes hide thy beauteous azure eye which gleamest.'

'Gleamest? thine eye which gleamest? Is that grammar?' thought Rosa, who had puzzled her little brains for some time with this absurd question, when the baby woke; then the cook came up to ask about dinner; then Mrs Fundy slipped over from No. 27, (they are opposite neighbours, and made an acquaintance through Mrs Fundy's macaw): and a thousand things happened. Finally there was no rhyme to babe except Tippo Saib (against whom Major Gashleigh, Rosa's grandfather, had distinguished himself), and so she gave up the little poem about her De Bracy.

Nevertheless, when Fitzroy returned from Chambers to take a walk with his wife in the Park, as he peeped through the rich tapestry hanging which divided the two drawing-rooms, he found his dear girl still seated at the desk, and writing, writing away with her ruby pen as fast as it could scribble.

'What a genius that child has!' he said; 'why, she is a second Mrs Norton!' and advanced smiling to peep over her shoulder and see what pretty thing Rosa was composing.

It was not poetry, though, that she was writing, and Fitz read as follows: –

LILLIPUT STREET, *Tuesday, 22nd May.*

Mr and Mrs Fitzroy Tymmyns request the pleasure of Sir Thomas and Lady Kicklebury's company at dinner on Wednesday, at 7½ o'clock.

'My dear!' exclaimed the barrister, pulling a long face.

'Law, Fitzroy!' cried the beloved of his bosom, 'how you do startle one!'

'Give a dinner party with our means!' said he.

'Ain't you making a fortune, you miser?' Rosa said. 'Fifteen guineas a day is four thousand five hundred a year; I've calculated it.' And, so saying, she rose and taking hold of his whiskers, (which are as fine as those of any man of his circuit,) she put her mouth close up against his and did something to his long face, which quite changed the expression of it: and which the little page heard outside the door.

'Our dining-room won't hold ten,' he said.

'We'll only ask twenty,' my love; 'ten are sure to refuse in this season, when everybody is giving parties. Look, here is the list.'

'Earl and Countess of Bungay, and Lady Barbara Saint Mary's.'

'You are dying to get a Lord into the house,' Timmins said (*he* has not altered his name in Fig-tree Court yet, and therefore I am not so affected as to call him *Tymmyns*). 'Law, my dear, they are our cousins, and must be asked,' Rosa said.

'Let us put down my sister and Tom Crowder, then.'

'Blanche Crowder is really so *very* fat, Fitzroy,' his wife said, 'and our rooms are so *very* small.'

Fitz laughed. 'You little rogue,' he said, 'Lady Bungay weighs two of Blanche, even when she's not in the f—'

'Fiddlesticks!' Rose cried out. 'Doctor Crowder really cannot be admitted; he makes such a noise eating his soup, that it is really quite disagreeable;' and she imitated the gurgling noise performed by the doctor while inhausting his soup, in such a funny way, that Fitz saw inviting him was out of the question.

'Besides, we musn't have too many relations,' Rosa went on. 'Mamma, of course, is coming. She doesn't like to be asked in the evening; and she'll bring her silver bread-basket, and her candlesticks, which are very rich and handsome.'

'And you complain of Blanche for being too stout!' groaned out Timmins.

'Well, well, don't be in a pet,' said little Rosa. 'The girls won't come to dinner; but will bring their music afterwards.' And she went on with the list.

'Sir Thomas and Lady Kicklebury, 2. No saying no: we *must* ask them, Charles. They are rich people, and any room in their house in Brobdingnag Gardens would swallow up *our* humble cot. But to people in *our* position in *society*, they will be glad enough to come. The city people are glad to mix with the old families.'

'Very good,' said Fitz, with a sad face of assent – and Mrs Timmins went on reading her list.

'Mr and Mrs Topham Sawyer, Belgravine Place.'

'Mrs Sawyer hasn't asked you all the season. She gives herself the airs of an empress; and when—'

'One's member, you know, my dear, one must have,' Rosa replied, with much dignity; as if the presence of the representative of her native place would be a protection to her dinner; and a note was written and transported by the page early next morning to the mansion of the Sawyers, in Belgravine Place.

The Topham Sawyers had just come down to breakfast, Mrs T. in her large dust-coloured morning dress and Madonna front (she looks rather scraggy of a morning, but I promise you her ringlets and figure will stun you of an evening); and having read the note, the following dialogue passed: –

Mrs Topham Sawyer. 'Well, upon my word, I don't know where things will end. Mr Sawyer, the Timminses have asked us to dinner.'

Mr Topham Sawyer. 'Ask us to dinner! What d— impudence!'

Mrs Topham Sawyer. 'The most dangerous and insolent revolutionary principles are abroad, Mr Sawyer; and I shall write and hint as much to these persons.'

Mr Topham Sawyer. 'No, d— it, Joanna, they are my constituents, and we must go. Write a civil note, and say we will come to their party.' (*He resumes the perusal of the 'Times,' and Mrs Topham Sawyer writes*) –

MY DEAR ROSA,

We shall have *great pleasure* in joining your little party. I do not reply in the third person, as *we are old friends*, you know, and *country neigh-bours*. I hope your mamma is well: present my *kindest remembrances* to her, and I hope we shall see much MORE of each other in the summer, when we go down to the Sawpits (for going abroad is out of the question in these *dreadful times*). With a hundred kisses to your dear little *pet*,

Believe me your attached

J. T. S.

She said *Pet*, because she did not know whether Rosa's child was a girl or boy: and Mrs Timmins was very much pleased with the kind and gracious nature of the reply to her invitation.

II

The next persons whom little Mrs Timmins was bent upon asking, were Mr and Mrs John Rowdy, of the firm of Stumpy, Rowdy, and Co., of Brobdingnag Gardens, of the Prairie, Putney, and of Lombard Street, City.

Mrs Timmins and Mrs Rowdy had been brought up at the same school together, and there was always a little rivalry between them, from the day when they contended for the French prize at school, to last week, when each had a stall at the Fancy Fair for the benefit of the Daughters of Decayed Muffin-men; and when Mrs Timmins danced against Mrs Rowdy in the Scythe Mazurka at the Polish Ball, headed by Mrs Hugh Slasher. Rowdy took twenty-three pounds more than Timmins in the Muffin transaction (for she had possession of a kettle-holder worked by the hands of R–y–lty, which brought crowds to her stall); but in the Mazourk Rosa conquered; she has the prettiest little foot possible (which in a red boot and silver heel looked so lovely that even the Chinese ambassador remarked it), whereas Mrs Rowdy's foot is no trifle, as Lord Cornbury acknowledged when it came down on his lordship's boot tip as they danced together amongst the Scythes.

'These people are ruining themselves,' said Mrs John Rowdy to her husband, on receiving the pink note. It was carried round by that rogue of a buttony page in the evening, and he walked to Brobdingnag Gardens and in the Park afterwards, with a young lady who is kitchen-maid at 27, and who is not more than fourteen years older than little Buttons.

'Those people are ruining themselves,' said Mrs John to her husband. 'Rosa says she has asked the Bungays.'

'Bungays, indeed! Timmins was always a tuft-hunter,' said Rowdy, who had been at college with the barrister, and who, for his own part, has no more objection to a lord than you or I have; and adding, 'Hang him, what business has *he* to be giving parties?' allowed Mrs Rowdy, nevertheless, to accept Rosa's invitation.

'When I go to business to-morrow, I will just have a look at Mr Fitz's account,' Mr Rowdy thought, 'and if it is overdrawn, as it usually is, why' . . . The announcement of Mrs Rowdy's brougham here put an end to this agreeable train of thought, and the banker and his lady stepped into it to join a snug little family party of two-and-twenty, given by Mr and Mrs Secondchop, at their great house on the other side of the Park.

'Rowdys 2, Bungays 3, ourselves and mamma 3, 2 Sawyers,' calculated little Rosa.

'General Gulpin,' Rosa continued, 'eats a great deal, and is very stupid, but he looks well at table, with his star and ribbon; let us put *him* down!' and she noted down 'Sir Thomas and Lady Gulpin, 2. Lord Castlenoodle, 1.'

'You will make your party abominably genteel and stupid,' groaned Timmins. 'Why don't you ask some of our old friends? Old Mrs Portman has asked us twenty times, I am sure, within the last two years.'

'And the last time we went there, there was pea-soup for dinner!' Mrs Timmins said, with a look of ineffable scorn.

'Nobody can have been kinder than the Hodges have always been to us; and some sort of return we might make, I think.'

'Return, indeed! A pretty sound it is on the staircase to hear Mr and Mrs Odge and Miss Odges, pronounced by Billiter, who always leaves his h's out. No, no; see attornies at your chambers, my dear – but what could the poor creatures do in *our* society?' And so, one by one, Timmins's old friends were tried and eliminated by Mrs Timmins, just as if she had been an Irish attorney-general, and they so many Catholics on Mr Mitchel's jury.

Mrs Fitzroy insisted that the party should be of her very best company. Funnyman, the great wit, was asked, because of his jokes; and Mrs Butt, on whom he practises; and Potter, who is asked because everybody else asks him; and Mr Ranville Ranville of the Foreign Office, who might give some news of the Spanish squabble; and Botherby, who has suddenly sprung up into note because he is intimate with the French Revolution, and visits Ledru-Rollin and Lamartine. And these, with a couple more who are *amis de la maison*, made up the twenty, whom Mrs Timmins thought she might safely invite to her little dinner.

But the deuce of it was, that when the answers to the invitations came back, everybody accepted! Here was a pretty quandary. How they were to get twenty into their dining-room, was a calculation which poor Timmins could not solve at all; and he paced up and down the little room in dismay.

'Pooh!' said Rosa with a laugh; 'your sister Blanche looked very well in one of my dresses, last year; and you know how stout she is. We will find some means to accommodate them all, depend upon it.'

Mrs John Rowdy's note to dear Rosa, accepting the latter's invitation, was a very gracious and kind one: and Mrs Fitz showed it to her husband when he came back from chambers. But there was another note which had arrived for him by this time from Mr Rowdy – or rather from the firm: and to the effect that Mr F. Timmins had overdrawn his account £28 18s. 6d., and was requested to pay that sum to his obedient servants, Stumpy, Rowdy, and Co.

And Timmins did not like to tell his wife that the contending parties in the Lough Neagh and Lough Corrib Railroad had come to a settlement, and that the fifteen guineas a day had consequently determined. 'I have had seven days of it, though,' he thought; 'and that will be enough to pay for the desk, the dinner, and the glasses, and make all right with Stumpy and Rowdy.'

III

The cards for dinner having been issued, it became the duty of Mrs Timmins to make further arrangements respecting the invitations to the tea-party which was to follow the more substantial meal.

These arrangements are difficult, as any lady knows who is in the habit of entertaining her friends. There are –

People who are offended if you ask them to tea whilst others have been asked to dinner –

People who are offended if you ask them to tea at all; and cry out furiously, 'Good Heavens! Jane, my love, why do these Timminses suppose that I am to leave my dinner-table to attend their —— *soirée?*' (the dear reader my fill up the —— to any strength, according to his liking) – or, 'Upon my word, William, my dear, it is too much to ask us to pay twelve shillings for a brougham, and to spend I don't know how much in gloves, just to make our curtsies in Mrs Timmins's little drawing-room.' Mrs Moser made the latter remark about the Timmins affair, while the former was uttered by Mr Grumpley, barrister-at-law, to his lady, in Gloucester Place.

That there are people who are offended if you don't ask them at all, is a point which I suppose nobody will question. Timmins's earliest friend in life was Simmins, whose wife and family have taken a cottage at Mortlake for the season.

'We can't ask them to come out of the country,' Rosa said to her Fitzroy – (between ourselves, she was delighted that Mrs Simmins was out of the way, and was as jealous of her as every well-regulated woman should be of her husband's female friends) – 'we can't ask them to come so far for the evening.'

'Why no, certainly,' said Fitzroy, who has himself no very great opinion of a tea-party; and so the Simminses were cut out of the list.

And what was the consequence? The consequence was, that Simmins and Timmins cut when they meet at Westminster; that Mrs Simmins sent back all the books which she had borrowed from Rosa, with a withering note of thanks; that Rosa goes about saying that Mrs Simmins squints; that Mrs S., on her side, declares that Rosa is crooked, and behaved shamefully to Captain Hicks, in marrying Fitzroy over him, though she was forced to do it by her mother, and prefers the captain to her husband to this day. If, in a word, these two men could be made to fight, I believe their wives would not be displeased; and the reason of all this misery, rage, and dissension, lies in a poor little twopenny dinner-party in Lilliput Street.

Well, the guests, both for before and after meat, having been asked – old Mrs Gashleigh, Rosa's mother – (and, by consequence, Fitzroy's *dear* mother-in-law, though I promise you that 'dear' is particularly sarcastic) – Mrs Gashleigh of course was sent for, and came with Miss Eliza Gashleigh who plays on the guitar, and Emily, who limps a little, but plays sweetly on the concertina. They live close by – trust them for that. Your mother-in-law is always within hearing, thank our stars for the attention of the dear women. The Gashleighs, I say, live close by, and came early on the morning after Rosa's notes had been issued for the dinner.

When Fitzroy, who was in his little study, which opens into his little dining-room – one of those absurd little rooms which ought to be called a gentleman's pantry, and is scarcely bigger than a shower-bath, or a state cabin in a ship – when Fitzroy heard his mother-in-law's knock, and her well-known scuffling and chattering in the passage, in which she squeezed up young Buttons, the page, while she put questions to him regarding baby, and the cook's health, and whether she had taken what Mrs Gashleigh had sent over night, and the housemaid's health, and whether Mr Timmins had gone to chambers or not? and when, after this preliminary chatter, Buttons flung open the door, announcing – 'Mrs Gashleigh and the young ladies,' Fitzroy laid down his 'Times' newspaper with an expression that had best not be printed in a journal which young people read, and took his hat and walked away.

Mrs Gashleigh has never liked him since he left off calling her mamma, and kissing her. But he said he could not stand it any longer – he was hanged if he would. So he went away to Chambers, leaving the field clear to Rosa, mamma, and the two dear girls.

– Or to one of them, rather; for before leaving the house, he thought he would have a look at little Fitzroy up-stairs in the nursery, and he found the child in the hands of his maternal aunt Eliza, who was holding him and pinching him as if he had been her guitar, I suppose; so that the little fellow bawled pitifully – and his father finally quitted the premises.

No sooner was he gone, and although the party was still a fortnight off, yet the women pounced upon his little Study, and began to put it in order. Some of his papers they pushed up over the bookcase, some they put behind the Encyclopædia, some they crammed into the drawers, where Mrs Gashleigh found three cigars, which she pocketed, and some letters, over which she cast her eye; and by Fitz's return they had the room as neat as possible, and the best glass and dessert-service mustered on the study-table.

It was a very neat and handsome service, as you may be sure Mrs Gashleigh thought, whose rich uncle had purchased it for the young couple, at Spode and Copeland's: but it was only for twelve persons.

It was agreed that it would be, in all respects, cheaper and better to purchase a dozen more dessert plates; and with 'my silver basket in the centre,' Mrs G. said (she is always bragging about that confounded bread-basket), 'we need not have any extra china dishes, and the table will look very pretty.'

On making a roll-call of the glass, it was calculated that at least a dozen or so tumblers, four or five dozen wines, eight water-bottles, and a proper quantity of ice-plates, were requisite; and that, as they would always be useful, it would be best to purchase the articles immediately. Fitz tumbled over the basket containing them, which stood in the hall, as he came in from Chambers, and over the boy who had brought them – and the little bill.

The women had had a long debate, and something like a quarrel, it must be owned, over the bill of fare. Mrs Gashleigh, who had lived a great part of her life in Devonshire, and kept house in great state there, was famous for making some dishes, without which, she thought, no dinner could be perfect. When she proposed her mock-turtle, and stewed pigeons, and gooseberry-cream, Rosa turned up her nose – a pretty little nose it was, by the way, and with a natural turn in that direction.

'Mock-turtle in June, mamma!' said she.

'It was good enough for your grandfather, Rosa,' the mamma replied: 'it was good enough for the Lord High Admiral, when he was at Plymouth; it was good enough for the first men in the county, and relished by Lord Fortyskewer and Lord Rolls; Sir Lawrence Porker ate twice of it after Exeter Races; and I think it might be good enough for—'

'I will *not* have it, mamma!' said Rosa, with a stamp of her foot – and Mrs Gashleigh knew what resolution there was in that; once, when she had tried to physic the baby, there had been a similar fight between them.

So Mrs Gashleigh made out a *carte*, in which the soup was left with a dash – a melancholy vacuum; and in which the pigeons were certainly thrust in amongst the *entrées*; but Rosa determined they never should make an *entrée* at all into *her* dinner-party, but that she would have the dinner her own way.

When Fitz returned, then, and after he had paid the little bill of £6 14*s*. 6*d*. for the glass, Rosa flew to him with her sweetest smiles, and the baby in her arms. And after she had made him remark how the child grew every day more and more like him, and after she had treated him to a number of compliments and caresses, which it were positively fulsome to exhibit in public, and after she had soothed him into good humour by her artless tenderness, she began to speak to him about some little points which she had at heart.

She pointed out with a sigh how shabby the old curtains looked since the dear new glasses which her darling Fitz had given her had been put up in the drawing-room. Muslin curtains cost nothing, and she must and would have them.

The muslin curtains were accorded. She and Fitz went and bought them at Shoolbred's, when you may be sure she treated herself likewise to a neat, sweet, pretty half-mourning (for the Court, you know, is in mourning) – a neat sweet *barège*, or calimanco, or bombazine, or tiffany, or some such thing; but Madame Camille of Regent Street, made it up, and Rosa looked like an angel in it on the night of her little dinner.

'And my sweet,' she continued, after the curtains had been given in, 'mamma and I have been talking about the dinner. She wants to make it very expensive, which I cannot allow. I have been thinking of a delightful and economical plan, and you, my sweetest Fitz, must put it into execution.'

'I have cooked a mutton-chop when I was in chambers,' Fitz said with a laugh. 'Am I to put on a cap and an apron?'

'No; but you are to go to the Megatherium Club (where, you wretch, you are always going without my leave), and you are to beg Monsieur Mirobolant, your famous cook, to send you one of his best aides-de-camp, as I know he will, and with his aid we can dress the dinner and the confectionery at home for *almost nothing*, and we can show those purse-proud Topham Sawyers and Rowdys that the *humble cottage* can furnish forth an elegant entertainment as well as the gilded halls of wealth.'

Fitz agreed to speak to Monsieur Mirobolant. If Rosa had had a fancy for the cook of the prime minister, I believe the deluded creature of a husband would have asked Lord John for the loan of him.

IV

Fitzroy Timmins, whose taste for wine is remarkable for so young a man, is a member of the committee of the Megatherium Club, and the great Mirobolant, good-natured as all great men are, was only too happy to oblige him. A young friend and *protégé* of his, of considerable merit, M. Cavalcadour, happened to be disengaged through the lamented death of Lord Hauncher, with whom young Cavalcadour had made his *début* as an artist. He had nothing to refuse to his master, Mirobolant, and would impress himself to be useful to a *gourmé* so distinguished as Monsieur Timmins. Fitz went away as pleased as Punch with this encomium of the great Mirobolant, and was one of those who voted against the decreasing of Mirobolant's salary, when the measure was proposed by Mr Parings, Colonel Close, and the Screw party in the committee of the club.

Faithful to the promise of his great master, the youthful Cavalcadour called in Lilliput Street the next day. A rich crimson velvet waistcoat, with buttons of blue glass and gold, a variegated blue satin stock, over which a graceful mosaic chain hung in glittering folds, a white hat worn on one side of his long curling ringlets, redolent with the most delightful hair oil – one of those white hats which looks as if it had been just skinned – and a pair of gloves not exactly of the colour of *beurre frais*, but of *beurre* that has been up the chimney, with a natty cane with a gilt knob, completed the upper part, at any rate, of the costume of the young fellow whom the page introduced to Mrs Timmins.

Her mamma and she had been just having a dispute about the gooseberry-cream when Cavalcadour arrived. His presence silenced Mrs Gashleigh; and Rosa, in carrying on a conversation with him in the French language, which she had acquired perfectly in an elegant finishing establishment in Kensington Square, had a great advantage over her mother, who could only pursue the dialogue with very much difficulty, eyeing one or other interlocutor with an alarmed and suspicious look, and gasping out 'We' whenever she thought a proper opportunity arose for the use of that affirmative.

'I have two leetl menus weez me,' said Cavalcadour to Mrs Gashleigh.

'Minews – yes, O indeed,' answered the lady.

'Two little cartes.'

'O two carts! O we,' she said – 'coming, I suppose;' and she looked out of the window to see if they were there.

Cavalcadour smiled; he produced from a pocket-book a pink paper and a blue paper, on which he had written two bills of fare, the last two which he had composed for the lamented Hauncher, and he handed these over to Mrs Fitzroy.

The poor little woman was dreadfully puzzled with these documents, (she has them in her possession still,) and began to read from the pink one as follows: –

DINER POUR 16 PERSONNES.

Potage (clair) à la Rigodon.
Do. à la Prince de Tombuctou.

Deux Poissons.

Saumon de Severne,   Rougets Gratinés
à la Boadicée.   à la Cléopâtre.

Deux Relevés.

Le Chapeau-à-trois-cornes farci à la Robespierre.
Le Tire-botte à l'Odalisque.

Six Entrées.
Sauté de Hannetons à l'Epinglière.
Cotelettes à la Megatherium.
Bourrasque de Veau à la Palsambleu.
Laitances de Carpe en goguette à la Reine Pomaré.
Turban de Volaille à l'Archévêque de Cantorbéry.

And so on with the *entremets*, and *hors d'œuvre*, and the *rotis*, and the *relevés*.

'Madame will see that the dinners are quite simple,' said M. Cavalcadour.

'O quite!' said Rosa, dreadfully puzzled.

'Which would madame like?'

'Which would we like, mamma?' Rosa asked; adding, as if after a little thought, 'I think, sir, we should prefer the blue one.' At which Mrs Gashleigh nodded as knowingly as she could; though pink or blue, I defy anybody to know what these cooks mean by their jargon.

'If you please, madam, we will go down below and examine the scene of operations,' Monsieur Cavalcadour said; and so he was marshalled down the stairs to the kitchen, which he didn't like to name, and appeared before the cook in all his splendour.

He cast a rapid glance round the premises, and a smile of something like contempt lighted up his features. 'Will you bring pen and ink, if you please, and I will write down a few of the articles which will be necessary for us? We shall require, if you please, eight more stew-pans, a couple of braising pans, eight sauté pans, six bain-marie pans, a freezing-pot with accessories, and a few more articles of which I will inscribe the names'; and Mr Cavalcadour did so, dashing down, with the rapidity of genius, a tremendous list of ironmongery goods, which he handed over to Mrs Timmins. She and her mamma were quite frightened by the awful catalogue.

'I will call three days hence and superintend the progress of matters; and we will make the stock for the soup the day before the dinner.'

'Don't you think, sir,' here interposed Mrs Gashleigh, 'that one soup – a fine rich mock-turtle, such as I have seen in the best houses in the West of England, and such as the late Lord Fortyskewer—'

'You will get what is wanted for the soups, if you please,'

Mr Cavalcadour continued, not heeding this interruption, and as bold as a captain on his own quarter-deck; 'for the stock of clear soup, you will get a leg of beef, a leg of veal, and a ham.'

'We munseer,' said the cook, dropping a terrified curtsey. 'A leg of beef, a leg of veal, and a ham.'

'You can't serve a leg of veal at a party,' said Mrs Gashleigh; 'and a leg of beef is not a company dish.'

'Madam, they are to make the stock of the clear soup,' Mr Cavalcadour said.

'*What?*' cried Mrs Gashleigh; and the cook repeated his former expression.

'Never, whilst *I* am in this house,' cried out Mrs Gashleigh, indignantly; 'never in a Christian *English* household; never shall such sinful waste be permitted by *me*. If you wish me to dine, Rosa, you must get a dinner less *expensive*. The Right Honourable Lord Fortyskewer could dine, sir, without these wicked luxuries, and I presume my daughter's guests can.'

'Madame is perfectly at liberty to decide,' said M. Cavalcadour. 'I came to oblige madame and my good friend Mirobolant, not myself.'

'Thank you, sir, I think it *will* be too expensive,' Rosa stammered in a great flutter; 'but I am very much obliged to you.'

'*Il n'y a point d'obligation, madame,*' said Monsieur Alcide Camile Cavalcadour in his most superb manner; and, making a splendid bow to the lady of the house, was respectfully conducted to the upper regions by little Buttons, leaving Rosa frightened, the cook amazed and silent, and Mrs Gashleigh boiling with indignation against the dresser.

Up to that moment, Mrs Blowser, the cook, who had come out of Devonshire with Mrs Gashleigh (of course that lady garrisoned her daughter's house with servants, and expected them to give her information of everything which took place there); up to that moment, I say, the cook had been quite contented with that subterraneous station which she occupied in life, and had a pride in keeping her kitchen neat, bright, and clean. It was, in her opinion, the comfortablest room in the house (we all thought so when we came down of a night to smoke there); and the handsomest kitchen in Lilliput Street.

But after the visit of Cavalcadour, the cook became quite discontented and uneasy in her mind. She talked in a melancholy manner over the area railings to the cooks at twenty-three and twenty-five. She stepped over the way, and conferred with the cook there. She made inquiries at the baker's and at other places about the kitchens in the great houses in Brobdingnag Gardens, and how many spits, bangmarry pans, and stoo pans they had. She thought she could not do with an occasional help, but must have a kitchen-maid. And she was often discovered by a gentleman of the police force, who was, I believe, her cousin, and occasionally visited her when Mrs Gashleigh was not in the house or spying it: – she was discovered, seated with *Mrs Rundell* in her lap, its leaves bespattered with her tears. 'My pease be gone, Pelisse,' she said, 'zins I zaw that ther Franchman': and it was all the faithful fellow could do to console her.

'—the dinner,' said Timmins, in a rage at last: 'having it cooked in the house is out of the question: the bother of it: and the row your mother makes are enough to drive one mad. It won't happen again, I can promise you, Rosa – order it at Fubsby's at one. You can have everything from Fubsby's – from footmen to saltspoons. Let's go and order it at Fubsby's.' 'Darling, if you don't mind the expense, and it will be any relief to you, let us do as you wish,' Rosa said; and she put on her bonnet, and they went off to the grand cook and confectioner of the Brobdingnag quarter.

V

On the arm of her Fitzroy, Rosa went off to Fubsby's, that magnificent shop at the corner of Parliament Place and Alycompayne Square, – a shop into which the rogue had often cast a glance of approbation as he passed; for there are not only the most wonderful and delicious cakes and confections in the window, but at the counter there are almost sure to be three or four of the prettiest women in the whole of this world, with little darling caps of the last French make, with beautiful wavy hair, and the neatest possible waists and aprons.

Yes, there they sit; and, others, perhaps, besides Fitz have cast a sheep's eye through those enormous plate-glass window panes. I suppose it is the fact of perpetually living amongst such a quantity of good things that makes those young ladies so beautiful. They come into the place, let us say, like ordinary people, and gradually grow handsomer and handsomer, until they grow out into the perfect angels you see. It can't be otherwise: if you and I, my dear fellow, were to have a course of that place, we should become beautiful too. They live in an atmosphere of the most delicious pine-apples, blancmanges, creams, (some whipt, and some so good that of course they don't want whipping,) jellies, tipsy-cakes, cherry-brandy – one hundred thousand sweet and lovely things. Look at the preserved fruits, look at the golden ginger, the outspreading ananas, the darling little rogues of China oranges, ranged in the gleaming crystal cylinders. *Mon Dieu!* Look at the strawberries in the leaves. Each of them is as large nearly as a lady's reticule, and looks as if it had been brought up in a nursery to itself. One of those strawberries is a meal for those young ladies behind the counter; they nibble off a little from the side, and if they are very hungry, which can scarcely ever happen, they are allowed to go to the crystal canisters and take out a rout-cake or macaroon. In the evening they sit and tell each other little riddles out of the bon-bons; and when they wish to amuse themselves, they read the most delightful remarks, in the French language, about Love, and Cupid, and Beauty, before they place them inside the crackers. They always are writing down good things into Mr Fubsby's ledgers. It must be a perfect feast to read them. Talk of the Garden of Eden! I believe it was nothing to Mr Fubsby's house; and I have no doubt that after those young ladies have been there a certain time, they get to such a pitch of loveliness at last, that they become complete angels, with wings sprouting out of their lovely shoulders, when (after giving just a preparatory balance or two) they fly up to the counter and perch there for a minute, hop down again, and affectionately kiss the other young ladies, and say 'Good bye, dears, we shall meet again *la haut*,' and then with a whirr of their deliciously scented wings, away they fly for good, whisking over the trees of Brobdingnag Square, and up into the sky, as the policeman touches his hat.

It is up there that they invent the legends for the crackers, and the wonderful riddles and remarks on the bonbons. No mortal, I am sure, could write them.

I never saw a man in such a state as Fitzroy Timmins in the presence of those ravishing houris. Mrs Fitz having explained that they required a dinner for twenty persons, the chief young lady asked what Mr and

Mrs Fitz would like, and named a thousand things, each better than the other, to all of which Fitz instantly said yes. The wretch was in such a state of infatuation that I believe if that lady had proposed to him a frica-seed elephant, or a boa-constrictor in jelly, he would have said, 'Oh yes, certainly; put it down.'

That Peri wrote down in her album a list of things which it would make your mouth water to listen to. But she took it all quite calmly. Heaven bless you! *They* don't care about things that are no delicacies to them! But whatever she chose to write down, Fitzroy let her.

After the dinner and dessert were ordered (at Fubsby's they furnish everything; dinner and dessert, plate and china, servants in your own livery, and if you please, guests of title too), the married couple retreated from that shop of wonders; Rosa delighted that the trouble of the dinner was all off their hands, but she was afraid it would be rather expensive.

'Nothing can be too expensive which pleases *you*, dear,' Fitz said.

'By the way, one of those young women was rather good-looking,' Rosa remarked; 'the one in the cap with the blue ribbons.' (And she cast about the shape of the cap in her mind, and determined to have exactly such another.)

'Think so? I didn't observe,' said the miserable hypocrite by her side; and when he had seen Rosa home, he went back, like an infamous fiend, to order something else which he had forgotten, he said, at Fubsby's. Get out of that Paradise, you cowardly, creeping, vile serpent, you!

Until the day of the dinner, the infatuated fop was *always* going to Fubsby's. *He was remarked there.* He used to go before he went to chambers in the morning, and sometimes on his return from the Temple: but the morning was the time which he preferred; and one day, when he went on one of his eternal pretexts, and was chattering and flirting at the counter, a lady who had been reading yesterday's paper and eating a half-penny bun for an hour in the back shop (if that paradise may be called a shop) – a lady stepped forward, laid down the 'Morning Herald', and con-fronted him.

That lady was Mrs Gashleigh. From that day the miserable Fitzroy was in her power; and she resumed a sway over his house, to shake off which had been the object of his life, and the result of many battles. And for a mere freak – (for, on going into Fubsby's a week afterwards he found the Peris drinking tea out of blue cups, and eating stale bread and butter, when his absurd passion instantly vanished) – I say, for a mere freak, the most intolerable burden of his life was put on his shoulders again – his mother-in-law.

On the day before the little dinner took place – and I promise you we shall come to it in the very next chapter – a tall and elegant middle-aged gentleman, who might have passed for an earl, but that there was a slight incompleteness about his hands and feet, the former being uncommonly red, and the latter large and irregular, was introduced to Mrs Timmins by the page, who announced him as Mr Truncheon.

'I'm Truncheon, ma'am,' he said, with a low bow.

'Indeed!' said Rosa.

'About the dinner, m'm, from Fubsby's, m'm. As you have no butler, m'm, I presume you will wish me to act as sich. I shall bring two persons as haids to-morrow; both answers to the name of John. I'd best, if you please, inspect the premisis, and will think you to allow your young man to show me the pantry and kitching.'

Truncheon spoke in a low voice, and with the deepest, and most respectful melancholy. There is not much expression in his eyes, but from what there is, you would fancy that he was oppressed by a secret sorrow. Rosa trembled as she surveyed this gentleman's size, his splendid appearance, and gravity. 'I am sure,' she said, 'I never shall dare to ask him to hand a glass of water.' Even Mrs Gashleigh, when she came on the morning of the actual dinner-party, to superintend matters, was cowed, and retreated from the kitchen before the calm majesty of Truncheon.

And yet that great man was, like all the truly great – affable.

He put aside his coat and waistcoat (both of evening cut, and looking prematurely splendid as he walked the streets in noonday), and did not disdain to rub the glasses and polish the decanters, and to show young Buttons the proper mode of preparing these articles for a dinner. And while he operated, the maids, and Buttons, and cook, when she could – and what had she but the vegetables to boil? – crowded round him, and listened with wonder as he talked of the great families as he had lived with. That man, as they saw him there before them, had been cab-boy to Lord Tantallan, valet to the Earl of Bareacres, and groom of the chambers to the Duchess Dowager of Fitzbattleaxe. O, it was delightful to hear Mr Truncheon!

VI

On the great, momentous, stupendous day of the dinner, my beloved female reader may imagine that Fitzroy Timmins was sent about his business at an early hour in the morning, while the women began to make preparations to receive their guests. 'There will be no need of your going to Fubsby's,' Mrs Gashleigh said to him, with a look that drove him out of doors. 'Every thing that we require has been ordered *there!* You will please to be back here at 6 o'clock, and not sooner: and I presume you will acquiesce in my arrangements about the *wine.*'

'O yes, mamma,' said the prostrate son-in-law.

'In so large a party – a party beyond some folks' *means* – expensive *wines* are *absurd.* The light sherry at 26*s.*, the champagne at 42*s.*; and you are not to go beyond 36*s.* for the claret and port after dinner. Mind, coffee will be served; and you come upstairs after two rounds of the claret.'

'Of course, of course,' acquiesced the wretch: and hurried out of the house to his chambers, and to discharge the commissions with which the womankind had intrusted him.

As for Mrs Gashleigh, you might have heard her bawling over the house the whole day long. That admirable woman was everywhere; in the kitchen until the arrival of Truncheon, before whom she would not retreat without a battle; on the stairs; in Fitzroy's dressing-room; and in Fitzroy minor's nursery, to whom she gave a dose of her own composition, while the nurse was sent out on a pretext to make purchases of garnish for the dishes to be served for the little dinner. Garnish for the dishes! As if the folks at Fubsby's could not garnish dishes better than Gashleigh, with her stupid old-world devices of laurel leaves, parsley, and cut turnips! Why, there was not a dish served that day that was not covered over with skewers, on which troufles, crayfish mushrooms, and forced-meat were impaled. When old Gashleigh went down with her barbarian bunches of holly and greens to stick about the meats, even the cook saw their incongruity, and, at Truncheon's orders, flung the whole shrubbery into the dust-house, where, while poking about the premises, you may be sure Mrs G. saw it.

Every candle which was to be burned that night (including the tallow candle, which she said was a good enough bed-light for Fitzroy) she stuck into the candlesticks with her own hands, giving her own high-shouldered plated candlesticks of the year 1798 the place of honour. She upset all poor Rosa's floral arrangements, turning the nosegays from one vase into the other without any pity, and was never tired of beating, and pushing, and patting, and *wapping* the curtain and sofa draperies into shape in the little drawing-room.

In Fitz's own apartments she revelled with peculiar pleasure. It has been described how she had sacked his Study and pushed away his papers, some of which, including three cigars, and the commencement of an article for the 'Law Magazine', 'Lives of the Sheriff's Officers', he has never been able to find to this day. Mamma now went into the little room in the back regions, which is Fitz's dressing-room, (and was destined to be a cloak-room,) and here she rummaged to her heart's delight.

In an incredibly short space of time she examined all his outlying pockets, drawers, and letters; she inspected his socks and handkerchiefs in the top drawers; and on the dressing-table, his razors, shaving-strop, and hair-oil. She carried off his silver-topped scent-bottle out of his dressing-case, and a half-dozen of his favourite pills (which Fitz possesses in common with every well-regulated man), and probably administered them to her own family. His boots, glossy pumps, and slippers, she pushed into the shower-bath, where the poor fellow stepped into them the next morning, in the midst of a pool in which they were lying. The baby was found sucking his boot-hooks the next day in the nursery; and as for the bottle of varnish for his shoes, (which he generally paints upon the trees himself, having a pretty taste in that way,) it could never be found to the present hour; but it was remarked that the young Master Gashleighs, when they came home for the holidays, always wore lacquered highlows; and the reader may draw his conclusions from *that* fact.

In the course of the day all the servants gave Mrs Timmins warning.

The cook said she coodn't abear it no longer, aving Mrs G. always about her kitching, with her fingers in all the saucepans. Mrs G. had got her the place, but she preferred one as Mrs G. didn't get for her.

The nurse said she was come to nuss Master Fitzroy, and knew her duty; his grandmamma wasn't his nuss, and was always aggrawating her, – Missus must shoot herself elsewhere.

The housemaid gave utterance to the same sentiments in language more violent.

Little Buttons bounced up to his mistress, said he was butler of the family, Mrs G. was always poking about his pantry, and dam if he'd stand it.

At every moment Rosa grew more and more bewildered. The baby howled a great deal during the day. His large china Christening-bowl was cracked by Mrs Gashleigh altering the flowers in it, and pretending to be very cool, whilst her hands shook with rage.

'Pray go on, mamma,' Rosa said with tears in her eyes. 'Should you like to break the chandelier?'

'Ungrateful, unnatural child!' bellowed the other; 'only that I know you couldn't do without me, I'd leave the house this minute.'

'As you wish,' said Rosa; but Mrs G. *didn't* wish: and in this juncture Truncheon arrived.

That officer surveyed the dining-room, laid the cloth there with admirable precision and neatness; ranged the plate on the side-board with graceful accuracy, but objected to that old thing in the centre, as he called Mrs Gashleigh's silver basket, as cumbrous and useless for the table, where they would want all the room they could get.

Order was not restored to the house, nor, indeed, any decent progress made, until this great man came: but where there was a revolt before, and a general disposition to strike work and to yell out defiance against Mrs Gashleigh, who was sitting bewildered and furious in the drawing-room – where there was before commotion, at the appearance of the master-spirit, all was peace and unanimity: the cook went back to her pans, the housemaid busied herself with the china and glass, cleaning some articles and breaking others, Buttons sprang up and down the stairs, obedient to the orders of his chief, and all things went well and in their season.

At six, the man with the wine came from Binney and Latham's. At a quarter-past six, Timmins himself arrived.

At half-past six, he might have been heard shouting out for his varnished boots – but we know where *those* had been hidden – and for his dressing things; but Mrs Gashleigh had put them away.

As in his vain inquiries for these articles he stood shouting, 'Nurse! Buttons! Rosa, my dear!' and the most fearful execrations up and down the stairs, Mr Truncheon came out on him.

'Igscuse me, sir,' says he, 'but it's impawsable. We can't dine twenty at that table – not if you set 'em out awinder, we can't.'

'What's to be done?' asked Fitzroy, in an agony; 'they've all said they'd come.'

'Can't do it,' said the other; 'with two top and bottom – and your table is as narrow as a bench – we can't hold more than heighteen, and then each person's helbows will be into his neighbour's cheer.'

'Rosa! Mrs Gashleigh!' cried out Timmins, 'come down and speak to this gentl— this –'

'Truncheon, sir,' said the man.

The women descended from the drawing-room. 'Look and see, ladies,' he said, inducting them into the dinning-room; 'there's the room, there's the table laid for heighteen, and I defy you to squeege in more.'

'One person in a party always fails,' said Mrs Gashleigh, getting alarmed.

'That's nineteen,' Mr Truncheon remarked; 'we must knock another hoff, mam'; and he looked her hard in the face.

Mrs Gashleigh was very red and nervous, and paced, or rather squeezed round the table (it was as much as she could do) – the chairs could not be put any closer than they were. It was impossible, unless the *convive* sat as a centre-piece in the middle, to put another guest at that table.

'Look at that lady movin round, sir. You see now the difficklty; if my men wasn't thinner, they couldn't hoperate at all,' Mr Truncheon observed, who seemed to have a spite to Mrs Gashleigh.

'What is to be done?' she said, with purple accents.

'My dearest mamma,' Rosa cried out, 'you must stop at home – how sorry I am!' And she shot one glance at Fitzroy, who shot another at the great Truncheon, who held down his eyes.

'We could manage with heighteen,' he said, mildly.

Mrs Gashleigh gave a hideous laugh.

She went away. At eight o'clock she was pacing at the corner of the street, and actually saw the company arrive. First came the Topham Sawyers in their light blue carriage, with the white hammer-cloth, and blue and white ribbons – their footmen drove the house down with the knocking.

Then followed the ponderous and snuff-coloured vehicle, with faded gilded wheels and brass earl's coronets all over it, the conveyance of the House of Bungay. The Countess of Bungay and daughter stepped out of the carriage. The fourteenth Earl of Bungay couldn't come.

Sir Thomas and Lady Gulpin's fly made its appearance, from which issued the general with his star, and Lady Gulpin in yellow satin. The Rowdy's brougham followed next; after which Mrs Butt's handsome equipage drove up.

The two friends of the house, young gentlemen from the Temple, now arrived in cab No. 9996. We tossed up, in fact, which should pay the fare.

Mr Ranville Ranville walked, and was dusting his boots as the Templars drove up. Lord Castlenoddy came out of a twopenny omnibus. Funnyman, the wag, came last, whirling up rapidly in a Hansom, just as Mrs Gashleigh, with rage in her heart, was counting that two people had failed, and that there were only seventeen after all.

Mr Truncheon passed our names to Mr Billiter, who bawled them out on the stairs. Rosa was smiling in a pink dress, and looking as fresh as an angel, and received her company with that grace which has always characterised her.

The moment of the dinner arrived, old Lady Bungay scuffled off on the arm of Fitzroy, while the rear was brought up by Rosa and Lord Castlemouldy, of Ballyshanvanvoght Castle, Co. Tipperary. Some fellows who had the luck, took down ladies to dinner. I was not sorry to be out of the way of Mrs Rowdy with her dandyfied airs, or of that high and mighty county princess, Mrs Topham Sawyer.

VII

Of course it does not become the present writer, who has partaken of the best entertainment which his friends could supply, to make fun of their (somewhat ostentatious, as it must be confessed) hospitality. If they gave a dinner beyond their means, it is no business of mine. I hate a man who goes and eats a friend's meat, and then blabs the secrets of the mahogany.

Such a man deserves never to be asked to dinner again; and, though at the close of a London season that seems no great loss, and you sicken of a white-bait as you would of a whale – yet we must always remember that there's another season coming, and hold our tongues for the present.

As for describing, then, the mere victuals on Timmins's table, that would be absurd. Everybody – (I mean of the genteel world, of course, of which I make no doubt the reader is a polite ornament) – everybody has the same everything in London. You see the same coats, the same dinners, the same boiled fowls and mutton, the same cutlets, fish, and cucumbers, the same lumps of Wenham-lake ice, &c. The waiters, with white neck-cloths, are as like each other everywhere as the peas which they hand round with the ducks of the second course. Can't any one invent anything new?

The only difference between Timmins's dinner and his neighbour's was, that he had hired, as we have said, the greater part of the plate, and that his cowardly conscience magnified faults and disasters of which no one else probably took heed.

But Rosa thought, from the supercilious air with which Mrs Topham Sawyer was eyeing the plate and other arrangements, that she was remarking the difference of the ciphers on the forks and spoons – (which had, in fact, been borrowed from every one of Fitzroy's friends – I know, for instance, that he had my six, among others, and only returned five, along with a battered, old, black-pronged, plated abomination, which I have no doubt belongs to Mrs Gashleigh, whom I hereby request to send back mine in exchange) – their guilty consciences, I say, made them fancy that every one was spying out their domestic deficiencies; whereas, it is probable that nobody present thought of their failings at all. People never do; they never see holes in their neighbours' coats – they are too indolent, simple, and charitable.

Some things, however, one could not help remarking; for instance, though Fitz is my closest friend, yet could I avoid seeing and being amused by his perplexity and his dismal efforts to be facetious? His eye wandered all round the little room with quick uneasy glances, very different from those frank and jovial looks with which he is accustomed to welcome you to a leg of mutton; and Rosa, from the other end of the table, and over the flowers, *entrée* dishes, and wine-coolers, telegraphed him with signals of corresponding alarm. Poor devils! why did they ever go beyond that leg of mutton?

Funnyman was not brilliant in conversation, scarcely opening his mouth, except for the purposes of feasting. The fact is our friend Tom Dawson was at table, who knew all his stories, and in his presence the greatest wag is always silent and uneasy.

Fitz has a very pretty wit of his own, and a good reputation on Circuit; but he is timid before great people. And indeed the presence of that awful Lady Bungay on his right hand, was enough to damp him. She was in Court-mourning (for the late Prince of Schlippen-schloppen). She had on a large black funereal turban and appurtenances, and a vast breast-plate of twinkling, twiddling, black bugles. No wonder a man could not be gay in talking to *her.*

Mrs Rowdy and Mrs Topham Sawyer love each other as women do who have the same receiving nights, and ask the same society; they were only separated by Ranville Ranville, who tries to be well with both: and they talked at each other across him.

Topham and Rowdy growled out a conversation about Rum, Ireland, and the Navigation Laws, quit unfit for print. Sawyer never speaks three words without mentioning the House and the Speaker.

The Irish Peer said nothing (which was a comfort); but he ate and drank of everything which came in his way; and cut his usual absurd figure in dyed whiskers and a yellow under-waistcoat.

General Gulpin sported his star, and looked fat and florid, but melancholy. His wife ordered away his dinner, just like honest Sancho's physician at Barataria.

Botherby's stories about Lamartine are as old as the hills, since the barricades of last month; and he could not get in a word or cut the slightest figure. And as for Tom Dawson, he was carrying on an undertoned small talk with Lady Barbara St Mary's, so that there was not much conversation worth record going on *within* the dining-room.

Outside, it was different. Those houses in Lilliput Street are so uncommonly compact, that you can hear everything which takes place all over the tenement; and so,

In the awful pauses of the banquet, and the hall-door being furthermore open, we had the benefit of hearing

The cook, and the occasional cook, below stairs, exchanging rapid phrases regarding the dinner;

The smash of the soup-tureen, and swift descent of the kitchen-maid and soup-ladle down the stairs to the lower regions. This accident created a laugh, and rather amused Fitzroy and the company, and caused Funny-man to say, bowing to Rosa, that she was mistress of herself, though China fall. But she did not heed him, for at that moment another noise commenced, namely, that of

The baby in the upper rooms, who commenced a series of piercing yells, which, though stopped by the sudden clapping to of the nursery-door, were only more dreadful to the mother when suppressed. She would have given a guinea to go upstairs and have done with the whole entertainment.

A thundering knock came at the door very early after the dessert, and the poor soul took a speedy opportunity of summoning the ladies to depart, though you may be sure it was only old Mrs Gashleigh, who had come with her daughters – of course the first person to come. I saw her red gown whisking up the stairs, which were covered with plates and dishes, over which she trampled.

Instead of having any quiet after the retreat of the ladies, the house was kept in a rattle, and the glasses jingled on the table as the flymen and coachmen plied the knocker, and the *soirée* came in. From my place I could see everything; the guests as they arrived (I remarked very few carriages, mostly cabs and flies), and a little crowd of blackguard boys and children, who were formed round the door, and gave ironical cheers to the folks as they stepped out of their vehicles.

As for the evening party, if a crowd in the dog-days is pleasant, poor Mrs Timmins certainly had a successful *soirée*. You could hardly move on the stair. Mrs Sternhold broke in the banisters, and nearly fell through. There was such a noise and chatter you could not hear the singing of the Miss Gashleighs, which was no great loss. Lady Bungay could hardly get to her carriage, being entangled with Colonel Wedgewood in the passage. An absurd attempt was made to get up a dance of some kind, but before Mrs Crowder had got round the room, the hanging-lamp in the dining-room below was stove in, and fell with a crash on the table, now prepared for refreshment.

Why, in fact, did the Timminses give that party at all? It was quite beyond their means. They have offended a score of their old friends, and pleased none of their acquaintances. So angry were many who were not asked, that poor Rosa says she must now give a couple more parties and take in those not previously invited. And I know for a fact that Fubsby's bill is not yet paid; nor Binney and Latham's, the wine-merchants; that the breakage and hire of glass and china cost ever so much money; that every true friend of Timmins has cried out against his absurd extravagance, and that now, when every one is going out of town Fitz has hardly money to pay his Circuit, much more to take Rosa to a watering-place, as he wished and promised.

As for Mrs Gashleigh, the only feasible plan of economy which she can suggest, is that she should come and live with her daughter and son-in-law, and that they should keep house together. If he agrees to this, she has a little sum at the banker's, with which she would not mind easing his present difficulties; and the poor wretch is so utterly bewildered and crest-fallen that it is very likely he will become her victim.

The Topham Sawyers, when they go down into the country, will represent Fitz as a ruined man and reckless prodigal; his uncle, the attorney, from whom he has expectations, will most likely withdraw his business, and adopt some other member of his family – Blanche Crowder for instance, whose husband, the doctor, has had high words with poor Fitzroy already, of course at the women's instigation – and all these accumulated miseries fall upon the unfortunate wretch because he was good-natured, and his wife would have a Little Dinner.

ELIZABETH GASKELL

Six Weeks at Heppenheim

After I left Oxford, I determined to spend some months in travel before settling down in life. My father had left me a few thousands, the income arising from which would be enough to provide for all the necessary requirements of a lawyer's education; such as lodgings in a quiet part of London, fees and payment to the distinguished barrister with whom I was to read; but there would be small surplus left over for luxuries or amusements; and as I was rather in debt on leaving college, since I had forestalled my income, and the expenses of my travelling would have to be defrayed out of my capital, I determined that they should not exceed fifty pounds. As long as that sum would last me I would remain abroad; when it was spent my holiday should be over, and I would return and settle down somewhere in the neighbourhood of Russell Square, in order to be near Mr —'s chambers in Lincoln's-inn. I had to wait in London for one day while my passport was being made out, and I went to examine the streets in which I purposed to live; I had picked them out, from studying a map, as desirable; and so they were, if judged entirely by my reason; but their aspect was very depressing to one country-bred, and just fresh from the beautiful street-architecture of Oxford. The thought of living in such a monotonous gray district for years made me all the more anxious to prolong my holiday by all the economy which could eke out my fifty pounds. I thought I could make it last for one hundred days at least. I was a good walker, and had no very luxurious tastes in the matter of accommodation or food; I had as fair a knowledge of German and French as any untravelled Englishman can have; and I resolved to avoid expensive hotels such as my own countrymen frequented.

I have stated this much about myself to explain how I fell in with the little story that I am going to record, but with which I had not much to do, – my part in it being little more than that of a sympathizing spectator. I had been through France into Switzerland, where I had gone beyond my strength in the way of walking, and I was on my way home, when one evening I came to the village of Heppenheim, on the Berg-Strasse. I had strolled about the dirty town of Worms all morning, and dined in a filthy hotel; and after that I had crossed the Rhine, and walked through Lorsch to Heppenheim. I was unnaturally tired and languid as I dragged myself up the rough-paved and irregular village street to the inn recommended to me. It was a large building, with a green court before it. A cross-looking but scrupulously clean hostess received me, and showed me into a large room with a dinner-table in it, which, though it might have accommo-dated thirty or forty guests, only stretched down half the length of the eating-room. There were windows at each end of the room; two looked to the front of the house, on which the evening shadows had already fallen; the opposite two were partly doors, opening into a large garden full of trained fruit-trees and beds of vegetables, amongst which rose-bushes and other flowers seemed to grow by permission, not by original intention. There was a stove at each end of the room, which, I suspect, had originally been divided into two. The door by which I had entered was exactly in the middle, and opposite to it was another, leading to a great bed-chamber, which my hostess showed me as my sleeping quarters for the night.

If the place had been much less clean and inviting, I should have remained there; I was almost surprised myself at my vis inertia; once seated in the last warm rays of the slanting sun by the garden window, I was disinclined to move, or even to speak. My hostess had taken my orders as to my evening meal, and had left me. The sun went down, and I grew shivery. The vast room looked cold and bare; the darkness brought out shadows that perplexed me, because I could not fully make out the objects that produced them after dazzling my eyes by gazing out into the crim-son light.

Some one came in; it was the maiden to prepare for my supper. She began to lay the cloth at one end of the large table. There was a smaller one close by me. I mustered up my voice, which seemed a little as if it was getting beyond my control, and called to her, –

'Will you let me have my supper here on this table?'

She came near; the light fell on her while I was in shadow. She was a tall young woman, with a fine strong figure, a pleasant face, expressive of goodness and sense, and with a good deal of comeliness about it, too, although the fair complexion was bronzed and reddened by weather, so as to have lost much of its delicacy, and the features, as I had afterwards opportunity enough of observing, were anything but regular. She had white teeth, however, and well-opened blue eyes – grave-looking eyes which had shed tears for past sorrow – plenty of light-brown hair, rather elaborately plaited, and fastened up by two great silver pins. That was all – perhaps more than all – I noticed that first night. She began to lay the cloth where I had directed. A shiver passed over me: she looked at me, and then said, –

'The gentleman is cold: shall I light the stove?'

Something vexed me – I am not usually so impatient: it was the coming-on of serious illness – I did not like to be noticed so closely; I believed that food would restore me, and I did not want to have my meal delayed, as I feared it might be by the lighting of the stove; and most of all I was feverishly annoyed by movement. I answered sharply and abruptly, –

'No; bring supper quickly; that is all I want.'

Her quiet, sad eyes met mine for a moment; but I saw no change in their expression, as if I had vexed her by my rudeness: her countenance did not for an instant lose its look of patient sense, and that is pretty nearly all I can remember of Thekla that first evening at Heppenheim.

I suppose I ate my supper, or tried to do so, at any rate; and I must have gone to bed, for days after I became conscious of lying there, weak as a new-born babe, and with a sense of past pain in all my weary limbs. As is the case in recovering from fever, one does not care to connect facts, much less to reason upon them; so how I came to be lying in that strange bed, in that large, half-furnished room; in what house that room was; in what town, in what country, I did not take the trouble to recal. It was of much more consequence to me then to discover what was the well-known herb that gave the scent to the clean, coarse sheets in which I lay. Gradually I extended my observations, always confining myself to the present. I must have been well cared-for by some one, and that lately, too, for the window was shaded, so as to prevent the morning sun from coming in upon the bed; there was the crackling of fresh wood in the great white china stove, which must have been newly replenished within a short time.

By-and-by the door opened slowly. I cannot tell why, but my impulse was to shut my eyes as if I were still asleep. But I could see through my apparently closed eyelids. In came, walking on tip-toe, with a slow care that defeated its object, two men. The first was aged from thirty to forty, in the dress of a Black Forest peasant, – old-fashioned coat and knee-breeches of strong blue cloth, but of a thoroughly good quality; he was followed by an older man, whose dress, of more pretension as to cut and colour (it was all black), was, nevertheless, as I had often the opportunity of observing afterwards, worn threadbare.

Their first sentences, in whispered German, told me who they were: the landlord of the inn where I was lying a helpless log, and the village doctor who had been called in. The latter felt my pulse, and nodded his head repeatedly in approbation. I had instinctively known that I was getting better, and hardly cared for this confirmation; but it seemed to give the truest pleasure to the landlord, who shook the hand of the doctor, in a pantomime expressive of as much thankfulness as if I had been his brother. Some low-spoken remarks were made, and then some question was asked, to which, apparently, my host was unable to reply. He left the room, and in a minute or two returned, followed by Thekla, who was questioned by the doctor, and replied with a quiet clearness, showing how carefully the details of my illness had been observed by her. Then she left the room, and, as if every minute had served to restore to my brain its power of combining facts, I was suddenly prompted to open my eyes, and ask in the best German I could muster what day of the month it was; not that I clearly remembered the date of my arrival at Heppenheim, but I knew it was about the beginning of September.

Again the doctor conveyed his sense of extreme satisfaction in a series of rapid pantomimic nods, and then replied in deliberate but tolerable English, to my great surprise, –

'It is the 29th of September, my dear sir. You must thank the dear God. Your fever has made its course of twenty-one days. Now patience and care must be practised. The good host and his household will have the care; you must have the patience. If you have relations in England, I will do my endeavours to tell them the state of your health.'

'I have no near relations,' said I, beginning in my weakness to cry, as I remembered, as if it had been a dream, the days when I had father, mother, sister.

'Chut, chut!' said he; then, turning to the landlord, he told him in German to make Thekla bring me one of her good bouillons; after which I was to have certain medicines, and to sleep as undisturbedly as possible. For days, he went on, I should require constant watching and careful feeding; every twenty minutes I was to have something, either wine or soup, in small quantities.

A dim notion came into my hazy mind that my previous husbandry of my fifty pounds, by taking long walks and scanty diet, would prove in the end very bad economy; but I sank into dozing unconsciousness before I could quite follow out my idea. I was roused by the touch of a spoon on my lips; it was Thekla feeding me. Her sweet, grave face had something approaching to a mother's look of tenderness upon it, as she gave me spoonful after spoonful with gentle patience and dainty care: and then I fell asleep once more. When next I wakened it was night; the stove was lighted, and the burning wood made a pleasant crackle, though I could only see the outlines and edges of red flame through the crevices of the small iron door. The uncurtained window on my left looked into the purple, solemn night. Turning a little, I saw Thekla sitting near a table, sewing diligently at some great white piece of household work. Every now and then she stopped to snuff the candle; sometimes she began to ply her needle again immediately; but once or twice she let her busy hands lie idly in her lap, and looked into the darkness and thought deeply for a moment or two; these pauses always ended in a kind of sobbing sigh, the sound of which seemed to restore her to self-consciousness, and she took to her sewing even more diligently than before. Watching her had a sort of dreamy interest for me; this diligence of hers was a pleasant contrast to my repose; it seemed to enhance the flavour of my rest. I was too much of an animal just then to have my sympathy, or even my curiosity, strongly excited by her look of sad remembrance, or by her sighs.

After a while she gave a little start, looked at a watch lying by her on the table, and came, shading the candle by her hand, softly to my bedside. When she saw my open eyes she went to a porringer placed at the top of the stove, and fed me with soup. She did not speak while doing this. I was half aware that she had done it many times since the doctor's visit, although this seemed to be the first time that I was fully awake. She passed her arm under the pillow on which my head rested, and raised me a very little; her support was as firm as a man's could have been. Again back to her work, and I to my slumbers, without a word being exchanged.

It was broad daylight when I wakened again; I could see the sunny atmosphere of the garden outside stealing in through the nicks at the side of the shawl hung up to darken the room – a shawl which I was sure had not been there when I had observed the window in the night. How gently my nurse must have moved about while doing her thoughtful act!

My breakfast was brought me by the hostess; she who had received me on my first arrival at this hospitable inn. She meant to do everything kindly, I am sure; but a sick room was not her place; by a thousand little mal-adroitnesses she fidgeted me past bearing; her shoes creaked, her dress rustled; she asked me questions about myself which it irritated me to answer; she congratulated me on being so much better, while I was faint for want of the food which she delayed giving me in order to talk. My host had more sense in him when he came in, although his shoes creaked as well as hers. By this time I was somewhat revived, and could talk a little; besides, it seemed churlish to be longer without acknowledging so much kindness received.

'I am afraid I have been a great trouble,' said I. 'I can only say that I am truly grateful.'

His good broad face reddened, and he moved a little uneasily.

'I don't see how I could have done otherwise than I – than we, did,' replied he, in the soft German of the district. 'We were all glad enough to do what we could; I don't say it was a pleasure, because it is our busiest time of year, – but then,' said he, laughing a little awkwardly, as if he feared his expression might have been misunderstood, 'I don't suppose it has been a pleasure to you either, sir, to be laid up so far from home.'

'No, indeed.'

'I may as well tell you now, sir, that we had to look over your papers and clothes. In the first place, when you were so ill I would fain have let your kinsfolk know, if I could have found a clue; and besides, you needed linen.'

'I am wearing a shirt of yours though,' said I, touching my sleeve.

'Yes, sir!' said he again, reddening a little. 'I told Thekla to take the finest out of the chest; but I am afraid you find it coarser than your own.'

For all answer I could only lay my weak hand on the great brown paw resting on the bed-side. He gave me a sudden squeeze in return that I thought would have crushed my bones.

'I beg your pardon, sir,' said he, misinterpreting the sudden look of pain which I could not repress; 'but watching a man come out of the shadow of death into life makes one feel very friendly towards him.'

'No old or true friend that I have had could have done more for me than you, and your wife, and Thekla, and the good doctor.'

'I am a widower,' said he, turning round the great wedding-ring that decked his third finger. 'My sister keeps house for me, and takes care of the children, – that is to say, she does it with the help of Thekla, the house-maiden. But I have other servants,' he continued. 'I am well to do, the good God be thanked! I have land, and cattle, and vineyards. It will soon be our vintage-time, and then you must go and see my grapes as they come into the village. I have a *"chasse"*, too, in the Odenwald; perhaps one day you will be strong enough to go and shoot the *"chevreuil"* with me.'

His good, true heart was trying to make me feel like a welcome guest. Some time afterwards I learnt from the doctor that – my poor fifty pounds being nearly all expended – my host and he had been brought to believe in my poverty, as the necessary examination of my clothes and papers showed so little evidence of wealth. But I myself have but little to do with my story; I only name these things, and repeat these conversations, to show what a true, kind, honest man my host was. By the way, I may as well call him by his name henceforward, Fritz Müller. The doctor's name, Wiedermann.

I was tired enough with this interview with Fritz Müller; but when Dr Wiedermann came he pronounced me to be much better; and through the day much the same course was pursued as on the previous one: being fed, lying still, and sleeping, were my passive and active occupations. It was a hot, sunshiny day, and I craved for air. Fresh air does not enter into the pharmacopœia of a German doctor; but somehow I obtained my wish. During the morning hours the window through which the sun streamed – the window looking on to the front court – was opened a little;

and through it I heard the sounds of active life, which gave me pleasure and interest enough. The hen's cackle, the cock's exultant call when he had found the treasure of a grain of corn, – the movements of a tethered donkey, and the cooing and whirring of the pigeons which lighted on the window-sill, gave me just subjects enough for interest. Now and then a cart or carriage drove up, – I could hear them ascending the rough village street long before they stopped at the 'Halbmond', the village inn. Then there came a sound of running and haste in the house; and Thekla was always called for in sharp, imperative tones. I heard little children's foot-steps, too, from time to time; and once there must have been some childish accident or hurt, for a shrill, plaintive little voice kept calling out, 'Thekla, Thekla, liebe Thekla.' Yet, after the first early morning hours, when my hostess attended on my wants, it was always Thekla who came to give me my food or my medicine; who redded up my room; who arranged the degree of light, shifting the temporary curtain with the shifting sun; and always as quietly and deliberately as though her attendance upon me were her sole work. Once or twice my hostess came into the large eating-room (out of which my room opened), and called Thekla away from whatever was her occupation in my room at the time, in a sharp, injured, imperative whisper. Once I remember it was to say that sheets were wanted for some stranger's bed, and to ask where she, the speaker, could have put the keys, in a tone of irritation, as though Thekla were responsible for Fräulein Müller's own forgetfulness.

Night came on; the sounds of daily life died away into silence; the children's voices were no more heard; the poultry were all gone to roost; the beasts of burden to their stables; and travellers were housed. Then Thekla came in softly and quietly, and took up her appointed place, after she had done all in her power for my comfort. I felt that I was in no state to be left all those weary hours which intervened between sunset and sunrise; but I did feel ashamed that this young woman, who had watched by me all the previous night, and for aught I knew, for many before, and had worked hard, been run off her legs, as English servants would say, all day long, should come and take up her care of me again; and it was with a feeling of relief that I saw her head bend forwards, and finally rest on her arms, which had fallen on the white piece of sewing spread before her on the table. She slept; and I slept. When I wakened dawn was stealing into the room, and making pale the lamplight. Thekla was standing by the stove, where she had been preparing the bouillon I should require on wakening. But she did not notice my half-open eyes, although her face was turned towards the bed. She was reading a letter slowly, as if its words were familiar to her, yet as though she were trying afresh to extract some fuller or some different meaning from their construction. She folded it up softly and slowly, and replaced it in her pocket with the quiet movement habitual to her. Then she looked before her, not at me, but at vacancy filled up by memories; and as the enchanter brought up the scenes and people which she saw, but I could not, her eyes filled with tears – tears that gathered almost imperceptibly to herself as it would seem – for when one large drop fell on her hands (held slightly together before her as she stood) she started a little, and brushed her eyes with the back of her hand, and then came towards the bed to see if I was awake. If I had not witnessed her previous emotion, I could never have guessed that she had any hidden sorrow or pain from her manner; tranquil, self-restrained as usual. The thought of this letter haunted me, especially as more than once I, wakeful or watchful during the ensuing nights, either saw it in her hands, or suspected that she had been recurring to it from noticing the same sorrowful, dreamy look upon her face when she thought herself unobserved. Most likely every one has noticed how inconsistently out of proportion some ideas become when one is shut up in any place without change of scene or thought. I really grew quite irritated about this letter. If I did not see it, I suspected it lay *perdu* in her pocket. What was in it? Of course it was a love-letter; but if so, what was going wrong in the course of her love? I became like a spoilt child in my recovery; every one whom I saw for the time being was thinking only of me, so it was perhaps no wonder that I became my sole object of thought; and at last the gratification of my curiosity about this letter seemed to me a duty that I owed to myself. As long as my fidgety inquisitiveness remained ungratified, I felt as if I could not get well. But to do myself justice, it was more than inquisitiveness. Thekla had tended me with the gentle, thoughtful care of a sister, in the midst of her busy life. I could often hear the Fräulein's sharp voice outside blaming her for something that had gone wrong; but I never heard much from Thekla in reply. Her name was called in various tones by different people, more frequently than I could count, as if her services were in perpetual requisition, yet I was never neglected, or even long uncared-for. The doctor was kind and attentive; my host friendly and really generous; his sister subdued her acerbity of manner when in my room, but Thekla was the one of all to whom I owed my comforts, if not my life. If I could do anything to smooth her path (and a little money goes a great way in these primitive parts of Germany), how willingly would I give it? So one night I began – she was no longer needed to watch by my bedside, but she was arranging my room before leaving me for the night –

'Thekla,' said I, 'you don't belong to Heppenheim, do you?'

She looked at me, and reddened a little.

'No. Why do you ask?'

'You have been so good to me that I cannot help wanting to know more about you. I must needs feel interested in one who has been by my side through my illness as you have. Where do your friends live? Are your parents alive?'

All this time I was driving at the letter.

'I was born at Altenahr. My father is an innkeeper there. He owns the "Golden Stag". My mother is dead, and he has married again, and has many children.'

'And your stepmother is unkind to you,' said I, jumping to a conclusion.

'Who said so?' asked she, with a shade of indignation in her tone. 'She is a right good woman, and makes my father a good wife.'

'Then why are you here living so far from home?'

Now the look came back to her face which I had seen upon it during the night hours when I had watched her by stealth; a dimming of the grave frankness of her eyes, a light quiver at the corners of her mouth. But all she said was, 'It was better.'

Somehow, I persisted with the wilfulness of an invalid. I am half ashamed of it now.

'But why better, Thekla? Was there—' How should I put it? I stopped a little, and then rushed blindfold at my object: 'Has not that letter which you read so often something to do with your being here?'

She fixed me with her serious eyes till I believe I reddened far more than she; and I hastened to pour out, incoherently enough, my conviction that she had some secret care, and my desire to help her if she was in any trouble.

'You cannot help me,' said she, a little softened by my explanation, though some shade of resentment at having been thus surreptitiously watched yet lingered in her manner. 'It is an old story; a sorrow gone by, past, at least it ought to be, only sometimes I am foolish' – her tones were softening now – 'and it is punishment enough that you have seen my folly.'

'If you had a brother here, Thekla, you would let him give you his sympathy if he could not give you his help, and you would not blame yourself if you had shown him your sorrow, should you? I tell you again, let me be as a brother to you.'

'In the first place, sir' – this 'sir' was to mark the distinction between me and the imaginary brother – 'I should have been ashamed to have shown even a brother my sorrow, which is also my reproach and my disgrace.' These were strong words; and I suppose my face showed that I attributed to them a still stronger meaning than they warranted; but *honi soit qui mal y pense* – for she went on dropping her eyes and speaking hurriedly.

'My shame and my reproach is this: I have loved a man who has not loved me' – she grasped her hands together till the fingers made deep white dents in the rosy flesh – 'and I can't make out whether he ever did, or whether he did once and is changed now; if only he did once love me, I could forgive myself.'

With hasty, trembling hands she began to rearrange the tisane and medicines for the night on the little table at my bed-side. But, having got thus far, I was determined to persevere.

'Thekla,' said I, 'tell me all about it, as you would to your mother, if she were alive. There are often misunderstandings which, never set to rights, make the misery and desolation of a life-time.'

She did not speak at first. Then she pulled out the letter, and said, in a quiet, hopeless tone of voice: –

'You can read German writing? Read that, and see if I have any reason for misunderstanding.'

The letter was signed 'Franz Weber,' and dated from some small town in Switzerland – I forget what – about a month previous to the time when I read it. It began with acknowledging the receipt of some money which had evidently been requested by the writer, and for which the thanks were almost fulsome; and then, by the quietest transition in the world, he went on to consult her as to the desirability of his marrying some girl in the place from which he wrote, saying that this Anna Somebody was only eighteen and very pretty, and her father a well-to-do shopkeeper, and adding, with coarse coxcombry, his belief that he was not indifferent to the maiden herself. He wound up by saying that, if this marriage did take place, he should certainly repay the various sums of money which Thekla had lent him at different times.

I was some time in making out all this. Thekla held the candle for me to read it; held it patiently and steadily, not speaking a word till I had folded up the letter again, and given it back to her. Then our eyes met.

'There is no misunderstanding possible, is there, sir?' asked she, with a faint smile.

'No,' I replied; 'but you are well rid of such a fellow.'

She shook her head a little. 'It shows his bad side, sir. We have all our bad sides. You must not judge him harshly; at least, I cannot. But then we were brought up together.'

'At Altenahr?'

'Yes; his father kept the other inn, and our parents, instead of being rivals, were great friends. Franz is a little younger than I, and was a delicate child. I had to take him to school, and I used to be so proud of it and of my charge. Then he grew strong, and was the handsomest lad in the village. Our fathers used to sit and smoke together, and talk of our marriage, and Franz must have heard as much as I. Whenever he was in trouble, he would come to me for what advice I could give him; and he danced twice as often with me as with any other girl at all the dances, and always brought his nosegay to me. Then his father wished him to travel, and learn the ways at the great hotels on the Rhine before he settled down in Altenahr. You know that is the custom in Germany, sir. They go from town to town as journeymen, learning something fresh everywhere, they say.'

'I knew that was done in trades,' I replied.

'Oh, yes; and among inn-keepers, too,' she said. 'Most of the waiters at the great hotels in Frankfort, and Heidelberg, and Mayence, and, I daresay, at all the other places, are the sons of innkeepers in small towns, who go out into the world to learn new ways, and perhaps to pick up a little English and French; otherwise, they say, they should never get on. Franz went off from Altenahr on his journeyings four years ago next May-day; and before he went, he brought me back a ring from Bonn, where he bought his new clothes. I don't wear it now; but I have got it upstairs, and it comforts me to see something that shows me it was not all my silly fancy. I suppose he fell among bad people, for he soon began to play for money, – and then he lost more than he could always pay – and sometimes I could help him a little, for we wrote to each other from time to time, as we knew each other's addresses; for the little ones grew around my father's hearth, and I thought that I, too, would go forth into the world and earn my own living, so that – well, I will tell the truth – I thought that by going into service, I could lay by enough for buying a handsome stock of household linen, and plenty of pans and kettles against – against what will never come to pass now.'

'Do the German women buy the pots and kettles, as you call them, when they are married?' asked I, awkwardly, laying hold of a trivial question to conceal the indignant sympathy with her wrongs which I did not like to express.

'Oh, yes; the bride furnishes all that is wanted in the kitchen, and all the store of house-linen. If my mother had lived, it would have been laid by for me, as she could have afforded to buy it, but my stepmother will have hard enough work to provide for her own four little girls. However,' she continued, brightening up, 'I can help her, for now I shall never marry; and my master here is just and liberal, and pays me sixty florins a year, which is high wages.' (Sixty florins are about five pounds sterling.) 'And now, goodnight, sir. This cup to the left holds the tisane, that to the right the acorn-tea.' She shaded the candle, and was leaving the room. I raised myself on my elbow, and called her back.

'Don't go on thinking about this man,' said I. 'He was not good enough for you. You are much better unmarried.'

'Perhaps so,' she answered gravely. 'But you cannot do him justice; you do not know him.'

A few minutes after, I heard her soft and cautious return; she had taken her shoes off, and came in her stockinged feet up to my bedside, shading the light with her hand. When she saw that my eyes were open, she laid down two letters on the table, close by my night-lamp.

'Perhaps, some time, sir, you would take the trouble to read these letters; you would then see how noble and clever Franz really is. It is I who ought to be blamed, not he.'

No more was said that night.

Some time the next morning I read the letters. They were filled with vague, inflated, sentimental descriptions of his inner life and feelings; entirely egotistical, and intermixed with quotations from second-rate philosophers and poets. There was, it must be said, nothing in them offensive to good principle or good feeling, however much they might be opposed to good taste. I was to go into the next room that afternoon for the first time of leaving my sick chamber. All morning I lay and ruminated. From time to time I thought of Thekla and Franz Weber. She was the strong, good, helpful character, he the weak and vain; how strange it seemed that she should have cared for one so dissimilar; and then I remembered the various happy marriages when to an outsider it seemed as if one was so inferior to the other that their union would have appeared a subject for despair if it had been looked at prospectively. My host came in, in the midst of these meditations, bringing a great flowered dressing-gown, lined with flannel, and the embroidered smoking-cap which he evidently considered as belonging to this Indian-looking robe. They had been his father's, he told me; and as he helped me to dress, he went on with his communications on small family matters. His inn was flourishing; the numbers increased every year of those who came to see the church at Heppenheim: the church which was the pride of the place, but which I had never yet seen. It was built by the great Kaiser Karl. And there was the Castle of Starkenburg, too, which the Abbots of Lorsch had often defended, stalwart churchmen as they were, against the temporal power of the emperors. And Melibocus was not beyond a walk either. In fact, it was the work of one person to superintend the inn alone; but he had his farm and his vineyards beyond, which of themselves gave him enough to do. And his sister was oppressed with the perpetual calls made upon her patience and her nerves in an inn; and would rather go back and live at Worms. And his children wanted so much looking after. By the time he had placed himself in a condition for requiring my full sympathy, I had finished my slow toilette; and I had to interrupt his confidences, and accept the help of his good strong arm to lead me into the great eating-room, out of which my chamber opened. I had a dreamy recollection of the vast apartment. But how pleasantly it was changed! There was the bare half of the room, it is true, looking as it had done on that first afternoon, sunless and cheerless, with the long, unoccupied table, and the necessary chairs for the possible visitors; but round the windows that opened on the garden a part of the room was enclosed by the house-hold clothes'-horses hung with great pieces of the blue homespun cloth of which the dress of the Black Forest peasant is made. This shut-in space was warmed by the lighted stove, as well as by the lowering rays of the October sun. There was a little round walnut table with some flowers upon it, and a great cushioned armchair placed so as to look out upon the garden and the hills beyond. I felt sure that this was all Thekla's arrangement; I had rather wondered that I had seen so little of her this day. She had come once or twice on necessary errands into my room in the morning, but had appeared to be in great haste, and had avoided meeting my eye. Even when I had returned the letters, which she had entrusted to me with so evident a purpose of placing the writer in my good opinion, she had never inquired as to how far they had answered her design; she had merely taken them with some low word of thanks, and put them hurriedly into her pocket. I suppose she shrank from remembering how fully she had given me her confidence the night before, now that daylight and actual life pressed close around her. Besides, there surely never was any one in such constant request as Thekla. I did not like this estrangement, though it was the natural consequence of my improved health, which would daily make me less and less require services which seemed so urgently claimed by others. And, moreover, after my host left me – I fear I had cut him a little short in the recapitulation of his domestic difficulties, but he was too thorough and good-hearted a man to bear malice – I wanted to be amused or interested. So I rang my little hand-bell, hoping that Thekla would answer it, when I could have fallen into conversation with her, without specifying any decided want. Instead of Thekla the Fräulein came, and I had to invent a wish; for I could not act as a baby, and say that I wanted my nurse. However, the Fräulein was better than no one, so I asked her if I could have some grapes, which had been provided for me on every day but this, and which were especially grateful to my feverish palate. She was a good, kind woman, although, perhaps, her temper was not the best in the world; and she expressed the sincerest regret as she told me that there were no more in the house. Like an invalid I fretted at my wish not being granted, and spoke out.

'But Thekla told me the vintage was not till the fourteenth; and you have a vineyard close beyond the garden on the slope of the hill out there, have you not?'

'Yes; and grapes for the gathering. But perhaps the gentleman does not know our laws. Until the vintage – (the day of beginning the vintage is fixed by the Grand Duke, and advertised in the public papers) – until the vintage, all owners of vineyards may only go on two appointed days in every week to gather their grapes; on those two days (Tuesdays and Fridays this year) they must gather enough for the wants of their families; and if they do not reckon rightly, and gather short measure, why they have to go without. And these two last days the Half-Moon has been besieged with visitors, all of whom have asked for grapes. But to-morrow the gentleman can have as many as he will; it is the day for gathering them.'

'What a strange kind of paternal law,' I grumbled out. 'Why is it so ordained? Is it to secure the owners against pilfering from their unfenced vineyards?'

'I am sure I cannot tell,' she replied. 'Country people in these villages have strange customs in many ways, as I daresay the English gentleman has perceived. If he would come to Worms he would see a different kind of life.'

'But not a view like this,' I replied, caught by a sudden change of light – some cloud passing away from the sun, or something. Right outside of the windows was, as I have so often said, the garden. Trained plum-trees with golden leaves, great bushes of purple, Michaelmas daisy, late flowering roses, apple-trees partly stripped of their rosy fruit, but still with enough left on their boughs to require the props set to support the luxuriant burden; to the left an arbour covered over with honeysuckle and other sweet-smelling creepers – all bounded by a low gray stone wall which opened out upon the steep vineyard, that stretched up the hill beyond, one hill of a series rising higher and higher into the purple distance. 'Why is there a rope with a bunch of straw tied in it stretched across the opening of the garden into the vineyard?' I inquired, as my eye suddenly caught upon the object.

'It is the country way of showing that no one must pass along that path. To-morrow the gentleman will see it removed; and then he shall have the grapes. Now I will go and prepare his coffee.' With a curtsey, after the fashion of Worms gentility, she withdrew. But an under-servant brought me my coffee; and with her I could not exchange a word: she spoke in such an execrable patois. I went to bed early, weary, and depressed. I must have fallen asleep immediately, for I never heard any one come to arrange my bed-side table; yet in the morning I found that every usual want or wish of mine had been attended to.

I was wakened by a tap at my door, and a pretty piping child's voice asking, in broken German, to come in. On giving the usual permission, Thekla entered, carrying a great lovely boy of two years old, or there-abouts, who had only his little night-shirt on, and was all flushed with sleep. He held tight in his hands a great cluster of muscatel and noble grapes. He seemed like a little Bacchus, as she carried him towards me with an expression of pretty loving pride upon her face as she looked at him. But when he came close to me – the grim, wasted, unshorn – he turned quick away, and hid his face in her neck, still grasping tight his bunch of grapes. She spoke to him rapidly and softly, coaxing him as I could tell full well, although I could not follow her words; and in a minute or two the little fellow obeyed her, and turned and stretched himself almost to overbalancing out of her arms, and half-dropped the fruit on the bed by me. Then he clutched at her again, burying his face in her kerchief, and fastening his little fists in her luxuriant hair.

'It is my master's only boy,' said she, disentangling his fingers with quiet patience, only to have them grasp her braids afresh. 'He is my little Max, my heart's delight, only he must not pull so hard. Say his "to-meet again", and kiss his hand lovingly, and we will go.' The promise of a speedy departure from my dusky room proved irresistible; he babbled out his Aufwiedersehen, and kissing his chubby hand, he was borne away joyful and chattering fast in his infantile half-language. I did not see Thekla again until late afternoon, when she brought me in my coffee. She was not like the same creature as the blooming, cheerful maiden whom

I had seen in the morning; she looked wan and care-worn, older by several years.

'What is the matter, Thekla?' said I, with true anxiety as to what might have befallen my good, faithful nurse.

She looked round before answering. 'I have seen him,' she said. 'He has been here, and the Fräulein has been so angry! She says she will tell my master. Oh, it has been such a day!' The poor young woman, who was usually so composed and self-restrained, was on the point of bursting into tears; but by a strong effort she checked herself, and tried to busy herself with rearranging the white china cup, so as to place it more conveniently to my hand.

'Come, Thekla,' said I, 'tell me all about it. I have heard loud voices talking, and I fancied something had put the Fräulein out; and Lottchen looked flurried when she brought me my dinner. Is Franz here? How has he found you out?'

'He is here. Yes, I am sure it is he; but four years makes such a difference in a man; his whole look and manner seemed so strange to me; but he knew me at once, and called me all the old names which we used to call each other when we were children; and he must needs tell me how it had come to pass that he had not married that Swiss Anna. He said he had never loved her; and that now he was going home to settle, and he hoped that I would come too, and—' There she stopped short.

'And marry him, and live at the inn at Altenahr,' said I, smiling, to reassure her, though I felt rather disappointed about the whole affair.

'No,' she replied. 'Old Weber, his father, is dead; he died in debt, and Franz will have no money. And he was always one that needed money. Some are, you know; and while I was thinking, and he was standing near me, the Fräulein came in; and – and – I don't wonder – for poor Franz is not a pleasant-looking man now-a-days – she was very angry, and called me a bold, bad girl, and said she could have no such goings on at the "Halbmond", but would tell my master when he came home from the forest.'

'But you could have told her that you were old friends.' I hesitated, before saying the word lovers, but, after a pause, out it came.

'Franz might have said so,' she replied, a little stiffly. 'I could not; but he went off as soon as she bade him. He went to the "Adler" over the way, only saying he would come for my answer to-morrow morning. I think it was he that should have told her what we were – neighbours' children and early friends – not have left it all to me. Oh,' said she, clasping her hands tight together, 'she will make such a story of it to my master.'

'Never mind,' said I, 'tell the master I want to see him, as soon as he comes in from the forest, and trust me to set him right before the Fräulein has the chance to set him wrong.'

She looked up at me gratefully, and went away without any more words. Presently the fine burly figure of my host stood at the opening to my enclosed sitting-room. He was there, three-cornered hat in hand, looking tired and heated as a man does after a hard day's work, but as kindly and genial as ever, which is not what every man is who is called to business after such a day, before he has had the necessary food and rest.

I had been reflecting a good deal on Thekla's story; I could not quite interpret her manner to-day to my full satisfaction; but yet the love which had grown with her growth, must assuredly have been called forth by her lover's sudden reappearance; and I was inclined to give him some credit for having broken off an engagement to Swiss Anna, which had promised so many worldly advantages; and, again, I had considered that if he was a little weak and sentimental, it was Thekla, who would marry him by her own free will, and perhaps she had sense and quiet resolution enough for both. So I gave the heads of the little history I have told you to my good friend and host, adding that I should like to have a man's opinion of this man; but that if he were not an absolute good-for-nothing, and if Thekla still loved him, as I believed, I would try and advance them the requisite money towards establishing themselves in the hereditary inn at Altenahr.

Such was the romantic ending to Thekla's sorrows, I had been planning and brooding over for the last hour. As I narrated my tale, and hinted at the possible happy conclusion that might be in store, my host's face changed. The ruddy colour faded, and his look became almost stern – certainly very grave in expression. It was so unsympathetic, that I instinctively cut my words short. When I had done, he paused a little, and then said: 'You would wish me to learn all I can respecting this stranger now at the "Adler", and give you the impression I receive of the fellow.'

'Exactly so,' said I; 'I want to learn all I can about him for Thekla's sake.'

'For Thekla's sake I will do it,' he gravely repeated.

'And come to me to-night, even if I am gone to bed?'

'Not so,' he replied. 'You must give me all the time you can in a matter like this.'

'But he will come for Thekla's answer in the morning.'

'Before he comes you shall know all I can learn.'

I was resting during the fatigues of dressing the next day, when my host tapped at my door. He looked graver and sterner than I had ever seen him do before; he sat down almost before I had begged him to do so.

'He is not worthy of her,' he said. 'He drinks brandy right hard; he boasts of his success at play, and' – here he set his teeth hard – 'he boasts of the women who have loved him. In a village like this, sir, there are always those who spend their evenings in the gardens of the inns; and this man, after he had drank his fill, made no secrets; it needed no spying to find out what he was, else I should not have been the one to do it.'

'Thekla must be told of this,' said I. 'She is not the woman to love any one whom she cannot respect.'

Herr Müller laughed a low bitter laugh, quite unlike himself. Then he replied, –

'As for that matter, sir, you are young; you have had no great experience of women. From what my sister tells me there can be little doubt of Thekla's feeling towards him. She found them standing together by the window; his arm round Thekla's waist, and whispering in her ear – and to do the maiden justice she is not the one to suffer such familiarities from every one. No' – continued he, still in the same contemptuous tone – 'you'll find she will make excuses for his faults and vices; or else, which is per-haps more likely, she will not believe your story, though I who tell it you can vouch for the truth of every word I say.' He turned short away and left the room. Presently I saw his stalwart figure in the hill-side vineyard, before my windows, scaling the steep ascent with long regular steps, going to the forest beyond. I was otherwise occupied than in watching his pro-gress during the next hour; at the end of that time he re-entered my room, looking heated and slightly tired, as if he had been walking fast, or labouring hard; but with the cloud off his brows, and the kindly light shining once again out of his honest eyes.

'I ask your pardon, sir,' he began, 'for troubling you afresh. I believe I was possessed by the devil this morning. I have been thinking it over. One has perhaps no right to rule for another person's happiness. To have such a' – here the honest fellow choked a little – 'such a woman as Thekla to love him ought to raise any man. Besides, I am no judge for him or for her. I have found out this morning that I love her myself, and so the end of it is, that if you, sir, who are so kind as to interest yourself in the matter, and if you think it is really her heart's desire to marry this man – which ought to be his salvation both for earth and heaven – I shall be very glad to go halves with you in any place for setting them up in the inn at Altenahr; only allow me to see that whatever money we advance is well and legally tied up, so that it is secured to her. And be so kind as to take no notice of what I have said about my having found out that I have loved her; I named it as a kind of apology for my hard words this morning, and as a reason why I was not a fit judge of what was best.' He had hurried on, so that I could not have stopped his eager speaking even had I wished to do so; but I was too much interested in the revelation of what was passing in his brave tender heart to desire to stop him. Now, however, his rapid words tripped each other up, and his speech ended in an unconscious sigh.

'But,' I said, 'since you were here Thekla has come to me, and we have had a long talk. She speaks now as openly to me as she would if I were her brother; with sensible frankness, where frankness is wise, with modest reticence, where confidence would be unbecoming. She came to ask me if I thought it her duty to marry this fellow, whose very appearance, changed for the worse, as she says it is, since she last saw him four years ago, seemed to have repelled her.'

'She could let him put his arm round her waist yesterday,' said Herr Müller, with a return of his morning's surliness.

'And she would marry him now if she could believe it to be her duty. For some reason of his own, this Franz Weber has tried to work upon this feeling of hers. He says it would be the saving of him.'

'As if a man had not strength enough in him – a man who is good for aught – to save himself, but needed a woman to pull him through life!'

'Nay,' I replied, hardly able to keep from smiling. 'You yourself said not five minutes ago, that her marrying him might be his salvation both for earth and heaven.'

'That was when I thought she loved the fellow,' he answered quick. 'Now – but what did you say to her, sir?'

'I told her, what I believe to be as true as gospel, that as she owned she did not love him any longer now his real self had come to displace his remembrance, that she would be sinning in marrying him; doing evil that possible good might come. I was clear myself on this point, though I should have been perplexed how to advise, if her love had still continued.'

'And what answer did she make?'

'She went over the history of their lives; she was pleading against her wishes to satisfy her conscience. She said that all along through their childhood she had been his strength; that while under her personal influence he had been negatively good; away from her, he had fallen into mischief—'

'Not to say vice,' put in Herr Müller.

'And now he came to her penitent, in sorrow, desirous of amendment, asking her for the love she seems to have considered as tacitly plighted to him in years gone by—'

'And which he has slighted and insulted. I hope you told her of his words and conduct last night in the "Adler" gardens?'

'No. I kept myself to the general principle, which, I am sure, is a true one. I repeated it in different forms; for the idea of the duty of self-sacrifice had taken strong possession of her fancy. Perhaps, if I had failed in setting her notion of her duty in the right aspect, I might have had recourse to the statement of facts, which would have pained her severely, but would have proved to her how little his words of penitence and promises of amendment were to be trusted to.'

'And it ended?'

'Ended by her being quite convinced that she would be doing wrong instead of right if she married a man whom she had entirely ceased to love, and that no real good could come from a course of action based on wrong-doing.'

'That is right and true,' he replied, his face broadening into happiness again.

'But she says she must leave your service, and go elsewhere.'

'Leave my service she shall; go elsewhere she shall not.'

'I cannot tell what you may have the power of inducing her to do; but she seems to me very resolute.'

'Why?' said he, firing round at me, as if I had made her resolute.

'She says your sister spoke to her before the maids of the household, and before some of the townspeople, in a way that she could not stand; and that you yourself by your manner to her last night showed how she had lost your respect. She added, with her face of pure maidenly truth, that he had come into such close contact with her only the instant before your sister had entered the room.'

'With your leave, sir,' said Herr Müller, turning towards the door, 'I will go and set all that right at once.'

It was easier said than done. When I next saw Thekla, her eyes were swollen up with crying, but she was silent, almost defiant towards me. A look of resolute determination had settled down upon her face. I learnt afterwards that parts of my conversation with Herr Müller had been injudiciously quoted by him in the talk he had had with her. I thought I would leave her to herself, and wait till she unburdened herself of the feeling of unjust resentment towards me. But it was days before she spoke to me with anything like her former frankness. I had heard all about it from my host long before.

He had gone to her straight on leaving me; and like a foolish, impetuous lover, had spoken out his mind and his wishes to her in the presence of his sister, who, it must be remembered, had heard no explanation of the conduct which had given her propriety so great a shock the day before. Herr Müller thought to re-instate Thekla in his sister's good opinion by giving her in the Fräulein's very presence the highest possible mark of his own love and esteem. And there in the kitchen, where the Fräulein was deeply engaged in the hot work of making some delicate preserve on the stove, and ordering Thekla about with short, sharp displeasure in her tones, the master had come in, and possessing himself of the maiden's hand, had, to her infinite surprise – to his sister's infinite indignation – made her the offer of his heart, his wealth, his life; had begged of her to marry him. I could gather from his account that she had been in a state of trembling discomfiture at first; she had not spoken, but had twisted her hand out of his, and had covered her face with her apron. And then the Fräulein had burst forth – 'accursed words' he called her speech. Thekla uncovered her face to listen; to listen to the end; to listen to the passionate recrimination between the brother and the sister. And then she went up, close up to the angry Fräulein, and had said quite quietly, but with a manner of final determination which had evidently sunk deep into her suitor's heart, and depressed him into hopelessness, that the Fräulein had no need to disturb herself; that on this very day she had been thinking of marrying another man, and that her heart was not like a room to let, into which as one tenant went out another might enter. Nevertheless, she felt the master's goodness. He had always treated her well from the time when she had entered the house as his servant. And she should be sorry to leave him; sorry to leave the children; very sorry to leave little Max: yes, she should even be sorry to leave the Fräulein, who was a good woman, only a little too apt to be hard on other women. But she had already been that very day and deposited her warning at the police office; the busy time would be soon over, and she should be glad to leave their service on All Saints' Day. Then (he thought) she had felt inclined to cry, for she suddenly braced herself up, and said, yes, she should be very glad; for somehow, though they had been kind to her, she had been very unhappy at Heppenheim; and she would go back to her home for a time, and see her old father and kind step-mother, and her nursling half-sister Ida, and be among her own people again.

I could see it was this last part that most of all rankled in Herr Müller's mind. In all probability Franz Weber was making his way back to Heppenheim too; and the bad suspicion would keep welling up that some lingering feeling for her old lover and disgraced playmate was making her so resolute to leave and return to Altenahr.

For some days after this I was the confidant of the whole household, excepting Thekla. She, poor creature, looked miserable enough; but the hardy, defiant expression was always on her face. Lottchen spoke out freely enough; the place would not be worth having if Thekla left it; it was she who had the head for everything, the patience for everything; who stood between all the under-servants and the Fräulein's tempers. As for the children, poor motherless children! Lottchen was sure that the master did not know what he was doing when he allowed his sister to turn Thekla away – and all for what? for having a lover, as every girl had who could get one. Why, the little boy Max slept in the room which Lottchen shared with Thekla; and she heard him in the night as quickly as if she was his mother; when she had been sitting up with me, when I was so ill, Lottchen had had to attend to him; and it was weary work after a hard day to have to get up and soothe a teething child; she knew she had been cross enough sometimes; but Thekla was always good and gentle with him, however tired he was. And as Lottchen left the room I could hear her repeating that she thought she should leave when Thekla went, for that her place would not be worth having.

Even the Fräulein had her word of regret – regret mingled with self-justification. She thought she had been quite right in speaking to Thekla for allowing such familiarities; how was she to know that the man was an old friend and playmate? He looked like a right profligate good-for-nothing. And to have a servant take up her scolding as an unpardonable offence, and persist in quitting her place, just when she had learnt all her work, and was so useful in the household – so useful that the Fräulein could never put up with any fresh, stupid house-maiden, but, sooner than take the trouble of teaching the new servant where everything was, and how to give out the stores if she was busy, she would go back to Worms. For, after all, housekeeping for a brother was thankless work; there was no satisfying men; and Heppenheim was but a poor ignorant village compared to Worms.

She must have spoken to her brother about her intention of leaving him, and returning to her former home; indeed a feeling of coolness had evidently grown up between the brother and sister during these latter days. When one evening Herr Müller brought in his pipe, and, as his custom had sometimes been, sat down by my stove to smoke, he looked gloomy and annoyed. I let him puff away, and take his own time. At length he began, –

'I have rid the village of him at last. I could not bear to have him here disgracing Thekla with speaking to her whenever she went to the vineyard or the fountain. I don't believe she likes him a bit.'

'No more do I,' I said. He turned on me.

'Then why did she speak to him at all? Why cannot she like an honest man who likes her? Why is she so bent on going home to Altenahr?'

'She speaks to him because she has known him from a child, and has a faithful pity for one whom she has known so innocent, and who is now so lost in all good men's regard. As for not liking an honest man – (though I may have my own opinion about that) – liking goes by fancy, as we say in English; and Altenahr is her home; her father's house is at Altenahr, as you know.'

'I wonder if he will go there,' quoth Herr Müller, after two or three more puffs. 'He was fast at the "Adler"; he could not pay his score, so he kept on staying here, saying that he should receive a letter from a friend with money in a day or two; lying in wait, too, for Thekla, who is well-known and respected all through Heppenheim: so his being an old friend of hers made him have a kind of standing. I went in this morning and paid his score, on condition that he left the place this day; and he left the village as merrily as a cricket, caring no more for Thekla than for the Kaiser who built our church: for he never looked back at the "Halbmond", but went whistling down the road.'

'That is a good riddance,' said I.

'Yes. But my sister says she must return to Worms. And Lottchen has given notice; she says the place will not be worth having when Thekla leaves. I wish I could give notice too.'

'Try Thekla again.'

'Not I,' said he, reddening. 'It would seem now as if I only wanted her for a housekeeper. Besides, she avoids me at every turn, and will not even look at me. I am sure she bears me some ill-will about that ne'er-do-well.'

There was silence between us for some time, which he at length broke.

'The pastor has a good and comely daughter. Her mother is a famous housewife. They often have asked me to come to the parsonage and smoke a pipe. When the vintage is over, and I am less busy, I think I will go there, and look about me.'

'When is the vintage?' asked I. 'I hope it will take place soon, for I am growing so well and strong I fear I must leave you shortly; but I should like to see the vintage first.'

'Oh, never fear! you must not travel yet awhile; and Government has fixed the grape-gathering to begin on the fourteenth.'

'What a paternal Government! How does it know when the grapes will be ripe? Why cannot every man fix his own time for gathering his own grapes?'

'That has never been our way in Germany. There are people employed by the Government to examine the vines, and report when the grapes are ripe. It is necessary to make laws about it; for, as you must have seen, there is nothing but the fear of the law to protect our vineyards and fruit-trees; there are no enclosures along the Berg-Strasse, as you tell me you have in England; but, as people are only allowed to go into the vineyards on stated days, no one, under pretence of gathering his own produce, can stray into his neighbour's grounds and help himself, without some of the duke's foresters seeing him.'

'Well,' said I, 'to each country its own laws.'

I think it was on that very evening that Thekla came in for something. She stopped arranging the table-cloth and the flowers, as if she had something to say, yet did not know how to begin. At length I found that her sore, hot heart, wanted some sympathy; her hand was against every one's, and she fancied every one had turned against her. She looked up at me, and said, a little abruptly, –

'Does the gentleman know that I go on the fifteenth?'

'So soon?' said I, with surprise. 'I thought you were to remain here till All Saints' Day.'

'So I should have done – so I must have done – if the Fräulein had not kindly given me leave to accept of a place – a very good place too – of housekeeper to a widow lady at Frankfort. It is just the sort of situation I have always wished for. I expect I shall be so happy and comfortable there.'

'Methinks the lady doth profess too much,' came into my mind. I saw she expected me to doubt the probability of her happiness, and was in a defiant mood.

'Of course,' said I, 'you would hardly have wished to leave Heppenheim if you had been happy here; and every new place always promises fair, whatever its performance may be. But wherever you go, remember you have always a friend in me.'

'Yes,' she replied, 'I think you are to be trusted. Though, from my experience, I should say that of very few men.'

'You have been unfortunate,' I answered; 'many men would say the same of women.'

She thought a moment, and then said, in a changed tone of voice, 'The Fräulein here has been much more friendly and helpful of these late days than her brother; yet I have served him faithfully, and have cared for his little Max as though he were my own brother. But this morning he spoke to me for the first time for many days, – he met me in the passage, and, suddenly stopping, he said he was glad I had met with so comfortable a place, and that I was at full liberty to go whenever I liked: and then he went quickly on, never waiting for my answer.'

'And what was wrong in that? It seems to me he was trying to make you feel entirely at your ease, to do as you thought best, without regard to his own interests.'

'Perhaps so. It is silly, I know,' she continued, turning full on me her grave, innocent eyes; 'but one's vanity suffers a little when every one is so willing to part with one.'

'Thekla! I owe you a great debt – let me speak to you openly. I know that your master wanted to marry you, and that you refused him. Do not deceive yourself. You are sorry for that refusal now?'

She kept her serious look fixed upon me; but her face and throat reddened all over.

'No,' said she, at length; 'I am not sorry. What can you think I am made of; having loved one man ever since I was a little child until a fortnight ago, and now just as ready to love another? I know you do not rightly consider what you say, or I should take it as an insult.'

'You loved an ideal man; he disappointed you, and you clung to your remembrance of him. He came, and the reality dispelled all illusions.'

'I do not understand philosophy,' said she. 'I only know that I think that Herr Müller had lost all respect for me from what his sister had told him; and I know that I am going away; and I trust I shall be happier in Frankfort than I have been here of late days.' So saying, she left the room.

I was wakened up on the morning of the fourteenth by the merry ringing of church bells, and the perpetual firing and popping off of guns and pistols. But all this was over by the time I was up and dressed, and seated at breakfast in my partitioned room. It was a perfect October day; the dew not yet off the blades of grass, glistening on the delicate gossamer webs, which stretched from flower to flower in the garden, lying in the morning shadow of the house. But beyond the garden, on the sunny hill-side, men, women, and children were clambering up the vineyards like ants, – busy, irregular in movement, clustering together, spreading wide apart, – I could hear the shrill merry voices as I sat, – and all along the valley, as far as I could see, it was much the same; for every one filled his house for the day of the vintage, that great annual festival. Lottchen, who had brought in my breakfast, was all in her Sunday best, having risen early to get her work done and go abroad to gather grapes. Bright colours seemed to abound; I could see dots of scarlet, and crimson, and orange through the fading leaves; it was not a day to languish in the house; and I was on the point of going out by myself, when Herr Müller came in to offer me his sturdy arm, and help me in walking to the vineyard. We crept through the garden scented with late flowers and sunny fruit, – we passed through the gate I had so often gazed at from the easy-chair, and were in the busy vineyard; great baskets lay on the grass already piled nearly full of purple and yellow grapes. The wine made from these was far from pleasant to my taste; for the best Rhine wine is made from a smaller grape, growing in closer, harder clusters; but the larger and less profitable grape is by far the most picturesque in its mode of growth, and far the best to eat into the bargain. Wherever we trod, it was on fragrant, crushed vine-leaves; every one we saw had his hands and face stained with the purple juice. Presently I sat down on a sunny bit of grass, and my host left me to go farther afield, to look after the more distant vineyards. I watched his progress. After he left me, he took off coat and waistcoat, displaying his snowy shirt and gaily-worked braces; and presently he was as busy as any one. I looked down on the village; the gray and orange and crimson roofs lay glowing in the noonday sun. I could see down into the streets; but they were all empty – even the old people came toiling up the hill-side to share in the general festivity. Lottchen had brought up cold dinners for a regiment of men; every one came and helped himself. Thekla was there, leading the little Karoline, and helping the toddling steps of Max; but she kept aloof from me; for I knew, or suspected, or had probed too much. She alone looked sad and grave, and spoke so little, even to her friends, that it was evident to see that she was trying to wean herself finally from the place. But I could see that she had lost her short, defiant manner. What she did say was kindly and gently spoken. The Fräulein came out late in the morning, dressed, I suppose, in the latest Worms fashion – quite different to anything I had ever seen before. She came up to me, and talked very graciously to me for some time.

'Here comes the proprietor (squire) and his lady, and their dear children. See, the vintagers have tied bunches of the finest grapes on to a stick, heavier than the children or even the lady can carry. Look! look! how he bows! – one can tell he has been an *attaché* at Vienna. That is the court way of bowing there – holding the hat right down before them, and bending the back at right angles. How graceful! And here is the doctor! I thought he would spare time to come up here. Well, doctor, you will go all the more cheerfully to your next patient for having been up into the vineyards. Nonsense, about grapes making other patients for you. Ah, here is the pastor and his wife, and the Fräulein Anna. Now, where is my brother, I wonder? Up in the far vineyard, I make no doubt. Mr Pastor, the view up above is far finer than what it is here, and the best grapes grow there; shall I accompany you and madame, and the dear Fräulein? The gentleman will excuse me.'

I was left alone. Presently I thought I would walk a little farther, or at any rate change my position. I rounded a corner in the pathway, and there I found Thekla, watching by little sleeping Max. He lay on her shawl; and over his head she had made an arching canopy of broken vine-branches, so that the great leaves threw their cool, flickering shadows on his face. He was smeared all over with grape-juice, his sturdy fingers grasped a half-eaten bunch even in his sleep. Thekla was keeping Lina quiet by teaching her how to weave a garland for her head out of field-flowers and autumn-tinted leaves. The maiden sat on the ground, with her back to the valley beyond, the child kneeling by her, watching the busy fingers with eager intentness. Both looked up as I drew near, and we exchanged a few words.

'Where is the master?' I asked. 'I promised to await his return; he wished to give me his arm down the wooden steps; but I do not see him.'

'He is in the higher vineyard,' said Thekla, quietly, but not looking round in that direction. 'He will be some time there, I should think. He went with the pastor and his wife; he will have to speak to his labourers and his friends. My arm is strong, and I can leave Max in Lina's care for five minutes. If you are tired, and want to go back, let me help you down the steps; they are steep and slippery.'

I had turned to look up the valley. Three or four hundred yards off, in the higher vineyard, walked the dignified pastor, and his homely, decorous wife. Behind came the Fräulein Anna, in her short-sleeved Sunday gown, daintily holding a parasol over her luxuriant brown hair. Close behind her came Herr Müller, stopping now to speak to his men, – again, to cull out a bunch of grapes to tie on to the Fräulein's stick; and by my feet sate the proud serving-maid in her country dress, waiting for my answer, with serious, upturned eyes, and sad, composed face.

'No, I am much obliged to you, Thekla; and if I did not feel so strong I would have thankfully taken your arm. But I only wanted to leave a message for the master, just to say that I have gone home.'

'Lina will give it to the father when he comes down,' said Thekla.

I went slowly down into the garden. The great labour of the day was over, and the younger part of the population had returned to the village, and were preparing the fireworks and pistol-shootings for the evening. Already one or two of those well-known German carts (in the shape of a V) were standing near the vineyard gates, the patient oxen meekly waiting while basketful after basketful of grapes were being emptied into the leaf-lined receptacle.

As I sat down in my easy-chair close to the open window through which I had entered, I could see the men and women on the hill-side drawing to a centre, and all stand round the pastor, bareheaded, for a minute or so. I guessed that some words of holy thanksgiving were being said, and I wished that I had stayed to hear them, and mark my especial gratitude for having been spared to see that day. Then I heard the distant voices, the deep tones of the men, the shriller pipes of women and children, join in the German harvest-hymn, which is generally sung on such occasions;* then silence, while I concluded that a blessing was spoken by

* Wir pflügen und wir streuen,
Den Saamen auf das Land;
Das Wachsen und Gedeihen steht,
In des höchsten Hand.
Er sendet Thau und Regen,
Und Sonn und Mondeschein;
Von Ihm kommt aller Segen,
Von unserm Gott allein:

the pastor, with outstretched arms; and then they once more dispersed, some to the village, some to finish their labours for the day among the vines. I saw Thekla coming through the garden with Max in her arms, and Lina clinging to her woollen skirts. Thekla made for my open window; it was rather a shorter passage into the house than round by the door. 'I may come through, may I not?' she asked, softly. 'I fear Max is not well; I cannot understand his look, and he wakened up so strange!' She paused to let me see the child's face; it was flushed almost to a crimson look of heat, and his breathing was laboured and uneasy, his eyes half-open and filmy.

'Something is wrong, I am sure,' said I. 'I don't know anything about children, but he is not in the least like himself.'

She bent down and kissed the cheek so tenderly that she would not have bruised the petal of a rose. 'Heart's darling,' she murmured. He quivered all over at her touch, working his fingers in an unnatural kind of way, and ending with a convulsive twitching all over his body. Lina began to cry at the grave, anxious look on our faces.

'You had better call the Fräulein to look at him,' said I. 'I feel sure he ought to have a doctor; I should say he was going to have a fit.'

'The Fräulein and the master are gone to the pastor's for coffee, and Lottchen is in the higher vineyard, taking the men their bread and beer. Could you find the kitchen girl, or old Karl? he will be in the stables, I think. I must lose no time.' Almost without waiting for my reply, she had passed through the room, and in the empty house I could hear her firm, careful footsteps going up the stair; Lina's pattering beside her; and the one voice wailing, the other speaking low comfort.

I was tired enough, but this good family had treated me too much like one of their own for me not to do what I could in such a case as this. I made my way out into the street, for the first time since I had come to the house on that memorable evening six weeks ago. I bribed the first person I met to guide me to the doctor's, and sent him straight down to the 'Halbmond', not staying to listen to the thorough scolding he fell to

Alle gute Gabe kommt her
Von Gott dem Hern,
Drum dankt und hofft auf Ihn.

giving me; then on to the parsonage, to tell the master and the Fräulein of the state of things at home.

I was sorry to be the bearer of bad news into such a festive chamber as the pastor's. There they sat, resting after heat and fatigue, each in their best gala dress, the table spread with 'Dicker-milch', potato-salad, cakes of various shapes and kinds – all the dainty cates dear to the German palate. The pastor was talking to Herr Müller, who stood near the pretty young Fräulein Anna, in her fresh white chemisette, with her round white arms, and her youthful coquettish airs, as she prepared to pour out the coffee; our Fräulein was talking busily to the Frau Mama; the younger boys and girls of the family filling up the room. A ghost would have startled the assembled party less than I did, and would probably have been more welcome, considering the news I brought. As he listened, the master caught up his hat and went forth, without apology or farewell. Our Fräulein made up for both, and questioned me fully; but now she, I could see, was in haste to go, although restrained by her manners, and the kind-hearted Frau Pastorin soon set her at liberty to follow her inclination. As for me I was dead-beat, and only too glad to avail myself of the hospitable couple's pressing request that I would stop and share their meal. Other magnates of the village came in presently, and relieved me of the strain of keeping up a German conversation about nothing at all with entire strangers. The pretty Fräulein's face had clouded over a little at Herr Müller's sudden departure; but she was soon as bright as could be, giving private chase and sudden little scoldings to her brothers, as they made raids upon the dainties under her charge. After I was duly rested and refreshed, I took my leave; for I, too, had my quieter anxieties about the sorrow in the Müller family.

The only person I could see at the 'Halbmond' was Lottchen; every one else was busy about the poor little Max, who was passing from one fit into another. I told Lottchen to ask the doctor to come in and see me before he took his leave for the night, and tired as I was, I kept up till after his visit, though it was very late before he came; I could see from his face how anxious he was. He would give me no opinion as to the child's chances of recovery, from which I guessed that he had not much hope. But when I expressed my fear he cut me very short.

'The truth is, you know nothing about it; no more do I, for that matter.

It is enough to try any man, much less a father, to hear his perpetual moans – not that he is conscious of pain, poor little worm; but if she stops for a moment in her perpetual carrying him backwards and forwards, he plains so piteously it is enough to – enough to make a man bless the Lord who never led him into the pit of matrimony. To see the father up there, following her as she walks up and down the room, the child's head over her shoulder, and Müller trying to make the heavy eyes recognize the old familiar ways of play, and the chirruping sounds which he can scarce make for crying— I shall be here to-morrow early, though before that either life or death will have come without the old doctor's help.'

All night long I dreamt my feverish dream – of the vineyard – the carts, which held little coffins instead of baskets of grapes – of the pastor's daughter, who would pull the dying child out of Thekla's arms; it was a bad, weary night! I slept long into the morning; the broad daylight filled my room, and yet no one had been near to waken me! Did that mean life or death? I got up and dressed as fast as I could; for I was aching all over with the fatigue of the day before. Out into the sitting-room; the table was laid for breakfast, but no one was there. I passed into the house beyond, up the stairs, blindly seeking for the room where I might know whether it was life or death. At the door of a room I found Lottchen crying; at the sight of me in that unwonted place she started, and began some kind of apology, broken both by tears and smiles as she told me that the doctor said the danger was over – past, and that Max was sleeping a gentle peaceful slumber in Thekla's arms – arms that had held him all through the livelong night.

'Look at him, sir; only go in softly; it is a pleasure to see the child to-day; tread softly, sir.'

She opened the chamber-door. I could see Thekla sitting, propped up by cushions and stools, holding her heavy burden, and bending over him with a look of tenderest love. Not far off stood the Fräulein, all disordered and tearful, stirring or seasoning some hot soup, while the master stood by her impatient. As soon as it was cooled or seasoned enough he took the basin and went to Thekla, and said something very low; she lifted up her head, and I could see her face; pale, weary with watching, but with a soft peaceful look upon it, which it had not worn for weeks. Fritz Müller began to feed her, for her hands were occupied in holding his child; I could not help remembering Mrs Inchbald's pretty description of Dor-riforth's anxiety in feeding Miss Milner; she compares it, if I remember rightly, to that of a tender-hearted boy, caring for his darling bird, the loss of which would embitter all the joys of his holidays. We closed the door without noise, so as not to waken the sleeping child. Lottchen brought me my coffee and bread; she was ready either to laugh or to weep on the slightest occasion. I could not tell if it was in innocence or mischief. She asked me the following question, –

'Do you think Thekla will leave to-day, sir?'

In the afternoon I heard Thekla's step behind my extemporary screen. I knew it quite well. She stopped for a moment before emerging into my view.

She was trying to look as composed as usual, but, perhaps because her steady nerves had been shaken by her night's watching, she could not help faint touches of dimples at the corners of her mouth, and her eyes were veiled from any inquisitive look by their drooping lids.

'I thought you would like to know that the doctor says Max is quite out of danger now. He will only require care.'

'Thank you, Thekla; Doctor — has been in already this afternoon to tell me so, and I am truly glad.'

She went to the window, and looked out for a moment. Many people were in the vineyards again to-day; although we, in our household anxiety, had paid them but little heed. Suddenly she turned round into the room, and I saw that her face was crimson with blushes. In another instant Herr Müller entered by the window.

'Has she told you, sir?' said he, possessing himself of her hand, and looking all a-glow with happiness. 'Hast thou told our good friend?' addressing her.

'No. I was going to tell him, but I did not know how to begin.'

'Then I will prompt thee. Say after me – "I have been a wilful, foolish woman—"'

She wrenched her hand out of his, half-laughing – 'I am a foolish woman, for I have promised to marry him. But he is a still more foolish man, for he wishes to marry me. That is what I say.'

'And I have sent Babette to Frankfort with the pastor. He is going there, and will explain all to Frau v. Schmidt; and Babette will serve her for a time. When Max is well enough to have the change of air the doctor prescribes for him, thou shalt take him to Altenahr, and thither will I also go; and become known to thy people and thy father. And before Christmas the gentleman here shall dance at our wedding.'

'I must go home to England, dear friends, before many days are over. Perhaps we may travel together as far as Remagen. Another year I will come back to Heppenheim and see you.'

As I planned it, so it was. We left Heppenheim all together on a lovely All-Saints' Day. The day before – the day of All-Souls – I had watched Fritz and Thekla lead little Lina up to the Acre of God, the Field of Rest, to hang the wreath of immortelles on her mother's grave. Peace be with the dead and the living.

ANTHONY TROLLOPE

An Unprotected Female at the Pyramids

In the happy days when we were young, no description conveyed to us so complete an idea of mysterious reality as that of an Oriental city. We knew it was actually there, but had such vague notions of its ways and looks! Let any one remember his early impressions as to Bagdad or Grand Cairo, and then say if this was not so. It was probably taken from the 'Arabian Nights', and the picture produced was one of strange, fantastic, luxurious houses; of women who were either very young and very beautiful, or else very old and very cunning, but in either state exercising much more influence on life than women in the East do now; of good-natured, capricious, though sometimes tyrannical monarchs; and of life full of quaint mysteries, quite unintelligible in every phasis, and on that account the more picturesque.

And perhaps Grand Cairo has thus filled us with more wonder even than Bagdad. We have been in a certain manner at home at Bagdad, but have only visited Grand Cairo occasionally. I know no place which was to me, in early years, so delightfully mysterious as Grand Cairo.

But the route to India and Australia has changed all this. Men from all countries, going to the East, now pass through Cairo, and its streets and costumes are no longer strange to us. It has become also a resort for invalids, or rather for those who fear that they may become invalids if they remain in a cold climate during the winter months. And thus at Cairo there is always to be found a considerable population of French, Americans, and English. Oriental life is brought home to us, dreadfully diluted by Western customs, and the delights of the 'Arabian Nights' are shorn of half their value. When we have seen a thing, it is never so magnificent to us as when it was half unknown.

188

It is not much that we deign to learn from these Orientals – we who glory in our civilization. We do not copy their silence or their abstemiousness, nor that invariable mindfulness of his own personal dignity which always adheres to a Turk or to an Arab. We chatter as much at Cairo as elsewhere, and eat as much, and drink as much, and dress ourselves generally in the same old ugly costume. But we do usually take upon ourselves to wear red caps, and we do ride on donkeys.

Nor are the visitors from the West to Cairo by any means confined to the male sex. Ladies are to be seen in the streets, quite regardless of the Mohammedan custom which presumes a veil to be necessary for an appearance in public; and, to tell the truth, the Mohammedans in general do not appear to be much shocked by their effrontery.

A quarter of the town has in this way become inhabited by men wearing coats and waistcoats, and by women who are without veils; but the English tongue in Egypt finds its centre at Shepheard's Hotel. It is here that people congregate who are looking out for parties to visit with them the Upper Nile, and who are generally all smiles and courtesy; and here also are to be found they who have just returned from this journey, and who are often in a frame of mind towards their companions that is much less amiable. From hence, during the winter, a *cortège* proceeds almost daily to the Pyramids, or to Memphis, or to the petrified forest, or to the City of the Sun. And then, again, four or five times a month the house is filled with young aspirants going out to India, male and female, full of valour and bloom; or with others coming home, no longer young, no longer aspiring, but laden with children and grievances.

The party with whom we are at present concerned is not about to proceed further than the Pyramids, and we shall be able to go with them and return in one and the same day.

It consisted chiefly of an English family, Mr and Mrs Damer, their daughter, and two young sons – of these chiefly, because they were the nucleus to which the others had attached themselves as adherents; they had originated the journey, and in the whole management of it Mr Damer regarded himself as the master.

The adherents were, firstly, M. de la Bordeau, a Frenchman, now resident in Cairo, who had given out that he was in some way concerned in the canal about to be made between the Mediterranean and the Red Sea.

In discussion on this subject he had become acquainted with Mr Damer; and although the latter gentleman, true to English interests, perpetually declared that the canal would never be made, and thus irritated M. de la Bordeau not a little – nevertheless, some measure of friendship had grown up between them.

There was also an American gentleman, Mr Jefferson Ingram, who was comprising all countries and all nations in one grand tour, as American gentlemen so often do. He was young and good-looking, and had made himself especially agreeable to Mr Damer, who had declared, more than once, that Mr Ingram was by far the most rational American he had ever met. Mr Ingram would listen to Mr Damer by the half-hour as to the virtue of the British Constitution, and had even sat by almost with patience when Mr Damer had expressed a doubt as to the good working of the United States scheme of policy – which, in an American, was most wonderful. But some of the sojourners at Shepheard's had observed that Mr Ingram was in the habit of talking with Miss Damer almost as much as with her father, and had argued from that, that fond as the young man was of politics, he did sometimes turn his mind to other things also.

And then there was Miss Dawkins. Now, Miss Dawkins was an important person, both as to herself and as to her line of life, and she must be described. She was, in the first place, an unprotected female of about thirty years of age. As this is becoming an established profession, setting itself up as it were in opposition to the old-world idea that women, like green peas, cannot come to perfection without supporting sticks, it will be understood at once what were Miss Dawkins' sentiments. She considered – or at any rate so expressed herself – that peas could grow very well without sticks, and could not only grow thus unsupported, but could also make their way about the world without any incumbrance of sticks whatsoever. She did not intend, she said, to rival Ida Pfeiffer, seeing that she was attached in a moderate way to bed and board, and was attached to society in a manner almost more than moderate; but she had no idea of being prevented from seeing anything she wished to see because she had neither father, nor husband, nor brothers available for the purpose of escort. She was a human creature, with arms and legs, she said; and she intended to use them. And this was all very well; but nevertheless she had a strong inclination to use the arms and legs of other people when she could make them serviceable.

In person Miss Dawkins was not without attraction. I should exaggerate if I were to say that she was beautiful and elegant; but she was good-looking, and not usually ill-mannered. She was tall, and gifted with features rather sharp, and with eyes very bright. Her hair was of the darkest shade of brown, and was always worn in *bandeaux*, very neatly. She appeared generally in black, though other circumstances did not lead one to suppose that she was in mourning; but then, no other travelling costume is so convenient! She always wore a dark broad-brimmed straw hat, as to the ribbons on which she was rather particular. She was very neat about her gloves and boots; and though it cannot be said that her dress was got up without reference to expense, there can be no doubt that it was not effected without considerable outlay, and more than considerable thought.

Miss Dawkins – Sabrina Dawkins was her name, but she seldom had friends about her intimate enough to use the word Sabrina – was certainly a clever young woman. She could talk on most subjects, if not well, at least well enough to amuse. If she had not read much, she never showed any lamentable deficiency; she was good-humoured, as a rule, and could on occasions be very soft and winning. People who had known her long would sometimes say that she was selfish; but with new acquaintances she was forbearing and self-denying.

With what income Miss Dawkins was blessed no one seemed to know. She lived like a gentlewoman, as far as outward appearance went, and never seemed to be in want; but some people would say that she knew very well how many sides there were to a shilling, and some enemy had once declared that she was an 'old soldier'. Such was Miss Dawkins.

She also, as well as Mr Ingram and M. de la Bordeau, had laid herself out to find the weak side of Mr Damer. Mr Damer, with all his family, was going up the Nile, and it was known that he had room for two in his boat over and above his own family. Miss Dawkins had told him that she had not quite made up her mind to undergo so great a fatigue, but that, nevertheless, she had a longing of the soul to see something of Nubia. To this Mr Damer had answered nothing but 'Oh!' which Miss Dawkins had not found to be encouraging.

But she had not on that account despaired. To a married man there are always two sides, and in this instance there was Mrs Damer as well as Mr Damer. When Mr Damer said 'Oh!' Miss Dawkins sighed, and said, 'Yes, indeed,' then smiled, and be-took herself to Mrs Damer.

Now Mrs Damer was soft-hearted, and also somewhat old-fashioned. She did not conceive any violent affection for Miss Dawkins, but she told her daughter that 'the single lady by herself was a very nice young woman, and that it was a thousand pities she should have to go about so much alone like.'

Miss Damer had turned up her pretty nose, thinking, perhaps, how small was the chance that it ever should be her own lot to be an unprotected female. But Miss Dawkins carried her point, at any rate as regarded the expedition to the Pyramids.

Miss Damer, I have said, had a pretty nose. I may also say that she had pretty eyes, mouth, and chin, with other necessary appendages, all pretty. As to the two Master Damers, who were respectively of the ages of fifteen and sixteen, it may be sufficient to say that they were conspicuous for red caps and for the constancy with which they raced their donkeys.

And now the donkeys, and the donkey-boys, and the dragomen were all standing at the steps of Shepheard's Hotel. To each donkey there was a donkey-boy, and to each gentleman there was a dragoman, so that a goodly *cortège* was assembled, and a goodly noise was made. It may here be remarked, perhaps with some little pride, that not half the noise is given in Egypt to persons speaking any other language as is bestowed on those whose vocabulary is English.

This lasted for half-an-hour. Had the party been French, the donkeys would have arrived only fifteen minutes before the appointed time. And then out came Damer *père* and Damer *mère*, Damer *fille* and Damer *fils*. Damer *mère* was leaning on her husband, as was her wont. She was not an unprotected female, and had no desire to make any attempts in that line. Damer *fille* was attended sedulously by Mr Ingram, for whose demolishment, however, Mr Damer still brought up, in a loud voice, the fag ends of certain political arguments, which he would fain have poured direct into the ears of his opponent, had not his wife been so persistent in claiming her privileges. M. de la Bordeau should have followed with Miss Dawkins, but his French politeness, or else his fear of the unprotected female, taught him to walk on the other side of the mistress of the party.

Miss Dawkins left the house with an eager young Damer yelling on each side of her; but nevertheless, though thus neglected by the gentlemen of the party, she was all smiles and prettiness, and looked so sweetly on Mr Ingram when that gentleman stayed a moment to help her to her donkey, that his heart almost misgave him for leaving her as soon as she was in her seat.

And then they were off. In going from the hotel to the Pyramids, our party had not to pass through any of the queer old narrow streets of the true Cairo – Cairo the Oriental. They all lay behind them as they went down by the back of the hotel by the barracks of the Pasha and the College of Dervishes, to the village of old Cairo and the banks of the Nile.

Here they were kept half an hour, while their dragomans made a bargain with the ferryman, a stately *reis*, or captain of a boat, who declared with much dignity, that he could not carry them over for a sum less than six times the amount to which he was justly entitled; while the dragomans, with great energy on behalf of their masters, offered him only five times that sum. As far as the *reis* was concerned, the contest might soon have been at an end, for the man was not without a conscience, and would have been content with five times and a half; but then the three dragomans quarrelled among themselves as to which should have the paying of the money, and the affair became very tedious.

'What horrid, odious men!' said Miss Dawkins, appealing to Mr Damer. 'Do you think they will let us go over at all?'

'Well, I suppose they will; people do get over generally, I believe. Abdallah! Abdallah! why don't you pay the man? That fellow is always striving to save half a piastre for me.'

'I wish he wasn't quite so particular,' said Mrs Damer, who was already becoming rather tired; 'but I'm sure he's a very honest man in trying to protect us from being robbed.'

'That he is,' said Miss Dawkins; 'what a delightful trait of national character it is, to see these men so faithful to their employers!' And then at last they got over the ferry, Mr Ingram having descended among the combatants, and settled the matter in dispute by threats and shouts, and an uplifted stick.

They crossed the broad Nile exactly at the spot where the Nilometer, or river gauge, measures from day to day, and from year to year, the increasing or decreasing treasures of the stream, and landed at a village where thousands of eggs are made into chickens by the process of artificial incubation.

Mrs Damer thought that it was very hard upon the maternal hens – the hens which should have been maternal – that they should be thus robbed of the delights of motherhood.

'So unnatural, you know,' said Miss Dawkins; 'so opposed to the fostering principles of creation. Don't you think so, Mr Ingram?'

Mr Ingram said he didn't know. He was again seating Miss Damer on her donkey, and it must be presumed that he performed this feat clumsily; for Fanny Damer could jump on and off the animal with hardly a finger to help her, when her brother or her father was her escort; but now, under the hands of Mr Ingram, this work of mounting was one which required considerable time and care. All which Miss Dawkins observed with precision.

'It's all very well talking,' said Mr Damer, bringing up his donkey nearly alongside of that of Mr Ingram, and ignoring his daughter's presence, just as he would have done that of his boys, or his dog; 'but you must admit that political power is more equally distributed in England than it is in America.'

'Perhaps it is,' said Mr Ingram, 'equally distributed among, we will say, three dozen families,' and he made a feint as though to hold in his impetuous donkey, using the spur, however, at the same time on the side that was unseen by Mr Damer. As he did so, Fanny's donkey became equally impetuous, and the two cantered on in advance of the whole party. It was quite in vain that Mr Damer, at the top of his voice, shouted out something about 'three dozen corruptible demagogues'. Mr Ingram found it quite impossible to restrain his donkey so as to listen to the sarcasm.

'I do believe papa would talk politics,' said Fanny, 'if he were at the top of Mont Blanc, or under the falls of Niagara. I do hate politics, Mr Ingram.'

'I am sorry for that, very,' said Mr Ingram, almost sadly.

'Sorry, why! You don't want me to talk politics, do you!'

'In America, we are all politicians, more or less; and therefore, I suppose, you would hate us all.'

'Well, I rather think I should,' said Fanny; 'you would be such bores.' But there was something in her eye, as she spoke, which atoned for the harshness of her words.

'A very nice young man is Mr Ingram; don't you think so?' said Miss Dawkins to Mrs Damer. Mrs Damer was going along upon her donkey, not altogether comfortably. She much wished to have her lord and legitimate protector by her side, but he had left her to the care of a dragoman, whose English was not intelligible to her, and she was rather cross.

'Indeed, Miss Dawkins, I don't know who are nice and who are not. This nasty donkey stumbles at every step. There! I know I shall be down directly.'

'You need not be at all afraid of that; they are perfectly safe, I believe, always,' said Miss Dawkins, rising in her stirrup and handling her reins quite triumphantly. 'A very little practice will make you quite at home.'

'I don't know what you mean by a very little practice. I have been here six weeks. Why did you put me on such a bad donkey as this?' and she turned to Abdallah, the dragoman.

'Him berry good donkey, my lady; berry good – best of all. Call him Jack in Cairo. Him go to Pyramid and back, and mind noting.'

'What does he say, Miss Dawkins?'

'He says that that donkey is one called Jack. If so, I've had him myself many times, and Jack is a very good donkey.'

'I wish you had him now with all my heart,' said Mrs Damer. Upon which Miss Dawkins offered to change, but those perils of mounting and dismounting were to Mrs Damer a great deal too severe to admit of this.

'Seven miles of canal to be carried out into the sea, at a minimum depth of twenty-three feet, and the stone to be fetched from Heaven knows where. All the money in France wouldn't do it.' This was addressed by Mr Damer to M. de la Bordeau, whom he had caught after the abrupt flight of Mr Ingram.

'Den we will borrow a leetle from England,' said M. de la Bordeau.

'Precious little, I can tell you. Such stock would not hold its price in our markets for twenty-four hours. If it were made, the freights would be too heavy to allow of merchandise passing through. The heavy goods would all go round; and as for passengers and mails, you don't expect to get them, I suppose, while there is a railroad ready made to their hand?'

'Ve vill carry all your ships through vidout any transportation. Think of that, my friend.'

'Pshaw! You are worse than Ingram. Of all the plans I ever heard it is the most monstrous, the most impracticable, the most —' But here he was interrupted by the entreaties of his wife, who had, in absolute deed and fact, slipped from her donkey, and was now calling lustily for her husband's aid. Whereupon Miss Dawkins allied herself to the Frenchman, and listened with an air of strong conviction to those arguments which were so weak in the ears of Mr Damer. M. de la Bordeau was about to ride across the Great Desert to Jerusalem; and it might perhaps be quite as well to do that with him, as to go up the Nile as far as the second cataract with the Damers.

'And so, M. de la Bordeau, you intend really to start for Mount Sinai?'

'Yes, mees; ve intend to make one start on Monday veek.'

'And so on to Jerusalem. You are quite right. It would be a thousand pities to be in these countries, and to return without going over such ground as that. I shall certainly go to Jerusalem myself by that route.'

'Vat, mees! you! Vould you not find it too much fatigante?'

'I care nothing for fatigue, if I like the party I am with – nothing at all, literally. You will hardly understand me, perhaps, M. de la Bordeau; but I do not see any reason why I, as a young woman, should not make any journey that is practicable for a young man.'

'Ah! dat is great resolution for you, mees.'

'I mean as far as fatigue is concerned. You are a Frenchman, and belong to the nation that is at the head of all human civilization—'

M. de la Bordeau took off his hat, and bowed low, to the peak of his donkey saddle. He dearly loved to hear his country praised – as Miss Dawkins was aware.

'And I am sure you must agree with me,' continued Miss Dawkins, 'that the time is gone by for women to consider themselves helpless animals, or to be so considered by others.'

'Mees Dawkins vould never be considered, not in any times at all, to be one helpless animal,' said M. de la Bordeau, civilly.

'I do not, at any rate, intend to be so regarded,' said she. 'It suits me to travel alone; not that I am averse to society; quite the contrary; if I meet pleasant people, I am always ready to join them. But it suits me to travel without any permanent party, and I do not see why false shame should prevent my seeing the world as thoroughly as though I belonged to the other sex. Why should it, M. de la Bordeau?'

M. de la Bordeau declared that he did not see any reason why it should.

'I am passionately anxious to stand upon Mount Sinai,' continued Miss Dawkins; 'to press with my feet the earliest spot in sacred history, of the identity of which we are certain; to feel within me the awe-inspiring thrill of that thrice sacred hour.'

The Frenchman looked as though he did not quite understand her, but he said that it would be *magnifique*.

'You have already made up your party, I suppose, M. de la Bordeau?'

M. de la Bordeau gave the names of two Frenchmen and one Englishman, who were going with him.

'Upon my word, it is a great temptation to join you,' said Miss Dawkins, 'only for that horrid Englishman.'

'Vat, Mr Stanley?'

'Oh, I don't mean any disrespect to Mr Stanley. The horridness I speak of does not attach to him personally, but to his stiff, respectable, ungainly, well-behaved, irrational, and uncivilized country. You see I am not very patriotic.'

'Not quite so much as my dear friend Mr Damer.'

'Ha! ha! ha! an excellent creature, isn't he? And so they all are, dear creatures. But then they are so backward. They are most anxious that I should join them up the Nile, but—' and then Miss Dawkins shrugged her shoulders gracefully, and, as she flattered herself, like a Frenchwoman. After that they rode on in silence for a few moments.

'Yes, I must see Mount Sinai,' said Miss Dawkins, and then sighed deeply. M. de la Bordeau, notwithstanding that his country does stand at the head of all human civilisation, was not courteous enough to declare that if Miss Dawkins would join his party across the desert, nothing would be wanting to make his beatitude in this world perfect.

Their road from the village of the chicken-hatching ovens lay up along the left bank of the Nile, through an immense grove of lofty palm trees, looking out from among which our visitors could ever and anon see the heads of the two great Pyramids; that is, such of them could see it as felt any solicitude in the matter.

It is astonishing how much things lose their great interest as men find themselves in their close neighbourhood. To one living in New York or London, how ecstatic is the interest inspired by these huge structures. One feels that no price would be too high to pay for seeing them, as long as time and distance, and the world's inexorable task-work, forbid such a visit. How intense would be the delight of climbing over the wondrous handiwork of those wondrous architects so long since dead; how thrilling the awe with which one would penetrate down into their interior caves – those caves in which lay buried the bones of ancient kings, whose very names seem to have come to us almost from another world!

But all these feelings become strangely dim, their acute edges wonderfully worn, as the subjects which inspired them are brought near to us. 'Ah! so those are the Pyramids, are they?' says the traveller, when the first glimpse of them is shown to him from the window of a railway carriage. 'Dear me; they don't look so very high, do they? For Heaven's sake put the blind down, or we shall be destroyed by the sand.' And then the ecstacy and keen delight of the Pyramids has vanished, and forever.

Our friends, therefore, who for weeks past had seen them from a distance, though they had not yet visited them, did not seem to have any strong feeling on the subject as they trotted through the grove of palm-trees. Mr Damer had not yet escaped from his wife, who was still fretful from the result of her little accident.

'It was all the chattering of that Miss Dawkins,' said Mrs Damer. 'She would not let me attend to what I was doing.'

'Miss Dawkins is an ass,' said her husband.

'It is a pity she has no one to look after her,' said Mrs Damer.

M. de la Bordeau was still listening to Miss Dawkins's raptures about Mount Sinai. 'I wonder whether she has got any money,' said M. de la Bordeau to himself. 'It can't be much,' he went on thinking, 'or she would not be left in this way by herself.' And the result of his thoughts was that Miss Dawkins, if undertaken, might probably become more plague than profit. As to Miss Dawkins herself, though she was ecstatic about Mount Sinai – which was not present – she seemed to have forgotten the poor Pyramids, which were then before her nose.

The two lads were riding races along the dusty path, much to the disgust of their donkey-boys. Their time for enjoyment was to come. There were hampers to be opened; and then the absolute climbing of the Pyramids would actually be a delight to them.

As for Miss Damer and Mr Ingram, it was clear that they had forgotten palm-trees, Pyramids, the Nile, and all Egypt. They had escaped to a much fairer paradise.

'Could I bear to live among Republicans?' said Fanny, repeating the last words of her American lover, and looking down from her donkey to the ground as she did so. 'I hardly know what Republicans are, Mr Ingram.'

'Let me teach you,' said he.

'You do talk such nonsense. I declare there is that Miss Dawkins looking at us as though she had twenty eyes. Could you not teach her, Mr Ingram?'

And so they emerged from the palm-tree grove, through a village crowded with dirty, straggling, Arab children, on to the cultivated plain, beyond which the Pyramids stood, now full before them; the two large Pyramids, a smaller one, and the huge sphynx's head all in a group together.

'Fanny,' said Bob Damer, riding up to her, 'mamma wants you; so toddle back.'

'Mamma wants me! What can she want me for now?' said Fanny, with a look of anything but filial duty in her face.

'To protect her from Miss Dawkins, I think. She wants you to ride at her side, so that Dawkins mayn't get at her. Now, Mr Ingram, I'll bet you half-a-crown I'm at the top of the big Pyramid before you.'

Poor Fanny! She obeyed, however; doubtless feeling that it would not do as yet to show too plainly that she preferred Mr Ingram to her mother. She arrested her donkey, therefore, till Mrs Damer overtook her; and Mr Ingram, as he paused for a moment with her while she did so, fell into the hands of Miss Dawkins.

'I cannot think, Fanny, how you get on so quick,' said Mrs Damer. 'I'm always last; but then my donkey is such a very nasty one. Look there, now; he's always trying to get me off.'

'We shall soon be at the Pyramids now, mamma.'

'How on earth I am ever to get back again I cannot think. I am so tired now that I can hardly sit.'

'You'll be better, mamma, when you get your luncheon and a glass of wine.'

'How on earth we are to eat and drink with those nasty Arab people around us, I can't conceive. They tell me we shall be eaten up by them. But, Fanny, what has Mr Ingram been saying to you all day?'

'What has he been saying, mamma? Oh! I don't know – a hundred things, I dare say. But he has not been talking to me all the time.'

'I think he has, Fanny, nearly, since we crossed the river. Oh, dear! oh, dear! this animal does hurt me so! Every time he moves he flings his head about, and that gives me such a bump.' And then Fanny commiserated her mother's sufferings, and in her commiseration contrived to elude any further questioning as to Mr Ingram's conversation.

'Majestic piles, are they not?' said Miss Dawkins, who, having changed her companion, allowed her mind to revert from Mount Sinai to the Pyramids. They were now riding through cultivated grounds, with the vast extent of the sands of Lybia before them. The two Pyramids were standing on the margin of the sand, with the head of the recumbent sphynx plainly visible between them. But no idea can be formed of the size of this immense figure till it is visited much more closely. The body is covered with sand, and the head and neck alone stand above the surface of the ground. They were still two miles distant, and the sphynx as yet was but an obscure mound between the two vast Pyramids.

'Immense piles!' said Miss Dawkins, repeating her own words.

'Yes, they are large,' said Mr Ingram, who did not choose to indulge in enthusiasm in the presence of Miss Dawkins.

'Enormous! What a grand idea – eh, Mr Ingram? The human race does not create such things as those now-a-days!'

'No, indeed,' he answered; 'but perhaps we create better things.'

'Better! You do not mean to say, Mr Ingram, that you are a utilitarian. I do, in truth, hope better things of you than that. Yes! steam mills are better, no doubt, and mechanics' institutes, and penny newspapers. But is nothing to be valued but what is useful?' and Miss Dawkins, in the height of her enthusiasm, switched her donkey severely over the shoulder.

'I might, perhaps, have said also that we create more beautiful things,' said Mr Ingram.

'But we cannot create older things.'

'No, certainly; we cannot do that.'

'Nor can we imbue what we do create with the grand associations which environ those piles with so intense an interest. Think of the mighty dead, Mr Ingram, and of their great power when living. Think of the hands which it took to raise those huge blocks—'

'And of the lives which it cost.'

'Doubtless. The tyranny and invincible power of the royal architects add to the grandeur of the idea. One would not perhaps wish to have back the kings of Egypt—'

'Well, no; they would be neither useful nor beautiful.'

'Perhaps not; and I do not wish to be picturesque at the expense of my fellow-creatures.'

'I doubt even whether the kings of Egypt would be picturesque.'

'You know what I mean, Mr Ingram. But the associations of such names, and the presence of the stupendous works with which they are connected, fill the soul with awe. Such, at least, is the effect with mine.'

'I fear that my tendencies, Miss Dawkins, are more realistic than your own.'

'You belong to a young country, Mr Ingram, and are naturally prone to think of material life. The necessity of living looms large before you.'

'Very large, indeed, Miss Dawkins.'

'Whereas with us, with some of us at least, the material aspect has given place to one in which poetry and enthusiasm prevail. To such among us the associations of past times are very dear. Cheops, to me, is more than Napoleon Bonaparte.'

'That is more than most of your countrymen can say – at any rate, just at present.'

'I am a woman,' continued Miss Dawkins.

Mr Ingram took off his hat in acknowledgement both of the announcement and of the fact.

'And to us it is not given – not given as yet – to share in the great deeds of the present. The envy of your sex has driven us from the paths which lead to honour. But the deeds of the past are as much ours as yours.'

'Oh, quite as much.'

''Tis to your country that we look for enfranchisement from this thraldom. Yes, Mr Ingram, the women of America have that strength of mind which has been wanting to those of Europe. In the United States woman will at last learn to exercise her proper mission.'

Mr Ingram expressed a sincere wish that such might be the case; and then wondering at the ingenuity with which Miss Dawkins had travelled round from Cheops and his Pyramid to the rights of women in America, he contrived to fall back, under the pretence of asking after the ailments of Mrs Damer.

And now at last they were on the sand, in the absolute desert, making their way up to the very foot of the most northern of the two Pyramids. They were by this time surrounded by a crowd of Arab guides, or Arabs professing to be guides, who had already ascertained that Mr Damer was the chief of the party, and were accordingly driving him almost to madness by the offers of their services, and their assurance that he could not possibly see the outside or the inside of either structure, or even remain alive upon the ground, unless he at once accepted their offers made at their own prices.

'Get away, will you?' said he. 'I don't want any of you, and I won't have you! If you take hold of me, I'll shoot you!' This was said to one specially energetic Arab, who, in his efforts to secure his prey, had caught hold of Mr Damer by the leg.

'Yes, yes, I say! Englishman always take me; me – me – me, and than no break him leg. Yes – yes – yes – I go. Master say, yes. Only one leetle ten shilling!'

'Abdallah!' shouted Mr Damer, 'why don't you take this man away? Why don't you make him understand that if all the Pyramids depended on it, I would not give him sixpence!'

And then Abdallah, thus invoked, came up, and explained to the man in Arabic that he would gain his object more surely if he would behave himself a little more quietly: a hint which the man took for one minute, and for one minute only.

And then poor Mrs Damer replied to an application for backsheish by the gift of a sixpence. Unfortunate woman! The word backsheish means, I believe, a gift; but it has come in Egypt to signify money, and is eternally dinned into the ears of strangers by Arab suppliants. Mrs Damer ought to have known better, as, during the last six weeks, she had never shown her face out of Shepheard's Hotel without being pestered for backsheish; but she was tired and weak, and foolishly thought to rid herself of the man who was annoying her.

No sooner had the coin dropped from her hand into that of the Arab, than she was surrounded by a cluster of beggars, who loudly made their petitions, as though they would, each of them, individually be injured if treated with less liberality than that first comer. They took hold of her donkey, her bridle, her saddle, her legs, and at last her arms and hands, screaming for backsheish in voices that were neither sweet nor mild.

In her dismay, she did give away sundry small coins – all, probably, that she had about her; but this only made the matter worse. Money was going, and each man, by sufficient energy, might hope to get some of it. They were very energetic, and so frightened the poor lady, that she would certainly have fallen, had she not been kept on her seat by their pressure around her.

'Oh, dear! oh, dear! get away,' she cried. 'I haven't got any more; indeed, I haven't. Go away, I tell you! Mr Damer, oh, Mr Damer!' and then, in the excess of her agony, she uttered one loud, long, and continuous shriek.

Up came Mr Damer; up came Abdallah; up came M. de la Bordeau; up came Mr Ingram; and at last she was rescued. 'You shouldn't go away, and leave me to the mercy of these nasty people. As to that Abdallah, he is of no use to anybody.'

'Why you bodder de good lady, you dam blackguard?' said Abdallah, raising his stick, as though he were going to lay them all low with a blow. 'Now you get noting, you tief!'

The Arabs for a moment retired to a little distance, like flies driven from a sugar bowl; but it was easy to see that, like the flies, they would return at the first vacant moment.

Our party, whom we left on their road, had now reached the very foot of the Pyramids, and proceeded to dismount from their donkeys. Their intention was first to ascend to the top, then to come down to their banquet, and after that to penetrate into the interior. And all this would seem to be easy of performance. The Pyramid is undoubtedly high, but it is so constructed as to admit of climbing without difficulty. A lady mounting it would undoubtedly need some assistance, but any man possessed of moderate activity would require no aid at all.

But our friends were at once alarmed at the tremendous nature of the task before them. A sheikh of the Arabs came forth, who communicated with them through Abdallah. The work could be done, no doubt, he said; but a great many men would be wanted to assist. Each lady must have four Arabs, and each gentleman three; and then, seeing that the work would be peculiarly severe on this special day, each of these numerous Arabs must be remunerated by some very large number of piastres.

Mr Damer, who was by no means a close man in his money dealings, opened his eyes with surprise, and mildly expostulated; M. de la Bordeau, who was rather a close man in his reckonings, immediately buttoned up his breeches pocket, and declared that he should decline to mount the Pyramid at all at that price; and then Mr Ingram descended to the combat.

The protestations of the men were fearful. They declared with loud voices, eager actions, and manifold English oaths, that an attempt was being made to rob them. They had a right to demand the sums which they were charging, and it was a shame that English gentlemen should come and take the bread out of their mouths. And so they screeched, gesticulated, and swore, and frightened poor Mrs Damer almost into fits.

But at last it was settled, and away they started, the sheikh declaring that the bargain had been made at so low a rate as to leave him not one piastre for himself. Each man had an Arab on each side of him, and Miss Dawkins and Miss Damer had each in addition one behind. Mrs Damer was so frightened as altogether to have lost all ambition to ascend. She sat below on a fragment of stone, with the three dragomans standing around her as guards; but even with the three dragomans the attacks on her were frequent; and as she declared afterwards, she was so bewildered, that she never had time to remember that she had come there from England to see the Pyramids, and that she was now immediately under them.

The boys, utterly ignoring their guards, scrambled up quicker than the Arabs could follow them. Mr Damer started off at a pace which soon brought him to the end of his tether, and from that point was dragged up by the sheer strength of his assistants; thereby accomplishing the wishes of the men, who induce their victims to start as rapidly as possible, in order that they may soon find themselves helpless from want of wind. Mr Ingram endeavoured to attach himself to Fanny, and she would have been nothing loth to have had him at her right hand, instead of the hideous brown, shrieking, one-eyed Arab who took hold of her. But it was soon found that any such arrangement was impossible. Each guide felt that if he lost his own peculiar hold he would lose his prey, and held on, therefore, with invincible tenacity. Miss Dawkins looked, too, as though she ought to be attended by some Christian cavalier, but no Christian cavalier was forthcoming. M. de la Bordeau was the wisest, for he took the matter quietly, did as he was bid, and allowed the guides nearly to carry him to the top of the edifice.

'Ha! so this is the top of the Pyramid, is it?' said Mr Damer, bringing out his words one by one, being terribly out of breath. 'Very wonderful, very wonderful indeed!'

'It is wonderful!' said Miss Dawkins, whose breath had not failed her in the least, 'very wonderful indeed! Only think, Mr Damer, you might travel on for days and days, till days became months, through those interminable sands, and yet you would never come to the end of them! Is it not quite stupendous?'

'Ah, yes, quite,' – puff, puff – said Mr Damer, striving to regain his breath.

Mr Damer was now at her disposal – weak, and worn with toil and travel, out of breath, and with half his manhood gone; if ever she might prevail over him so as to procure from his mouth an assent to that Nile proposition, it would be now. And after all, that Nile proposition was the best one now before her. She did not quite like the idea of starting off across the Great Desert without any lady, and was not sure that she was prepared to be fallen in love with by M. de la Bordeau, even if there should ultimately be any readiness on the part of that gentleman to perform the *rôle* of lover. With Mr Ingram the matter was different; nor was she so diffident of her own charms as to think it altogether impossible that she might succeed, in the teeth of that little chit, Fanny Damer. That Mr Ingram would join the party up the Nile she had very little doubt; and then there would be one place left for her. She would thus, at any rate, become commingled with a most respectable family, who might be of material service to her.

Thus actuated, she commenced an earnest attack upon Mr Damer.

'Stupendous!' she said again, for she was fond of repeating favourite words. 'What a wondrous race must have been those Egyptian kings of old!'

'I dare say they were,' said Mr Damer, wiping his brow as he sat upon a large loose stone, a fragment lying on the flat top of the Pyramid, one of those stones with which the complete apex was once made, or was once about to be made.

'A magnificent race! so gigantic in their conceptions! Their ideas altogether overwhelm us, poor, insignificant, latter-day mortals. They built these vast Pyramids; but for us, it is task enough to climb to their top.'

'Quite enough,' ejaculated Mr Damer.

But Mr Damer would not always remain weak and out of breath, and it was absolutely necessary for Miss Dawkins to hurry away from Cheops and his tomb, to Thebes and Karnac.

'After seeing this it is impossible for any one, with a spark of imagination, to leave Egypt without going further a-field.'

Mr Damer merely wiped his brow and grunted. This Miss Dawkins took as a signal of weakness, and went on with her task perseveringly.

'For myself, I have resolved to go up, at any rate, as far as Asouan and the first cataract. I had thought of acceding to the wishes of a party who are going across the Great Desert by Mount Sinai to Jerusalem; but the kindness of yourself and Mrs Damer is so great, and the prospect of joining in your boat is so pleasurable, that I have made up my mind to accept your very kind offer.'

This, it will be acknowledged, was bold on the part of Miss Dawkins; but what will not audacity effect? To use the slang of modern language, cheek carries everything now-a-days. And whatever may have been Miss Dawkins' deficiencies, in this virtue she was not deficient.

'I have made up my mind to accept your very kind offer,' she said, shining on Mr Damer with her blandest smile.

What was a stout, breathless, perspiring, middle-aged gentleman to do under such circumstances? Mr Damer was a man who, in most matters, had his own way. That his wife should have given such an invitation without consulting him, was, he knew, quite impossible. She would as soon have thought of asking all those Arab guides to accompany them. Nor was it to be thought of, that he should allow himself to be kidnapped into such an arrangement by the impudence of any Miss Dawkins. But there was, he felt, a difficulty in answering such a proposition from a young lady with a direct negative, especially while he was so scant of breath. So he wiped his brow again, and looked at her.

'But I can only agree to this on one understanding,' continued Miss Dawkins, 'and that is, that I am allowed to defray my own full share of the expense of the journey.'

Upon hearing this Mr Damer thought that he saw his way out of the wood. 'Wherever I go, Miss Dawkins, I am always the paymaster myself,' and this he contrived to say with some sternness, palpitating though he still was; and the sternness which was deficient in his voice he endeavoured to put into his countenance.

But he did not know Miss Dawkins. 'Oh, Mr Damer,' she said – and as she spoke her smile became almost blander than it was before – 'oh, Mr Damer, I could not think of suffering you to be so liberal; I could not, indeed. But I shall be quite content that you should pay everything and let me settle with you in one sum afterwards.'

Mr Damer's breath was now rather more under his own command. 'I am afraid, Miss Dawkins,' he said, 'that Mrs Damer's weak state of health will not admit of such an arrangement.'

'What, about the paying?'

'Not only as to that, but we are a family party, Miss Dawkins; and great as would be the benefit to all of us of your society, in Mrs Damer's present state of health, I am afraid – in short, you would not find it agreeable. And therefore' – this he added, seeing that she was still about to persevere – 'I fear that we must forego the advantage you offer.'

And then, looking into his face, Miss Dawkins did perceive that even her audacity would not prevail.

'Oh, very well,' she said, and moving from the stone on which she had been sitting, she walked off, carrying her head very high, to a corner of the Pyramid from which she could look forth alone towards the sands of Lybia.

In the meantime another little overture was being made at the top of the same Pyramid – an overture which was not received quite in the same spirit. While Mr Damer was recovering his breath for the sake of answering Miss Dawkins, Miss Damer had walked to the further corner of the square platform on which they were placed, and there sat herself down with her face turned towards Cairo. Perhaps it was not singular that Mr Ingram should have followed her.

This would have been very well if a dozen Arabs had not also followed them. But as this was the case, Mr Ingram had to play his game under some difficulty. He had no sooner seated himself beside her than they came and stood directly in front of the seat, shutting out the view, and by no means improving the fragrance of the air around them.

'And this, then, Miss Damer, will be our last excursion,' he said, in his tenderest, softest tone.

'De good Englishman will gib de poor Arab one little backsheesh,' said an Arab, putting out his hand and shaking Mr Ingram's shoulder.

'Yes, yes, yes; him gib backsheesh,' said another.

'Him berry good man,' said a third, putting up a filthy hand, and touching Mr Ingram's face.

'And young lady berry good, too; she gib backsheesh to poor Arab.'

'Yes,' said a fourth, preparing to take a similar liberty with Miss Damer.

This was too much for Mr Ingram. He had already used very positive language in his endeavour to assure his tormentors that they would not get a piastre from him. But this only changed their soft persuasions into threats. Upon hearing which, and upon seeing what the man attempted to do in his endeavour to get money from Miss Damer, he raised his stick, and struck first one and then another as violently as he could upon their heads.

Any ordinary civilised men would have been stunned by such blows, for they fell on the bare foreheads of the Arabs; but the objects of the American's wrath merely skulked away; and the others, convinced by the only arguments which they understood, followed in pursuit of victims who might be less pugnacious.

It is hard for a man to be at once tender and pugnacious – to be sentimental, while he is putting forth his physical strength with all the violence in his power. It is difficult, also, for him to be gentle instantly after having been in a rage. So he changed his tactics at the moment, and came to the point at once in a manner befitting his present state of mind.

'Those vile wretches have put me in such a heat,' he said, 'that I hardly know what I am saying. But the fact is this, Miss Damer, I cannot leave Cairo without knowing— You understand what I mean, Miss Damer.'

'Indeed I do not, Mr Ingram; except that I am afraid you mean nonsense.'

'Yes, you do; you know that I love you. I am sure you must know it. At any rate you know it now.'

'Mr Ingram, you should not talk in such a way.'

'Why should I not? But the truth is, Fanny, I can talk in no other way. I do love you very dearly. Can you love me well enough to go and be my wife in a country far away from your own?'

Before she left the top of the Pyramid, Fanny Damer had said that she would try.

Mr Ingram was now a proud and happy man, and seemed to think the steps of the Pyramid too small for his elastic energy. But Fanny feared that her troubles were to come. There was papa – that terrible bugbear on all such occasions! What would papa say? She was sure her papa would not allow her to marry and go so far away from her own family and country. For herself, she liked the Americans – always had liked them, so she said; would desire nothing better than to live among them. But papa! And Fanny sighed as she felt that all the recognised miseries of a young lady in love were about to fall upon her.

Nevertheless, at her lover's instance, she promised and declared, in twenty different loving phrases, that nothing on earth should ever make her false to her love or to her lover.

'Fanny, where are you? Why are you not ready to come down?' shouted Mr Damer, not in the best of tempers. He felt that he had almost been unkind to an unprotected female, and his heart misgave him. And yet it would have misgiven him more had he allowed himself to be entrapped by Miss Dawkins.

'I am quite ready, papa,' said Fanny running up to him – for it may be understood that there is quite room enough for a young lady to run on the top of the Pyramid.

'I am sure I don't know where you have been all the time,' said Mr Damer; 'and where are those two boys?'

Fanny pointed to the top of the other Pyramid, and there they were, conspicuous with their red caps.

'And M. de la Bordeau?'

'Oh! he has gone down, I think – no, he is there with Miss Dawkins.'

And in truth Miss Dawkins was leaning on his arm most affectionately, as she stooped over and looked down upon the ruins below her.

'And where is that fellow, Ingram?' said Mr Damer, looking about him. 'He is always out of the way when he's wanted.'

To this Fanny said nothing. Why should she? She was not Mr Ingram's keeper.

And then they all descended, each again with his proper number of Arabs to hurry and embarrass him; and they found Mrs Damer at the bottom, like a piece of sugar covered with flies. She was heard to declare afterwards that she would not go to the Pyramids again, not if they were to be given to her for herself, as ornaments for her garden.

The pic-nic lunch among the big stones at the foot of the Pyramids was not a very gay affair. Miss Dawkins talked more than any one else, being determined to show that she bore her defeat gallantly. Her conversation, however, was chiefly addressed to M. de la Bordeau, and he seemed to think more of his cold chicken and ham than he did of her wit and attention.

Fanny hardly spoke a word. There was her father before her, and she could not eat, much less talk, as she thought of all that she would have to go through. What would he say to the idea of having an American son-in-law?

Nor was Mr Ingram very lively. A young man, when he has been just accepted, never is so. His happiness under the present circumstances was, no doubt, intense, but it was of a silent nature.

And then the interior of the building had to be visited. To tell the truth, none of the party would have cared to perform this feat, had it not been for the honour of the thing. To have come from Paris, New York, or London, to the Pyramids, and then not to have visited the very tomb of Cheops, would have shown on the part of all of them an indifference to subjects of interest which would have been altogether fatal to their character as travellers. And so a party for the interior was made up.

Miss Damer, when she saw the aperture through which it was expected that she should descend, at once declared for staying with her mother. Miss Dawkins, however, was enthusiastic for the journey. 'Persons with so very little command over their nerves might really as well stay at home,' she said to Mr Ingram, who glowered at her dreadfully for expressing such an opinion about his Fanny.

This entrance into the Pyramids is a terrible task, which should be undertaken by no lady. Those who perform it have to creep down, and then to be dragged up through infinite dirt, foul smells, and bad air; and when they have done it, they see nothing. But they do earn the gratification of saying that they have been inside a Pyramid.

'Well, I've done that once,' said Mr Damer, coming out, 'and I do not think that anyone will catch me doing it again. I never was in such a filthy place in my life.'

'Oh, Fanny! I am so glad you did not go; I am sure it is not fit for ladies,' said poor Mrs Damer, forgetful of her friend Miss Dawkins.

'I should have been ashamed of myself,' said Miss Dawkins, bristling up, and throwing back her head as she stood, 'if I had allowed any consideration to have prevented my visiting such a spot. If it be not improper for men to go there, how can it be improper for women?'

'I did not say improper, my dear,' said Mrs Damer, apologetically.

'And as for the fatigue, what can a woman be worth who is afraid to encounter as much as I have now gone through for the sake of visiting the last resting-place of such a king as Cheops?' And Miss Dawkins, as she pronounced the last words, looked round her with disdain upon poor Fanny Damer.

'But I meant the dirt,' said Mrs Damer.

'Dirt!' ejaculated Miss Dawkins, and then walked away. Why should she now submit her high tone of feeling to the Damers, or why care longer for their good opinion? Therefore she scattered contempt around her as she ejaculated the last word, 'dirt.'

'And then the return home! I know I shall never get there,' said Mrs Damer, looking piteously up into her husband's face.

'Nonsense, my dear; nonsense; you must get there.' Mrs Damer groaned, and acknowledged in her heart that she must – either dead or alive.

'And, Jefferson,' said Fanny, whispering – for there had been a moment since their descent in which she had been instructed to call him by his Christian name – 'never mind talking to me going home. I will ride by mamma. Do you go with papa, and put him in a good humour; and if he says anything about the lords and the bishops, don't you contradict him, you know.'

What will not a man do for love? Mr Ingram promised. And in this way they started: the two boys led the van; then came Mr Damer and Mr Ingram, unusually and unpatriotically acquiescent as to England's aristocratic propensities; then Miss Dawkins, riding, alas! alone; after her, M. de la Bordeau, also alone – the ungallant Frenchman! And the rear was brought up by Mrs Damer and her daughter, flanked on each side by a dragoman, with a third dragoman behind him.

And in this order they went back to Cairo, riding their donkeys and crossing the ferry solemnly, and, for the most part, silently. Mr Ingram did talk, as he had an important object in view – that of putting Mr Damer into a good humour.

In this he succeeded so well, that, by the time they had remounted, after crossing the Nile, Mr Damer opened his heart to his companion on the subject that was troubling him, and told him all about Miss Dawkins.

'I don't see why we should have a companion that we don't like for eight or ten weeks, merely because it seems rude to refuse a lady.'

'Indeed, I agree with you,' said Mr Ingram; 'I should call it weak-minded to give way in such a case.'

'My daughter does not like her at all,' continued Mr Damer.

'Nor would she be a nice companion for Miss Damer; not according to my way of thinking,' said Mr Ingram.

'And as to my having asked her, or Mrs Damer having asked her – why, God bless my soul, it is pure invention on the woman's part!'

'Ha! ha! ha!' laughed Mr Ingram; 'I must say she plays her game well; but then she is an old soldier, and has the benefit of experience.' What would Miss Dawkins have said had she known that Mr Ingram called her an old soldier?

'I don't like the kind of thing at all,' said Mr Damer, who was very serious upon the subject. 'You see the position in which I am placed. I am forced to be very rude, or—'

'I don't call it rude at all.'

'Disobliging, then; or else I must have all my comfort invaded and pleasure destroyed by, by, by—' And Mr Damer paused, being at a loss for an appropriate name for Miss Dawkins.

'By an unprotected female,' suggested Mr Ingram.

'Yes; just so. I am as fond of pleasant company as anybody; but then I like to choose it myself.'

'So do I,' said Mr Ingram, thinking of his own choice.

'Now, Ingram, if you would join us, we should be delighted.'

'Upon my word, sir, the offer is too flattering,' said Ingram, hesitatingly; for he felt that he could not undertake such a journey until Mr Damer knew on what terms he stood with Fanny.

'You are a terrible democrat,' said Mr Damer, laughing; 'but then, on that matter, you know, we could agree to differ.'

'Exactly so,' said Mr Ingram, who had not collected his thoughts or made up his mind as to what he had better say and do, on the spur of the moment.

'Well, what do you say to it?' said Mr Damer, encouragingly. But Ingram paused before he answered.

'For Heaven's sake, my dear fellow, don't have the slightest hesitation in refusing, if you don't like the plan.'

'The fact is, Mr Damer, I should like it too well.'

'Like it too well?'

'Yes, sir, and I may as well tell you now as later. I had intended this evening to have asked for your permission to address your daughter.'

'God bless my soul!' said Mr Damer, looking as though a totally new idea had now been opened to him.

'And under these circumstances, I will now wait and see whether or not you will renew your offer.'

'God bless my soul!' said Mr Damer again. It often does strike an old gentleman as very odd that any man should fall in love with his daughter, whom he has not ceased to look upon as a child. The case is generally quite different with mothers. They seem to think that every young man must fall in love with their girls.

'And have you said anything to Fanny about this?' asked Mr Damer.

'Yes, sir; I have her permission to speak to you.'

'God bless my soul!' said Mr Damer; and by this time they had arrived at Shepheard's Hotel.

'Oh, mamma,' said Fanny, as soon as she found herself alone with her mother that evening, 'I have something that I must tell you.'

'Oh, Fanny, don't tell me anything to-night, for I am a great deal too tired to listen.'

'But oh, mamma, pray – you must listen to this; indeed you must.' And Fanny knelt down at her mother's knee, and looked beseechingly up into her face.

'What is it, Fanny? You know that all my bones are sore, and that I am so tired that I am almost dead.'

'Mamma, Mr Ingram has—'

'Has what, my dear? has he done anything wrong?'

'No, mamma; but he has – he has proposed to me.' And Fanny, bursting into tears, hid her face in her mother's lap.

And thus the story was told on both sides of the house. On the next day, as a matter of course, all the difficulties and dangers of such a marriage as that which was now projected, were insisted on by both father and mother. It was improper; it would cause a severing of the family not to be thought of; it would be an alliance of a dangerous nature, and not at all calculated to insure happiness; and, in short, it was impossible. On that day, therefore, they all went to bed very unhappy. But on the next day, as was also a matter of course, seeing that there were no pecuniary difficulties, the mother and father were talked over, and Mr Ingram was accepted as a son-in-law. It need hardly be said that the offer of a place in Mr Damer's boat was again made, and that on this occasion it was accepted without hesitation.

There was an American Protestant clergyman resident in Cairo, with whom among other persons, Miss Dawkins had become acquainted. Upon this gentleman, or upon his wife, Miss Dawkins called a few days after the journey to the Pyramids, and finding him in his study, thus performed her duty to her neighbour:

'You know your countryman, Mr Ingram, I think?' said she.

'Oh, yes; very intimately.'

'If you have any regard for him, Mr Burton,' such was the gentleman's name, 'I think you should put him on his guard.'

'On his guard against what?' said Mr Burton, with a serious air, for there was something solemn in the threat of impending misfortune as conveyed by Miss Dawkins.

'Why,' said she, 'those Damers, I fear, are dangerous people.'

'Do you mean that they will borrow money of him?'

'Oh, no; not that exactly; but they are clearly setting their cap at him.'

'Setting their cap at him?'

'Yes; there is a daughter, you know; a little chit of a thing; and I fear Mr Ingram may be caught before he knows where he is. It would be such a pity, you know. He is going up the river with them, I hear. That, in his place, is very foolish. They asked me, but I positively refused.'

Mr Burton remarked that 'in such a matter as that Mr Ingram would be perfectly able to take care of himself.'

'Well, perhaps so; but seeing what was going on, I thought it my duty to tell you.' And so Miss Dawkins took her leave.

Mr Ingram did go up the Nile with the Damers, as did an old friend of the Damers who arrived from England. And a very pleasant trip they had of it. And as far as the present historian knows, the two lovers were shortly afterwards married in England.

Poor Miss Dawkins was left in Cairo for some time on her beam ends. But she was one of those who are not easily vanquished. After an interval of ten days she made acquaintance with an Irish family – having utterly failed in moving the hard heart of M. de la Bordeau – and with them she proceeded to Constantinople. They consisted of two brothers and a sister, and were, therefore, very convenient for matrimonial purposes. But, nevertheless, when I last heard of Miss Dawkins, she was still an un-protected female.

WILKIE COLLINS

Mrs Badgery

Is there any law in England which will protect me from Mrs Badgery?

I am a bachelor, and Mrs Badgery is a widow. Let nobody rashly imagine that I am about to relate a common-place grievance, because I have suffered that first sentence to escape my pen. My objection to Mrs Badgery is, not that she is too fond of me, but that she is too fond of the memory of her late husband. She has not attempted to marry me; she would not think of marrying me, even if I asked her. Understand, therefore, if you please, at the outset, that my grievance in relation to this widow lady is a grievance of an entirely new kind.

Let me begin again. I am a bachelor of a certain age. I have a large circle of acquaintance; but I solemnly declare that the late Mr Badgery was never numbered on the list of my friends. I never heard of him in my life; I never knew that he had left a relict; I never set eyes on Mrs Badgery until one fatal morning when I went to see if the fixtures were all right in my new house.

My new house is in the suburbs of London. I looked at it, liked it, took it. Three times I visited it before I sent my furniture in. Once with a friend, once with a surveyor, once by myself, to throw a sharp eye, as I have already intimated, over the fixtures. The third visit marked the fatal occasion on which I first saw Mrs Badgery. A deep interest attaches to this event, and I shall go into details in describing it.

I rang at the bell of the garden-door. The old woman appointed to keep the house answered it. I directly saw something strange and confused in her face and manner. Some men would have pondered a little and questioned her. I am by nature impetuous and a rusher at conclusions. 'Drunk,' I said to myself, and walked on into the house perfectly satisfied.

I looked into the front parlour. Grate all right, curtain-pole all right, gas chandelier all right. I looked into the back parlour – ditto, ditto, ditto, as we men of business say. I mounted the stairs. Blind on back window right? Yes; blind on back window right. I opened the door of the front drawing-room – and there, sitting in the middle of the bare floor, was a large woman on a little camp-stool! She was dressed in the deepest mourning; her face was hidden by the thickest crape veil I ever saw; and she was groaning softly to herself in the desolate solitude of my new unfurnished house.

What did I do? Do! I bounced back into the landing as if I had been shot, uttering the national exclamation of terror and astonishment, 'Hullo!' (And here I particularly beg, in parenthesis, that the printer will follow my spelling of the word, and not put Hillo or Halloa instead, both of which are senseless compromises which represent no sound that ever yet issued from an Englishman's lips.) I said, 'Hullo!' and then I turned round fiercely upon the old woman who kept the house, and said 'Hullo!' again.

She understood the irresistible appeal that I had made to her feelings, and curtseyed, and looked towards the drawing-room, and humbly hoped that I was not startled or put out. I asked who the crape-covered woman on the camp-stool was, and what she wanted there. Before the old woman could answer, the soft groaning in the drawing-room ceased, and a muffled voice, speaking from behind the crape veil, addressed me reproachfully, and said:

'I am the widow of the late Mr Badgery.'

What did I say in answer? Exactly the words which, I flatter myself, any other sensible man in my situation would have said. And what words were they? These two:

'Oh, indeed?'

'Mr Badgery and myself were the last tenants who inhabited this house,' continued the muffled voice. 'Mr Badgery died here.' The voice ceased, and the soft groans began again.

It was perhaps not necessary to answer this; but I did answer it. How? In one word:

'Ha!'

'Our house has been long empty,' resumed the voice, choked by sobs. 'Our establishment has been broken up. Being left in reduced circum-stances, I now live in a cottage near; but it is not home to me. This is home. However long I live, wherever I go, whatever changes may happen to this beloved house, nothing can ever prevent me from looking on it as *my* home. I came here, sir, with Mr Badgery after our honey-moon. All the brief happiness of my life was once contained within these four walls. Every dear remembrance that I fondly cherish is shut up in these sacred rooms.'

Again the voice ceased, and again the soft groans echoed round my empty walls, and oozed out past me down my uncarpeted staircase.

I reflected. Mrs Badgery's brief happiness and dear remembrances were not included in the list of fixtures. Why could she not take them away with her? Why should she leave them littered about in the way of my furniture? I was just thinking how I could put this view of the case strongly to Mrs Badgery, when she suddenly left off groaning and addressed me once more.

'While this house has been empty,' she said, 'I have been in the habit of looking in from time to time, and renewing my tender associations with the place. I have lived, as it were, in the sacred memories of Mr Badgery and of the past, which these dear, these priceless rooms call up, dismantled and dusty as they are at the present moment. It has been my practice to give a remuneration to the attendant for any slight trouble that I might occasion—'

'Only sixpence, sir,' whispered the old woman, close at my ear.

'And to ask nothing in return,' continued Mrs Badgery, 'but the permission to bring my camp-stool with me, and to meditate on Mr Badgery in the empty rooms, with every one of which some happy thought, or eloquent word, or tender action of his, is so sweetly associated. I came here on my usual errand to-day. I am discovered, I presume, by the new proprietor of the house – discovered, I am quite ready to admit, as an intruder. I am willing to go, if you wish it after hearing my explanation. My heart is full, sir; I am quite incapable of contending with you. You would hardly think it, but I am sitting on the spot once occupied by our ottoman. I am looking towards the window in which my flower-stand once stood. In this very place Mr Badgery first sat down and clasped me to his heart, when we came back from our honey-moon trip. "Matilda," he said, "your drawing-room has been expensively papered, carpeted, and furnished for a month; but it has only been adorned, love, since you entered it." If you have no sympathy, sir, for such remembrances as these; if you see nothing pitiable in my position, taken in connection with my presence here; if you cannot enter into my feelings, and thoroughly understand that this is not a house, but a Shrine – you have only to say so, and I am quite willing to go.'

She spoke with the air of a martyr – a martyr to my insensibility. If she had been the proprietor and I had been the intruder, she could not have been more mournfully magnanimous. All this time, too, she never raised her veil – she never has raised it, in my presence, from that time to this. I have no idea whether she is young or old, dark or fair, handsome or ugly: my impression is, that she is in every respect a finished and perfect Gorgon; but I have no basis of fact on which I can support that dismal idea. A moving mass of crape and a muffled voice – that, if you drive me to it, is all I know, in a personal point of view, of Mrs Badgery.

'Ever since my irreparable loss, this has been the shrine of my pilgrimage, and the altar of my worship,' proceeded the voice. 'One man may call himself a landlord, and say that he will let it; another man may call himself a tenant, and say that he will take it. I don't blame either of those two men; I don't wish to intrude on either of those two men; I only tell them that this is my home; that my heart is still in possession, and that no mortal laws, landlords, or tenants can ever turn it out. If you don't understand this, sir; if the holiest feelings that do honour to our common nature have no particular sanctity in your estimation, pray do not scruple to say so; pray tell me to go.'

'I don't wish to do anything uncivil, ma'am,' said I. 'But I am a single man, and I am not sentimental.' (Mrs Badgery groaned.) 'Nobody told me I was coming into a Shrine when I took this house; nobody warned me, when I first went over it, that there was a Heart in possession. I regret to have disturbed your meditations, and I am sorry to hear that Mr Badgery is dead. That is all I have to say about it; and, now, with your kind permission, I will do myself the honour of wishing you good morning, and will go up-stairs to look after the fixtures on the second floor.'

Could I have given a gentler hint than this? Could I have spoken more compassionately to a woman whom I sincerely believe to be old and ugly? Where is the man to be found who can lay his hand on his heart and honestly say that he ever really pitied the sorrows of a Gorgon? Search through the whole surface of the globe, and you will discover human phenomena of all sorts; but you will not find that man.

To resume. I made her a bow, and left her on the camp-stool in the middle of the drawing-room floor, exactly as I had found her. I ascended to the second floor, walked into the back room first, and inspected the grate. It appeared to be a little out of repair, so I stooped down to look at it closer. While I was kneeling over the bars, I was violently startled by the fall of one large drop of warm water, from a great height, exactly in the middle of a bald place, which has been widening a great deal of late years on the top of my head. I turned on my knees, and looked round. Heaven and earth! the crape-covered woman had followed me up-stairs – the source from which the drop of warm water had fallen was no other than Mrs Badgery's eye!

'I wish you could contrive not to cry over the top of my head, ma'am,' said I. My patience was becoming exhausted, and I spoke with considerable asperity. The curly-headed youth of the present age may not be able to sympathise with my feelings on this occasion; but my bald brethren know as well as I do that the most unpardonable of all liberties is a liberty taken with the unguarded top of the human head.

Mrs Badgery did not seem to hear me. When she had dropped the tear, she was standing exactly over me, looking down at the grate; and she never stirred an inch after I had spoken. 'Don't cry over my head, ma'am,' I repeated, more irritably than before.

'This was his dressing-room,' said Mrs Badgery, indulging in muffled soliloquy. 'He was singularly particular about his shaving-water. He always liked to have it in a little tin pot, and he invariably desired that it might be placed on this hob.' She groaned again, and tapped one side of the grate with the leg of her camp-stool.

If I had been a woman, or if Mrs Badgery had been a man, I should now have proceeded to extremities, and should have vindicated my right to my own house by an appeal to physical force. Under existing circumstances, all that I could do was to express my indignation by a glance. The glance produced not the slightest result – and no wonder. Who can look at a woman with any effect through a crape veil?

I retreated into the second-floor front room, and instantly shut the door after me. The next moment I heard the rustling of the crape garments outside, and the muffled voice of Mrs Badgery poured lamentably through the keyhole. 'Do you mean to make that your bedroom?' asked the voice on the other side of the door. 'Oh, don't, don't make that your bedroom! I am going away directly – but, oh pray, pray let that one room be sacred! Don't sleep there! If you can possibly help it, don't sleep there!'

I opened the window, and looked up and down the road. If I had seen a policeman within hail I should certainly have called him in. No such person was visible. I shut the window again, and warned Mrs Badgery, through the door, in my sternest tones, not to interfere with my domestic arrangements. 'I mean to have my bedstead put up here,' I said. 'And what is more, I mean to sleep here. And what is more, I mean to snore here!' Severe, I think, that last sentence? It completely crushed Mrs Badgery for the moment. I heard the crape garments rustling away from the door; I heard the muffled groans going slowly and solemnly down the stairs again.

In due course of time I also descended to the ground-floor. Had Mrs Badgery really left the premises? I looked into the front parlour – empty. Back parlour – empty. Any other room on the ground-floor? Yes; a long room at the end of the passage. The door was closed. I opened it cautiously, and peeped in. A faint scream, and a smack of two distractedly-clasped hands saluted my appearance. There she was, again on the camp-stool, again sitting exactly in the middle of the floor.

'Don't, don't look in, in that way!' cried Mrs Badgery, wringing her hands. 'I could bear it in any other room, but I can't bear it in this. Every Monday morning I looked out the things for the wash in this room. He was difficult to please about his linen; the washerwoman never put starch enough into his collars to satisfy him. Oh, how often and often has he popped his head in here, as you popped yours just now; and said, in his amusing way, "More starch!" Oh, how droll he always was – how very, very droll in this dear little back room!'

I said nothing. The situation had now got beyond words. I stood with the door in my hand, looking down the passage towards the garden, and waiting doggedly for Mrs Badgery to go out. My plan succeeded. She rose, sighed, shut up the camp-stool, stalked along the passage, paused on the hall mat, said to herself, 'Sweet, sweet spot!' descended the steps, groaned along the gravel-walk, and disappeared from view at last through the garden-door.

'Let her in again at your peril!' said I to the woman who kept the house. She curtseyed and trembled. I left the premises, satisfied with my own conduct under very trying circumstances; delusively convinced also that I had done with Mrs Badgery.

The next day I sent in the furniture. The most unprotected object on the face of this earth is a house when the furniture is going in. The doors must be kept open; and employ as many servants as you may, nobody can be depended on as a domestic sentry so long as the van is at the gate. The confusion of 'moving in' demoralises the steadiest disposition, and there is no such thing as a properly-guarded post from the top of the house to the bottom. How the invasion was managed, how the surprise was effected, I know not; but it is certainly the fact that, when my furniture went in, the inevitable Mrs Badgery went in along with it.

I have some very choice engravings, after the old masters; and I was first awakened to a consciousness of Mrs Badgery's presence in the house while I was hanging up my proof impression of Titian's Venus over the front-parlour fireplace. 'Not there!' cried the muffled voice, imploringly. '*His* portrait used to hang there. Oh, what a print – what a dreadful, dreadful print to put where *his* dear portrait used to be!' I turned round in a fury. There she was, still muffled up in crape, still carrying her abominable camp-stool. Before I could say a word in remonstrance, six men in green baize aprons staggered in with my sideboard, and Mrs Badgery suddenly disappeared. Had they trampled her under foot, or crushed her in the doorway? Though not an inhuman man by nature, I asked myself those questions quite composedly. No very long time elapsed before they were practically answered in the negative by the re-appearance of Mrs Badgery herself, in a perfectly unruffled condition of chronic grief. In the course of the day I had my toes trodden on, I was knocked about by my own furniture, the six men in baize aprons dropped all sorts of small articles over me in going up and down stairs; but Mrs Badgery escaped unscathed. Every time I thought she had been turned out of the house she proved, on the contrary, to be groaning close behind me. She wept over Mr Badgery's memory in every room, perfectly undisturbed to the last by the chaotic confusion of moving in. I am not sure, but I think she brought a tin box of sandwiches with her, and celebrated a tearful pic-nic of her own in the groves of my front garden. I say I am not sure of this; but I am positively certain that I never entirely got rid of her all day; and I know to my cost that she insisted on making me as well acquainted with Mr Badgery's favourite notions and habits as I am with my own. It may interest the reader if I report that my taste in carpets is not equal to Mr Badgery's; that my ideas on the subject of servants' wages are not so generous as Mr Badgery's; and that I ignorantly persisted in placing a sofa in the position which Mr Badgery, in his time, considered to be particularly fitted for an arm-chair. I could go nowhere, look nowhere, do nothing, say nothing, all that day, without bringing the widowed incubus in the crape garments down upon me immediately. I tried civil remonstrances, I tried rude speeches, I tried sulky silence – nothing had the least effect on her. The memory of Mr Badgery was the shield of proof with which she warded off my fiercest attacks. Not till the last article of furniture had been moved in did I lose sight of her; and even then she had not really left the house. One of my six men in green baize aprons routed her out of the back-garden area, where she was telling my servants, with floods of tears, of Mr Badgery's virtuous strictness with his housemaid in the matter of followers. My admirable man in green baize courageously saw her out, and shut the garden-door after her. I gave him half-a-crown on the spot; and if anything happens to him, I am ready to make the future prosperity of his fatherless family my own peculiar care.

The next day was Sunday, and I attended morning service at my new parish church. A popular preacher had been announced, and the building was crowded. I advanced a little way up the nave, and looked to my right, and saw no room. Before I could look to my left, I felt a hand laid persuasively on my arm. I turned round – and there was Mrs Badgery, with her pew-door open, solemnly beckoning me in. The crowd had closed up behind me; the eyes of a dozen members of the congregation, at least, were fixed on me. I had no choice but to save appearances, and accept the dreadful invitation. There was a vacant place next to the door of the pew. I tried to drop into it, but Mrs Badgery stopped me. '*His* seat,' she whispered, and signed to me to place myself on the other side of her. It is unnecessary to say that I had to climb over a hassock, and that I knocked down all Mrs Badgery's devotional books before I succeeded in passing between her and the front of the pew. She cried uninterruptedly through the service; composed herself when it was over; and began to tell me what Mr Badgery's opinions had been on points of abstract theology. Fortunately there was great confusion and crowding at the door of the church; and I escaped, at the hazard of my life, by running round the back of the carriages. I passed the interval between the services alone in the fields, being deterred from going home by the fear that Mrs Badgery might have got there before me.

Monday came. I positively ordered my servants to let no lady in deep mourning pass inside the garden-door without first consulting me. After that, feeling tolerably secure, I occupied myself in arranging my books and prints. I had not pursued this employment much more than an hour, when one of the servants burst excitably into the room, and informed me that a lady in deep mourning had been taken faint, just outside my door, and had requested leave to come in and sit down for a few moments. I ran down the garden-path to bolt the door, and arrived just in time to see it violently pushed open by an officious and sympathising crowd. They drew away on either side as they saw me. There she was, leaning on the grocer's shoulder, with the butcher's boy in attendance, carrying her camp-stool! Leaving my servants to do what they liked with her, I ran back and locked myself up in my bedroom. When she evacuated the premises, some hours afterwards, I received a message of apology, informing me that this particular Monday was the sad anniversary of her wedding-day, and that she had been taken faint, in consequence, at the sight of her lost husband's house.

Tuesday forenoon passed away happily, without any new invasion. After lunch I thought I would go out and take a walk. My garden-door has a sort of peep-hole in it, covered with a wire grating. As I got close to this grating, I thought I saw something mysteriously dark on the outer side of it. I bent my head down to look through, and instantly found myself face to face with the crape veil. 'Sweet, sweet spot!' said the muffled voice, speaking straight into my eyes through the grating. The usual groans followed, and the name of Mr Badgery was plaintively pronounced before I could recover myself sufficiently to retreat to the house.

Wednesday is the day on which I am writing this narrative. It is not twelve o'clock yet, and there is every probability that some new form of sentimental persecution is in store for me before the evening. Thus far, these lines contain a perfectly true statement of Mrs Badgery's conduct towards me since I entered on the possession of *my* house and *her* shrine. What am I to do? – that is the point I wish to insist on – what am I to do? How am I to get away from the memory of Mr Badgery, and the unappeasable grief of his disconsolate widow? Any other species of invasion it is possible to resist; but how is a man placed in my unhappy and unparalleled circumstances to defend himself? I can't keep a dog ready to fly at Mrs Badgery. I can't charge her at a police-court with being oppressively fond of the house in which her husband died. I can't set man-traps for a woman, or prosecute a weeping widow as a trespasser and a nuisance. I am helplessly involved in the unrelaxing folds of Mrs Badgery's crape veil. Surely there was no exaggeration in my language when I said that I was a sufferer under a perfectly new grievance! Can anybody advise me? Has anybody had even the faintest and remotest experience of the peculiar form of persecution under which I am now suffering? If nobody has, is there any legal gentleman in the united kingdom who can answer the all-important question which appears at the head of this narrative? I began by asking that question because it was uppermost in my mind. It is uppermost in my mind still, and I therefore beg leave to conclude appropriately by asking it again:

Is there any law in England which will protect me from Mrs Badgery?

CHARLES DICKENS

Mrs Lirriper's Lodgings

How Mrs Lirriper Carried on the Business

Whoever would begin to be worried with letting Lodgings that wasn't a lone woman with a living to get is a thing inconceivable to me, my dear; excuse the familiarity, but it comes natural to me in my own little room, when wishing to open my mind to those that I can trust, and I should be truly thankful if they were all mankind, but such is not so, for have but a Furnished bill in the window and your watch on the mantelpiece, and farewell to it if you turn your back for but a second, however gentlemanly the manners; nor is being of your own sex any safeguard, as I have reason, in the form of sugar-tongs to know, for that lady (and a fine woman she was) got me to run for a glass of water, on the plea of going to be confined, which certainly turned out true, but it was in the Station-house.

Number Eighty-one Norfolk Street, Strand – situated midway between the City and St James's, and within five minutes' walk of the principal places of public amusement – is my address. I have rented this house many years, as the parish rate-books will testify; and I could wish my landlord was as alive to the fact as I am myself; but no, bless you, not a half a pound of paint to save his life, nor so much, my dear, as a tile upon the roof, though on your bended knees.

My dear, you never have found Number Eighty-one Norfolk Street Strand advertised in Bradshaw's Railway Guide, and with the blessing of Heaven you never will or shall so find it. Some there are who do not think it lowering themselves to make their names that cheap, and even going the lengths of a portrait of the house not like it with a blot in every window and a coach and four at the door, but what will suit Wozenham's lower down on the other side of the way will not suit me, Miss Wozenham having her opinions and me having mine, though when it comes to systematic underbidding capable of being proved on oath in a court of justice and taking the form of 'If Mrs Lirriper names eighteen shillings a week, I name fifteen and six,' it then comes to a settlement between yourself and your conscience, supposing for the sake of argument your name to be Wozenham, which I am well aware it is not or my opinion of you would be greatly lowered, and as to airy bedrooms and a night-porter in constant attendance the less said the better, the bedrooms being stuffy and the porter stuff.

It is forty years ago since me and my poor Lirriper got married at St Clement's Danes, where I now have a sitting in a very pleasant pew with genteel company and my own hassock, and being partial to evening service not too crowded. My poor Lirriper was a handsome figure of a man, with a beaming eye and a voice as mellow as a musical instrument made of honey and steel, but he had ever been a free liver being in the commercial travelling line and travelling what he called a limekiln road – 'a dry road, Emma my dear,' my poor Lirriper says to me, 'where I have to lay the dust with one drink or another all day long and half the night, and it wears me Emma' – and this led to his running through a good deal and might have run through the turnpike too when that dreadful horse that never would stand still for a single instant set off, but for its being night and the gate shut and consequently took his wheel, my poor Lirriper and the gig smashed to atoms and never spoke afterwards. He was a handsome figure of a man, and a man with a jovial heart and a sweet temper; but if they had come up then they never could have given you the mellowness of his voice, and indeed I consider photographs wanting in mellowness as a general rule and making you look like a new-ploughed field.

My poor Lirriper being behindhand with the world and being buried at Hatfield church in Hertfordshire, not that it was his native place but that he had a liking for the Salisbury Arms where we went upon our wedding-day and passed as happy a fortnight as ever happy was, I went round to the creditors and I says 'Gentlemen I am acquainted with the fact that I am not answerable for my late husband's debts but I wish to pay them for I am his lawful wife and his good name is dear to me. I am going into the Lodgings gentlemen as a business and if I prosper every farthing that my late husband owed shall be paid for the sake of the love I bore him, by this right hand.' It took a long time to do but it was done, and the silver cream-jug which is between ourselves and the bed and the mattress in my room up-stairs (or it would have found legs so sure as ever the Furnished bill was up) being presented by the gentlemen engraved 'To Mrs Lirriper a mark of grateful respect for her honourable conduct' gave me a turn which was too much for my feelings, till Mr Betley which at that time had the parlours and loved his joke says 'Cheer up Mrs Lir-riper, you should feel as if it was only your christening and they were your godfathers and godmothers which did promise for you.' And it brought me round, and I don't mind confessing to you my dear that I then put a sandwich and a drop of sherry in a little basket and went down to Hatfield church-yard outside the coach and kissed my hand and laid it with a kind of proud and swelling love on my husband's grave, though bless you it had taken me so long to clear his name that my wedding-ring was worn quite fine and smooth when I laid it on the green green waving grass.

I am an old woman now and my good looks are gone but that's me my dear over the plate-warmer and considered like in the times when you used to pay two guineas on ivory and took your chance pretty much how you came out, which made you very careful how you left it about after-wards because people were turned so red and uncomfortable by mostly guessing it was somebody else quite different, and there was once a certain person that had put his money in a hop business that came in one morning to pay his rent and his respects being the second floor that would have taken it down from its hook and put it in his breast-pocket – you under-stand my dear – for the L, he says, of the original – only there was no mellowness in *his* voice and I wouldn't let him, but his opinion of it you may gather from his saying to it 'Speak to me Emma!' which was far from a rational observation no doubt but still a tribute to its being a likeness, and I think myself it *was* like me when I was young and wore that sort of stays.

But it was about the Lodgings that I was intending to hold forth and certainly I ought to know something of the business having been in it so long, for it was early in the second year of my married life that I lost my poor Lirriper and I set up at Islington directly afterwards and afterwards came here, being two houses and eight-and-thirty years and some losses and a deal of experience.

Girls are your first trial after fixtures and they try you even worse than what I call the Wandering Christians, though why *they* should roam the earth looking for bills and then coming in and viewing the apartments and stickling about terms and never at all wanting them or dreaming of taking them being already provided, is a mystery I should be thankful to have explained if by any miracle it could be. It's wonderful they live so long and thrive so on it but I suppose the exercise makes it healthy, knocking so much and going from house to house and up and down stairs all day, and then their pretending to be so particular and punctual is a most astonishing thing, looking at their watches and saying 'Could you give me the refusal of the rooms till twenty minutes past eleven the day after to-morrow in the forenoon, and supposing it to be considered essential by my friend from the country could there be a small iron bedstead put in the little room upon the stairs?' Why when I was new to it my dear I used to consider before I promised and to make my mind anxious with calculations and to get quite wearied out with disappointments, but now I says 'Certainly by all means' well knowing it's a Wandering Christian and I shall hear no more about it, indeed by this time I know most of the Wandering Christians by sight as well as they know me, it being the habit of each individual revolving round London in that capacity to come back about twice a year, and it's very remarkable that it runs in families and the children grow up to it, but even were it otherwise I should no sooner hear of the friend from the country which is a certain sign than I should nod and say to myself You're a Wandering Christian, though whether they are (as I *have* heard) persons of small property with a taste for regular employment and frequent change of scene I cannot undertake to tell you.

Girls as I was beginning to remark are one of your first and your lasting troubles, being like your teeth which begin with convulsions and never cease tormenting you from the time you cut them till they cut you, and then you don't want to part with them which seems hard but we must all succumb or buy artificial, and even where you get a will nine times out of ten you'll get a dirty face with it and naturally lodgers do not like good society to be shown in with a smear of black across the nose or a smudgy eyebrow. Where they pick the black up is a mystery I cannot solve, as in the case of the willingest girl that ever came into a house half-starved poor thing, a girl so willing that I called her Willing Sophy down upon her knees scrubbing early and late and ever cheerful but always smiling with a black face. And I says to Sophy, 'Now Sophy my good girl have a regular day for your stoves and keep the width of the Airy between yourself and the blacking and do not brush your hair with the bottoms of the saucepans and do not meddle with the snuffs of the candles and it stands to reason that it can no longer be' yet there it was and always on her nose, which turning up and being broad at the end seemed to boast of it and caused warning from a steady gentleman and excellent lodger with breakfast by the week but a little irritable and use of a sitting-room when required, his words being 'Mrs Lirriper I have arrived at the point of admitting that the Black is a man and a brother, but only in a natural form and when it can't be got off.' Well consequently I put poor Sophy on to other work and forbid her answering the door or answering a bell on any account but she was so unfortunately willing that nothing would stop her flying up the kitchen-stairs whenever a bell was heard to tingle. I put it to her 'O Sophy Sophy for goodness' goodness' sake where does it come from?' To which that poor unlucky willing mortal bursting out crying to see me so vexed replied 'I took a deal of black into me ma'am when I was a small child being much neglected and I think it must be, that it works out,' so it continuing to work out of that poor thing and not having another fault to find with her I says 'Sophy what do you seriously think of my helping you away to New South Wales where it might not be noticed?' Nor did I ever repent the money which was well spent, for she married the ship's cook on the voyage (himself a Mulotter) and did well and lived happy, and so far as ever I heard it was *not* noticed in a new state of society to her dying day.

In what way Miss Wozenham lower down on the other side of the way reconciled it to her feelings as a lady (which she is not) to entice Mary Anne Perkinsop from my service is best known to herself, I do not know and I do not wish to know how opinions are formed at Wozenham's on any point. But Mary Anne Perkinsop although I behaved handsomely to her and she behaved unhandsomely to me was worth her weight in gold as overawing lodgers without driving them away, for lodgers would be far more sparing of their bells with Mary Anne than I ever knew them to be with Maid or Mistress, which is a great triumph especially when accompanied with a cast in the eye and a bag of bones, but it was the steadiness of her way with them through her father's having failed in Pork. It was Mary Anne's looking so respectable in her person and being so strict in her spirits that conquered the tea-and-sugarest gentleman (for he weighed them both in a pair of scales every morning) that I have ever had to deal with and no lamb grew meeker, still it afterwards came round to me that Miss Wozenham happening to pass and seeing Mary Anne take in the milk of a milkman that made free in a rosy-faced way (I think no worse of him) with every girl in the street but was quite frozen up like the statue at Charing-cross by her, saw Mary Anne's value in the lodging business and went as high as one pound per quarter more, consequently Mary Anne with not a word betwixt us says 'If *you* will provide yourself Mrs Lirriper in a month from this day *I* have already done the same,' which hurt me and I said so, and she then hurt me more by insinuating that her father having failed in Pork had laid her open to it.

My dear I do assure you it's a harassing thing to know what kind of girls to give the preference to, for if they are lively they get bell'd off their legs and if they are sluggish you suffer from it yourself in complaints and if they are sparkling-eyed they get made love to, and if they are smart in their persons they try on your Lodgers' bonnets and if they are musical I defy you to keep them away from bands and organs, and allowing for any difference you like in their heads their heads will be always out of window just the same. And then what the gentlemen like in girls the ladies don't, which is fruitful hot water for all parties, and then there's temper though such a temper as Caroline Maxey's I hope not often. A good-looking black-eyed girl was Caroline and a comely-made girl to your cost when she did break out and laid about her, as took place first and last through a new-married couple come to see London in the first floor and the lady very high and it *was* supposed not liking the good looks of Caroline having none of her own to spare, but anyhow she did try Caroline though that was no excuse. So one afternoon Caroline comes down into the kitchen flushed and flashing, and she says to me 'Mrs Lirriper that woman in the first has aggravated me past bearing,' I says 'Caroline keep your temper,' Caroline says with a curdling laugh 'Keep my temper? You're

right Mrs Lirriper, so I will. Capital D her!' bursts out Caroline (you
might have struck me into the centre of the earth with a feather when she
said it) 'I'll give her a touch of the temper that *I* keep!' Caroline downs
with her hair my dear, screeches and rushes up-stairs, I following as fast
as my trembling legs could bear me, but before I got into the room the
dinner-cloth and pink-and-white service all dragged off upon the floor
with a crash and the new-married couple on their backs in the firegrate,
him with the shovel and tongs and a dish of cucumber across him and a
mercy it was summer-time. 'Caroline' I says 'be calm,' but she catches off
my cap and tears it in her teeth as she passes me, then pounces on the
new-married lady makes her a bundle of ribbons takes her by the two ears
and knocks the back of her head upon the carpet Murder screaming all
the time Policemen running down the street and Wozenham's windows
(judge of my feelings when I came to know it) thrown up and Miss Wozenham calling out from the balcony with crocodile's tears 'It's Mrs Lirriper
been overcharging somebody to madness – she'll be murdered – I always
thought so – Pleeseman save her!' My dear four of them and Caroline
behind the chiffoniere attacking with the poker and when disarmed
prize-fighting with her double fists, and down and up and up and down
and dreadful! But I couldn't bear to see the poor young creature roughly
handled and her hair torn when they got the better of her, and I says
'Gentlemen Policemen pray remember that her sex is the sex of your
mothers and sisters and your sweethearts, and God bless them and you!'
And there she was sitting down on the ground handcuffed, taking breath
against the skirting-board and them cool with their coats in strips, and
all she says was 'Mrs Lirriper I'm sorry as ever I touched *you*, for you're a
kind motherly old thing,' and it made me think that I had often wished
I had been a mother indeed and how would my heart have felt if I had
been the mother of that girl! Well you know it turned out at the
Police-office that she had done it before, and she had her clothes away
and was sent to prison, and when she was to come out I trotted off to the
gate in the evening with just a morsel of jelly in that little basket of mine
to give her a mite of strength to face the world again, and there I met
with a very decent mother waiting for her son through bad company and
a stubborn one he was with his half-boots not laced. So out came Caroline
and I says 'Caroline come along with me and sit down under the wall

where it's retired and eat a little trifle that I have brought with me to do you good,' and she throws her arms round my neck and says sobbing 'O why were you never a mother when there are such mothers as there are!' she says, and in half a minute more she begins to laugh and says 'Did I really tear your cap to shreds?' and when I told her 'You certainly did so Caroline' she laughed again and said while she patted my face 'Then why do you wear such queer old caps you dear old thing? If you hadn't worn such queer old caps I don't think I should have done it even then.' Fancy the girl! Nothing could get out of her what she was going to do except O she would do well enough, and we parted she being very thankful and kissing my hands, and I nevermore saw or heard of that girl, except that I shall always believe that a very genteel cap which was brought anonymous to me one Saturday night in an oilskin basket by a most impertinent young sparrow of a monkey whistling with dirty shoes on the clean steps and playing the harp on the Airy railings with a hoop-stick came from Caroline.

What you lay yourself open to my dear in the way of being the object of uncharitable suspicions when you go into the Lodging business I have not the words to tell you, but never was I so dishonourable as to have two keys nor would I willingly think it even of Miss Wozenham lower down on the other side of the way sincerely hoping that it may not be, though doubtless at the same time money cannot come from nowhere and it is not reason to suppose that Bradshaws put it in for love be it blotty as it may. It *is* a hardship hurting to the feelings that Lodgers open their minds so wide to the idea that you are trying to get the better of them and shut their minds so close to the idea that they are trying to get the better of you, but as Major Jackman says to me 'I know the ways of this circular world Mrs Lirriper, and that's one of 'em all round it' and many is the little ruffle in my mind that the Major has smoothed, for he is a clever man who has seen much. Dear dear, thirteen years have passed though it seems but yesterday since I was sitting with my glasses on at the open front parlour window one evening in August (the parlours being then vacant) reading yesterday's paper my eyes for print being poor though still I am thankful to say a long sight at a distance, when I hear a gentleman come posting across the road and up the street in a dreadful rage talking to himself in a fury and d'ing and c'ing somebody. 'By George!' says he out loud and clutching his walking-stick, 'I'll go to Mrs Lirriper's. Which is Mrs Lirriper's?' Then looking round and seeing me he flourishes his hat right off his head as if I had been the queen and he says, 'Excuse the intrusion Madam, but pray Madam can you tell me at what number in this street there resides a well-known and much-respected lady by the name of Lirriper?' A little flustered though I must say gratified I took off my glasses and courtesied and said 'Sir, Mrs Lirriper is your humble servant.' 'Astonishing!' says he. 'A million pardons! Madam, may I ask you to have the kindness to direct one of your domestics to open the door to a gentleman in search of apartments, by the name of Jackman?' I had never heard the name but a politer gentleman I never hope to see, for says he 'Madam I am shocked at your opening the door yourself to no worthier a fellow than Jemmy Jackman. After you Madam. I never precede a lady.' Then he comes into the parlours and he sniffs, and he says 'Hah! These are parlours! Not musty cupboards' he says 'but parlours, and no smell of coal-sacks.' Now my dear it having been remarked by some inimical to the whole neighbourhood that it always smells of coal-sacks which might prove a drawback to Lodgers if encouraged, I says to the Major gently though firmly that I think he is referring to Arundel or Surrey or Howard but not Norfolk. 'Madam' says he 'I refer to Wozenham's lower down over the way – Madam you can form no notion what Wozenham's is – Madam it is a vast coal-sack, and Miss Wozenham has the principles and manners of a female heaver – Madam from the manner in which I have heard her mention you I know she has no appreciation of a lady, and from the manner in which she has conducted herself towards me I know she has no appreciation of a gentleman – Madam my name is Jackman – should you require any other reference than what I have already said, I name the Bank of England – perhaps you know it!' Such was the beginning of the Major's occupying the parlours and from that hour to this the same and a most obliging Lodger and punctual in all respects except one irregular which I need not particularly specify, but made up for by his being a protection and at all times ready to fill in the papers of the Assessed Taxes and Juries and that, and once collared a young man with the drawing-room clock under his coat, and once on the parapets with his own hands and blankets put out the kitchen chimney and afterwards attending the summons made a most eloquent speech against the Parish before the magistrates and saved the engine, and ever quite the gentleman though passionate. And certainly Miss Wozenham's detaining the trunks and umbrella was not in a liberal spirit though it may have been according to her rights in law or an act *I* would myself have stooped to, the Major being so much the gentleman that though he is far from tall he seems almost so when he has his shirt-frill out and his frock-coat on and his hat with the curly brims, and in what service he was I cannot truly tell you my dear whether Militia or Foreign, for I never heard him even name himself as Major but always simple 'Jemmy Jackman' and once soon after he came when I felt it my duty to let him know that Miss Wozenham had put it about that he was no Major and I took the liberty of adding 'which you are sir' his words were 'Madam at any rate I am not a Minor, and sufficient for the day is the evil thereof' which cannot be denied to be the sacred truth, nor yet his military ways of having his boots with only the dirt brushed off taken to him in the front parlour every morning on a clean plate and varnishing them himself with a little sponge and a saucer and a whistle in a whisper so sure as ever his breakfast is ended, and so neat his ways that it never soils his linen which is scrupulous though more in quality than quantity, neither that nor his mustachios which to the best of my belief are done at the same time and which are as black and shining as his boots, his head of hair being a lovely white.

It was the third year nearly up of the Major's being in the parlours that early one morning in the month of February when Parliament was coming on and you may therefore suppose a number of impostors were about ready to take hold of anything they could get, a gentleman and a lady from the country came in to view the Second, and I well remember that I had been looking out of window and had watched them and the heavy sleet driving down the street together looking for bills. I did not quite take to the face of the gentleman though he was good-looking too but the lady was a very pretty young thing and delicate, and it seemed too rough for her to be out at all though she had only come from the Adelphi Hotel which would not have been much above a quarter of a mile if the weather had been less severe. Now it did so happen my dear that I had been forced to put five shillings weekly additional on the second in consequence of a loss from running away full dressed as if going out to a dinner-party, which was very artful and had made me rather suspicious taking it along with

Parliament, so when the gentleman proposed three months certain and the money in advance and leave then reserved to renew on the same terms for six months more, I says I was not quite certain but that I might have engaged myself to another party but would step down-stairs and look into it if they would take a seat. They took a seat and I went down to the handle of the Major's door that I had already began to consult finding it a great blessing, and I knew by his whistling in a whisper that he was varnishing his boots which was generally considered private, however he kindly calls out 'If it's you, Madam, come in,' and I went in and told him.

'Well, Madam,' says the Major rubbing his nose – as I did fear at the moment with the black sponge but it was only his knuckle, he being always neat and dexterous with his fingers – 'well, Madam, I suppose you would be glad of the money?'

I was delicate of saying 'Yes' too out, for a little extra colour rose into the Major's cheeks and there was irregularity which I will not particularly specify in a quarter which I will not name.

'I am of opinion, Madam,' says the Major 'that when money is ready for you – when it is ready for you, Mrs Lirriper – you ought to take it. What is there against it, Madam, in this case up-stairs?'

'I really cannot say there is anything against it, sir, still I thought I would consult you.'

'You said a newly-married couple, I think, Madam?' says the Major.

I says 'Ye-es. Evidently. And indeed the young lady mentioned to me in a casual way that she had not been married many months.'

The Major rubbed his nose again and stirred the varnish round and round in its little saucer with his piece of sponge and took to his whistling in a whisper for a few moments. Then he says 'You would call it a Good Let, Madam?'

'O certainly a Good Let sir.'

'Say they renew for the additional six months. Would it put you about very much Madam if – if the worst was to come to the worst?' said the Major.

'Well I hardly know,' I says to the Major. 'It depends upon circumstances. Would *you* object Sir for instance?'

'I?' says the Major. 'Object? Jemmy Jackman? Mrs Lirriper close with the proposal.'

So I went up-stairs and accepted, and they came in next day which was Saturday and the Major was so good as to draw up a Memorandum of an agreement in a beautiful round hand and expressions that sounded to me equally legal and military, and Mr Edson signed it on the Monday morning and the Major called upon Mr Edson on the Tuesday and Mr Edson called upon the Major on the Wednesday and the Second and the parlours were as friendly as could be wished.

The three months paid for had run out and we had got without any fresh overtures as to payment into May my dear, when there came an obligation upon Mr Edson to go a business expedition right across the Isle of Man, which fell quite unexpected upon that pretty little thing and is not a place that according to my views is particularly in the way to anywhere at any time but that may be a matter of opinion. So short a notice was it that he was to go next day, and dreadfully she cried poor pretty, and I am sure I cried too when I saw her on the cold pavement in the sharp east wind – it being a very backward spring that year – taking a last leave of him with her pretty bright hair blowing this way and that and her arms clinging round his neck and him saying 'There there there. Now let me go Peggy.' And by that time it was plain that what the Major had been so accommodating as to say he would not object to happening in the house, would happen in it, and I told her as much when he was gone while I comforted her with my arm up the staircase, for I says 'You will soon have others to keep up for my pretty and you must think of that.'

His letter never came when it ought to have come and what she went through morning after morning when the postman brought none for her the very postman himself compassionated when she ran down to the door, and yet we cannot wonder at its being calculated to blunt the feelings to have all the trouble of other people's letters and none of the pleasure and doing it oftener in the mud and mizzle than not and at a rate of wages more resembling Little Britain than Great. But at last one morning when she was too poorly to come running down-stairs he says to me with a pleased look in his face that made me next to love the man in his uniform coat though he was dripping wet 'I have taken you first in the street this morning Mrs Lirriper, for here's the one for Mrs Edson.' I went up to her bedroom with it as fast as ever I could go, and she sat up in bed when she saw it and kissed it and tore it open and then a blank stare came upon her. 'It's very short!' she says lifting her large eyes to my face. 'O Mrs Lirriper it's very short!' I says 'My dear Mrs Edson no doubt that's because your husband hadn't time to write more just at that time.' 'No doubt, no doubt,' says she, and puts her two hands on her face and turns round in her bed.

I shut her softly in and I crept down-stairs and I tapped at the Major's door, and when the Major having his thin slices of bacon in his own Dutch oven saw me he came out of his chair and put me down on the sofa. 'Hush!' says he, 'I see something's the matter. Don't speak – take time.' I says 'O Major I'm afraid there's cruel work up-stairs.' 'Yes yes' says he 'I had begun to be afraid of it – take time.' And then in opposition to his own words he rages out frightfully, and says 'I shall never forgive myself Madam, that I, Jemmy Jackman, didn't see it all that morning – didn't go straight upstairs when my boot-sponge was in my hand – didn't force it down his throat – and choke him dead with it on the spot!'

The Major and me agreed when we came to ourselves that just at present we could do no more than take on to suspect nothing and use our best endeavours to keep that poor young creature quiet, and what I ever should have done without the Major when it got about among the organ-men that quiet was our object is unknown, for he made lion and tiger war upon them to that degree that without seeing it I could not have believed it was in any gentleman to have such a power of bursting out with fire-irons walking-sticks water-jugs coals potatoes off his table the very hat off his head, and at the same time so furious in foreign languages that they would stand with their handles half-turned fixed like the Sleeping Ugly – for I cannot say Beauty.

Ever to see the postman come near the house now gave me such a fear that it was a reprieve when he went by, but in about another ten days or a fortnight he says again, 'Here's one for Mrs Edson. – Is she pretty well?' 'She is pretty well postman, but not well enough to rise so early as she used' which was so far gospel-truth.

I carried the letter in to the Major at his breakfast and I says tottering 'Major I have not the courage to take it up to her.'

'It's an ill-looking villain of a letter,' says the Major.

'I have not the courage Major' I says again in a tremble 'to take it up to her.'

After seeming lost in consideration for some moments the Major says, raising his head as if something new and useful had occurred to his mind 'Mrs Lirriper, I shall never forgive myself that I, Jemmy Jackman, didn't go straight up-stairs that morning when my boot-sponge was in my hand – and force it down his throat – and choke him dead with it.'

'Major' I says a little hasty 'you didn't do it which is a blessing, for it would have done no good and I think your sponge was better employed on your own honourable boots.'

So we got to be rational, and planned that I should tap at her bedroom door and lay the letter on the mat outside and wait on the upper landing for what might happen, and never was gunpowder cannon balls or shells or rockets more dreaded than that dreadful letter was by me as I took it to the second floor.

A terrible loud scream sounded through the house the minute after she had opened it, and I found her on the floor lying as if her life was gone. My dear I never looked at the face of the letter which was lying open by her, for there was no occasion.

Everything I needed to bring her round the Major brought up with his own hands, besides running out to the chemist's for what was not in the house and likewise having the fiercest of all his many skirmishes with a musical instrument representing a ball-room I do not know in what particular country and company waltzing in and out at folding-doors with rolling eyes. When after a long time I saw her coming to, I slipped on the landing till I heard her cry, and then I went in and says cheerily 'Mrs Edson you're not well my dear and it's not to be wondered at,' as if I had not been in before. Whether she believed or disbelieved I cannot say and it would signify nothing if I could, but I stayed by her for hours and then she God ever blesses me! and says she will try to rest for her head is bad.

'Major,' I whispers, looking in at the parlours, 'I beg and pray of you don't go out.'

The Major whispers, 'Madam, trust me I will do no such a thing. How is she?'

I says 'Major the good Lord above us only knows what burns and rages in her poor mind. I left her sitting at her window. I am going to sit at mine.'

It came on afternoon and it came on evening. Norfolk is a delightful street to lodge in – provided you don't go lower down – but of a summer evening when the dust and waste paper lie in it and stray children play in it and a kind of a gritty calm and bake settles on it and a peal of church-bells is practising in the neighbourhood it is a trifle dull, and never have I seen it since at such a time and never shall I see it evermore at such a time without seeing the dull June evening when that forlorn young creature sat at her open corner window on the second and me at my open corner window (the other corner) on the third. Something merciful, something wiser and better far than my own self, had moved me while it was yet light to sit in my bonnet and shawl, and as the shadows fell and the tide rose I could sometimes – when I put out my head and looked at her window below – see that she leaned out a little looking down the street. It was just settling dark when I saw *her* in the street.

So fearful of losing sight of her that it almost stops my breath while I tell it, I went down-stairs faster than I ever moved in all my life and only tapped with my hand at the Major's door in passing it and slipping out. She was gone already. I made the same speed down the street and when I came to the corner of Howard Street I saw that she had turned it and was there plain before me going towards the west. O with what a thankful heart I saw her going along!

She was quite unacquainted with London and had very seldom been out for more than an airing in our own street where she knew two or three little children belonging to neighbours and had sometimes stood among them at the street looking at the water. She must be going at hazard I knew, still she kept the by-streets quite correctly as long as they would serve her, and then turned up into the Strand. But at every corner I could see her head turned one way, and that way was always the river way.

It may have been only the darkness and quiet of the Adelphi that caused her to strike into it but she struck into it much as readily as if she had set out to go there, which perhaps was the case. She went straight down to the Terrace and along it and looked over the iron rail, and I often woke afterwards in my own bed with the horror of seeing her do it. The desertion of the wharf below and the flowing of the high water there seemed to settle her purpose. She looked about as if to make out the way down, and she struck out the right way or the wrong way – I don't know which, for I don't know the place before or since – and I followed her the way she went.

It was noticeable that all this time she never once looked back. But there was now a great change in the manner of her going, and instead of going at a steady quick walk with her arms folded before her – among the dark dismal arches she went in a wild way with her arms opened wide, as if they were wings and she was flying to her death.

We were on the wharf and she stopped. I stopped. I saw her hands at her bonnet-strings, and I rushed between her and the brink and took her round the waist with both my arms. She might have drowned me, I felt then, but she could never have got quit of me.

Down to that moment my mind had been all in a maze and not half an idea had I had in it what I should say to her, but the instant I touched her it came to me like magic and I had my natural voice and my senses and even almost my breath.

'Mrs Edson!' I says 'My dear! Take care. How ever did you lose your way and stumble on a dangerous place like this? Why you must have come here by the most perplexing streets in all London. No wonder you are lost, I'm sure. And this place too! Why I thought nobody ever got here, except me to order my coals and the Major in the parlours to smoke his cigar!' – for I saw that blessed man close by, pretending to it.

'Hah – Hah – Hum!' coughs the Major.

'And good gracious me' I says, 'why here he is!'

'Halloa! who goes there?' says the Major in a military manner.

'Well!' I says, 'if this don't beat everything! Don't you know us Major Jackman?'

'Halloa!' says the Major. 'Who calls on Jemmy Jackman?' (and more out of breath he was, and did it less like life than I should have expected.)

'Why here's Mrs Edson Major' I says, 'strolling out to cool her poor head which has been very bad, has missed her way and got lost, and Goodness knows where she might have got to but for me coming here to drop an order into my coal merchant's letter-box and you coming here to smoke your cigar! – And you really are not well enough my dear' I says to her 'to be half so far from home without me. – And your arm will be very acceptable I am sure Major' I says to him 'and I know she may lean upon it as heavy as she likes.' And now we had both got her – thanks be Above! – one on each side.

She was all in a cold shiver and she so continued till I laid her on her own bed, and up to the early morning she held me by the hand and moaned and moaned 'O wicked, wicked, wicked!' But when at last I made believe to droop my head and be overpowered with a dead sleep, I heard that poor young creature give such touching and such humble thanks for being preserved from taking her own life in her madness that I thought I should have cried my eyes out on the counterpane and I knew she was safe.

Being well enough to do and able to afford it, me and the Major laid our little plans next day while she was asleep worn out, and so I says to her as soon as I could do it nicely:

'Mrs Edson my dear, when Mr Edson paid me the rent for these farther six months—'

She gave a start and I felt her large eyes look at me, but I went on with it and with my needlework.

'— I can't say that I am quite sure I dated the receipt right. Could you let me look at it?'

She laid her frozen cold hand upon mine and she looked through me when I was forced to look up from my needlework, but I had taken the precaution of having on my spectacles.

'I have no receipt' says she.

'Ah! Then he has got it' I says in a careless way. 'It's of no great consequence. A receipt's a receipt.'

From that time she always had hold of my hand when I could spare it which was generally only when I read to her, for of course she and me had our bits of needlework to plod at and neither of us was very handy at those little things, though I am still rather proud of my share in them too considering. And though she took to all I read to her, I used to fancy that next to what was taught upon the Mount she took most of all to His gentle compassion for us poor women and to His young life and to how His mother was proud of Him and treasured His sayings in her heart. She had a grateful look in her eyes that never never never will be out of mine until they are closed in my last sleep, and when I chanced to look at her without thinking of it I would always meet that look, and she would often offer me her trembling lip to kiss, much more like a little affectionate half broken-hearted child than ever I can imagine any grown person.

One time the trembling of this poor lip was so strong and her tears ran down so fast that I thought she was going to tell me all her woe, so I takes her two hands in mine and I says:

'No my dear not now, you had best not try to do it now. Wait for better times when you have got over this and are strong, and then you shall tell me whatever you will. Shall it be agreed?'

With our hands still joined she nodded her head many times, and she lifted my hands and put them to her lips and to her bosom. 'Only one word now my dear' I says. 'Is there any one?'

She looked inquiringly 'Any one?'

'That I can go to?'

She shook her head.

'No one that I can bring?'

She shook her head.

'No one is wanted by *me* my dear. Now that may be considered past and gone.'

Not much more than a week afterwards – for this was far on in the time of our being so together – I was bending over at her bedside with my ear down to her lips, by turns listening for her breath and looking for a sign of life in her face. At last it came in a solemn way – not in a flash but like a kind of pale faint light brought very slow to the face.

She said something to me that had no sound in it, but I saw she asked me:

'Is this death?'

And I says:

'Poor dear poor dear, I think it is.'

Knowing somehow that she wanted me to move her weak right hand, I took it and laid it on her breast and then folded her other hand upon it, and she prayed a good good prayer and I joined in it poor me though there were no words spoke. Then I brought the baby in its wrappers from where it lay, and I says:

'My dear this is sent to a childless old woman. This is for me to take care of.'

The trembling lip was put up towards my face for the last time, and I dearly kissed it.

'Yes my dear,' I says. 'Please God! Me and the Major.'

I don't know how to tell it right, but I saw her soul brighten and leap up, and get free and fly away in the grateful look.

So this is the why and wherefore of its coming to pass my dear that we called him Jemmy, being after the Major his own godfather with Lirriper for a surname being after myself, and never was a dear child such a brightening thing in a Lodgings or such a playmate to his grandmother as Jemmy to this house and me, and always good and minding what he was told (upon the whole) and soothing for the temper and making everything pleasanter except when he grew old enough to drop his cap down Wozenham's Airy and they wouldn't hand it up to him, and being worked into a state I put on my best bonnet and gloves and parasol with the child in my hand and I says 'Miss Wozenham I little thought ever to have entered your house but unless my grandson's cap is instantly restored, the laws of this country regulating the property of the Subject shall at length decide betwixt yourself and me, cost what it may.' With a sneer upon her face which did strike me I must say as being expressive of two keys but it may have been a mistake and if there is any doubt let Miss Wozenham have the full benefit of it as is but right, she rang the bell and she says 'Jane, is there a street-child's old cap down our Airy?' I says 'Miss Wozenham before your housemaid answers that question you must allow me to inform you to your face that my grandson is *not* a street-child and is *not* in the habit of wearing old caps. In fact' I says 'Miss Wozenham I am far from sure that my grandson's cap may not be newer than your own' which was perfectly savage in me, her lace being the commonest machine-make washed and torn besides, but I had been put into a state to begin with fomented by impertinence. Miss Wozenham says red in the face 'Jane you heard my question, is there any child's cap down our Airy?' 'Yes Ma'am' says Jane 'I think I did see some such rubbish a-lying there.' 'Then' says Miss Wozenham 'let these visitors out, and then throw up that worthless article out of my premises.' But here the child who had been staring at Miss Wozenham with all his eyes and more, frowns down his little eyebrows purses up his little mouth puts his chubby legs far apart turns his little dimpled fists round and round slowly over one another like a little coffee-mill, and says to her 'Oo impdent to mi Gran, me tut oor hi!' 'O!' says Miss Wozenham looking down scornfully at the Mite 'this is not a street-child is it not! Really!' I bursts out laughing and I says 'Miss Wozenham if this ain't a pretty sight to you I don't envy your feelings and I wish you good-day. Jemmy come along with Gran.' And I was still in the best of humours though his cap came flying up into the street as if it had been just turned on out of the water-plug, and I went home laughing all the way, all owing to that dear boy.

The miles and miles that me and the Major have travelled with Jemmy in the dusk between the lights are not to be calculated, Jemmy driving on the coach-box which is the Major's brass-bound writing desk on the table, me inside in the easy-chair and the Major Guard up behind with a brown-paper horn doing it really wonderful. I do assure you my dear that sometimes when I have taken a few winks in my place inside the coach and have come half awake by the flashing light of the fire and have heard that precious pet driving and the Major blowing up behind to have the change of horses ready when we got to the Inn, I have half believed we were on the old North Road that my poor Lirriper knew so well. Then to see that child and the Major both wrapped up getting down to warm their feet and going stamping about and having glasses of ale out of the paper matchboxes on the chimney-piece is to see the Major enjoying it fully as much as the child I am very sure, and it's equal to any play when Coachee opens the coach-door to look in at me inside and say 'Wery 'past that 'tage. – 'Prightened old lady?'

But what my inexpressible feelings were when we lost that child can only be compared to the Major's which were not a shade better, through his straying out at five years old and eleven o'clock in the forenoon and never heard of by word or sign or deed till half-past nine at night, when the Major had gone to the Editor of the Times newspaper to put in an advertisement, which came out next day four-and-twenty hours after he was found, and which I mean always carefully to keep in my lavender drawer as the first printed account of him. The more the day got on, the more I got distracted and the Major too and both of us made worse by the composed ways of the police though very civil and obliging and what I must call their obstinacy in not entertaining the idea that he was stolen. 'We mostly find Mum' says the sergeant who came round to comfort me, which he didn't at all and he had been one of the private constables in Caroline's time to which he referred in his opening words when he said 'Don't give way to uneasiness in your mind Mum, it'll all come as right as my nose did when I got the same barked by that young woman in your second floor' – says this sergeant 'we mostly find Mum as people ain't over-anxious to have what I may call second-hand children. *You'll* get him back Mum.' 'O but my dear good sir' I says clasping my hands and wringing them and clasping them again 'he is such an uncommon child!' 'Yes Mum' says the sergeant, 'we mostly find that too Mum. The question is what his clothes were worth.' 'His clothes' I says 'were not worth much sir for he had only got his playing-dress on, but the dear child!—' 'All right Mum' says the sergeant. 'You'll get him back Mum. And even if he'd had his best clothes on, it wouldn't come to worse than his being found wrapped up in a cabbage-leaf, a shivering in a lane.' His words pierced my heart like daggers and daggers, and me and the Major ran in and out like wild things all day long till the Major returning from his interview with the Editor of the Times at night rushes into my little room hysterical and squeezes my hand and wipes his eyes and says 'Joy joy – officer in plain clothes came up on the steps as I was letting myself in – compose your feelings – Jemmy's found.' Consequently I fainted away and when I came to, embraced the legs of the officer in plain clothes who seemed to be taking a kind of a quiet inventory in his mind of the property in my little room with brown whiskers, and I says 'Blessings on you sir where is the Darling!' and he says 'In Kennington Station House.' I was dropping at his feet Stone at the image of that Innocence in cells with murderers when he adds 'He followed the Monkey.' I says deeming it slang language 'O sir explain for a loving grandmother what Monkey!' He says 'Him in the spangled cap with the strap under the chin, as won't keep on – him as sweeps the crossings on a round table and don't want to draw his sabre more than he can help.' Then I understood it all and most thankfully thanked him, and me and the Major and him drove over to Kennington and there we found our boy lying quite comfortable before a blazing fire having sweetly played himself to sleep upon a small accordion nothing like so big as a flat-iron which they had been so kind as to lend him for the purpose and which it appeared had been stopped upon a very young person.

My dear the system upon which the Major commenced and as I may say perfected Jemmy's learning when he was so small that if the dear was on the other side of the table you had to look under it instead of over it to see him with his mother's own bright hair in beautiful curls, is a thing that ought to be known to the Throne and Lords and Commons and then might obtain some promotion for the Major which he well deserves and would be none the worse for (speaking between friends) L. S. D.-ically. When the Major first undertook his learning he says to me:

'I'm going Madam', he says, 'to make our child a Calculating Boy.'

'Major', I says, 'you terrify me and may do the pet a permanent injury you would never forgive yourself.'

'Madam', says the Major, 'next to my regret that when I had my boot-sponge in my hand, I didn't choke that scoundrel with it – on the spot—'

'There! For Gracious' sake,' I interrupts, 'let his conscience find him without sponges.'

'—I say next to that regret, Madam,' says the Major 'would be the regret with which my breast,' which he tapped, 'would be surcharged if this fine mind was not early cultivated. But mark me Madam,' says the Major holding up his forefinger 'cultivated on a principle that will make it a delight.'

'Major' I says 'I will be candid with you and tell you openly that if ever I find the dear child fall off in his appetite I shall know it is his calculations and shall put a stop to them at two minutes' notice. Or if I find them mounting to his head' I says, 'or striking anyways cold to his stomach or leading to anything approaching flabbiness in his legs, the result will be the same, but Major you are a clever man and have seen much and you love the child and are his own godfather, and if you feel a confidence in trying try.'

'Spoken Madam' says the Major 'like Emma Lirriper. All I have to ask, Madam, is that you will leave my godson and myself to make a week or two's preparations for surprising you, and that you will give me leave to have up and down any small articles not actually in use that I may require from the kitchen.'

'From the kitchen Major?' I says half feeling as if he had a mind to cook the child.

'From the kitchen' says the Major, and smiles and swells, and at the same time looks taller.

So I passed my word and the Major and the dear boy were shut up together for half an hour at a time through a certain while, and never could I hear anything going on betwixt them but talking and laughing and Jemmy clapping his hands and screaming out numbers, so I says to myself 'it has not harmed him yet' nor could I on examining the dear find any signs of it anywhere about him which was likewise a great relief. At last one day Jemmy brings me a card in joke in the Major's neat writing 'The Messrs. Jemmy Jackman' for we had given him the Major's other name too 'request the honour of Mrs Lirriper's company at the Jackman Institution in the front parlour this evening at five, military time, to witness a few slight feats of elementary arithmetic.' And if you'll believe me there in the front parlour at five punctual to the moment was the Major behind the Pembroke table with both leaves up and a lot of things from the kitchen tidily set out on old newspapers spread atop of it, and there was the Mite stood upon a chair with his rosy cheeks flushing and his eyes sparkling clusters of diamonds.

'Now Gran' says he, 'oo tit down and don't oo touch ler poople' – for he saw with every one of those diamonds of his that I was going to give him a squeeze.

'Very well sir' I says 'I am obedient in this good company I am sure.' And I sits down in the easy-chair that was put for me, shaking my sides.

But picture my admiration when the Major going on almost as quick as if he was conjuring sets out all the articles he names, and says 'Three saucepans, an Italian iron, a hand-bell, a toasting-fork, a nutmeg-grater, four potlids, a spice-box, two egg-cups, and a chopping-board – how many?' and when that Mite instantly cries 'Tifteen, tut down tive and carry ler 'toppin-board' and then claps his hands draws up his legs and dances on his chair.

My dear with the same astonishing ease and correctness him and the Major added up the tables chairs and sofy, the picters fenders and fire-irons their own selves me and the cat and the eyes in Miss Wozenham's head, and whenever the sum was done Young Roses and Diamonds claps his hands and draws up his legs and dances on his chair.

The pride of the Major! (*'Here's* a mind Ma'am!' he says to me behind his hand.)

Then he says aloud, 'We now come to the next elementary rule – which is called—'

'Umtraction!' cries Jemmy.

'Right', says the Major. 'We have here a toasting-fork, a potato in its natural state, two potlids, one egg-cup, a wooden spoon, and two skewers, from which it is necessary for commercial purposes to subtract a sprat-gridiron, a small pickle-jar, two lemons, one pepper-castor, a blackbeetle-trap, and a knob of the dresser-drawer – what remains?'

'Toatin-fork!' cries Jemmy.

'In numbers how many?' says the Major.

'One!' cries Jemmy.

(*'Here's* a boy, Ma'am!' says the Major to me behind his hand.)

Then the Major goes on:

'We now approach the next elementary rule – which is entitled—'

'Tickleication' cries Jemmy.

'Correct' says the Major.

But my dear to relate to you in detail the way in which they multiplied fourteen sticks of firewood by two bits of ginger and a larding needle, or divided pretty well everything else there was on the table by the heater of the Italian iron and a chamber candlestick, and got a lemon over, would make my head spin round and round and round as it did at the time. So I says 'if you'll excuse my addressing the chair Professor Jackman I think the period of the lecture has now arrived when it becomes necessary that I should take a good hug of this young scholar.' Upon which Jemmy calls out from his station on the chair, 'Gran oo open oor arms and me'll make a 'pring into 'em.' So I opened my arms to him as I had opened my sorrowful heart when his poor young mother lay a dying, and he had his jump and we had a good long hug together and the Major prouder than any peacock says to me behind his hand, 'You need not let him know it Madam' (which I certainly need not for the Major was quite audible) 'but he is a boy!'

In this way Jemmy grew and grew and went to day-school and continued under the Major too, and in summer we were as happy as the days were long, and in winter we were as happy as the days were short and there seemed to rest a Blessing on the Lodgings for they as good as Let themselves and would have done it if there had been twice the accommodation, when sore and hard against my will I one day says to the Major:

'Major you know what I am going to break to you. Our boy must go to boarding-school.'

It was a sad sight to see the Major's countenance drop, and I pitied the good soul with all my heart.

'Yes Major' I says, 'though he is as popular with the Lodgers as you are yourself and though he is to you and me what only you and me know, still it is in the course of things and Life is made of partings and we must part with our Pet.'

Bold as I spoke, I saw two Majors and half-a-dozen fireplaces, and when the poor Major put one of his neat bright-varnished boots upon the fender and his elbow on his knee and his head upon his hand and rocked himself a little to and fro, I was dreadfully cut up.

'But' says I clearing my throat 'you have so well prepared him Major – he has had such a Tutor in you – that he will have none of the first drudgery to go through. And he is so clever besides that he'll soon make his way to the front rank.'

'He is a boy' says the Major – having sniffed – 'that has not his like on the face of the earth.'

'True as you say Major, and it is not for us merely for our own sakes to do anything to keep him back from being a credit and an ornament wherever he goes and perhaps even rising to be a great man, is it Major? He will have all my little savings when my work is done (being all the world to me) and we must try to make him a wise man and a good man, mustn't we Major?'

'Madam' says the Major rising 'Jemmy Jackman is becoming an older file than I was aware of, and you put him to shame. You are thoroughly right Madam. You are simply and undeniably right. – And if you'll excuse me, I'll take a walk.'

So the Major being gone out and Jemmy being at home, I got the child into my little room here and I stood him by my chair and I took his mother's own curls in my hand and I spoke to him loving and serious. And when I had reminded the darling how that he was now in his tenth year and when I had said to him about his getting on in life pretty much what I had said to the Major I broke to him how that we must have this same parting, and there I was forced to stop for there I saw of a sudden the well-remembered lip with its tremble, and it so brought back that time! But with the spirit that was in him he controlled it soon and he says gravely nodding through his tears, 'I understand Gran – I know it *must* be, Gran – go on Gran, don't be afraid of *me*.' And when I had said all that ever I could think of, he turned his bright steady face to mine and he says just a little broken here and there 'You shall see Gran that I can be a man and that I can do anything that is grateful and loving to you – and if I don't grow up to be what you would like to have me – I hope it will be – because I shall die.' And with that he sat down by me and I went on to tell him of the school of which I had excellent recommendations and where it was and how many scholars and what games they played as I had heard and what length of holidays, to all of which he listened bright and clear. And so it came that at last he says 'And now dear Gran let me kneel down here where I have been used to say my prayers and let me fold my face for just a minute in your gown and let me cry, for you have been more than father – more than mother – more than brothers sisters friends – to me!' And so he did cry and I too and we were both much the better for it.

From that time forth he was true to his word and ever blithe and ready, and even when me and the Major took him down into Lincolnshire he was far the gayest of the party though for sure and certain he might easily have been that, but he really was and put life into us only when it came to the last Good-bye, he says with a wistful look, 'You wouldn't have me not really sorry would you Gran?' and when I says 'No dear, Lord forbid!' he says 'I am glad of that!' and ran in out of sight.

But now that the child was gone out of the Lodgings the Major fell into a regularly moping state. It was taken notice of by all the Lodgers that the Major moped. He hadn't even the same air of being rather tall that he used to have, and if he varnished his boots with a single gleam of interest it was as much as he did.

One evening the Major came into my little room to take a cup of tea and a morsel of buttered toast and to read Jemmy's newest letter which had arrived that afternoon (by the very same postman more than middle-aged upon the Beat now), and the letter raising him up a little I says to the Major:

'Major you mustn't get into a moping way.'

The Major shook his head. 'Jemmy Jackman Madam,' he says with a deep sigh, 'is an older file than I thought him.'

'Moping is not the way to grow younger Major.'

'My dear Madam,' says the Major, 'is there *any* way of growing younger?'

Feeling that the Major was getting rather the best of that point I made a diversion to another.

'Thirteen years! Thir-teen years! Many Lodgers have come and gone, in the thirteen years that you have lived in the parlours Major.'

'Hah!' says the Major warming. 'Many Madam, many.'

'And I should say you have been familiar with them all?'

'As a rule (with its exceptions like all rules) my dear Madam' says the Major, 'they have honoured me with their acquaintance, and not unfrequently with their confidence.'

Watching the Major as he drooped his white head and stroked his black mustachios and moped again, a thought which I think must have been going about looking for an owner somewhere dropped into my old noddle if you will excuse the expression.

'The walls of my Lodgings' I says in a casual way – for my dear it is of no use going straight at a man who mopes – 'might have something to tell if they could tell it.'

The Major neither moved nor said anything but I saw he was attending with his shoulders my dear – attending with his shoulders to what I said. In fact I saw that his shoulders were struck by it.

'The dear boy was always fond of story-books' I went on, like as if I was talking to myself. 'I am sure this house – his own home – might write a story or two for his reading one day or another.'

The Major's shoulders gave a dip and a curve and his head came up in his shirt-collar. The Major's head came up in his shirt-collar as I hadn't seen it come up since Jemmy went to school.

'It is unquestionable that in intervals of cribbage and a friendly rubber, my dear Madam,' says the Major, 'and also over what used to be called in my young times – in the salad days of Jemmy Jackman – the social glass, I have exchanged many a reminiscence with your Lodgers.'

My remark was – I confess I made it with the deepest and artfullest of intentions – 'I wish our dear boy had heard them!'

'Are you serious Madam?' asked the Major starting and turning full round.

'Why not Major?'

'Madam' says the Major, turning up one of his cuffs, 'they shall be written for him.'

'Ah! Now you speak' I says giving my hands a pleased clap. 'Now you are in a way out of moping Major!'

'Between this and my holidays – I mean the dear boy's' says the Major turning up his other cuff, 'a good deal may be done towards it.'

'Major you are a clever man and you have seen much and not a doubt of it.'

'I'll begin,' says the Major looking as tall as ever he did, 'to-morrow.'

My dear the Major was another man in three days and he was himself again in a week and he wrote and wrote and wrote with his pen scratching like rats behind the wainscot, and whether he had many grounds to go upon or whether he did at all romance I cannot tell you, but what he has written is in the left-hand glass closet of the little bookcase close behind you.

How the Parlours Added a Few Words

I have the honour of presenting myself by the name of Jackman. I esteem it a proud privilege to go down to posterity through the instrumentality of the most remarkable boy that ever lived – by the name of JEMMY JACKMAN LIRRIPER – and of my most worthy and most highly respected friend, Mrs Emma Lirriper, of Eighty-one, Norfolk Street, Strand, in the County of Middlesex, in the United Kingdom of Great Britain and Ireland.

It is not for me to express the rapture with which we received that dear and eminently remarkable boy, on the occurrence of his first Christmas holidays. Suffice it to observe that when he came flying into the house with two splendid prizes (Arithmetic, and Exemplary Conduct), Mrs Lirriper and myself embraced with emotion, and instantly took him to the Play, where we were all three admirably entertained.

Nor is it to render homage to the virtues of the best of her good and honoured sex – whom, in deference to her unassuming worth, I will only here designate by the initials E. L. – that I add this record to the bundle of papers with which our, in a most distinguished degree, remarkable boy has expressed himself delighted, before re-consigning the same to the left-hand glass closet of Mrs Lirriper's little bookcase.

Neither is it to obtrude the name of the old original superannuated obscure Jemmy Jackman, once (to his degradation) of Wozenham's, long (to his elevation) of Lirriper's. If I could be consciously guilty of that piece of bad taste, it would indeed be a work of supererogation, now that the name is borne by JEMMY JACKMAN LIRRIPER.

No, I take up my humble pen to register a little record of our strikingly remarkable boy, which my poor capacity regards as presenting a pleasant little picture of the dear boy's mind. The picture may be interesting to himself when he is a man.

Our first reunited Christmas-day was the most delightful one we have ever passed together. Jemmy was never silent for five minutes, except in church-time. He talked as we sat by the fire, he talked when we were out walking, he talked as we sat by the fire again, he talked incessantly at dinner, though he made a dinner almost as remarkable as himself. It was the spring of happiness in his fresh young heart flowing and flowing, and it fertilised (if I may be allowed so bold a figure) my much-esteemed friend, and J. J. the present writer.

There were only we three. We dined in my esteemed friend's little room, and our entertainment was perfect. But everything in the establishment is, in neatness, order, and comfort, always perfect. After dinner our boy slipped away to his old stool at my esteemed friend's knee, and there, with his hot chestnuts and his glass of brown sherry (really, a most excellent wine!) on a chair for a table, his face outshone the apples in the dish.

We talked of these jottings of mine, which Jemmy had read through and through by that time; and so it came about that my esteemed friend remarked, as she sat smoothing Jemmy's curls:

'And as you belong to the house too, Jemmy – and so much more than the Lodgers, having been born in it – why, your story ought to be added to the rest, I think, one of these days.'

Jemmy's eyes sparkled at this, and he said, 'So *I* think, Gran.'

Then he sat looking at the fire, and then he began to laugh in a sort of confidence with the fire, and then he said, folding his arms across my esteemed friend's lap, and raising his bright face to hers: 'Would you like to hear a boy's story, Gran?'

'Of all things,' replied my esteemed friend.

'Would you, godfather?'

'Of all things,' I too replied.

'Well, then,' said Jemmy, 'I'll tell you one.'

Here our indisputably remarkable boy gave himself a hug, and laughed again, musically, at the idea of his coming out in that new line. Then he once more took the fire into the same sort of confidence as before, and began:

'Once upon a time, When pigs drank wine, And monkeys chewed tobaccer, 'Twas neither in your time nor mine, But that's no macker—'

'Bless the child!' cried my esteemed friend, 'what's amiss with his brain?'

'It's poetry, Gran,' returned Jemmy, shouting with laughter. 'We always begin stories that way at school.'

'Gave me quite a turn, Major,' said my esteemed friend, fanning herself with a plate. 'Thought he was light-headed!'

'In those remarkable times, Gran and godfather, there was once a boy – not me, you know.'

'No, no,' says my respected friend, 'not you. Not him, Major, you understand?'

'No, no,' says I.

'And he went to school in Rutlandshire—'

'Why not Lincolnshire?' says my respected friend.

'Why not, you dear old Gran? Because I go to school in Lincolnshire, don't I?'

'Ah, to be sure!' says my respected friend. 'And it's not Jemmy, you understand, Major?'

'No, no,' says I.

'Well!' our boy proceeded, hugging himself comfortably, and laughing merrily (again in confidence with the fire), before he again looked up in Mrs Lirriper's face, 'and so he was tremendously in love with his schoolmaster's daughter, and she was the most beautiful creature that ever was seen, and she had brown eyes, and she had brown hair all curling beautifully, and she had a delicious voice, and she was delicious altogether, and her name was Seraphina.'

'What's the name of *your* schoolmaster's daughter, Jemmy?' asks my respected friend.

'Polly!' replied Jemmy, pointing his forefinger at her. 'There now! Caught you! Ha, ha, ha!'

When he and my respected friend had had a laugh and a hug together, our admittedly remarkable boy resumed with a great relish:

'Well! And so he loved her. And so he thought about her, and dreamed about her, and made her presents of oranges and nuts, and would have made her presents of pearls and diamonds if he could have afforded it out of his pocket-money, but he couldn't. And so her father – O, he WAS a Tartar! Keeping the boys up to the mark, holding examinations once a month, lecturing upon all sorts of subjects at all sorts of times, and knowing everything in the world out of book. And so this boy—'

'Had he any name?' asks my respected friend.

'No, he hadn't, Gran. Ha, ha! There now! Caught you again!'

After this, they had another laugh and another hug, and then our boy went on.

'Well! And so this boy, he had a friend about as old as himself at the same school, and his name (for He *had* a name, as it happened) was – let me remember – was Bobbo.'

'Not Bob,' says my respected friend.

'Of course not,' says Jemmy. 'What made you think it was, Gran? Well! And so this friend was the cleverest and bravest and best-looking and most generous of all the friends that ever were, and so he was in love with Seraphina's sister, and so Seraphina's sister was in love with him, and so they all grew up.'

'Bless us!' says my respected friend. 'They were very sudden about it.'

'So they all grew up,' our boy repeated, laughing heartily, 'and Bobbo and this boy went away together on horseback to seek their fortunes, and they partly got their horses by favour, and partly in a bargain; that is to say, they had saved up between them seven and fourpence, and the two horses, being Arabs, were worth more, only the man said he would take that, to favour them. Well! And so they made their fortunes and came prancing back to the school, with their pockets full of gold, enough to last for ever. And so they rang at the parents' and visitors' bell (not the back gate), and when the bell was answered they proclaimed "The same as if it was scarlet fever! Every boy goes home for an indefinite period!" And then there was great hurrahing, and then they kissed Seraphina and her sister – each his own love, and not the other's on any account – and then they ordered the Tartar into instant confinement.'

'Poor man!' said my respected friend.

'Into instant confinement, Gran,' repeated Jemmy, trying to look severe and roaring with laughter; 'and he was to have nothing to eat but the boys' dinners, and was to drink half a cask of their beer every day. And so then the preparations were made for the two weddings, and there were hampers, and potted things, and sweet things, and nuts, and postage-stamps, and all manner of things. And so they were so jolly, that they let the Tartar out, and he was jolly too.'

'I am glad they let him out,' says my respected friend, 'because he had only done his duty.'

'O, but hadn't he overdone it, though!' cried Jemmy. 'Well! And so then this boy mounted his horse, with his bride in his arms, and cantered away, and cantered on and on till he came to a certain place where he had a certain Gran and a certain godfather – not you two, you know.'

'No, no,' we both said.

'And there he was received with great rejoicings, and he filled the cupboard and the bookcase with gold, and he showered it out on his Gran and his godfather because they were the two kindest and dearest people that ever lived in this world. And so while they were sitting up to their knees in gold, a knocking was heard at the street door, and who should it be but Bobbo, also on horseback with his bride in his arms, and what had he come to say but that he would take (at double rent) all the Lodgings for ever, that were not wanted by this boy and this Gran and this godfather, and that they would all live together, and all be happy! And so they were, and so it never ended!'

'And was there no quarrelling?' asked my respected friend, as Jemmy sat upon her lap and hugged her.

'No! Nobody ever quarrelled.'

'And did the money never melt away?'

'No! Nobody could ever spend it all.'

'And did none of them ever grow older?'

'No! Nobody ever grew older after that.'

'And did none of them ever die?'

'O, no, no, no, Gran!' exclaimed our dear boy, laying his cheek upon her breast, and drawing her closer to him. 'Nobody ever died.'

'Ah, Major, Major!' says my respected friend, smiling benignly upon me, 'this beats our stories. Let us end with the Boy's story, Major, for the Boy's story is the best that is ever told!'

In submission to which request on the part of the best of women, I have here noted it down as faithfully as my best abilities, coupled with my best intentions, would admit, subscribing it with my name,

J. JACKMAN.

THE PARLOURS.
MRS LIRRIPER'S LODGINGS.

THOMAS HARDY

The Three Strangers

Among the few features of agricultural England which retain an appearance but little modified by the lapse of centuries, may be reckoned the high, grassy, and furzy downs, coombs, or ewe-leases, as they are indifferently called, that fill a large area of certain counties in the south and south-west. If any mark of human occupation is met with hereon, it usually takes the form of the solitary cottage of some shepherd.

Fifty years ago such a lonely cottage stood on such a down, and may possibly be standing there now. In spite of its loneliness, however, the spot, by actual measurement, was not more than five miles from a county-town. Yet that affected it little. Five miles of irregular upland, during the long inimical seasons, with their sleets, snows, rains, and mists, afford withdrawing space enough to isolate a Timon or a Nebuchadnezzar; much less, in fair weather, to please that less repellent tribe, the poets, philosophers, artists, and others who 'conceive and meditate of pleasant things'.

Some old earthen camp or barrow, some clump of trees, at least some starved fragment of ancient hedge, is usually taken advantage of in the erection of these forlorn dwellings. But, in the present case, such a kind of shelter had been disregarded. Higher Crowstairs, as the house was called, stood quite detached and undefended. The only reason for its precise situation seemed to be the crossing of two footpaths at right angles hard by, which may have crossed there and thus for a good five hundred years. Hence the house was exposed to the elements on all sides. But, though the wind up here blew unmistakably when it did blow, and the rain hit hard whenever it fell, the various weathers of the winter season were not quite so formidable on the coomb as they were imagined to be by dwellers on low ground. The raw rimes were not so pernicious as in the hollows, and the frosts were scarcely so severe. When the shepherd and his family who tenanted the house were pitied for their sufferings from the exposure, they said that upon the whole they were less inconvenienced by 'wuzzes and flames' (hoarses and phlegms) than when they had lived by the stream of a snug neighbouring valley.

The night of March 28, 182–, was precisely one of the nights that were wont to call forth these expressions of commiseration. The level rainstorm smote walls, slopes, and hedges like the clothyard shafts of Senlac and Crecy. Such sheep and outdoor animals as had no shelter stood with their buttocks to the winds; while the tails of little birds trying to roost on some scraggy thorn were blown inside-out like umbrellas. The gable-end of the cottage was stained with wet, and the eavesdroppings flapped against the wall. Yet never was commiseration for the shepherd more misplaced. For that cheerful rustic was entertaining a large party in glorification of the christening of his second girl.

The guests had arrived before the rain began to fall, and they were all now assembled in the chief or living room of the dwelling. A glance into the apartment at eight o'clock on this eventful evening would have resulted in the opinion that it was as cosy and comfortable a nook as could be wished for in boisterous weather. The calling of its inhabitant was proclaimed by a number of highly-polished sheep-crooks without stems that were hung ornamentally over the fireplace, the curl of each shining crook varying from the antiquated type engraved in the patriarchal pictures of old family Bibles to the most approved fashion of the last local sheep-fair. The room was lighted by half a dozen candles, having wicks only a trifle smaller than the grease which enveloped them, in candlesticks that were never used but at high-days, holy-days, and family feasts. The lights were scattered about the room, two of them standing on the chimney-piece. This position of candles was in itself significant. Candles on the chimney-piece always meant a party.

On the hearth, in front of a back-brand to give substance, blazed a fire of thorns, that crackled 'like the laughter of the fool'.

Nineteen persons were gathered here. Of these, five women, wearing gowns of various bright hues, sat in chairs along the wall; girls shy and not shy filled the window-bench; four men, including Charley Jake the hedge-carpenter, Elijah New the parish-clerk, and John Pitcher, a neighbouring dairyman, the shepherd's father-in-law, lolled in the settle; a young man and maid, who were blushing over tentative *pourparlers* on a life-companionship, sat beneath the corner-cupboard; and an elderly engaged man of fifty or upward moved restlessly about from spots where his betrothed was not to the spot where she was. Enjoyment was pretty general, and so much the more prevailed in being unhampered by conventional restrictions. Absolute confidence in each other's good opinion begat perfect ease, while the finishing stroke of manner, amounting to a truly princely serenity, was lent to the majority by the absence of any expression or trait denoting that they wished to get on in the world, enlarge their minds, or do any eclipsing thing whatever – which nowadays so generally nips the bloom and *bonhomie* of all except the two extremes of the social scale.

Shepherd Fennel had married well, his wife being a dairyman's daughter from the valley below, who brought fifty guineas in her pocket – and kept them there, till they should be required for ministering to the needs of a coming family. This frugal woman had been somewhat exercised as to the character that should be given to the gathering. A sit-still party had its advantages; but an undisturbed position of ease in chairs and settles was apt to lead on the men to such an unconscionable deal of toping that they would sometimes fairly drink the house dry. A dancing-party was the alternative; but this, while avoiding the foregoing objection on the score of good drink, had a counterbalancing disadvantage in the matter of good victuals, the ravenous appetites engendered by the exercise causing immense havoc in the buttery. Shepherdess Fennel fell back upon the intermediate plan of mingling short dances with short periods of talk and singing, so as to hinder any ungovernable rage in either. But this scheme was entirely confined to her own gentle mind: the shepherd himself was in the mood to exhibit the most reckless phases of hospitality.

The fiddler was a boy of those parts, about twelve years of age, who had a wonderful dexterity in jigs and reels, though his fingers were so small and short as to necessitate a constant shifting for the high notes, from which he scrambled back to the first position with sounds not of unmixed purity of tone. At seven the shrill tweedle-dee of this youngster had begun, accompanied by a booming ground-bass from Elijah New, the parish-clerk, who had thoughtfully brought with him his favourite musical instrument, the serpent. Dancing was instantaneous, Mrs Fennel privately enjoining the players on no account to let the dance exceed the length of a quarter of an hour.

But Elijah and the boy, in the excitement of their position, quite forgot the injunction. Moreover, Oliver Giles, a man of seventeen, one of the dancers, who was enamoured of his partner, a fair girl of thirty-three rolling years, had recklessly handed a new crown-piece to the musicians, as a bribe to keep going as long as they had muscle and wind. Mrs Fennel, seeing the steam begin to generate on the countenances of her guests, crossed over and touched the fiddler's elbow and put her hand on the serpent's mouth. But they took no notice, and fearing she might lose her character of genial hostess if she were to interfere too markedly, she retired and sat down helpless. And so the dance whizzed on with cumulative fury, the performers moving in their planet-like courses, direct and retrograde, from apogee to perigee, till the hand of the well-kicked clock at the bottom of the room had travelled over the circumference of an hour.

While these cheerful events were in course of enactment within Fennel's pastoral dwelling, an incident having considerable bearing on the party had occurred in the gloomy night without. Mrs Fennel's concern about the growing fierceness of the dance corresponded in point of time with the ascent of a human figure to the solitary hill of Higher Crowstairs from the direction of the distant town. This personage strode on through the rain without a pause, following the little-worn path which, farther on in its course, skirted the shepherd's cottage.

It was nearly the time of full moon, and on this account, though the sky was lined with a uniform sheet of dripping cloud, ordinary objects out of doors were readily visible. The sad wan light revealed the lonely pedestrian to be a man of supple frame; his gait suggested that he had somewhat passed the period of perfect and instinctive agility, though not so far as to be otherwise than rapid of motion when occasion required. In point of fact, he might have been about forty years of age. He appeared tall, but a recruiting sergeant, or other person accustomed to the judging of men's heights by the eye, would have discerned that this was chiefly owing to his gauntness, and that he was not more than five-feet-eight or nine.

Notwithstanding the regularity of his tread, there was caution in it, as in that of one who mentally feels his way; and despite the fact that it was not a black coat nor a dark garment of any sort that he wore, there was something about him which suggested that he naturally belonged to the black-coated tribes of men. His clothes were of fustian, and his boots hobnailed, yet in his progress he showed not the mud-accustomed bearing of hobnailed and fustianed peasantry.

By the time that he had arrived abreast of the shepherd's premises the rain came down, or rather came along, with yet more determined violence. The outskirts of the little settlement partially broke the force of wind and rain, and this induced him to stand still. The most salient of the shepherd's domestic erections was an empty sty at the forward corner of his hedgeless garden, for in these latitudes the principle of masking the homelier features of your establishment by a conventional frontage was unknown. The traveller's eye was attracted to this small building by the pallid shine of the wet slates that covered it. He turned aside, and, finding it empty, stood under the pent-roof for shelter.

While he stood, the boom of the serpent within the adjacent house, and the lesser strains of the fiddler, reached the spot as an accompaniment to the surging hiss of the flying rain on the sod, its louder beating on the cabbage-leaves of the garden, on the eight or ten beehives just discernible by the path, and its dripping from the eaves into a row of buckets and pans that had been placed under the walls of the cottage. For at Higher Crowstairs, as at all such elevated domiciles, the grand difficulty of house-keeping was an insufficiency of water; and a casual rainfall was utilized by turning out, as catchers, every utensil that the house contained. Some queer stories might be told of the contrivances for economy in suds and dish-waters that are absolutely necessitated in upland habitations during the droughts of summer. But at this season there were no such exigencies: a mere acceptance of what the skies bestowed was sufficient for an abundant store.

At last the notes of the serpent ceased and the house was silent. This cessation of activity aroused the solitary pedestrian from the reverie into which he had lapsed, and, emerging from the shed, with an apparently new intention, he walked up the path to the house-door. Arrived here, his first act was to kneel down on a large stone beside the row of vessels, and to drink a copious draught from one of them. Having quenched his thirst he rose and lifted his hand to knock, but paused with his eye upon the panel. Since the dark surface of the wood revealed absolutely nothing, it was evident that he must be mentally looking through the door, as if he wished to measure thereby all the possibilities that a house of this sort might include, and how they might bear upon the question of his entry.

In his indecision he turned and surveyed the scene around. Not a soul was anywhere visible. The garden-path stretched downward from his feet, gleaming like the track of a snail; the roof of the little well (mostly dry), the well cover, the top rail of the garden-gate, were varnished with the same dull liquid glaze; while, far away in the vale, a faint whiteness of more than usual extent showed that the rivers were high in the meads. Beyond all this winked a few bleared lamplights through the beating drops, lights that denoted the situation of the county-town from which he had appeared to come. The absence of all notes of life in that direction seemed to clinch his intentions, and he knocked at the door.

Within, a desultory chat had taken the place of movement and musical sound. The hedge-carpenter was suggesting a song to the company, which nobody just then was inclined to undertake, so that the knock afforded a not unwelcome diversion.

'Walk in!' said the shepherd promptly.

The latch clicked upward, and out of the night our pedestrian appeared upon the door-mat. The shepherd arose, snuffed two of the nearest candles, and turned to look at him.

Their light disclosed that the stranger was dark in complexion and not unprepossessing as to feature. His hat, which for a moment he did not remove, hung low over his eyes, without concealing that they were large, open, and determined, moving with a flash rather than a glance round the room. He seemed pleased with the survey, and, baring his shaggy head, said, in a rich deep voice, 'The rain is so heavy, friends, that I ask leave to come in and rest awhile.'

'To be sure, stranger,' said the shepherd. 'And faith, you've been lucky in choosing your time, for we are having a bit of a fling for a glad cause – though, to be sure, a man could hardly wish that glad cause to happen more than once a year.'

'Nor less,' spoke up a woman. 'For 'tis best to get your family over and done with, as soon as you can, so as to be all the earlier out of the fag o't.'

'And what may be this glad cause?' asked the stranger.

'A birth and christening,' said the shepherd.

The stranger hoped his host might not be made unhappy either by too many or too few of such episodes, and being invited by a gesture to a pull at the mug, he readily acquiesced. His manner, which, before entering, had been so dubious, was now altogether that of a careless and candid man.

'Late to be traipsing athwart this coomb – hey?' said the engaged man of fifty.

'Late it is, master, as you say. – I'll take a seat in the chimney-corner, if you have nothing to urge against it, ma'am; for I am a little moist on the side that was next the rain.'

Mrs Shepherd Fennel assented, and made room for the self-invited comer, who, having got completely inside the chimney-corner, stretched out his legs and his arms with the expansiveness of a person quite at home.

'Yes, I am rather thin in the vamp,' he said freely, seeing that the eyes of the shepherd's wife fell upon his boots, 'and I am not well fitted either. I have had some rough times lately, and have been forced to pick up what I can get in the way of wearing, but I must find a suit better fit for working-days when I reach home.'

'One of hereabouts?' she inquired.

'Not quite that – farther up the country.'

'I thought so. And so am I; and by your tongue you come from my neighbourhood.'

'But you would hardly have heard of me,' he said quickly. 'My time would be long before yours, ma'am, you see.'

This testimony to the youthfulness of his hostess had the effect of stopping her cross-examination.

'There is only one thing more wanted to make me happy,' continued the new-comer. 'And that is a little baccy, which I am sorry to say I am out of.'

'I'll fill your pipe,' said the shepherd.

'I must ask you to lend me a pipe likewise.'

'A smoker, and no pipe about ye?'

'I have dropped it somewhere on the road.'

The shepherd filled and handed him a new clay pipe, saying, as he did so, 'Hand me your baccy-box – I'll fill that too, now I am about it.'

The man went through the movement of searching his pockets.

'Lost that too?' said his entertainer, with some surprise.

'I am afraid so,' said the man with some confusion. 'Give it to me in a screw of paper.' Lighting his pipe at the candle with a suction that drew the whole flame into the bowl, he resettled himself in the corner, and bent his looks upon the faint steam from his damp legs, as if he wished to say no more.

Meanwhile the general body of guests had been taking little notice of this visitor by reason of an absorbing discussion in which they were engaged with the band about a tune for the next dance. The matter being settled, they were about to stand up, when an interruption came in the shape of another knock at the door.

At sound of the same the man in the chimney-corner took up the poker and began stirring the fire as if doing it thoroughly were the one aim of his existence; and a second time the shepherd said 'Walk in!' In a moment another man stood upon the straw-woven door-mat. He too was a stranger.

This individual was one of a type radically different from the first. There was more of the commonplace in his manner, and a certain jovial cosmopolitanism sat upon his features. He was several years older than the first arrival, his hair being slightly frosted, his eyebrows bristly, and his whiskers cut back from his cheeks. His face was rather full and flabby, and yet it was not altogether a face without power. A few grog-blossoms marked the neighbourhood of his nose. He flung back his long drab greatcoat, revealing that beneath it he wore a suit of cinder-grey shade throughout, large heavy seals, of some metal or other that would take a polish, dangling from his fob as his only personal ornament. Shaking the water-drops from his low-crowned glazed hat, he said, 'I must ask for a few minutes' shelter, comrades, or I shall be wetted to my skin before I get to Casterbridge.'

'Make yourself at home, master,' said the shepherd, perhaps a trifle less heartily than on the first occasion. Not that Fennel had the least tinge of niggardliness in his composition; but the room was far from large, spare chairs were not numerous, and damp companions were not altogether desirable at close quarters for the women and girls in their bright-coloured gowns.

However, the second comer, after taking off his greatcoat, and hanging his hat on a nail in one of the ceiling-beams as if he had been specially invited to put it there, advanced and sat down at the table. This had been pushed so closely into the chimney-corner, to give all available room to the dancers, that its inner edge grazed the elbow of the man who had ensconced himself by the fire; and thus the two strangers were brought into close companionship. They nodded to each other by way of breaking the ice of unacquaintance, and the first stranger handed his neighbour the family mug – a huge vessel of brown ware, having its upper edge worn away like a threshold by the rub of whole generations of thirsty lips that had gone the way of all flesh, and bearing the following inscription burnt upon its rotund side in yellow letters: –

THERE IS NO FUN

UNTILL I CUM.

The other man, nothing loth, raised the mug to his lips, and drank on, and on, and on – till a curious blueness overspread the countenance of the shepherd's wife, who had regarded with no little surprise the first stranger's free offer to the second of what did not belong to him to dispense.

'I knew it!' said the toper to the shepherd with much satisfaction. 'When I walked up your garden before coming in, and saw the hives all of a row, I said to myself, "Where there's bees there's honey, and where there's honey there's mead." But mead of such a truly comfortable sort as this I really didn't expect to meet in my older days.' He took yet another pull at the mug, till it assumed an ominous elevation.

'Glad you enjoy it!' said the shepherd warmly.

'It is goodish mead,' assented Mrs Fennel with an absence of enthusiasm, which seemed to say that it was possible to buy praise for one's cellar at too heavy a price. 'It is trouble enough to make – and really I hardly think we shall make any more. For honey sells well, and we ourselves can make shift with a drop o' small mead and metheglin for common use from the comb-washings.'

'Oh, but you'll never have the heart!' reproachfully cried the stranger in cinder-grey, after taking up the mug a third time and setting it down empty. 'I love mead, when 'tis old like this, as I love to go to church o' Sundays, or to relieve the needy any day of the week.'

'Ha, ha, ha!' said the man in the chimney-corner, who, in spite of the taciturnity induced by the pipe of tobacco, could not or would not refrain from this slight testimony to his comrade's humour.

Now the old mead of those days, brewed of the purest first-year or maiden honey, four pounds to the gallon – with its due complement of white of eggs, cinnamon, ginger, cloves, mace, rosemary, yeast, and processes of working, bottling, and cellaring – tasted remarkably strong, but it did not taste so strong as it actually was. Hence, presently, the stranger in cinder-grey at the table, moved by its creeping influence, unbuttoned his waistcoat, threw himself back in his chair, spread his legs, and made his presence felt in various ways.

'Well, well, as I say,' he resumed, 'I am going to Casterbridge, and to Casterbridge I must go. I should have been almost there by this time; but the rain drove me into your dwelling, and I'm not sorry for it.'

'You don't live in Casterbridge?' said the shepherd.

'Not as yet; though I shortly mean to move there.'

'Going to set up in trade, perhaps?'

'No, no,' said the shepherd's wife. 'It is easy to see that the gentleman is rich, and don't want to work at anything.'

The cinder-grey stranger paused, as if to consider whether he would accept that definition of himself. He presently rejected it by answering, 'Rich is not quite the word for me, dame. I do work, and I must work. And even if I only get to Casterbridge by midnight I must begin work there at eight tomorrow morning. Yes, het or wet, blow or snow, famine or sword, my day's work tomorrow must be done.'

'Poor man! Then, in spite o' seeming, you be worse off than we?' replied the shepherd's wife.

''Tis the nature of my trade, men and maidens. 'Tis the nature of my trade more than my poverty . . . But really and truly I must up and off, or I shan't get a lodging in the town.' However, the speaker did not move, and directly added, 'There's time for one more draught of friendship before I go; and I'd perform it at once if the mug were not dry.'

'Here's a mug o' small,' said Mrs Fennel. 'Small, we call it, though to be sure 'tis only the first wash o' the combs.'

'No,' said the stranger disdainfully. 'I won't spoil your first kindness by partaking o' your second.'

'Certainly not,' broke in Fennel. 'We don't increase and multiply every day, and I'll fill the mug again.' He went away to the dark place under the stairs where the barrel stood. The shepherdess followed him.

'Why should you do this?' she said reproachfully, as soon as they were alone. 'He's emptied it once, though it held enough for ten people; and now he's not contented wi' the small, but must needs call for more o' the strong! And a stranger unbeknown to any of us. For my part, I don't like the look o' the man at all.'

'But he's in the house, my honey; and 'tis a wet night, and a christening. Daze it, what's a cup of mead more or less? there'll be plenty more next bee-burning.'

'Very well – this time, then,' she answered, looking wistfully at the barrel. 'But what is the man's calling, and where is he one of, that he should come in and join us like this?'

'I don't know. I'll ask him again.'

The catastrophe of having the mug drained dry at one pull by the stranger in cinder-grey was effectually guarded against this time by Mrs Fennel. She poured out his allowance in a small cup, keeping the large one at a discreet distance from him. When he had tossed off his portion the shepherd renewed his inquiry about the stranger's occupation.

The latter did not immediately reply, and the man in the chimney-corner, with sudden demonstrativeness, said, 'Anybody may know my trade – I'm a wheelwright.'

'A very good trade for these parts,' said the shepherd.

'And anybody may know mine – if they've the sense to find it out,' said the stranger in cinder-grey.

'You may generally tell what a man is by his claws,' observed the hedge-carpenter, looking at his own hands. 'My fingers be as full of thorns as an old pin-cushion is of pins.'

The hands of the man in the chimney-corner instinctively sought the shade, and he gazed into the fire as he resumed his pipe. The man at the table took up the hedge-carpenter's remark, and added smartly, 'True; but the oddity of my trade is that, instead of setting a mark upon me, it sets a mark upon my customers.'

No observation being offered by anybody in elucidation of this enigma, the shepherd's wife once more called for a song. The same obstacles presented themselves as at the former time – one had no voice, another had forgotten the first verse. The stranger at the table, whose soul had now risen to a good working temperature, relieved the difficulty by exclaiming that, to start the company, he would sing himself. Thrusting one thumb into the arm-hole of his waistcoat, he waved the other hand in the air, and, with an extemporizing gaze at the shining sheep-crooks above the mantelpiece, began: –

> Oh my trade it is the rarest one,
>   Simple shepherds all –
>   My trade is a sight to see;
> For my customers I tie, and take them up on high,
>   And waft 'em to a far countree!

The room was silent when he had finished the verse – with one exception, that of the man in the chimney-corner, who, at the singer's word, 'Chorus!' joined him in a deep bass voice of musical relish –

> And waft 'em to a far countree!

Oliver Giles, John Pitcher the dairyman, the parish-clerk, the engaged man of fifty, the row of young women against the wall, seemed lost in thought not of the gayest kind. The shepherd looked meditatively on the ground, the shepherdess gazed keenly at the singer, and with some suspicion; she was doubting whether this stranger were merely singing an old song from recollection, or was composing one there and then for the occasion. All were as perplexed at the obscure revelation as the guests at Belshazzar's Feast, except the man in the chimney-corner, who quietly said, 'Second verse, stranger,' and smoked on.

The singer thoroughly moistened himself from his lips inwards, and went on with the next stanza as requested: –

My tools are but common ones,
  Simple shepherds all,
My tools are no sight to see:
A little hempen string, and a post whereon to swing,
  Are implements enough for me!

Shepherd Fennel glanced round. There was no longer any doubt that the stranger was answering his question rhythmically. The guests one and all started back with suppressed exclamations. The young woman engaged to the man of fifty fainted half-way, and would have proceeded, but finding him wanting in alacrity for catching her she sat down trembling.

'Oh, he's the ——!' whispered the people in the background, mentioning the name of an ominous public officer. 'He's come to do it. 'Tis to be at Casterbridge jail tomorrow – the man for sheep-stealing – the poor clock-maker we heard of, who used to live away at Shottsford and had no work to do – Timothy Sommers, whose family were a-starving, and so he went out of Shottsford by the high-road, and took a sheep in open daylight, defying the farmer and the farmer's wife and the farmer's lad, and every man jack among 'em. He' (and they nodded towards the stranger of the deadly trade) 'is come from up the country to do it because there's not enough to do in his own country-town, and he's got the place here now our own county man's dead; he's going to live in the same cottage under the prison wall.'

The stranger in cinder-grey took no notice of this whispered string of observations, but again wetted his lips. Seeing that his friend in the chimney-corner was the only one who reciprocated his joviality in any way, he held out his cup towards that appreciative comrade, who also held out his own. They clinked together, the eyes of the rest of the room hanging upon the singer's actions. He parted his lips for the third verse; but at that moment another knock was audible upon the door. This time the knock was faint and hesitating.

The company seemed scared; the shepherd looked with consternation towards the entrance, and it was with some effort that he resisted his alarmed wife's deprecatory glance, and uttered for the third time the welcoming words, 'Walk in!'

The door was gently opened, and another man stood upon the mat. He, like those who had preceded him, was a stranger. This time it was a short, small personage, of fair complexion, and dressed in a decent suit of dark clothes.

'Can you tell me the way to —— ?' he began; when, gazing round the room to observe the nature of the company amongst whom he had fallen, his eyes lighted on the stranger in cinder-grey. It was just at the instant when the latter, who had thrown his mind into his song with such a will that he scarcely heeded the interruption, silenced all whispers and inquiries by bursting into his third verse: –

> Tomorrow is my working day,
>   Simple shepherds all –
> Tomorrow is a working day for me:
> For the farmer's sheep is slain, and the lad who did it ta'en,
>   And on his soul may God ha' merc-y!

The stranger in the chimney-corner, waving cups with the singer so heartily that his mead splashed over on the hearth, repeated in his bass voice as before: –

> And on his soul may God ha' merc-y!

All this time the third stranger had been standing in the doorway. Finding now that he did not come forward or go on speaking, the guests particularly regarded him. They noticed to their surprise that he stood before them the picture of abject terror – his knees trembling, his hand shaking so violently that the door-latch by which he supported himself rattled audibly; his white lips were parted, and his eyes fixed on the merry officer of justice in the middle of the room. A moment more and he had turned, closed the door, and fled.

'What a man can it be?' said the shepherd.

The rest, between the awfulness of their late discovery and the odd conduct of this third visitor, looked as if they knew not what to think, and said nothing. Instinctively they withdrew farther and farther from the grim gentleman in their midst, whom some of them seemed to take for the Prince of Darkness himself, till they formed a remote circle, an empty space of floor being left between them and him –

. . . circulus, cujus centrum diabolus

The room was so silent – though there were more than twenty people in it – that nothing could be heard but the patter of the rain against the window-shutters, accompanied by the occasional hiss of a stray drop that fell down the chimney into the fire, and the steady puffing of the man in the corner, who had now resumed his pipe of long clay.

The stillness was unexpectedly broken. The distant sound of a gun reverberated through the air – apparently from the direction of the county-town.

'Be jiggered!' cried the stranger who had sung the song, jumping up.

'What does that mean?' asked several.

'A prisoner escaped from the jail – that's what it means.'

All listened. The sound was repeated, and none of them spoke but the man in the chimney-corner, who said quietly, 'I've often been told that in this county they fire a gun at such times; but I never heard it till now.'

'I wonder if it is *my* man?' murmured the personage in cinder-gray.

'Surely it is!' said the shepherd involuntarily. 'And surely we've seen him! That little man who looked in at the door by now, and quivered like a leaf when he seed ye and heard your song!'

'His teeth chattered, and the breath went out of his body,' said the dairyman.

'And his heart seemed to sink within him like a stone,' said Oliver Giles.

'And he bolted as if he'd been shot at,' said the hedge-carpenter.

'True – his teeth chattered, and his heart seemed to sink; and he bolted as if he's been shot at,' slowly summed up the man in the chimney-corner.

'I didn't notice it,' remarked the hangman.

'We were all a-wondering what made him run off in such a fright,' faltered one of the women against the wall, 'and now 'tis explained.'

The firing of the alarm-gun went on at intervals, low and sullenly, and their suspicions became a certainty. The sinister gentleman in cinder-grey roused himself. 'Is there a constable here?' he asked in thick tones. 'If so, let him step forward.'

The engaged man of fifty stepped quavering out of the corner, his betrothed beginning to sob on the back of the chair.

'You are a sworn constable?'

'I be, sir.'

'Then pursue the criminal at once, with assistance, and bring him back here. He can't have gone far.'

'I will, sir, I will – when I've got my staff. I'll go home and get it, and come sharp here, and start in a body.'

'Staff! – never mind your staff; the man 'll be gone!'

'But I can't do nothing without my staff – can I, William, and John, and Charles Jake? No; for there's the king's royal crown a painted on en in yaller and gold, and the lion and the unicorn, so as when I raise en up and hit my prisoner, 'tis made a lawful blow thereby. I wouldn't 'tempt to take up a man without my staff – no, not I. If I hadn't the law to gie me courage, why, instead o' my taking up him he might take up me!'

'Now, I'm a king's man myself, and can give you authority enough for this,' said the formidable officer in grey. 'Now then, all of ye, be ready. Have ye any lanterns?'

'Yes – have ye any lanterns? – I demand it!' said the constable.

'And the rest of you able-bodied—'

'Able-bodied men – yes – the rest of ye!' said the constable.

'Have you some good stout staves and pitchforks—'

'Staves and pitchforks – in the name o' the law! And take 'em in yer hands and go in quest, and do as we in authority tell ye!'

Thus aroused, the men prepared to give chase. The evidence was, indeed, though circumstantial, so convincing, that but little argument was needed to show the shepherd's guests that after what they had seen it would look very much like connivance if they did not instantly pursue the unhappy third stranger, who could not as yet have gone more than a few hundred yards over such uneven country.

A shepherd is always well provided with lanterns; and, lighting these hastily, and with hurdle-staves in their hands, they poured out of the door, taking a direction along the crest of the hill, away from the town, the rain having fortunately a little abated.

Disturbed by the noise, or possibly by unpleasant dreams of her baptism, the child who had been christened began to cry heart-brokenly in the room overhead. These notes of grief came down through the chinks of the floor to the ears of the women below, who jumped up one by one, and seemed glad of the excuse to ascend and comfort the baby, for the incidents of the last half-hour greatly oppressed them. Thus in the space of two or three minutes the room on the ground-floor was deserted quite.

But it was not for long. Hardly had the sound of footsteps died away when a man returned round the corner of the house from the direction the pursuers had taken. Peeping in at the door, and seeing nobody there, he entered leisurely. It was the stranger of the chimney-corner, who had gone out with the rest. The motive of his return was shown by his helping himself to a cut piece of skimmer-cake that lay on a ledge beside where he had sat, and which he had apparently forgotten to take with him. He also poured out half a cup more mead from the quantity that remained, ravenously eating and drinking these as he stood. He had not finished when another figure came in just as quietly – his friend in cinder-grey.

'Oh – you here?' said the latter, smiling. 'I thought you had gone to help in the capture.' And this speaker also revealed the object of his return by looking solicitously round for the fascinating mug of old mead.

'And I thought you had gone,' said the other, continuing his skimmer-cake with some effort.

'Well, on second thoughts, I felt there were enough without me,' said the first confidentially, 'and such a night as it is, too. Besides, 'tis the business o' the Government to take care of its criminals – not mine.'

'True; so it is. And I felt as you did, that there were enough without me.'

'I don't want to break my limbs running over the humps and hollows of this wild country.'

'Nor I neither, between you and me.'

'These shepherd-people are used to it – simple-minded souls, you know, stirred up to anything in a moment. They'll have him ready for me before the morning, and no trouble to me at all.'

'They'll have him, and we shall have saved ourselves all labour in the matter.'

'True, true. Well, my way is to Casterbridge; and 'tis as much as my legs will do to take me that far. Going the same way?'

'No, I am sorry to say! I have to get home over there' (he nodded indefinitely to the right), 'and I feel as you do, that it is quite enough for my legs to do before bedtime.'

The other had by this time finished the mead in the mug, after which, shaking hands heartily at the door, and wishing each other well, they went their several ways.

In the meantime the company of pursuers had reached the end of the hog's-back elevation which dominated this part of the coomb. They had decided on no particular plan of action; and, finding that the man of the baleful trade was no longer in their company, they seemed quite unable to form any such plan now. They descended in all directions down the hill, and straightway several of the party fell into the snare set by Nature for all misguided midnight ramblers over this part of the cretaceous formation. The 'lynchets', or flint slopes, which belted the escarpment at intervals of a dozen yards, took the less cautious ones unawares, and losing their footing on the rubbly steep they slid sharply downwards, the lanterns rolling from their hands to the bottom, and there lying on their sides till the horn was scorched through.

When they had again gathered themselves together, the shepherd, as the man who knew the country best, took the lead, and guided them round these treacherous inclines. The lanterns, which seemed rather to dazzle their eyes and warn the fugitive than to assist them in the exploration, were extinguished, due silence was observed; and in this more rational order they plunged into the vale. It was a grassy, briery, moist defile, affording some shelter to any person who had sought it; but the party perambulated it in vain, and ascended on the other side. Here they wandered apart, and after an interval closed together again to report progress. At the second time of closing in they found themselves near a lonely ash, the single tree on this part of the upland, probably sown there by a passing bird some fifty years before. And here, standing a little to one side of the trunk, as motionless as the trunk itself, appeared the man they were in quest of, his outline being well defined against the sky beyond. The band noiselessly drew up and faced him.

'Your money or your life!' said the constable sternly to the still figure.

'No, no,' whispered John Pitcher. "Tisn't our side ought to say that.

That's the doctrine of vagabonds like him, and we be on the side of the law.'

'Well, well,' replied the constable impatiently; 'I must say something, mustn't I? and if you had all the weight o' this undertaking upon your mind, perhaps you'd say the wrong thing too! – Prisoner at the bar, surrender, in the name of the Father – the Crown, I mane!'

The man under the tree seemed now to notice them for the first time, and, giving them no opportunity whatever for exhibiting their courage, he strolled slowly towards them. He was, indeed, the little man, the third stranger; but his trepidation had in a great measure gone.

'Well, travellers,' he said, 'did I hear ye speak to me?'

'You did: you've got to come and be our prisoner at once,' said the constable. 'We arrest ye on the charge of not biding in Casterbridge jail in a decent proper manner to be hung tomorrow morning. Neighbours, do your duty, and seize the culpet!'

On hearing the charge, the man seemed enlightened, and, saying not another word, resigned himself with preternatural civility to the search-party, who, with their staves in their hands, surrounded him on all sides, and marched him back towards the shepherd's cottage.

It was eleven o'clock by the time they arrived. The light shining from the open door, a sound of men's voices within, proclaimed to them as they approached the house that some new events had arisen in their absence. On entering they discovered the shepherd's living-room to be invaded by two officers from Casterbridge jail, and a well-known magistrate who lived at the nearest country-seat, intelligence of the escape having become generally circulated.

'Gentlemen,' said the constable, 'I have brought back your man – not without risk and danger; but every one must do his duty! He is inside this circle of able-bodied persons, who have lent me useful aid, considering their ignorance of Crown work. Men, bring forward your prisoner!' And the third stranger was led to the light.

'Who is this?' said one of the officials.

'The man,' said the constable.

'Certainly not,' said the turnkey; and the first corroborated his statement.

'But how can it be otherwise?' asked the constable. 'Or why was he so terrified at sight o' the singing instrument of the law who sat there?' Here he related the strange behaviour of the third stranger on entering the house during the hangman's song.

'Can't understand it,' said the officer coolly. 'All I know is that it is not the condemned man. He's quite a different character from this one; a gauntish fellow, with dark hair and eyes, rather good-looking, and with a musical bass voice that if you heard it once you'd never mistake as long as you lived.'

'Why, souls – 'twas the man in the chimney-corner!'

'Hey – what?' said the magistrate, coming forward after inquiring particulars from the shepherd in the background. 'Haven't you got the man after all?'

'Well, sir,' said the constable, 'he's the man we were in search of, that's true; and yet he's not the man we were in search of. For the man we were in search of was not the man we wanted, sir, if you understand my everyday way; for 'twas the man in the chimney-corner!'

'A pretty kettle of fish altogether!' said the magistrate. 'You had better start for the other man at once.'

The prisoner now spoke for the first time. The mention of the man in the chimney-corner seemed to have moved him as nothing else could do. 'Sir,' he said, stepping forward to the magistrate, 'take no more trouble about me. The time is come when I may as well speak. I have done nothing; my crime is that the condemned man is my brother. Early this afternoon I left home at Shottsford to tramp it all the way to Casterbridge jail to bid him farewell. I was benighted, and called here to rest and ask the way. When I opened the door I saw before me the very man, my brother, that I thought to see in the condemned cell at Casterbridge. He was in this chimney-corner; and jammed close to him, so that he could not have got out if he had tried, was the executioner who'd come to take his life, singing a song about it and not knowing that it was his victim who was close by, joining in to save appearances. My brother looked a glance of agony at me, and I knew he meant, "Don't reveal what you see; my life depends on it." I was so terror-struck that I could hardly stand, and, not knowing what I did, I turned and hurried away.'

The narrator's manner and tone had the stamp of truth, and his story made a great impression on all around. 'And do you know where your brother is at the present time?' asked the magistrate.

'I do not. I have never seen him since I closed this door.'

'I can testify to that, for we've been between ye ever since,' said the constable.

'Where does he think to fly to? – what is his occupation?'

'He's a watch-and-clock-maker, sir.'

''A said 'a was a wheelwright – a wicked rogue,' said the constable.

'The wheels of clocks and watches he meant, no doubt,' said Shepherd Fennel. 'I thought his hands were palish for's trade.'

'Well, it appears to me that nothing can be gained by retaining this poor man in custody,' said the magistrate; 'your business lies with the other, unquestionably.'

And so the little man was released off-hand; but he looked nothing the less sad on that account, it being beyond the power of magistrate or constable to raze out the written troubles in his brain, for they concerned another whom he regarded with more solicitude than himself. When this was done, and the man had gone his way, the night was found to be so far advanced that it was deemed useless to renew the search before the next morning.

Next day, accordingly, the quest for the clever sheep-stealer became general and keen, to all appearance at least. But the intended punishment was cruelly disproportioned to the transgression, and the sympathy of a great many country-folk in that district was strongly on the side of the fugitive. Moreover, his marvellous coolness and daring in hob-and-nobbing with the hangman, under the unprecedented circumstances of the shepherd's party, won their admiration. So that it may be questioned if all those who ostensibly made themselves so busy in exploring woods and fields and lanes were quite so thorough when it came to the private examination of their own lofts and outhouses. Stories were afloat of a mysterious figure being occasionally seen in some old overgrown trackway or other, remote from turnpike-roads; but when a search was instituted in any of these suspected quarters nobody was found. Thus the days and weeks passed without tidings.

In brief, the bass-voiced man of the chimney-corner was never recaptured. Some said that he went across the sea, others that he did not, but buried himself in the depths of a populous city. At any rate, the gentleman in cinder-grey never did his morning's work at Casterbridge, nor met anywhere at all, for business purposes, the genial comrade with whom he had passed an hour of relaxation in the lonely house on the coomb.

The grass has long been green on the graves of Shepherd Fennel and his frugal wife; the guests who made up the christening party have mainly followed their entertainers to the tomb; the baby in whose honour they all had met is a matron in the sere and yellow leaf. But the arrival of the three strangers at the shepherd's that night, and the details connected therewith, is a story as well known as ever in the country about Higher Crowstairs.

MARGARET OLIPHANT

The Library Window

I

I was not aware at first of the many discussions which had gone on about that window. It was almost opposite one of the windows of the large old-fashioned drawing-room of the house in which I spent that summer, which was of so much importance in my life. Our house and the library were on opposite sides of the broad High Street of St Rule's, which is a fine street, wide and ample, and very quiet, as strangers think who come from noisier places; but in a summer evening there is much coming and going, and the stillness is full of sound – the sound of footsteps and pleasant voices, softened by the summer air. There are even exceptional moments when it is noisy: the time of the fair, and on Saturday nights sometimes, and when there are excursion trains. Then even the softest sunny air of the evening will not smooth the harsh tones and the stumbling steps; but at these unlovely moments we shut the windows, and even I, who am so fond of that deep recess where I can take refuge from all that is going on inside, and make myself a spectator of all the varied story out of doors, withdraw from my watch-tower. To tell the truth, there never was very much going on inside. The house belonged to my aunt, to whom (she says, Thank God!) nothing ever happens. I believe that many things have happened to her in her time; but that was all over at the period of which I am speaking, and she was old, and very quiet. Her life went on in a routine never broken. She got up at the same hour every day, and did the same things in the same rotation, day by day the same. She said that this was the greatest support in the world, and that routine is a kind of salvation. It may be so; but it is a very dull salvation, and I used to feel that I would rather have incident, whatever kind of incident it might be. But then at that time I was not old, which makes all the difference.

At the time of which I speak the deep recess of the drawing-room window was a great comfort to me. Though she was an old lady (perhaps because she was so old) she was very tolerant, and had a kind of feeling for me. She never said a word, but often gave me a smile when she saw how I had built myself up, with my books and my basket of work. I did very little work, I fear – now and then a few stitches when the spirit moved me, or when I had got well afloat in a dream, and was more tempted to follow it out than to read my book, as sometimes happened. At other times, and if the book were interesting, I used to get through volume after volume sitting there, paying no attention to anybody. And yet I did pay a kind of attention. Aunt Mary's old ladies came in to call, and I heard them talk, though I very seldom listened; but for all that, if they had anything to say that was interesting, it is curious how I found it in my mind afterwards, as if the air had blown it to me. They came and went, and I had the sensation of their old bonnets gliding out and in, and their dresses rustling; and now and then had to jump up and shake hands with some one who knew me, and asked after my papa and mamma. Then Aunt Mary would give me a little smile again, and I slipped back to my window. She never seemed to mind. My mother would not have let me do it, I know. She would have remembered dozens of things there were to do. She would have sent me up-stairs to fetch something which I was quite sure she did not want, or down-stairs to carry some quite unnecessary message to the housemaid. She liked to keep me running about. Perhaps that was one reason why I was so fond of Aunt Mary's drawing-room, and the deep recess of the window, and the curtain that fell half over it, and the broad window-seat where one could collect so many things without being found fault with for untidiness. Whenever we had anything the matter with us in these days, we were sent to St Rule's to get up our strength. And this was my case at the time of which I am going to speak.

Everybody had said, since ever I learned to speak, that I was fantastic and fanciful and dreamy, and all the other words with which a girl who may happen to like poetry, and to be fond of thinking, is so often made uncomfortable. People don't know what they mean when they say fantastic. It sounds like Madge Wildfire or something of that sort. My mother thought I should always be busy, to keep nonsense out of my head. But really I was not at all fond of nonsense. I was rather serious than otherwise. I would have been no trouble to anybody if I had been left to myself. It was only that I had a sort of second-sight, and was conscious of things to which I paid no attention. Even when reading the most interesting book, the things that were being talked about blew in to me; and I heard what the people were saying in the streets as they passed under the window. Aunt Mary always said I could do two or indeed three things at once – both read and listen, and see. I am sure that I did not listen much, and seldom looked out, of set purpose – as some people do who notice what bonnets the ladies in the street have on; but I did hear what I couldn't help hearing, even when I was reading my book, and I did see all sorts of things, though often for a whole half-hour I might never lift my eyes.

This does not explain what I said at the beginning, that there were many discussions about that window. It was, and still is, the last window in the row, of the College Library, which is opposite my aunt's house in the High Street. Yet it is not exactly opposite, but a little to the west, so that I could see it best from the left side of my recess. I took it calmly for granted that it was a window like any other till I first heard the talk about it which was going on in the drawing-room. 'Have you never made up your mind, Mrs Balcarres,' said old Mr Pitmilly, 'whether that window opposite is a window or no?' He said Mistress Balcarres – and he was always called Mr Pitmilly, Morton: which was the name of his place.

'I am never sure of it, to tell the truth,' said Aunt Mary, 'all these years.'

'Bless me!' said one of the old ladies, 'and what window may that be?'

Mr Pitmilly had a way of laughing as he spoke, which did not please me; but it was true that he was not perhaps desirous of pleasing me. He said, 'Oh, just the window opposite,' with his laugh running through his words; 'our friend can never make up her mind about it, though she has been living opposite it since—'

'You need never mind the date,' said another; 'the Leebrary window! Dear me, what should it be but a window? up at that height it could not be a door.'

'The question is,' said my aunt, 'if it is a real window with glass in it, or if it is merely painted, or if it once was a window, and has been built up. And the oftener people look at it, the less they are able to say.'

'Let me see this window,' said old Lady Carnbee, who was very active and strong-minded; and then they all came crowding upon me – three or four old ladies, very eager, and Mr Pitmilly's white hair appearing over their heads, and my aunt sitting quiet and smiling behind.

'I mind the window very well,' said Lady Carnbee; 'ay: and so do more than me. But in its present appearance it is just like any other window; but has not been cleaned, I should say, in the memory of man.'

'I see what ye mean,' said one of the others. 'It is just a very dead thing without any reflection in it; but I've seen as bad before.'

'Ay, it's dead enough,' said another, 'but that's no rule; for these hizzies of women-servants in this ill age—'

'Nay, the women are well enough,' said the softest voice of all, which was Aunt Mary's. 'I will never let them risk their lives cleaning the outside of mine. And there are no women-servants in the Old Library: there is maybe something more in it than that.'

They were all pressing into my recess, pressing upon me, a row of old faces, peering into something they could not understand. I had a sense in my mind how curious it was, the wall of old ladies in their old satin gowns all glazed with age, Lady Carnbee with her lace about her head. Nobody was looking at me or thinking of me; but I felt unconsciously the contrast of my youngness to their oldness, and stared at them as they stared over my head at the Library window. I had given it no attention up to this time. I was more taken up with the old ladies than with the thing they were looking at.

'The framework is all right at least, I can see that, and pented black—'

'And the panes are pented black too. It's no window, Mrs Balcarres. It has been filled in, in the days of the window duties: you will mind, Leddy Carnbee.'

'Mind!' said that oldest lady. 'I mind when your mother was marriet, Jeanie: and that's neither the day nor yesterday. But as for the window, it's just a delusion: and that is my opinion of the matter, if you ask me.'

'There's a great want of light in that muckle room at the college,' said another. 'If it was a window, the Leebrary would have more light.'

'One thing is clear,' said one of the younger ones, 'it cannot be a window to see through. It may be filled in or it may be built up, but it is not a window to give light.'

'And who ever heard of a window that was no to see through?' Lady Carnbee said. I was fascinated by the look on her face, which was a curious scornful look as of one who knew more than she chose to say: and then my wandering fancy was caught by her hand as she held it up, throwing back the lace that dropped over it. Lady Carnbee's lace was the chief thing about her – heavy black Spanish lace with large flowers. Everything she wore was trimmed with it. A large veil of it hung over her old bonnet. But her hand coming out of this heavy lace was a curious thing to see. She had very long fingers, very taper, which had been much admired in her youth; and her hand was very white, or rather more than white, pale, bleached, and bloodless, with large blue veins standing up upon the back; and she wore some fine rings, among others a big diamond in an ugly old claw setting. They were too big for her, and were wound round and round with yellow silk to make them keep on: and this little cushion of silk, turned brown with long wearing, had twisted round so that it was more conspicuous than the jewels; while the big diamond blazed underneath in the hollow of her hand, like some dangerous thing hiding and sending out darts of light. The hand, which seemed to come almost to a point, with this strange ornament underneath, clutched at my half-terrified imagination. It too seemed to mean far more than was said. I felt as if it might clutch me with sharp claws, and the lurking, dazzling creature bite – with a sting that would go to the heart.

Presently, however, the circle of the old faces broke up, the old ladies returned to their seats, and Mr Pitmilly, small but very erect, stood up in the midst of them, talking with mild authority like a little oracle among the ladies. Only Lady Carnbee always contradicted the neat, little, old gentleman. She gesticulated, when she talked, like a Frenchwoman, and darted forth that hand of hers with the lace hanging over it, so that I always caught a glimpse of the lurking diamond. I thought she looked like a witch among the comfortable little group which gave such attention to everything Mr Pitmilly said.

'For my part, it is my opinion there is no window there at all,' he said. 'It's very like the thing that's called in scientific language an optical illusion. It arises generally, if I may use such a word in the presence of ladies, from a liver that is not just in the perfitt order and balance that organ demands – and then you will see things – a blue dog, I remember, was the thing in one case, and in another—'

'The man has gane gyte,' said Lady Carnbee; 'I mind the windows in the Auld Leebrary as long as I mind anything. Is the Leebrary itself an optical illusion too?'

'Na, na,' and 'No, no,' said the old ladies; 'a blue dogue would be a strange vagary: but the Library we have all kent from our youth,' said one. 'And I mind when the Assemblies were held there one year when the Town Hall was building,' another said.

'It is just a great divert to me,' said Aunt Mary: but what was strange was that she paused there, and said in a low tone, 'now': and then went on again, 'for whoever comes to my house, there are aye discussions about that window. I have never just made up my mind about it myself. Sometimes I think it's a case of these wicked window duties, as you said, Miss Jeanie, when half the windows in our houses were blocked up to save the tax. And then, I think, it may be due to that blank kind of building like the great new buildings on the Earthen Mound in Edinburgh, where the windows are just ornaments. And then whiles I am sure I can see the glass shining when the sun catches it in the afternoon.'

'You could so easily satisfy yourself, Mrs Balcarres, if you were to—'

'Give a laddie a penny to cast a stone, and see what happens,' said Lady Carnbee.

'But I am not sure that I have any desire to satisfy myself,' Aunt Mary said. And then there was a stir in the room, and I had to come out from my recess and open the door for the old ladies and see them down-stairs, as they all went away following one another. Mr Pitmilly gave his arm to Lady Carnbee, though she was always contradicting him; and so the tea-party dispersed. Aunt Mary came to the head of the stairs with her guests in an old-fashioned gracious way, while I went down with them to see that the maid was ready at the door. When I came back Aunt Mary was still standing in the recess looking out. Returning to my seat she said, with a kind of wistful look, 'Well, honey: and what is your opinion?'

'I have no opinion. I was reading my book all the time,' I said.

'And so you were, honey, and no' very civil; but all the same I ken well you heard every word we said.'

II

It was a night in June; dinner was long over, and had it been winter the maids would have been shutting up the house, and my Aunt Mary preparing to go upstairs to her room. But it was still clear daylight, that daylight out of which the sun has been long gone, and which has no longer any rose reflections, but all has sunk into a pearly neutral tint – a light which is daylight yet is not day. We had taken a turn in the garden after dinner, and now we had returned to what we called our usual occupations. My aunt was reading. The English post had come in, and she had got her 'Times', which was her great diversion. The 'Scotsman' was her morning reading, but she liked her 'Times' at night.

As for me, I too was at my usual occupation, which at that time was doing nothing. I had a book as usual, and was absorbed in it: but I was conscious of all that was going on all the same. The people strolled along the broad pavement, making remarks as they passed under the open window which came up into my story or my dream, and sometimes made me laugh. The tone and the faint sing-song, or rather chant, of the accent, which was 'a wee Fifish', was novel to me, and associated with holiday, and pleasant; and sometimes they said to each other something that was amusing, and often something that suggested a whole story; but presently they began to drop off, the footsteps slackened, the voices died away. It was getting late, though the clear soft daylight went on and on. All through the lingering evening, which seemed to consist of interminable hours, long but not weary, drawn out as if the spell of the light and the outdoor life might never end, I had now and then, quite unawares, cast a glance at the mysterious window which my aunt and her friends had discussed, as I felt, though I dared not say it even to myself, rather foolishly. It caught my eye without any intention on my part, as I paused, as it were, to take breath, in the flowing and current of undistinguishable thoughts and things from without and within which carried me along. First it occurred to me, with a little sensation of discovery, how absurd to say it was not a window, a living window, one to see through! Why, then, had they never *seen* it, these old folk? I saw as I looked up suddenly the faint greyness as of visible space within – a room behind, certainly dim, as it was natural a room should be on the other side of the street – quite indefinite: yet so clear that if some one were to come to the window there would be nothing surprising in it. For certainly there was a feeling of space behind the panes which these old half-blind ladies had disputed about whether they were glass or only fictitious panes marked on the wall. How silly! when eyes that could see could make it out in a minute. It was only a greyness at present, but it was unmistakable, a space that went back into gloom, as every room does when you look into it across a street. There were no curtains to show whether it was inhabited or not; but a room – oh, as distinctly as ever room was! I was pleased with myself, but said nothing, while Aunt Mary rustled her paper, waiting for a favourable moment to announce a discovery which settled her problem at once. Then I was carried away upon the stream again, and forgot the window, till somebody threw unawares a word from the outer world, 'I'm goin' hame; it'll soon be dark.' Dark! what was the fool thinking of? it never would be dark if one waited out, wandering in the soft air for hours longer; and then my eyes, acquiring easily that new habit, looked across the way again.

Ah, now! nobody indeed had come to the window; and no light had been lighted, seeing it was still beautiful to read by – a still, clear, colourless light; but the room inside had certainly widened. I could see the grey space and air a little deeper, and a sort of vision, very dim, of a wall, and something against it; something dark, with the blackness that a solid article, however indistinctly seen, takes in the lighter darkness that is only space – a large, black, dark thing coming out into the grey. I looked more intently, and made sure it was a piece of furniture, either a writing-table or perhaps a large book-case. No doubt it must be the last, since this was part of the old library. I never visited the old College Library, but I had seen such places before, and I could well imagine it to myself. How curious that for all the time these old people had looked at it, they had never seen this before!

It was more silent now, and my eyes, I suppose, had grown dim with gazing, doing my best to make it out, when suddenly Aunt Mary said, 'Will you ring the bell, my dear? I must have my lamp.'

'Your lamp?' I cried, 'when it is still daylight.' But then I gave another look at my window, and perceived with a start that the light had indeed changed: for now I saw nothing. It was still light, but there was so much change in the light that my room, with the grey space and the large shadowy bookcase, had gone out, and I saw them no more: for even a Scotch night in June, though it looks as if it would never end, does darken at the last. I had almost cried out, but checked myself, and rang the bell for Aunt Mary, and made up my mind I would say nothing till next morning, when to be sure naturally it would be more clear.

Next morning I rather think I forgot all about it – or was busy: or was more idle than usual: the two things meant nearly the same. At all events I thought no more of the window, though I still sat in my own, opposite to it, but occupied with some other fancy. Aunt Mary's visitors came as usual in the afternoon; but their talk was of other things, and for a day or two nothing at all happened to bring back my thoughts into this channel. It might be nearly a week before the subject came back, and once more it was old Lady Carnbee who set me thinking; not that she said anything upon that particular theme. But she was the last of my aunt's afternoon guests to go away, and when she rose to leave she threw up her hands, with those lively gesticulations which so many old Scotch ladies have. 'My faith!' said she, 'there is that bairn there still like a dream. Is the creature bewitched, Mary Balcarres? and is she bound to sit there by night and by day for the rest of her days? You should mind that there's things about, uncanny for women of our blood.'

I was too much startled at first to recognise that it was of me she was speaking. She was like a figure in a picture, with her pale face the colour of ashes, and the big pattern of the Spanish lace hanging half over it, and her hand held up, with the big diamond blazing at me from the inside of her uplifted palm. It was held up in surprise, but it looked as if it were raised in malediction; and the diamond threw out darts of light and glared and twinkled at me. If it had been in its right place it would not have mattered; but there, in the open of the hand! I started up, half in terror, half in wrath. And then the old lady laughed, and her hand dropped. 'I've wakened you to life, and broke the spell,' she said, nodding her old head at me, while the large black silk flowers of the lace waved and threatened. And she took my arm to go downstairs, laughing and bidding me be steady, and no' tremble and shake like a broken reed. 'You should be as steady as a rock at your age. I was like a young tree,' she said, leaning so heavily that my willowy girlish frame quivered – 'I was a support to virtue, like Pamela, in my time.'

'Aunt Mary, Lady Carnbee is a witch!' I cried, when I came back.

'Is that what you think, honey? well: maybe she once was,' said Aunt Mary, whom nothing surprised.

And it was that night once more after dinner, and after the post came in, and the 'Times', that I suddenly saw the Library window again. I had seen it every day and noticed nothing; but to-night, still in a little tumult of mind over Lady Carnbee and her wicked diamond which wished me harm, and her lace which waved threats and warnings at me, I looked across the street, and there I saw quite plainly the room opposite, far more clear than before. I saw dimly that it must be a large room, and that the big piece of furniture against the wall was a writing-desk. That in a moment, when first my eyes rested upon it, was quite clear: a large old-fashioned escritoire, standing out into the room: and I knew by the shape of it that it had a great many pigeon-holes and little drawers in the back, and a large table for writing. There was one just like it in my father's library at home. It was such a surprise to see it all so clearly that I closed my eyes, for the moment almost giddy, wondering how papa's desk could have come here – and then when I reminded myself that this was non-sense, and that there were many such writing-tables besides papa's, and looked again – lo! it had all become quite vague and indistinct as it was at first; and I saw nothing but the blank window, of which the old ladies could never be certain whether it was filled up to avoid the window-tax, or whether it had ever been a window at all.

This occupied my mind very much, and yet I did not say anything to Aunt Mary. For one thing, I rarely saw anything at all in the early part of the day; but then that is natural: you can never see into a place from outside, whether it is an empty room or a looking-glass, or people's eyes, or anything else that is mysterious, in the day. It has, I suppose, something to do with the light. But in the evening in June in Scotland – then is the time to see. For it is daylight, yet it is not day, and there is a quality in it which I cannot describe, it is so clear, as if every object was a reflection of itself.

I used to see more and more of the room as the days went on. The large escritoire stood out more and more into the space: with sometimes white glimmering things, which looked like papers, lying on it: and once or twice I was sure I saw a pile of books on the floor close to the writing-table, as if they had gilding upon them in broken specks, like old books. It was always about the time when the lads in the street began to call to each other that they were going home, and sometimes a shriller voice would come from one of the doors, bidding somebody to 'cry upon the laddies' to come back to their suppers. That was always the time I saw best, though it was close upon the moment when the veil seemed to fall and the clear radiance became less living, and all the sounds died out of the street, and Aunt Mary said in her soft voice, 'Honey! will you ring for the lamp?' She said honey as people say darling: and I think it is a prettier word.

Then finally, while I sat one evening with my book in my hand, looking straight across the street, not distracted by anything, I saw a little movement within. It was not any one visible – but everybody must know what it is to see the stir in the air, the little disturbance – you cannot tell what it is, but that it indicates some one there, even though you can see no one. Perhaps it is a shadow making just one flicker in the still place. You may look at an empty room and the furniture in it for hours, and then suddenly there will be the flicker, and you know that something has come into it. It might only be a dog or a cat; it might be, if that were possible, a bird flying across; but it is some one, something living, which is so different, so completely different, in a moment from the things that are not living. It seemed to strike quite through me, and I gave a little cry. Then Aunt Mary stirred a little, and put down the huge newspaper that almost covered her from sight, and said, 'What is it, honey?' I cried 'Nothing,' with a little gasp, quickly, for I did not want to be disturbed just at this moment when somebody was coming! But I suppose she was not satisfied, for she got up and stood behind to see what it was, putting her hand on my shoulder. It was the softest touch in the world, but I could have flung it off angrily: for that moment everything was still again, and the place grew grey and I saw no more.

'Nothing,' I repeated, but I was so vexed I could have cried. 'I told you it was nothing, Aunt Mary. Don't you believe me, that you come to look – and spoil it all!'

I did not mean of course to say these last words; they were forced out of me. I was so much annoyed to see it all melt away like a dream: for it was no dream, but as real as – as real as – myself or anything I ever saw.

She gave my shoulder a little pat with her hand. 'Honey,' she said, 'were you looking at something? Is't that? is't that?' 'Is it what?' I wanted to say, shaking off her hand, but something in me stopped me: for I said nothing at all, and she went quietly back to her place. I suppose she must have rung the bell herself, for immediately I felt the soft flood of the light behind me, and the evening outside dimmed down, as it did every night, and I saw nothing more.

It was next day, I think, in the afternoon that I spoke. It was brought on by something she said about her fine work. 'I get a mist before my eyes,' she said; 'you will have to learn my old lace stitches, honey – for I soon will not see to draw the threads.'

'Oh, I hope you will keep your sight,' I cried, without thinking what I was saying. I was then young and very matter-of-fact. I had not found out that one may mean something, yet not half or a hundredth part of what one seems to mean: and even then probably hoping to be contradicted if it is anyhow against one's self.

'My sight!' she said, looking up at me with a look that was almost angry; 'there is no question of losing my sight – on the contrary, my eyes are very strong. I may not see to draw fine threads, but I see at a distance as well as ever I did – as well as you do.'

'I did not mean any harm, Aunt Mary,' I said. 'I thought you said— But how can your sight be as good as ever when you are in doubt about that window? I can see into the room as clear as—' My voice wavered, for I had just looked up and across the street, and I could have sworn that there was no window at all, but only a false image of one painted on the wall.

'Ah!' she said, with a little tone of keenness and of surprise: and she half rose up, throwing down her work hastily, as if she meant to come to me: then, perhaps seeing the bewildered look on my face, she paused and hesitated – 'Ay, honey!' she said, 'have you got so far ben as that?'

What did she mean? Of course I knew all the old Scotch phrases as well as I knew myself; but it is a comfort to take refuge in a little ignorance, and I know I pretended not to understand whenever I was put out. 'I don't know what you mean by "far ben",' I cried out, very impatient. I don't know what might have followed, but some one just then came to call, and she could only give me a look before she went forward, putting out her hand to her visitor. It was a very soft look, but anxious, and as if she did not know what to do: and she shook her head a very little, and I thought, though there was a smile on her face, there was something wet about her eyes. I retired into my recess, and nothing more was said.

But it was very tantalising that it should fluctuate so; for sometimes I saw that room quite plain and clear – quite as clear as I could see papa's library, for example, when I shut my eyes. I compared it naturally to my father's study, because of the shape of the writing-table, which, as I tell you, was the same as his. At times I saw the papers on the table quite plain, just as I had seen his papers many a day. And the little pile of books on the floor at the foot – not ranged regularly in order, but put down one above the other, with all their angles going different ways, and a speck of the old gilding shining here and there. And then again at other times I saw nothing, absolutely nothing, and was no better than the old ladies who had peered over my head, drawing their eyelids together, and arguing that the window had been shut up because of the old long-abolished window tax, or else that it had never been a window at all. It annoyed me very much at those dull moments to feel that I too puckered up my eyelids and saw no better than they.

Aunt Mary's old ladies came and went day after day while June went on. I was to go back in July, and I felt that I should be very unwilling indeed to leave until I had quite cleared up – as I was indeed in the way of doing – the mystery of that window which changed so strangely and appeared quite a different thing, not only to different people, but to the same eyes at different times. Of course I said to myself it must simply be an effect of the light. And yet I did not quite like that explanation either, but would have been better pleased to make out to myself that it was some superiority in me which made it so clear to me, if it were only the great superiority of young eyes over old – though that was not quite enough to satisfy me, seeing it was a superiority which I shared with every little lass and lad in the street. I rather wanted, I believe, to think that there was some particular insight in me which gave clearness to my sight – which was a most impertinent assumption, but really did not mean half the harm it seems to mean when it is put down here in black and white. I had several times again, however, seen the room quite plain, and made out that it was a large room, with a great picture in a dim gilded frame hanging on the farther wall, and many other pieces of solid furniture making a blackness here and there, besides the great escritoire against the wall, which had evidently been placed near the window for the sake of the light. One thing became visible to me after another, till I almost thought I should end by being able to read the old lettering on one of the big volumes which projected from the others and caught the light; but this was all preliminary to the great event which happened about Midsummer Day – the day of St John, which was once so much thought of as a festival, but now means nothing at all in Scotland any more than any other of the saints' days: which I shall always think a great pity and loss to Scotland, whatever Aunt Mary may say.

III

It was about midsummer, I cannot say exactly to a day when, but near that time, when the great event happened. I had grown very well acquainted by this time with that large dim room. Not only the escritoire, which was very plain to me now, with the papers upon it, and the books at its foot, but the great picture that hung against the farther wall, and various other shadowy pieces of furniture, especially a chair which one evening I saw had been moved into the space before the escritoire, – a little change which made my heart beat, for it spoke so distinctly of some one who must have been there, the some one who had already made me start, two or three times before, by some vague shadow of him or thrill of him which made a sort of movement in the silent space: a movement which made me sure that next minute I must see something or hear something which would explain the whole – if it were not that something always happened outside to stop it, at the very moment of its accomplishment. I had no warning this time of movement or shadow. I had been looking into the room very attentively a little while before, and had made out everything almost clearer than ever; and then had bent my attention again on my book, and read a chapter or two at a most exciting period of the story: and consequently had quite left St Rule's, and the High Street, and the College Library, and was really in a South American forest, almost throttled by the flowery creepers, and treading softly lest I should put my foot on a scorpion or a dangerous snake. At this moment something suddenly calling my attention to the outside, I looked across, and then, with a start, sprang up, for I could not contain myself. I don't know what I said, but enough to startle the people in the room, one of whom was old Mr Pitmilly. They all looked round upon me to ask what was the matter. And when I gave my usual answer of 'Nothing', sitting down again shamefaced but very much excited, Mr Pitmilly got up and came forward, and looked out, apparently to see what was the cause. He saw nothing, for he went back again, and I could hear him telling Aunt Mary not to be alarmed, for Missy had fallen into a doze with the heat, and had startled herself waking up, at which they all laughed: another time I could have killed him for his impertinence, but my mind was too much taken up now to pay any attention. My head was throbbing and my heart beating. I was in such high excitement, however, that to restrain myself completely, to be perfectly silent, was more easy to me then than at any other time of my life. I waited until the old gentleman had taken his seat again, and then I looked back. Yes, there he was! I had not been deceived. I knew then, when I looked across, that this was what I had been looking for all the time – that I had known he was there, and had been waiting for him, every time there was that flicker of movement in the room – him and no one else. And there at last, just as I had expected, he was. I don't know that in reality I ever had expected him, or any one: but this was what I felt when, suddenly looking into that curious dim room, I saw him there.

He was sitting in the chair, which he must have placed for himself, or which some one else in the dead of night when nobody was looking must have set for him, in front of the escritoire – with the back of his head towards me, writing. The light fell upon him from the left hand, and therefore upon his shoulders and the side of his head, which, however, was too much turned away to show anything of his face. Oh, how strange that there should be some one staring at him as I was doing, and he never to turn his head, to make a movement! If any one stood and looked at me, were I in the soundest sleep that ever was, I would wake, I would jump up, I would feel it through everything. But there he sat and never moved. You are not to suppose, though I said the light fell upon him from the left hand, that there was very much light. There never is in a room you are looking into like that across the street; but there was enough to see him by – the outline of his figure dark and solid, seated in the chair, and the fairness of his head visible faintly, a clear spot against the dimness. I saw this outline against the dim gilding of the frame of the large picture which hung on the farther wall.

I sat all the time the visitors were there, in a sort of rapture, gazing at this figure. I knew no reason why I should be so much moved. In an ordinary way, to see a student at an opposite window quietly doing his work might have interested me a little, but certainly it would not have moved me in any such way. It is always interesting to have a glimpse like this of an unknown life – to see so much and yet know so little, and to wonder, perhaps, what the man is doing, and why he never turns his head. One would go to the window – but not too close, lest he should see you and think you were spying upon him – and one would ask, Is he still there? is he writing, writing always? I wonder what he is writing! And it would be a great amusement: but no more. This was not my feeling at all in the present case. It was a sort of breathless watch, an absorption. I did not feel that I had eyes for anything else, or any room in my mind for another thought. I no longer heard, as I generally did, the stories and the wise remarks (or foolish) of Aunt Mary's old ladies or Mr Pitmilly. I heard only a murmur behind me, the interchange of voices, one softer, one sharper; but it was not as in the time when I sat reading and heard every word, till the story in my book, and the stories they were telling (what they said almost always shaped into stories), were all mingled into each other, and the hero in the novel became somehow the hero (or more likely heroine) of them all. But I took no notice of what they were saying now. And it was not that there was anything very interesting to look at, except the fact that he was there. He did nothing to keep up the absorption of my thoughts. He moved just so much as a man will do when he is very busily writing, thinking of nothing else. There was a faint turn of his head as he went from one side to another of the page he was writing; but it appeared to be a long long page which never wanted turning. Just a little inclination when he was at the end of the line, outward, and then a little inclination inward when he began the next. That was little enough to keep one gazing. But I suppose it was the gradual course of events leading up to this, the finding out of one thing after another as the eyes got accustomed to the vague light: first the room itself, and then the writing-table, and then the other furniture, and last of all the human inhabitant who gave it all meaning. This was all so interesting that it was like a country which one had discovered. And then the extraordinary blindness of the other people who disputed among themselves whether it was a window at all! I did not, I am sure, wish to be disrespectful, and I was very fond of my Aunt Mary, and I liked Mr Pitmilly well enough, and I was afraid of Lady Carnbee. But yet to think of the – I know I ought not to say stupidity – the blindness of them, the foolishness, the insensibility! discussing it as if a thing that your eyes could see was a thing to discuss! It would have been unkind to think it was because they were old and their faculties dimmed. It is so sad to think that the faculties grow dim, that such a woman as my Aunt Mary should fail in seeing, or hearing, or feeling, that I would not have dwelt on it for a moment, it would have seemed so cruel! And then such a clever old lady as Lady Carnbee, who could see through a millstone, people said – and Mr Pitmilly, such an old man of the world. It did indeed bring tears to my eyes to think that all those clever people, solely by reason of being no longer young as I was, should have the simplest things shut out from them; and for all their wisdom and their knowledge be unable to see what a girl like me could see so easily. I was too much grieved for them to dwell upon that thought, and half ashamed, though perhaps half proud too, to be so much better off than they.

All those thoughts flitted through my mind as I sat and gazed across the street. And I felt there was so much going on in that room across the street! He was so absorbed in his writing, never looked up, never paused for a word, never turned round in his chair, or got up and walked about the room as my father did. Papa is a great writer, everybody says: but he would have come to the window and looked out, he would have drummed with his fingers on the pane, he would have watched a fly and helped it over a difficulty, and played with the fringe of the curtain, and done a dozen other nice, pleasant, foolish things, till the next sentence took shape. 'My dear, I am waiting for a word,' he would say to my mother when she looked at him, with a question why he was so idle, in her eyes;

and then he would laugh, and go back again to his writing-table. But He over there never stopped at all. It was like a fascination. I could not take my eyes from him and that little scarcely perceptible movement he made, turning his head. I trembled with impatience to see him turn the page, or perhaps throw down his finished sheet on the floor, as somebody looking into a window like me once saw Sir Walter do, sheet after sheet. I should have cried out if this Unknown had done that. I should not have been able to help myself, whoever had been present; and gradually I got into such a state of suspense waiting for it to be done that my head grew hot and my hands cold. And then, just when there was a little movement of his elbow, as if he were about to do this, to be called away by Aunt Mary to see Lady Carnbee to the door! I believe I did not hear her till she had called me three times, and then I stumbled up, all flushed and hot, and nearly crying. When I came out from the recess to give the old lady my arm (Mr Pitmilly had gone away some time before), she put up her hand and stroked my cheek. 'What ails the bairn?' she said; 'she's fevered. You must not let her sit her lane in the window, Mary Balcarres. You and me know what comes of that.' Her old fingers had a strange touch, cold like something not living, and I felt that dreadful diamond sting me on the cheek.

I do not say that this was not just a part of my excitement and suspense; and I know it is enough to make any one laugh when the excitement was all about an unknown man writing in a room on the other side of the way, and my impatience because he never came to an end of the page. If you think I was not quite as well aware of this as any one could be! but the worst was that this dreadful old lady felt my heart beating against her arm that was within mine. 'You are just in a dream,' she said to me, with her old voice close at my ear as we went down-stairs. 'I don't know who it is about, but it's bound to be some man that is not worth it. If you were wise you would think of him no more.'

'I am thinking of no man!' I said, half crying. 'It is very unkind and dreadful of you to say so, Lady Carnbee. I never thought of – any man, in all my life!' I cried in a passion of indignation. The old lady clung tighter to my arm, and pressed it to her, not unkindly.

'Poor little bird,' she said, 'how it's strugglin' and flutterin'! I'm not saying but what it's more dangerous when it's all for a dream.'

She was not at all unkind; but I was very angry and excited, and would scarcely shake that old pale hand which she put out to me from her carriage window when I had helped her in. I was angry with her, and I was afraid of the diamond, which looked up from under her finger as if it saw through and through me; and whether you believe me or not, I am certain that it stung me again – a sharp malignant prick, oh full of meaning! She never wore gloves, but only black lace mittens, through which that horrible diamond gleamed.

I ran up-stairs – she had been the last to go and Aunt Mary too had gone to get ready for dinner, for it was late. I hurried to my place, and looked across, with my heart beating more than ever. I made quite sure I should see the finished sheet lying white upon the floor. But what I gazed at was only the dim blank of that window which they said was no window. The light had changed in some wonderful way during that five minutes I had been gone, and there was nothing, nothing, not a reflection, not a glimmer. It looked exactly as they all said, the blank form of a window painted on the wall. It was too much: I sat down in my excitement and cried as if my heart would break. I felt that they had done something to it, that it was not natural, that I could not bear their unkindness – even Aunt Mary. They thought it not good for me! not good for me! and they had done something – even Aunt Mary herself – and that wicked diamond that hid itself in Lady Carnbee's hand. Of course I knew all this was ridiculous as well as you could tell me; but I was exasperated by the disappointment and the sudden stop to all my excited feelings, and I could not bear it. It was more strong than I.

I was late for dinner, and naturally there were some traces in my eyes that I had been crying when I came into the full light in the dining-room, where Aunt Mary could look at me at her pleasure, and I could not run away. She said, 'Honey, you have been shedding tears. I'm loth, loth that a bairn of your mother's should be made to shed tears in my house.'

'I have not been made to shed tears,' cried I; and then, to save myself another fit of crying, I burst out laughing and said, 'I am afraid of that dreadful diamond on old Lady Carnbee's hand. It bites – I am sure it bites! Aunt Mary, look here.'

'You foolish lassie,' Aunt Mary said; but she looked at my cheek under the light of the lamp, and then she gave it a little pat with her soft hand.

'Go away with you, you silly bairn. There is no bite; but a flushed cheek, my honey, and a wet eye. You must just read out my paper to me after dinner when the post is in: and we'll have no more thinking and no more dreaming for tonight.'

'Yes, Aunt Mary,' said I. But I knew what would happen; for when she opens up her 'Times', all full of the news of the world, and the speeches and things which she takes an interest in, though I cannot tell why – she forgets. And as I kept very quiet and made not a sound, she forgot to-night what she had said, and the curtain hung a little more over me than usual, and I sat down in my recess as if I had been a hundred miles away. And my heart gave a great jump, as if it would have come out of my breast; for he was there. But not as he had been in the morning – I suppose the light, perhaps, was not good enough to go on with his work without a lamp or candles – for he had turned away from the table and was fronting the window, sitting leaning back in his chair, and turning his head to me. Not to me – he knew nothing about me. I thought he was not looking at anything; but with his face turned my way. My heart was in my mouth: it was so unexpected, so strange! though why it should have seemed strange I know not, for there was no communication between him and me that it should have moved me; and what could be more natural than that a man, wearied of his work, and feeling the want perhaps of more light, and yet that it was not dark enough to light a lamp, should turn round in his own chair, and rest a little, and think – perhaps of nothing at all? Papa always says he is thinking of nothing at all. He says things blow through his mind as if the doors were open, and he has no responsibility. What sort of things were blowing through this man's mind? or was he thinking, still thinking, of what he had been writing and going on with it still? The thing that troubled me most was that I could not make out his face. It is very difficult to do so when you see a person only through two windows, your own and his. I wanted very much to recognise him afterwards if I should chance to meet him in the street. If he had only stood up and moved about the room, I should have made out the rest of his figure, and then I should have known him again; or if he had only come to the window (as papa always did), then I should have seen his face clearly enough to have recognised him. But, to be sure, he did not see any need to do anything in order that I might recognise him, for he did not know I existed; and probably if he had known I was watching him, he would have been annoyed and gone away.

But he was as immovable there facing the window as he had been seated at the desk. Sometimes he made a little faint stir with a hand or a foot, and I held my breath, hoping he was about to rise from his chair – but he never did it. And with all the efforts I made I could not be sure of his face. I puckered my eyelids together as old Miss Jeanie did who was short-sighted, and I put my hands on each side of my face to concentrate the light on him: but it was all in vain. Either the face changed as I sat staring, or else it was the light that was not good enough, or I don't know what it was. His hair seemed to me light – certainly there was no dark line about his head, as there would have been had it been very dark – and I saw, where it came across the old gilt frame on the wall behind, that it must be fair: and I am almost sure he had no beard. Indeed I am sure that he had no beard, for the outline of his face was distinct enough; and the daylight was still quite clear out of doors, so that I recognised perfectly a baker's boy who was on the pavement opposite, and whom I should have known again whenever I had met him: as if it was of the least importance to recognise a baker's boy! There was one thing, however, rather curious about this boy. He had been throwing stones at something or somebody. In St Rule's they have a great way of throwing stones at each other, and I suppose there had been a battle. I suppose also that he had one stone in his hand left over from the battle, and his roving eye took in all the incidents of the street to judge where he could throw it with most effect and mischief. But apparently he found nothing worthy of it in the street, for he suddenly turned round with a flick under his leg to show his cleverness, and aimed it straight at the window. I remarked without remarking that it struck with a hard sound and without any breaking of glass, and fell straight down on the pavement. But I took no notice of this even in my mind, so intently was I watching the figure within, which moved not nor took the slightest notice, and remained just as dimly clear, as perfectly seen, yet as indistinguishable, as before. And then the light began to fail a little, not diminishing the prospect within, but making it still less distinct than it had been.

Then I jumped up, feeling Aunt Mary's hand upon my shoulder. 'Honey,' she said, 'I asked you twice to ring the bell; but you did not hear me.'

'Oh, Aunt Mary!' I cried in great penitence, but turning again to the window in spite of myself.

'You must come away from there: you must come away from there,' she said, almost as if she were angry: and then her soft voice grew softer, and she gave me a kiss: 'never mind about the lamp, honey; I have rung myself, and it is coming; but, silly bairn, you must not aye be dreaming – your little head will turn.'

All the answer I made, for I could scarcely speak, was to give a little wave with my hand to the window on the other side of the street.

She stood there patting me softly on the shoulder for a whole minute or more, murmuring something that sounded like, 'She must go away, she must go away.' Then she said, always with her hand soft on my shoulder, 'Like a dream when one awaketh.' And when I looked again, I saw the blank of an opaque surface and nothing more.

Aunt Mary asked me no more questions. She made me come into the room and sit in the light and read something to her. But I did not know what I was reading, for there suddenly came into my mind and took possession of it, the thud of the stone upon the window, and its descent straight down, as if from some hard substance that threw it off: though I had myself seen it strike upon the glass of the panes across the way.

IV

I am afraid I continued in a state of great exaltation and commotion of mind for some time. I used to hurry through the day till the evening came, when I could watch my neighbour through the window opposite. I did not talk much to any one, and I never said a word about my own questions and wonderings. I wondered who he was, what he was doing, and why he never came till the evening (or very rarely); and I also wondered much to what house the room belonged in which he sat. It seemed to form a portion of the old College Library, as I have often said. The window was one of the line of windows which I understood lighted the large hall; but whether this room belonged to the library itself, or how its occupant gained access to it, I could not tell. I made up my mind that it must open out of the hall, and that the gentleman must be the Librarian or one of his assistants, perhaps kept busy all the day in his official duties, and only able to get to his desk and do his own private work in the evening. One has heard of so many things like that – a man who had to take up some other kind of work for his living, and then when his leisure-time came, gave it all up to something he really loved – some study or some book he was writing. My father himself at one time had been like that. He had been in the Treasury all day, and then in the evening wrote his books, which made him famous. His daughter, however little she might know of other things, could not but know that! But it discouraged me very much when somebody pointed out to me one day in the street an old gentleman who wore a wig and took a great deal of snuff, and said, That's the Librarian of the old College. It gave me a great shock for a moment; but then I remembered that an old gentleman has generally assistants, and that it must be one of them.

Gradually I became quite sure of this. There was another small window above, which twinkled very much when the sun shone, and looked a very kindly bright little window, above that dullness of the other which hid so much. I made up my mind this was the window of his other room, and that these two chambers at the end of the beautiful hall were really beautiful for him to live in, so near all the books, and so retired and quiet, that nobody knew of them. What a fine thing for him! and you could see what use he made of his good fortune as he sat there, so constant at his writing for hours together. Was it a book he was writing, or could it be perhaps Poems? This was a thought which made my heart beat; but I concluded with much regret that it could not be Poems, because no one could possibly write Poems like that, straight off, without pausing for a word or a rhyme. Had they been Poems he must have risen up, he must have paced about the room or come to the window as papa did – not that papa wrote Poems: he always said, 'I am not worthy even to speak of such prevailing mysteries,' shaking his head – which gave me a wonderful admiration and almost awe of a Poet, who was thus much greater even than papa. But I could not believe that a poet could have kept still for hours and hours like that. What could it be then? perhaps it was history; that is a great thing to work at, but you would not perhaps need to move nor to stride up and down, or look out upon the sky and the wonderful light.

He did move now and then, however, though he never came to the window. Sometimes, as I have said, he would turn round in his chair and turn his face towards it, and sit there for a long time musing when the light had begun to fail, and the world was full of that strange day which was night, that light without colour, in which everything was so clearly visible, and there were no shadows. 'It was between the night and the day, when the fairy folk have power.' This was the after-light of the wonderful, long, long summer evening, the light without shadows. It had a spell in it, and sometimes it made me afraid: and all manner of strange thoughts seemed to come in, and I always felt that if only we had a little more vision in our eyes we might see beautiful folk walking about in it, who were not of our world. I thought most likely he saw them, from the way he sat there looking out: and this made my heart expand with the most curious sensation, as if of pride that, though I could not see, he did, and did not even require to come to the window, as I did, sitting close in the depth of the recess, with my eyes upon him, and almost seeing things through his eyes.

I was so much absorbed in these thoughts and in watching him every evening – for now he never missed an evening, but was always there – that people began to remark that I was looking pale and that I could not be well, for I paid no attention when they talked to me, and did not care to go out, nor to join the other girls for their tennis, nor to do anything that others did; and some said to Aunt Mary that I was quickly losing all the ground I had gained, and that she could never send me back to my mother with a white face like that. Aunt Mary had begun to look at me anxiously for some time before that, and, I am sure, held secret consultations over me, sometimes with the doctor, and sometimes with her old ladies, who thought they knew more about young girls than even the doctors. And I could hear them saying to her that I wanted diversion, that I must be diverted, and that she must take me out more, and give a party, and that when the summer visitors began to come there would perhaps be a ball or two, or Lady Carnbee would get up a picnic. 'And there's my young lord coming home,' said the old lady whom they called Miss Jeanie, 'and I never knew the young lassie yet that would not cock up her bonnet at the sight of a young lord.'

But Aunt Mary shook her head. 'I would not lippen much to the young lord,' she said. 'His mother is sore set upon siller for him; and my poor bit honey has no fortune to speak of. No, we must not fly so high as the young lord; but I will gladly take her about the country to see the old castles and towers. It will perhaps rouse her up a little.'

'And if that does not answer we must think of something else,' the old lady said.

I heard them perhaps that day because they were talking of me, which is always so effective a way of making you hear – for latterly I had not been paying any attention to what they were saying; and I thought to myself how little they knew, and how little I cared about even the old castles and curious houses, having something else in my mind. But just about that time Mr Pitmilly came in, who was always a friend to me, and, when he heard them talking, he managed to stop them and turn the conversation into another channel. And after a while, when the ladies were gone away, he came up to my recess, and gave a glance right over my head. And then he asked my Aunt Mary if ever she had settled her question about the window opposite, 'that you thought was a window sometimes, and then not a window, and many curious things,' the old gentleman said.

My Aunt Mary gave me another very wistful look; and then she said, 'Indeed, Mr Pitmilly, we are just where we were, and I am quite as unsettled as ever; and I think my niece she has taken up my views, for I see her many a time looking across and wondering, and I am not clear now what her opinion is.'

'My opinion!' I said, 'Aunt Mary.' I could not help being a little scornful, as one is when one is very young. 'I have no opinion. There is not only a window but there is a room, and I could show you' I was going to say, 'show you the gentleman who sits and writes in it,' but I stopped, not knowing what they might say, and looked from one to another. 'I could tell you – all the furniture that is in it,' I said. And then I felt something like a flame that went over my face, and that all at once my cheeks were burning. I thought they gave a little glance at each other, but that may have been folly. 'There is a great picture, in a big dim frame,' I said, feeling a little breathless, 'on the wall opposite the window—'

'Is there so?' said Mr Pitmilly, with a little laugh. And he said, 'Now I will tell you what we'll do. You know that there is a conversation party, or whatever they call it, in the big room to-night, and it will be all open and lighted up. And it is a handsome room, and two-three things well worth looking at. I will just step along after we have all got our dinner, and take you over to the pairty, madam – Missy and you—'

'Dear me!' said Aunt Mary. 'I have not gone to a pairty for more years than I would like to say – and never once to the Library Hall.' Then she gave a little shiver, and said quite low, 'I could not go there.'

'Then you will just begin again to-night, madam,' said Mr Pitmilly, taking no notice of this, 'and a proud man will I be leading in Mistress Balcarres that was once the pride of the ball!'

'Ah, once!' said Aunt Mary, with a low little laugh and then a sigh. 'And we'll not say how long ago;' and after that she made a pause, looking always at me: and then she said, 'I accept your offer, and we'll put on our braws; and I hope you will have no occasion to think shame of us. But why not take your dinner here?'

That was how it was settled, and the old gentleman went away to dress, looking quite pleased. But I came to Aunt Mary as soon as he was gone, and besought her not to make me go. 'I like the long bonnie night and the light that lasts so long. And I cannot bear to dress up and go out, wasting it all in a stupid party. I hate parties, Aunt Mary!' I cried, 'and I would far rather stay here.'

'My honey,' she said, taking both my hands, 'I know it will maybe be a blow to you, but it's better so.'

'How could it be a blow to me?' I cried; 'but I would far rather not go.'

'You'll just go with me, honey, just this once: it is not often I go out. You will go with me this one night, just this one night, my honey sweet.'

I am sure there were tears in Aunt Mary's eyes, and she kissed me between the words. There was nothing more that I could say; but how I grudged the evening! A mere party, a conversazione (when all the College was away, too, and nobody to make conversation!), instead of my enchanted hour at my window and the soft strange light, and the dim face looking out, which kept me wondering and wondering what was he thinking of, what was he looking for, who was he? all one wonder and mystery and question, through the long, long, slowly fading night!

It occurred to me, however, when I was dressing – though I was so sure that he would prefer his solitude to everything – that he might perhaps, it was just possible, be there. And when I thought of that, I took out my white frock though Janet had laid out my blue one – and my little pearl necklace which I had thought was too good to wear. They were not very large pearls, but they were real pearls, and very even and lustrous though they were small; and though I did not think much of my appearance then, there must have been something about me – pale as I was but apt to colour in a moment, with my dress so white, and my pearls so white, and my hair all shadowy perhaps, that was pleasant to look at: for even old Mr Pitmilly had a strange look in his eyes, as if he was not only pleased but sorry too, perhaps thinking me a creature that would have troubles in this life, though I was so young and knew them not. And when Aunt Mary looked at me, there was a little quiver about her mouth. She herself had on her pretty lace and her white hair very nicely done, and looking her best. As for Mr Pitmilly, he had a beautiful fine French cambric frill to his shirt, plaited in the most minute plaits, and with a diamond pin in it which sparkled as much as Lady Carnbee's ring; but this was a fine frank kindly stone, that looked you straight in the face and sparkled, with the light dancing in it as if it were pleased to see you, and to be shining on that old gentleman's honest and faithful breast: for he had been one of Aunt Mary's lovers in their early days, and still thought there was nobody like her in the world.

I had got into quite a happy commotion of mind by the time we set out across the street in the soft light of the evening to the Library Hall. Perhaps, after all, I should see him, and see the room which I was so well acquainted with, and find out why he sat there so constantly and never was seen abroad. I thought I might even hear what he was working at, which would be such a pleasant thing to tell papa when I went home. A friend of mine at St Rule's – oh, far, far more busy than you ever were, papa! – and then my father would laugh as he always did, and say he was but an idler and never busy at all.

The room was all light and bright, flowers wherever flowers could be, and the long lines of the books that went along the walls on each side, lighting up wherever there was a line of gilding or an ornament, with a little response. It dazzled me at first all that light: but I was very eager, though I kept very quiet, looking round to see if perhaps in any corner, in the middle of any group, he would be there. I did not expect to see him among the ladies. He would not be with them, – he was too studious, too silent: but, perhaps among that circle of grey heads at the upper end of the room – perhaps—

No: I am not sure that it was not half a pleasure to me to make quite sure that there was not one whom I could take for him, who was at all like my vague image of him. No: it was absurd to think that he would be here, amid all that sound of voices, under the glare of that light. I felt a little proud to think that he was in his room as usual, doing his work, or thinking so deeply over it, as when he turned round in his chair with his face to the light.

I was thus getting a little composed and quiet in my mind, for now that the expectation of seeing him was over, though it was a disappointment, it was a satisfaction too – when Mr Pitmilly came up to me, holding out his arm. 'Now,' he said, 'I am going to take you to see the curiosities.' I thought to myself that after I had seen them and spoken to everybody I knew, Aunt Mary would let me go home, so I went very willingly, though I did not care for the curiosities. Something, however, struck me strangely as we walked up the room. It was the air, rather fresh and strong, from an open window at the east end of the hall. How should there be a window there? I hardly saw what it meant for the first moment, but it blew in my face as if there was some meaning in it, and I felt very uneasy without seeing why.

Then there was another thing that startled me. On that side of the wall which was to the street there seemed no windows at all. A long line of bookcases filled it from end to end. I could not see what that meant either, but it confused me. I was altogether confused. I felt as if I was in a strange country, not knowing where I was going, not knowing what I might find out next. If there were no windows on the wall to the street, where was my window? My heart, which had been jumping up and calming down again all this time, gave a great leap at this, as if it would have come out of me – but I did not know what it could mean.

Then we stopped before a glass case, and Mr Pitmilly showed me some things in it. I could not pay much attention to them. My head was going round and round. I heard his voice going on, and then myself speaking with a queer sound that was hollow in my ears; but I did not know what I was saying or what he was saying. Then he took me to the very end of the room, the east end, saying something that I caught – that I was pale, that the air would do me good. The air was blowing full on me, lifting the lace of my dress, lifting my hair, almost chilly. The window opened into the pale daylight, into the little lane that ran by the end of the building. Mr Pitmilly went on talking, but I could not make out a word he said. Then I heard my own voice, speaking through it, though I did not seem to be aware that I was speaking. 'Where is my window? – where, then, is my window?' I seemed to be saying, and I turned right round, dragging him with me, still holding his arm. As I did this my eye fell upon something at last which I knew. It was a large picture in a broad frame, hanging against the farther wall.

What did it mean? Oh, what did it mean? I turned round again to the open window at the east end, and to the daylight, the strange light without any shadow, that was all round about this lighted hall, holding it like a bubble that would burst, like something that was not real. The real place was the room I knew, in which that picture was hanging, where the writing-table was, and where he sat with his face to the light. But where was the light and the window through which it came? I think my senses must have left me. I went up to the picture which I knew, and then I walked straight across the room, always dragging Mr Pitmilly, whose face was pale, but who did not struggle but allowed me to lead him, straight across to where the window was – where the window was not; – where there was no sign of it. 'Where is my window? – where is my window?' I said. And all the time I was sure that I was in a dream, and these lights were all some theatrical illusion, and the people talking; and nothing real but the pale, pale, watching, lingering day standing by to wait until that foolish bubble should burst.

'My dear,' said Mr Pitmilly, 'my dear! Mind that you are in public. Mind where you are. You must not make an outcry and frighten your Aunt Mary. Come away with me. Come away, my dear young lady! and you'll take a seat for a minute or two and compose yourself; and I'll get you an ice or a little wine.' He kept patting my hand, which was on his arm, and looking at me very anxiously. 'Bless me! bless me! I never thought it would have this effect,' he said.

But I would not allow him to take me away in that direction. I went to the picture again and looked at it without seeing it: and then I went across the room again, with some kind of wild thought that if I insisted I should find it. 'My window – my window!' I said.

There was one of the professors standing there, and he heard me. 'The window!' said he. 'Ah, you've been taken in with what appears outside. It was put there to be in uniformity with the window on the stair. But it never was a real window. It is just behind that bookcase. Many people are taken in by it,' he said.

His voice seemed to sound from somewhere far away, and as if it would go on for ever; and the hall swam in a dazzle of shining and of noises round me; and the daylight through the open window grew greyer, waiting till it should be over, and the bubble burst.

V

It was Mr Pitmilly who took me home; or rather it was I who took him, pushing him on a little in front of me, holding fast by his arm, not waiting for Aunt Mary or any one. We came out into the daylight again outside, I, without even a cloak or a shawl, with my bare arms, and uncovered head, and the pearls round my neck. There was a rush of the people about, and a baker's boy, that baker's boy, stood right in my way and cried, 'Here's a braw ane!' shouting to the others: the words struck me somehow, as his stone had struck the window, without any reason. But I did not mind the people staring, and hurried across the street, with Mr Pitmilly half a step in advance. The door was open, and Janet standing at it, looking out to see what she could see of the ladies in their grand dresses. She gave a shriek when she saw me hurrying across the street; but I brushed past her, and pushed Mr Pitmilly up the stairs, and took him breathless to the recess, where I threw myself down on the seat, feeling as if I could not have gone another step farther, and waved my hand across to the window. 'There! there!' I cried. Ah! there it was – not that senseless mob – not the theatre and the gas, and the people all in a murmur and clang of talking. Never in all these days had I seen that room so clearly. There was a faint tone of light behind, as if it might have been a reflection from some of those vulgar lights in the hall, and he sat against it, calm, wrapped in his thoughts, with his face turned to the window. Nobody but must have seen him. Janet could have seen him had I called her up-stairs. It was like a picture, all the things I knew, and the same attitude, and the atmosphere, full of quietness, not disturbed by anything. I pulled Mr Pitmilly's arm before I let him go, – 'You see, you see!' I cried. He gave me the most bewildered look, as if he would have liked to cry. He saw nothing! I was sure of that from his eyes. He was an old man, and there was no vision in him. If I had called up Janet, she would have seen it all. 'My dear!' he said. 'My dear!' waving his hands in a helpless way. 'He has been there all these nights,' I cried, 'and I thought you could tell me who he was and what he was doing; and that he might have taken me in to that room, and showed me, that I might tell papa. Papa would understand, he would like to hear. Oh, can't you tell me what work he is doing, Mr Pitmilly? He never lifts his head as long as the light throws a shadow, and then when it is like this he turns round and thinks, and takes a rest!'

Mr Pitmilly was trembling, whether it was with cold or I know not what. He said, with a shake in his voice, 'My dear young lady – my dear—' and then stopped and looked at me as if he were going to cry. 'It's peetiful, it's peetiful,' he said; and then in another voice, 'I am going across there again to bring your Aunt Mary home; do you understand, my poor little thing, my— I am going to bring her home – you will be better when she is here.' I was glad when he went away, as he could not see anything: and I sat alone in the dark which was not dark, but quite clear light – a light like nothing I ever saw. How clear it was in that room! not glaring like the gas and the voices, but so quiet, everything so visible, as if it were in another world. I heard a little rustle behind me, and there was Janet, standing staring at me with two big eyes wide open. She was only a little older than I was. I called to her, 'Janet, come here, come here, and you will see him, – come here and see him!' impatient that she should be so shy and keep behind. 'Oh, my bonnie young leddy!' she said, and burst out crying. I stamped my foot at her, in my indignation that she would not come, and she fled before me with a rustle and swing of haste, as if she were afraid. None of them, none of them! not even a girl like myself, with the sight in her eyes, would understand. I turned back again, and held out my hands to him sitting there, who was the only one that knew. 'Oh,' I said, 'say something to me! I don't know who you are, or what you are: but you're lonely and so am I; and I only – feel for you. Say something to me!' I neither hoped that he would hear, nor expected any answer. How could he hear, with the street between us, and his window shut, and all the murmuring of the voices and the people standing about? But for one moment it seemed to me that there was only him and me in the whole world.

But I gasped with my breath, that had almost gone from me, when I saw him move in his chair! He had heard me, though I knew not how. He rose up, and I rose too, speechless, incapable of anything but this mechanical movement. He seemed to draw me as if I were a puppet moved by his will. He came forward to the window, and stood looking across at me. I was sure that he looked at me. At last he had seen me: at last he had found out that somebody, though only a girl, was watching him, looking for him, believing in him. I was in such trouble and commotion of mind and trembling, that I could not keep on my feet, but dropped kneeling on the window-seat, supporting myself against the window, feeling as if my heart were being drawn out of me. I cannot describe his face. It was all dim, yet there was a light on it: I think it must have been a smile; and as closely as I looked at him he looked at me. His hair was fair, and there was a little quiver about his lips. Then he put his hands upon the window to open it. It was stiff and hard to move; but at last he forced it open with a sound that echoed all along the street. I saw that the people heard it, and several looked up. As for me, I put my hands together, leaning with my face against the glass, drawn to him as if I could have gone out of myself, my heart out of my bosom, my eyes out of my head. He opened the window with a noise that was heard from the West Port to the Abbey. Could any one doubt that?

And then he leaned forward out of the window, looking out. There was not one in the street but must have seen him. He looked at me first, with a little wave of his hand, as if it were a salutation – yet not exactly that either, for I thought he waved me away; and then he looked up and down in the dim shining of the ending day, first to the east, to the old Abbey towers, and then to the west, along the broad line of the street where so many people were coming and going, but so little noise, all like enchanted folk in an enchanted place. I watched him with such a melting heart, with such a deep satisfaction as words could not say; for nobody could tell me now that he was not there, – nobody could say I was dreaming any more.

I watched him as if I could not breathe – my heart in my throat, my eyes upon him. He looked up and down, and then he looked back to me. I was the first, and I was the last, though it was not for long: he did know, he did see, who it was that had recognised him and sympathised with him all the time. I was in a kind of rapture, yet stupor too; my look went with his look, following it as if I were his shadow; and then suddenly he was gone, and I saw him no more.

I dropped back again upon my seat, seeking something to support me, something to lean upon. He had lifted his hand and waved it once again to me. How he went I cannot tell, nor where he went I cannot tell; but in a moment he was away, and the window standing open, and the room fading into stillness and dimness, yet so clear, with all its space, and the great picture in its gilded frame upon the wall. It gave me no pain to see him go away. My heart was so content, and I was so worn out and satisfied – for what doubt or question could there be about him now? As I was lying back as weak as water, Aunt Mary came in behind me, and flew to me with a little rustle as if she had come on wings, and put her arms round me, and drew my head on to her breast. I had begun to cry a little, with sobs like a child. 'You saw him, you saw him!' I said. To lean upon her, and feel her so soft, so kind, gave me a pleasure I cannot describe, and her arms round me, and her voice saying 'Honey, my honey!' – as if she were nearly crying too. Lying there I came back to myself, quite sweetly, glad of everything. But I wanted some assurance from them that they had seen him too. I waved my hand to the window that was still standing open, and the room that was stealing away into the faint dark. 'This time you saw it all?' I said, getting more eager. 'My honey!' said Aunt Mary, giving me a kiss: and Mr Pitmilly began to walk about the room with short little steps behind, as if he were out of patience. I sat straight up and put away Aunt Mary's arms. 'You cannot be so blind, so blind!' I cried. 'Oh, not to-night, at least not to-night!' But neither the one nor the other made any reply. I shook myself quite free, and raised myself up. And there, in the middle of the street, stood the baker's boy like a statue, staring up at the open window, with his mouth open and his face full of wonder – breathless, as if he could not believe what he saw. I darted forward, calling to him, and beckoned him to come to me. 'Oh, bring him up! bring him, bring him to me!' I cried.

Mr Pitmilly went out directly, and got the boy by the shoulder. He did not want to come. It was strange to see the little old gentleman, with his beautiful frill and his diamond pin, standing out in the street, with his hand upon the boy's shoulder, and the other boys round, all in a little crowd. And presently they came towards the house, the others all following, gaping and wondering. He came in unwilling, almost resisting, looking as if we meant him some harm. 'Come away, my laddie, come and speak to the young lady,' Mr Pitmilly was saying. And Aunt Mary took my hands to keep me back. But I would not be kept back.

'Boy,' I cried, 'you saw it too: you saw it: tell them you saw it! It is that I want, and no more.'

He looked at me as they all did, as if he thought I was mad. 'What's she wantin' wi' me?' he said; and then, 'I did nae harm, even if I did throw a bit stane at it – and it's nae sin to throw a stane'.

'You rascal!' said Mr Pitmilly, giving him a shake; 'have you been throwing stones? You'll kill somebody some of these days with your stones.' The old gentleman was confused and troubled, for he did not understand what I wanted, nor anything that had happened. And then Aunt Mary, holding my hands and drawing me close to her, spoke. 'Laddie,' she said, 'answer the young lady, like a good lad. There's no intention of finding fault with you. Answer her, my man, and then Janet will give ye your supper before you go.'

'Oh speak, speak!' I cried; 'answer them and tell them! you saw that window opened, and the gentleman look out and wave his hand?'

'I saw nae gentleman,' he said, with his head down, 'except this wee gentleman here.'

'Listen, laddie,' said Aunt Mary. 'I saw ye standing in the middle of the street staring. What were ye looking at?'

'It was naething to make a wark about. It was just yon windy yonder in the library that is nae windy. And it was open as sure's death. You may laugh if you like. Is that a' she's wantin' wi' me?'

'You are telling a pack of lies, laddie,' Mr Pitmilly said.

'I'm tellin' nae lees – it was standin' open just like ony ither windy. It's as sure's death. I couldna believe it mysel'; but it's true.'

'And there it is,' I cried, turning round and pointing it out to them with great triumph in my heart. But the light was all grey, it had faded, it had changed. The window was just as it had always been, a sombre break upon the wall.

I was treated like an invalid all that evening, and taken upstairs to bed, and Aunt Mary sat up in my room the whole night through. Whenever I opened my eyes she was always sitting there close to me, watching. And there never was in all my life so strange a night. When I would talk in my excitement, she kissed me and hushed me like a child. 'Oh, honey, you are not the only one!' she said. 'Oh whisht, whisht, bairn! I should never have let you be there!'

'Aunt Mary, Aunt Mary, you have seen him too?'

'Oh whisht, whisht, honey!' Aunt Mary said: her eyes were shining – there were tears in them. 'Oh whisht, whisht! Put it out of your mind, and try to sleep. I will not speak another word,' she cried.

But I had my arms round her, and my mouth at her ear. 'Who is he there? – tell me that and I will ask no more—'

'Oh honey, rest, and try to sleep! It is just – how can I tell you? – a dream, a dream! Did you not hear what Lady Carnbee said? – the women of our blood—'

'What? what? Aunt Mary, oh Aunt Mary—'

'I canna tell you,' she cried in her agitation, 'I canna tell you! How can I tell you, when I know just what you know and no more? It is a longing all your life after – it is a looking – for what never comes.'

'He will come,' I cried. 'I shall see him to-morrow – that I know, I know!'

She kissed me and cried over me, her cheek hot and wet like mine. 'My honey, try if you can sleep – try if you can sleep: and we'll wait to see what to-morrow brings.'

'I have no fear,' said I; and then I suppose, though it is strange to think of, I must have fallen asleep – I was so worn-out, and young, and not used to lying in my bed awake. From time to time I opened my eyes, and sometimes jumped up remembering everything: but Aunt Mary was always there to soothe me, and I lay down again in her shelter like a bird in its nest.

But I would not let them keep me in bed next day. I was in a kind of fever, not knowing what I did. The window was quite opaque, without the least glimmer in it, flat and blank like a piece of wood. Never from the first day had I seen it so little like a window. 'It cannot be wondered at,' I said to myself, 'that seeing it like that, and with eyes that are old, not so clear as mine, they should think what they do.' And then I smiled to myself to think of the evening and the long light, and whether he would look out again, or only give me a signal with his hand. I decided I would like that best: not that he should take the trouble to come forward and open it again, but just a turn of his head and a wave of his hand. It would be more friendly and show more confidence, – not as if I wanted that kind of demonstration every night.

I did not come down in the afternoon, but kept at my own window up-stairs alone, till the tea-party should be over. I could hear them making a great talk; and I was sure they were all in the recess staring at the window, and laughing at the silly lassie. Let them laugh! I felt above all that now. At dinner I was very restless, hurrying to get it over; and I think Aunt Mary was restless too. I doubt whether she read her 'Times' when it came; she opened it up so as to shield her, and watched from a corner. And I settled myself in the recess, with my heart full of expectation. I wanted nothing more than to see him writing at his table, and to turn his head and give me a little wave of his hand, just to show that he knew I was there. I sat from half-past seven o'clock to ten o'clock: and the daylight grew softer and softer, till at last it was as if it was shining through a pearl, and not a shadow to be seen. But the window all the time was as black as night, and there was nothing, nothing there.

Well: but other nights it had been like that: he would not be there every night only to please me. There are other things in a man's life, a great learned man like that. I said to myself I was not disappointed. Why should I be disappointed? There had been other nights when he was not there. Aunt Mary watched me, every movement I made, her eyes shining, often wet, with a pity in them that almost made me cry: but I felt as if I were more sorry for her than for myself. And then I flung myself upon her, and asked her, again and again, what it was, and who it was, imploring her to tell me if she knew? and when she had seen him, and what had happened? and what it meant about the women of our blood? She told me that how it was she could not tell, nor when: it was just at the time it had to be; and that we all saw him in our time – 'that is,' she said, 'the ones that are like you and me.' What was it that made her and me different from the rest? but she only shook her head and would not tell me. 'They say,' she said, and then stopped short. 'Oh, honey, try and forget all about it – if I had but known you were of that kind! They say – that once there was one that was a Scholar, and liked his books more than any lady's love. Honey, do not look at me like that. To think I should have brought all this on you!'

'He was a Scholar?' I cried.

'And one of us, that must have been a light woman, not like you and me—But maybe it was just in innocence; for who can tell? She waved to him and waved to him to come over: and yon ring was the token: but he would not come. But still she sat at her window and waved and waved – till at last her brothers heard of it, that were stirring men; and then – oh, my honey, let us speak of it no more!'

'They killed him!' I cried, carried away. And then I grasped her with my hands, and gave her a shake, and flung away from her. 'You tell me that to throw dust in my eyes – when I saw him only last night: and he as living as I am, and as young!'

'My honey, my honey!' Aunt Mary said.

After that I would not speak to her for a long time; but she kept close to me, never leaving me when she could help it, and always with that pity in her eyes. For the next night it was the same; and the third night. That third night I thought I could not bear it any longer. I would have to do something if only I knew what to do! If it would ever get dark, quite dark, there might be something to be done. I had wild dreams of stealing out of the house and getting a ladder, and mounting up to try if I could not open that window, in the middle of the night – if perhaps I could get the baker's boy to help me; and then my mind got into a whirl, and it was as if I had done it; and I could almost see the boy put the ladder to the window, and hear him cry out that there was nothing there. Oh, how slow it was, the night! and how light it was, and everything so clear – no darkness to cover you, no shadow, whether on one side of the street or on the other side! I could not sleep, though I was forced to go to bed. And in the deep midnight, when it is dark dark in every other place, I slipped very softly down-stairs, though there was one board on the landing-place that creaked – and opened the door and stepped out. There was not a soul to be seen, up or down, from the Abbey to the West Port: and the trees stood like ghosts, and the silence was terrible, and everything as clear as day. You don't know what silence is till you find it in the light like that, not morning but night, no sunrising, no shadow, but everything as clear as the day.

It did not make any difference as the slow minutes went on: one o'clock, two o'clock. How strange it was to hear the clocks striking in that dead light when there was nobody to hear them! But it made no difference. The window was quite blank; even the marking of the panes seemed to have melted away. I stole up again after a long time, through the silent house, in the clear light, cold and trembling, with despair in my heart.

I am sure Aunt Mary must have watched and seen me coming back, for after a while I heard faint sounds in the house; and very early, when there had come a little sunshine into the air, she came to my bedside with a cup of tea in her hand; and she, too, was looking like a ghost. 'Are you warm, honey – are you comfortable?' she said. 'It doesn't matter,' said I. I did not feel as if anything mattered; unless if one could get into the dark somewhere – the soft, deep dark that would cover you over and hide you – but I could not tell from what. The dreadful thing was that there was nothing, nothing to look for, nothing to hide from – only the silence and the light.

That day my mother came and took me home. I had not heard she was coming; she arrived quite unexpectedly, and said she had no time to stay, but must start the same evening so as to be in London next day, papa having settled to go abroad. At first I had a wild thought I would not go. But how can a girl say I will not, when her mother has come for her, and there is no reason, no reason in the world, to resist, and no right! I had to go, whatever I might wish or any one might say. Aunt Mary's dear eyes were wet; she went about the house drying them quietly with her hand-kerchief, but she always said, 'It is the best thing for you, honey – the best thing for you!' Oh, how I hated to hear it said that it was the best thing, as if anything mattered, one more than another! The old ladies were all there in the afternoon, Lady Carnbee looking at me from under her black lace, and the diamond lurking, sending out darts from under her finger. She patted me on the shoulder, and told me to be a good bairn. 'And never lippen to what you see from the window,' she said. 'The eye is deceitful as well as the heart.' She kept patting me on the shoulder, and I felt again as if that sharp wicked stone stung me. Was that what Aunt Mary meant when she said yon ring was the token? I thought afterwards I saw the mark on my shoulder. You will say why? How can I tell why? If I had known, I should have been contented, and it would not have mattered any more.

I never went back to St Rule's, and for years of my life I never again looked out of a window when any other window was in sight. You ask me did I ever see him again? I cannot tell: the imagination is a great deceiver, as Lady Carnbee said: and if he stayed there so long, only to punish the race that had wronged him, why should I ever have seen him again? for I had received my share. But who can tell what happens in a heart that often, often, and so long as that, comes back to do its errand? If it was he whom I have seen again, the anger is gone from him, and he means good and no longer harm to the house of the woman that loved him. I have seen his face looking at me from a crowd. There was one time when I came home a widow from India, very sad, with my little children: I am certain I saw him there among all the people coming to welcome their friends. There was nobody to welcome me, – for I was not expected: and very sad was I, without a face I knew: when all at once I saw him, and he waved his hand to me. My heart leaped up again: I had forgotten who he was, but only that it was a face I knew, and I landed almost cheerfully, thinking here was some one who would help me. But he had disappeared, as he did from the window, with that one wave of his hand.

And again I was reminded of it all when old Lady Carnbee died – an old, old woman – and it was found in her will that she had left me that diamond ring. I am afraid of it still. It is locked up in an old sandal-wood box in the lumber-room in the little old country-house which belongs to me, but where I never live. If any one would steal it, it would be a relief to my mind. Yet I never knew what Aunt Mary meant when she said, 'Yon ring was the token,' nor what it could have to do with that strange window in the old College Library of St Rule's.

ROBERT LOUIS STEVENSON

The Body Snatcher

Every night in the year, four of us sat together in the small parlour of the
George, at Debenham; the undertaker, and the landlord, and Fettes, and
myself. Sometimes there would be more; but blow high, blow low, come
rain, or snow, or frost, we four would be each planted in his own particular
armchair. Fettes was an old drunken Scotchman, a man of education obviously, and a man of some property; since he lived in idleness. He had come
to Debenham years ago, while still young; and by mere continuance of
living had grown to be an adopted townsman. His blue camlet cloak was
a local antiquity, like the church spire. His place in the parlour at the
George, his absence from church, his old, crapulous, disreputable vices,
were all things of course in Debenham. He had some vague Radical opinions and some fleeting infidelities, which he would now and again set forth
and emphasize with tottering slaps upon the table. He drank rum – five
glasses regularly every evening; and for the greater portion of his nightly
visit to the George sat, with his glass in his right hand, in a state of melancholy, alcoholic saturation. We called him the Doctor; for he was supposed
to have some special knowledge of medicine, and had been known, upon
a pinch, to set a fracture or reduce a dislocation; but beyond these slight
particulars, we had no knowledge of his character and antecedents.

One dark winter night, it had struck nine some time before the landlord joined us. There was a sick man in the George, a great neighbouring
proprietor suddenly struck down with apoplexy on his way to Parliament;
and the great man's still greater London doctor had been telegraphed to
his bedside. It was the first time such a thing had happened in Debenham,
for the railway was but newly open, and we were all proportionately moved
by the occurrence.

'He's come,' said the landlord, after he had filled and lighted his pipe.

'He?' said I. 'Who? – not the doctor?'

'Himself,' replied our host.

'What is his name?'

'Dr Macfarlane,' said the landlord.

Fettes was far through his third tumbler, stupidly fuddled, now nodding over, now staring mazily around him; but at the last word he seemed to awaken, and repeated the name 'Macfarlane' twice, quietly enough the first time, but with a sudden emotion at the second.

'Yes,' said the landlord, 'that's his name, Doctor Wolfe Macfarlane.'

Fettes became instantly sober; his eyes awoke, his voice became clear, loud, and steady, his language forcible and earnest; we were all startled by the transformation, as if a man had risen from the dead.

'I beg your pardon,' he said; 'I am afraid I have not been paying much attention to your talk. Who is this Wolfe Macfarlane?' And then, when he had heard the landlord out, 'It cannot be, it cannot be,' he added; 'and yet I would like well to see him face to face.'

'Do you know him, Doctor?' asked the undertaker, with a gasp.

'God forbid,' was the reply. 'And yet the name is a strange one; it were too much to fancy two. Tell me, landlord, is he old?'

'Well,' said the host, 'he's not a young man, to be sure, and his hair is white; but he looks younger than you.'

'He is older, though; years older. But' – with a slap upon the table – 'it's the rum you see in my face, rum and sin. This man, perhaps, may have an easy conscience and a good digestion. Conscience! hear me speak. You would think I was some good, old, decent Christian; would you not? But no, not I; I never canted. Voltaire might have canted if he'd stood in my shoes; but the brains' – with a rattling fillip on his bald head – 'the brains were clear and active; and I saw and I made no deductions.'

'If you know this doctor,' I ventured to remark after a somewhat awful pause, 'I should gather that you do not share the landlord's good opinion.'

Fettes paid no regard to me. 'Yes,' he said, with sudden decision, 'I must see him face to face.'

There was another pause, and then a door was closed rather sharply on the first floor and a step was heard upon the stair.

'That's the doctor,' cried the landlord; 'look sharp, and you can catch him.'

It was but two steps from the small parlour to the door of the old George inn; the wide oak staircase landed almost in the street; there was room for a Turkey rug and nothing more between the threshold and the last round of the descent; but this little space was every evening brilliantly lit up, not only by the light upon the stair and the great signal lamp below the sign, but by the warm radiance of the bar-room window. The George thus brightly advertised itself to passers-by in the cold street. Fettes walked steadily to the spot, and we, who were hanging behind, beheld the two men meet, as one of them had phrased it, face to face. Dr Macfarlane was alert and vigorous. His white hair set off his pale and placid although energetic countenance; he was richly dressed in the finest of broadcloth and the whitest of linen, with a great gold watch chain and studs and spectacles of the same precious material; he wore a broad folded tie, white and speckled with lilac, and he carried on his arm a comfortable driving-coat of fur. There was no doubt but he became his years, breathing, as he did, of wealth and consideration; and it was a surprising contrast to see our parlour sot, bald, dirty, pimpled, and robed in his old camlet cloak, confront him at the bottom of the stairs.

'Macfarlane,' he said, somewhat loudly, more like a herald than a friend.

The great doctor pulled up short on the fourth step, as though the familiarity of the address surprised and somewhat shocked his dignity.

'Toddy Macfarlane,' repeated Fettes.

The London man almost staggered; he stared for the swiftest of seconds at the man before him, glanced behind him with a sort of scare, and then in a startled whisper, 'Fettes!' he said, 'you!'

'Ay,' said the other, 'me. Did you think I was dead, too? We are not so easy shot of our acquaintance.'

'Hush, hush!' exclaimed the Doctor. 'Hush, hush! this meeting is so unexpected – I can see you are unmanned. I hardly knew you, I confess, at first; but I am overjoyed, overjoyed, to have this opportunity. For the present it must be how-d'ye-do and good-bye in one; for my fly is waiting, and I must not fail the train; but you shall – let me see – yes – you shall give me your address, and you can count on early news of me. We must do something for you, Fettes; I fear you are out at elbows; but we must see to that – for auld lang syne, as once we sang at suppers.'

'Money!' cried Fettes; 'money from you! The money that I had of you is lying where I cast it in the rain.'

Dr Macfarlane had talked himself into some measure of superiority and confidence; but the uncommon energy of this refusal cast him back into his first confusion. A horrible, ugly look came and went across his almost venerable countenance. 'My dear fellow,' he said, 'be it as you please; my last thought is to offend you. I would intrude on none. I will leave you my address, however—'

'I do not wish it; I do not wish to know the roof that shelters you,' interrupted the other. 'I heard your name; I feared it might be you; I wished to know if, after all, there were a God; I know now that there is none. Begone!'

He still stood in the middle of the rug, between the stair and doorway; and the great London physician, in order to escape, would be forced to step upon one side. It was plain that he hesitated before the thought of this humiliation. White as he was, there was a dangerous glitter in his spectacles; but while he still paused uncertain he became aware that the driver of his fly was peering in from the street at this unusual scene, and caught a glimpse at the same time of our little body from the parlour, huddled by the corner of the bar. The presence of so many witnesses decided him at once to flee. He crouched together, brushing on the wainscot, and made a dart, like a serpent, striking for the door. But his tribulation was not yet entirely at an end; for even as he was passing Fettes clutched him by the arm, and these words came in a whisper, and yet painfully distinct, 'Have you seen it again?'

The great, rich London doctor cried out aloud with a sharp, throttling cry; he dashed his questioner across the open space, and, with his hands over his head, fled out of the door like a detected thief. Before it had occurred to one of us to make a movement the fly was already rattling towards the station. The scene was over like a dream; but the dream had left proofs and traces of its passage. Next day the servant found the fine gold spectacles crushed and broken on the threshold, and that very night were we not all standing breathless by the bar-room window, and Fettes at our side, sober, pale, and resolute in look?

'God protect us, Mr Fettes!' said the landlord, coming first into possession of his customary senses. 'What in the universe is all this? These are strange things you have been saying.'

Fettes turned towards us: he looked us each in succession in the face. 'See if you can hold your tongues,' said he. 'That man, Macfarlane, is not safe to cross; those that have done so already, have repented it too late.'

And then, without so much as finishing his third glass, far less waiting for the other two, he bade us a good-bye and went forth, under the lamp of the hotel, into the black night.

We three returned to our places in the parlour, with the big red fire and four clear candles; and as we recapitulated what had passed the first chill of our surprise soon changed into a glow of curiosity. We sat late; it was the latest session I have known in the old George; each man, before we parted, had his theory that he was bound to prove; and none of us had any nearer business in this world than to track out the past of our contemned companion, and surprise the secret that he shared with the great London doctor. It is no great boast; but I believe I was a better hand at worming out a story than either of my fellows at the George; and perhaps there is now no other man alive who could narrate to you the following foul and unnatural events:

In his young days Fettes studied medicine in the schools of Edinburgh. He had talent of a kind, the talent that picks up swiftly what it hears and readily retails it for its own. He worked little at home; but he was civil, attentive, and intelligent in the presence of his masters. They soon picked him out as a lad who listened closely and remembered well; nay, strange as it seemed to me when first I heard it, he was in those days well favoured and pleased by his exterior. There was, at this period, a certain extramural teacher of anatomy, whom I shall here designate by the letter K—. His name was subsequently too well known. The man who bore it skulked through the streets of Edinburgh in disguise, while the mob that applauded at the execution of Burke called loudly for the blood of his employer. But Mr K— was then at the top of his vogue; he enjoyed a popularity due partly to his own talent and address, partly to the incapacity of his rival, the university professor. The students, at least, swore by his name, and Fettes believed himself, and was believed by others, to have laid the foundations of success when he had acquired the favour of this meteorically famous man. Mr K— was a *bon vivant* as well as an accomplished teacher; he liked a sly allusion no less than a careful preparation. In both capacities Fettes enjoyed and deserved his notice, and by the second year of his attendance he held the half-irregular position of second demonstrator or sub-assistant in the class.

In this capacity, the charge of the theatre and lecture-room devolved in particular upon his shoulders; he had to answer for the cleanliness of the premises and the conduct of the other students; and it was a part of his duty to supply, receive, and divide the various subjects. It was with a view to this last – at that time very delicate – affair that he was lodged by Mr K— in the same wynd, and at last in the same building, with the dissecting rooms. Here, after a night of turbulent pleasures, his hand still tottering, his sight still misty and confused, he would be called out of bed in the black hours before the winter dawn by the unclean and desperate interlopers who supplied the table; he would open the door to these men, since infamous throughout the land; he would help them with their tragic burden, pay them their sordid price, and remain alone when they were gone with the unfriended relics of humanity. From such a scene he would return to snatch another hour or two of slumber, to repair the abuses of the night and refresh himself for the labours of the day.

Few lads could have been more insensible to the impressions of a life thus passed among the ensigns of mortality. His mind was closed against all general considerations; he was incapable of interest in the fate and fortunes of another, the slave of his own desires and low ambitions. Cold, light, and selfish in the last resort, he had that modicum of prudence, miscalled morality, which keeps a man from inconvenient drunkenness or punishable theft. He coveted besides a measure of consideration from his masters and his fellow-pupils, and he had no desire to fail conspicuously in the external parts of life. Thus he made it his pleasure to gain some distinction in his studies, and day after day rendered unimpeachable eye service to his employer, Mr K—. For his day of work he indemnified himself by nights of roaring blackguardly enjoyment; and, when that balance had been struck, the organ that he called his conscience declared itself content.

The supply of subjects was a continual trouble to him as well as to his master. In that large and busy class, the raw material of the anatomists kept perpetually running out; and the business thus rendered necessary was not only unpleasant in itself, but threatened dangerous consequences to all who were concerned. It was the policy of Mr K— to ask no question in his dealings with the trade. 'They bring the body, and we pay the price,' he used to say – dwelling on the alliteration – '*quid pro quo.*' And again, and somewhat profanely, 'Ask no questions,' he would tell his assistants, 'for conscience's sake.' There was no understanding that the subjects were provided by the crime of murder; had that idea been broached to him in words he would have recoiled in horror; but the lightness of his speech upon so grave a matter was, in itself, an offence against good manners, and a temptation to the men with whom he dealt. Fettes, for instance, had often remarked to himself upon the singular freshness of the bodies; he had been struck again and again by the hangdog, abominable looks of the ruffians who came to him before the dawn; and, putting things together clearly in his private thoughts, he perhaps attributed a meaning too immoral and too categorical to the unguarded counsels of his master. He understood his duty, in short, to have three branches: to take what was brought, to pay the price, and to avert the eye from any evidence of crime.

One November morning this policy of silence was put sharply to the test. He had been awake all night with racking toothache – pacing his room like a caged beast, or throwing himself in fury on his bed – and had fallen at last into that profound, uneasy slumber that so often follows on a night of pain, when he was awakened by the third or fourth angry repetition of the concerted signal. There was a thin, bright moonshine; it was bitter cold, windy, and frosty; the town had not yet awakened, but an indefinable stir already preluded the noise and business of the day. The ghouls had come later than usual, and they seemed more than usually eager to be gone. Fettes, sick with sleep, lighted them upstairs; he heard their grumbling Irish voices through a dream; as they stripped the sack from their sad merchandise, he leaned, dozing, with his shoulder propped against the wall. He had to shake himself to find the men their money. As he did so his eyes lighted on the dead face. He started; he took two steps nearer, with the candle raised.

'God Almighty,' he cried, 'that is Jane Galbraith!'

The men answered nothing, but they shuffled nearer towards the door.

'I know her, I tell you,' he continued. 'She was alive and hearty yesterday. It's impossible she can be dead; it's impossible you should have got this body fairly.'

'Sure, sir, you're mistaken entirely,' said one of the men.

But the other looked Fettes darkly in the eyes, and demanded his money on the spot.

It was impossible to misconceive the threat or to exaggerate the danger. The lad's heart failed him; he stammered some excuses, counted out the sum, and saw his hateful visitors depart. No sooner were they gone than he hastened to confirm his doubts; by a dozen unquestionable marks he identified the girl he had jested with the day before; he saw with horror, marks upon her body that might well betoken violence. A panic seized him, and he took refuge in his room. There he reflected at length over the discovery that he had made; considered soberly the bearing of Mr K—'s instructions, and the danger to himself of interference in so serious a business; and at last, in sore perplexity, determined to wait for the advice of his immediate superior, the class assistant.

This was a young doctor, Wolfe Macfarlane, a high favourite among all the reckless students, clever, dissipated, and unscrupulous to the last degree. He had travelled and studied abroad; his manners were agreeable and a little forward; he was an authority upon the stage, skilful on the ice or the links with skate or golf club; he dressed with nice audacity, and, to put the finishing touch upon his glory, he kept a gig and a strong, trotting horse. With Fettes he was on terms of intimacy; indeed, their relative positions called for some community of life; and when subjects were scarce, the pair would drive far into the country in Macfarlane's gig, visit and desecrate some lonely graveyard, and return before dawn with their booty to the door of the dissecting room.

On that particular morning Macfarlane arrived somewhat earlier than his wont. Fettes heard him, and met him on the stairs, told him his story, and showed him the cause of his alarm. Macfarlane examined the ecchymoses.

'Yes,' he said with a nod, 'it looks fishy.'

'Well, what should I do?' asked Fettes.

'Do?' repeated the other. 'Do you want to do anything? Least said, soonest mended, I should say.'

'Someone else might recognize her,' objected Fettes. 'She was as well known as the Castle Rock.'

'We'll hope not,' said Macfarlane, 'and if anybody does – well, you didn't, don't you see, and there's an end. The fact is, this has been going on too long. Stir up the mud, and you'll get K— into the most unholy trouble; you'll be in a shocking box yourself, so will I, if you come to that. I should like to know how anyone of us would look, or what the devil we should have to say for ourselves, in any Christian witness-box. For me, you know, there's one thing certain; that, practically speaking, all our subjects have been murdered.'

'Macfarlane!' cried Fettes.

'Come now!' sneered the other. 'As if you hadn't suspected it yourself!'

'Suspecting is one thing—'

'And proof another. Yes, I know; and I'm as sorry as you are *this* should have come here,' tapping the body with his cane. 'The next best thing for me is not to recognize it; and,' he added coolly, 'I don't. You may, if you please. I don't dictate, but I think a man of the world would do as I do; and I may add I fancy that is what K— would look for at our hands. The question is, why did he choose us two for his assistants? And I answer, because he didn't want old wives.'

This was the tone of all others to affect the mind of a lad like Fettes; he agreed to imitate Macfarlane; the body of the unfortunate girl was duly dissected, and no one remarked or appeared to recognize her.

One afternoon, when his day's work was over, Fettes dropped into a popular tavern, and found Macfarlane sitting with a stranger. This was a small man, very pale and dark, with cold black eyes. The cut of his features gave a promise of intellect and refinement which was but feebly realized in his manners; for he proved, upon a nearer acquaintance, coarse, vulgar and stupid. He exercised, however, a very remarkable control over Macfarlane; issued orders like the Great Bashaw; became inflamed at the least discussion or delay, and commented rudely on the servility with which he was obeyed. This most offensive person took a fancy to Fettes on the spot, plied him with drinks, and honoured him with unusual confidences on his past career. If a tenth part of what he confessed were true, he was a very loathsome rogue; and the lad's vanity was tickled by the attention of so experienced a man.

'I'm a pretty bad fellow myself,' the stranger remarked; 'but Macfarlane is the boy – Toddy Macfarlane, I call him. Toddy, order your friend another glass.' Or it might be, 'Toddy, you jump up and shut that door.' 'Toddy hates me,' he said again; 'oh, yes, Toddy, you do.'

'Don't you call me that confounded name,' growled Macfarlane.

'Hear him! Did you ever see the lads play knife? He would like to do that all over my body,' remarked the stranger.

'We medicals have a better way than that,' said Fettes. 'When we dislike a dear friend of ours, we dissect him.'

Macfarlane looked up sharply, as though this jest were scarcely to his mind.

The afternoon passed. Gray, for that was the stranger's name, invited Fettes to join them at dinner, ordered a feast so sumptuous that the tavern was thrown into commotion; and when all was done commanded Macfarlane to settle the bill. It was late before they separated; the man Gray was incapably drunk; Macfarlane, sobered by his fury, chewed the end of the money he had been forced to squander and the slights he had been obliged to swallow; Fettes, with various liquors singing in his head, returned home with devious footsteps and a mind entirely in abeyance. Next day Macfarlane was absent from the class; and Fettes smiled to himself as he imagined him still squiring the intolerable Gray from tavern to tavern. As soon as the hour of liberty had struck, he posted from place to place in quest of his last night's companions; he could find them, however, nowhere, returned early to his rooms, went early to bed, and slept the sleep of the just.

At four in the morning he was wakened by the well-known signal. Descending to the door, he was filled with astonishment to find Macfarlane with his gig, and, in the gig, one of those long and ghastly packages with which he was so well acquainted.

'What?' he cried. 'Have you been out alone? How did you manage?'

But Macfarlane silenced him roughly, bidding him turn to business. When they had got the body upstairs and laid it on the table, Macfarlane made at first as if he were going away; then he paused and seemed to hesitate; and then, 'You had better look at the face,' said he, in tones of some constraint. 'You had better,' he repeated, as Fettes only stared at him in wonder.

'But where and how and when did you come by it?' cried the other.

'Look at the face,' was the only answer.

Fettes was staggered; strange doubts assailed him; he looked from the young doctor to the body, and then back again; at last with a start, he did as he was bidden. He had almost expected the sight that met his eyes, and yet the shock was cruel. To see, fixed in the rigidity of death and naked on that coarse layer of sackcloth, the man whom he had left well clad and full of meat and sin, upon the threshold of a tavern, awoke, even in the thoughtless Fettes, some of the terrors of the conscience. It was a *cras tibi* which re-echoed in his soul, that two whom he had known should have come to lie upon these icy tables. Yet these were only secondary thoughts. His first concern regarded Wolfe. Unprepared for a challenge so momentous, he knew not how to look his comrade in the face; he durst not meet his eye, and he had neither words nor voice at his command.

It was Macfarlane himself who made the first advance. He came up quietly behind and laid his hand gently but firmly on the other's shoulder.

'Richardson,' said he, 'may have the head.'

Now, Richardson was a student who had long been anxious for that portion of the human subject to dissect. There was no answer, and the murderer resumed: 'Talking of business, you must pay me; your accounts, you see, must tally.'

Fettes found a voice, the ghost of his own: 'Pay you!' he cried. 'Pay you for that!'

'Why, yes, of course you must; by all means and on every possible account you must,' returned the other. 'I dare not give it for nothing; you dare not take it for nothing: it would compromise us both. This is another case like Jane Galbraith's; the more things are wrong, the more we must act as if all were right. Where does old K— keep his money?'

'There,' answered Fettes hoarsely, pointing to a cupboard in the corner.

'Give me the key, then,' said the other calmly, holding out his hand.

There was an instant's hesitation, and the die was cast. Macfarlane could not suppress a nervous twitch, the infinitesimal mark of an immense relief, as he felt the key between his fingers. He opened the cupboard, brought out pen and ink and a paper book that stood in one compartment, and separated from the funds in a drawer a sum suitable to the occasion.

'Now, look here,' he said, 'there is the payment made. First proof of your good faith; first step to your security. You have now to clinch it by a second. Enter the payment in your book, and then you for your part may defy the devil.'

The next few seconds were for Fettes an agony of thought; but in balancing his terrors it was the most immediate that triumphed. Any future difficulty seemed almost welcome if he could avoid a present quarrel with Macfarlane. He set down the candle which he had been carrying all this time, and with a steady hand entered the date, the nature, and the amount of the transaction.

'And now,' said Macfarlane, 'it's only fair that you should pocket the lucre. I've had my share already. By-the-by, when a man of the world falls into a bit of luck, has a few extra shillings in his pocket – I'm ashamed to speak of it, but there's a rule of conduct in the case. No treating, no purchase of expensive class-books, no squaring of old debts; borrow, don't lend.'

'Macfarlane,' began Fettes, still somewhat hoarsely, 'I have put my neck in a halter to oblige you.'

'To oblige me?' cried Wolfe. 'Oh, come! You did, as near as I can see the matter, what you downright had to do in self-defence. Suppose I got into trouble, where would you be? This second little matter flows clearly from the first; Mr Gray is the continuation of Miss Galbraith; you can't begin and then stop; if you begin, you must keep on beginning; that's the truth. No rest for the wicked.'

A horrible sense of blackness and the treachery of fate seized hold upon the soul of the unhappy student.

'My God!' he cried, 'but what have *I* done? and when did *I* begin? To be made a class assistant – in the name of reason, where's the harm in that? Service wanted the position; Service might have got it. Would *he* have been where *I* am now?'

'My dear fellow,' said Macfarlane, 'what a boy you are! What harm *has* come to you? What harm *can* come to you if you hold your tongue? Why, man, do you know what this life is? There are two squads of us – the lions and the lambs. If you're a lamb, you'll come to lie upon these tables like Gray or Jane Galbraith; if you're a lion, you'll live and drive a horse like me, like K—, like all the world with any wit or courage. You're staggered at the first. But look at K—! My dear fellow, you're clever, you have pluck. I like you, and K— likes you; you were born to lead the hunt; and I tell you, on my honour and my experience of life, three days from now you'll laugh at all these scarecrows like a high-school boy at a farce.'

And with that Macfarlane took his departure, and drove off up the wynd in his gig to get under cover before daylight. Fettes was thus left alone with his regrets. He saw the miserable peril in which he stood involved; he saw, with inexpressible dismay, that there was no limit to his weakness, and that, from concession to concession, he had fallen from the arbiter of Macfarlane's destiny to his paid and helpless accomplice. He would have given the world to have been a little braver at the time, but it did not occur to him that he might still be brave. The secret of Jane Galbraith and the cursed entry in the day book closed his mouth.

Hours passed; the class began to arrive; the members of the unhappy Gray were dealt out to one and to another, and received without remark; Richardson was made happy with the head; and before the hour of freedom rang Fettes trembled with exultation to perceive how far they had already gone towards safety. For two days he continued to watch, with increasing joy, the dreadful process of disguise. On the third day Macfarlane made his appearance – he had been ill, he said; but he made up for lost time by the energy with which he directed the students; to Richardson, in particular, he extended the most valuable assistance and advice, and that student, encouraged by the praise of the demonstrator, burned high with ambitious hopes, and saw the medal already in his grasp.

Before the week was out Macfarlane's prophecy had been fulfilled. Fettes had outlived his terrors and forgotten his abasement. He began to plume himself upon his courage; and had so arranged the story in his mind that he could look back on these events with an unhealthy pride. Of his accomplice he saw but little. They met, of course, in the business of the class; they received their orders together from Mr K—; at times they had a word or two in private, and Macfarlane was from first to last particularly kind and jovial. But it was plain that he avoided any reference to their common secret; and even when Fettes whispered to him that he had cast in his lot with the lions and forsworn the lambs, he only signed to him smilingly to hold his peace.

At length an occasion arose which threw the pair once more into a closer union. Mr K— was again short of subjects; pupils were eager; and it was a part of this teacher's pretensions to be always well supplied. At the same time there came the news of a burial in the rustic graveyard of Glencorse. Time has little changed the place in question. It stood, then as now, upon a cross road, out of call of human habitations, and buried fathom deep in the foliage of six cedar trees. The cries of the sheep upon the neighbouring hills, the streamlets upon either hand, one loudly singing among pebbles, the other dripping furtively from pond to pond, the stir of the wind in mountainous old flowering chestnuts, and, once in seven days, the voice of the bell and the old tunes of the precentor, were the only sounds that disturbed the silence round the rural church. The Resurrection Man – to use a by-name of the period – was not to be deterred by any of the sanctities of customary piety. It was part of his trade to despise and desecrate the scrolls and trumpets of old tombs, the paths worn by the feet of worshippers and mourners, and the offerings and the inscriptions of bereaved affection. To rustic neighbourhoods, where love is more than commonly tenacious, and where some bonds of blood or fellowship unite the entire society of a parish, the body snatcher, far from being repelled by natural respect, was attracted by the ease and safety of his task. To bodies that had been laid in the earth in joyful expectation of a far different awakening, there came that hasty, lamp-lit, terror-haunted resurrection of the spade and mattock; the coffin was forced, the cerements torn, and the melancholy relics, clad in sackcloth, after being rattled for hours on moonless byways, were at length exposed to uttermost indignities before a class of gaping boys.

Somewhat as two vultures may swoop upon a dying lamb, Fettes and Macfarlane were to be let loose upon a grave in that green and quiet resting-place. The wife of a farmer, a woman who had lived for sixty years, and been known for nothing but good butter and a godly conversation, was to be rooted from her grave at midnight, and carried, dead and naked, to that far-away city that she had always honoured with her Sunday's best; the place beside her family was to be empty till the crack of doom; her innocent and almost venerable members to be exposed to that last curiosity of the anatomist.

Late one afternoon the pair set forth, well wrapped in cloaks, and furnished with a formidable bottle. It rained without remission; a cold, dense, lashing rain; now and again there blew a puff of wind, but these sheets of falling water kept it down. Bottle and all, it was a sad and silent drive as far as Penicuik, where they were to spend the evening. They stopped once, to hide their implements in a thick bush not far from the churchyard; and once again at the Fisher's Tryst, to have a toast before the kitchen fire, and vary their nips of whisky with a glass of ale. When they reached their journey's end the gig was housed, the horse was fed and comforted, and the two young doctors, in a private room, sat down to the best dinner and the best wine the house afforded. The lights, the fire, the beating rain upon the window, the cold, incongruous work that lay before them, added zest to their enjoyment of the meal. With every glass their cordiality increased. Soon Macfarlane handed a little pile of gold to his companion.

'A compliment,' he said. 'Between friends these little d—d accommodations ought to fly like pipe-lights.'

Fettes pocketed the money, and applauded the sentiment to the echo. 'You are a philosopher,' he cried. 'I was an ass till I knew you. You and K— between you, by the Lord Harry, but you'll make a man of me.'

'Of course we shall,' applauded Macfarlane. 'A man? I'll tell you it required a man to back me up the other morning. There are some big, brawling, forty-year-old cowards would have turned sick at the look of the d—d thing; but not you – you kept your head. I watched you.'

'Well, and why not?' Fettes thus vaunted himself. 'It was no affair of mine. There was nothing to gain on the one side but disturbance, and on the other I could count on your gratitude, don't you see?' And he slapped his pocket till the gold pieces rang.

Macfarlane somehow felt a certain touch of alarm at these unpleasant words; he may have regretted that he had taught his young companion so successfully; but he had no time to interfere, for the other noisily continued in this boastful strain.

'The great thing is not to be afraid. Now, between you and me, I don't want to hang – that's practical – but for all cant, Macfarlane, I was born with a contempt. Hell, God, devil, right, wrong, sin, crime, and all that old gallery of curiosities – they may frighten boys, but men of the world, like you and me, despise them. Here's to the memory of Gray!'

It was by this time growing somewhat late. The gig, according to order, was brought round to the door with both lamps brightly shining, and the young men had to pay their bill and take the road. They announced that they were bound for Peebles, drove in that direction till they were clear of the last houses of the town; then, extinguishing the lamps, returned upon their course, and followed a by-road towards Glencorse. There was no sound but that of their own passage, and the incessant, strident pouring of the rain. It was pitch dark; here and there a white gate or a white stone in the wall guided them for a short space across the night; but for the most part it was at a foot's pace, and almost groping, that they picked their way through that resonant blackness to their solemn and isolated destination. In the sunken roads that traverse the neighbourhood of the burying-ground the last glimmer failed them, and it became necessary to kindle a match and reillume one of the lanterns of the gig. Thus, under the dripping trees, and environed by huge and moving shadows, they reached the scene of their unhallowed labours.

They were both experienced in such affairs, and powerful with the spade; and they had scarce been twenty minutes at their task before they were rewarded by a dull rattle on the coffin lid. At the same moment Macfarlane, having hurt his hand upon a stone, flung it carelessly above his head. The grave, in which they now stood almost to the shoulders, was close to the edge of the plateau of the graveyard; and the gig lamp had been propped, the better to illuminate their labours, against a tree, and on the immediate verge of the steep bank descending to the stream. Chance had taken a sure aim with the stone. Then came a clang of broken glass; night fell upon them; sounds alternately dull and ringing announced the bounding of the lantern down the bank, and its occasional collision with the trees; a stone or two, which it had dislodged in its descent, rattled behind it into the profundities of the glen; and then silence, like night, resumed its sway; and they might bend their hearing to its utmost pitch but nought was to be heard except the rain, now marching to the wind, now steadily falling over miles of open country.

They were so nearly at an end of their abhorred task that they judged it wiser to complete it in the dark. The coffin was exhumed and broken open; the body inserted in the dripping sack and carried between them to the gig; one mounted, to keep it in its place, and the other, taking the horse by the mouth, groped along by wall and bush, until they reached the wider road by the Fisher's Tryst. Here was a faint, diffused radiancy which they hailed like daylight; by that they pushed the horse to a good pace and began to rattle almost merrily in the direction of the town.

They had both been wetted to the skin during their operations, and now, as the gig jumped among the deep ruts, the thing that stood propped between them fell now upon the one and now upon the other. At every repetition of the horrid contact each instinctively repelled it with the greater haste; and the process, natural although it was, began to tell upon the nerves of the companions. Macfarlane made some ill-favoured jest about the farmer's wife, but it came hollowly from his lips, and was allowed to drop in silence. Still their unnatural burden bumped from side to side, and now the head would be laid, as if in confidence, upon their shoulders, and now the drenching sackcloth would flap icily about their faces. A creeping chill began to possess the soul of Fettes. He peered at the bundle, and it seemed somehow larger than at first. All over the countryside, and from every degree of distance, the farm dogs accompanied their passage with tragic ululations; and it grew and grew upon his mind that some unnatural miracle had been accomplished, that some nameless change had befallen the dead body, and that it was in fear of their unholy burden that the dogs were howling.

'For God's sake,' said he, making a great effort to arrive at speech, 'for God's sake let's have a light.'

Seemingly Macfarlane was affected in the same direction; for, though he made no reply, he stopped the horse, passed the reins to his companion, got down, and proceeded to kindle the remaining lamp. They had by that time got no farther than the cross road down to Auchenclinny. The rain still poured, as though the deluge were returning, and it was no easy matter to make a light in such a world of wet and darkness. When at last the flickering blue flame had been transferred to the wick, and began to expand and clarify, and shed a wide circle of misty brightness round the gig, it became possible for the two young men to see each other and the thing they had along with them. The rain had moulded the rough sacking to the outlines of the body underneath; the head was distinct from the trunk, the shoulders plainly modelled; something at once spectral and human riveted their eyes upon the ghastly comrade of their drive.

For some time Macfarlane stood motionless, holding up the hand. A nameless dread was swathed, like a wet sheet, about the body, and tightened the white skin upon the face of Fettes; a fear that was meaningless, a horror of what could not be, kept mounting in his brain. Another beat of the watch, and he had spoken; but his comrade forestalled him.

'That is not a woman,' said Macfarlane, in a hushed voice.

'It was a woman when we put her in,' whispered Fettes.

'Hold that lamp,' said the other; 'I must see her face.'

And as Fettes took the lamp his companion untied the fastenings of the sack and drew down the cover from the head. The light fell very clear upon the dark, well-moulded features and smooth-shaven cheeks of a too familiar countenance, often beheld in dreams by both of these young men. A wild yell rang up into the night; each leaped from his own side into the roadway; the lamp fell, broke, and was extinguished; and the horse, terrified by this unusual commotion, bounded and went off towards Edinburgh at the gallop, bearing along with it, sole occupant of the gig, the body of the long dead and long dissected Gray.

ARTHUR CONAN DOYLE

Silver Blaze

'I am afraid, Watson, that I shall have to go,' said Holmes as we sat down together to our breakfast one morning.

'Go! Where to?'

'To Dartmoor; to King's Pyland.'

I was not surprised. Indeed, my only wonder was that he had not already been mixed up in this extraordinary case, which was the one topic of conversation through the length and breadth of England. For a whole day my companion had rambled about the room with his chin upon his chest and his brows knitted, charging and recharging his pipe with the strongest black tobacco, and absolutely deaf to any of my questions or remarks. Fresh editions of every paper had been sent up by our news agent, only to be glanced over and tossed down into a corner. Yet, silent as he was, I knew perfectly well what it was over which he was brooding. There was but one problem before the public which could challenge his powers of analysis, and that was the singular disappearance of the favourite for the Wessex Cup, and the tragic murder of its trainer. When, therefore, he suddenly announced his intention of setting out for the scene of the drama, it was only what I had both expected and hoped for.

'I should be most happy to go down with you if I should not be in the way,' said I.

'My dear Watson, you would confer a great favour upon me by coming. And I think that your time will not be misspent, for there are points about the case which promise to make it an absolutely unique one. We have, I think, just time to catch our train at Paddington, and I will go further into the matter upon our journey. You would oblige me by bringing with you your very excellent field-glass.'

And so it happened that an hour or so later I found myself in the corner of a first-class carriage flying along en route for Exeter, while Sherlock Holmes, with his sharp, eager face framed in his ear-flapped travelling-cap, dipped rapidly into the bundle of fresh papers which he had procured at Paddington. We had left Reading far behind us before he thrust the last one of them under the seat and offered me his cigar-case.

'We are going well,' said he, looking out of the window and glancing at his watch. 'Our rate at present is fifty-three and a half miles an hour.'

'I have not observed the quarter-mile posts,' said I.

'Nor have I. But the telegraph posts upon this line are sixty yards apart, and the calculation is a simple one. I presume that you have looked into this matter of the murder of John Straker and the disappearance of Silver Blaze?'

'I have seen what the *Telegraph* and the *Chronicle* have to say.'

'It is one of those cases where the art of the reasoner should be used rather for the sifting of details than for the acquiring of fresh evidence. The tragedy has been so uncommon, so complete, and of such personal importance to so many people that we are suffering from a plethora of surmise, conjecture, and hypothesis. The difficulty is to detach the frame-work of fact – of absolute undeniable fact – from the embellishments of theorists and reporters. Then, having established ourselves upon this sound basis, it is our duty to see what inferences may be drawn and what are the special points upon which the whole mystery turns. On Tuesday evening I received telegrams from both Colonel Ross, the owner of the horse, and from Inspector Gregory, who is looking after the case, inviting my coöperation.'

'Tuesday evening!' I exclaimed. 'And this is Thursday morning. Why didn't you go down yesterday?'

'Because I made a blunder, my dear Watson – which is, I am afraid, a more common occurrence than anyone would think who only knew me through your memoirs. The fact is that I could not believe it possible that the most remarkable horse in England could long remain concealed, espe-cially in so sparsely inhabited a place as the north of Dartmoor. From hour to hour yesterday I expected to hear that he had been found, and that his abductor was the murderer of John Straker. When, however, another morning had come and I found that beyond the arrest of young

Fitzroy Simpson nothing had been done, I felt that it was time for me to take action. Yet in some ways I feel that yesterday has not been wasted.'

'You have formed a theory, then?'

'At least I have got a grip of the essential facts of the case. I shall enumerate them to you, for nothing clears up a case so much as stating it to another person, and I can hardly expect your coöperation if I do not show you the position from which we start.'

I lay back against the cushions, puffing at my cigar, while Holmes, leaning forward, with his long, thin forefinger checking off the points upon the palm of his left hand, gave me a sketch of the events which had led to our journey.

'Silver Blaze,' said he, 'is from the Somomy stock and holds as brilliant a record as his famous ancestor. He is now in his fifth year and has brought in turn each of the prizes of the turf to Colonel Ross, his fortunate owner. Up to the time of the catastrophe he was the first favourite for the Wessex Cup, the betting being three to one on him. He has always, however, been a prime favourite with the racing public and has never yet disappointed them, so that even at those odds enormous sums of money have been laid upon him. It is obvious, therefore, that there were many people who had the strongest interest in preventing Silver Blaze from being there at the fall of the flag next Tuesday.

'The fact was, of course, appreciated at King's Pyland, where the colonel's training-stable is situated. Every precaution was taken to guard the favourite. The trainer, John Straker, is a retired jockey who rode in Colonel Ross's colours before he became too heavy for the weighing-chair. He has served the colonel for five years as jockey and for seven as trainer, and has always shown himself to be a zealous and honest servant. Under him were three lads, for the establishment was a small one, containing only four horses in all. One of these lads sat up each night in the stable, while the others slept in the loft. All three bore excellent characters. John Straker, who is a married man, lived in a small villa about two hundred yards from the stables. He has no children, keeps one maidservant, and is comfortably off. The country round is very lonely, but about half a mile to the north there is a small cluster of villas which have been built by a Tavistock contractor for the use of invalids and others who may wish to enjoy the pure Dartmoor air. Tavistock itself lies two miles to the west, while across the moor, also about two miles distant, is the larger training establishment of Mapleton, which belongs to Lord Backwater and is managed by Silas Brown. In every other direction the moor is a complete wilderness, inhabited only by a few roaming gypsies. Such was the general situation last Monday night when the catastrophe occurred.

'On that evening the horses had been exercised and watered as usual, and the stables were locked up at nine o'clock. Two of the lads walked up to the trainer's house, where they had supper in the kitchen, while the third, Ned Hunter, remained on guard. At a few minutes after nine the maid, Edith Baxter, carried down to the stables his supper, which consisted of a dish of curried mutton. She took no liquid, as there was a water-tap in the stables, and it was the rule that the lad on duty should drink nothing else. The maid carried a lantern with her, as it was very dark and the path ran across the open moor.

'Edith Baxter was within thirty yards of the stables when a man appeared out of the darkness and called to her to stop. As he stepped into the circle of yellow light thrown by the lantern she saw that he was a person of gentlemanly bearing, dressed in a gray suit of tweeds, with a cloth cap. He wore gaiters and carried a heavy stick with a knob to it. She was most impressed, however, by the extreme pallor of his face and by the nervousness of his manner. His age, she thought, would be rather over thirty than under it.

'"Can you tell me where I am?" he asked. "I had almost made up my mind to sleep on the moor when I saw the light of your lantern."

'"You are close to the King's Pyland training stables," said she.

'"Oh, indeed! What a stroke of luck!" he cried. "I understand that a stable-boy sleeps there alone every night. Perhaps that is his supper which you are carrying to him. Now I am sure that you would not be too proud to earn the price of a new dress, would you?" He took a piece of white paper folded up out of his waistcoat pocket. "See that the boy has this to-night, and you shall have the prettiest frock that money can buy."

'She was frightened by the earnestness of his manner and ran past him to the window through which she was accustomed to hand the meals. It was already opened, and Hunter was seated at the small table inside. She had begun to tell him of what had happened when the stranger came up again.

341

'"Good-evening," said he, looking through the window. "I wanted to have a word with you." The girl has sworn that as he spoke she noticed the corner of the little paper packet protruding from his closed hand.

'"What business have you here?" asked the lad.

'"It's business that may put something into your pocket," said the other. "You've two horses in for the Wessex Cup – Silver Blaze and Bayard. Let me have the straight tip and you won't be a loser. Is it a fact that at the weights Bayard could give the other a hundred yards in five furlongs, and that the stable have put their money on him?"

'"So, you're one of those damned touts!" cried the lad. "I'll show you how we serve them in King's Pyland." He sprang up and rushed across the stable to unloose the dog. The girl fled away to the house, but as she ran she looked back and saw that the stranger was leaning through the window. A minute later, however, when Hunter rushed out with the hound he was gone, and though he ran all round the buildings he failed to find any trace of him.'

'One moment,' I asked. 'Did the stable-boy, when he ran out with the dog, leave the door unlocked behind him?'

'Excellent, Watson, excellent!' murmured my companion. 'The importance of the point struck me so forcibly that I sent a special wire to Dartmoor yesterday to clear the matter up. The boy locked the door before he left it. The window, I may add, was not large enough for a man to get through.

'Hunter waited until his fellow-grooms had returned, when he sent a message to the trainer and told him what had occurred. Straker was excited at hearing the account, although he does not seem to have quite realized its true significance. It left him, however, vaguely uneasy, and Mrs Straker, waking at one in the morning, found that he was dressing. In reply to her inquiries, he said that he could not sleep on account of his anxiety about the horses, and that he intended to walk down to the stables to see that all was well. She begged him to remain at home, as she could hear the rain pattering against the window, but in spite of her entreaties he pulled on his large mackintosh and left the house.

'Mrs Straker awoke at seven in the morning to find that her husband had not yet returned. She dressed herself hastily, called the maid, and set off for the stables. The door was open; inside, huddled together upon a chair, Hunter was sunk in a state of absolute stupor, the favourite's stall was empty, and there were no signs of his trainer.

'The two lads who slept in the chaff-cutting loft above the harness-room were quickly aroused. They had heard nothing during the night, for they are both sound sleepers. Hunter was obviously under the influence of some powerful drug, and as no sense could be got out of him, he was left to sleep it off while the two lads and the two women ran out in search of the absentees. They still had hopes that the trainer had for some reason taken out the horse for early exercise, but on ascending the knoll near the house, from which all the neighbouring moors were visible, they not only could see no signs of the missing favourite, but they perceived something which warned them that they were in the presence of a tragedy.

'About a quarter of a mile from the stables John Straker's overcoat was flapping from a furze-bush. Immediately beyond there was a bowl-shaped depression in the moor, and at the bottom of this was found the dead body of the unfortunate trainer. His head had been shattered by a savage blow from some heavy weapon, and he was wounded on the thigh, where there was a long, clean cut, inflicted evidently by some very sharp instrument. It was clear, however, that Straker had defended himself vigorously against his assailants, for in his right hand he held a small knife, which was clotted with blood up to the handle, while in his left he clasped a red and black silk cravat, which was recognized by the maid as having been worn on the preceding evening by the stranger who had visited the stables. Hunter, on recovering from his stupor, was also quite positive as to the ownership of the cravat. He was equally certain that the same stranger had, while standing at the window, drugged his curried mutton, and so deprived the stables of their watchman. As to the missing horse, there were abundant proofs in the mud which lay at the bottom of the fatal hollow that he had been there at the time of the struggle. But from that morning he has disappeared, and although a large reward has been offered, and all the gypsies of Dartmoor are on the alert, no news has come of him. Finally, an analysis has shown that the remains of his supper left by the stable-lad contained an appreciable quantity of powdered opium, while the people at the house partook of the same dish on the same night without any ill effect.

'Those are the main facts of the case, stripped of all surmise, and stated as baldly as possible. I shall now recapitulate what the police have done in the matter.

'Inspector Gregory, to whom the case has been committed, is an extremely competent officer. Were he but gifted with imagination he might rise to great heights in his profession. On his arrival he promptly found and arrested the man upon whom suspicion naturally rested. There was little difficulty in finding him, for he inhabited one of those villas which I have mentioned. His name, it appears, was Fitzroy Simpson. He was a man of excellent birth and education, who had squandered a fortune upon the turf, and who lived now by doing a little quiet and genteel book-making in the sporting clubs of London. An examination of his betting-book shows that bets to the amount of five thousand pounds had been registered by him against the favourite. On being arrested he volunteered the statement that he had come down to Dartmoor in the hope of getting some information about the King's Pyland horses, and also about Desborough, the second favourite, which was in charge of Silas Brown at the Mapleton stables. He did not attempt to deny that he had acted as described upon the evening before, but declared that he had no sinister designs and had simply wished to obtain first-hand information. When confronted with his cravat he turned very pale and was utterly unable to account for its presence in the hand of the murdered man. His wet clothing showed that he had been out in the storm of the night before, and his stick, which was a penang-lawyer weighted with lead, was just such a weapon as might, by repeated blows, have inflicted the terrible injuries to which the trainer had succumbed. On the other hand, there was no wound upon his person, while the state of Straker's knife would show that one at least of his assailants must bear his mark upon him. There you have it all in a nutshell, Watson, and if you can give me any light I shall be infinitely obliged to you.'

I had listened with the greatest interest to the statement which Holmes, with characteristic clearness, had laid before me. Though most of the facts were familiar to me, I had not sufficiently appreciated their relative importance, nor their connection to each other.

'Is it not possible,' I suggested, 'that the incised wound upon Straker may have been caused by his own knife in the convulsive struggles which follow any brain injury?'

'It is more than possible; it is probable,' said Holmes. 'In that case one of the main points in favour of the accused disappears.'

'And yet,' said I, 'even now I fail to understand what the theory of the police can be.'

'I am afraid that whatever theory we state has very grave objections to it,' returned my companion. 'The police imagine, I take it, that this Fitzroy Simpson, having drugged the lad, and having in some way obtained a duplicate key, opened the stable door and took out the horse, with the intention, apparently, of kidnapping him altogether. His bridle is missing, so that Simpson must have put this on. Then, having left the door open behind him, he was leading the horse away over the moor when he was either met or overtaken by the trainer. A row naturally ensued. Simpson beat out the trainer's brains with his heavy stick without receiving any injury from the small knife which Straker used in self-defence, and then the thief either led the horse on to some secret hiding-place, or else it may have bolted during the struggle, and be now wandering out on the moors. That is the case as it appears to the police, and improbable as it is, all other explanations are more improbable still. However, I shall very quickly test the matter when I am once upon the spot, and until then I cannot really see how we can get much further than our present position.'

It was evening before we reached the little town of Tavistock, which lies, like the boss of a shield, in the middle of the huge circle of Dartmoor. Two gentlemen were awaiting us in the station – the one a tall, fair man with lion-like hair and beard and curiously penetrating light blue eyes; the other a small, alert person, very neat and dapper, in a frock-coat and gaiters, with trim little side-whiskers and an eyeglass. The latter was Colonel Ross, the well-known sportsman; the other, Inspector Gregory, a man who was rapidly making his name in the English detective service.

'I am delighted that you have come down, Mr Holmes,' said the colonel. 'The inspector here has done all that could possibly be suggested, but I wish to leave no stone unturned in trying to avenge poor Straker and in recovering my horse.'

'Have there been any fresh developments?' asked Holmes.

'I am sorry to say that we have made very little progress,' said the inspector. 'We have an open carriage outside, and as you would no doubt like to see the place before the light fails, we might talk it over as we drive.'

A minute later we were all seated in a comfortable landau and were rattling through the quaint old Devonshire city. Inspector Gregory was full of his case and poured out a stream of remarks, while Holmes threw in an occasional question or interjection. Colonel Ross leaned back with his arms folded and his hat tilted over his eyes, while I listened with interest to the dialogue of the two detectives. Gregory was formulating his theory, which was almost exactly what Holmes had foretold in the train.

'The net is drawn pretty close round Fitzroy Simpson,' he remarked, 'and I believe myself that he is our man. At the same time I recognize that the evidence is purely circumstantial, and that some new development may upset it.'

'How about Straker's knife?'

'We have quite come to the conclusion that he wounded himself in his fall.'

'My friend Dr Watson made that suggestion to me as we came down. If so, it would tell against this man Simpson.'

'Undoubtedly. He has neither a knife nor any sign of a wound. The evidence against him is certainly very strong. He had a great interest in the disappearance of the favourite. He lies under suspicion of having poisoned the stable-boy; he was undoubtedly out in the storm; he was armed with a heavy stick, and his cravat was found in the dead man's hand. I really think we have enough to go before a jury.'

Holmes shook his head. 'A clever counsel would tear it all to rags,' said he. 'Why should he take the horse out of the stable? If he wished to injure it, why could he not do it there? Has a duplicate key been found in his possession? What chemist sold him the powdered opium? Above all, where could he, a stranger to the district, hide a horse, and such a horse as this? What is his own explanation as to the paper which he wished the maid to give to the stable-boy?'

'He says that it was a ten-pound note. One was found in his purse. But your other difficulties are not so formidable as they seem. He is not a stranger to the district. He has twice lodged at Tavistock in the summer. The opium was probably brought from London. The key, having served its purpose, would be hurled away. The horse may be at the bottom of one of the pits or old mines upon the moor.'

'What does he say about the cravat?'

'He acknowledges that it is his and declares that he had lost it. But a new element has been introduced into the case which may account for his leading the horse from the stable.'

Holmes pricked up his ears.

'We have found traces which show that a party of gypsies encamped on Monday night within a mile of the spot where the murder took place. On Tuesday they were gone. Now, presuming that there was some understanding between Simpson and these gypsies, might he not have been leading the horse to them when he was overtaken, and may they not have him now?'

'It is certainly possible.'

'The moor is being scoured for these gypsies. I have also examined every stable and outhouse in Tavistock, and for a radius of ten miles.'

'There is another training-stable quite close, I understand?'

'Yes, and that is a factor which we must certainly not neglect. As Desborough, their horse, was second in the betting, they had an interest in the disappearance of the favourite. Silas Brown, the trainer, is known to have had large bets upon the event, and he was no friend to poor Straker. We have, however, examined the stables, and there is nothing to connect him with the affair.'

'And nothing to connect this man Simpson with the interests of the Mapleton stables?'

'Nothing at all.'

Holmes leaned back in the carriage, and the conversation ceased. A few minutes later our driver pulled up at a neat little red-brick villa with overhanging eaves which stood by the road. Some distance off, across a paddock, lay a long gray-tiled outbuilding. In every other direction the low curves of the moor, bronze-coloured from the fading ferns, stretched away to the sky-line, broken only by the steeples of Tavistock, and by a cluster of houses away to the westward which marked the Mapleton stables. We all sprang out with the exception of Holmes, who continued to lean back with his eyes fixed upon the sky in front of him, entirely absorbed in his own thoughts. It was only when I touched his arm that he roused himself with a violent start and stepped out of the carriage.

'Excuse me,' said he, turning to Colonel Ross, who had looked at him in some surprise. 'I was day-dreaming.' There was a gleam in his eyes and a suppressed excitement in his manner which convinced me, used as I was to his ways, that his hand was upon a clue, though I could not imagine where he had found it.

'Perhaps you would prefer at once to go on to the scene of the crime, Mr Holmes?' said Gregory.

'I think that I should prefer to stay here a little and go into one or two questions of detail. Straker was brought back here, I presume?'

'Yes, he lies upstairs. The inquest is to-morrow.'

'He has been in your service some years, Colonel Ross?'

'I have always found him an excellent servant.'

'I presume that you made an inventory of what he had in his pockets at the time of his death, Inspector?'

'I have the things themselves in the sitting-room if you would care to see them.'

'I should be very glad.' We all filed into the front room and sat round the central table while the inspector unlocked a square tin box and laid a small heap of things before us. There was a box of vestas, two inches of tallow candle, an A D P brier-root pipe, a pouch of sealskin with half an ounce of long-cut Cavendish, a silver watch with a gold chain, five sovereigns in gold, an aluminum pencil-case, a few papers, and an ivory-handled knife with a very delicate, inflexible blade marked Weiss & Co., London.

'This is a very singular knife,' said Holmes, lifting it up and examining it minutely. 'I presume, as I see blood-stains upon it, that it is the one which was found in the dead man's grasp. Watson, this knife is surely in your line?'

'It is what we call a cataract knife,' said I.

'I thought so. A very delicate blade devised for very delicate work. A strange thing for a man to carry with him upon a rough expedition, especially as it would not shut in his pocket.'

'The tip was guarded by a disc of cork which we found beside his body,' said the inspector. 'His wife tells us that the knife had lain upon the dressing-table, and that he had picked it up as he left the room. It was a poor weapon, but perhaps the best that he could lay his hands on at the moment.'

'Very possibly. How about these papers?'

'Three of them are receipted hay-dealers' accounts. One of them is a letter of instructions from Colonel Ross. This other is a milliner's account for thirty-seven pounds fifteen made out by Madame Lesurier, of Bond Street, to William Derbyshire. Mrs Straker tells us that Derbyshire was a friend of her husband's, and that occasionally his letters were addressed here.'

'Madame Derbyshire had somewhat expensive tastes,' remarked Holmes, glancing down the account. 'Twenty-two guineas is rather heavy for a single costume. However, there appears to be nothing more to learn, and we may now go down to the scene of the crime.'

As we emerged from the sitting-room a woman, who had been waiting in the passage, took a step forward and laid her hand upon the inspector's sleeve. Her face was haggard and thin and eager, stamped with the print of a recent horror.

'Have you got them? Have you found them?' she panted.

'No, Mrs Straker. But Mr Holmes here has come from London to help us, and we shall do all that is possible.'

'Surely I met you in Plymouth at a garden-party some little time ago, Mrs Straker?' said Holmes.

'No, sir; you are mistaken.'

'Dear me! Why, I could have sworn to it. You wore a costume of dove-coloured silk with ostrich-feather trimming.'

'I never had such a dress, sir,' answered the lady.

'Ah, that quite settles it,' said Holmes. And with an apology he followed the inspector outside. A short walk across the moor took us to the hollow in which the body had been found. At the brink of it was the furze-bush upon which the coat had been hung.

'There was no wind that night, I understand,' said Holmes.

'None, but very heavy rain.'

'In that case the overcoat was not blown against the furze-bush, but placed there.'

'Yes, it was laid across the bush.'

'You fill me with interest. I perceive that the ground has been trampled up a good deal. No doubt many feet have been here since Monday night.'

'A piece of matting has been laid here at the side, and we have all stood upon that.'

'Excellent.'

'In this bag I have one of the boots which Straker wore, one of Fitzroy Simpson's shoes, and a cast horseshoe of Silver Blaze.'

'My dear Inspector, you surpass yourself!' Holmes took the bag, and, descending into the hollow, he pushed the matting into a more central position. Then stretching himself upon his face and leaning his chin upon his hands, he made a careful study of the trampled mud in front of him. 'Hullo!' said he suddenly. 'What's this?' It was a wax vesta, half burned, which was so coated with mud that it looked at first like a little chip of wood.

'I cannot think how I came to overlook it,' said the inspector with an expression of annoyance.

'It was invisible, buried in the mud. I only saw it because I was looking for it.'

'What! you expected to find it?'

'I thought it not unlikely.'

He took the boots from the bag and compared the impressions of each of them with marks upon the ground. Then he clambered up to the rim of the hollow and crawled about among the ferns and bushes.

'I am afraid that there are no more tracks,' said the inspector. 'I have examined the ground very carefully for a hundred yards in each direction.'

'Indeed!' said Holmes, rising. 'I should not have the impertinence to do it again after what you say. But I should like to take a little walk over the moor before it grows dark that I may know my ground to-morrow, and I think that I shall put this horseshoe into my pocket for luck.'

Colonel Ross, who had shown some signs of impatience at my companion's quiet and systematic method of work, glanced at his watch. 'I wish you would come back with me, Inspector,' said he. 'There are several points on which I should like your advice, and especially as to whether we do not owe it to the public to remove our horse's name from the entries for the cup.'

'Certainly not,' cried Holmes with decision. 'I should let the name stand.'

The colonel bowed. 'I am very glad to have had your opinion, sir,' said he. 'You will find us at poor Straker's house when you have finished your walk, and we can drive together into Tavistock.'

He turned back with the inspector, while Holmes and I walked slowly across the moor. The sun was beginning to sink behind the stable of Mapleton, and the long, sloping plain in front of us was tinged with gold, deepening into rich, ruddy browns where the faded ferns and brambles caught the evening light. But the glories of the landscape were all wasted upon my companion, who was sunk in the deepest thought.

'It's this way, Watson,' said he at last. 'We may leave the question of who killed John Straker for the instant and confine ourselves to finding out what has become of the horse. Now, supposing that he broke away during or after the tragedy, where could he have gone to? The horse is a very gregarious creature. If left to himself his instincts would have been either to return to King's Pyland or go over to Mapleton. Why should he run wild upon the moor? He would surely have been seen by now. And why should gypsies kidnap him? These people always clear out when they hear of trouble, for they do not wish to be pestered by the police. They could not hope to sell such a horse. They would run a great risk and gain nothing by taking him. Surely that is clear.'

'Where is he, then?'

'I have already said that he must have gone to King's Pyland or to Mapleton. He is not at King's Pyland. Therefore he is at Mapleton. Let us take that as a working hypothesis and see what it leads us to. This part of the moor, as the inspector remarked, is very hard and dry. But it falls away towards Mapleton, and you can see from here that there is a long hollow over yonder, which must have been very wet on Monday night. If our supposition is correct, then the horse must have crossed that, and there is the point where we should look for his tracks.'

We had been walking briskly during this conversation, and a few more minutes brought us to the hollow in question. At Holmes's request I walked down the bank to the right, and he to the left, but I had not taken fifty paces before I heard him give a shout and saw him waving his hand to me. The track of a horse was plainly outlined in the soft earth in front of him, and the shoe which he took from his pocket exactly fitted the impression.

'See the value of imagination,' said Holmes. 'It is the one quality which

Gregory lacks. We imagined what might have happened, acted upon the supposition, and find ourselves justified. Let us proceed.'

We crossed the marshy bottom and passed over a quarter of a mile of dry, hard turf. Again the ground sloped, and again we came on the tracks. Then we lost them for half a mile, but only to pick them up once more quite close to Mapleton. It was Holmes who saw them first, and he stood pointing with a look of triumph upon his face. A man's track was visible beside the horse's.

'The horse was alone before,' I cried.

'Quite so. It was alone before. Hullo, what is this?'

The double track turned sharp off and took the direction of King's Pyland. Holmes whistled, and we both followed along after it. His eyes were on the trail, but I happened to look a little to one side and saw to my surprise the same tracks coming back again in the opposite direction.

'One for you, Watson,' said Holmes when I pointed it out. 'You have saved us a long walk, which would have brought us back on our own traces. Let us follow the return track.'

We had not to go far. It ended at the paving of asphalt which led up to the gates of the Mapleton stables. As we approached, a groom ran out from them.

'We don't want any loiterers about here,' said he.

'I only wished to ask a question,' said Holmes, with his finger and thumb in his waistcoat pocket. 'Should I be too early to see your master, Mr Silas Brown, if I were to call at five o'clock to-morrow morning?'

'Bless you, sir, if anyone is about he will be, for he is always the first stirring. But here he is, sir, to answer your questions for himself. No, sir, no, it is as much as my place is worth to let him see me touch your money. Afterwards, if you like.'

As Sherlock Holmes replaced the half-crown which he had drawn from his pocket, a fierce-looking elderly man strode out from the gate with a hunting-crop swinging in his hand.

'What's this, Dawson!' he cried. 'No gossiping! Go about your business! And you, what the devil do you want here?'

'Ten minutes' talk with you, my good sir,' said Holmes in the sweetest of voices.

'I've no time to talk to every gadabout. We want no strangers here. Be off, or you may find a dog at your heels.'

Holmes leaned forward and whispered something in the trainer's ear. He started violently and flushed to the temples.

'It's a lie!' he shouted. 'An infernal lie!'

'Very good. Shall we argue about it here in public or talk it over in your parlour?'

'Oh, come in if you wish to.'

Holmes smiled. 'I shall not keep you more than a few minutes, Watson,' said he. 'Now, Mr Brown, I am quite at your disposal.'

It was twenty minutes, and the reds had all faded into grays before Holmes and the trainer reappeared. Never have I seen such a change as had been brought about in Silas Brown in that short time. His face was ashy pale, beads of perspiration shone upon his brow, and his hands shook until the hunting-crop wagged like a branch in the wind. His bullying, overbearing manner was all gone too, and he cringed along at my companion's side like a dog with its master.

'Your instructions will be done. It shall all be done,' said he.

'There must be no mistake,' said Holmes, looking round at him. The other winced as he read the menace in his eyes.

'Oh, no, there shall be no mistake. It shall be there. Should I change it first or not?'

Holmes thought a little and then burst out laughing. 'No, don't,' said he, 'I shall write to you about it. No tricks, now, or—'

'Oh, you can trust me, you can trust me!'

'Yes, I think I can. Well, you shall hear from me to-morrow.' He turned upon his heel, disregarding the trembling hand which the other held out to him, and we set off for King's Pyland.

'A more perfect compound of the bully, coward, and sneak than Master Silas Brown I have seldom met with,' remarked Holmes as we trudged along together.

'He has the horse, then?'

'He tried to bluster out of it, but I described to him so exactly what his actions had been upon that morning that he is convinced that I was watching him. Of course you observed the peculiarly square toes in the impressions, and that his own boots exactly corresponded to them. Again, of course no subordinate would have dared to do such a thing. I described to him how, when according to his custom he was the first down, he perceived a strange horse wandering over the moor. How he went out to it, and his astonishment at recognizing, from the white forehead which has given the favourite its name, that chance had put in his power the only horse which could beat the one upon which he had put his money. Then I described how his first impulse had been to lead him back to King's Pyland, and how the devil had shown him how he could hide the horse until the race was over, and how he had led it back and concealed it at Mapleton. When I told him every detail he gave it up and thought only of saving his own skin.'

'But his stables had been searched?'

'Oh, an old horse-faker like him has many a dodge.'

'But are you not afraid to leave the horse in his power now, since he has every interest in injuring it?'

'My dear fellow, he will guard it as the apple of his eye. He knows that his only hope of mercy is to produce it safe.'

'Colonel Ross did not impress me as a man who would be likely to show much mercy in any case.'

'The matter does not rest with Colonel Ross. I follow my own methods and tell as much or as little as I choose. That is the advantage of being unofficial. I don't know whether you observed it, Watson, but the colonel's manner has been just a trifle cavalier to me. I am inclined now to have a little amusement at his expense. Say nothing to him about the horse.'

'Certainly not without your permission.'

'And of course this is all quite a minor point compared to the question of who killed John Straker.'

'And you will devote yourself to that?'

'On the contrary, we both go back to London by the night train.'

I was thunderstruck by my friend's words. We had only been a few hours in Devonshire, and that he should give up an investigation which he had begun so brilliantly was quite incomprehensible to me. Not a word more could I draw from him until we were back at the trainer's house. The colonel and the inspector were awaiting us in the parlour.

'My friend and I return to town by the night-express,' said Holmes. 'We have had a charming little breath of your beautiful Dartmoor air.'

The inspector opened his eyes, and the colonel's lip curled in a sneer.

'So you despair of arresting the murderer of poor Straker,' said he.

Holmes shrugged his shoulders. 'There are certainly grave difficulties in the way,' said he. 'I have every hope, however, that your horse will start upon Tuesday, and I beg that you will have your jockey in readiness. Might I ask for a photograph of Mr John Straker?'

The inspector took one from an envelope and handed it to him.

'My dear Gregory, you anticipate all my wants. If I might ask you to wait here for an instant, I have a question which I should like to put to the maid.'

'I must say that I am rather disappointed in our London consultant,' said Colonel Ross bluntly as my friend left the room. 'I do not see that we are any further than when he came.'

'At least you have his assurance that your horse will run,' said I.

'Yes, I have his assurance,' said the colonel with a shrug of his shoulders. 'I should prefer to have the horse.'

I was about to make some reply in defence of my friend when he entered the room again.

'Now, gentlemen,' said he, 'I am quite ready for Tavistock.'

As we stepped into the carriage one of the stable-lads held the door open for us. A sudden idea seemed to occur to Holmes, for he leaned forward and touched the lad upon the sleeve.

'You have a few sheep in the paddock,' he said. 'Who attends to them?'

'I do, sir.'

'Have you noticed anything amiss with them of late?'

'Well, sir, not of much account, but three of them have gone lame, sir.'

I could see that Holmes was extremely pleased, for he chuckled and rubbed his hands together.

'A long shot, Watson, a very long shot,' said he, pinching my arm. 'Gregory, let me recommend to your attention this singular epidemic among the sheep. Drive on, coachman!'

Colonel Ross still wore an expression which showed the poor opinion which he had formed of my companion's ability, but I saw by the inspector's face that his attention had been keenly aroused.

'You consider that to be important?' he asked.

'Exceedingly so.'

'Is there any point to which you would wish to draw my attention?'

'To the curious incident of the dog in the night-time.'

'The dog did nothing in the night-time.'

'That was the curious incident,' remarked Sherlock Holmes.

Four days later Holmes and I were again in the train, bound for Winchester to see the race for the Wessex Cup. Colonel Ross met us by appointment outside the station, and we drove in his drag to the course beyond the town. His face was grave, and his manner was cold in the extreme.

'I have seen nothing of my horse,' said he.

'I suppose that you would know him when you saw him?' asked Holmes.

The colonel was very angry. 'I have been on the turf for twenty years and never was asked such a question as that before,' said he. 'A child would know Silver Blaze with his white forehead and his mottled off-foreleg.'

'How is the betting?'

'Well, that is the curious part of it. You could have got fifteen to one yesterday, but the price has become shorter and shorter, until you can hardly get three to one now.'

'Hum!' said Holmes. 'Somebody knows something, that is clear.'

As the drag drew up in the enclosure near the grandstand I glanced at the card to see the entries.

Wessex Plate [it ran] 50 sovs. each h ft with 1000 sovs. added, for four and five year olds. Second, £300. Third, £200. New course (one mile and five furlongs).

1. Mr Heath Newton's The Negro. Red cap. Cinnamon jacket.
2. Colonel Wardlaw's Pugilist. Pink cap. Blue and black jacket.
3. Lord Backwater's Desborough. Yellow cap and sleeves.
4. Colonel Ross's Silver Blaze. Black cap. Red jacket.
5. Duke of Balmoral's Iris. Yellow and black stripes.
6. Lord Singleford's Rasper. Purple cap. Black sleeves.

'We scratched our other one and put all hopes on your word,' said the colonel. 'Why, what is that? Silver Blaze favourite?'

'Five to four against Silver Blaze!' roared the ring. 'Five to four against Silver Blaze! Five to fifteen against Desborough! Five to four on the field!'

'There are the numbers up,' I cried. 'They are all six there.'

'All six there? Then my horse is running,' cried the colonel in great agitation. 'But I don't see him. My colours have not passed.'

'Only five have passed. This must be he.'

As I spoke a powerful bay horse swept out from the weighing enclosure and cantered past us, bearing on its back the well-known black and red of the colonel.

'That's not my horse,' cried the owner. 'That beast has not a white hair upon its body. What is this that you have done, Mr Holmes?'

'Well, well, let us see how he gets on,' said my friend imperturbably. For a few minutes he gazed through my field-glass. 'Capital! An excellent start!' he cried suddenly. 'There they are, coming round the curve!'

From our drag we had a superb view as they came up the straight. The six horses were so close together that a carpet could have covered them, but halfway up the yellow of the Mapleton stable showed to the front. Before they reached us, however, Desborough's bolt was shot, and the colonel's horse, coming away with a rush, passed the post a good six lengths before its rival, the Duke of Balmoral's Iris making a bad third.

'It's my race, anyhow,' gasped the colonel, passing his hand over his eyes. 'I confess that I can make neither head nor tail of it. Don't you think that you have kept up your mystery long enough, Mr Holmes?'

'Certainly, Colonel, you shall know everything. Let us all go round and have a look at the horse together. Here he is,' he continued as we made our way into the weighing enclosure, where only owners and their friends find admittance. 'You have only to wash his face and his leg in spirits of wine, and you will find that he is the same old Silver Blaze as ever.'

'You take my breath away!'

'I found him in the hands of a faker and took the liberty of running him just as he was sent over.'

'My dear sir, you have done wonders. The horse looks very fit and well. It never went better in its life. I owe you a thousand apologies for having doubted your ability. You have done me a great service by recovering my horse. You would do me a greater still if you could lay your hands on the murderer of John Straker.'

'I have done so,' said Holmes quietly.

The colonel and I stared at him in amazement. 'You have got him! Where is he, then?'

'He is here.'

'Here! Where?'

'In my company at the present moment.'

The colonel flushed angrily. 'I quite recognize that I am under obligations to you, Mr Holmes,' said he, 'but I must regard what you have just said as either a very bad joke or an insult.'

Sherlock Holmes laughed. 'I assure you that I have not associated you with the crime, Colonel,' said he. 'The real murderer is standing immediately behind you.' He stepped past and laid his hand upon the glossy neck of the thoroughbred.

'The horse!' cried both the colonel and myself.

'Yes, the horse. And it may lessen his guilt if I say that it was done in self-defence, and that John Straker was a man who was entirely unworthy of your confidence. But there goes the bell, and as I stand to win a little on this next race, I shall defer a lengthy explanation until a more fitting time.'

We had the corner of a Pullman car to ourselves that evening as we whirled back to London, and I fancy that the journey was a short one to Colonel Ross as well as to myself as we listened to our companion's narrative of the events which had occurred at the Dartmoor training-stables upon that Monday night, and the means by which he had unravelled them.

'I confess,' said he, 'that any theories which I had formed from the newspaper reports were entirely erroneous. And yet there were indications there, had they not been overlaid by other details which concealed their true import. I went to Devonshire with the conviction that Fitzroy Simpson was the true culprit, although, of course, I saw that the evidence against him was by no means complete. It was while I was in the carriage, just as we reached the trainer's house, that the immense significance of the curried mutton occurred to me. You may remember that I was distrait and remained sitting after you had all alighted. I was marvelling in my own mind how I could possibly have overlooked so obvious a clue.'

'I confess,' said the colonel, 'that even now I cannot see how it helps us.'

'It was the first link in my chain of reasoning. Powdered opium is by no means tasteless. The flavour is not disagreeable, but it is perceptible. Were it mixed with any ordinary dish the eater would undoubtedly detect it and would probably eat no more. A curry was exactly the medium which would disguise this taste. By no possible supposition could this stranger, Fitzroy Simpson, have caused curry to be served in the trainer's family that night, and it is surely too monstrous a coincidence to suppose that he happened to come along with powdered opium upon the very night when a dish happened to be served which would disguise the flavour. That is unthinkable. Therefore Simpson becomes eliminated from the case, and our attention centres upon Straker and his wife, the only two people who could have chosen curried mutton for supper that night. The opium was added after the dish was set aside for the stable-boy, for the others had the same for supper with no ill effects. Which of them, then, had access to that dish without the maid seeing them?

'Before deciding that question I had grasped the significance of the silence of the dog, for one true inference invariably suggests others. The Simpson incident had shown me that a dog was kept in the stables, and yet, though someone had been in and had fetched out a horse, he had not barked enough to arouse the two lads in the loft. Obviously the midnight visitor was someone whom the dog knew well.

'I was already convinced, or almost convinced, that John Straker went down to the stables in the dead of the night and took out Silver Blaze. For what purpose? For a dishonest one, obviously, or why should he drug his own stable-boy? And yet I was at a loss to know why. There have been cases before now where trainers have made sure of great sums of money by laying against their own horses through agents and then preventing them from winning by fraud. Sometimes it is a pulling jockey. Sometimes it is some surer and subtler means. What was it here? I hoped that the contents of his pockets might help me to form a conclusion.

'And they did so. You cannot have forgotten the singular knife which was found in the dead man's hand, a knife which certainly no sane man would choose for a weapon. It was, as Dr Watson told us, a form of knife which is used for the most delicate operations known in surgery. And it was to be used for a delicate operation that night. You must know, with your wide experience of turf matters, Colonel Ross, that it is possible to make a slight nick upon the tendons of a horse's ham, and to do it subcutaneously, so as to leave absolutely no trace. A horse so treated would develop a slight lameness, which would be put down to a strain in exercise or a touch of rheumatism, but never to foul play.'

'Villain! Scoundrel!' cried the colonel.

'We have here the explanation of why John Straker wished to take the horse out on to the moor. So spirited a creature would have certainly roused the soundest of sleepers when it felt the prick of the knife. It was absolutely necessary to do it in the open air.'

'I have been blind!' cried the colonel. 'Of course that was why he needed the candle and struck the match.'

'Undoubtedly. But in examining his belongings I was fortunate enough to discover not only the method of the crime but even its motives. As a man of the world, Colonel, you know that men do not carry other people's bills about in their pockets. We have most of us quite enough to do to settle our own. I at once concluded that Straker was leading a double life and keeping a second establishment. The nature of the bill showed that there was a lady in the case, and one who had expensive tastes. Liberal as you are with your servants, one can hardly expect that they can buy twenty-guinea walking dresses for their ladies. I questioned Mrs Straker as to the dress without her knowing it, and, having satisfied myself that it had never reached her, I made a note of the milliner's address and felt that by calling there with Straker's photograph I could easily dispose of the mythical Derbyshire.

'From that time on all was plain. Straker had led out the horse to a hollow where his light would be invisible. Simpson in his flight had dropped his cravat, and Straker had picked it up – with some idea, perhaps, that he might use it in securing the horse's leg. Once in the hollow, he had got behind the horse and had struck a light; but the creature, frightened at the sudden glare, and with the strange instinct of animals feeling that some mischief was intended, had lashed out, and the steel shoe had struck Straker full on the forehead. He had already, in spite of the rain, taken off his overcoat in order to do his delicate task, and so, as he fell, his knife gashed his thigh. Do I make it clear?'

'Wonderful!' cried the colonel. 'Wonderful! You might have been there!'

'My final shot was, I confess, a very long one. It struck me that so astute a man as Straker would not undertake this delicate tendon-nicking without a little practice. What could he practise on? My eyes fell upon the sheep, and I asked a question which, rather to my surprise, showed that my surmise was correct.

'When I returned to London I called upon the milliner, who had recognized Straker as an excellent customer of the name of Derbyshire, who had a very dashing wife, with a strong partiality for expensive dresses. I have no doubt that this woman had plunged him over head and ears in debt, and so led him into this miserable plot.'

'You have explained all but one thing,' cried the colonel. 'Where was the horse?'

'Ah, it bolted, and was cared for by one of your neighbours. We must have an amnesty in that direction, I think. This is Clapham Junction, if I am not mistaken, and we shall be in Victoria in less than ten minutes. If you care to smoke a cigar in our rooms, Colonel, I shall be happy to give you any other details which might interest you.'

ARTHUR MORRISON

Behind the Shade

The street was the common East End street – two parallels of brick pierced with windows and doors. But at the end of one, where the builder had found a remnant of land too small for another six-roomer, there stood an odd box of a cottage, with three rooms and a wash-house. It had a green door with a well-blacked knocker round the corner; and in the lower window in front stood a 'shade of fruit' – a cone of waxen grapes and apples under a glass cover.

Although the house was smaller than the others, and was built upon a remnant, it was always a house of some consideration. In a street like this mere independence of pattern gives distinction. And a house inhabited by one sole family makes a figure among houses inhabited by two or more, even though it be the smallest of all. And here the seal of respectability was set by the shade of fruit – a sign accepted in those parts. Now, when people keep a house to themselves, and keep it clean; when they neither stand at the doors nor gossip across back-fences; when, moreover, they have a well-dusted shade of fruit in the front window; and, especially, when they are two women who tell nobody their business: they are known at once for well-to-do, and are regarded with the admixture of spite and respect that is proper to the circumstances. They are also watched.

Still, the neighbours knew the history of the Perkinses, mother and daughter, in its main features, with little disagreement: having told it to each other, filling in the details when occasion seemed to serve. Perkins, ere he died, had been a shipwright; and this was when the shipwrights were the aristocracy of the work-shops, and he that worked more than three or four days a week was counted a mean slave: it was long (in fact) before depression, strikes, iron plates, and collective blindness had driven shipbuilding to the Clyde. Perkins had laboured no harder than his fellows, had married a tradesman's daughter, and had spent his money with freedom; and some while after his death his widow and daughter came to live in the small house, and kept a school for tradesmen's little girls in a back room over the wash-house. But as the School Board waxed in power, and the tradesmen's pride in regard thereunto waned, the attendance, never large, came down to twos and threes. Then Mrs Perkins met with her accident. A dweller in Stidder's Rents overtook her one night, and, having vigorously punched her in the face and the breast, kicked her and jumped on her for five minutes as she lay on the pavement. (In the dark, it afterwards appeared, he had mistaken her for his mother.) The one distinct opinion the adventure bred in the street was Mrs Webster's, the Little Bethelite, who considered it a judgment for sinful pride – for Mrs Perkins had been a Church-goer. But the neighbours never saw Mrs Perkins again. The doctor left his patient 'as well as she ever would be,' but bed-ridden and helpless. Her daughter was a scraggy, sharp-faced woman of thirty or so, whose black dress hung from her hips as from a wooden frame; and some people got into the way of calling her Mrs Perkins, seeing no other thus to honour. And meantime, the school had ceased, although Miss Perkins essayed a revival, and joined a Dissenting chapel to that end.

Then, one day, a card appeared in the window, over the shade of fruit, with the legend 'Pianoforte Lessons'. It was not approved by the street. It was a standing advertisement of the fact that the Perkinses had a piano, which others had not. It also revealed a grasping spirit on the part of people able to keep a house to themselves, with red curtains and a shade of fruit in the parlour window; who, moreover, had been able to give up keeping a school because of ill-health. The pianoforte lessons were eight-and-sixpence a quarter, two a week. Nobody was ever known to take them but the relieving officer's daughter, and she paid sixpence a lesson, to see how she got on, and left off in three weeks. The card stayed in the window a fortnight longer, and none of the neighbours saw the cart that came in the night and took away the old cabinet piano with the channelled keys, that had been fourth-hand when Perkins bought it twenty years ago. Mrs Clark, the widow who sewed far into the night, may possibly have heard a noise and looked; but she said nothing if she did. There was no card in the window next morning, but the shade of fruit stood primly respectable as ever. The curtains were drawn a little closer across, for some of the children playing in the street were used to flatten their faces against the lower panes, and to discuss the piano, the stuff-bottomed chairs, the antimacassars, the mantelpiece ornaments, and the loo table with the family Bible and the album on it.

It was soon after this that the Perkinses altogether ceased from shopping – ceased, at any rate, in that neighbourhood. Trade with them had already been dwindling, and it was said that Miss Perkins was getting stingier than her mother – who had been stingy enough herself. Indeed, the Perkins demeanour began to change for the worse, to be significant of a miserly retirement and an offensive alienation from the rest of the street. One day the deacon called, as was his practice now and then; but, being invited no further than the doorstep, he went away in dudgeon, and did not return. Nor, indeed, was Miss Perkins seen again at chapel.

Then there was a discovery. The spare figure of Miss Perkins was seldom seen in the streets, and then almost always at night; but on these occasions she was observed to carry parcels, of varying wrappings and shapes. Once, in broad daylight, with a package in newspaper, she made such haste past a shop-window where stood Mrs Webster and Mrs Jones, that she tripped on the broken sole of one shoe, and fell headlong. The newspaper broke away from its pins, and although the woman reached and recovered her parcel before she rose, it was plain to see that it was made up of cheap shirts, cut out ready for the stitching. The street had the news the same hour, and it was generally held that such a taking of the bread out of the mouths of them that wanted it by them that had plenty was a scandal and a shame, and ought to be put a stop to. And Mrs Webster, foremost in the setting right of things, undertook to find out whence the work came, and to say a few plain words in the right quarter.

All this while nobody watched closely enough to note that the parcels brought in were fewer than the parcels taken out. Even a hand-truck, late one evening, went unremarked: the door being round the corner, and most people within. One morning, though, Miss Perkins, her best foot foremost, was venturing along a near street with an outgoing parcel – large and triangular and wrapped in white drugget – when the relieving officer turned the corner across the way.

The relieving officer was a man in whose system of etiquette the Perkinses had caused some little disturbance. His ordinary female acquaintances (not, of course, professional) he was in the habit of recognising by a gracious nod. When he met the minister's wife he lifted his hat, instantly assuming an intense frown, in the event of irreverent observation. Now he quite felt that the Perkinses were entitled to some advance upon the nod, although it would be absurd to raise them to a level with the minister's wife. So he had long since established a compromise: he closed his finger and thumb upon the brim of his hat, and let his hand fall forthwith. Preparing now to accomplish this salute, he was astounded to see that Miss Perkins, as soon as she was aware of his approach, turned her face, which was rather flushed, away from him, and went hurrying onward, looking at the wall on her side of the street. The relieving officer, checking his hand on its way to his hat, stopped and looked after her as she turned the corner, hugging her parcel on the side next the wall. Then he shouldered his umbrella and pursued his way, holding his head high, and staring fiercely straight before him; for a relieving officer is not used to being cut.

It was a little after this that Mr Crouch, the landlord, called. He had not been calling regularly, because of late Miss Perkins had left her five shillings of rent with Mrs Crouch every Saturday evening. He noted with satisfaction the whitened sills and the shade of fruit, behind which the curtains were now drawn close and pinned together. He turned the corner and lifted the bright knocker. Miss Perkins half opened the door, stood in the opening, and began to speak.

His jaw dropped. 'Beg pardon – forgot something. Won't wait – call next week – do just as well'; and he hurried round the corner and down the street, puffing and blowing and staring. 'Why, the woman frightened me,' he afterward explained to Mrs Crouch. 'There's something wrong with her eyes, and she looked like a corpse. The rent wasn't ready – I could see that before she spoke; so I cleared out.'

'P'r'aps something's happened to the old lady,' suggested Mrs Crouch. 'Anyhow, I should think the rent 'ud be all right.' And he thought it would.

Nobody saw the Perkinses that week. The shade of fruit stood in its old place, but was thought not to have been dusted after Tuesday. Certainly the sills and the doorstep were neglected. Friday, Saturday and

Sunday were swallowed up in a choking brown fog, wherein men lost their bearings, and fell into docks, and stepped over embankment edges. It was as though a great blot had fallen, and had obliterated three days from the calendar. It cleared on Monday morning, and, just as the women in the street were sweeping their steps, Mr Crouch was seen at the green door. He lifted the knocker, dull and sticky now with the foul vapour, and knocked a gentle rat-tat. There was no answer. He knocked again, a little louder, and waited, listening. But there was neither voice nor movement within. He gave three heavy knocks, and then came round to the front window. There was the shade of fruit, the glass a little duller on the top, the curtains pinned close about it, and nothing to see beyond them. He tapped at the window with his knuckles, and backed into the roadway to look at the one above. This was a window with a striped holland blind and a short net curtain; but never a face was there.

The sweepers stopped to look, and one from opposite came and reported that she had seen nothing of Miss Perkins for a week, and that certainly nobody had left the house that morning. And Mr Crouch grew excited, and bellowed through the keyhole.

In the end they opened the sash-fastening with a knife, moved the shade of fruit, and got in. The room was bare and empty, and their steps and voices resounded as those of people in an unfurnished house. The wash-house was vacant, but it was clean, and there was a little net curtain in the window. The short passage and the stairs were bare boards. In the back room by the stair-head was a drawn window-blind, and that was all. In the front room with the striped blind and the short curtain there was a bed of rags and old newspapers; also a wooden box; and on each of these was a dead woman.

Both deaths, the doctor found, were from syncope, the result of inanition; and the better-nourished woman – she on the bed – had died the sooner; perhaps by a day or two. The other case was rather curious; it exhibited a degree of shrinkage in the digestive organs unprecedented in his experience. After the inquest the street had an evening's fame: for the papers printed coarse drawings of the house, and in leaderettes demanded the abolition of something. Then it became its wonted self. And it was doubted if the waxen apples and the curtains fetched enough to pay Mr Crouch his fortnight's rent.

'MRS ERNEST LEVERSON'

Suggestion

If Lady Winthrop had not spoken of me as 'that intolerable, effeminate boy,' she might have had some chance of marrying my father. She was a middle-aged widow; prosaic, fond of domineering, and an alarmingly excellent housekeeper; the serious work of her life was paying visits; in her lighter moments she collected autographs. She was highly suitable and altogether insupportable; and this unfortunate remark about me was, as people say, the last straw. Some encouragement from father Lady Winthrop must, I think, have received; for she took to calling at odd hours, asking my sister Marjorie sudden abrupt questions, and being generally impossible. A tradition existed that her advice was of use to our father in his household, and when, last year, he married his daughter's school-friend, a beautiful girl of twenty, it surprised every one except Marjorie and myself.

The whole thing was done, in fact, by suggestion. I shall never forget that summer evening when father first realised, with regard to Laura Egerton, the possible. He was giving a little dinner of eighteen people. *Through a mistake of Marjorie's* (my idea) Lady Winthrop did not receive her invitation till the very last minute. Of course she accepted – we knew she would – but unknowing that it was a dinner party, she came without putting on evening-dress.

Nothing could be more trying to the average woman than such a *contretemps*; and Lady Winthrop was not one to rise, sublimely, and laughing, above the situation. I can see her now, in a plaid blouse and a vile temper, displaying herself, mentally and physically, to the utmost disadvantage, while Marjorie apologised the whole evening, in pale blue crêpe-de-chine; and Laura, in yellow, with mauve orchids, sat – an adorable contrast – on my father's other side, with a slightly conscious air that was perfectly fascinating. It is quite extraordinary what trifles have their little effect in these matters. *I* had sent Laura the orchids, anonymously; I could not help it if she chose to think they were from my father. Also, I had hinted of his secret affection for her, and lent her Verlaine. I said I had found it in his study, turned down at her favourite page. Laura has, like myself, the artistic temperament; she is cultured, rather romantic, and in search of the *au-delà*. My father has at times – never to me – rather charming manners; also he is still handsome, with that look of having suffered that comes from enjoying oneself too much. That evening his really sham melancholy and apparently hollow gaiety were delightful for a son to witness, and appealed evidently to her heart. Yes, strange as it may seem, while the world said that pretty Miss Egerton married old Carington for his money, she was really in love, or thought herself in love, with our father. Poor girl! She little knew what an irritating, ill-tempered, absent-minded person he is in private life; and at times I have pangs of remorse.

A fortnight after the wedding, father forgot he was married, and began again treating Laura with a sort of *distrait* gallantry as Marjorie's friend, or else ignoring her altogether. When, from time to time, he remembers she is his wife, he scolds her about the houskeeping in a fitful, perfunctory way, for he does not know that Marjorie does it still. Laura bears the rebukes like an angel; indeed, rather than take the slightest practical trouble she would prefer to listen to the strongest language in my father's vocabulary.

But she is sensitive; and when father, speedily resuming his bachelor manners, recommended his visits to an old friend who lives in one of the little houses opposite the Oratory, she seemed quite vexed. Father is horribly careless, and Laura found a letter. They had a rather serious explanation, and for a little time after, Laura seemed depressed. She soon tried to rouse herself, and is at times cheerful enough with Marjorie and myself, but I fear she has had a disillusion. They never quarrel now, and I think we all three dislike father about equally, though Laura never owns it, and is gracefully attentive to him in a gentle, filial sort of way.

We are fond of going to parties – not father – and Laura is a very nice chaperone for Marjorie. They are both perfectly devoted to me. 'Cecil knows everything,' they are always saying, and they do nothing – not even choosing a hat – without asking my advice.

Since I left Eton I am supposed to be reading with a tutor, but as a matter of fact I have plenty of leisure; and am very glad to be of use to the girls, of whom I'm, by the way, quite proud. They are rather a sweet contrast; Marjorie has the sort of fresh rosy prettiness you see in the park and on the river. She is tall, and slim as a punt-pole, and if she were not very careful how she dresses, she would look like a drawing by Pilotelle in the *Lady's Pictorial*. She is practical and lively, she rides and drives and dances; skates, and goes to some mysterious haunt called *The Stores*, and is, in her own way, quite a modern English type.

Laura has that exotic beauty so much admired by Philistines; dreamy dark eyes, and a wonderful white complexion. She loves music and poetry and pictures and admiration in a lofty sort of way; she has a morbid fondness for mental gymnastics, and a dislike to physical exertion, and never takes any exercise except waving her hair. Sometimes she looks bored, and I have heard her sigh.

'Cissy,' Marjorie said, coming one day into my study, 'I want to speak to you about Laura.'

'Do you have pangs of conscience too?' I asked, lighting a cigarette.

'Dear, we took a great responsibility. Poor girl! Oh, couldn't we make Papa more—'

'Impossible,' I said; 'no one has any influence with him. He can't bear even me, though if he had a shade of decency he would dash away an unbidden tear every time I look at him with my mother's blue eyes.'

My poor mother was a great beauty, and I am supposed to be her living image.

'Laura has no object in life,' said Marjorie. 'I have, all girls have, I suppose. By the way, Cissy, I am quite sure Charlie Winthrop is serious.'

'How sweet of him! I am so glad. I got father off my hands last season.'

'Must I really marry him, Cissy? He bores me.'

'What has that to do with it? Certainly you must. You are not a beauty, and I doubt your ever having a better chance.'

Marjorie rose and looked at herself in the long pier-glass that stands opposite my writing-table. I could not resist the temptation to go and stand beside her.

'I am just the style that is admired now,' said Marjorie, dispassionately.

'So am I,' I said reflectively. 'But *you* will soon be out of date.'

Every one says I am strangely like my mother. Her face was of that pure and perfect oval one so seldom sees, with delicate features, rosebud mouth, and soft flaxen hair. A blondness without insipidity, for the dark-blue eyes are fringed with dark lashes, and from their languorous depths looks out a soft mockery. I have a curious ideal devotion to my mother; she died when I was quite young – only two months old – and I often spend hours thinking of her, as I gaze at myself in the mirror.

'Do come down from the clouds,' said Marjorie impatiently, for I had sunk into a reverie. 'I came to ask you to think of something to amuse Laura – to interest her.'

'We ought to make it up to her in some way. Haven't you tried anything?'

'Only palmistry; and Mrs Wilkinson prophesied her all that she detests, and depressed her dreadfully.'

'What do you think she really needs most?' I asked.

Our eyes met.

'Really, Cissy, you're too disgraceful,' said Marjorie. There was a pause. 'And so I'm to accept Charlie?'

'What man do you like better?' I asked.

'I don't know what you mean,' said Marjorie, colouring.

'*I* thought Adrian Grant would have been more sympathetic to Laura than to you. I have just had a note from him, asking me to tea at his studio to-day.' I threw it to her. 'He says I'm to bring you both. Would that amuse Laura?'

'Oh,' cried Marjorie, enchanted, 'of course we'll go. I wonder what he thinks of me,' she added wistfully.

'He didn't say. He is going to send Laura his verses, "Hearts-ease and Heliotrope".'

She sighed. Then she said, 'Father was complaining again to-day of your laziness.'

'I, lazy! Why, I've been swinging the censer in Laura's boudoir because she wants to encourage the religious temperament, and I've designed your dress for the Clives' fancy ball.'

'Where's the design?'

'In my head. You're not to wear white; Miss Clive must wear white.'

'I wonder you don't marry her,' said Marjorie, 'you admire her so much.'

'I never marry. Besides, I know she's pretty, but that furtive Slade-school manner of hers gets on my nerves. You don't know how dreadfully I suffer from my nerves.'

She lingered a little, asking me what I advised her to choose for a birthday present for herself – an American organ, a black poodle, or an *édition de luxe* of Browning. I advised the last, as being least noisy. Then I told her I felt sure that in spite of her admiration for Adrian, she was far too good-natured to interfere with Laura's prospects. She said I was incorrigible, and left the room with a smile of resignation.

And I returned to my reading. On my last birthday – I was seventeen – my father – who has his gleams of dry humour – gave me *Robinson Crusoe*! I prefer Pierre Loti, and intend to have an onyx-paved bath-room, with soft apricot-coloured light shimmering through the blue-lined green curtains in my chambers, as soon as I get Margery married, and Laura more – settled down.

I met Adrian Grant first at a luncheon party at the Clives'. I seemed to amuse him; he came to see me, and became at once obviously enamoured of my step-mother. He is rather an impressionable impressionist, and a delightful creature, tall and graceful and beautiful, and altogether most interesting. Every one admits he's fascinating; he is very popular and very much disliked. He is by way of being a painter; he has a little money of his own – enough for his telegrams, but not enough for his buttonholes – and nothing could be more incongruous than the idea of his marrying. I have never seen Marjorie so much attracted. But she is a good loyal girl, and will accept Charlie Winthrop, who is a dear person, good-natured and ridiculously rich – just the sort of man for a brother-in-law. It will annoy my old enemy Lady Winthrop – he is her nephew, and she wants him to marry that little Miss Clive. Dorothy Clive has her failings, but she could not – to do her justice – be happy with Charlie Winthrop.

Adrian's gorgeous studio gives one the complex impression of being at once the calm retreat of a mediæval saint and the luxurious abode of a modern Pagan. One feels that everything could be done there, everything from praying to flirting – everything except painting. The tea-party amused me, I was pretending to listen to a brown person who was talking absurd worn-out literary clichés – as that the New Humour is not funny, or that Bourget understood women, when I overheard this fragment of conversation.

'But don't you like Society?' Adrian was saying.

'I get rather tired of it. People are so much alike. They all say the same things,' said Laura.

'Of course they all say the same things to *you*,' murmured Adrian, as he affected to point out a rather curious old silver crucifix.

'That,' said Laura, 'is one of the things they say.'

About three weeks later I found myself dining alone with Adrian Grant, at one of the two restaurants in London. (The cooking is better at the other, this one is the more becoming.) I had lilies-of-the-valley in my button-hole, Adrian was wearing a red carnation. Several people glanced at us. Of course he is very well known in Society. Also, I was looking rather nice, and I could not help hoping, while Adrian gazed rather absently over my head, that the shaded candles were staining to a richer rose the waking wonder of my face.

Adrian was charming of course, but he seemed worried and a little preoccupied, and drank a good deal of champagne.

Towards the end of dinner, he said – almost abruptly for him – 'Carington.'

'Cecil,' I interrupted. He smiled.

'Cissy . . . it seems an odd thing to say to you, but though you are so young, I think you know everything. I am sure you know everything. You know about me. I am in love. I am quite miserable. What on earth am I to do !' He drank more champagne. 'Tell me,' he said, 'what to do.' For a few minutes, while we listened to that interminable hackneyed *Intermezzo*, I reflected; asking myself by what strange phases I had risen to the extraordinary position of giving advice to Adrian on such a subject?

Laura was not happy with our father. From a selfish motive, Marjorie and I had practically arranged that monstrous marriage. That very day he had been disagreeable, asking me with a clumsy sarcasm to raise his allowance, so that he could afford my favourite cigarettes. If Adrian were free, Marjorie might refuse Charlie Winthrop. I don't want her to refuse him. Adrian has treated me as a friend. I like him – I like him enormously. I am quite devoted to him. And how can I rid myself of the feeling of responsibility, the sense that I owe some compensation to poor beautiful Laura?

We spoke of various matters. Just before we left the table, I said, with what seemed, but was not, irrelevance, 'Dear Adrian, Mrs Carington—'

'Go on, Cissy.'

'She is one of those who must be appealed to, at first, by her imagination. She married our father because she thought he was lonely and misunderstood.'

'*I* am lonely and misunderstood,' said Adrian, his eyes flashing with delight.

'Ah, not twice! She doesn't like that now.'

I finished my coffee slowly, and then I said,

'Go to the Clives' fancy-ball as Tristan.'

Adrian pressed my hand . . .

At the door of the restaurant we parted, and I drove home through the cool April night, wondering, wondering. Suddenly I thought of my mother – my beautiful sainted mother, who would have loved me, I am convinced, had she lived, with an extraordinary devotion. What would she have said to all this? What would she have thought? I know not why, but a mad reaction seized me. I felt recklessly conscientious. My father! After all, he was my father. I was possessed by passionate scruples. If I went back now to Adrian – if I went back and implored him, supplicated him never to see Laura again!

I felt I could persuade him. I have sufficient personal magnetism to do that, if I make up my mind. After one glance in the looking-glass, I put up my stick and stopped the hansom. I had taken a resolution. I told the man to drive to Adrian's rooms.

He turned round with a sharp jerk. In another second a brougham passed us – a swift little brougham that I knew. It slackened – it stopped – we passed it – I saw my father. He was getting out at one of the little houses opposite the Brompton Oratory.

'Turn round again,' I shouted to the cabman. And he drove me straight home.

EVELYN SHARP

In Dull Brown

'All the same,' said Nancy, who was lazily sipping her coffee in bed, 'brown doesn't suit you a bit.'

'No,' said Jean sadly, 'and I should not be wearing it at all if my other skirt did not want brushing. Nevertheless, a russet-brown frock demands adventures. The girls in novels always wear russet-brown, whatever their complexion is, and they always have adventures. Now—'

'Isn't it time you started?' asked the gentle voice of her sister. Jean glanced at the clock and said something in English that was not classical.

'I shall have to take an omnibus. Bother!' she said, and the heroine of the russet-brown frock made an abrupt and undignified exit.

It was a fine warm morning in November, the sort of day that follows a week of stormy wet weather as though to cheat the unwary into imagining that the spring instead of the winter is on its way. The pavements were still wet from yesterday's rain, the trees in the park stood stripped by yesterday's gale; only the sun and the sparrows kept up the illusion that it was never going to rain any more. But the caprices of the atmosphere made no impression on the people who cannot help being out; and Jean, as she made the fourteenth passenger on the top of an omnibus, had a vague feeling of contempt for the other thirteen who were engrossed in their morning papers.

'Just imagine missing that glorious effect,' she thought to herself, as they rumbled along the edge of the Green Park where the mist was slowly yielding to the warmth of the sun and allowing itself to be coaxed out of growing into a fog. And almost simultaneously she became as material as the rest, in her annoyance with her neighbour for taking more than his share of the seat.

'Nice morning!' he said at that moment, and folded up his *Telegraph*.

'Yes,' said Jean, in a tone that was not encouraging. That the morning was 'nice' would never have occurred to her; and it seemed unfair to sacrifice the effect over the Green Park, even for conversational purposes. Then she caught sight of his face, which was a harmless one, and in an ordinary way good-looking, and she accused herself of priggishness, and stared at the unconscious passenger in front, preparatory to cultivating the one at her side.

'We deserve some compensation for yesterday,' she continued, more graciously.

'Yesterday? Oh, it was beastly wet, wasn't it? I suppose you don't like wet weather, eh?' said the man, with a suspicion of familiarity in his tone. Jean frowned a little.

'That comes of the simple russet gown,' she thought; 'of course he thinks I am a little shop-girl.' But the sun was shining, and life had been very dull lately, and she would be getting down at Piccadilly Circus. Besides, he was little more than a boy, and she liked boys, and there would be no harm in having five minutes' conversation with this one.

'I suppose no one does. I wasn't trying to be particularly original,' she replied carelessly.

He smiled and glanced at her with more interest. Her identity was beginning to puzzle him.

'Going to business?' he asked tentatively.

'Well, yes, I suppose so. At least, I am going to teach three children all sorts of things they don't want to learn a bit.'

'How awfully clever of you!'

The little obvious remark made her laugh. In spite of the humble brown dress that did not suit her, she looked very pretty when she threw back her head and laughed.

'That is because you have never taught,' she said; 'to be a really good teacher you must systematically forget quite half of what you do know. For instance, I can teach German better than anything else in the world, because I know less about it. Perhaps that is why I always won the German prizes at school,' she added reflectively.

'You are very paradoxical – or very cynical, which is it?' asked her neighbour, smiling.

'Oh, I don't know. Am I? But did you ever try to teach?'

'Not I. Gives one the hump, doesn't it? I should just whack the little beasts when they didn't work. Don't you feel like that sometimes?'

'Clearly you never tried to teach,' she said, and laughed again.

'Those are lucky pupils of yours,' he observed.

'Why?' she asked abruptly, and flashed a stern look at him sideways.

'Oh, because you – seem right on it, don't you know,' he answered hastily. The adroitness of his answer pleased her, and she put him down as a gentleman, and felt justified in going a little further.

'I like teaching, yes,' she went on gravely. 'But all the same I am glad that I only teach for my living and can draw for my pleasure. Now whatever made me tell you that I wonder?'

'It was awfully decent of you to tell me,' he said; 'I suppose you thought I should be interested, eh?'

'I suppose I did,' she assented, and this time she laughed for no reason whatever.

'Will you let me say something very personal?' he asked, waxing bolder. But his tone was still humble, and she felt more kindly towards him now that he evidently knew she was not to be patronised. Besides, she was curious. So she said nothing to dissuade him, and he went on.

'Why do you look so beastly happy, and all that, don't you know? Is it because you work so hard?'

'I look happy!' she exclaimed. 'I suppose it is the sun, then, or the jolly day, or – or the *feel* of everything after the rain. Yes, I suppose it must be that.'

'I don't, then. Lots of girls might feel all that and not look as you do. I think it is because you have such a bally lot to do.'

'I should stop thinking that, if I were you,' said Jean a little bitterly; 'I know that is the usual idea about women who work – among those who don't. They should try it for a time, and see.'

'I believe you are cynical after all,' observed her companion. 'Don't you like being called happy?'

'Oh, yes, I like it. But I hate humbug, and it is all nonsense to pretend that working hard for one's living is rather an amusing thing to do. Because it isn't, and if it has never been so for a man, why should it be for a woman? If anything, it is worse for women. For one happy hour it gives us two sad ones; it makes us hard – what you call cynical. It builds up our characters at the expense of our hearts. It makes heroines of us and spoils the woman in us. We learn to look the world in the face, and it teaches us to be prigs. We probe into its realities for the first time, and the disclosure is too much for us. Working hard to get enough bread and butter to eat is a sordid, demoralising thing, and the people who talk cant about it never had to do it themselves. *You* don't like the kind of woman who works, you know you don't!'

The omnibus was slowing at the Circus. Jean stopped suddenly and glanced up at her companion with an amused, half shamefaced look.

'I am so sorry. You see how objectionable it has made *me*. Aren't you glad you will never see me again?'

And before he had time to speak she had slipped away, and the omnibus was turning ruthlessly down Waterloo Place.

'What deuced odd things women are,' he reflected, by way of deluding himself into the belief that amusement and not interest was the predominant sensation in his mind. But the next morning saw him waiting carefully in West Kensington for the same City omnibus as before; and when it rumbled on its way to Piccadilly Circus and no one in russet-brown got up to relieve the monotony of black coats and umbrellas round him, he was quite unreasonably disappointed, though he told himself savagely at the same time that of course he had never expected to see her at all.

'And if I had, she would have avoided me at once. Women are always like that,' he thought, and just as the reflection shaped itself in his mind he caught a glimpse of Air Street that sent his usual composure to the winds and brought him down the steps at a pace that upset the descent of all the other passengers who had no similar desire to rush in the direction of Air Street.

'Did yer expect us to take yer to Timbuctoo?' scoffed the conductor, with the usual contempt of his kind for the passenger who gets into the wrong omnibus. But the victim of his scorn was as regardless of it as of the pink ticket he was grinding into pulp in his hand; and he stood on the pavement with his underlip drawn tightly inwards, until he had regained his customary air of gentlemanly indifference. Then he turned up into Regent Street and made a cross cut through the slums that lie on the borders of Soho.

And as Jean was hastening along Oxford Street, ten minutes later, she met him coming towards her with a superb expression of pleased surprise on his face, which deceived her so completely that she bowed at once and held out her hand to him, although, as she said afterwards to Nancy, 'he was being most dreadfully unconventional, and I couldn't help wondering if he would have spoken to me again, if I had worn my new tailor-made gown and looked ordinary.' At the time she only felt that Oxford Street, even on a damp and muggy morning, was quite a nice place for a walk.

'Beastly day for you to be out,' he began, taking away her umbrella and holding his own over her head. To be looked after was a novel experience to Jean, and she found herself half resenting his air of protection.

'Oh, it's all right. You get used to it when you have to,' she said with a short laugh. It was not at all what she wanted to say to him, but the perversity of her nature was uppermost and she had to say it.

'All the same, it is beastly rough on you,' he persisted.

'Why? Some one must do the work,' she said defiantly.

'Is it so important, then?' he asked with a smile that was half a sneer. Jean blushed hotly.

'It means my living to me,' she said; and he winced at her unpleasant frankness.

'You were quite different yesterday, weren't you?' he complained gently.

'You speak as though my being one thing or another ought to depend on your pleasure,' she retorted; 'of course, you think like everybody else that a woman is only to be tolerated as long as she is cheerful. How can you be cheerful when the weather is dreary, and you are tired out with yesterday's work? You don't know what it is like. You should keep to the women who don't work; they will always look pretty, and smile sweetly and behave in a domesticated manner.'

'I don't think I said anything to provoke all that, did I?'

'Yes, you did,' she answered unreasonably. 'I said – I mean *you* said, oh never mind! But you do like domesticated women best, don't you? On your honour now?'

There was no doubt that he did, especially at that moment. But he lied, smilingly, and well.

'I like all women. But most of all, women like you. Didn't I tell you yesterday how happy you looked? You are such a rum little girl – oh hang, please forgive me. But without any rotting, I wish you'd tell me what you do want me to say. When I said how jolly you looked, you were offended; and now I pity you for being out in the rain, you don't like that any better. What am I to do?'

'I don't see why you should do anything,' she said curtly. They had reached the corner of Berners Street, and she came to a standstill. 'I am glad I met you again,' she added very quickly, without meeting his eyes. And then she ran down the street, and disappeared inside a doorway.

Tom Unwin stepped into a hansom with two umbrellas and an unsatisfactory impression of the last quarter of an hour. And for the next two mornings he went to the City by train. But the third saw him again in Oxford Street shortly before nine o'clock, and he held a small and elegant umbrella in his hand, although it was a cloudless day, and there was hoar frost beneath the gravel on the wood pavement.

'How very odd that we should meet again,' she exclaimed, blushing in spite of the self-possession on which she prided herself.

'Not so very odd,' he replied; 'I believe I am responsible for this meeting.'

'I feel sure there is a suitable reply to that, but you mustn't expect me to make it. I am never any good at making suitable replies,' said Jean; and she laughed as she had done the first time they met.

'I don't want suitable replies from you,' he rejoined, just as lightly; 'tell me what you really think instead.'

'That it was quite charming of you to come this particular way to the City on this particular morning,' said Jean demurely. 'Now, do you know, I should have thought it was ever so much quicker to go along the Strand.'

'On the contrary, I find it very much quicker when I come along Oxford Street.'

'At all events, *you* know how to make suitable replies.'

'Then you thought that was a suitable reply? Got you there, didn't I?' and he laughed, which pleased her immensely, although she pretended to be hurt.

'Isn't it queer how one can live two perfectly different lives at the same time?' she said irrelevantly.

'Two? I live half a dozen. But let's hear yours first.'

'I was only thinking,' continued Jean, 'that if the mother of my pupils knew I was walking along Oxford Street with some one I had never been introduced to—'

'Well?' he said, as she paused.

'Oh, well, it isn't exactly an ordinary thing to do, is it?'

'Why not?'

'Well, it isn't, is it?'

'But must one be ordinary?'

'People won't forgive you for being anything else, unless you are in a history book, where you can't do any harm.'

'People be hanged! When shall I see you again?'

'Next time you take a short cut to the City, I suppose. Good-bye.'

'Stop!' he cried. And when she did stop, with an air of innocent inquiry on her face, he found he had nothing whatever to say.

'You – you haven't told me your name,' he stammered lamely.

'Is that all? You needn't make me any later just for *that*,' she exclaimed, turning away again. 'Besides, you haven't told me yours,' she added, over her shoulder.

'Do you want to know it?'

'Why, no; it doesn't matter to me. But I thought you wanted to make some more conversation. Good-bye, again.'

'Well, I'm hanged! Look here, if I tell you mine, will you tell me yours?'

'But I don't mind a bit if you *don't* tell me yours.'

'Will you, though?'

'Oh, make haste, or else I can't wait to hear it.'

'Here you are, then. It is – Tom.'

She faced him sternly.

'Why don't you go on?'

'Unwin,' he added, hastily. 'Now yours, please.'

But the only answer he got was a mocking smile; and he was again left at the corner of Berners Street with a lady's umbrella in his hand.

The next morning there was a dull yellow fog, and Jean was in a perverse mood.

'I think you are very mistaken to walk to business on a day like this, when you might go by train,' she said, as she reluctantly gave up her books to be carried by him. The fog was making her eyes smart, and she felt cross.

'But I shall get my reward,' he said, with elaborate courtesy.

'Oh, please don't. The fog is bad enough without allusions to the hymn-book. Besides, I can't stand being used as a means for somebody else to get into heaven. It is very selfish of me, I suppose, but I don't like it.'

'I am afraid you mistake me. I never for a moment associated you with my chances of salvation.'

'Then why didn't you?' she cried indignantly. 'I should like to know why you come and bother me every morning like this if you think I am as hopelessly bad as all that! I didn't ask you to come, did I? Please give me my books and let me go.'

'I think you hopelessly bad? Why, I assure you—'

'Give me my books. Can't you see how late I am?' she said, stamping her foot impetuously. And she seized Bright's English History and Cornwall's Geography out of his hand, and left him precipitately, without another word.

'You are a most unreasonable little girl,' he exclaimed hotly; and the policeman to whom he said it smiled patiently.

He started with the intention of going by train on the following morning; then he changed his mind, and ran back to take an omnibus. After that he found it was getting late, so he took a cab to Oxford Circus, and then strolled on towards Holborn as though nothing but chance or necessity had brought him there. But, although he walked as far as Berners Street and back again to the Circus, he met no one in a dull brown frock. And he was just as unsuccessful the next morning, and the one after, and at the end of a week he found himself the sad possessor of a slender silk umbrella, a regretful remembrance, and a fresh store of cynicism.

'She is like all the others,' he told himself, with a shrug of his shoulders; 'they play the very devil with you until they begin to get frightened of the consequences, and then they fight shy. And I'm hanged if I even know her name!'

And the days wore on, and the autumn grew into winter, and Oxford Street no longer saw the playing of a comedy at nine o'clock in the morning. And Tom Unwin found other interests in life, and if a chance occurrence reminded him of a determined little figure in russet brown, the passing thought brought nothing but an amused smile to his lips.

Then the spring came, suddenly and completely, on the heels of a six weeks' frost; and chance took him down Piccadilly one morning in March, where the budding freshness of the trees drew him into the Green Park. The impression of spring met him everywhere, in the fragrance of the almond-trees, and the quarrelling of the sparrows, and the transparency of the blue haze over Westminster; and, indifferent though he was to such things, there was a note of familiarity in it all that affected him strangely, and left him with a lazy sensation of pleasure. What that something was he did not realise until his eyes fell on one of the chairs under the trees, and then, as he stood quite still and wondered whether she would know him again, he discovered what there was in the air that had seemed to him so familiar and so pleasant.

'I was just thinking about you,' he said deliberately, when she had shown very decidedly that she did mean to know him. He spoke with an easy indifference that she showed no signs of sharing.

'Oh, I have been wondering—' she began, in a voice that trembled with eagerness.

'Yes? Supposing we sit down. That's better. You have been wondering—?'

She leaned back in her chair, and looked up through the branches at the pale blue sky beyond. There was an odd little look of defiance on her face.

'So, after all, you did find that the Strand was the quickest way,' she said abruptly.

'Possibly. And you?' he asked, with his customary smile.

'How often did you go down Oxford Street after – the last time I saw you?'

'As far as I can remember, the measure of my endurance was a week. And how much longer did you take the precaution of avoiding such a dangerous person as myself?'

She turned round and stared at him with great wondering eyes, into which a look of comprehension was slowly creeping.

'You actually thought I did that? And all the time I was ill, I was having visions of you—'

'Ill? You never told me you had been ill,' he interrupted.

'You didn't exactly give me the chance, did you? It was the fog, I suppose. I am all right now. They thought I should never go down Oxford

Street again. But I take a good deal of killing, and so here I am again.' She ended with a cynical smile. He was making holes in the soft turf with his walking-stick. She went on speaking to the pale blue sky and the network of branches above her.

'And the odd part is that I did not mind the illness so much as—' And she paused again.

'Yes?' he said, in a voice that had lost some of its jauntiness.

'I think it won't interest you.'

'How can you say that unless you tell me?'

'I am sure it won't,' she said decidedly. 'And I couldn't possibly tell you, really.'

'Go on, please,' he said, looking round at her; and she went on meekly.

'The thing that bothered me was my having been cross the last time we met. You see, it was not the being cross that I minded exactly; *that* wouldn't have mattered a bit if I had seen you again the next day, but—'

'I quite understand. Bad temper is a luxury we keep for our most familiar friends. I am honoured by the distinction,' he said, and his smile was not a sneer.

'I wish you wouldn't laugh at me,' she said, a little wistfully.

'I am not laughing at you, child,' he hastened to assure her, and he took one of her hands in his. 'I have missed you, too,' he went on, in a low tone that he strove to make natural.

'Did you *really*? I thought you would at first, perhaps, and then I thought you would just laugh, and forget. And you really did think of me sometimes? I am so glad.'

He had a twinge of conscience. But a reputation once acquired is a tender thing, and must be handled with delicacy.

'I have not forgotten,' he said, and tried to change the conversation. 'And you never even told me your name, you perverse little person,' he added playfully.

'You told me yours,' she said, and laughed triumphantly.

'And yours, please?'

'It will quite spoil it all,' she objected.

'Is it so bad as that, then? Never mind, I can bear a good deal. What is it – Susan, Jemima, Emmelina?'

There was a little pause, and then she nodded at the pale blue sky above and said 'Jean' in a hurried whisper. And he was less exigent than she had been, for he did not ask for any more.

When he left her on her own doorstep she lingered for a moment in the sunlight before she went in to Nancy.

'And he really is coming to see me to-morrow,' she said out loud with a joyous laugh; 'I wonder, shall I tell Nancy or not?' After mature consideration she decided not to tell Nancy, though if Nancy had been less unsuspicious she would certainly have noticed something unusual in the manner of her practical little eldest sister, when she started for Berners Street on the following morning, and twice repeated that she would be back to tea should any one call and ask for her.

'Nobody is likely to ask for you,' said Nancy with sisterly frankness, 'nobody ever does. You needn't bother to be back to tea unless you like,' she added with a self-conscious smile. 'Jimmy said he might look in.'

'So much the better,' thought Jean; 'I can bring in a cake without exciting suspicion.' And she started gaily on her way, and wondered ingenuously why all the people in the street seemed so indifferent to her happiness. At Berners Street, a shock was awaiting her. Would Miss Moreen kindly stay till five to-day as the children's mother was obliged to go out, and nurse had a holiday? And as the children's mother had already gone out and nurse's holiday had begun before breakfast, there was no appeal left to poor Jean, and she settled down to her day's work with a sense of injustice in her mind and a queer feeling in her throat that had to be overcome during an arithmetic lesson. But as the day wore on her spirits rose to an unnatural pitch; she spent the afternoon in romping furiously with her pupils; and when five o'clock came, she was standing outside in the street counting the coins in her little purse.

'I can just do it, and I shall!' she cried, and a passing cabby pulled up in answer to her graphic appeal and carried her away westwards. He whistled when she paid him an extravagant fare, and watched her with a chuckle as she flew up the steps and fumbled nervously at the keyhole before she was able to unlock the door. He would have wondered more, or perhaps less, had he seen her standing on the mat outside the front room on the first floor, giving her hat and hair certain touches which did not affect their appearance in the least, and listening breathlessly to the sound of voices that came from within. Then she turned the handle suddenly and went in.

The lamp was not yet lighted and the daylight was waning. The room was in partial darkness, but the fire was burning brightly, and it shone on the face of a man as he leaned forward in a low chair, and talked to the beautiful girl who lay on the sofa, smiling up at him in a gentle deprecating manner, as if his homage were new and overwhelming to her.

The man was not the expected Jimmy, and Jean took two swift little steps into the room. The spell was broken and they looked round with a start.

'Oh, here you are,' cried Nancy, gliding off the sofa and putting her arms round her in her pretty affectionate manner. 'Poor Mr Unwin has been waiting quite an hour for you. Whatever made you so late?'

Jean disengaged herself a little roughly, and held out her hand to Tom.

'Have you been very bored?' she asked him with a slight curl of her lip.

'That could hardly be the case in Miss Nancy's company,' he replied in his best manner; 'but if she had not been so kind to me your tardiness in coming would certainly have been harder to bear.'

The carefully picked words did not come naturally from the boyish fellow who had talked slang to her on the top of the omnibus, but Tom Unwin never talked slang when there was a situation of any kind. Jean was bitterly conscious of being the only one of the three who was not behaving in a picturesque manner. The other two vied with each other in showing her little attentions, a fact that entirely failed to deceive her.

'Do they think I am a fool?' she thought scornfully. 'Why should they suppose that I need propitiating?'

And she insisted curtly on pouring out her own cup of tea, and sat down obstinately on a high chair, without noticing the low one he was pulling forward for her.

'Don't let me disturb you,' she said calmly; 'you made such a charming picture when I came in.'

They only seemed to her to be making a ridiculous picture now. She was conscious of nothing but the satirical view of the situation, and she had a mad desire to point at them and scream with laughter at their fatuity in supposing that she did not see through their discomfiture.

'We thought you were never coming,' began Nancy in her gentle tired voice; 'I was afraid you had been taken ill or something.'

'Yes, indeed,' added Tom with strained jocularity; 'it was all I could do to restrain Miss Nancy from sending a telegram to somebody about you. She only gave up the idea when I got her to acknowledge that she didn't even know where to send it.'

'Now, that is really too bad of you,' exclaimed Nancy with a carefully studied pout; 'you know quite well—'

'Indeed, I appeal to you, Miss Moreen—'

'Don't listen to him, Jean.'

'It doesn't seem to me to matter very much,' said Jean with much composure; 'I am very glad that I gave you so much to talk about.'

They made another attempt to conciliate her.

'Do have some cake. It isn't bad,' said Nancy invitingly.

'Or some more tea?' added Tom anxiously. 'You must be so played out with your long day's work. Have the little brats been very trying?'

'Oh, you needn't worry about the little brats, thanks,' said Jean, eating bread and butter voraciously for the sake of an occupation.

'Come nearer the fire,' said Nancy coaxingly; 'Mr Unwin will move up that other chair.'

'Of course,' said Mr Unwin with alacrity, glad of any excuse that removed him for a moment from the unpleasant scrutiny of her large cold eyes.

'You are both very kind to bother about me like this. I am really not used to it,' said Jean with a hard little laugh. 'Won't you go on with your conversation while I write a postcard?'

She made a place for her cup on the tea-tray, strolled across the room to the bureau, and sat down to look vacantly at a blank postcard. The other two seated themselves stiffly at opposite ends of the hearthrug, and manufactured stilted phrases for the ears of Jean.

'Your sister draws, I believe?'

'Oh, yes. Jean is fearfully clever, you know. She used to win prizes and things. I never won a prize in my life. Oh, yes; Jean is certainly very clever indeed.'

'I am sure of it. It must be charming to be so clever.'

'Yes. Nothing else matters if you are as clever as all that. It doesn't affect Jean in the least if things happen to go wrong, because she always has her cleverness to console her, don't you see.'

'Brains are a perennial consolation,' said Tom solemnly; 'I always knew, Miss Nancy, that your sister was very exceptional.'

'Exceptional! Yes, I suppose I am that,' thought Jean with a curious feeling of dissatisfaction. The burden of her own cleverness was almost too much for her, and she would have given worlds, just then, to have been as ordinary as Nancy – and as beautiful.

'Will you forgive me if I go upstairs and finish a drawing?' she said, coming forward into the firelight again. They uttered some conventional regrets, and Tom held the door open for her. 'Good-bye,' she said, smiling, 'I am sorry my drawing won't wait. It has to go in to-morrow morning.'

'I envy you your charming talent,' he said with a sigh that was a little overdone.

'Do you? It prevents me from being domesticated, you know, and that is always a pity, isn't it?' she said, and drew her hand away quickly.

Upstairs with her head on an old brown cloak she lay and listened to the hum of voices below.

'Why wasn't I born a fool with a pretty face?' she murmured. 'Fools are the only really happy people in the world, for they are the only people the rest of us have the capacity to understand. And to be understood by the majority of people is the whole secret of happiness. No one would take the trouble to understand *me*. Of course, it is unbearably conceited to say so, but there is no one to hear.'

When Nancy came up to bed, she found her sister working away steadily at her drawing.

'It was very mean of you to leave me so long with that man, Jean; he stayed quite an hour after you left,' she said, suppressing a yawn.

'Oh, I thought you wouldn't mind; I don't get on with him half so well as you do. Stand out of the light, will you?'

'He thinks you're immensely clever,' said Nancy; 'he says he never met any one so determined and plucky in his life. Of course you will get on, he says.'

'Yes,' said Jean with a strange smile, as she nibbled the top of her pencil; 'I suppose I shall get on. And to the end of my days people will admire me from a distance, and talk about my talent and my determination, just as they talk about your beauty and your womanly ways. That is so like the world; it always associates us with a certain atmosphere and never admits the possibility of any other.'

Nancy was perched on the end of the bed in her white peignoir, with her knees up to her chin and a puzzled expression on her face.

'How queer you are to-night, Jean,' she said; 'I don't think I understand.'

'My atmosphere,' continued Jean in the same passionless tone, 'is the clever and capable one. It is the one that is always reserved for the unattractive people who have understanding, the sort of people who know all there is to know, from observation, and never get the chance of experiencing one jot of it. They are the people who learn about life from the outside, and remain half alive themselves to the end of time. Nobody would think of falling in love with them, and they don't even know how to be lovable. It is a very clinging atmosphere,' she added sadly; 'I shall never shake it off.'

Nancy stopped making a becoming wreck of her coils of hair, and looked more bewildered than before.

'I don't understand, Jean,' she said again.

Jean looked at her for a moment with eyes full of admiration.

'Don't worry about it, child,' she said slowly; 'you will never have to understand.'

T. BARON RUSSELL

A Guardian of the Poor

I

Borlase and Company did not aspire, like certain other drapers in the Southern Suburbs, to be universal providers. Neither did they seek, otherwise than passively, to rival these powerful neighbours in the esteem of villadom and the superior order of suburban society. The wares that changed hands across Borlase's many counters were modestly content to assimilate, at a respectful interval, those examples of last year's mode which found their way to the more ambitious emporia, where they were exhibited to the wives and daughters of retired tradesmen and head-clerks, as Parisian innovations, almost sinfully novel. The raw material of feminine adornment was what Borlase and Company dealt in, uncostly chiffons and faced ribbons, which with the *Penny Dressmaker* and the *Amateur Bonnet Journal* to aid, produced under deft hands a sort of jerry-built finery, whose characteristic a sensitive instinct might divine, in a sympathetic glance, from the 'groves' of dingy two-storeyed houses, which sent forth their hundreds a-Saturday's to Borlase's shop. The possibilities latent in shoddy (or débris of old cloth) and of cotton warps in a fabric guaranteed 'all wool', and so demonstrated to unconfiding customers, on a triumphant withdrawal of weft by Mr Borlase, had been deeply explored by the mercers who supplied him; for the acts of Parliament which forbid adulteration do not apply to wares otherwise than edible, and the later statute against fraudulent misdescription is beneficently evasible, as having no particular officer to set it in motion. Thus, 'full-fashioned' stockings, owing their form to judicious blocking after manufacture, and double-width calicoes at four pence three farthings, which yield on agitation a rich dressing of clay-like powder, are quite securely vendible, without danger to the repute of the retailer as a pillar of society and a local vestryman.

Since you cannot be a vestryman and a guardian of the poor, even in the suburbs, for nothing, it is to be gathered that Mr Borlase – the sole constituent of Borlase and Company – went not unrewarded, even in this world's corruptible profit, for the benefits which he bestowed on society. It was his pride to be referred to as the cheapest draper in the neighbourhood. You could purchase at his shop, on astonishingly economical terms, goods which only a very acute and highly trained perception could distinguish at sight from others, which, in less favoured markets, were priced at twice those rates, an advantage secured by the frequent conferences of Borlase and Company with hungry looking German wholesalers in Jewin Street and other recondite thoroughfares of the E.C. district.

The purchasing capacity in the individual, among Mr Borlase's clientage, being small, it follows that the number of his transactions, to be lucrative, must be also large. Hence the sixty-odd 'young people' ('who,' as a local paper worded it 'constituted the *personnel* of Messrs. Borlase and Co's staff') had all their work cut out for them on a Saturday night. But practice, and the consciousness that lapse or error entailed fines not conveniently spared from scanty wages, soon taught new-comers the art of managing two customers at a time, and four on Saturday. Thus the crowded shop full of buyers was kept pretty constantly on the move, even at the busiest of times. Lest any should go empty away, Borlase and Company in person – pompous, full-fed, and evaporating venality at every pore – mingled with his patrons near the exit; and woe to the shop girl who had failed to cajole her customer! This duty of shop-walking Mr Borlase divided at busy times with a lean man, grey-headed and stooping at the shoulders, who rubbed lank hands together when addressed by a customer (he never ventured to accost one, in the Borlasian manner) and was summoned quickly from counter to counter to 'sign'. From Monday to Friday he docketed invoices, checked sales-books, and drudged through the other routine of account-keeping, day by day; on Saturday, from two o'clock onward, he relieved his proprietor of the duty of initialling bills, so that the latter might stand guard at the door. He picked up the arrears of his afternoon work after the shop closed at eleven-thirty.

Alone, of all Borlase and Company's people, he slept at home, living at a house in Denmark Street, near the back of the shop. He had grown to the lean, grey pantaloon he was, in Borlase and Company's service, and rising to a proud stipend of two pounds a week, had taken to his arms the faded little wife who had waited for him. His position was deemed one of the plums of the establishment.

On an afternoon, early in January, the eyes of this John Hunt strayed often to the clock. Not that he longed for tea-time: had it not been Saturday he might have wished for five o'clock to come round, but on Saturdays he was not allowed to go home, but shared the bounty of Borlase and Company with the twenty-four young men and twenty-nine 'young persons' of the counters. He knew very well that to-day there could be no hurried home-going; and however he might weary to assure himself that all was well in the shabby little six-roomed house, where the shabby little wife was moving about her work, not quite so actively as usual, he must await, with what patience he might, the end of the day's work. And having an occasion for anxiety, he found the hours, busy as they were, long in passing. There was a little more work during the half hour which the assistants divided among them, in thirds, for tea. Customers were many, and with the best will in the world to keep them in hand, the men and girls had to bear frequent complaints from impatient buyers, and Hunt, hurrying at the call of 'sign' – he had no other name in the shop – was summoned hither and thither to stay the departure of patrons who 'really couldn't wait about any longer'. To suffer a customer to go away unsupplied was the cardinal sin at Borlase's: 'getting the swop' the young people called it. The rule of the place required that, on this emergency threatening, Mr Borlase, or the temporary shop walker, must be called in. Three 'swops' involved 'the sack'; every one knew that: and it is wonderful what patience that knowledge imparted to the assistants at the various counters.

The grand rush of the week, however, came after tea on Saturday evening, when the shop grew hot and gassy even in January, and a vague odour of damp umbrellas pervaded everything. Customers waited, row upon row. It was not easy to move among them: and to keep them good humoured required endless resource and tact. The day's meridian was at nine o'clock. After that, the tide of purchasers would slacken, by degrees, until closing time. The night was inclement, but as the critical opportunity of Sunday morning chapel would soon be at hand, the rain could not keep folk at home. On one side of the door, the shop-window was dull with drops. By some oversight, the grating overhead had not been opened on this side to let the steam out. Every one in the shop was damp, cross, and sticky at the fingers.

A stout inhabitant entered at ten, and spent a happy hour inspecting the entire stock of bonnet ribbons. She decided a dozen times on this or that: a dozen times she altered her mind, at the reflection that each colour of the solar spectrum failed to suit 'her style.' No, nothing would do. She must go somewhere else, that was all; if the young lady hadn't got what she wanted, it was no use of the young lady for to try for to put her off with something else. It was all very well, she added, to say they had shown her everything. If it was too much trouble to get it down (here the rotund lady raised her voice), why, better say so at once.

'Sign!' said the shop girl, wearily.

'What is it, Miss?'

'Lady wishes for a dark 'eliotrope ribbon, shot with cerise.' (Such atrocities were common at Borlase's.)

'Well, haven't you shown the lady—?'

'We haven't the width.' Hunt vainly endeavoured to still the rising storm: the customer was inexorable. No, she would go; it was quite plain they didn't *mean* to serve her; she had been kept waiting—'

'Very sorry we cannot suit you, Madam, now; but we shall be having some new ribbons in on Monday.' The outraged dame departed.

At the door she encountered the swift eye of Borlase and Company, which at once detected something wrong. No, she was *not* suited. Mr Borlase was quite sure if— No, they had admitted they hadn't got it; it was no good wasting any more of her time. She would just be off.

'May I ask who said that we were out of stock?' Mr Borlase asked. The tone was suave, but the look dangerous.

'The young person at the counter said so; so did that shabby-looking man that signs the bills,' he was answered. Mr Borlase looked more dangerous still.

By this time the shutters were being put up by the junior assistants, the collars of their black coats turned up to keep off a little of the fine rain. Only the side door remained open, and a man stood by it to let the customers out, one by one. Hunt had slipped off to his desk and was already rapidly adding up counterfoils, before the lights were put out in the shop. Mr Borlase rolled pompously into the little office about this time, and began to pay the staff, who were waiting, in a long *queue*, to file past him. He recited in the tone of a patron the pay of each assistant, as he shoved it through the little cash window, distracting Hunt's calculations horribly.

The latter was working rapidly. It was not easy to keep his mind on the figures. He was tired and anxious; as the time for going home came nearer, he grew even excited. Finally, the last book was made up, and the grand total, verified by comparison with the till, happily 'came out' right. Mr Borlase, who had lit a cigar, laid it cautiously down, and checked the money. Then he gave Hunt his forty shillings, and the drudge, buttoning up his shabby frockcoat, prepared to go. This operation attracting Mr Borlase's attention, recalled the words of the angry customer. He called Hunt back and surveyed him coldly. The coat was faded and shiny. It dragged in creases at the buttonholes, and the buttons showed an edge of metal, where the cloth covering had worn out. The braid down the front was threadbare, and showed grey in places. Certainly his shop-walker was inexcusably shabby.

'How is it that your coat is so unsightly, Hunt?' Mr Borlase at length demanded, querulously. 'It's a disgrace to my establishment, and customers remark upon it. Just look to it that you make yourself presentable. I can't have a scarecrow walking my shop; it reflects upon me – upon me, mind you!'

Hunt murmured something to the effect that the coat certainly *was* rather old; but his master interrupted him impatiently. 'Old,' he said; 'of course it's old – much too old. If you can't dress yourself properly, I shall find some one who can. And, Hunt,' he added, reminiscently, 'another thing. I've once or twice noticed on week-days that you smell of tobacco – shag tobacco. That's another thing I must have mended. I can't have my customers disgusted by your filthy habits. Look to that also'; and he turned away, leaving Hunt to shuffle off homeward under an inefficient umbrella.

II

Hunt paused on the doorstep of the little house in Denmark Street, and looked up, anxiously, at the first-floor window. All dark – and, so far, so good. He opened the door noiselessly with a latch-key and listened. Everything was quiet. The little wife had gone to bed then, and he made his way on tiptoe to the kitchen, lit a paraffin lamp, spread the discreditable coat wide open on two nails, that it might dry, and put on his slippers. A scratching at the back door, mingled with faint whines, made him step quickly across the kitchen, to admit a mongrel fox-terrier. 'What, Joey!' he cried, in the high-pitched voice which some men use to dogs and children – 'What, Joey! What the little bow-wow – didn't they let you in?' He sat down as the animal frisked around him, jumping at last into his lap, to lick his face, and nuzzle its cold nose against his neck, while he pulled its ears caressingly and tried to look into the eager, welcoming eyes. To a man humbled, lonely, and as yet childless, the demonstrative admiration of the dog was precious: this one living thing, and the tired woman upstairs, looked up to him, and he could not spare even the dog's homage.

Presently he turned to the deal table – spotless, and scrubbed until the harder fibres of the wood stood out in ridges where the softer parts had worn away. On one corner a piece of coarse tablecloth, oft darned, had been spread and turned over, to cover something that lay under it. He turned it back and began to eat his supper of bread and cheese, cutting off snips of rind to throw to the dog, sitting alert on its haunches with anticipatory wags. Supper finished, Hunt took his money, in a dirty canvas bag, from his pocket, and laid it out on the table. Seven shillings for the rent, three shillings to complete the guinea that was hoarding for a certain other purpose; that left thirty shillings. Two shillings for his own pocket; eighteen shillings, Mary's housekeeping money; two shillings for the old mother who lived down in Camberwell, to be near the workhouse, whence came a small weekly relief that helped to keep her. Eight shillings over: John thought he knew of a shop where a second-hand frockcoat (his strict official costume as shop-walker) was offered for ten shillings, but might be compassed, with discretion, for eight. He gathered up the money, and looked wistfully at the tin tobacco-box on the dresser shelf.

No; it was empty, he remembered. He had not been able to save the threepence halfpenny this week. Still – there might be a few grains of dust in it. He took down a blackened clay pipe, ran his little finger round the bowl, and shook the box tentatively. Something rustled within; he put his thumb nail to the lid. Half an ounce of shag screwed up in paper! So the little wife had thought of him, and prepared this surprise. Dear girl. The old man's eyes moistened – he *was* an old man, though only forty by the calendar – as he unwrapped the tobacco, carefully shaking particles of the dust from folds in the paper, and filled himself half a pipe. Then he smoked, fingering the dog's ears reflectively and mentally adding up afresh his scanty moneys. Certainly it was good that he should be able to put by the three shillings this Saturday: that guinea might be wanted, any day; and after that there would be at least half-a-crown a week, and beer-money, needed for the charwoman who was to 'do for' the missus and give an eye to the house, presently.

III

When he blew out the lamp, and crept, slippers in hand, upstairs, he was shivering a little. He stood a moment outside the bedroom door and lit a match for the candle, to avoid disturbing the sleeping wife. He undressed very quietly; but the woman moved at some slight sound, and sat up at once on seeing him, smiling, and holding out her arms. He put them down very gently.

'Careful, dearie,' he said; 'careful, you know,' and took her head in his arm. 'How have you been?'

'Oh, very bobbish. So you found the bit o' smoke?' – his breath being her informant.

'Yes, dear. But you oughtn't to scrape—'

She put her hand over his mouth. 'Hush,' she said, 'you old stupid. I couldn't let you go without the only little bit of comfort. But look here,' she added gravely; 'look what's come.' She drew a folded buff paper from under the pillow. She had brought it upstairs in her hand, that the sight of it might not vex him before supper. It was a printed circular from the local police station, remarking that Mr Hunt had taken out a license to keep one dog the year before, but had not renewed it this year at its expiration. If Mr Hunt had now ceased to keep one dog, the circular politely concluded, this notice might be disregarded.

He looked blank. Seven-and-sixpence for Joey. The little doggy never appeared in the light of an extravagance except at license-time; he was an economical quadruped, subsisting on the scraps, and such treasure-trove as he could pick up in the gutter. But the notice meant good-bye to the frock-coat, for the present week at least; and Hunt knew that it might be long enough before he had eight shillings in his pocket again.

He brightened up, however, before the little woman had time to remark his depression.

'All right,' he said, cheerfully, 'I've got seven-and-six over, old girl. I'll go round to the post office and get the license, first thing on Monday morning.'

'You'd better let me get it; you'll be late if you go yourself. I can just as well pop round, in the morning.'

'Oh, I don't like you to go out any more than you're obliged to. I'll start a little earlier. I dare say Miss King'll be in the shop.'

The idea of discarding the dog never for an instant occurred to either.

In the morning – Sunday – John slipped early out of bed, lit the fire below stairs, and was at his wife's beside with a cup of tea when she awoke. In the meantime, he had been to a near chemist's where a painted tin plate proclaimed that medicines could be obtained on the Sabbath by ringing the bell, and procured a pennyworth of ammonia – he called it 'ahmonia' – from the grumbling apprentice. Then, laying the despised coat on the kitchen table, he had carefully brushed it, rubbed the pungent fluid into the cloth with a rag, and brushed yet again. Afterwards, using the handle of a pen, he inked the thread-bare places and the frayed buttonholes, spread the condemned garment on a clothes-line that the smell of the ammonia might evaporate, and stretched the sleeves and pulled the lappels, as well as he could, into better shape. This had been, in its time, a Sunday coat, purchased not secondhand but *new*, in some moment of temporary prosperity, though he had been obliged to depose it to every day wear long since, and had never replaced it. This half hour's work would give it a fresh lease of life, he reflected, as he stepped back to contemplate the effect – if only the buttons didn't happen to catch Borlase and Company's eye. And later on, he would manage to get another.

IV

Monday morning was a slack time at Borlase's – a time devoted to putting in order stock which had been disturbed on Saturday night, and which was allowed, perforce, to be put away hurriedly in the hey-day of harvest. Ribbons had to be re-rolled in their paper interlining, and neatly secured with tiny pins. Calicoes had to be refolded in tighter bales: hat trimmings and artificial flowers to be dusted with a sort of overgrown paint-brush, and laid carefully in their shiny black boxes. A general overhauling of wares, in short, had to be done, in the intervals of serving a few early callers, until, after dinner, the ladies of the suburb began to arrive, and the shop to assume its afternoon bustle. John checked invoices, entered up the bought ledger, and verified the charges of city warehousemen for goods newly delivered, crossing the narrow deep shop to reach the warehouse behind in search of various consignments, which needed to be 'passed' as correct and entered in the stock book, before being placed on the shelves for sale. Mr Borlase was 'signing' in the shop, as usual: this duty only devolved upon Hunt on the busy night of the seventh day.

Presently he detected an error in a piece of dress stuff, and drew his principal, by the eye, into the corner where it lay.

'Schweitzer and Brunn invoice this as three dozen and five,' he said, 'It's marked five dozen and three on the cover.'

'Well, which is it?'

'Five three, I should think, sir. The mistake's more likely to be in the bill than in the goods.'

'Well, take it out and measure it, can't you.'

'Very good, sir,' Hunt replied. As he shuffled off, Mr Borlase eyed his round shoulders and shining elbows with disapprobation. In the afternoon light, Hunt looked shabbier than ever. Customers would get the idea that he was underpaid. This must be looked to.

In a little while Hunt sought the master's eye again. 'It's five dozen and three, right enough,' he said: 'five three, good measure. Will you have it cut, or send for a corrected invoice?'

Mr Borlase glared. '*You've* nothing to do with the measure,' he said, sharply: 'what's it to do with you? All *you've* got to do is to see that it holds three dozen and five: stop there. I can't keep my books and Schweitzer's too. Mark it "query over" in the Stock Book. Haven't you got enough to fill your time without wasting it on other people's blunders as well as your own?'

'And, Hunt,' he added, sternly, 'what about that coat of yours? I told you on Saturday it wouldn't do. Why haven't you come in a better one?'

'I haven't got a better one, sir,' Hunt faltered.

'You – haven't – got – a better one, sir,' Borlase replied mocking him. 'Then why the devil haven't you bought yourself a better one, sir?'

Hunt answered that there hadn't been time: and besides, he had not the money.

'You haven't the money? What do you mean by "you haven't the money?" Weren't you paid on Saturday? "Yes you know" – but yes, you don't know' – the temper of Borlase and Company rose, or was affected to rise, higher: 'But yes, you don't know,' said the outraged draper, 'that you disgrace my shop.'

'I'm very sorry, sir: I shall try what I can do next Saturday: but I have a good many expenses just now; and I've had the dog license to pay this morning, and my wife—'

'Dog license? What do you want with dog licenses? What do you want with dogs? Put the brute in a bucket of water – that's the way to pay dog licenses! Why – the coat's absolutely falling to pieces: look at the braid, look at the elbows.' Mr Borlase in his wrath, seized one of the lappels in his finger, and gave it a pull. The worn braid, accustomed to more tender usage, yielded and ripped a foot or more down the front, showing the frayed edges beneath.

The situation was plainly impossible. On the one hand, Hunt could not be made to buy himself new clothes if he had no money. On the other, he was as plainly an eyesore in the present coat – and Mr Borlase had by his own act destroyed it. He was a man of quick decisions. 'Come with me,' he said. 'Mr Peters! Take the floor please,' and he pushed Hunt by the elbow to the staircase which led to the upper storeys.

The first floor was occupied by Mr Borlase and his family. At the end of a corridor was a wide hanging-cupboard, with sliding doors. Searching in this, Mr Borlase found a long-discarded frock-coat of his own. 'Put that on,' he said sternly. 'And don't let me see you disgracing my shop any more. How many men do you think would take the coat off their own backs to clothe you?'

Hunt broke into thanks: it is likely that this simple fellow was actually grateful for the thing thus flung to him. He walked homeward buoyantly at tea time, full of excitement and eager to show this great acquisition to Mary.

But something chilled him as he opened the door. Mary would have been in the passage at the first sound of his latch-key, ordinarily. The place was empty, now, and a strange hat hung on a walking-stick leaning against the casing of the parlour door.

So the hour had come, and the guinea was wanted already! He ran hurriedly upstairs to the bedroom. The doctor pushed him from the door, and came out on the landing with him. 'You can't come in, just yet,' he said.

'When was she "taken"?' John asked.

'About two o'clock, I understand. The woman happened to be with her, and has just fetched me.'

'How long—'

'Oh, an hour more yet I expect. All very nicely: no cause for alarm. Just keep quiet, and don't disturb her, there's a good fellow: it's all you can do.'

He pushed the reluctant John to the stair-head and re-entered the bedroom with a quick movement. Hunt crept downstairs, and choked over his tea: then rushed back to the shop. He had brought the old coat on his arm, and laid it carefully over the stair-railing. It could still be mended, and would do for house wear.

He made several mistakes that night: but as this concerned only himself (who had to ferret out and rectify them) it had no other effect than to keep him a little later than nine o'clock before he could leave. He ran home, and arrived panting. The frowsy charwoman met him in the passage.

'There, it's a good job you've come,' she said. 'She's been a-askin' for you. It's a boy. You can come up and speak to her, a minute, but you mustn't stop long. She's got to have her sleep. Then you can go and get me my beer. There isn't a drop in the 'ouse.'

Mary only lifted her eyes when he pressed his lips to her damp brow. She did not speak.

'Let me see him,' he whispered.

She turned back a corner of the quilt, where a shapeless face, inconceivably small, inconceivably red, lay on her arms. John stooped and kissed the scant, silky, black hair. The child threw up a tiny open hand, seizing the finger with which he touched it. A great emotion mastered and silenced him, and he stooped to kiss the baby finger-nails. Mary smiled again and closed her eyes.

V

Hunt fared irregularly during the next few days. His work, as it happened, was rather heavy – heavier than usual – and the accident saved him some anxious thoughts, for full hours are short hours. Every now and then, though, as he moved on some errand of his labour, came a new experience – the joy of sudden recollection. There was a baby! The remembrance gave him a fresh thrill of happiness each time that it recurred. An hour, each night, he sat alone with his wife in the bed-room, gazing silently at the little head, just hidden by the flannel it was wrapped in. They dared not speak, lest the child should rouse – and indeed, Mary was hardly strong enough to talk yet, though she described herself, in a whisper, as 'getting on famous'.

The charwoman departed early in each evening, now, and John slept, secretly, on the landing, that he might hear his wife's call, if she should need him in the night. He was supposed to lie on a couch in that mathematical-looking parlour, the use of which was so rigidly confined to Sunday afternoons: but this was a myth, loyally concealed by the charwoman, who was spared the trouble of a bed-making by the inscrutable whim of her patient's husband. He caught a severe cold in the process, which was not surprising.

Mary's progress did not satisfy the doctor. Ten days showed little or no recovery of strength. He ordered beef tea, and John provided it. But no success attended this time-honoured prescription. Possibly it was not skillfully prepared: anyway the patient grew worse. On Wednesday at dinner time, John found the doctor waiting for him. 'I don't like the looks of your wife, Mr Hunt,' he said, bluntly. 'She isn't picking up as fast as we should wish. I should like her to have some beef essence – a small quantity, every two hours.'

'What, Liebig?' asked John.

'No, no, not Liebig: *essence*, not extract. It is a kind of jelly. You get it at the chemists: lot of nourishment in a small space – very easily assimilated, you know.'

John didn't know, but he neglected his dinner and hurried to the drug stores. 'Fifteen pence,' said the man at the counter; and John's heart sank at the smallness of the tin that was handed him. On his return he met the landlord, demanding the rent. Three more visits to the chemists, at one and threepence, left him, by Thursday night, with an empty pocket; and there was only enough food in the house for the charwoman's meals next day. At noon on Friday he found the doctor in the house again.

'She has had no beef to-day I find,' said the man of science in reply to John's interrogative look. 'And she is sinking, besides. She must have a teaspoonful of brandy every two hours, as well as the essence: if you can, give her a few grapes.' He hurried off before John could recover his self-possession: for many shilling visits must be comprised in a day, by the small general practitioner who would make a living in Camberwell.

John sat down on the stairs in blank misery. He had not a farthing; and Mary was upstairs – perhaps – perhaps dying! He leaned on the wall for support – being weak with hunger himself – and his hat fell off. This reminded him that he was sitting on his coat tails, which would be creased, and he rose, unsteadily. The coat! It was his only removable asset; and Mary was dying. They had never used the pawnshop; but the coat had been a good one, and would certainly fetch a loan – half a sovereign, perhaps, thought the inexperienced John. He went into the kitchen, took down his old coat from its nail, and with needle and cotton hastily repaired the torn binding. Then he ran to the pawnbrokers, whence he emerged, after an interval rich in contumely, with three shillings (less a penny for the ticket) extracted with difficulty from the scornful Hebrew in the little box. But two and elevenpence produced two tins of beef, half a quartern of brandy, and a half-penny roll; the situation, for the moment, was saved.

He was late at the shop and was rebuked for it. Mr Borlase had been awaiting him, having an official appointment to keep. He had to meet his fellow Guardians and the Watch Committee.

VI

Mrs Hunt had rallied a little by night fall, and was reported 'decidedly better' by the doctor next morning. John began to be more hopeful; and he had breakfasted, also, the charwoman having brought in a loaf.

After dinner-time John took up his duties (this being Saturday) as shop walker, privately resolving to make the most of tea at Borlase's. Presently the customary rush of business set in, absorbing all his attention. He did not see that Mr Borlase was eyeing him with a puzzled air, as if he missed something. He did not see either that the fat woman who had gone empty away a fortnight since, entered the shop, and that the sight of her woke up a sudden recollection in his proprietor, who looked over her substantial shoulders at John with a highly unfriendly eye.

VII

A few hours later, he was at home, in the bare kitchen – his chin resting on one hand and his vacant glance fixed on the window opposite.

He had sat there an hour – his mind blank, save for the one dull impression of misery. The detail of his trouble was absent from his thoughts: only the dull, aching consequence of it remained.

Mr Borlase has paid the assistants as usual, checked the cash and received the accounts in silence. But when the shop was empty and dark he had turned upon Hunt in fury.

'What the devil do you mean, by turning up on a Saturday again, in those scarecrow clothes?' he had asked. 'Eh? What the hell do you mean by it? Didn't I take my coat off my own back to give you, eh? And you,

you ungrateful hound, you come to me that figure, to disgrace me! What do you mean by it? Where's my coat?'

'I'm very sorry, sir, I shall have it—'

'Where's my coat, I ask you?'

'If you'll let me explain, sir, I – you see my wife—'

'Where's my coat?'

'I was about to explain, sir. I—'

'Where's my coat?'

'I – I've put it away sir: I have pledged it.'

Mr Borlase staggered.

'You pledged it! You pledged *my coat!* You—'

'My wife was dying, sir: and I had to get—'

'You pledged my coat! The coat I *gave* you! . . . Not a word! Not a word! You have stolen my coat. That is what it amounts to. I've a great mind to give you into custody. It's a gross breach of confidence. A great many men *would* have given you into custody before this. Well, well! So it has come to this! Very well, Mr Blasted Hunt. You have pawned my property; well, this is the end. You can take a week's notice, and go: go, you THIEF!'

It was with difficulty that the angry Borlase abstained from physical assault.

Hunt had slunk away, the disgraceful epithet burning in his ears. But the scene, that he had lived over again and again in the interval, was almost forgotten now. In a week he would be out of work. In a week, Mary must starve; this was the one dull agony that obscured all other consciousness. A leaking gutter-spout outside dripped – dop – dop – dop – on the stones; the recurrent sound impressed itself dully on his brain. Even the questions: 'How can I tell her? How long can I keep it from her?' had passed away. His mind was empty of thought – it could only ache.

The dog crept up to him and licked his hand. He started up. Yes! In two weeks' time they would be parted; they would have to go into the workhouse.

And Mr Borlase was a Guardian of the Poor.

JOSEPH CONRAD

Amy Foster

Kennedy is a country doctor, and lives in Colebrook, on the shores of Eastbay. The high ground rising abruptly behind the red roofs of the little town crowds the quaint High Street against the wall which defends it from the sea. Beyond the sea-wall there curves for miles in a vast and regular sweep the barren beach of shingle, with the village of Brenzett standing out darkly across the water, a spire in a clump of trees; and still further out the perpendicular column of a lighthouse, looking in the distance no bigger than a lead pencil, marks the vanishing-point of the land. The country at the back of Brenzett is low and flat, but the bay is fairly well sheltered from the seas, and occasionally a big ship, windbound or through stress of weather, makes use of the anchoring-ground a mile and a half due north from you as you stand at the back door of the Ship Inn in Brenzett. A dilapidated windmill nearby lifting its shattered arms from a mound no loftier than a rubbish-heap, and a Martello tower squatting at the water's edge half a mile to the south of the Coast-guard cottages, are familiar to the skippers of small craft. These are the official sea-marks for the patch of trustworthy bottom represented on the Admiralty charts by an irregular oval of dots enclosing several figures six, with a tiny anchor engraved among them, and the legend 'mud and shells' over all.

The brow of the upland overtops the square tower of the Colebrook Church. The slope is green and looped by a white road. Ascending along this road, you open a valley broad and shallow, a wide green trough of pastures and hedges merging inland into a vista of purple tints and flowing lines closing the view.

In this valley down to Brenzett and Colebrook and up to Darnford, the market town fourteen miles away, lies the practice of my friend

Kennedy. He had begun life as surgeon in the Navy, and afterwards had been the companion of a famous traveller, in the days when there were continents with unexplored interiors. His papers on the fauna and flora made him known to scientific societies. And now he had come to a country practice – from choice. The penetrating power of his mind, acting like a corrosive fluid, had destroyed his ambition, I fancy. His intelligence is of a scientific order, of an investigating habit, and of that unappeasable curiosity which believes that there is a particle of a general truth in every mystery.

A good many years ago now, on my return from abroad, he invited me to stay with him. I came readily enough, and as he could not neglect his patients to keep me company, he took me on his rounds – thirty miles or so of an afternoon, sometimes. I waited for him on the roads; the horse reached after the leafy twigs, and, sitting high in the dog-cart, I could hear Kennedy's laugh through the half-open door left open of some cottage. He had a big, hearty laugh that would have fitted a man twice his size, a brisk manner, a bronzed face, and a pair of grey, profoundly attentive eyes. He had the talent of making people talk to him freely, and an inexhaustible patience in listening to their tales.

One day, as we trotted out of a large village into a shady bit of road, I saw on our left hand a low brick cottage, with diamond panes in the windows, a creeper on the end wall, a roof of shingle, and some roses climbing on the rickety trellis-work of the tiny porch. Kennedy pulled up to a walk. A woman, in full sunlight, was throwing a dripping blanket over a line stretched between two old apple-trees. And as the bobtailed, long-necked chestnut, trying to get his head, jerked the left hand, covered by a thick dogskin glove, the doctor raised his voice over the hedge: 'How's your child, Amy?'

I had the time to see her dull face, red, not with a mantling blush, but as if her flat cheeks had been vigorously slapped, and to take in the squat figure, the scanty, dusty brown hair drawn into a tight knot at the back of the head. She looked quite young. With a distinct catch in her breath, her voice sounded low and timid.

'He's well, thank you.'

We trotted again. 'A young patient of yours,' I said; and the doctor, flicking the chestnut absently, muttered, 'Her husband used to be.'

'She seems a dull creature,' I remarked listlessly.

'Precisely,' said Kennedy. 'She is very passive. It's enough to look at the red hands hanging at the end of those short arms, at those slow, prominent brown eyes, to know the inertness of her mind – an inertness that one would think made it everlastingly safe from all the surprises of imagination. And yet which of us is safe? At any rate, such as you see her, she had enough imagination to fall in love. She's the daughter of one Isaac Foster, who from a small farmer has sunk into a shepherd; the beginning of his misfortunes dating from his runaway marriage with the cook of his widowed father – a well-to-do, apoplectic grazier, who passionately struck his name off his will, and had been heard to utter threats against his life. But this old affair, scandalous enough to serve as a motive for a Greek tragedy, arose from the similarity of their characters. There are other tragedies, less scandalous and of a subtler poignancy, arising from irreconcilable differences and from that fear of the Incomprehensible that hangs over all our heads – over all our heads . . .'

The tired chestnut dropped into a walk; and the rim of the sun, all red in a speckless sky, touched familiarly the smooth top of a ploughed rise near the road as I had seen it times innumerable touch the distant horizon of the sea. The uniform brownness of the harrowed field glowed with a rosy tinge, as though the powdered clods had sweated out in minute pearls of blood the toil of uncounted ploughmen. From the edge of a copse a waggon with two horses was rolling gently along the ridge. Raised above our heads upon the sky-line, it loomed up against the red sun, triumphantly big, enormous, like a chariot of giants drawn by two slow-stepping steeds of legendary proportions. And the clumsy figure of the man plodding at the head of the leading horse projected itself on the background of the Infinite with a heroic uncouthness. The end of his carter's whip quivered high up in the blue. Kennedy discoursed.

'She's the eldest of a large family. At the age of fifteen they put her out to service at the New Barns Farm. I attended Mrs Smith, the tenant's wife, and saw that girl there for the first time. Mrs Smith, a genteel person with a sharp nose, made her put on a black dress every afternoon. I don't know what induced me to notice her at all. There are faces that call your attention by a curious want of definiteness in their whole aspect, as, walking in a mist, you peer attentively at a vague shape which, after all, may be nothing more curious or strange than a signpost. The only peculiarity I perceived in her was a slight hesitation in her utterance, a sort of preliminary stammer which passes away with the first word. When sharply spoken to, she was apt to lose her head at once; but her heart was of the kindest. She had never been heard to express a dislike for a single human being, and she was tender to every living creature. She was devoted to Mrs Smith, to Mr Smith, to their dogs, cats, canaries; and as to Mrs Smith's grey parrot, its peculiarities exercised upon her a positive fascination. Nevertheless, when that outlandish bird, attacked by the cat, shrieked for help in human accents, she ran out into the yard stopping her ears, and did not prevent the crime. For Mrs Smith this was another evidence of her stupidity; on the other hand, her want of charm, in view of Smith's well-known frivolousness, was a great recommendation. Her short-sighted eyes would swim with pity for a poor mouse in a trap, and she had been seen once by some boys on her knees in the wet grass helping a toad in difficulties. If it's true, as some German fellow has said, that without phosphorus there is no thought, it is still more true that there is no kindness of heart without a certain amount of imagination. She had some. She had even more than is necessary to understand suffering and to be moved by pity. She fell in love under circumstances that leave no room for doubt in the matter; for you need imagination to form a notion of beauty at all, and still more to discover your ideal in an unfamiliar shape.

'How this aptitude came to her, what it did feed upon, is an inscrutable mystery. She was born in the village, and had never been further away from it than Colebrook or perhaps Darnford. She lived for four years with the Smiths. New Barns is an isolated farmhouse a mile away from the road, and she was content to look day after day at the same fields, hollows, rises; at the trees and the hedgerows; at the faces of the four men about the farm, always the same – day after day, month after month, year after year. She never showed a desire for conversation, and, as it seemed to me, she did not know how to smile. Sometimes of a fine Sunday afternoon she would put on her best dress, a pair of stout boots, a large grey hat trimmed with a black feather (I've seen her in that finery), seize an absurdly slender parasol, climb over two stiles, tramp over three fields and along two hundred yards of road – never further. There stood Foster's cottage. She would help her mother to give their tea to the younger children, wash up the crockery, kiss the little ones, and go back to the farm. That was all. All the rest, all the change, all the relaxation. She never seemed to wish for anything more. And then she fell in love. She fell in love silently, obstinately – perhaps helplessly. It came slowly, but when it came it worked like a powerful spell; it was love as the Ancients understood it: an irresistible and fateful impulse – a possession! Yes, it was in her to become haunted and possessed by a face, by a presence, fatally, as though she had been a pagan worshipper of form under a joyous sky – and to be awakened at last from that mysterious forgetfulness of self, from that enchantment, from that transport, by a fear resembling the unaccountable terror of a brute . . .'

With the sun hanging low on its western limit, the expanse of the grass-lands framed in the counterscarps of the rising ground took on a gorgeous and sombre aspect. A sense of penetrating sadness, like that inspired by a grave strain of music, disengaged itself from the silence of the fields. The men we met walked past slow, unsmiling, with downcast eyes, as if the melancholy of an overburdened earth had weighted their feet, bowed their shoulders, borne down their glances.

'Yes,' said the doctor to my remark, 'one would think the earth is under a curse, since of all her children these that cling to her the closest are uncouth in body and as leaden of gait as if their very hearts were loaded with chains. But here on this same road you might have seen amongst these heavy men a being lithe, supple, and long-limbed, straight like a pine with something striving upwards in his appearance as though the heart within him had been buoyant. Perhaps it was only the force of the contrast, but when he was passing one of these villagers here, the soles of his feet did not seem to me to touch the dust of the road. He vaulted over the stiles, paced these slopes with a long elastic stride that made him noticeable at a great distance, and had lustrous black eyes. He was so different from the mankind around that, with his freedom of movement, his soft – a little startled – glance, his olive complexion and graceful bearing, his humanity suggested to me the nature of a woodland creature. He came from there.'

The doctor pointed with his whip, and from the summit of the descent seen over the rolling tops of the trees in a park by the side of the road, appeared the level sea far below us, like the floor of an immense edifice inlaid with bands of dark ripple, with still trails of glitter, ending in a belt of glassy water at the foot of the sky. The light blurr of smoke, from an invisible steamer, faded on the great clearness of the horizon like the mist of a breath on a mirror; and, inshore, the white sails of a coaster, with the appearance of disentangling themselves slowly from under the branches, floated clear of the foliage of the trees.

'Shipwrecked in the bay?' I said.

'Yes; he was a castaway. A poor emigrant from Central Europe bound to America and washed ashore here in a storm. And for him, who knew nothing of the earth, England was an undiscovered country. It was some time before he learned its name; and for all I know he might have expected to find wild beasts or wild men here, when, crawling in the dark over the sea-wall, he rolled down the other side into a dyke, where it was another miracle he didn't get drowned. But he struggled instinctively like an animal under a net, and this blind struggle threw him out into a field. He must have been, indeed, of a tougher fibre than he looked to withstand without expiring such buffetings, the violence of his exertions, and so much fear. Later on, in his broken English that resembled curiously the speech of a young child, he told me himself that he put his trust in God, believing he was no longer in this world. And truly – he would add – how was he to know? He fought his way against the rain and the gale on all fours, and crawled at last among some sheep huddled close under the lee of a hedge. They ran off in all directions, bleating in the darkness, and he welcomed the first familiar sound he heard on these shores. It must have been two in the morning then. And this is all we know of the manner of his landing, though he did not arrive unattended by any means. Only his grisly company did not begin to come ashore till much later in the day . . .'

The doctor gathered the reins, clicked his tongue; we trotted down the hill. Then turning, almost directly, a sharp corner into the High Street, we rattled over the stones and were home.

Late in the evening Kennedy, breaking a spell of moodiness that had come over him, returned to the story. Smoking his pipe, he paced the long room from end to end. A reading-lamp concentrated all its light upon the papers on his desk; and, sitting by the open window, I saw, after the windless, scorching day, the frigid splendour of a hazy sea lying motionless under the moon. Not a whisper, not a splash, not a stir of the shingle, not a footstep, not a sigh came up from the earth below – never a sign of life but the scent of climbing jasmine; and Kennedy's voice, speaking behind me, passed through the wide casement, to vanish outside in a chill and sumptuous stillness.

'. . . The relations of shipwrecks in the olden time tell us of much suffering. Often the castaways were only saved from drowning to die miserably from starvation on a barren coast; others suffered violent death or else slavery, passing through years of precarious existence with people to whom their strangeness was an object of suspicion, dislike, or fear. We read about these things, and they are very pitiful. It is indeed hard upon a man to find himself a lost stranger, helpless, incomprehensible, and of a mysterious origin, in some obscure corner of the earth. Yet amongst all the adventurers shipwrecked in all the wild parts of the world, there is not one, it seems to me, that ever had to suffer a fate so simply tragic as the man I am speaking of, the most innocent of adventurers cast out by the sea in the bight of this bay, almost within sight from this very window.

'He did not know the name of his ship. Indeed, in the course of time we discovered he did not even know that ships had names – "like Christian people"; and when, one day, from the top of the Talfourd Hill, he beheld the sea lying open to his view, his eyes roamed afar, lost in an air of wild surprise, as though he had never seen such a sight before. And probably he had not. As far as I could make out, he had been hustled together with many others on board an emigrant-ship lying at the mouth of the Elbe, too bewildered to take note of his surroundings, too weary to see anything, too anxious to care. They were driven below into the 'tween-deck and battened down from the very start. It was a low timber dwelling – he would say – with wooden beams overhead, like the houses in his country, but you went into it down a ladder. It was very large, very cold, damp and sombre, with places in the manner of wooden boxes where people had to sleep, one above another, and it kept on rocking all ways at once all the time. He crept into one of these boxes and lay down there in the clothes in which he had left his home many days before, keeping his bundle and his stick by his side. People groaned, children cried, water dripped, the lights went out, the walls of the place creaked, and everything was being shaken so that in one's little box one dared not lift one's head. He had lost touch with his only companion (a young man from the same valley, he said), and all the time a great noise of wind went on outside and heavy blows fell – boom! boom! An awful sickness overcame him, even to the point of making him neglect his prayers. Besides, one could not tell whether it was morning or evening. It seemed always to be night in that place.

'Before that he had been travelling a long, long time on the iron track. He looked out of the window, which had a wonderfully clear glass in it, and the trees, the houses, the fields, and the long roads seemed to fly round and round about him till his head swam. He gave me to understand that he had on his passage beheld uncounted multitudes of people – whole nations – all dressed in such clothes as the rich wear. Once he was made to get out of the carriage, and slept through a night on a bench in a house of bricks with his bundle under his head; and once for many hours he had to sit on a floor of flat stones dozing, with his knees up and with his bundle between his feet. There was a roof over him, which seemed made of glass, and was so high that the tallest mountain-pine he had ever seen would have had room to grow under it. Steam-machines rolled in at one end and out at the other. People swarmed more than you can see on a feast-day round the miraculous Holy Image in the yard of the Carmelite Convent down in the plains where, before he left his home, he drove his mother in a wooden cart – a pious old woman who wanted to offer prayers and make a vow for his safety. He could not give me an idea of how large and lofty and full of noise and smoke and gloom, and clang of iron, the place was, but some one had told him it was called Berlin. Then they rang a bell, and another steam-machine came in, and again he was taken on and on through a land that wearied his eyes by its flatness without a single bit of a hill to be seen anywhere. One more night he spent shut up in a building like a good stable with a litter of straw on the floor, guarding his bundle amongst a lot of men, of whom not one could understand a single word he said. In the morning they were all led down to the stony shores of an extremely broad muddy river, flowing not between hills but between houses that seemed immense. There was a steam-machine that went on the water, and they all stood upon it packed tight, only now there were with them many women and children who made much noise. A cold rain fell, the wind blew in his face; he was wet through, and his teeth chattered. He and the young man from the same valley took each other by the hand.

'They thought they were being taken to America straightaway, but suddenly the steam-machine bumped against the side of a thing like a house on the water. The walls were smooth and black, and there uprose, growing from the roof as it were, bare trees in the shape of crosses, extremely high. That's how it appeared to him then, for he had never seen a ship before. This was the ship that was going to swim all the way to America. Voices shouted, everything swayed; there was a ladder dipping up and down. He went up on his hands and knees in mortal fear of falling into the water below, which made a great splashing. He got separated from his companion, and when he descended into the bottom of that ship his heart seemed to melt suddenly within him.

'It was then also, as he told me, that he lost contact for good and all with one of those three men who the summer before had been going about through all the little towns in the foothills of his country. They would arrive on market-days driving in a peasant's cart, and would set up an office in an inn or some other Jew's house. There were three of them, of whom one with a long beard looked venerable; and they had red cloth collars round their necks and gold lace on their sleeves like Government officials. They sat proudly behind a long table; and in the next room, so that the common people shouldn't hear, they kept a cunning telegraph machine, through which they could talk to the Emperor of America. The fathers hung about the door, but the young men of the mountains would crowd up to the table asking many questions, for there was work to be got all the year round at three dollars a day in America, and no military service to do.

'But the American Kaiser would not take everybody. Oh no! He himself had a great difficulty in getting accepted, and the venerable man in uniform had to go out of the room several times to work the telegraph on his behalf. The American Kaiser engaged him at last at three dollars, he being young and strong. However, many able young men backed out, afraid of the great distance; besides, only those who had some money could be taken. There were some who sold their huts and their land because it cost a lot of money to get to America; but then, once there, you had three dollars a day, and if you were clever you could find places where true gold could be picked up on the ground. His father's house was getting over-full. Two of his brothers were married and had children. He promised to send money home from America by post twice a year. His father sold an old cow, a pair of piebald mountain ponies of his own raising, and a cleared plot of fair pasture land on the sunny slope of a pine-clad pass to a Jew inn-keeper, in order to pay the people of the ship that took men to America to get rich in a short time.

'He must have been a real adventurer at heart, for how many of the greatest enterprises in the conquest of the earth had for their beginning just such a bargaining away of the paternal cow for the mirage of true gold far away! I have been telling you more or less in my own words what I learned fragmentarily in the course of two or three years, during which I seldom missed an opportunity of a friendly chat with him. He told me this story of his adventure with many flashes of white teeth and lively glances of black eyes, at first in a sort of anxious baby-talk, then, as he acquired the language, with great fluency, but always with that singing, soft, and at the same time vibrating intonation that instilled a strangely penetrating power into the sound of the most familiar English words, as if they had been the words of an unearthly language. And he always would come to an end, with many emphatic shakes of his head, upon that awful sensation of his heart melting within him directly he set foot on board that ship. Afterwards there seemed to come for him a period of blank ignorance, at any rate as to facts. No doubt he must have been abominably sea-sick and abominably unhappy – this soft and passionate adventurer, taken thus out of his knowledge, and feeling bitterly as he lay in his emigrant bunk his utter loneliness; for his was a highly sensitive nature. The next thing we know of him for certain is that he had been hiding in Hammond's pig-pound by the side of the road to Norton, six miles, as the crow flies, from the sea. Of these experiences he was unwilling to speak; they seemed to have seared into his soul a sombre sort of wonder and indignation. Through the rumours of the countryside, which lasted for a good many days after his arrival, we know that the fishermen of West Colebrook had been disturbed and started by heavy knocks against the walls of weatherboard cottages, and by a voice crying piercingly strange words in the night. Several of them turned out even, but, no doubt, he had fled in sudden alarm at their rough angry tones hailing each other in the darkness. A sort of frenzy must have helped him up the steep Norton hill. It was he, no doubt, who early the following morning had been seen lying (in a swoon, I should say) on the roadside grass by the Brenzett carrier, who actually got down to have a nearer look, but drew back, intimidated by the perfect immobility, and by something queer in the aspect of that tramp, sleeping so still under the showers. As the day advanced, some children came dashing into school at Norton in such a fright that the schoolmistress went out and spoke indignantly to a "horrid-looking man" on the road. He edged away, hanging his head, for a few steps, and then suddenly ran off with extraordinary fleetness. The driver of Mr Bradley's milk-cart made no secret of it that he had lashed with his whip at a hairy sort of gipsy fellow who, jumping up at a turn of the road by the Vents, made a snatch at the pony's bridle. And he caught him a good one too, right over the face, he said, that made him drop down in the mud a jolly sight quicker than he had jumped up; but it was a good half a mile before he could stop the pony. Maybe that in his desperate endeavours to get help, and in his need to get in touch with some one, the poor devil had tried to stop the cart. Also three boys confessed afterwards to throwing stones at a funny tramp, knocking about all wet and muddy, and, it seemed, very drunk, in the narrow deep lane by the lime-kilns. All this was the talk of three villages for days; but we have Mrs Finn's (the wife of Smith's waggoner) unimpeachable testimony that she saw him get over the low wall of Hammond's pig-pound and lurch straight at her, babbling aloud in a voice that was enough to make one die of fright. Having the baby with her in a perambulator, Mrs Finn called out to him to go away, and as he persisted in coming nearer, she hit him courageously with her umbrella over the head, and, without once looking back, ran like the wind with the perambulator as far as the first house in the village. She stopped then, out of breath, and spoke to old Lewis, hammering there at a heap of stones; and the old chap, taking off his immense black wire goggles, got up on his shaky legs to look where she pointed. Together they followed with their eyes the figure of the man running over a field; they saw him fall down, pick himself up, and run on again, staggering and waving his long arms above his head, in the direction of the New Barns Farm. From that moment he is plainly in the toils of his obscure and touching destiny. There is no doubt after this of what happened to him. All is certain now: Mrs Smith's intense terror; Amy Foster's stolid conviction, held against the other's nervous attack, that the man "meant no harm"; Smith's exasperation (on his return from Darnford Market) at finding the dog barking himself into a fit, the back door locked, his wife in hysterics; and all for an unfortunate dirty tramp, supposed to be even then lurking in his stackyard. Was he? He would teach him to frighten women.

'Smith is notoriously hot-tempered, but the sight of some nondescript and miry creature sitting cross-legged amongst a lot of loose straw, and swinging itself to and fro like a bear in a cage, made him pause. Then this tramp stood up silently before him, one mass of mud and filth from head to foot. Smith, alone amongst his stacks with this apparition, in the stormy twilight ringing with the infuriated barking of the dog, felt the dread of an inexplicable strangeness. But when that being, parting with his black hands the long matted locks that hung before his face, as you part the two halves of a curtain, looked out at him with glistening, wild, black-and-white eyes, the weirdness of this silent encounter fairly staggered him. He has admitted since (for the story has been a legitimate subject of conversation about here for years) that he made more than one step backwards. Then a sudden burst of rapid, senseless speech persuaded him at once that he had to do with an escaped lunatic. In fact, that impression never wore off completely. Smith has not in his heart given up his secret conviction of the man's essential insanity to this very day.

'As the creature approached him, jabbering in a most discomposing manner, Smith (unaware that he was being addressed as "gracious lord", and adjured in God's name to afford food and shelter) kept on speaking firmly but gently to it, and retreating all the time into the other yard. At last, watching his chance, by a sudden charge he bundled him head-long into the wood-lodge, and instantly shot the bolt. Thereupon he wiped his brow, though the day was cold. He had done his duty to the community by shutting up a wandering and probably dangerous maniac. Smith isn't a hard man at all, but he had room in his brain only for that one idea of lunacy. He was not imaginative enough to ask himself whether the man might not be perishing with cold and hunger. Meantime, at first, the maniac made a great deal of noise in the lodge. Mrs Smith was screaming upstairs, where she had locked herself in her bedroom; but Amy Foster sobbed piteously at the kitchen-door, wringing her hands and muttering, "Don't! don't!" I daresay Smith had a rough time of it that evening with one noise and another, and this insane, disturbing voice crying obstinately through the door only added to his irritation. He couldn't possibly have connected this troublesome lunatic with the sinking of a ship in Eastbay, of which there had been a rumour in the Darnford market-place. And I daresay the man inside had been very near to insanity on that night. Before his excitement collapsed and he became unconscious he was throwing himself violently about in the dark, rolling on some dirty sacks, and biting his fists with rage, cold, hunger, amazement, and despair.

'He was a mountaineer of the eastern range of the Carpathians, and the vessel sunk the night before in Eastbay was the Hamburg emigrant-ship *Herzogin Sophia-Dorothea*, of appalling memory.

'A few months later we could read in the papers the accounts of the bogus "Emigration Agencies" among the Sclavonian peasantry in the more remote provinces of Austria. The object of these scoundrels was to get hold of the poor ignorant people's homesteads, and they were in league with the local usurers. They exported their victims through Hamburg mostly. As to the ship, I had watched her out of this very window, reaching close-hauled under short canvas into the bay on a dark, threatening afternoon. She came to an anchor, correctly by the chart, off the Brenzett Coastguard station. I remember before the night fell looking out again at the outlines of her spars and rigging that stood out dark and pointed on a background of ragged, slaty clouds like another and a slighter spire to the left of the Brenzett church-tower. In the evening the wind rose. At midnight I could hear in my bed the terrific gusts and the sounds of a driving deluge.

'About that time the Coastguardmen thought they saw the lights of a steamer over the anchoring-ground. In a moment they vanished; but it is clear that another vessel of some sort had tried for shelter in the bay on that awful, blind night, had rammed the German ship amidships (a breach – as one of the divers told me afterwards – "that you could sail a Thames barge through"), and then had gone out either scatheless or damaged, who shall say; but had gone out, unknown, unseen, and fatal, to perish mysteriously at sea. Of her nothing ever came to light, and yet the hue and cry that was raised all over the world would have found her out if she had been in existence anywhere on the face of the waters.

'A completeness without a clue, and a stealthy silence as of a neatly executed crime, characterise this murderous disaster, which, as you may remember, had its gruesome celebrity. The wind would have prevented the loudest outcries from reaching the shore; there had been evidently no time for signals of distress. It was death without any sort of fuss. The Hamburg ship, filling all at once, capsized as she sank, and at daylight there was not even the end of a spar to be seen above water. She was missed, of course, and at first the Coastguardmen surmised that she had either dragged her anchor or parted her cable some time during the night, and had been blown out to sea. Then, after the tide turned, the wreck must have shifted a little and released some of the bodies, because a child – a little fair-haired child in a red frock – came ashore abreast of the Martello tower. By the afternoon you could see along three miles of beach dark figures with bare legs dashing in and out of the tumbling foam, and rough-looking men, women with hard faces, children, mostly fair-haired, were being carried, stiff and dripping, on stretchers, on wattles, on ladders, in a long procession past the door of the Ship Inn, to be laid out in a row under the north wall of the Brenzett Church.

'Officially, the body of the little girl in the red frock is the first thing that came ashore from that ship. But I have patients amongst the seafaring population of West Colebrook, and, unofficially, I am informed that very early that morning two brothers, who went down to look after their cobble hauled up on the beach, found, a good way from Brenzett, an ordinary ship's hencoop lying high and dry on the shore, with eleven drowned ducks inside. Their families ate the birds, and the hencoop was split into firewood with a hatchet. It is possible that a man (supposing he happened to be on deck at the time of the accident) might have floated ashore on that hencoop. He might. I admit it is improbable, but there was the man – and for days, nay, for weeks – it didn't enter our heads that we had amongst us the only living soul that had escaped from that disaster. The man himself, even when he learned to speak intelligibly, could tell us very little. He remembered he had felt better (after the ship had anchored, I suppose), and that the darkness, the wind, and the rain took his breath away. This looks as if he had been on deck some time during that night.

But we mustn't forget he had been taken out of his knowledge, that he had been sea-sick and battened down below for four days, that he had no general notion of a ship or of the sea, and therefore could have no definite idea of what was happening to him. The rain, the wind, the darkness he knew; he understood the bleating of the sheep, and he remembered the pain of his wretchedness and misery, his heartbroken astonishment that it was neither seen nor understood, his dismay at finding all the men angry and all the women fierce. He had approached them as a beggar, it is true, he said; but in his country, even if they gave nothing, they spoke gently to beggars. The children in his country were not taught to throw stones at those who asked for compassion. Smith's strategy overcame him completely. The wood-lodge presented the horrible aspect of a dungeon. What would be done to him next? . . . No wonder that Amy Foster appeared to his eyes with the aureole of an angel of light. The girl had not been able to sleep for thinking of the poor man, and in the morning, before the Smiths were up, she slipped out across the back yard. Holding the door of the wood-lodge ajar, she looked in and extended to him half a loaf of white bread – "such bread as the rich eat in my country", he used to say.

At this he got up slowly from amongst all sorts of rubbish, stiff, hungry, trembling, miserable, and doubtful. "Can you eat this?" she asked in her soft and timid voice. He must have taken her for a "gracious lady". He devoured ferociously, and tears were falling on the crust. Suddenly he dropped the bread, seized her wrist, and imprinted a kiss on her hand. She was not frightened. Through his forlorn condition she had observed that he was good-looking. She shut the door and walked back slowly to the kitchen. Much later on, she told Mrs Smith, who shuddered at the bare idea of being touched by that creature.

'Through this act of impulsive pity he was brought back again within the pale of human relations with his new surroundings. He never forgot it – never.

'That very same morning old Mr Swaffer (Smith's nearest neighbour) came over to give his advice, and ended by carrying him off. He stood, unsteady on his legs, meek, and caked over in half-dried mud, while the two men talked around him in an incomprehensible tongue. Mrs Smith had refused to come downstairs till the madman was off the premises; Amy Foster, far from within the dark kitchen, watched through the open back door; and he obeyed the signs that were made to him to the best of his ability. But Smith was full of mistrust. "Mind, sir! It may be all his cunning," he cried repeatedly in a tone of warning. When Mr Swaffer started the mare, the deplorable being sitting humbly by his side, through weakness, nearly fell out over the back of the high two-wheeled cart. Swaffer took him straight home. And it is then that I come upon the scene.

'I was called in by the simple process of the old man beckoning to me with his forefinger over the gate of his house as I happened to be driving past. I got down, of course.

'"I've got something here," he mumbled, leading the way to an outhouse at a little distance from his other farm-buildings.

'It was there that I saw him first, in a long low room taken upon the space of that sort of coach-house. It was bare and whitewashed, with a small square aperture glazed with one cracked, dusty pane at its further end. He was lying on his back upon a straw pallet; they had given him a couple of horse-blankets, and he seemed to have spent the remainder of his strength in the exertion of cleaning himself. He was almost speechless; his quick breathing under the blankets pulled up to his chin, his glittering, restless black eyes reminded me of a wild bird caught in a snare. While I was examining him, old Swaffer stood silently by the door, passing the tips of his fingers along his shaven upper lip. I gave some directions, promised to send a bottle of medicine, and naturally made some inquiries.

'"Smith caught him in the stackyard at New Barns," said the old chap in his deliberate, unmoved manner, and as if the other had been indeed a sort of wild animal. "That's how I came by him. Quite a curiosity, isn't he? Now tell me, doctor – you've been all over the world – don't you think that's a bit of a Hindoo we've got hold of here?"

'I was greatly surprised. His long black hair scattered over the straw bolster contrasted with the olive pallor of his face. It occurred to me he might be a Basque. It didn't necessarily follow that he should understand Spanish; but I tried him with the few words I know, and also with some French. The whispered sounds I caught by bending my ear to his lips puzzled me utterly. That afternoon the young ladies from the Rectory (one of them read Goethe with a dictionary, and the other had struggled with Dante for years), coming to see Miss Swaffer, tried their German and Italian on him from the doorway. They retreated, just the least bit scared by the flood of passionate speech which, turning on his pallet, he let out at them. They admitted that the sound was pleasant, soft, musical – but, in conjunction with his looks perhaps, it was startling – so excitable, so utterly unlike anything one had ever heard. The village boys climbed up the bank to have a peep through the little square aperture. Everybody was wondering what Mr Swaffer would do with him.

'He simply kept him.

'Swaffer would be called eccentric were he not so much respected. They will tell you that Mr Swaffer sits up as late as ten o'clock at night to read books, and they will tell you also that he can write a cheque for two hundred pounds without thinking twice about it. He himself would tell you that the Swaffers had owned land between this and Darnford for these three hundred years. He must be eighty-five to-day, but he does not look a bit older than when I first came here. He is a great breeder of sheep, and deals extensively in cattle. He attends market-days for miles around in every sort of weather, and drives sitting bowed low over the reins, his lank grey hair curling over the collar of his warm coat, and with a green plaid rug round his legs. The calmness of advanced age gives a solemnity to his manner. He is clean-shaved; his lips are thin and sensitive; something rigid and monachal in the set of his features lends a certain elevation to the character of his face. He has been known to drive miles in the rain to see a new kind of rose in somebody's garden, or a monstrous cabbage grown by a cottager. He loves to hear tell of or to be shown something what he calls "outlandish". Perhaps it was just that outlandishness of the man which influenced old Swaffer. Perhaps it was only an inexplicable caprice. All I know is that at the end of three weeks I caught sight of Smith's lunatic digging in Swaffer's kitchen garden. They had found out he could use a spade. He dug barefooted.

'His black hair flowed over his shoulders. I suppose it was Swaffer who had given him the striped old cotton shirt; but he wore still the national brown cloth trousers (in which he had been washed ashore) fitting to the leg almost like tights; was belted with a broad leathern belt studded with little brass discs; and had never yet ventured into the village. The land he looked upon seemed to him kept neatly, like the grounds round a landowner's house; the size of the cart-horses struck him with astonishment;

the roads resembled garden walks, and the aspect of the people, especially on Sundays, spoke of opulence. He wondered what made them so hard-hearted and their children so bold. He got his food at the back door, carried it in both hands, carefully, to his outhouse, and, sitting alone on his pallet, would make the sign of the cross before he began. Beside the same pallet, kneeling in the early darkness of the short days, he recited aloud the Lord's Prayer before he slept. Whenever he saw old Swaffer he would bow with veneration from the waist, and stand erect while the old man, with his fingers over his upper lip, surveyed him silently. He bowed also to Miss Swaffer, who kept house frugally for her father – a broad-shouldered, big-boned woman of forty-five, with the pocket of her dress full of keys, and a grey, steady eye. She was Church – as people said (while her father was one of the trustees of the Baptist Chapel) – and wore a little steel cross at her waist. She dressed severely in black, in memory of one of the innumerable Bradleys of the neighbourhood, to whom she had been engaged some twenty-five years ago – a young farmer who broke his neck out hunting on the eve of the wedding-day. She had the unmoved countenance of the deaf, spoke very seldom, and her lips, thin like her father's, astonished one sometimes by a mysteriously ironic curl.

'These were the people to whom he owed allegiance, and an overwhelming loneliness seemed to fall from the leaden sky of that winter without sunshine. All the faces were sad. He could talk to no one, and had no hope of ever understanding anybody. It was as if these had been the faces of people from the other world – dead people – he used to tell me years afterwards. Upon my word, I wonder he did not go mad. He didn't know where he was. Somewhere very far from his mountains – somewhere over the water. Was this America, he wondered?

'If it hadn't been for the steel cross at Miss Swaffer's belt he would not, he confessed, have known whether he was in a Christian country at all. He used to cast stealthy glances at it, and feel comforted. There was nothing here the same as in his country! The earth and the water were different; there were no images of the Redeemer by the roadside. The very grass was different, and the trees. All the trees but the three old Norway-pines on the bit of lawn before Swaffer's house, and these reminded him of his country. He had been detected once, after dusk, with his forehead against the trunk of one of them, sobbing, and talking to himself. They had been like brothers to him at that time, he affirmed. Everything else was strange. Conceive you the kind of an existence overshadowed, oppressed, by the everyday material appearances, as if by the visions of a nightmare. At night, when he could not sleep, he kept on thinking of the girl who gave him the first piece of bread he had eaten in this foreign land. She had been neither fierce nor angry, nor frightened. Her face he remembered as the only comprehensible face amongst all these faces that were as closed, as mysterious, and as mute as the faces of the dead who are possessed of a knowledge beyond the comprehension of the living. I wonder whether the memory of her compassion prevented him from cutting his throat. But there! I suppose I am an old sentimentalist, and forget the instinctive love of life which it takes all the strength of an uncommon despair to overcome.

'He did the work which was given him with an intelligence which surprised old Swaffer. By-and-by it was discovered that he could help at the ploughing, could milk the cows, feed the bullocks in the cattle-yard, and was of some use with the sheep. He began to pick up words, too, very fast; and suddenly, one fine morning in spring, he rescued from an untimely death a grandchild of old Swaffer.

'Swaffer's younger daughter is married to Willcox, a solicitor and the Town Clerk of Colebrook. Regularly twice a year they come to stay with the old man for a few days. Their only child, a little girl not three years old at the time, ran out of the house alone in her little white pinafore, and, toddling across the grass of a terraced garden, pitched herself over a low wall head first into the horse-pond in the yard below.

'Our man was out with the waggoner and the plough in the field nearest to the house, and as he was leading the team round to begin a fresh furrow, he saw, through the gap of a gate, what for anybody else would have been a mere flutter of something white. But he had straight-glancing, quick, far-reaching eyes, that only seemed to flinch and lose their amazing power before the immensity of the sea. He was barefooted, and looking as outlandish as the heart of Swaffer could desire. Leaving the horses on the turn, to the inexpressible disgust of the waggoner he bounded off, going over the ploughed ground in long leaps, and suddenly appeared before the mother, thrust the child into her arms, and strode away.

'The pond was not very deep; but still, if he had not had such good eyes, the child would have perished – miserably suffocated in the foot or so of sticky mud at the bottom. Old Swaffer walked out slowly into the field, waited till the plough came over to his side, had a good look at him, and without saying a word went back to the house. But from that time they laid out his meals on the kitchen table; and at first, Miss Swaffer, all in black and with an inscrutable face, would come and stand in the doorway of the living-room to see him make a big sign of the cross before he fell to. I believe that from that day, too, Swaffer began to pay him regular wages.

'I can't follow step by step his development. He cut his hair short, was seen in the village and along the road going to and fro to his work like any other man. Children ceased to shout after him. He became aware of social differences, but remained for a long time surprised at the bare poverty of the churches among so much wealth. He couldn't understand either why they were kept shut up on week-days. There was nothing to steal in them. Was it to keep people from praying too often? The rectory took much notice of him about that time, and I believe the young ladies attempted to prepare the ground for his conversion. They could not, however, break him of his habit of crossing himself, but he went so far as to take off the string with a couple of brass medals the size of a sixpence, a tiny metal cross, and a square sort of scapulary which he wore round his neck. He hung them on the wall by the side of his bed, and he was still to be heard every evening reciting the Lord's Prayer, in incomprehensible words and in a slow, fervent tone, as he had heard his old father do at the head of all the kneeling family, big and little, on every evening of his life. And though he wore corduroys at work, and a slop-made pepper-and-salt suit on Sundays, strangers would turn round to look after him on the road. His foreignness had a peculiar and indelible stamp. At last people became used to see him. But they never became used to him. His rapid, skimming walk; his swarthy complexion; his hat cocked on the left ear; his habit, on warm evenings, of wearing his coat over one shoulder, like a hussar's dolman; his manner of leaping over the stiles, not as a feat of agility, but in the ordinary course of progression – all these peculiarities were, as one may say, so many causes of scorn and offence to the inhabitants of the village. They wouldn't in their dinner hour lie flat on their backs on the grass to stare at the sky. Neither did they go about the fields screaming dismal tunes. Many times have I heard his high-pitched voice from behind the ridge of some sloping sheep-walk, a voice light and soaring, like a lark's, but with a melancholy human note, over our fields that hear only the song of birds. And I should be startled myself. Ah! He was different: innocent of heart, and full of good-will, which nobody wanted, this castaway, that, like a man transplanted into another planet, was separated by an immense space from his past and by an immense ignorance from his future. His quick, fervent utterance positively shocked everybody. "An excitable devil", they called him. One evening, in the tap-room of the Coach and Horses, (having drunk some whisky), he upset them all by singing a love-song of his country. They hooted him down, and he was pained; but Preble, the lame wheelwright, and Vincent, the fat blacksmith, and the other notables, too, wanted to drink their evening beer in peace. On another occasion he tried to show them how to dance. The dust rose in clouds from the sanded floor; he leaped straight up amongst the deal tables, struck his heels together, squatted on one heel in front of old Preble, shooting out the other leg, uttered wild and exulting cries, jumped up to whirl on one foot, snapping his fingers above his head – and a strange carter who was having a drink in there began to swear, and cleared out with his half-pint in his hand into the bar. But when suddenly he sprang upon a table and continued to dance among the glasses, the landlord interfered. He didn't want any "acrobat tricks in the tap-room". They laid their hands on him. Having had a glass or two, Mr Swaffer's foreigner tried to expostulate; was ejected forcibly; got a black eye.

'I believe he felt the hostility of his human surroundings. But he was tough – tough in spirit, too, as well as in body. Only the memory of the sea frightened him, with that vague terror that is left by a bad dream. His home was far away; and he did not want now to go to America. I had often explained to him that there is no place on earth where true gold can be found lying ready and to be got for the trouble of the picking up. How then, he asked, could he ever return home with empty hands when there had been sold a cow, two ponies, and a bit of land to pay for his going? His eyes would fill with tears, and, averting them from the immense shimmer of the sea, he would throw himself face down on the grass. But sometimes, cocking his hat with a little conquering air, he would defy my wisdom. He had found his bit of true gold. That was Amy Foster's heart, which was "a golden heart, and soft to people's misery", he would say in the accents of overwhelming conviction.

'He was called Yanko. He had explained that this meant Little John; but as he would also repeat very often that he was a mountaineer (some word sounding in the dialect of his country like Goorall) he got it for his surname. And this is the only trace of him that the succeeding ages may find in the marriage register of the parish. There it stands – Yanko Goorall – in the rector's handwriting. The crooked cross made by the castaway, a cross whose tracing no doubt seemed to him the most solemn part of the whole ceremony, is all that remains now to perpetuate the memory of his name.

'His courtship had lasted some time – ever since he got his precarious footing in the community. It began by his buying for Amy Foster a green satin ribbon in Darnford. This was what you did in his country. You bought a ribbon at a Jew's stall on a fair-day. I don't suppose the girl knew what to do with it, but he seemed to think that his honourable intentions could not be mistaken.

'It was only when he declared his purpose to get married that I fully understood how, for a hundred futile and inappreciable reasons, how – shall I say odious? – he was to all the countryside. Every old woman in the village was up in arms. Smith, coming upon him near the farm, promised to break his head for him if he found him about again. But he twisted his little black moustache with such a bellicose air and rolled such big, black fierce eyes at Smith that this promise came to nothing. Smith, however, told the girl that she must be mad to take up with a man who was surely wrong in his head. All the same, when she heard him in the gloaming whistle from beyond the orchard a couple of bars of a weird and mournful tune, she would drop whatever she had in her hand – she would leave Mrs Smith in the middle of a sentence – and she would run out to his call. Mrs Smith called her a shameless hussy. She answered nothing. She said nothing at all to anybody, and went on her way as if she had been deaf. She and I alone in all the land, I fancy, could see his very real beauty. He was very good-looking, and most graceful in his bearing, with that something wild as of a woodland creature in his aspect. Her mother moaned over her dismally whenever the girl came to see her on her day out. The father was surly, but pretended not to know; and Mrs Finn once told her plainly that "this man, my dear, will do you some harm some day yet". And so it went on. They could be seen on the roads, she tramping stolidly in her finery – grey dress, black feather, stout boots, prominent white cotton gloves that caught your eye a hundred yards away; and he, his coat slung picturesquely over one shoulder, pacing by her side, gallant of bearing and casting tender glances upon the girl with the golden heart. I wonder whether he saw how plain she was. Perhaps among types so different from what he had ever seen, he had not the power to judge; or perhaps he was seduced by the divine quality of her pity.

'Yanko was in great trouble meantime. In his country you get an old man for an ambassador in marriage affairs. He did not know how to proceed. However, one day in the midst of sheep in a field (he was now Swaffer's under-shepherd with Foster) he took off his hat to the father and declared himself humbly. "I daresay she's fool enough to marry you," was all Foster said. "And then," he used to relate, "he puts his hat on his head, looks black at me as if he wanted to cut my throat, whistles the dog, and off he goes, leaving me to do the work." The Fosters, of course, didn't like to lose the wages the girl earned; Amy used to give all her money to her mother. But there was in Foster a very genuine aversion to that match. He contended that the fellow was very good with sheep, but was not fit for any girl to marry. For one thing, he used to go along the hedges muttering to himself like a dam' fool; and then, these foreigners behave very queerly to women sometimes. And perhaps he would want to carry her off somewhere – or run off himself. It was not safe. He preached it to his daughter that the fellow might ill-use her in some way. She made no answer. It was, they said in the village, as if the man had done something to her. People discussed the matter. It was quite an excitement, and the two went on "walking out" together in the face of opposition. Then something unexpected happened.

'I don't know whether old Swaffer ever understood how much he was regarded in the light of a father by his foreign retainer. Anyway the relation was curiously feudal. So when Yanko asked formally for an interview – "and the Miss too" (he called the severe, deaf Miss Swaffer simply *Miss*) – it was to obtain their permission to marry. Swaffer heard him unmoved, dismissed him by a nod, and then shouted the intelligence into

Miss Swaffer's best ear. She showed no surprise, and only remarked grimly, in a veiled blank voice, "He certainly won't get any other girl to marry him."

'It is Miss Swaffer who has all the credit of the munificence; but in a very few days it came out that Mr Swaffer had presented Yanko with a cottage (the cottage you've seen this morning) and something like an acre of ground – had made it over to him in absolute property. Willcox expedited the deed, and I remember him telling me he had a great pleasure in making it ready. It recited: "In consideration of saving the life of my beloved grandchild, Bertha Willcox."

'Of course, after that no power on earth could prevent them from getting married.

'Her infatuation endured. People saw her going out to meet him in the evening. She stared with unblinking, fascinated eyes up the road where he was expected to appear, walking freely, with a swing from the hip, and humming one of the love-tunes of his country. When the boy was born, he got elevated at the Coach and Horses, essayed again a song and a dance, and was again ejected. People expressed their commiseration for a woman married to that Jack-in-the-box. He didn't care. There was a man now (he told me boastfully) to whom he could sing and talk in the language of his country, and show how to dance by-and-by.

'But I don't know. To me he appeared to have grown less springy of step, heavier in body, less keen of eye. Imagination, no doubt; but it seems to me now as if the net of fate had been drawn closer round him already.

'One day I met him on the footpath over the Talfourd Hill. He told me that "women were funny". I had heard already of domestic differences. People were saying that Amy Foster was beginning to find out what sort of man she had married. He looked upon the sea with indifferent, unseeing eyes. His wife had snatched the child out of his arms one day as he sat on the doorstep crooning to it a song such as the mothers sing to babies in his mountains. She seemed to think he was doing it some harm. Women are funny. And she had objected to him praying aloud in the evening. Why? He expected the boy to repeat the prayer aloud after him by-and-by, as he used to do after his old father when he was a child – in his own country. And I discovered he longed for their boy to grow up so that he could have a man to talk with in that language that to our ears sounded so disturbing, so passionate, and so bizarre. Why his wife should dislike the idea he couldn't tell. But that would pass, he said. And tilting his head knowingly, he tapped his breastbone to indicate that she had a good heart: not hard, not fierce, open to compassion, charitable to the poor!

'I walked away thoughtfully; I wondered whether his difference, his strangeness, were not penetrating with repulsion that dull nature they had begun by irresistibly attracting. I wondered . . .'

The doctor came to the window and looked out at the frigid splendour of the sea, immense in the haze, as if enclosing all the earth with all the hearts lost among the passions of love and fear.

'Physiologically, now,' he said, turning away abruptly, 'it was possible. It was possible.'

He remained silent. Then went on –

'At all events, the next time I saw him he was ill – lung trouble. He was tough, but I daresay he was not acclimatized as well as I had supposed. It was a bad winter; and, of course, these mountaineers do get fits of home-sickness; and a state of depression would make him vulnerable. He was lying half-dressed on a couch downstairs.

'A table covered with a dark oilcloth took up all the middle of the little room. There was a wicker cradle on the floor, a kettle spouting steam on the hob, and some child's linen lay drying on the fender. The room was warm, but the door opens right into the garden, as you noticed perhaps.

'He was very feverish, and kept on muttering to himself. She sat on a chair and looked at him fixedly across the table with her brown, blurred eyes. "Why don't you have him upstairs?" I asked. With a start and a confused stammer she said, "Oh! ah! I couldn't sit with him upstairs, sir."

'I gave her certain directions; and going outside, I said again that he ought to be in bed upstairs. She wrung her hands. "I couldn't. I couldn't. He keeps on saying something – I don't know what." With the memory of all the talk against the man that had been dinned into her ears, I looked at her narrowly. I looked into her short-sighted eyes, at her dumb eyes that once in her life had seen an enticing shape, but seemed, staring at me, to see nothing at all now. But I saw she was uneasy.

'"What's the matter with him?" she asked in a sort of vacant trepidation. "He doesn't look very ill. I never did see anybody look like this before . . ."

'"Do you think," I asked indignantly, "he is shamming?"

'"I can't help it, sir," she said stolidly. And suddenly she clapped her hands and looked right and left. "And there's the baby. I am so frightened. He wanted me just now to give him the baby. I can't understand what he says to it."

'"Can't you ask a neighbour to come in to-night?" I asked.

'"Please, sir, nobody seems to care to come," she muttered, dully resigned all at once.

'I impressed upon her the necessity of the greatest care, and then had to go. There was a good deal of sickness that winter. "Oh, I hope he won't talk!" she exclaimed softly just as I was going away.

'I don't know how it is I did not see – but I didn't. And yet, turning in my trap, I saw her lingering before the door, very still, and as if meditating a flight up the miry road.

'Towards the night his fever increased.

'He tossed, moaned, and now and then muttered a complaint. And she sat with the table between her and the couch, watching every movement and every sound, with the terror, the unreasonable terror, of that man she could not understand creeping over her. She had drawn the wicker cradle close to her feet. There was nothing in her now but the maternal instinct and that unaccountable fear.

'Suddenly coming to himself, parched, he demanded a drink of water. She did not move. She had not understood, though he may have thought he was speaking in English. He waited, looking at her, burning with fever, amazed at her silence and immobility, and then he shouted impatiently, "Water! Give me water!"

'She jumped to her feet, snatched up the child, and stood still. He spoke to her, and his passionate remonstrances only increased her fear of that strange man. I believe he spoke to her for a long time, entreating, wondering, pleading, ordering, I suppose. She says she bore it as long as she could. And then a gust of rage came over him.

'He sat up and called out terribly one word – some word. Then he got up as though he hadn't been ill at all, she says. And as in fevered dismay, indignation, and wonder he tried to get to her round the table, she simply opened the door and ran out with the child in her arms. She heard him call twice after her down the road in a terrible voice – and fled . . . Ah!

but you should have seen stirring behind the dull, blurred glance of these eyes the spectre of the fear which had haunted her on that night three miles and a half to the door of Foster's cottage! I did the next day.

'And it was I who found him lying face down and his body in a puddle, just outside the little wicket-gate.

'I had been called out that night to an urgent case in the village, and on my way home at daybreak passed by the cottage. The door stood open. My man helped me to carry him in. We laid him on the couch. The lamp smoked, the fire was out, the chill of the stormy night oozed from the cheerless yellow paper on the wall. "Amy!" I called aloud, and my voice seemed to lose itself in the emptiness of this tiny house as if I had cried in a desert. He opened his eyes. "Gone!" he said distinctly. "I had only asked for water – only for a little water . . ."

'He was muddy. I covered him up and stood waiting in silence, catching a painfully gasped word now and then. They were no longer in his own language. The fever had left him, taking with it the heat of life. And with his panting breast and lustrous eyes he reminded me again of a wild creature under the net; of a bird caught in a snare. She had left him. She had left him – sick – helpless – thirsty. The spear of the hunter had entered his very soul. "Why?" he cried in the penetrating and indignant voice of a man calling to a responsible Maker. A gust of wind and a swish of rain answered.

'And as I turned away to shut the door he pronounced the word "Merciful!" and expired.

'Eventually I certified heart-failure as the immediate cause of death. His heart must have indeed failed him, or else he might have stood this night of storm and exposure, too. I closed his eyes and drove away. Not very far from the cottage I met Foster walking sturdily between the dripping hedges with his collie at his heels.

'"Do you know where your daughter is?" I asked.

'"Don't I!" he cried. "I am going to talk to him a bit. Frightening a poor woman like this."

'"He won't frighten her any more," I said. 'He is dead.'

'He struck with his stick at the mud.

'"And there's the child."

'Then, after thinking deeply for a while –

"'I don't know that it isn't for the best."

'That's what he said. And she says nothing at all now. Not a word of him. Never. Is his image as utterly gone from her mind as his lithe and striding figure, his carolling voice are gone from our fields? He is no longer before her eyes to excite her imagination into a passion of love or fear; and his memory seems to have vanished from her dull brain as a shadow passes away upon a white screen. She lives in the cottage and works for Miss Swaffer. She is Amy Foster for everybody, and the child is "Amy Foster's boy." She calls him Johnny – which means Little John.

'It is impossible to say whether this name recalls anything to her. Does she ever think of the past? I have seen her hanging over the boy's cot in a very passion of maternal tenderness. The little fellow was lying on his back, a little frightened at me, but very still, with his big black eyes, with his fluttered air of a bird in a snare. And looking at him I seemed to see again the other one – the father, cast out mysteriously by the sea to perish in the supreme disaster of loneliness and despair.'

H. G. WELLS

The Magic Shop

I had seen the Magic Shop from afar several times; I had passed it once or twice, a shop window of alluring little objects, magic balls, magic hens, wonderful cones, ventriloquist dolls, the material of the basket trick, packs of cards that *looked* all right, and all that sort of thing, but never had I thought of going in until one day, almost without warning, Gip hauled me by my finger right up to the window, and so conducted himself that there was nothing for it but to take him in. I had not thought the place was there, to tell the truth – a modest-sized frontage in Regent Street, between the picture shop and the place where the chicks run about just out of patent incubators, but there it was sure enough. I had fancied it was down nearer the Circus, or round the corner in Oxford Street, or even in Holborn; always over the way and a little inaccessible it had been, with something of the mirage in its position; but there it was now quite indisputably, and the fat end of Gip's pointing finger made a noise upon the glass.

'If I was rich,' said Gip, dabbing a finger at the Disappearing Egg, 'I'd buy myself that. And that' – which was The Crying Baby, Very Human – 'and that,' which was a mystery, and called, so a neat card asserted, 'Buy One and Astonish Your Friends.'

'Anything,' said Gip, 'will disappear under one of those cones. I have read about it in a book.

'And there, dadda, is the Vanishing Halfpenny – only they've put it this way up so's we can't see how it's done.'

Gip, dear boy, inherits his mother's breeding, and he did not propose to enter the shop or worry in any way; only, you know, quite unconsciously he lugged my finger doorward, and he made his interest clear.

'That,' he said, and pointed to the Magic Bottle.

'If you had that?' I said; at which promising inquiry he looked up with a sudden radiance.

'I could show it to Jessie,' he said, thoughtful as ever of others.

'It's less than a hundred days to your birthday, Gibbles,' I said, and laid my hand on the door-handle.

Gip made no answer, but his grip tightened on my finger, and so we came into the shop.

It was no common shop this; it was a magic shop, and all the prancing precedence Gip would have taken in the matter of mere toys was wanting. He left the burthen of the conversation to me.

It was a little, narrow shop, not very well lit, and the door-bell pinged again with a plaintive note as we closed it behind us. For a moment or so we were alone and could glance about us. There was a tiger in papier-mâché on the glass case that covered the low counter – a grave, kind-eyed tiger that waggled his head in a methodical manner; there were several crystal spheres, a china hand holding magic cards, a stock of magic fish-bowls in various sizes, and an immodest magic hat that shamelessly displayed its springs. On the floor were magic mirrors; one to draw you out long and thin, one to swell your head and vanish your legs, and one to make you short and fat like a draught; and while we were laughing at these the shopman, as I suppose, came in.

At any rate, there he was behind the counter – a curious, sallow, dark man, with one ear larger than the other and a chin like the toe-cap of a boot.

'What can we have the pleasure?' he said, spreading his long, magic fingers on the glass case; and so with a start we were aware of him.

'I want,' I said, 'to buy my little boy a few simple tricks.'

'Legerdemain?' he asked. 'Mechanical? Domestic?'

'Anything amusing?' said I.

'Um!' said the shopman, and scratched his head for a moment as if thinking. Then, quite distinctly, he drew from his head a glass ball. 'Something in this way?' he said, and held it out.

The action was unexpected. I had seen the trick done at entertainments endless times before – it's part of the common stock of conjurers – but I had not expected it here. 'That's good,' I said, with a laugh.

'Isn't it?' said the shopman.

Gip stretched out his disengaged hand to take this object and found merely a blank palm.

'It's in your pocket,' said the shopman, and there it was!

'How much will that be?' I asked.

'We make no charge for glass balls,' said the shopman politely. 'We get them' – he picked one out of his elbow as he spoke – 'free.' He produced another from the back of his neck, and laid it beside its predecessor on the counter. Gip regarded his glass ball sagely, then directed a look of inquiry at the two on the counter, and finally brought his round-eyed scrutiny to the shopman, who smiled. 'You may have those too,' said the shopman, 'and, if you *don't* mind, one from my mouth. *So!*'

Gip counselled me mutely for a moment, and then in a profound silence put away the four balls, resumed my reassuring finger, and nerved himself for the next event.

'We get all our smaller tricks in that way,' the shopman remarked.

I laughed in the manner of one who subscribes to a jest. 'Instead of going to the wholesale shop,' I said. 'Of course, it's cheaper.'

'In a way,' the shopman said. 'Though we pay in the end. But not so heavily – as people suppose . . . Our larger tricks, and our daily provisions and all the other things we want, we get out of that hat . . . And you know, sir, if you'll excuse my saying it, there *isn't* a wholesale shop, not for Genuine Magic goods, sir. I don't know if you noticed our inscription – the Genuine Magic shop.' He drew a business-card from his cheek and handed it to me. 'Genuine,' he said, with his finger on the word, and added, 'There is absolutely no deception, sir.'

He seemed to be carrying out the joke pretty thoroughly, I thought.

He turned to Gip with a smile of remarkable affability. 'You, you know, are the Right Sort of Boy.'

I was surprised at his knowing that, because, in the interests of discipline, we keep it rather a secret even at home; but Gip received it in unflinching silence, keeping a steadfast eye on him.

'It's only the Right Sort of Boy gets through that doorway.'

And, as if by way of illustration, there came a rattling at the door, and a squeaking little voice could be faintly heard. 'Nyar! I *warn* 'a go in there, dadda, I WARN 'a go in there. Ny-a-a-ah!' and then the accents of a down-trodden parent, urging consolations and propitiations. 'It's locked, Edward,' he said.

'But it isn't,' said I.

'It is, sir,' said the shopman, 'always – for that sort of child,' and as he spoke we had a glimpse of the other youngster, a little, white face, pallid from sweet-eating and over-sapid food, and distorted by evil passions, a ruthless little egotist, pawing at the enchanted pane. 'It's no good, sir,' said the shopman, as I moved, with my natural helpfulness, doorward, and presently the spoilt child was carried off howling.

'How do you manage that?' I said, breathing a little more freely.

'Magic!' said the shopman, with a careless wave of the hand, and behold! sparks of coloured fire flew out of his fingers and vanished into the shadows of the shop.

'You were saying,' he said, addressing himself to Gip, 'before you came in, that you would like one of our "Buy One and Astonish your Friends" boxes?'

Gip, after a gallant effort, said 'Yes.'

'It's in your pocket.'

And leaning over the counter – he really had an extraordinarily long body – this amazing person produced the article in the customary conjurer's manner. 'Paper,' he said, and took a sheet out of the empty hat with the springs; 'string,' and behold his mouth was a string-box, from which he drew an unending thread, which when he had tied his parcel he bit off – and, it seemed to me, swallowed the ball of string. And then he lit a candle at the nose of one of the ventriloquist's dummies, stuck one of his fingers (which had become sealing-wax red) into the flame, and so sealed the parcel. 'Then there was the Disappearing Egg,' he remarked, and produced one from within my coat-breast and packed it, and also The Crying Baby, Very Human. I handed each parcel to Gip as it was ready, and he clasped them to his chest.

He said very little, but his eyes were eloquent; the clutch of his arms was eloquent. He was the playground of unspeakable emotions. These, you know, were *real* Magics.

Then, with a start, I discovered something moving about in my hat – something soft and jumpy. I whipped it off, and a ruffled pigeon – no doubt a confederate – dropped out and ran on the counter, and went, I fancy, into a cardboard box behind the papier-mâché tiger.

'Tut, tut!' said the shopman, dexterously relieving me of my headdress; 'careless bird, and – as I live – nesting!'

He shook my hat, and shook out into his extended hand two or three eggs, a large marble, a watch, about half-a-dozen of the inevitable glass balls, and then crumpled, crinkled paper, more and more and more, talking all the time of the way in which people neglect to brush their hats *inside* as well as out, politely, of course, but with a certain personal application. 'All sorts of things accumulate, sir . . . Not *you*, of course, in particular . . . Nearly every customer . . . Astonishing what they carry about with them . . .' The crumpled paper rose and billowed on the counter more and more and more, until he was nearly hidden from us, until he was altogether hidden, and still his voice went on and on. 'We none of us know what the fair semblance of a human being may conceal, sir. Are we all then no better than brushed exteriors, whited sepulchres—'

His voice stopped – exactly like when you hit a neighbour's gramophone with a well-aimed brick, the same instant silence, and the rustle of the paper stopped, and everything was still . . .

'Have you done with my hat?' I said, after an interval.

There was no answer.

I stared at Gip, and Gip stared at me, and there were our distortions in the magic mirrors, looking very rum, and grave, and quiet . . .

'I think we'll go now,' I said. 'Will you tell me how much all this comes to? . . .

'I say,' I said, on a rather louder note, 'I want the bill; and my hat, please.'

It might have been a sniff from behind the paper pile . . .

'Let's look behind the counter, Gip,' I said. 'He's making fun of us.'

I led Gip round the head-wagging tiger, and what do you think there was behind the counter? No one at all! Only my hat on the floor, and a common conjurer's lop-eared white rabbit lost in meditation, and looking as stupid and crumpled as only a conjurer's rabbit can do. I resumed my hat, and the rabbit lolloped a lollop or so out of my way.

'Dadda!' said Gip, in a guilty whisper.

'What is it, Gip?' said I.

'I *do* like this shop, dadda.'

'So should I,' I said to myself, 'if the counter wouldn't suddenly extend itself to shut one off from the door.' But I didn't call Gip's attention to that. 'Pussy!' he said, with a hand out to the rabbit as it came lolloping past us; 'Pussy, do Gip a magic!' and his eyes followed it as it squeezed through a door I had certainly not remarked a moment before. Then this door opened wider, and the man with one ear larger than the other appeared again. He was smiling still, but his eye met mine with something between amusement and defiance. 'You'd like to see our show-room, sir,' he said, with an innocent suavity. Gip tugged my finger forward. I glanced at the counter and met the shopman's eye again. I was beginning to think the magic just a little too genuine. 'We haven't *very* much time,' I said. But somehow we were inside the show-room before I could finish that.

'All goods of the same quality,' said the shopman, rubbing his flexible hands together, 'and that is the Best. Nothing in the place that isn't genuine Magic, and warranted thoroughly rum. Excuse me, sir!'

I felt him pull at something that clung to my coat-sleeve, and then I saw he held a little, wriggling red demon by the tail – the little creature bit and fought and tried to get at his hand – and in a moment he tossed it carelessly behind a counter. No doubt the thing was only an image of twisted indiarubber, but for the moment—! And his gesture was exactly that of a man who handles some petty biting bit of vermin. I glanced at Gip, but Gip was looking at a magic rocking-horse. I was glad he hadn't seen the thing. 'I say,' I said, in an undertone, and indicating Gip and the red demon with my eyes, 'you haven't many things like *that* about, have you?'

'None of ours! Probably brought it with you,' said the shopman – also in an undertone, and with a more dazzling smile than ever. 'Astonishing what people *will* carry about with them unawares!' And then to Gip, 'Do you see anything you fancy here?'

There were many things that Gip fancied there.

He turned to this astonishing tradesman with mingled confidence and respect. 'Is that a Magic Sword?' he said.

'A Magic Toy Sword. It neither bends, breaks, nor cuts the fingers. It renders the bearer invincible in battle against any one under eighteen. Half-a-crown to seven and sixpence, according to size. These panoplies on cards are for juvenile knights-errant and very useful – shield of safety, sandals of swiftness, helmet of invisibility.'

'Oh, daddy!' gasped Gip.

I tried to find out what they cost, but the shopman did not heed me. He had got Gip now; he had got him away from my finger; he had embarked upon the exposition of all his confounded stock, and nothing was going to stop him. Presently I saw with a qualm of distrust and something very like jealousy that Gip had hold of this person's finger as usually he has hold of mine. No doubt the fellow was interesting, I thought, and had an interestingly faked lot of stuff, really *good* faked stuff, still—

I wandered after them, saying very little, but keeping an eye on this prestidigital fellow. After all, Gip was enjoying it. And no doubt when the time came to go we should be able to go quite easily.

It was a long, rambling place, that show-room, a gallery broken up by stands and stalls and pillars, with archways leading off to other departments, in which the queerest-looking assistants loafed and stared at one, and with perplexing mirrors and curtains. So perplexing, indeed, were these that I was presently unable to make out the door by which we had come.

The shopman showed Gip magic trains that ran without steam or clockwork, just as you set the signals, and then some very, very valuable boxes of soldiers that all came alive directly you took off the lid and said ——. I myself haven't a very quick ear and it was a tongue-twisting sound, but Gip – he has his mother's ear – got it in no time. 'Bravo!' said the shopman, putting the men back into the box unceremoniously and handing it to Gip. 'Now,' said the shopman, and in a moment Gip had made them all alive again.

'You'll take that box?' asked the shopman.

'We'll take that box,' said I, 'unless you charge its full value. In which case it would need a Trust Magnate—'

'Dear heart! *No!*' and the shopman swept the little men back again, shut the lid, waved the box in the air, and there it was, in brown paper, tied up and – *with Gip's full name and address on the paper!*

The shopman laughed at my amazement.

'This is the genuine magic,' he said. 'The real thing.'

'It's a little too genuine for my taste,' I said again.

After that he fell to showing Gip tricks, odd tricks, and still odder the way they were done. He explained them, he turned them inside out, and there was the dear little chap nodding his busy bit of a head in the sagest manner.

I did not attend as well as I might. 'Hey, presto!' said the Magic Shopman, and then would come the clear, small 'Hey, presto!' of the boy. But I was distracted by other things. It was being borne in upon me just how tremendously rum this place was; it was, so to speak, inundated by a sense of rumness. There was something a little rum about the fixtures even, about the ceiling, about the floor, about the casually distributed chairs. I had a queer feeling that whenever I wasn't looking at them straight they went askew, and moved about, and played a noiseless puss-in-the-corner behind my back. And the cornice had a serpentine design with masks – masks altogether too expressive for proper plaster.

Then abruptly my attention was caught by one of the odd-looking assistants. He was some way off and evidently unaware of my presence – I saw a sort of three-quarter length of him over a pile of toys and through an arch – and, you know, he was leaning against a pillar in an idle sort of way doing the most horrid things with his features! The particular horrid thing he did was with his nose. He did it just as though he was idle and wanted to amuse himself. First of all it was a short, blobby nose, and then suddenly he shot it out like a telescope, and then out it flew and became thinner and thinner until it was like a long, red, flexible whip. Like a thing in a nightmare it was! He flourished it about and flung it forth as a fly-fisher flings his line.

My instant thought was that Gip mustn't see him. I turned about, and there was Gip quite preoccupied with the shopman, and thinking no evil. They were whispering together and looking at me. Gip was standing on a little stool, and the shopman was holding a sort of big drum in his hand.

'Hide and seek, dadda!' cried Gip. 'You're He!'

And before I could do anything to prevent it, the shopman had clapped the big drum over him.

I saw what was up directly. 'Take that off,' I cried, 'this instant! You'll frighten the boy. Take it off!'

The shopman with the unequal ears did so without a word, and held the big cylinder towards me to show its emptiness. And the little stool was vacant! In that instant my boy had utterly disappeared? . . .

You know, perhaps, that sinister something that comes like a hand out of the unseen and grips your heart about. You know it takes your common self away and leaves you tense and deliberate, neither slow nor hasty, neither angry nor afraid. So it was with me.

I came up to this grinning shopman and kicked his stool aside.

'Stop this folly!' I said. 'Where is my boy?'

'You see,' he said, still displaying the drum's interior, 'there is no deception—'

I put out my hand to grip him, and he eluded me by a dexterous movement. I snatched again, and he turned from me and pushed open a door to escape. 'Stop!' I said, and he laughed, receding. I leapt after him – into utter darkness.

Thud!

'Lor' bless my 'eart! I didn't see you coming, sir!'

I was in Regent Street, and I had collided with a decent-looking working man; and a yard away, perhaps, and looking a little perplexed with himself, was Gip. There was some sort of apology, and then Gip had turned and come to me with a bright little smile, as though for a moment he had missed me.

And he was carrying four parcels in his arm!

He secured immediate possession of my finger.

For the second I was rather at a loss. I stared round to see the door of the magic shop, and, behold, it was not there! There was no door, no shop, nothing, only the common pilaster between the shop where they sell pictures and the window with the chicks! . . .

I did the only thing possible in that mental tumult; I walked straight to the kerbstone and held up my umbrella for a cab.

''Ansoms,' said Gip, in a note of culminating exultation.

I helped him in, recalled my address with an effort, and got in also. Something unusual proclaimed itself in my tail-coat pocket, and I felt and discovered a glass ball. With a petulant expression I flung it into the street.

Gip said nothing.

For a space neither of us spoke.

'Dada!' said Gip, at last, 'that *was* a proper shop!'

I came round with that to the problem of just how the whole thing had seemed to him. He looked completely undamaged – so far, good; he was neither scared nor unhinged, he was simply tremendously satisfied with the afternoon's entertainment, and there in his arms were the four parcels.

Confound it! what could be in them?

'Um!' I said. 'Little boys can't go to shops like that every day.'

He received this with his usual stoicism, and for a moment I was sorry I was his father and not his mother, and so couldn't suddenly there, *coram publico*, in our hansom, kiss him. After all, I thought, the thing wasn't so very bad.

But it was only when we opened the parcels that I really began to be reassured. Three of them contained boxes of soldiers, quite ordinary lead soldiers, but of so good a quality as to make Gip altogether forget that originally these parcels had been Magic Tricks of the only genuine sort, and the fourth contained a kitten, a little living white kitten, in excellent health and appetite and temper.

I saw this unpacking with a sort of provisional relief. I hung about in the nursery for quite an unconscionable time . . .

That happened six months ago. And now I am beginning to believe it is all right. The kitten had only the magic natural to all kittens, and the soldiers seem as steady a company as any colonel could desire. And Gip—?

The intelligent parent will understand that I have to go cautiously with Gip.

But I went so far as this one day. I said, 'How would you like your soldiers to come alive, Gip, and march about by themselves?'

'Mine do,' said Gip. 'I just have to say a word I know before I open the lid.'

'Then they march about alone?'

'Oh, *quite*, dadda. I shouldn't like them if they didn't do that.'

I displayed no unbecoming surprise, and since then I have taken occasion to drop in upon him once or twice, unannounced, when the soldiers were about, but so far I have never discovered them performing in anything like a magical manner . . .

It's so difficult to tell.

There's also a question of finance. I have an incurable habit of paying bills. I have been up and down Regent Street several times, looking for that shop. I am inclined to think, indeed, that in that matter honour is satisfied, and that, since Gip's name and address are known to them, I may very well leave it to these people, whoever they may be, to send in their bill in their own time.

M. R. JAMES

The Stalls of Barchester Cathedral

This matter began, as far as I am concerned, with the reading of a notice in the obituary section of the *Gentleman's Magazine* for an early year in the nineteenth century:

'On February 26th, at his residence in the Cathedral Close of Barchester, the Venerable John Benwell Haynes, D.D., aged 57, Archdeacon of Sowerbridge and Rector of Pickhill and Candley. He was of —— College, Cambridge, and where, by talent and assiduity, he commanded the esteem of his seniors; when, at the usual time, he took his first degree, his name stood high in the list of *wranglers*. These academical honours procured for him within a short time a Fellowship of his College. In the year 1783 he received Holy Orders, and was shortly afterwards presented to the perpetual Curacy of Ranxton-sub-Ashe by his friend and patron the late truly venerable Bishop of Lichfield . . . His speedy preferments, first to a Prebend, and subsequently to the dignity of Precentor in the Cathedral of Barchester, form an eloquent testimony to the respect in which he was held and to his eminent qualifications. He succeeded to the Archdeaconry upon the sudden decease of Archdeacon Pulteney in 1810. His sermons, ever conformable to the principles of the religion and Church which he adorned, displayed in no ordinary degree, without the least trace of enthusiasm, the refinement of the scholar united with the graces of the Christian. Free from sectarian violence, and informed by the spirit of the truest charity, they will long dwell in the memories of his hearers. (Here a further omission.) The productions of his pen include an able defence of Episcopacy, which, though often perused by the author of this tribute to his memory, afford but one additional instance of the want of liberality and enterprise which is a too common characteristic of the publishers of our generation. His published works are, indeed, confined to a spirited and elegant version of the *Argonautica* of Valerius Flaccus, a volume of *Discourses upon the Several Events in the Life of Joshua*, delivered in his Cathedral, and a number of the charges which he pronounced at various visitations to the clergy of his Archdeaconry. These are distinguished by etc., etc. The urbanity and hospitality of the subject of these lines will not readily be forgotten by those who enjoyed his acquaintance. His interest in the venerable and awful pile under whose hoary vault he was so punctual an attendant, and particularly in the musical portion of its rites, might be termed filial, and formed a strong and delightful contrast to the polite indifference displayed by too many of our Cathedral dignitaries at the present time.'

The final paragraph, after informing us that Dr Haynes died a bachelor, says:

'It might have been augured that an existence so placid and benevolent would have been terminated in a ripe old age by a dissolution equally gradual and calm. But how unsearchable are the workings of Providence! The peaceful and retired seclusion amid which the honoured evening of Dr Haynes' life was mellowing to its close was destined to be disturbed, nay, shattered, by a tragedy as appalling as it was unexpected. The morning of the 26th of February—'

But perhaps I shall do better to keep back the remainder of the narrative until I have told the circumstances which led up to it. These, as far as they are now accessible, I have derived from another source.

I had read the obituary notice which I have been quoting, quite by chance, along with a great many others of the same period. It had excited some little speculation in my mind, but, beyond thinking that, if I ever had an opportunity of examining the local records of the period indicated, I would try to remember Dr Haynes, I made no effort to pursue his case.

Quite lately I was cataloguing the manuscripts in the library of the college to which he belonged. I had reached the end of the numbered volumes on the shelves, and I proceeded to ask the librarian whether there were any more books which he thought I ought to include in my description. 'I don't think there are,' he said, 'but we had better come and look at the manuscript class and make sure. Have you time to do that now?' I had time. We went to the library, checked off the manuscripts, and, at the end of our survey, arrived at a shelf of which I had seen nothing. Its contents consisted for the most part of sermons, bundles of fragmentary papers, college exercises, *Cyrus*, an epic poem in several cantos, the product of a country clergyman's leisure, mathematical tracts by a deceased professor, and other similar material of a kind with which I am only too familiar. I took brief notes of these. Lastly, there was a tin box, which was pulled out and dusted. Its label, much faded, was thus inscribed: 'Papers of the Ven. Archdeacon Haynes. Bequeathed in 1834 by his sister, Miss Letitia Haynes.'

I knew at once that the name was one which I had somewhere encountered, and could very soon locate it. 'That must be the Archdeacon Haynes who came to a very odd end at Barchester. I've read his obituary in the *Gentleman's Magazine*. May I take the box home? Do you know if there is anything interesting in it?'

The librarian was very willing that I should take the box and examine it at leisure. 'I never looked inside it myself,' he said, 'but I've always been meaning to. I am pretty sure that is the box which our old Master once said ought never to have been accepted by the college. He said that to Martin years ago; and he said also that as long as he had control over the library it should never be opened. Martin told me about it, and said that he wanted terribly to know what was in it; but the Master was librarian, and always kept the box in the lodge, so there was no getting at it in his time, and when he died it was taken away by mistake by his heirs, and only returned a few years ago. I can't think why I haven't opened it; but, as I have to go away from Cambridge this afternoon, you had better have first go at it. I think I can trust you not to publish anything undesirable in our catalogue.'

I took the box home and examined its contents, and thereafter consulted the librarian as to what should be done about publication, and, since I have his leave to make a story out of it, provided I disguise the identity of the people concerned, I will try what can be done.

The materials are, of course, mainly journals and letters. How much I shall quote and how much epitomize must be determined by considerations of space. The proper understanding of the situation has necessitated a little – not very arduous – research, which has been greatly facilitated by the excellent illustrations and text of the Barchester volume in Bell's *Cathedral Series*.

When you enter the choir of Barchester Cathedral now, you pass through a screen of metal and coloured marbles, designed by Sir Gilbert

Scott, and find yourself in what I must call a very bare and odiously furnished place. The stalls are modern; without canopies. The places of the dignitaries and the names of the prebends have fortunately been allowed to survive, and are inscribed on small brass plates affixed to the stalls. The organ is in the triforium, and what is seen of the case is Gothic. The reredos and its surroundings are like every other.

Careful engravings of a hundred years ago show a very different state of things. The organ is on a massive classical screen. The stalls are also classical and very massive. There is a baldacchino of wood over the altar, with urns upon its corners. Farther east is a solid altar screen, classical in design, of wood, with a pediment, in which is a triangle surrounded by rays, enclosing certain Hebrew letters in gold. Cherubs contemplate these. There is a pulpit with a great sounding-board at the eastern end of the stalls on the north side, and there is a black and white marble pavement. Two ladies and a gentleman are admiring the general effect. From other sources I gather that the archdeacon's stall then, as now, was next to the bishop's throne at the south-eastern end of the stalls. His house almost faces the west front of the church, and is a fine red-brick building of William the Third's time.

Here Dr Haynes, already a mature man, took up his abode with his sister in the year 1810. The dignity had long been the object of his wishes, but his predecessor refused to depart until he had attained the age of ninety-two. About a week after he had held a modest festival in celebration of that ninety-second birthday, there came a morning, late in the year, when Dr Haynes, hurrying cheerfully into his breakfast-room, rubbing his hands and humming a tune, was greeted, and checked in his genial flow of spirits, by the sight of his sister, seated, indeed, in her usual place behind the tea-urn, but bowed forward and sobbing unrestrainedly into her handkerchief. 'What – what is the matter? What bad news?' he began. 'Oh, Johnny, you've not heard? The poor dear archdeacon!' 'The archdeacon, yes? What is it – ill, is he?' 'No, no; they found him on the staircase this morning; it is so shocking.' 'Is it possible! Dear, dear, poor Pulteney! Had there been any seizure?' 'They don't think so, and that is almost the worst thing about it. It seems to have been all the fault of that stupid maid of theirs, Jane.' Dr Haynes paused. 'I don't quite understand, Letitia. How was the maid at fault?' 'Why, as far as I can make out, there was a stair-rod missing, and she never mentioned it, and the poor archdeacon set his foot quite on the edge of the step – you know how slippery that oak is – and it seems he must have fallen almost the whole flight and broken his neck. It *is* so sad for poor Miss Pulteney. Of course, they will get rid of the girl at once. I never liked her.' Miss Haynes's grief resumed its sway, but eventually relaxed so far as to permit of her taking some breakfast. Not so her brother, who, after standing in silence before the window for some minutes, left the room, and did not appear again that morning.

I need only add that the careless maid-servant was dismissed forthwith, but that the missing stair-rod was very shortly afterwards found *under* the stair-carpet – an additional proof, if any were needed, of extreme stupidity and carelessness on her part.

For a good many years Dr Haynes had been marked out by his ability, which seems to have been really considerable, as the likely successor of Archdeacon Pulteney, and no disappointment was in store for him. He was duly installed, and entered with zeal upon the discharge of those functions which are appropriate to one in his position. A considerable space in his journals is occupied with exclamations upon the confusion in which Archdeacon Pulteney had left the business of his office and the documents appertaining to it. Dues upon Wringham and Barnswood have been uncollected for something like twelve years, and are largely irrecoverable; no visitation has been held for seven years; four chancels are almost past mending. The persons deputized by the archdeacon have been nearly as incapable as himself. It was almost a matter for thankfulness that this state of things had not been permitted to continue, and a letter from a friend confirms this view. 'ὁ κατέχων,' it says (in rather cruel allusion to the Second Epistle to the Thessalonians), 'is removed at last. My poor friend! Upon what a scene of confusion will you be entering! I give you my word that, on the last occasion of my crossing his threshold, there was no single paper that he could lay hands upon, no syllable of mine that he could hear, and no fact in connection with my business that he could remember. But now, thanks to a negligent maid and a loose stair-carpet, there is some prospect that necessary business will be transacted without a complete loss alike of voice and temper.' This letter was tucked into a pocket in the cover of one of the diaries.

There can be no doubt of the new archdeacon's zeal and enthusiasm. 'Give me but time to reduce to some semblance of order the innumerable errors and complications with which I am confronted, and I shall gladly and sincerely join with the aged Israelite in the canticle which too many, I fear, pronounce but with their lips.' This reflection I find, not in a diary, but a letter; the doctor's friends seem to have returned his correspondence to his surviving sister. He does not confine himself, however, to reflections. His investigation of the rights and duties of his office are very searching and business-like, and there is a calculation in one place that a period of three years will just suffice to set the business of the Archdeaconry upon a proper footing. The estimate appears to have been an exact one. For just three years he is occupied in reforms; but I look in vain at the end of that time for the promised *Nunc dimittis*. He has now found a new sphere of activity. Hitherto his duties have precluded him from more than an occasional attendance at the Cathedral services. Now he begins to take an interest in the fabric and the music. Upon his struggles with the organist, an old gentleman who had been in office since 1786, I have no time to dwell; they were not attended with any marked success. More to the purpose is his sudden growth of enthusiasm for the Cathedral itself and its furniture. There is a draft of a letter to Sylvanus Urban (which I do not think was ever sent) describing the stalls in the choir. As I have said, these were of fairly late date – of about the year 1700, in fact.

'The archdeacon's stall, situated at the south-east end, west of the episcopal throne (now so worthily occupied by the truly excellent prelate who adorns the See of Barchester), is distinguished by some curious ornamentation. In addition to the arms of Dean West, by whose efforts the whole of the internal furniture of the choir was completed, the prayer-desk is terminated at the eastern extremity by three small but remarkable statuettes in the grotesque manner. One is an exquisitely modelled figure of a cat, whose crouching posture suggests with admirable spirit the suppleness, vigilance, and craft of the redoubted adversary of the genus *Mus*. Opposite to this is a figure seated upon a throne and invested with the attributes of royalty; but it is no earthly monarch whom the carver has sought to portray. His feet are studiously concealed by the long robe in which he is draped; but neither the crown nor the cap which he wears suffice to hide the prick-ears and curving horns which betray his Tartarean origin; and the hand which rests upon his knee is armed with talons of horrifying length and sharpness. Between these two figures stands a shape muffled in a long mantle. This might at first sight be mistaken for a monk or "friar of orders gray", for the head is cowled and a knotted cord depends from somewhere about the waist. A slight inspection, however, will lead to a very different conclusion. The knotted cord is quickly seen to be a halter, held by a hand all but concealed within the draperies; while the sunken features and, horrid to relate, the rent flesh upon the cheek-bones, proclaim the King of Terrors. These figures are evidently the production of no unskilled chisel; and should it chance that any of your correspondents are able to throw light upon their origin and significance, my obligations to your valuable miscellany will be largely increased.'

There is more description in the paper, and, seeing that the woodwork in question has now disappeared, it has a considerable interest. A paragraph at the end is worth quoting:

'Some late researches among the Chapter accounts have shown me that the carving of the stalls was not, as was very usually reported, the work of Dutch artists, but was executed by a native of this city or district named Austin. The timber was procured from an oak copse in the vicinity, the property of the Dean and Chapter, known as Holywood. Upon a recent visit to the parish within whose boundaries it is situated, I learned from the aged and truly respectable incumbent that traditions still lingered amongst the inhabitants of the great size and age of the oaks employed to furnish the materials of the stately structure which has been, however imperfectly, described in the above lines. Of one in particular, which stood near the centre of the grove, it is remembered that it was known as the Hanging Oak. The propriety of that title is confirmed by the fact that a quantity of human bones was found in the soil about its roots, and that at certain times of the year it was the custom for those who wished to secure a successful issue to their affairs, whether of love or the ordinary business of life, to suspend from its boughs small images or puppets rudely fashioned of straw, twigs, or the like rustic materials.'

So much for the archdeacon's archæological investigations. To return to his career as it is to be gathered from his diaries. Those of his first three years of hard and careful work show him throughout in high spirits, and, doubtless, during this time, that reputation for hospitality and urbanity which is mentioned in his obituary notice was well deserved. After that, as time goes on, I see a shadow coming over him – destined to develop into utter blackness – which I cannot but think must have been reflected in his outward demeanour. He commits a good deal of his fears and troubles to his diary; there was no other outlet for them. He was unmarried, and his sister was not always with him. But I am much mistaken if he has told all that he might have told. A series of extracts shall be given:

Aug. 30, 1816. – The days begin to draw in more perceptibly than ever. Now that the Archdeaconry papers are reduced to order, I must find some further employment for the evening hours of autumn and winter. It is a great blow that Letitia's health will not allow her to stay through these months. Why not go on with my *Defence of Episcopacy?* It may be useful.

Sept. 15. – Letitia has left me for Brighton.

Oct. 11. – Candles lit in the choir for the first time at evening prayers. It came as a shock: I find that I absolutely shrink from the dark season.

Nov. 17. – Much struck by the character of the carving on my desk: I do not know that I had ever carefully noticed it before. My attention was called to it by an accident. During the *Magnificat* I was, I regret to say, almost overcome with sleep. My hand was resting on the back of the carved figure of a cat which is the nearest to me of the three figures on the end of my stall. I was not aware of this, for I was not looking in that direction, until I was startled by what seemed a softness, a feeling as of rather rough and coarse fur, and a sudden movement, as if the creature were twisting round its head to bite me. I regained complete consciousness in an instant, and I have some idea that I must have uttered a suppressed exclamation, for I noticed that Mr Treasurer turned his head quickly in my direction. The impression of the unpleasant feeling was so strong that I found myself rubbing my hand upon my surplice. This accident led me to examine the figures after prayers more carefully than I had done before, and I realized for the first time with what skill they are executed.

Dec. 6. – I do indeed miss Letitia's company. The evenings, after I have worked as long as I can at my *Defence*, are very trying. The house is too large for a lonely man, and visitors of any kind are too rare. I get an uncomfortable impression when going to my room that there *is* company of some kind. The fact is (I may as well formulate it to myself) that I hear voices. This, I am well aware, is a common symptom of incipient decay of the brain – and I believe that I should be less disquieted than I am if I had any suspicion that this was the cause. I have none – none whatever, nor is there anything in my family history to give colour to such an idea. Work, diligent work, and a punctual attention to the duties which fall to me is my best remedy, and I have little doubt that it will prove efficacious.

Jan. 1. – My trouble is, I must confess it, increasing upon me. Last night, upon my return after midnight from the Deanery, I lit my candle to go upstairs. I was nearly at the top when something whispered to me, 'Let me wish you a happy New Year.' I could not be mistaken: it spoke distinctly and with a peculiar emphasis. Had I dropped my candle, as I all but did, I tremble to think what the consequences must have been. As it was, I managed to get up the last flight, and was quickly in my room with the door locked, and experienced no other disturbance.

Jan. 15. – I had occasion to come downstairs last night to my workroom for my watch, which I had inadvertently left on my table when I went up to bed. I think I was at the top of the last flight when I had a sudden impression of a sharp whisper in my ear *'Take care.'* I clutched the balusters and naturally looked round at once. Of course, there was nothing. After a moment I went on – it was no good turning back – but I had as nearly as possible fallen: a cat – a large one by the feel of it – slipped between my feet, but again, of course, I saw nothing. It *may* have been the kitchen cat, but I do not think it was.

Feb. 27. – A curious thing last night, which I should like to forget. Perhaps if I put it down here I may see it in its true proportion. I worked in the library from about 9 to 10. The hall and staircase seemed to be unusually full of what I can only call movement without sound: by this I mean that there seemed to be continuous going and coming, and that whenever I ceased writing to listen, or looked out into the hall, the stillness was absolutely unbroken. Nor, in going to my room at an earlier hour than usual – about half-past ten – was I conscious of anything that I could call a noise. It so happened that I had told John to come to my room for the letter to the bishop which I wished to have delivered early in the morning at the Palace. He was to sit up, therefore, and come for it when he heard me retire. This I had for the moment forgotten, though I had remembered to carry the letter with me to my room. But when, as I was winding up my watch, I heard a light tap at the door, and a low voice saying, 'May I come in?' (which I most undoubtedly did hear), I recollected the fact, and took up the letter from my dressing-table, saying, 'Certainly: come in.' No one, however, answered my summons, and it was now that, as I strongly suspect, I committed an error: for I opened the door and held the letter out. There was certainly no one at that moment in the passage, but, in the instant of my standing there, the door at the end opened and John appeared carrying a candle. I asked him whether he had come to the door earlier; but am satisfied that he had not. I do not like the situation; but although my senses were very much on the alert, and though it was some time before I could sleep, I must allow that I perceived nothing further of an untoward character.

With the return of spring, when his sister came to live with him for some months, Dr Haynes's entries become more cheerful, and, indeed, no symptom of depression is discernible until the early part of September, when he was again left alone. And now, indeed, there is evidence that he was incommoded again, and that more pressingly. To this matter I will return in a moment, but I digress to put in a document which, rightly or wrongly, I believe to have a bearing on the thread of the story.

The account-books of Dr Haynes, preserved along with his other papers, show, from a date but little later than that of his institution as archdeacon, a quarterly payment of £25 to J. L. Nothing could have been made of this, had it stood by itself. But I connect with it a very dirty and ill-written letter, which, like another that I have quoted, was in a pocket in the cover of a diary. Of date or postmark there is no vestige, and the decipherment was not easy. It appears to run:

Dr Sr.

I have bin expctin to her off you theis last wicks, and not Haveing done so must supose you have not got mine witch was saying how me and my man had met in with bad times this season all seems to go cross with us on the farm and which way to look for the rent we have no knowledge of it this been the sad case with us if you would have the great [liberality *probably, but the exact spelling defies reproduction*] to send fourty pounds otherwise steps will have to be took which I should not wish. Has you was the Means of me losing my place with Dr Pulteney

I think it is only just what I am asking and you know best what I could say if I was Put to it but I do not wish anything of that unpleasant Nature being one that always wish to have everything Pleasant about me.

Your obedt Servt,
JANE LEE.

About the time at which I suppose this letter to have been written there is, in fact, a payment of £40 to J. L.

We return to the diary:

Oct. 22. – At evening prayers, during the Psalms, I had that same experience which I recollect from last year. I was resting my hand on one of the carved figures, as before (I usually avoid that of the cat now), and – I was going to have said – a change came over it, but that seems attributing too much importance to what must, after all, be due to some physical affection in myself: at any rate, the wood seemed to become chilly and soft as if made of wet linen. I can assign the moment at which I became sensible of this. The choir were singing the words (*Set thou an ungodly man to be ruler over him and*) *let Satan stand at his right hand.*

The whispering in my house was more persistent to-night. I seemed not to be rid of it in my room. I have not noticed this before. A nervous man, which I am not, and hope I am not becoming, would have been much annoyed, if not alarmed, by it. The cat was on the stairs to-night. I think it sits there always. There *is* no kitchen cat.

Nov. 15. – Here again I must note a matter I do not understand. I am much troubled in sleep. No definite image presented itself, but I was pursued by the very vivid impression that wet lips were whispering into my ear with great rapidity and emphasis for some time together. After this, I suppose, I fell asleep, but was awakened with a start by a feeling as if a hand were laid on my shoulder. To my intense alarm I found myself standing at the top of the lowest flight of the first staircase. The moon was shining brightly enough through the large window to let me see that there was a large cat on the second or third step. I can make no comment. I crept up to bed again, I do not know how. Yes, mine is a heavy burden. [Then follows a line or two which has been scratched out. I fancy I read something like 'acted for the best'.]

Not long after this it is evident to me that the archdeacon's firmness began to give way under the pressure of these phenomena. I omit as unnecessarily painful and distressing the ejaculations and prayers which, in the months of December and January, appear for the first time and become increasingly frequent. Throughout this time, however, he is obstinate in clinging to his post. Why he did not plead ill-health and take refuge at Bath or Brighton I cannot tell; my impression is that it would have done him no good; that he was a man who, if he had confessed himself beaten by the annoyances, would have succumbed at once, and that he was conscious of this. He did seek to palliate them by inviting visitors to his house. The result he has noted in this fashion:

Jan. 7. – I have prevailed on my cousin Allen to give me a few days, and he is to occupy the chamber next to mine.

Jan. 8. – A still night. Allen slept well, but complained of the wind. My own experiences were as before: still whispering and whispering: what is it that he wants to say?

Jan. 9. – Allen thinks this a very noisy house. He thinks, too, that my cat is an unusually large and fine specimen, but very wild.

Jan. 10. – Allen and I in the library until 11. He left me twice to see what the maids were doing in the hall: returning the second time he told me he had seen one of them passing through the door at the end of the passage, and said if his wife were here she would soon get them into better order. I asked him what coloured dress the maid wore; he said grey or white. I supposed it would be so.

Jan. 11. – Allen left me to-day. I must be firm.'

These words, *I must be firm*, occur again and again on subsequent days; sometimes they are the only entry. In these cases they are in an unusually large hand, and dug into the paper in a way which must have broken the pen that wrote them.

Apparently the archdeacon's friends did not remark any change in his behaviour, and this gives me a high idea of his courage and determination. The diary tells us nothing more than I have indicated of the last days of his life. The end of it all must be told in the polished language of the obituary notice:

The morning of the 26th of February was cold and tempestuous. At an early hour the servants had occasion to go into the front hall of the residence occupied by the lamented subject of these lines. What was their horror upon observing the form of their beloved and respected master lying upon the landing of the principal staircase in an attitude which inspired the gravest fears. Assistance was procured, and an universal consternation was experienced upon the discovery that he had been the object of a brutal and a murderous attack. The vertebral column was fractured in more than one place. This might have been the result of a fall: it appeared that the stair-carpet was loosened at one point. But, in addition to this, there were injuries inflicted upon the eyes, nose and mouth, as if by the agency of some savage animal, which, dreadful to relate, rendered those features unrecognizable. The vital spark was, it is needless to add, completely extinct, and had been so, upon the testimony of respectable medical authorities, for several hours. The author or authors of this mysterious outrage are alike buried in mystery, and the most active conjecture has hitherto failed to suggest a solution of the melancholy problem afforded by this appalling occurrence.

The writer goes on to reflect upon the probability that the writings of Mr Shelley, Lord Byron, and M. Voltaire may have been instrumental in bringing about the disaster, and concludes by hoping, somewhat vaguely, that this event may 'operate as an example to the rising generation'; but this portion of his remarks need not be quoted in full.

I had already formed the conclusion that Dr Haynes was responsible for the death of Dr Pulteney. But the incident connected with the carved figure of death upon the archdeacon's stall was a very perplexing feature. The conjecture that it had been cut out of the wood of the Hanging Oak was not difficult, but seemed impossible to substantiate. However, I paid a visit to Barchester, partly with the view of finding out whether there were any relics of the woodwork to be heard of. I was introduced by one of the canons to the curator of the local museum, who was, my friend said, more likely to be able to give me information on the point than anyone else. I told this gentleman of the description of certain carved figures and arms formerly on the stalls, and asked whether any had survived. He was able to show me the arms of Dean West and some other fragments. These, he said, had been got from an old resident, who had also once owned a figure – perhaps one of those which I was inquiring for. There was a very odd thing about that figure, he said. 'The old man who had it told me that he picked it up in a woodyard, whence he had obtained the still extant pieces, and had taken it home for his children. On the way home he was fiddling about with it and it came in two in his hands, and a bit of paper dropped out. This he picked up and, just noticing that there was writing on it, put it into his pocket, and subsequently into a vase on his mantelpiece. I was at his house not very long ago, and happened to pick up the vase and turn it over to see whether there were any marks on it, and the paper fell into my hand. The old man, on my handing it to him, told me the story I have told you, and said I might keep the paper. It was crumpled and rather torn, so I have mounted it on a card, which I have here. If you can tell me what it means I shall be very glad, and also, I may say, a good deal surprised.'

He gave me the card. The paper was quite legibly inscribed in an old hand, and this is what was on it:

> When I grew in the Wood
> I was water'd wth Blood
> Now in the Church I stand
> Who that touches me with his Hand
> If a Bloody hand he bear
> I councell him to be ware
> Lest he be fetcht away
> Whether by night or day,
> But chiefly when the wind blows high
> In a night of February.
> This I drempt, 26 Febr. A° 1699.   JOHN AUSTIN.

'I suppose it is a charm or a spell: wouldn't you call it something of that kind?' said the curator.

'Yes,' I said, 'I suppose one might. What became of the figure in which it was concealed?'

'Oh, I forgot,' said he. 'The old man told me it was so ugly and frightened his children so much that he burnt it.'

'SAKI'

The Unrest-Cure

On the rack in the railway carriage immediately opposite Clovis was a solidly wrought travelling bag, with a carefully written label, on which was inscribed, 'J. P. Huddle, The Warren, Tilfield, near Slowborough.' Immediately below the rack sat the human embodiment of the label, a solid, sedate individual, sedately dressed, sedately conversational. Even without his conversation (which was addressed to a friend seated by his side, and touched chiefly on such topics as the backwardness of Roman hyacinths and the prevalence of measles at the Rectory), one could have gauged fairly accurately the temperament and mental outlook of the travelling bag's owner. But he seemed unwilling to leave anything to the imagination of a casual observer, and his talk grew presently personal and introspective.

'I don't know how it is,' he told his friend, 'I'm not much over forty, but I seem to have settled down into a deep groove of elderly middle-age. My sister shows the same tendency. We like everything to be exactly in its accustomed place; we like things to happen exactly at their appointed times; we like everything to be usual, orderly, punctual, methodical, to a hair's breadth, to a minute. It distresses and upsets us if it is not so. For instance, to take a very trifling matter, a thrush has built its nest year after year in the catkin-tree on the lawn; this year, for no obvious reason, it is building in the ivy on the garden wall. We have said very little about it, but I think we both feel that the change is unnecessary, and just a little irritating.'

'Perhaps,' said the friend, 'it is a different thrush.'

'We have suspected that,' said J. P. Huddle, 'and I think it gives us even more cause for annoyance. We don't feel that we want a change of thrush at our time of life; and yet, as I have said, we have scarcely reached an age when these things should make themselves seriously felt.'

457

'What you want,' said the friend, 'is an Unrest-cure.'

'An Unrest-cure? I've never heard of such a thing.'

'You've heard of Rest-cures for people who've broken down under stress of too much worry and strenuous living; well, you're suffering from over-much repose and placidity, and you need the opposite kind of treatment.'

'But where would one go for such a thing?'

'Well, you might stand as an Orange candidate for Kilkenny, or do a course of district visiting in one of the Apache quarters of Paris, or give lectures in Berlin to prove that most of Wagner's music was written by Gambetta; and there's always the interior of Morocco to travel in. But, to be really effective, the Unrest-cure ought to be tried in the home. How you would do it I haven't the faintest idea.'

It was at this point in the conversation that Clovis became galvanized into alert attention. After all, his two days' visit to an elderly relative at Slowborough did not promise much excitement. Before the train had stopped he had decorated his sinister shirt-cuff with the inscription, 'J. P. Huddle, The Warren, Tilfield, near Slowborough.'

Two mornings later Mr Huddle broke in on his sister's privacy as she sat reading *Country Life* in the morning room. It was her day and hour and place for reading *Country Life*, and the intrusion was absolutely irregular; but he bore in his hand a telegram, and in that household telegrams were recognized as happening by the hand of God. This particular telegram partook of the nature of a thunderbolt. 'Bishop examining confirmation class in neighbourhood unable stay rectory on account measles invokes your hospitality sending secretary arrange.'

'I scarcely know the Bishop; I've only spoken to him once,' exclaimed J. P. Huddle, with the exculpating air of one who realizes too late the indiscretion of speaking to strange Bishops. Miss Huddle was the first to rally; she disliked thunderbolts as fervently as her brother did, but the womanly instinct in her told her that thunderbolts must be fed.

'We can curry the cold duck,' she said. It was not the appointed day for curry, but the little orange envelope involved a certain departure from rule and custom. Her brother said nothing, but his eyes thanked her for being brave.

'A young gentleman to see you,' announced the parlour-maid.

'The secretary!' murmured the Huddles in unison; they instantly stiff-ened into a demeanour which proclaimed that, though they held all strangers to be guilty, they were willing to hear anything they might have to say in their defence. The young gentleman, who came into the room with a certain elegant haughtiness, was not at all Huddle's idea of a bishop's secretary; he had not supposed that the episcopal establishment could have afforded such an expensively upholstered article when there were so many other claims on its resources. The face was fleetingly famil-iar; if he had bestowed more attention on the fellow-traveller sitting opposite him in the railway carriage two days before he might have rec-ognized Clovis in his present visitor.

'You are the Bishop's secretary?' asked Huddle, becoming consciously deferential.

'His confidential secretary,' answered Clovis. 'You may call me Stanis-laus; my other name doesn't matter. The Bishop and Colonel Alberti may be here to lunch. I shall be here in any case.'

It sounded rather like the programme of a Royal visit.

'The Bishop is examining a confirmation class in the neighbourhood, isn't he?' asked Miss Huddle.

'Ostensibly,' was the dark reply, followed by a request for a large-scale map of the locality.

Clovis was still immersed in a seemingly profound study of the map when another telegram arrived. It was addressed to 'Prince Stanislaus, care of Huddle, The Warren, etc.' Clovis glanced at the contents and announced: 'The Bishop and Alberti won't be here till late in the after-noon.' Then he returned to his scrutiny of the map.

The luncheon was not a very festive function. The princely secretary ate and drank with fair appetite, but severely discouraged conversation. At the finish of the meal he broke suddenly into a radiant smile, thanked his hostess for a charming repast, and kissed her hand with deferential rapture. Miss Huddle was unable to decide in her mind whether the action savoured of Louis Quatorzian courtliness or the reprehensible Roman attitude towards the Sabine women. It was not her day for having a head-ache, but she felt that the circumstances excused her, and retired to her room to have as much headache as was possible before the Bishop's arrival. Clovis, having asked the way to the nearest telegraph office, disappeared presently down the carriage drive. Mr Huddle met him in the hall some two hours later, and asked when the Bishop would arrive.

'He is in the library with Alberti,' was the reply.

'But why wasn't I told? I never knew he had come!' exclaimed Huddle.

'No one knows he is here,' said Clovis; 'the quieter we can keep matters the better. And on no account disturb him in the library. Those are his orders.'

'But what is all this mystery about? And who is Alberti? And isn't the Bishop going to have tea?'

'The Bishop is out for blood, not tea.'

'Blood!' gasped Huddle, who did not find that the thunderbolt improved on acquaintance.

'Tonight is going to be a great night in the history of Christendom,' said Clovis. 'We are going to massacre every Jew in the neighbourhood.'

'To massacre the Jews!' said Huddle indignantly. 'Do you mean to tell me there's a general rising against them?'

'No, it's the Bishop's own idea. He's in there arranging all the details now.'

'But – the Bishop is such a tolerant, humane man.'

'That is precisely what will heighten the effect of his action. The sensation will be enormous.'

That at least Huddle could believe.

'He will be hanged!' he exclaimed with conviction.

'A motor is waiting to carry him to the coast, where a steam yacht is in readiness.'

'But there aren't thirty Jews in the whole neighbourhood,' protested Huddle, whose brain, under the repeated shocks of the day, was operating with the uncertainty of a telegraph wire during earthquake disturbances.

'We have twenty-six on our list,' said Clovis, referring to a bundle of notes. 'We shall be able to deal with them all the more thoroughly.'

'Do you mean to tell me that you are meditating violence against a man like Sir Leon Birberry,' stammered Huddle; 'he's one of the most respected men in the country.'

'He's down on our list,' said Clovis carelessly; 'after all, we've got men we can trust to do our job, so we shan't have to rely on local assistance. And we've got some Boy-scouts helping us as auxiliaries.'

'Boy-scouts!'

'Yes; when they understood there was real killing to be done they were even keener than the men.'

'This thing will be a blot on the Twentieth Century!'

'And your house will be the blotting-pad. Have you realized that half the papers of Europe and the United States will publish pictures of it? By the way, I've sent some photographs of you and your sister, that I found in the library, to the *Martin* and *Die Woche;* I hope you don't mind. Also a sketch of the staircase; most of the killing will probably be done on the staircase.'

The emotions that were surging in J. P. Huddle's brain were almost too intense to be disclosed in speech, but he managed to gasp out: 'There aren't any Jews in this house.'

'Not at present,' said Clovis.

'I shall go to the police,' shouted Huddle with sudden energy.

'In the shrubbery,' said Clovis, 'are posted ten men, who have orders to fire on any one who leaves the house without my signal of permission. Another armed picquet is in ambush near the front gate. The Boy-scouts watch the back premises.'

At this moment the cheerful hoot of a motor-horn was heard from the drive. Huddle rushed to the hall door with the feeling of a man half-awakened from a nightmare, and beheld Sir Leon Birberry, who had driven himself over in his car. 'I got your telegram,' he said; 'what's up?'

Telegram? It seemed to be a day of telegrams.

'Come here at once. Urgent. James Huddle,' was the purport of the message displayed before Huddle's bewildered eyes.

'I see it all!' he exclaimed suddenly in a voice shaken with agitation, and with a look of agony in the direction of the shrubbery he hauled the astonished Birberry into the house. Tea had just been laid in the hall, but the now thoroughly panic-stricken Huddle dragged his protesting guest upstairs, and in a few minutes' time the entire household had been summoned to that region of momentary safety. Clovis alone graced the tea-table with his presence; the fanatics in the library were evidently too immersed in their monstrous machinations to dally with the solace of teacup and hot toast. Once the youth rose, in answer to the summons of the front-door bell, and admitted Mr Paul Isaacs, shoemaker and parish councillor, who had also received a pressing invitation to The Warren. With an atrocious assumption of courtesy, which a Borgia could hardly have outdone, the secretary escorted this new captive of his net to the head of the stairway, where his involuntary host awaited him.

And then ensued a long ghastly vigil of watching and waiting. Once or twice Clovis left the house to stroll across to the shrubbery, returning always to the library, for the purpose evidently of making a brief report. Once he took in the letters from the evening postman, and brought them to the top of the stairs with punctilious politeness. After his next absence he came half-way up the stairs to make an announcement.

'The Boy-scouts mistook my signal, and have killed the postman. I've had very little practice in this sort of thing, you see. Another time I shall do better.'

The housemaid, who was engaged to be married to the evening postman, gave way to clamorous grief.

'Remember that your mistress has a headache,' said J. P. Huddle. (Miss Huddle's headache was worse.)

Clovis hastened downstairs, and after a short visit to the library returned with another message:

'The Bishop is sorry to hear that Miss Huddle has a headache. He is issuing orders that as far as possible no firearms shall be used near the house; any killing that is necessary on the premises will be done with cold steel. The Bishop does not see why a man should not be a gentleman as well as a Christian.'

That was the last they saw of Clovis; it was nearly seven o'clock, and his elderly relative liked him to dress for dinner. But, though he had left them for ever, the lurking suggestion of his presence haunted the lower regions of the house during the long hours of the wakeful night, and every creak of the stairway, every rustle of wind through the shrubbery, was fraught with horrible meaning. At about seven next morning the gardener's boy and the early postman finally convinced the watchers that the Twentieth Century was still unblotted.

'I don't suppose,' mused Clovis, as an early train bore him townwards, 'that they will be in the least grateful for the Unrest-cure.'

G. K. CHESTERTON

The Honour of Israel Gow

A stormy evening of olive and silver was closing in, as Father Brown, wrapped in a grey Scotch plaid, came to the end of a grey Scotch valley and beheld the strange castle of Glengyle. It stopped one end of the glen or hollow like a blind alley; and it looked like the end of the world. Rising in steep roofs and spires of seagreen slate in the manner of the old French-Scottish châteaux, it reminded an Englishman of the sinister steeple-hats of witches in fairy tales; and the pine woods that rocked round the green turrets looked, by comparison, as black as numberless flocks of ravens. This note of a dreamy, almost a sleepy devilry, was no mere fancy from the landscape. For there did rest on the place one of those clouds of pride and madness and mysterious sorrow which lie more heavily on the noble houses of Scotland than on any other of the children of men. For Scotland has a double dose of the poison called heredity; the sense of blood in the aristocrat, and the sense of doom in the Calvinist.

The priest had snatched a day from his business at Glasgow to meet his friend Flambeau, the amateur detective, who was at Glengyle Castle with another more formal officer investigating the life and death of the late Earl of Glengyle. That mysterious person was the last representative of a race whose valour, insanity, and violent cunning had made them terrible even among the sinister nobility of their nation in the sixteenth century. None were deeper in that labyrinthine ambition, in chamber within chamber of that palace of lies that was built up around Mary Queen of Scots.

The rhyme in the country-side attested the motive and the result of their machinations candidly:

As green sap to the simmer trees
Is red gold to the Ogilvies.

For many centuries there had never been a decent lord in Glengyle Castle; and with the Victorian era one would have thought that all eccentricities were exhausted. The last Glengyle, however, satisfied his tribal tradition by doing the only thing that was left for him to do; he disappeared. I do not mean that he went abroad; by all accounts he was still in the castle, if he was anywhere. But though his name was in the church register and the big red Peerage, nobody ever saw him under the sun.

If anyone saw him it was a solitary man-servant, something between a groom and a gardener. He was so deaf that the more business-like assumed him to be dumb; while the more penetrating declared him to be half-witted. A gaunt, red-haired labourer, with a dogged jaw and chin, but quite blank blue eyes, he went by the name of Israel Gow, and was the one silent servant on that deserted estate. But the energy with which he dug potatoes, and the regularity with which he disappeared into the kitchen gave people an impression that he was providing for the meals of a superior, and that the strange earl was still concealed in the castle. If society needed any further proof that he was there, the servant persistently asserted that he was not at home. One morning the provost and the minister (for the Glengyles were Presbyterian) were summoned to the castle. There they found that the gardener, groom and cook had added to his many professions that of an undertaker, and had nailed up his noble master in a coffin. With how much or how little further inquiry this odd fact was passed, did not as yet very plainly appear; for the thing had never been legally investigated till Flambeau had gone north two or three days before. By then the body of Lord Glengyle (if it was the body) had lain for some time in the little churchyard on the hill.

As Father Brown passed through the dim garden and came under the shadow of the château, the clouds were thick and the whole air damp and thundery. Against the last stripe of the green-gold sunset he saw a black human silhouette; a man in a chimney-pot hat, with a big spade over his shoulder. The combination was queerly suggestive of a sexton; but when Brown remembered the deaf servant who dug potatoes, he thought it natural enough. He knew something of the Scotch peasant; he knew the respectability which might well feel it necessary to wear 'blacks' for an official inquiry; he knew also the economy that would not lose an hour's digging for that. Even the man's start and suspicious stare as the priest went by were consonant enough with the vigilance and jealousy of such a type.

The great door was opened by Flambeau himself, who had with him a lean man with iron-grey hair and papers in his hand: Inspector Craven from Scotland Yard. The entrance hall was mostly stripped and empty; but the pale, sneering faces of one or two of the wicked Ogilvies looked down out of the black periwigs and blackening canvas.

Following them into an inner room, Father Brown found that the allies had been seated at a long oak table, of which their end was covered with scribbled papers, flanked with whisky and cigars. Through the whole of its remaining length it was occupied by detached objects arranged at intervals; objects about as inexplicable as any objects could be. One looked like a small heap of glittering broken glass. Another looked like a high heap of brown dust. A third appeared to be a plain stick of wood.

'You seem to have a sort of geological museum here,' he said, as he sat down, jerking his head briefly in the direction of the brown dust and the crystalline fragments.

'Not a geological museum,' replied Flambeau; 'say a psychological museum.'

'Oh, for the Lord's sake,' cried the police detective, laughing, 'don't let's begin with such long words.'

'Don't you know what psychology means?' asked Flambeau with friendly surprise. 'Psychology means being off your chump.'

'Still I hardly follow,' replied the official.

'Well,' said Flambeau, with decision; 'I mean that we've only found out one thing about Lord Glengyle. He was a maniac.'

The black silhouette of Gow with his top hat and spade passed the window, dimly outlined against the darkening sky. Father Brown stared passively at it and answered:

'I can understand there must have been something odd about the man, or he wouldn't have buried himself alive – nor been in such a hurry to bury himself dead. But what makes you think it was lunacy?'

'Well,' said Flambeau; 'you just listen to the list of things Mr Craven has found in the house.'

'We must get a candle,' said Craven, suddenly. 'A storm is getting up, and it's too dark to read.'

'Have you found any candles,' asked Brown smiling, 'among your oddities?'

Flambeau raised a grave face, and fixed his dark eyes on his friend.

'That is curious, too,' he said. 'Twenty-five candles, and not a trace of a candlestick.'

In the rapidly darkening room and rapidly rising wind, Brown went along the table to where a bundle of wax candles lay among the other scrappy exhibits. As he did so he bent accidentally over the heap of red-brown dust; and a sharp sneeze cracked the silence.

'Hullo!' he said; 'snuff!'

He took one of the candles, lit it carefully, came back and stuck it in the neck of the whisky bottle. The unrestful night air, blowing through the crazy window, waved the long flame like a banner. And on every side of the castle they could hear the miles and miles of black pine wood seething like a black sea around a rock.

'I will read the inventory,' began Craven gravely, picking up one of the papers, 'the inventory of what we found loose and unexplained in the castle. You are to understand that the place generally was dismantled and neglected; but one or two rooms had plainly been inhabited in a simple but not squalid style by somebody; somebody who was not the servant Gow. The list is as follows:

'First item. A very considerable hoard of precious stones, nearly all diamonds, and all of them loose, without any setting whatever. Of course, it is natural that the Ogilvies should have family jewels; but those are exactly the jewels that are almost always set in particular articles of ornament. The Ogilvies would seem to have kept theirs loose in their pockets, like coppers.

'Second item. Heaps and heaps of loose snuff, not kept in a horn, or even a pouch, but lying in heaps on the mantelpieces, on the sideboard, on the piano, anywhere. It looks as if the old gentleman would not take the trouble to look in a pocket or lift a lid.

'Third item. Here and there about the house curious little heaps of minute pieces of metal, some like steel springs and some in the form of microscopic wheels. As if they had gutted some mechanical toy.

'Fourth item. The wax candles, which have to be stuck in bottle necks because there is nothing else to stick them in. Now I wish you to note how very much queerer all this is than anything we anticipated. For the central riddle we are prepared; we have all seen at a glance that there was something wrong about the last earl. We have come here to find out whether he really lived here, whether he really died here, whether that red-haired scarecrow who did his burying had anything to do with his dying. But suppose the worst in all this, the most lurid or melodramatic solution you like. Suppose the servant really killed the master, or suppose the master isn't really dead, or suppose the master is dressed up as the servant, or suppose the servant is buried for the master; invent what Wilkie Collins's tragedy you like, and you still have not explained a candle without a candlestick, or why an elderly gentleman of good family should habitually spill snuff on the piano. The core of the tale we could imagine; it is the fringes that are mysterious. By no stretch of fancy can the human mind connect together snuff and diamonds and wax and loose clockwork.'

'I think I see the connexion,' said the priest. 'This Glengyle was mad against the French Revolution. He was an enthusiast for the *ancien régime*, and was trying to re-enact literally the family life of the last Bourbons. He had snuff because it was the eighteenth century luxury; wax candles, because they were the eighteenth century lighting; the mechanical bits of iron represent the locksmith hobby of Louis XVI; the diamonds are for the Diamond Necklace of Marie Antoinette.'

Both the other men were staring at him with round eyes. 'What a perfectly extraordinary notion!' cried Flambeau. 'Do you really think that is the truth?'

'I am perfectly sure it isn't,' answered Father Brown, 'only you said that nobody could connect snuff and diamonds and clockwork and candles. I give you that connexion off-hand. The real truth, I am very sure, lies deeper.'

He paused a moment and listened to the wailing of the wind in the turrets. Then he said: 'The late Earl of Glengyle was a thief. He lived a second and darker life as a desperate house-breaker. He did not have any candlesticks because he only used these candles cut short in the lantern he carried. The snuff he employed as the fiercest French criminals have used pepper: to fling it suddenly in dense masses in the face of a captor or pursuer. But the final proof is in the curious coincidence of the diamonds and the small steel wheels. Surely that makes everything plain to you? Diamonds and small steel wheels are the only two instruments with which you can cut out a pane of glass.'

The bough of a broken pine tree lashed heavily in the blast against the window-pane behind them, as if in parody of a burglar, but they did not turn round. Their eyes were fastened on Father Brown.

'Diamonds and small wheels,' repeated Craven ruminating. 'Is that all that makes you think it the true explanation?'

'I don't think it the true explanation,' replied the priest placidly; 'but you said that nobody could connect the four things. The true tale, of course, is something much more humdrum. Glengyle had found, or thought he had found, precious stones on his estate. Somebody had bamboozled him with those loose brilliants, saying they were found in the castle caverns. The little wheels are some diamond-cutting affair. He had to do the thing very roughly and in a small way, with the help of a few shepherds or rude fellows on these hills. Snuff is the one great luxury of such Scotch shepherds; it's the one thing with which you can bribe them. They didn't have candlesticks because they didn't want them; they held the candles in their hands when they explored the caves.'

'Is that all?' asked Flambeau after a long pause. 'Have we got to the dull truth at last?'

'Oh, no,' said Father Brown.

As the wind died in the most distant pine woods with a long hoot as of mockery, Father Brown, with an utterly impassive face, went on:

'I only suggested that because you said one could not plausibly connect snuff with clockwork or candles with bright stones. Ten false philosophies will fit the universe; ten false theories will fit Glengyle Castle. But we want the real explanation of the castle and the universe. But are there no other exhibits?'

Craven laughed, and Flambeau rose smiling to his feet and strolled down the long table.

'Items five, six, seven, etc.,' he said, 'are certainly more varied than instructive. A curious collection, not of lead pencils, but of the lead out of lead pencils. A senseless stick of bamboo, with the top rather splintered. It might be the instrument of the crime. Only, there isn't any crime. The only other things are a few old missals and little Catholic pictures, which the Ogilvies kept, I suppose, from the Middle Ages – their family pride being stronger than their Puritanism. We only put them in the museum because they seem curiously cut about and defaced.'

The heady tempest without drove a dreadful wrack of clouds across Glengyle and threw the long room into darkness as Father Brown picked up the little illuminated pages to examine them. He spoke before the drift of darkness had passed; but it was the voice of an utterly new man.

'Mr Craven,' said he, talking like a man ten years younger: 'you have got a legal warrant, haven't you, to go up and examine that grave? The sooner we do it the better, and get to the bottom of this horrible affair. If I were you I should start now.'

'Now,' repeated the astonished detective, 'and why now?'

'Because this is serious,' answered Brown; 'this is not spilt snuff or loose pebbles, that might be there for a hundred reasons. There is only one reason I know of for *this* being done; and the reason goes down to the roots of the world. These religious pictures are not just dirtied or torn or scrawled over, which might be done in idleness or bigotry, by children or by Protestants. These have been treated very carefully – and very queerly. In every place where the great ornamented name of God comes in the old illuminations it has been elaborately taken out. The only other thing that has been removed is the halo round the head of the Child Jesus. Therefore, I say, let us get our warrant and our spade and our hatchet, and go up and break open that coffin.'

'What *do* you mean?' demanded the London officer.

'I mean,' answered the little priest, and his voice seemed to rise slightly in the roar of the gale. 'I mean that the great devil of the universe may be sitting on the top tower of this castle at this moment, as big as a hundred elephants, and roaring like the Apocalypse. There is black magic somewhere at the bottom of this.'

'Black magic,' repeated Flambeau in a low voice, for he was too enlightened a man not to know of such things; 'but what can these other things mean?'

'Oh, something damnable, I suppose,' replied Brown impatiently. 'How should I know? How can I guess all their mazes down below? Perhaps you can make a torture out of snuff and bamboo. Perhaps lunatics lust after wax and steel filings. Perhaps there is a maddening drug made of lead pencils! Our shortest cut to the mystery is up the hill to the grave.'

His comrades hardly knew that they had obeyed and followed him till a blast of the night wind nearly flung them on their faces in the garden. Nevertheless they had obeyed him like automata; for Craven found a hatchet in his hand, and the warrant in his pocket; Flambeau was carrying the heavy spade of the strange gardener; Father Brown was carrying the little gilt book from which had been torn the name of God.

The path up the hill to the churchyard was crooked but short; only under the stress of wind it seemed laborious and long. Far as the eye could see, farther and farther as they mounted the slope, were seas beyond seas of pines, now all aslope one way under the wind. And that universal gesture seemed as vain as it was vast, as vain as if that wind were whistling about some unpeopled and purposeless planet. Through all that infinite growth of grey-blue forests sang, shrill and high, that ancient sorrow that is in the heart of all heathen things. One could fancy that the voices from the underworld of unfathomable foliage were cries of the lost and wandering pagan gods: gods who had gone roaming in that irrational forest, and who will never find their way back to heaven.

'You see,' said Father Brown in a low but easy tone, 'Scotch people before Scotland existed were a curious lot. In fact, they're a curious lot still. But in the prehistoric times I fancy they really worshipped demons. That,' he added genially, 'is why they jumped at the Puritan theology.'

'My friend,' said Flambeau, turning in a kind of fury, 'what does all that snuff mean?'

'My friend,' replied Brown, with equal seriousness, 'there is one mark of all genuine religions: materialism. Now, devil-worship is a perfectly genuine religion.'

They had come up on the grassy scalp of the hill, one of the few bald spots that stood clear of the crashing and roaring pine forest. A mean enclosure, partly timber and partly wire, rattled in the tempest to tell them the border of the graveyard. But by the time Inspector Craven had come to the corner of the grave, and Flambeau had planted his spade point downwards and leaned on it, they were both almost as shaken as the shaky wood and wire. At the foot of the grave grew great tall thistles, grey and silver in their decay. Once or twice, when a ball of thistledown broke under the breeze and flew past him, Craven jumped slightly as if it had been an arrow.

Flambeau drove the blade of his spade through the whistling grass into the wet clay below. Then he seemed to stop and lean on it as on a staff.

'Go on,' said the priest very gently. 'We are only trying to find the truth. What are you afraid of?'

'I am afraid of finding it,' said Flambeau.

The London detective spoke suddenly in a high crowing voice that was meant to be conversational and cheery. 'I wonder why he really did hide himself like that. Something nasty, I suppose; was he a leper?'

'Something worse than that,' said Flambeau.

'And what do you imagine,' asked the other, 'would be worse than a leper?'

'I don't imagine it,' said Flambeau.

He dug for some dreadful minutes in silence, and then said in a choked voice: 'I'm afraid of his not being the right shape.'

'Nor was that piece of paper, you know,' said Father Brown quietly, 'and we survived even that piece of paper.'

Flambeau dug on with a blind energy. But the tempest had shouldered away the choking grey clouds that clung to the hills like smoke and revealed grey fields of faint starlight before he cleared the shape of a rude timber coffin, and somehow tipped it up upon the turf. Craven stepped forward with his axe; a thistle-top touched him, and he flinched. Then he took a firmer stride, and hacked and wrenched with an energy like Flambeau's till the lid was torn off, and all that was there lay glimmering in the grey starlight.

'Bones,' said Craven; and then he added, 'but it is a man,' as if that were something unexpected.

'Is he,' asked Flambeau in a voice that went oddly up and down, 'is he all right?'

'Seems so,' said the officer huskily, bending over the obscure and decaying skeleton in the box. 'Wait a minute.'

A vast heave went over Flambeau's huge figure. 'And now I come to think of it,' he cried, 'why in the name of madness shouldn't he be all right? What is it gets hold of a man on these cursed cold mountains? I think it's the black, brainless repetition; all these forests, and over all an ancient horror of unconsciousness. It's like the dream of an atheist. Pine-trees and more pine-trees and millions more pine-trees—'

'God!' cried the man by the coffin; 'but he hasn't got a head.'

While the others stood rigid the priest, for the first time, showed a leap of startled concern.

'No head!' he repeated. '*No head?*' as if he had almost expected some other deficiency.

Half-witted visions of a headless baby born to Glengyle, of a headless youth hiding himself in the castle, of a headless man pacing those ancient halls or that gorgeous garden, passed in panorama through their minds. But even in that stiffened instant the tale took no root in them and seemed to have no reason in it. They stood listening to the loud woods and the shrieking sky quite foolishly, like exhausted animals. Thought seemed to be something enormous that had suddenly slipped out of their grasp.

'There are three headless men,' said Father Brown, 'standing round this open grave.'

The pale detective from London opened his mouth to speak, and left it open like a yokel, while a long scream of wind tore the sky; then he looked at the axe in his hands as if it did not belong to him, and dropped it.

'Father,' said Flambeau in that infantile and heavy voice he used very seldom, 'what are we to do?'

His friend's reply came with the pent promptitude of a gun going off.

'Sleep!' cried Father Brown. 'Sleep. We have come to the end of the ways. Do you know what sleep is? Do you know that every man who sleeps believes in God? It is a sacrament; for it is an act of faith and it is a food. And we need a sacrament, if only a natural one. Something has fallen on us that falls very seldom on men; perhaps the worst thing that can fall on them.'

Craven's parted lips came together to say: 'What do you mean?'

The priest turned his face to the castle as he answered:

'We have found the truth; and the truth makes no sense.'

He went down the path in front of them with a plunging and reckless step very rare with him, and when they reached the castle again he threw himself upon sleep with the simplicity of a dog.

Despite his mystic praise of slumber, Father Brown was up earlier than anyone else except the silent gardener; and was found smoking a big pipe and watching that expert at his speechless labours in the kitchen garden. Towards daybreak the rocking storm had ended in roaring rains, and the day came with a curious freshness. The gardener seemed even to have been conversing, but at sight of the detectives he planted his spade sullenly in a bed and, saying something about his breakfast, shifted along the lines of cabbages and shut himself in the kitchen. 'He's a valuable man, that,' said Father Brown. 'He does the potatoes amazingly. Still,' he added, with a dispassionate charity, 'he has his faults; which of us hasn't? He doesn't dig this bank quite regularly. There, for instance,' and he stamped suddenly on one spot. 'I'm really very doubtful about that potato.'

'And why?' asked Craven, amused with the little man's new hobby.

'I'm doubtful about it,' said the other, 'because old Gow was doubtful about it himself. He put his spade in methodically in every place but just this. There must be a mighty fine potato just there.'

Flambeau pulled up the spade and impetuously drove it into the place. He turned up, under a load of soil, something that did not look like a potato, but rather like a monstrous, over-domed mushroom. But it struck the spade with a cold click; it rolled over like a ball, and grinned up at them.

'The Earl of Glengyle,' said Brown sadly, and looked down heavily at the skull.

Then, after a momentary meditation, he plucked the spade from Flambeau, and, saying: 'We must hide it again,' clamped the skull down in the earth. Then he learned his little body and huge head on the great handle of the spade, that stood up stiffly in the earth, and his eyes were empty and his forehead full of wrinkles. 'If one could only conceive,' he muttered, 'the meaning of this last monstrosity.' And leaning on the large spade handle, he buried his brows in his hands, as men do in church.

All the corners of the sky were brightening into blue and silver; the birds were chattering in the tiny garden trees; so loud it seemed as if the trees themselves were talking. But the three men were silent enough.

'Well, I give it all up,' said Flambeau at last boisterously. 'My brain and this world don't fit each other; and there's an end of it. Snuff, spoilt Prayer Books, and the insides of musical boxes – what—'

Brown threw up his bothered brow and rapped on the spade handle with an intolerance quite unusual with him. 'Oh, tut, tut, tut, tut!' he cried. 'All that is as plain as a pikestaff. I understood the snuff and clock-work, and so on, when I first opened my eyes this morning. And since then I've had it out with old Gow, the gardener, who is neither so deaf nor so stupid as he pretends. There's something amiss about the loose items. I was wrong about the torn mass-book, too; there's no harm in that. But it's this last business. Desecrating graves and stealing dead men's heads – surely there's harm in that? Surely there's black magic still in that? That doesn't fit in to the quite simple story of the snuff and the candles.' And, striding about again, he smoked moodily.

'My friend,' said Flambeau, with a grim humour, 'you must be careful with me and remember I was once a criminal. The great advantage of that estate was that I always made up the story myself, and acted it as quick as I chose. This detective business of waiting about is too much for my French impatience. All my life, for good or evil, I have done things at the instant; I always fought duels the next morning; I always paid bills on the nail; I never even put off a visit to the dentist—'

Father Brown's pipe fell out of his mouth and broke into three pieces on the gravel path. He stood rolling his eyes, the exact picture of an idiot. 'Lord, what a turnip I am!' he kept saying. 'Lord, what a turnip!' Then, in a somewhat groggy kind of way, he began to laugh.

'The dentist!' he repeated. 'Six hours in the spiritual abyss, and all because I never thought of the dentist! Such a simple, such a beautiful and peaceful thought! Friends, we have passed a night in hell; but now the sun is risen, the birds are singing, and the radiant form of the dentist consoles the world.'

'I will get some sense out of this,' cried Flambeau, striding forward, 'if I use the tortures of the Inquisition.'

Father Brown repressed what appeared to be a momentary disposition to dance on the now sunlit lawn and cried quite piteously, like a child: 'Oh, let me be silly a little. You don't know how unhappy I have been.

And now I know that there has been no deep sin in this business at all. Only a little lunacy, perhaps – and who minds that?'

He spun round once, then faced them with gravity.

'This is not a story of crime,' he said; 'rather it is the story of a strange and crooked honesty. We are dealing with the one man on earth, perhaps, who has taken no more than his due. It is a study in the savage living logic that has been the religion of this race.

'That old local rhyme about the house of Glengyle –

> As green sap to the simmer trees
> Is red gold to the Ogilvies –

was literal as well as metaphorical. It did not merely mean that the Glengyles sought for wealth; it was also true that they literally gathered gold; they had a huge collection of ornaments and utensils in that metal. They were, in fact, misers whose mania took that turn. In the light of that fact, run through all the things we found in the castle. Diamonds without their gold rings; candles without their gold candlesticks; snuff without the gold snuff-boxes; pencil-leads without the gold pencil-cases; a walking-stick without its gold top; clockwork without the gold clocks – or rather watches. And, mad as it sounds, because the halos and the name of God in the old missals were of real gold, these also were taken away.'

The garden seemed to brighten, the grass to grow gayer in the strengthening sun, as the crazy truth was told. Flambeau lit a cigarette as his friend went on.

'Were taken away,' continued Father Brown; 'were taken away – but not stolen. Thieves would never have left this mystery. Thieves would have taken the gold snuff-boxes, snuff and all; the gold pencil-cases, lead and all. We have to deal with a man with a peculiar conscience, but certainly a conscience. I found that mad moralist this morning in the kitchen garden yonder, and I heard the whole story.

'The late Archbishop Ogilvie was the nearest approach to a good man ever born at Glengyle. But his bitter virtue took the turn of the misanthrope; he moped over the dishonesty of his ancestors, from which, somehow, he generalized a dishonesty of all men. More especially he distrusted philanthropy or free-giving; and he swore if he could find one man who took his exact rights he should have all the gold of Glengyle. Having delivered this defiance to humanity he shut himself up, without the smallest expectation of its being answered. One day, however, a deaf and seemingly senseless lad from a distant village brought him a belated telegram; and Glengyle, in his acrid pleasantry, gave him a new farthing. At least he thought he had done so, but when he turned over his change he found the new farthing still there and a sovereign gone. The accident offered him vistas of sneering speculation. Either way, the boy would show the greasy greed of the species. Either he would vanish, a thief stealing a coin; or he would sneak back with it virtuously, a snob seeking a reward. In the middle of the night Lord Glengyle was knocked up out of his bed – for he lived alone – and forced to open the door to the deaf idiot. The idiot brought with him, not the sovereign, but exactly nineteen shillings and eleven-pence three-farthings in change.

'Then the wild exactitude of this action took hold on the mad lord's brain like fire. He swore he was Diogenes, that had long sought an honest man, and at last had found one. He made a new will, which I have seen. He took the literal youth into his huge, neglected house, and trained him up as his solitary servant and – after an odd manner – his heir. And whatever that queer creature understands, he understood absolutely his lord's two fixed ideas: first, that the letter of right is everything; and second, that he himself was to have the gold of Glengyle. So far, that is all; and that is simple. He has stripped the house of gold, and taken not a grain that was not gold; not so much as a grain of snuff. He lifted the gold leaf off an old illumination, fully satisfied that he left the rest unspoilt. All that I understood; but I could not understand this skull business. I was really uneasy about that human head buried among the potatoes. It distressed me – till Flambeau said the word.

'It will be all right. He will put the skull back in the grave, when he has taken the gold out of the tooth.'

And, indeed, when Flambeau crossed the hill that morning, he saw that strange being, the just miser, digging at the desecrated grave, the plaid round his throat thrashing out in the mountain wind; the sober top hat on his head.

MAX BEERBOHM

Enoch Soames

When a book about the literature of the eighteen-nineties was given by
Mr Holbrook Jackson to the world, I looked eagerly in the index for
SOAMES, ENOCH. I had feared he would not be there. He was not there.
But everybody else was. Many writers whom I had quite forgotten, or
remembered but faintly, lived again for me, they and their work, in
Mr Holbrook Jackson's pages. The book was as thorough as it was bril-
liantly written. And thus the omission found by me was an all the deadlier
record of poor Soames' failure to impress himself on his decade.

I daresay I am the only person who noticed the omission. Soames
had failed so piteously as all that! Nor is there a counterpoise in the thought
that if he had had some measure of success he might have passed, like those
others, out of my mind, to return only at the historian's beck. It is true that
had his gifts, such as they were, been acknowledged in his lifetime, he would
never have made the bargain I saw him make – that strange bargain whose
results have kept him always in the foreground of my memory. But it is from
those very results that the full piteousness of him glares out.

Not my compassion, however, impels me to write of him. For his sake,
poor fellow, I should be inclined to keep my pen out of the ink. It is ill
to deride the dead. And how can I write about Enoch Soames without
making him ridiculous? Or rather, how am I to hush up the horrid fact
that he *was* ridiculous? I shall not be able to do that. Yet, sooner or later,
write about him I must. You will see, in due course, that I have no option.
And I may as well get the thing done now.

In the Summer Term of '93 a bolt from the blue flashed down on Oxford.
It drove deep, it hurtlingly embedded itself in the soil. Dons and

477

undergraduates stood around, rather pale, discussing nothing but it. Whence came it, this meteorite? From Paris. Its name? Will Rothenstein. Its aim? To do a series of twenty-four portraits in lithograph. These were to be published from the Bodley Head, London. The matter was urgent. Already the Warden of A, and the Master of B, and the Regius Professor of C, had meekly 'sat'. Dignified and doddering old men, who had never consented to sit to any one, could not withstand this dynamic little stranger. He did not sue: he invited; he did not invite: he commanded. He was twenty-one years old. He wore spectacles that flashed more than any other pair ever seen. He was a wit. He was brimful of ideas. He knew Whistler. He knew Edmond de Goncourt. He knew every one in Paris. He knew them all by heart. He was Paris in Oxford. It was whispered that, so soon as he had polished off his selection of dons, he was going to include a few undergraduates. It was a proud day for me when I – I – was included. I liked Rothenstein not less than I feared him; and there arose between us a friendship that has grown ever warmer, and been more and more valued by me, with every passing year.

At the end of Term he settled in – or rather, meteoritically into – London. It was to him I owed my first knowledge of that forever enchanting little world-in-itself, Chelsea, and my first acquaintance with Walter Sickert and other august elders who dwelt there. It was Rothenstein that took me to see, in Cambridge Street, Pimlico, a young man whose drawings were already famous among the few – Aubrey Beardsley, by name. With Rothenstein I paid my first visit to the Bodley Head. By him I was inducted into another haunt of intellect and daring, the domino room of the Café Royal.

There, on that October evening – there, in that exuberant vista of gilding and crimson velvet set amidst all those opposing mirrors and upholding caryatids, with fumes of tobacco ever rising to the painted and pagan ceiling, and with the hum of presumably cynical conversation broken into so sharply now and again by the clatter of dominoes shuffled on marble tables, I drew a deep breath, and 'This indeed,' said I to myself, 'is life!'

It was the hour before dinner. We drank vermouth. Those who knew Rothenstein were pointing him out to those who knew him only by name. Men were constantly coming in through the swing-doors and wandering slowly up and down in search of vacant tables, or of tables occupied by friends. One of these rovers interested me because I was sure he wanted to catch Rothenstein's eye. He had twice passed our table, with a hesitating look; but Rothenstein, in the thick of a disquisition on Puvis de Chavannes, had not seen him. He was a stooping, shambling person, rather tall, very pale, with longish and brownish hair. He had a thin vague beard – or rather, he had a chin on which a large number of hairs weakly curled and clustered to cover its retreat. He was an odd-looking person; but in the 'nineties odd apparitions were more frequent, I think, than they are now. The young writers of that era – and I was sure this man was a writer – strove earnestly to be distinct in aspect. This man had striven unsuccessfully. He wore a soft black hat of clerical kind but of Bohemian intention, and a grey waterproof cape which, perhaps because it was waterproof, failed to be romantic. I decided that 'dim' was the *mot juste* for him. I had already essayed to write, and was immensely keen on the *mot juste*, that Holy Grail of the period.

The dim man was now again approaching our table, and this time he made up his mind to pause in front of it. 'You don't remember me,' he said in a toneless voice.

Rothenstein brightly focussed him. 'Yes, I do,' he replied after a moment, with pride rather than effusion – pride in a retentive memory. 'Edwin Soames.'

'Enoch Soames,' said Enoch.

'Enoch Soames,' repeated Rothenstein in a tone implying that it was enough to have hit on the surname. 'We met in Paris two or three times when you were living there. We met at the Café Groche.'

'And I came to your studio once.'

'Oh yes; I was sorry I was out.'

'But you were in. You showed me some of your paintings, you know . . . I hear you're in Chelsea now.'

'Yes.'

I almost wondered that Mr Soames did not, after this monosyllable, pass along. He stood patiently there, rather like a dumb animal, rather like a donkey looking over a gate. A sad figure, his. It occurred to me that 'hungry' was perhaps the *mot juste* for him; but – hungry for what? He looked as if he had little appetite for anything. I was sorry for him; and Rothenstein, though he had not invited him to Chelsea, did ask him to sit down and have something to drink.

Seated, he was more self-assertive. He flung back the wings of his cape with a gesture which – had not those wings been waterproof – might have seemed to hurl defiance at things in general. And he ordered an absinthe. '*Je me tiens toujours fidèle,*' he told Rothenstein, '*à la sorcière glauque.*'

'It is bad for you,' said Rothenstein drily.

'Nothing is bad for one,' answered Soames. '*Dans ce monde il n'y a ni de bien ni de mal.*'

'Nothing good and nothing bad? How do you mean?'

'I explained it all in the preface to "Negations".'

'"Negations"?'

'Yes; I gave you a copy of it.'

'Oh yes, of course. But did you explain – for instance – that there was no such thing as bad or good grammar?'

'N-no,' said Soames. 'Of course in Art there is the good and the evil. But in Life – no.' He was rolling a cigarette. He had weak white hands, not well washed, and with finger-tips much stained by nicotine. 'In Life there are illusions of good and evil, but' – his voice trailed away to a murmur in which the words 'vieux jeu' and 'rococo' were faintly audible. I think he felt he was not doing himself justice, and feared that Rothenstein was going to point out fallacies. Anyway, he cleared his throat and said '*Parlons d'autre chose.*'

It occurs to you that he was a fool? It didn't to me. I was young, and had not the clarity of judgment that Rothenstein already had. Soames was quite five or six years older than either of us. Also, he had written a book.

It was wonderful to have written a book.

If Rothenstein had not been there, I should have revered Soames. Even as it was, I respected him. And I was very near indeed to reverence when he said he had another book coming out soon. I asked if I might ask what kind of book it was to be.

'My poems,' he answered. Rothenstein asked if this was to be the title of the book. The poet meditated on this suggestion, but said he rather thought of giving the book no title at all. 'If a book is good in itself—' he murmured, waving his cigarette.

Rothenstein objected that absence of title might be bad for the sale of a book. 'If,' he urged, 'I went into a bookseller's and said simply "Have you got?" or "Have you a copy of?" how would they know what I wanted?'

'Oh, of course I should have my name on the cover,' Soames answered earnestly. 'And I rather want,' he added, looking hard at Rothenstein, 'to have a drawing of myself as frontispiece.' Rothenstein admitted that this was a capital idea, and mentioned that he was going into the country and would be there for some time. He then looked at his watch, exclaimed at the hour, paid the waiter, and went away with me to dinner. Soames remained at his post of fidelity to the glaucous witch.

'Why were you so determined not to draw him?' I asked.

'Draw him? Him? How can one draw a man who doesn't exist?'

'He is dim,' I admitted. But my *mot juste* fell flat. Rothenstein repeated that Soames was non-existent.

Still, Soames had written a book. I asked if Rothenstein had read 'Negations.' He said he had looked into it, 'but,' he added crisply, 'I don't profess to know anything about writing.' A reservation very characteristic of the period! Painters would not then allow that any one outside their own order had a right to any opinion about painting. This law (graven on the tablets brought down by Whistler from the summit of Fujiyama) imposed certain limitations. If other arts than painting were not utterly unintelligible to all but the men who practised them, the law tottered – the Monroe Doctrine, as it were, did not hold good. Therefore no painter would offer an opinion of a book without warning you at any rate that his opinion was worthless. No one is a better judge of literature than Rothenstein; but it wouldn't have done to tell him so in those days; and I knew that I must form an unaided judgment on 'Negations'.

Not to buy a book of which I had met the author face to face would have been for me in those days an impossible act of self-denial. When I returned to Oxford for the Christmas Term I had duly secured 'Negations'. I used to keep it lying carelessly on the table in my room, and whenever a friend took it up and asked what it was about I would say 'Oh, it's rather a remarkable book. It's by a man whom I know.' Just 'what it was about' I never was able to say. Head or tail was just what I hadn't made of that slim green volume. I found in the preface no clue to the exiguous labyrinth of contents, and in that labyrinth nothing to explain the preface.

Lean near to life. Lean very near – nearer.
Life is web, and therein nor warp nor woof is, but web only.

It is for this I am Catholick in church and in thought, yet do let swift
Mood weave there what the shuttle of Mood wills.

These were the opening phrases of the preface, but those which followed
were less easy to understand. Then came 'Stark: A *Conte*', about a midi-
nette who, so far as I could gather, murdered, or was about to murder, a
mannequin. It seemed to me like a story by Catulle Mendès in which the
translator had either skipped or cut out every alternate sentence. Next, a
dialogue between Pan and St Ursula – lacking, I rather felt, in 'snap'.
Next, some aphorisms (entitled ἀφορίσματα). Throughout, in fact, there
was a great variety of form; and the forms had evidently been wrought
with much care. It was rather the substance that eluded me. Was there,
I wondered, any substance at all? It did now occur to me: suppose Enoch
Soames was a fool! Up cropped a rival hypothesis: suppose *I* was! I inclined
to give Soames the benefit of the doubt. I had read 'L'Après-midi d'un
Faune' without extracting a glimmer of meaning. Yet Mallarmé – of
course – was a Master. How was I to know that Soames wasn't another?
There was a sort of music in his prose, not indeed arresting, but perhaps,
I thought, haunting, and laden perhaps with meanings as deep as Mal-
larmé's own. I awaited his poems with an open mind.

And I looked forward to them with positive impatience after I had had
a second meeting with him. This was on an evening in January. Going
into the aforesaid domino room, I passed a table at which sat a pale man
with an open book before him. He looked from his book to me, and I
looked back over my shoulder with a vague sense that I ought to have
recognized him. I returned to pay my respects. After exchanging a few
words, I said with a glance to the open book, 'I see I am interrupting you,'
and was about to pass on, but 'I prefer,' Soames replied in his toneless
voice, 'to be interrupted,' and I obeyed his gesture that I should sit down.

I asked him if he often read here. 'Yes; things of this kind I read here,'
he answered, indicating the title of his book – 'The Poems of Shelley'.

'Anything that you really' – and I was going to say 'admire?' But I cautiously left my sentence unfinished, and was glad that I had done so, for
he said, with unwonted emphasis, 'Anything second-rate.'

I had read little of Shelley, but 'Of course,' I murmured, 'he's very
uneven.'

'I should have thought evenness was just what was wrong with him. A deadly evenness. That's why I read him here. The noise of this place breaks the rhythm. He's tolerable here.' Soames took up the book and glanced through the pages. He laughed. Soames' laugh was a short, single and mirthless sound from the throat, unaccompanied by any movement of the face or brightening of the eyes. 'What a period!' he uttered, laying the book down. And 'What a country!' he added.

I asked rather nervously if he didn't think Keats had more or less held his own against the drawbacks of time and place. He admitted that there were 'passages in Keats', but did not specify them. Of 'the older men', as he called them, he seemed to like only Milton. 'Milton,' he said, 'wasn't sentimental.' Also, 'Milton had a dark insight.' And again, 'I can always read Milton in the reading-room.'

'The reading-room?'

'Of the British Museum. I go there every day.'

'You do? I've only been there once. I'm afraid I found it rather a depressing place. It – it seemed to sap one's vitality.'

'It does. That's why I go there. The lower one's vitality, the more sensitive one is to great art. I live near the Museum. I have rooms in Dyott Street.'

'And you go round to the reading-room to read Milton?'

'Usually Milton.' He looked at me. 'It was Milton,' he certificatively added, 'who converted me to Diabolism.'

'Diabolism? Oh yes? Really?' said I, with that vague discomfort and that intense desire to be polite which one feels when a man speaks of his own religion. 'You – worship the Devil?'

Soames shook his head. 'It's not exactly worship,' he qualified, sipping his absinthe. 'It's more a matter of trusting and encouraging.'

'Ah, yes . . . But I had rather gathered from the preface to "Negations" that you were a – a Catholic.'

'*Je l'étais à cette époque.* Perhaps I still am. Yes, I'm a Catholic Diabolist.'

This profession he made in an almost cursory tone. I could see that what was upmost in his mind was the fact that I had read 'Negations'. His pale eyes had for the first time gleamed. I felt as one who is about to be examined, *viva voce*, on the very subject in which he is shakiest. I hastily asked him how soon his poems were to be published. 'Next week,' he told me.

'And are they to be published without a title?'

'No. I found a title, at last. But I shan't tell you what it is,' as though I had been so impertinent as to inquire. 'I am not sure that it wholly satisfies me. But it is the best I can find. It does suggest something of the quality of the poems. . . . Strange growths, natural and wild; yet exquisite,' he added, 'and many-hued, and full of poisons.'

I asked him what he thought of Baudelaire. He uttered the snort that was his laugh, and 'Baudelaire,' he said, 'was a *bourgeois malgré lui*'. France had had only one poet: Villon; 'and two-thirds of Villon were sheer journalism.' Verlaine was 'an *épicier malgré lui*'. Altogether, rather to my surprise, he rated French literature lower than English. There were 'passages' in Villiers de l'Isle-Adam. But 'I,' he summed up, 'owe nothing to France.' He nodded at me. 'You'll see,' he predicted.

I did not, when the time came, quite see that. I thought the author of 'Fungoids' did – unconsciously, no doubt – owe something to the young Parisian décadents, or to the young English ones who owed something to *them*. I still think so. The little book – bought by me in Oxford – lies before me as I write. Its pale grey buckram cover and silver lettering have not worn well. Nor have its contents. Through these, with a melancholy interest, I have again been looking. They are not much. But at the time of their publication I had a vague suspicion that they *might* be. I suppose it is my capacity for faith, not poor Soames' work, that is weaker than it once was. . . .

To a Young Woman

Thou art, who hast not been!
    Pale tunes irresolute
    And traceries of old sounds
    Blown from a rotted flute
Mingle with noise of cymbals rouged with rust,
    Nor not strange forms and epicene
    Lie bleeding in the dust,
      Being wounded with wounds.

    For this it is
    That is thy counterpart
    Of age-long mockeries
    Thou hast not been nor art!

There seemed to me a certain inconsistency as between the first and last lines of this. I tried, with bent brows, to resolve the discord. But I did not take my failure as wholly incompatible with a meaning in Soames' mind. Might it not rather indicate the depth of his meaning? As for the craftsmanship, 'rouged with rust' seemed to me a fine stroke, and 'nor not' instead of 'and' had a curious felicity. I wondered who the Young Woman was, and what she had made of it all. I sadly suspect that Soames could not have made more of it than she. Yet, even now, if one doesn't try to make any sense at all of the poem, and reads it just for the sound, there is a certain grace of cadence. Soames was an artist – in so far as he was anything, poor fellow!

It seemed to me, when first I read 'Fungoids,' that, oddly enough, the Diabolistic side of him was the best. Diabolism seemed to be a cheerful, even a wholesome, influence in his life.

NOCTURNE

Round and round the shutter'd Square
I stroll'd with the Devil's arm in mine.
No sound but the scrape of his hoofs was there
And the ring of his laughter and mine.
We had drunk black wine.

I scream'd 'I will race you, Master!'
'What matter,' he shriek'd, 'to-night
Which of us runs the faster?
There is nothing to fear to-night
In the foul moon's light!'

Then I look'd him in the eyes,
And I laugh'd full shrill at the lie he told
And the gnawing fear he would fain disguise.
It was true, what I'd time and again been told:
He was old – old.

There was, I felt, quite a swing about that first stanza – a joyous and rollicking note of comradeship. The second was slightly hysterical perhaps. But I liked the third: it was so bracingly unorthodox, even according to the tenets of Soames' peculiar sect in the faith. Not much 'trusting and encouraging' here! Soames triumphantly exposing the Devil as a liar, and laughing 'full shrill', cut a quite heartening figure, I thought – then! Now, in the light of what befell, none of his poems depresses me so much as 'Nocturne'.

I looked out for what the metropolitan reviewers would have to say. They seemed to fall into two classes: those who had little to say and those who had nothing. The second class was the larger, and the words of the first were cold; insomuch that

Strikes a note of modernity throughout . . . These tripping numbers. – *Preston Telegraph*

was the sole lure offered in advertisements by Soames' publisher. I had hoped that when next I met the poet I could congratulate him on having made a stir; for I fancied he was not so sure of his intrinsic greatness as he seemed. I was but able to say, rather coarsely, when next I did see him, that I hoped 'Fungoids' was 'selling splendidly.' He looked at me across his glass of absinthe and asked if I had bought a copy. His publisher had told him that three had been sold. I laughed, as at a jest.

'You don't suppose I *care*, do you?' he said, with something like a snarl. I disclaimed the notion. He added that he was not a tradesman. I said mildly that I wasn't, either, and murmured that an artist who gave truly new and great things to the world had always to wait long for recognition. He said he cared not a sou for recognition. I agreed that the act of creation was its own reward.

His moroseness might have alienated me if I had regarded myself as a nobody. But ah! hadn't both John Lane and Aubrey Beardsley suggested that I should write an essay for the great new venture that was afoot – 'The Yellow Book'? And hadn't Henry Harland, as editor, accepted my essay? And wasn't it to be in the very first number? At Oxford I was still *in statu pupillari*. In London I regarded myself as very much indeed a graduate now – one whom no Soames could ruffle. Partly to show off, partly in sheer good-will, I told Soames he ought to contribute to 'The Yellow Book'. He uttered from the throat a sound of scorn for that publication.

Nevertheless, I did, a day or two later, tentatively ask Harland if he knew anything of the work of a man called Enoch Soames. Harland paused in the midst of his characteristic stride around the room, threw up his hands towards the ceiling, and groaned aloud: he had often met 'that absurd creature' in Paris, and this very morning had received some poems in manuscript from him.

'Has he *no* talent?' he asked.

'He has an income. He's all right.' Harland was the most joyous of men and most generous of critics, and he hated to talk of anything about which he couldn't be enthusiastic. So I dropped the subject of Soames. The news that Soames had an income did take the edge off solicitude. I learned afterwards that he was the son of an unsuccessful and deceased bookseller in Preston, but had inherited an annuity of £300 from a married aunt, and had no surviving relatives of any kind. Materially, then, he was 'all right.' But there was still a spiritual pathos about him, sharpened for me now by the possibility that even the praises of 'The Preston Telegraph' might not have been forthcoming had he not been the son of a Preston man. He had a sort of weak doggedness which I could not but admire. Neither he nor his work received the slightest encouragement; but he persisted in behaving as a personage: always he kept his dingy little flag flying. Wherever congregated the *jeunes féroces* of the arts, in whatever Soho restaurant they had just discovered, in whatever music-hall they were most frequenting, there was Soames in the midst of them, or rather on the fringe of them, a dim but inevitable figure. He never sought to propitiate his fellow-writers, never bated a jot of his arrogance about his own work or of his contempt for theirs. To the painters he was respectful, even humble; but for the poets and prosaists of 'The Yellow Book', and later of 'The Savoy', he had never a word but of scorn. He wasn't resented. It didn't occur to anybody that he or his Catholic Diabolism mattered. When, in the autumn of '96, he brought out (at his own expense, this time) a third book, his last book, nobody said a word for or against it. I meant, but forgot, to buy it. I never saw it, and am ashamed to say I don't even remember what it was called. But I did, at the time of its publication, say to Rothenstein that I thought poor old Soames was really a rather tragic figure, and that I believed he would literally die for want of recognition. Rothenstein scoffed. He said I was trying to get credit for a kind heart which I didn't possess; and perhaps this was so. But at the private view of the New English Art Club, a few weeks later, I beheld a pastel portrait of 'Enoch Soames, Esq.' It was very like him, and very like Roth-enstein to have done it. Soames was standing near it, in his soft hat and his waterproof cape, all through the afternoon. Anybody who knew him would have recognised the portrait at a glance, but nobody who didn't know him would have recognised the portrait from its bystander: it 'existed' so much more than he; it was bound to. Also, it had not that expression of faint happiness which on this day was discernible, yes, in Soames' countenance. Fame had breathed on him. Twice again in the course of the month I went to the New English, and on both occasions Soames himself was on view there. Looking back, I regard the close of that exhibition as having been virtually the close of his career. He had felt the breath of Fame against his cheek – so late, for such a little while; and at its withdrawal he gave in, gave up, gave out. He, who had never looked strong or well, looked ghastly now – a shadow of the shade he had once been. He still frequented the domino room, but, having lost all wish to excite curiosity, he no longer read books there. 'You read only at the Museum now?' asked I, with attempted cheerfulness. He said he never went there now. 'No absinthe there,' he muttered. It was the sort of thing that in the old days he would have said for effect; but it carried conviction now. Absinthe, erst but a point in the 'personality' he had striven so hard to build up, was solace and necessity now. He no longer called it 'la sorcière glauque'. He had shed away all his French phrases. He had become a plain, unvarnished, Preston man.

Failure, if it be a plain, unvarnished, complete failure, and even though it be a squalid failure, has always a certain dignity. I avoided Soames because he made me feel rather vulgar. John Lane had published, by this time, two little books of mine, and they had had a pleasant little success of esteem. I was a – slight but definite – 'personality'. Frank Harris had engaged me to kick up my heels in the *Saturday Review*, Alfred Harms-worth was letting me do likewise in the *Daily Mail*. I was just what Soames wasn't. And he shamed my gloss. Had I known that he really and firmly believed in the greatness of what he as an artist had achieved, I might not have shunned him. No man who hasn't lost his vanity can be held to have altogether failed. Soames' dignity was an illusion of mine. One day in the first week of June, 1897, that illusion went. But on the evening of that day Soames went too.

I had been out most of the morning, and, as it was too late to reach home in time for luncheon, I sought 'the Vingtième'. This little place – Restaurant du Vingtième Siècle, to give it its full title – had been discovered in '96 by the poets and prosaists, but had now been more or less abandoned in favour of some later find. I don't think it lived long enough to justify its name; but at that time there it still was, in Greek Street, a few doors from Soho Square, and almost opposite to that house where, in the first years of the century, a little girl, and with her a boy named De Quincey, made nightly encampment in darkness and hunger among dust and rats and old legal parchments. The Vingtième was but a small whitewashed room, leading out into the street at one end and into a kitchen at the other. The proprietor and cook was a Frenchman, known to us as Monsieur Vingtième; the waiters were his two daughters, Rose and Berthe; and the food, according to faith, was good. The tables were so narrow, and were set so close together, that there was space for twelve of them, six jutting from either wall.

Only the two nearest to the door, as I went in, were occupied. On one side sat a tall, flashy, rather Mephistophelian man whom I had seen from time to time in the domino room and elsewhere. On the other side sat Soames. They made a queer contrast in that sunlit room – Soames sitting haggard in that hat and cape which nowhere at any season had I seen him doff, and this other, this keenly vital man, at sight of whom I more than ever wondered whether he were a diamond merchant, a conjurer, or the head of a private detective agency. I was sure Soames didn't want my company; but I asked, as it would have seemed brutal not to, whether I might join him, and took the chair opposite to his. He was smoking a cigarette, with an untasted salmi of something on his plate and a half-empty bottle of Sauterne before him; and he was quite silent. I said that the preparations for the Jubilee made London impossible. (I rather liked them, really.) I professed a wish to go right away till the whole thing was over. In vain did I attune myself to his gloom. He seemed not to hear me nor even to see me. I felt that his behaviour made me ridiculous in the eyes of the other man. The gangway between the two rows of tables at the Vingtième was hardly more than two feet wide (Rose and Berthe, in their ministrations, had always to edge past each other, quarrelling in whispers as they did so), and any one at the table abreast of yours was practically at yours. I thought our neighbour was amused at my failure to interest Soames, and so, as I could not explain to him that my insistence was merely charitable, I became silent. Without turning my head, I had him well within my range of vision. I hoped I looked less vulgar than he in contrast with Soames. I was sure he was not an Englishman, but what *was* his nationality? Though his jet-black hair was *en brosse*, I did not think he was French. To Berthe, who waited on him, he spoke French fluently, but with a hardly native idiom and accent. I gathered that this was his first visit to the Vingtième; but Berthe was off-hand in her manner to him: he had not made a good impression. His eyes were handsome, but – like the Vingtième's tables – too narrow and set too close together. His nose was predatory, and the points of his moustache, waxed up beyond his nostrils, gave a fixity to his smile. Decidedly, he was sinister. And my sense of discomfort in his presence was intensified by the scarlet waistcoat which tightly, and so unseasonably in June, sheathed his ample chest. This waistcoat wasn't wrong merely because of the heat, either. It was somehow all wrong in itself. It wouldn't have done on Christmas morning. It would have struck a jarring note at the first night of 'Hernani'. I was trying to account for its wrongness when Soames suddenly and strangely broke silence. 'A hundred years hence!' he murmured, as in a trance.

'We shall not be here!' I briskly but fatuously added.

'We shall not be here. No,' he droned, 'but the Museum will still be just where it is. And the reading-room, just where it is. And people will be able to go and read there.' He inhaled sharply, and a spasm as of actual pain contorted his features.

I wondered what train of thought poor Soames had been following. He did not enlighten me when he said, after a long pause, 'You think I haven't minded.'

'Minded what, Soames?'

'Neglect. Failure.'

'*Failure?*' I said heartily. 'Failure?' I repeated vaguely. 'Neglect – yes, perhaps; but that's quite another matter. Of course you haven't been – appreciated. But what then? Any artist who – who gives –' What I wanted to say was, 'Any artist who gives truly new and great things to the world has always to wait long for recognition'; but the flattery would not out: in the face of his misery, a misery so genuine and so unmasked, my lips would not say the words.

And then – he said them for me. I flushed. 'That's what you were going to say, isn't it?' he asked.

'How did you know?'

'It's what you said to me three years ago, when "Fungoids" was published.' I flushed the more. I need not have done so at all, for 'It's the only important thing I ever heard you say,' he continued. 'And I've never forgotten it. It's a true thing. It's a horrible truth. But – d'you remember what I answered? I said "I don't care a sou for recognition." And you believed me. You've gone on believing I'm above that sort of thing. You're shallow. What should *you* know of the feelings of a man like me? You imagine that a great artist's faith in himself and in the verdict of posterity is enough to keep him happy . . . You've never guessed at the bitterness and loneliness, the' – his voice broke; but presently he resumed, speaking with a force that I had never known in him. 'Posterity! What use is it to *me*? A dead man doesn't know that people are visiting his grave – visiting his birthplace – putting up tablets to him – unveiling statues of him. A dead man can't read the books that are written about him. A hundred years hence! Think of it! If I could come back to life *then* – just for a few hours – and go to the reading-room, and *read*! Or better still: if I could be projected, now, at this moment, into that future, into that reading-room, just for this one after-noon! I'd sell myself body and soul to the devil, for that! Think of the pages and pages in the catalogue: "Soames, Enoch" endlessly – endless editions, commentaries, prolegomena, biographies' – but here he was interrupted by a sudden loud creak of the chair at the next table. Our neighbour had half risen from his place. He was leaning towards us, apologetically intrusive.

'Excuse – permit me,' he said softly. 'I have been unable not to hear. Might I take a liberty? In this little restaurant-sans-façon' – he spread wide his hands – 'might I, as the phrase is, "cut in"?'

I could but signify our acquiescence. Berthe had appeared at the kit-chen door, thinking the stranger wanted his bill. He waved her away with his cigar, and in another moment had seated himself beside me, com-manding a full view of Soames.

'Though not an Englishman,' he explained, 'I know my London well, Mr Soames. Your name and fame – Mr Beerbohm's too – very known to me. Your point is: who am *I*?' He glanced quickly over his shoulder, and in a lowered voice said 'I am the Devil.'

I couldn't help it: I laughed. I tried not to, I knew there was nothing to laugh at, my rudeness shamed me, but – I laughed with increasing volume. The Devil's quiet dignity, the surprise and disgust of his raised eyebrows, did but the more dissolve me. I rocked to and fro, I lay back aching. I behaved deplorably.

'I am a gentleman, and,' he said with intense emphasis, 'I thought I was in the company of *gentlemen*.'

'Don't!' I gasped faintly. 'Oh, don't!'

'Curious, *nicht wahr?*' I heard him say to Soames. 'There is a type of person to whom the very mention of my name is – oh-so-awfully-funny! In your theatres the dullest comédien needs only to say "The Devil!" and right away they give him "the loud laugh that speaks the vacant mind". Is it not so?'

I had now just breath enough to offer my apologies. He accepted them, but coldly, and readdressed himself to Soames.

'I am a man of business,' he said, 'and always I would put things through "right now", as they say in the States. You are a poet. *Les affaires* – you detest them. So be it. But with me you will deal, eh? What you have said just now gives me furiously to hope.'

Soames had not moved, except to light a fresh cigarette. He sat crouched forward, with his elbows squared on the table, and his head just above the level of his hands, staring up at the Devil. 'Go on,' he nodded. I had no remnant of laughter in me now.

'It will be the more pleasant, our little deal,' the Devil went on, 'because you are – I mistake not? – a Diabolist.'

'A Catholic Diabolist,' said Soames.

The Devil accepted the reservation genially. 'You wish,' he resumed, 'to visit now – this afternoon as-ever-is – the reading-room of the British Museum, yes? but of a hundred years hence, yes? *Parfaitement*. Time – an illusion. Past and future – they are as ever-present as the present, or at any rate only what you call "just-round-the-corner". I switch you on to any date. I project you – pouf! You wish to be in the reading-room just as it will be on the afternoon of June 3rd, 1997? You wish to find yourself standing in that room, just past the swing-doors, this very minute, yes? and to stay there till closing time? Am I right?'

Soames nodded.

The Devil looked at his watch. 'Ten past two,' he said. 'Closing time in summer same then as now: seven o'clock. That will give you almost five hours. At seven o'clock – pouf! – you find yourself again here, sitting at this table. I am dining to-night *dans le monde – dans le higlif.* That concludes my present visit to your great city. I come and fetch you here, Mr Soames, on my way home.'

'Home?' I echoed.

'Be it never so humble!' said the Devil lightly.

'All right,' said Soames.

'Soames!' I entreated. But my friend moved not a muscle.

The Devil had made as though to stretch forth his hand across the table and touch Soames' forearm; but he paused in his gesture.

'A hundred years hence, as now,' he smiled, 'no smoking allowed in the reading-room. You would better therefore—'

Soames removed the cigarette from his mouth and dropped it into his glass of Sauterne.

'Soames!' again I cried. 'Can't you' – but the Devil had now stretched forth his hand across the table. He brought it slowly down on – the table-cloth. Soames' chair was empty. His cigarette floated sodden in his wine-glass. There was no other trace of him.

For a few moments the Devil let his hand rest where it lay, gazing at me out of the corners of his eyes, vulgarly triumphant.

A shudder shook me. With an effort I controlled myself and rose from my chair. 'Very clever,' I said condescendingly. 'But – "The Time Machine" is a delightful book, don't you think? So entirely original!'

'You are pleased to sneer,' said the Devil, who had also risen, 'but it is one thing to write about a not possible machine; it is a quite other thing to be a Supernatural Power.' All the same, I had scored.

Berthe had come forth at the sound of our rising. I explained to her that Mr Soames had been called away, and that both he and I would be dining here. It was not until I was out in the open air that I began to feel giddy. I have but the haziest recollection of what I did, where I wandered, in the glaring sunshine of that endless afternoon. I remember the sound of carpenters' hammers all along Piccadilly, and the bare chaotic look of the half-erected 'stands'. Was it in the Green Park, or in Kensington Gardens, or *where* was it that I sat on a chair beneath a tree, trying to read an evening paper? There was a phrase in the leading article that went on repeating itself in my fagged mind – 'Little is hidden from this august Lady full of the garnered wisdom of sixty years of Sovereignty.' I remember wildly conceiving a letter (to reach Windsor by express messenger told to await answer):

MADAM, – Well knowing that your Majesty is full of the garnered wisdom of sixty years of Sovereignty, I venture to ask your advice in the following delicate matter. Mr Enoch Soames, whose poems you may or may not know, . . .

Was there *no* way of helping him – saving him? A bargain was a bargain, and I was the last man to aid or abet any one in wriggling out of a reasonable obligation. I wouldn't have lifted a little finger to save Faust. But poor Soames! – doomed to pay without respite an eternal price for nothing but a fruitless search and a bitter disillusioning . . .

Odd and uncanny it seemed to me that he, Soames, in the flesh, in the waterproof cape, was at this moment living in the last decade of the next century, poring over books not yet written, and seeing and seen by men not yet born. Uncannier and odder still, that to-night and evermore he would be in Hell. Assuredly, truth was stranger than fiction.

Endless that afternoon was. Almost I wished I had gone with Soames – not indeed to stay in the reading-room, but to sally forth for a brisk sight-seeing walk around a new London. I wandered restlessly out of the Park I had sat in. Vainly I tried to imagine myself an ardent tourist from the eighteenth century. Intolerable was the strain of the slow-passing and empty minutes. Long before seven o'clock I was back at the Vingtième.

I sat there just where I had sat for luncheon. Air came in listlessly through the open door behind me. Now and again Rose or Berthe appeared for a moment. I had told them I would not order any dinner till Mr Soames came. A hurdy-gurdy began to play, abruptly drowning the noise of a quarrel between some Frenchmen further up the street. Whenever the tune was changed I heard the quarrel still raging. I had bought another evening paper on my way. I unfolded it. My eyes gazed ever away from it to the clock over the kitchen door . . .

Five minutes, now, to the hour! I remembered that clocks in restaurants are kept five minutes fast. I concentrated my eyes on the paper. I vowed I would not look away from it again. I held it upright, at its full width, close to my face, so that I had no view of anything but it . . . Rather a tremulous sheet? Only because of the draught, I told myself.

My arms gradually became stiff; they ached; but I could not drop them – now. I had a suspicion, I had a certainty. Well, what then? . . . What else had I come for? Yet I held tight that barrier of newspaper. Only the sound of Berthe's brisk footstep from the kitchen enabled me, forced me, to drop it, and to utter:

'What shall we have to eat, Soames?'

'*Il est souffrant, ce pauvre Monsieur Soames?*' asked Berthe.

'He's only – tired.' I asked her to get some wine – Burgundy – and whatever food might be ready. Soames sat crouched forward against the table, exactly as when last I had seen him. It was as though he had never moved – he who had moved so unimaginably far. Once or twice in the afternoon it had for an instant occurred to me that perhaps his journey was not to be fruitless – that perhaps we had all been wrong in our esti-mate of the works of Enoch Soames. That we had been horribly right was horribly clear from the look of him. But 'Don't be discouraged,' I falter-ingly said. 'Perhaps it's only that you – didn't leave enough time. Two, three centuries hence, perhaps—'

'Yes,' his voice came. 'I've thought of that.'

'And now – now for the more immediate future! Where are you going to hide? How would it be if you caught the Paris express from Charing Cross? Almost an hour to spare. Don't go on to Paris. Stop at Calais. Live in Calais. He'd never think of looking for you in Calais.'

'It's like my luck,' he said, 'to spend my last hours on earth with an ass.' But I was not offended. 'And a treacherous ass,' he strangely added, tossing across to me a crumpled bit of paper which he had been holding in his hand. I glanced at the writing on it – some sort of gibberish, apparently. I laid it impatiently aside.

'Come, Soames! pull yourself together! This isn't a mere matter of life and death. It's a question of eternal torment, mind you! You don't mean to say you're going to wait limply here till the Devil comes to fetch you?'

'I can't do anything else. I've no choice.'

'Come! This is "trusting and encouraging" with a vengeance! This is

Diabolism run mad!' I filled his glass with wine. 'Surely, now that you've *seen* the brute—'

'It's no good abusing him.'

'You must admit there's nothing Miltonic about him, Soames.'

'I don't say he's not rather different from what I expected.'

'He's a vulgarian, he's a swell-mobsman, he's the sort of man who hangs about the corridors of trains going to the Riviera and steals ladies' jewel-cases. Imagine eternal torment presided over by *him*!'

'You don't suppose I look forward to it, do you?'

'Then why not slip quietly out of the way?'

Again and again I filled his glass, and always, mechanically, he emptied it; but the wine kindled no spark of enterprise in him. He did not eat, and I myself ate hardly at all. I did not in my heart believe that any dash for freedom could save him. The chase would be swift, the capture certain. But better anything than this passive, meek, miserable waiting. I told Soames that for the honour of the human race he ought to make some show of resistance. He asked what the human race had ever done for him. 'Besides,' he said, 'can't you understand that I'm in his power? You saw him touch me, didn't you? There's an end of it. I've no will. I'm sealed.'

I made a gesture of despair. He went on repeating the word 'sealed'. I began to realise that the wine had clouded his brain. No wonder! Foodless he had gone into futurity, foodless he still was. I urged him to eat at any rate some bread. It was maddening to think that he, who had so much to tell, might tell nothing. 'How was it all,' I asked, 'yonder? Come! Tell me your adventures.'

'They'd make first-rate "copy", wouldn't they?'

'I'm awfully sorry for you, Soames, and I make all possible allowances; but what earthly right have you to insinuate that I should make "copy", as you call it, out of you?'

The poor fellow pressed his hands to his forehead. 'I don't know,' he said. 'I had some reason, I'm sure . . . I'll try to remember.'

'That's right. Try to remember everything. Eat a little more bread. What did the reading-room look like?'

'Much as usual,' he at length muttered.

'Many people there?'

'Usual sort of number.'

'What did they look like?'

Soames tried to visualize them. 'They all,' he presently remembered, 'looked very like one another.'

My mind took a fearsome leap. 'All dressed in Jaeger?'

'Yes. I think so. Greyish-yellowish stuff.'

'A sort of uniform?' He nodded. 'With a number on it, perhaps? – a number on a large disc of metal sewn on to the left sleeve? DKF 78,910 – that sort of thing?' It was even so. 'And all of them – men and women alike – looking very well-cared-for? very Utopian? and smelling rather strongly of carbolic? and all of them quite hairless?' I was right every time. Soames was only not sure whether the men and women were hairless or shorn. 'I hadn't time to look at them very closely,' he explained.

'No, of course not. But—'

'They stared at *me*, I can tell you. I attracted a great deal of attention.' At last he had done that! 'I think I rather scared them. They moved away whenever I came near. They followed me about at a distance, wherever I went. The men at the round desk in the middle seemed to have a sort of panic whenever I went to make inquiries.'

'What did you do when you arrived?'

Well, he had gone straight to the catalogue, of course – to the S volumes, and had stood long before SN–SOF, unable to take this volume out of the shelf, because his heart was beating so . . . At first, he said, he wasn't disappointed – he only thought there was some new arrangement. He went to the middle desk and asked where the catalogue of *twentieth*-century books was kept. He gathered that there was still only one catalogue. Again he looked up his name, stared at the three little pasted slips he had known so well. Then he went and sat down for a long time . . .

'And then,' he droned, 'I looked up the "Dictionary of National Biography" and some encyclopædias . . . I went back to the middle desk and asked what was the best modern book on late nineteenth-century literature. They told me Mr T. K. Nupton's book was considered the best. I looked it up in the catalogue and filled in a form for it. It was brought to me. My name wasn't in the index, but— Yes!' he said with a sudden change of tone. 'That's what I'd forgotten. Where's that bit of paper? Give it me back.'

I, too, had forgotten that cryptic screed. I found it fallen on the floor, and handed it to him.

He smoothed it out, nodding and smiling at me disagreeably. 'I found myself glancing through Nupton's book,' he resumed. 'Not very easy reading. Some sort of phonetic spelling . . . All the modern books I saw were phonetic.'

'Then I don't want to hear any more, Soames, please.'

'The proper names seemed all to be spelt in the old way. But for that, I mightn't have noticed my own name.'

'Your own name? Really? Soames, I'm *very* glad.'

'And yours.'

'No!'

'I thought I should find you waiting here to-night. So I took the trouble to copy out the passage. Read it.'

I snatched the paper. Soames' handwriting was characteristically dim. It, and the noisome spelling, and my excitement, made me all the slower to grasp what T. K. Nupton was driving at.

The document lies before me at this moment. Strange that the words I here copy out for you were copied out for me by poor Soames just seventy-eight years hence. . . .

From p. 234 of 'Inglish Littracher 1890–1900,' bi T. K. Nupton, published bi th Stait, 1992:

Fr. egzarmpl, a riter ov th time, naimd Max Beerbohm, hoo woz stil alive in th twentieth senchri, rote a stauri in wich e pautraid an immajnari karrakter kauld "Enoch Soames" – a thurd-rait poit hoo beleevz imself a grate jeneus an maix a bargin with th Devvl in auder ter no wot posterriti thinx ov im! It iz a sumwot labud sattire but not without vallu az showing hou seriusli the yung men ov th aiteen-ninetiz took themselv. Nou that the littreri profeshn haz bin auganized az a department of publik servis, our riters hav found their levvl an hav lernt ter doo their duti without thort ov th morro. "Th laibrer iz werthi ov hiz hire, an that iz aul. Thank hevvn we hav no Enoch Soameses amung us to-dai!

I found that by murmuring the words aloud (a device which I commend to my reader) I was able to master them, little by little. The clearer they became, the greater was my bewilderment, my distress and horror. The whole thing was a nightmare. Afar, the great grisly background of what was in store for the poor dear art of letters; here, at the table, fixing on me a gaze that made me hot all over, the poor fellow whom – whom evidently . . . but no: whatever down-grade my character might take in coming years, I should never be such a brute as to—

Again I examined the screed. 'Immajnari' – but here Soames was, no more imaginary, alas! than I. And 'labud' – what on earth was that? (To this day, I have never made out that word.) 'It's all very – baffling,' I at length stammered.

Soames said nothing, but cruelly did not cease to look at me.

'Are you sure,' I temporised, 'quite sure you copied the thing out correctly?'

'Quite.'

'Well, then it's this wretched Nupton who must have made – must be going to make – some idiotic mistake . . . Look here, Soames! you know me better than to suppose that I . . . After all, the name "Max Beerbohm" is not at all an uncommon one, and there must be several Enoch Soameses running around – or rather, "Enoch Soames" is a name that might occur to any one writing a story. And I don't write stories: I'm an essayist, an observer, a recorder . . . I admit that it's an extraordinary coincidence. But you must see—'

'I see the whole thing,' said Soames quietly. And he added, with a touch of his old manner, but with more dignity than I had ever known in him, '*Parlons d'autre chose.*'

I accepted that suggestion very promptly. I returned straight to the more immediate future. I spent most of the long evening in renewed appeals to Soames to slip away and seek refuge somewhere. I remember saying at last that if indeed I was destined to write about him, the supposed 'stauri' had better have at least a happy ending. Soames repeated those last three words in a tone of intense scorn. 'In Life and in Art,' he said, 'all that matters is an *inevitable* ending.'

'But,' I urged, more hopefully than I felt, 'an ending that can be avoided *isn't* inevitable.'

'You aren't an artist,' he rasped. 'And you're so hopelessly not an artist that, so far from being able to imagine a thing and make it seem true, you're going to make even a true thing seem as if you'd made it up. You're a miserable bungler. And it's like my luck.'

I protested that the miserable bungler was not I – was not going to be I – but T. K. Nupton; and we had a rather heated argument, in the thick of which it suddenly seemed to me that Soames saw he was in the wrong: he had quite physically cowered. But I wondered why – and now I guessed with a cold throb just why – he stared so, past me. The bringer of that 'inevitable ending' filled the doorway.

I managed to turn in my chair and to say, not without a semblance of lightness, 'Aha, come in!' Dread was indeed rather blunted in me by his looking so absurdly like a villain in a melodrama. The sheen of his tilted hat and of his shirtfront, the repeated twists he was giving to his moustache, and most of all the magnificence of his sneer, gave token that he was there only to be foiled.

He was at our table in a stride. 'I am sorry,' he sneered witheringly, 'to break up your pleasant party, but—'

'You don't: you complete it,' I assured him. 'Mr Soames and I want to have a little talk with you. Won't you sit? Mr Soames got nothing – frankly nothing – by his journey this afternoon. We don't wish to say that the whole thing was a swindle – a common swindle. On the contrary, we believe you meant well. But of course the bargain, such as it was, is off.'

The Devil gave no verbal answer. He merely looked at Soames and pointed with rigid forefinger to the door. Soames was wretchedly rising from his chair when, with a desperate quick gesture, I swept together two dinner-knives that were on the table, and laid their blades across each other. The Devil stepped sharp back against the table behind him, averting his face and shuddering.

'You are not superstitious!' he hissed.

'Not at all,' I smiled.

'Soames!' he said as to an underling, but without turning his face, 'put those knives straight!'

With an inhibitive gesture to my friend, 'Mr Soames,' I said emphatically to the Devil, 'is a *Catholic* Diabolist'; but my poor friend did the Devil's bidding, not mine; and now, with his master's eyes again fixed on him, he arose, he shuffled past me. I tried to speak. It was he that spoke.

'Try,' was the prayer he threw back at me as the Devil pushed him roughly out through the door, '*try* to make them know that I did exist!'

In another instant I too was through that door. I stood staring all ways – up the street, across it, down it. There was moonlight and lamp-light, but there was not Soames nor that other.

Dazed, I stood there. Dazed, I turned back, at length, into the little room; and I suppose I paid Berthe or Rose for my dinner and luncheon, and for Soames': I hope so, for I never went to the Vingtième again. Ever since that night I have avoided Greek Street altogether. And for years I did not set foot even in Soho Square, because on that same night it was there that I paced and loitered, long and long, with some such dull sense of hope as a man has in not straying far from the place where he has lost something . . . 'Round and round the shutter'd Square' – that line came back to me on my lonely beat, and with it the whole stanza, ringing in my brain and bearing in on me how tragically different from the happy scene imagined by him was the poet's actual experience of that prince in whom of all princes we should put not our trust.

But – strange how the mind of an essayist, be it never so stricken, roves and ranges! – I remember pausing before a wide doorstep and wondering if perchance it was on this very one that the young De Quincey lay ill and faint while poor Ann flew as fast as her feet would carry her to Oxford Street, the 'stony-hearted stepmother' of them both, and came back bear-ing that 'glass of port wine and spices' but for which he might, so he thought, actually have died. Was this the very doorstep that the old De Quincey used to revisit in homage? I pondered Ann's fate, the cause of her sudden vanishing from the ken of her boy-friend; and presently I blamed myself for letting the past over-ride the present. Poor vanished Soames!

And for myself, too, I began to be troubled. What had I better do? Would there be a hue and cry – Mysterious Disappearance of an Author, and all that? He had last been seen lunching and dining in my company. Hadn't I better get a hansom and drive straight to Scotland Yard? . . . They would think I was a lunatic. After all, I reassured myself, London was a very large place, and one very dim figure might easily drop out of it unobserved – now especially, in the blinding glare of the near Jubilee. Better say nothing at all, I thought.

And I was right. Soames' disappearance made no stir at all. He was utterly forgotten before any one, so far as I am aware, noticed that he was no longer hanging around. Now and again some poet or prosaist may have said to another, 'What has become of that man Soames?' but I never heard any such question asked. The solicitor through whom he was paid his annuity may be presumed to have made inquiries, but no echo of these resounded. There was something rather ghastly to me in the general unconsciousness that Soames had existed, and more than once I caught myself wondering whether Nupton, that babe unborn, were going to be right in thinking him a figment of my brain.

In that extract from Nupton's repulsive book there is one point which perhaps puzzles you. How is it that the author, though I have here mentioned him by name and have quoted the exact words he is going to write, is not going to grasp the obvious corollary that I have invented nothing? The answer can but be this: Nupton will not have read the later passages of this memoir. Such lack of thoroughness is a serious fault in any one who undertakes to do scholar's work. And I hope these words will meet the eye of some contemporary rival to Nupton and be the undoing of Nupton.

I like to think that some time between 1992 and 1997 somebody will have looked up this memoir, and will have forced on the world his inevitable and startling conclusions. And I have reasons for believing that this will be so. You realise that the reading-room into which Soames was projected by the Devil was in all respects precisely as it will be on the afternoon of June 3rd, 1997. You realise, therefore, that on that afternoon, when it comes round, there the self-same crowd will be, and there Soames too will be, punctually, he and they doing precisely what they did before. Recall now Soames' account of the sensation he made. You may say that the mere difference of his costume was enough to make him sensational in that uniformed crowd. You wouldn't say so if you had ever seen him. I assure you that in no period could Soames be anything but dim. The fact that people are going to stare at him, and follow him around, and seem afraid of him, can be explained only on the hypothesis that they will somehow have been prepared for his ghostly visitation. They will have been awfully waiting to see whether he really would come. And when he does come the effect will of course be – awful.

An authentic, guaranteed, proven ghost, but – only a ghost, alas! Only that. In his first visit, Soames was a creature of flesh and blood, whereas the creatures into whose midst he was projected were but ghosts, I take it – solid, palpable, vocal, but unconscious and automatic ghosts, in a building that was itself an illusion. Next time, that building and those creatures will be real. It is of Soames that there will be but the semblance. I wish I could think him destined to revisit the world actually, physically, consciously. I wish he had this one brief escape, this one small treat, to look forward to. I never forget him for long. He is where he is, and forever. The more rigid moralists among you may say he has only himself to blame. For my part, I think he has been very hardly used. It is well that vanity should be chastened; and Enoch Soames' vanity was, I admit, above the average, and called for special treatment. But there was no need for vindictiveness. You say he contracted to pay the price he is paying; yes; but I maintain that he was induced to do so by fraud. Well-informed in all things, the Devil must have known that my friend would gain nothing by his visit to futurity. The whole thing was a very shabby trick. The more I think of it, the more detestable the Devil seems to me.

Of him I have caught sight several times, here and there, since that day at the Vingtième. Only once, however, have I seen him at close quarters. This was in Paris. I was walking, one afternoon, along the Rue d'Antin, when I saw him advancing from the opposite direction – over-dressed as ever, and swinging an ebony cane, and altogether behaving as though the whole pavement belonged to him. At thought of Enoch Soames and the myriads of other sufferers eternally in this brute's dominion, a great cold wrath filled me, and I drew myself up to my full height. But – well, one is so used to nodding and smiling in the street to anybody whom one knows, that the action becomes almost independent of oneself: to prevent it requires a very sharp effort and great presence of mind. I was miserably aware, as I passed the Devil, that I nodded and smiled to him. And my shame was the deeper and hotter because he, if you please, stared straight at me with the utmost haughtiness.

To be cut – deliberately cut – by *him*! I was, I still am, furious at having had that happen to me.

ARNOLD BENNETT

The Matador of the Five Towns

I

Mrs Brindley looked across the lunch-table at her husband with glinting, eager eyes, which showed that there was something unusual in the brain behind them.

'Bob,' she said, factitiously calm. 'You don't know what I've just remembered!'

'Well?' said he.

'It's only grandma's birthday to-day!'

My friend Robert Brindley, the architect, struck the table with a violent fist, making his little boys blink, and then he said quietly:

'*The* deuce!'

I gathered that grandmamma's birthday had been forgotten and that it was not a festival that could be neglected with impunity. Both Mr and Mrs Brindley had evidently a humorous appreciation of crises, contretemps, and those collisions of circumstances which are usually called 'junctures' for short. I could have imagined either of them saying to the other: 'Here's a funny thing! The house is on fire!' And then yielding to laughter as they ran for buckets. Mrs Brindley, in particular, laughed now; she gazed at the table-cloth and laughed almost silently to herself; though it appeared that their joint forgetfulness might result in temporary estrangement from a venerable ancestor who was also, birthdays being duly observed, a continual fount of rich presents in specie.

Robert Brindley drew a time-table from his breast-pocket with the rapid gesture of habit. All men of business in the Five Towns seem to carry that time-table in their breast-pockets. Then he examined his watch carefully.

'You'll have time to dress up your progeny and catch the 2.5. It makes the connection at Knype for Axe.'

The two little boys, aged perhaps four and six, who had been ladling the messy contents of specially deep plates on to their bibs, dropped their spoons and began to babble about grea'-granny, and one of them insisted several times that he must wear his new gaiters.

'Yes,' said Mrs Brindley to her husband, after reflection. 'And a fine old crowd there'll be in the train – with this football match!'

'Can't be helped! . . . Now, you kids, hook it upstairs to nurse.'

'And what about you?' asked Mrs Brindley.

'You must tell the old lady I'm kept by business.'

'I told her that last year, and you know what happened.'

'Well,' said Brindley. 'Here Loring's just come. You don't expect me to leave him, do you? Or have you had the beautiful idea of taking him over to Axe to pass a pleasant Saturday afternoon with your esteemed grandmother?'

'No,' said Mrs Brindley. 'Hardly that!'

'Well, then?'

The boys, having first revolved on their axes, slid down from their high chairs as though from horses.

'Look here,' I said. 'You mustn't mind me. I shall be all right.'

'Ha-ha!' shouted Brindley. 'I seem to see you turned loose alone in this amusing town on a winter afternoon. I seem to see you!'

'I could stop in and read,' I said, eyeing the multitudinous books on every wall of the dining-room. The house was dadoed throughout with books.

'Rot!' said Brindley.

This was only my third visit to his home and to the Five Towns, but he and I had already become curiously intimate. My first two visits had been occasioned by official pilgrimages as a British Museum expert in ceramics. The third was for a purely friendly week-end, and had no pre-text. The fact is, I was drawn to the astonishing district and its astonishing inhabitants. The Five Towns, to me, was like the East to those who have smelt the East: it 'called.'

'I'll tell you what we *could* do,' said Mrs Brindley. 'We could put him on to Dr Stirling.'

'So we could!' Brindley agreed. 'Wife, this is one of your bright, intelligent days. We'll put you on to the doctor, Loring. I'll impress on him that he must keep you constantly amused till I get back, which I fear it won't be early. This is what we call manners, you know – to invite a fellow-creature to travel a hundred and fifty miles to spend two days here, and then to turn him out before he's been in the house an hour. It's *us*, that is! But the truth of the matter is, the birthday business might be a bit serious. It might easily cost me fifty quid and no end of diplomacy. If you were a married man you'd know that the ten plagues of Egypt are simply nothing in comparison with your wife's relations. And she's over eighty, the old lady.'

'I'll give you ten plagues of Egypt!' Mrs Brindley menaced her spouse, as she wafted the boys from the room. 'Mr Loring, do take some more of that cheese if you fancy it.' She vanished.

Within ten minutes Brindley was conducting me to the doctor's, whose house was on the way to the station. In its spacious porch he explained the circumstances in six words, depositing me like a parcel. The doctor, who had once by mysterious medicaments saved my frail organism from the consequences of one of Brindley's Falstaffian 'nights,' hospitably protested his readiness to sacrifice patients to my pleasure.

'It'll be a chance for MacIlroy,' said he.

'Who's MacIlroy?' I asked.

'MacIlroy is another Scotchman,' growled Brindley. 'Extraordinary how they stick together! When he wanted an assistant, do you suppose he looked about for some one in the district, some one who understood us and loved us and could take a hand at bridge? Not he! Off he goes to Cupar, or somewhere, and comes back with another stage Scotchman, named MacIlroy. Now listen here, Doc! A charge to keep you have, and mind you keep it, or I'll never pay your confounded bill. We'll knock on the window to-night as we come back. In the meantime you can show Loring your etchings, and pray for me.' And to me: 'Here's a latchkey.' With no further ceremony he hurried away to join his wife and children at Bleakridge Station. In such singular manner was I transferred forcibly from host to host.

II

The doctor and I resembled each other in this: that there was no offensive affability about either of us. Though abounding in good-nature, we could not become intimate by a sudden act of volition. Our conversation was difficult, unnatural, and by gusts falsely familiar. He displayed to me his bachelor house, his etchings, a few specimens of modern *rouge flambé* ware made at Knype, his whisky, his celebrated prize-winning fox-terrier Titus, the largest collection of books in the Five Towns, and photographs of Marischal College, Aberdeen. Then we fell flat, socially prone. Sitting in his study, with Titus between us on the hearthrug, we knew no more what to say or do. I regretted that Brindley's wife's grandmother should have been born on a fifteenth of February. Brindley was a vivacious talker, he could be trusted to talk. I, too, am a good talker – with another good talker. With a bad talker I am just a little worse than he is. The doctor said abruptly after a nerve-trying silence that he had forgotten a most important call at Hanbridge, and would I care to go with him in the car? I was and still am convinced that he was simply inventing. He wanted to break the sinister spell by getting out of the house, and he had not the face to suggest a sortie into the streets of the Five Towns as a promenade of pleasure.

So we went forth, splashing warily through the rich mud and the dank mist of Trafalgar Road, past all those strange little Indian-red houses, and ragged empty spaces, and poster-hoardings, and rounded kilns, and high, smoking chimneys, up hill, down hill, and up hill again, encountering and overtaking many electric trams that dipped and rose like ships at sea, into Crown Square, the centre of Hanbridge, the metropolis of the Five Towns. And while the doctor paid his mysterious call I stared around me at the large shops and the banks and the gilded hotels. Down the radiating street-vistas I could make out the façades of halls, theatres, chapels. Trams rumbled continually in and out of the square. They seemed to enter casually, to hesitate a few moments as if at a loss, and then to decide with a nonchalant clang of bells that they might as well go off somewhere else in search of something more interesting. They were rather like human beings who are condemned to live for ever in a place of which they are sick beyond the expressiveness of words.

And indeed the influence of Crown Square, with its large effects of terra cotta, plate glass, and gold letters, all under a heavy skyscape of drab smoke, was depressing. A few very seedy men (sharply contrasting with the fine delicacy of costly things behind plate-glass) stood doggedly here and there in the mud, immobilized by the gloomy enchantment of the Square. Two of them turned to look at Stirling's motor-car and me. They gazed fixedly for a long time, and then one said, only his lips moving:

'Has Tommy stood thee that there quart o' beer as he promised thee?'

No reply, no response of any sort, for a further long period! Then the other said, with grim resignation:

'Ay!'

The conversation ceased, having made a little oasis in the dismal desert of their silent scrutiny of the car. Except for an occasional stamp of the foot they never moved. They just doggedly and indifferently stood, blown upon by all the nipping draughts of the square, and as it might be sinking deeper and deeper into its dejection. As for me, instead of desolating, the harsh disconsolateness of the scene seemed to uplift me; I savoured it with joy, as one savours the melancholy of a tragic work of art.

'We might go down to the *Signal* offices and worry Buchanan a bit,' said the doctor, cheerfully, when he came back to the car. This was the second of his inspirations.

Buchanan, of whom I had heard, was another Scotchman and the editor of the sole daily organ of the Five Towns, an evening newspaper cried all day in the streets and read by the entire population. Its green sheet appeared to be a permanent waving feature of the main thoroughfares. The offices lay round a corner close by, and as we drew up in front of them a crowd of tattered urchins interrupted their diversions in the sodden road to celebrate our glorious arrival by unanimously yelling at the top of their strident and hoarse voices:

'Hooray! Hoo—bl—dy—ray!'

Abashed, I followed my doctor into the shelter of the building, a new edifice, capacious and considerable but horribly faced with terra cotta, and quite unimposing, lacking in the spectacular effect; like nearly everything in the Five Towns, carelessly and scornfully ugly! The mean, swinging double-doors returned to the assault when you pushed them, and hit you viciously. In a dark, countered room marked 'Enquiries' there was nobody.

'Hi, there!' called the doctor.

A head appeared at a door.

'Mr Buchanan upstairs?'

'Yes,' snapped the head, and disappeared.

Up a dark staircase we went, and at the summit were half flung back again by another self-acting door.

In the room to which we next came an old man and a youngish one were bent over a large, littered table, scribbling on and arranging pieces of grey tissue paper and telegrams. Behind the old man stood a boy. Neither of them looked up.

'Mr Buchanan in his—' the doctor began to question. 'Oh! There you are!'

The editor was standing in hat and muffler at the window, gazing out. His age was about that of the doctor – forty or so; and like the doctor he was rather stout and clean-shaven. Their Scotch accents mingled in greeting, the doctor's being the more marked. Buchanan shook my hand with a certain courtliness, indicating that he was well accustomed to receive strangers. As an expert in small talk, however, he shone no brighter than his visitors, and the three of us stood there by the window awkwardly in the heaped disorder of the room, while the other two men scratched and fidgeted with bits of paper at the soiled table.

Suddenly and savagely the old man turned on the boy:

'What the hades are you waiting there for?'

'I thought there was something else, sir.'

'Sling your hook.'

Buchanan winked at Stirling and me as the boy slouched off and the old man blandly resumed his writing.

'Perhaps you'd like to look over the place?' Buchanan suggested politely to me. 'I'll come with you. It's all I'm fit for to-day . . . 'Flu!' He glanced at Stirling, and yawned.

'Ye ought to be in bed,' said Stirling.

'Yes. I know. I've known it for twelve years. I shall go to bed as soon as I get a bit of time to myself. Well, will you come? The half-time results are beginning to come in.'

A telephone-bell rang impatiently.

'You might just see what that is, boss,' said the old man without looking up.

Buchanan went to the telephone and replied into it: 'Yes? What? Oh! Myatt? Yes, he's playing . . . Of course I'm sure! Good-bye.' He turned to the old man: 'It's another of 'em wanting to know if Myatt is playing. Birmingham, this time.'

'Ah!' exclaimed the old man, still writing.

'It's because of the betting,' Buchanan glanced at me. 'The odds are on Knype now – three to two.'

'If Myatt is playing Knype have got me to thank for it,' said the doctor, surprisingly.

'You?'

'Me! He fetched me to his wife this morning. She's nearing her confinement. False alarm. I guaranteed him at least another twelve hours.'

'Oh! So that's it, is it?' Buchanan murmured.

Both the sub-editors raised their heads.

'That's it,' said the doctor.

'Some people were saying he'd quarrelled with the trainer again and was shamming,' said Buchanan. 'But I didn't believe that. There's no hanky-panky about Jos Myatt, anyhow.'

I learnt in answer to my questions that a great and terrible football match was at that moment in progress at Knype, a couple of miles away, between the Knype Club and the Manchester Rovers. It was conveyed to me that the importance of this match was almost national, and that the entire district was practically holding its breath till the result should be known. The half-time result was one goal each.

'If Knype lose,' said Buchanan, explanatorily, 'they'll find themselves pushed out of the First League at the end of the season. That's a cert . . . one of the oldest clubs in England! Semi-finalists for the English Cup in '78.'

''79,' corrected the elder sub-editor.

I gathered that the crisis was grave.

'And Myatt's the captain, I suppose?' said I.

'No. But he's the finest full-back in the League.'

I then had a vision of Myatt as a great man. By an effort of the imagination I perceived that the equivalent of the fate of nations depended upon him. I recollected, now, large yellow posters on the hoardings we had passed, with the names of Knype and of Manchester Rovers in letters a foot high and the legend 'League match at Knype' over all. It seemed to me that the heroic name of Jos Myatt, if truly he were the finest full-back in the League, if truly his presence or absence affected the betting as far off as Birmingham, ought also to have been on the posters, together with possibly his portrait. I saw Jos Myatt as a matador, with a long ribbon of scarlet necktie down his breast, and embroidered trousers.

'Why,' said Buchanan, 'if Knype drop into the Second Division they'll never pay another dividend! It'll be all up with first-class football in the Five Towns!'

The interests involved seemed to grow more complicated. And here I had been in the district nearly four hours without having guessed that the district was quivering in the tense excitement of gigantic issues! And here was this Scotch doctor, at whose word the great Myatt would have declined to play, never saying a syllable about the affair, until a chance remark from Buchanan loosened his tongue. But all doctors are strangely secretive. Secretiveness is one of their chief private pleasures.

'Come and see the pigeons, eh?' said Buchanan.

'Pigeons?' I repeated.

'We give the results of over a hundred matches in our Football Edition,' said Buchanan, and added: 'not counting Rugby.'

As we left the room two boys dodged round us into it, bearing telegrams.

In a moment we were, in the most astonishing manner, on a leaden roof of the *Signal* offices. High factory chimneys rose over the horizon of slates on every side, blowing thick smoke into the general murk of the afternoon sky, and crossing the western crimson with long pennons of black. And out of the murk there came from afar a blue-and-white pigeon which circled largely several times over the offices of the *Signal*. At length it descended, and I could hear the whirr of its strong wings. The wings ceased to beat and the pigeon slanted downwards in a curve, its head lower than its wide tail. Then the little head gradually rose and the tail fell; the curve had changed, the pace slackened; the pigeon was calculating with all its brain; eyes, wings, tail and feet were being co-ordinated to the resolution of an intricate mechanical problem. The pinkish claws seemed to grope – and after an instant of hesitation the thing was done, the problem solved; the pigeon, with delicious gracefulness, had established equilibrium on the ridge of a pigeon-cote, and folded its wings, and was peering about with strange motions of its extremely movable head. Presently it flew down to the leads, waddled to and fro with the ungainly gestures of a fat woman of sixty, and disappeared into the cote. At the same moment the boy who had been dismissed from the sub-editor's room ran forward and entered the cote by a wire-screened door.

'Handy things, pigeons!' said the doctor as we approached to examine the cote. Fifty or sixty pigeons were cooing and strutting in it. There was a protest of wings as the boy seized the last arriving messenger.

'Give it here!' Buchanan ordered.

The boy handed over a thin tube of paper which he had unfastened from the bird's leg. Buchanan unrolled it and showed it to me. I read: 'Midland Federation. Axe United, Macclesfield Town. Match abandoned after half-hour's play owing to fog. Three forty-five.'

'Three forty-five,' said Buchanan, looking at his watch. 'He's done the ten miles in half an hour, roughly. Not bad. First time we tried pigeons from as far off as Axe. Here, boy!' And he restored the paper to the boy, who gave it to another boy, who departed with it.

'Man,' said the doctor, eyeing Buchanan. 'Ye'd no business out here. Ye're not precisely a pigeon.'

Down we went, one after another, by the ladder, and now we fell into the composing-room, where Buchanan said he felt warmer. An immense, dirty, white-washed apartment crowded with linotypes and other machines, in front of which sat men in white aprons, tapping, tapping – gazing at documents pinned at the level of their eyes – and tapping, tapping. A kind of cavernous retreat in which monstrous iron growths rose out of the floor and were met half-way by electric flowers that had their roots in the ceiling! In this jungle there was scarcely room for us to walk. Buchanan explained the linotypes to me. I watched, as though romantically dreaming, the flashing descent of letter after letter, a rain of letters into the belly of the machine; then, going round to the back, I watched the same letters rising again in a close, slow procession, and sorting themselves by themselves at the top in readiness to answer again to the tapping, tapping of a man in a once-white apron. And while I was watching all that I could somehow, by a faculty which we have, at the same time see pigeons far overhead, arriving and arriving out of the murk from beyond the verge of chimneys.

'Ingenious, isn't it?' said Stirling.

But I imagine that he had not the faculty by which to see the pigeons.

A reverend, bearded, spectacled man, with his shirt-sleeves rolled up and an apron stretched over his hemispherical paunch, strolled slowly along an alley, glancing at a galley-proof with an ingenuous air just as if he had never seen a galley-proof before.

'It's a stick more than a column already,' said he confidentially, offering the long paper, and then gravely looking at Buchanan, with head bent forward, not through his spectacles but over them.

The editor negligently accepted the proof, and I read a series of titles: 'Knype *v.* Manchester Rovers. Record Gate. Fifteen thousand spectators. Two goals in twelve minutes. Myatt in form. Special Report.'

Buchanan gave the slip back without a word.

'There you are!' said he to me, as another compositor near us attached a piece of tissue paper to his machine. It was the very paper that I had seen come out of the sky, but its contents had been enlarged and amended by the sub-editorial pen. The man began tapping, tapping, and the letters began to flash downwards on their way to tell a quarter of a million people that Axe *v.* Macclesfield had been stopped by fog.

'I suppose that Knype match is over by now?' I said.

'Oh no!' said Buchanan. 'The second half has scarcely begun.'

'Like to go?' Stirling asked.

'Well,' I said, feeling adventurous, 'it's a notion, isn't it?'

'You can run Mr Loring down there in five or six minutes,' said Buchanan. 'And he's probably never seen anything like it before. You might call here as you come home and see the paper on the machines.'

III

We went on the Grand Stand, which was packed with men whose eyes were fixed, with an unconscious but intense effort, on a common object. Among the men were a few women in furs and wraps, equally absorbed. Nobody took any notice of us as we insinuated our way up a rickety flight of wooden stairs, but when by misadventure we grazed a human being the elbow of that being shoved itself automatically and fiercely outwards, to repel. I had an impression of hats, caps, and woolly overcoats stretched in long parallel lines, and of grimy raw planks everywhere presenting possibly dangerous splinters, save where use had worn them into smooth shininess. Then gradually I became aware of the vast field, which was more brown than green. Around the field was a wide border of infinitesimal hats and pale faces, rising in tiers, and beyond this border fences, hoardings, chimneys, furnaces, gasometers, telegraph-poles, houses, and dead trees. And here and there, perched in strange perilous places, even high up towards the sombre sky, were more human beings clinging. On the field itself, at one end of it, were a scattered handful of doll-like figures, motionless; some had white bodies, others red; and three were in black; all were so small and so far off that they seemed to be mere unimportant casual incidents in whatever recondite affair it was that was proceeding. Then a whistle shrieked, and all these figures began simultaneously to move, and then I saw a ball in the air. An obscure, uneasy murmuring rose from the immense multitude like an invisible but audible vapour. The next instant the vapour had condensed into a sudden shout. Now I saw the ball rolling solitary in the middle of the field, and a single red doll racing towards it; at one end was a confused group of red and white, and at the other two white dolls, rather lonely in the expanse. The single red doll overtook the ball and scudded along with it at his twinkling toes. A great voice behind me bellowed with an incredible volume of sound:

'Now, Jos!'

And another voice, further away, bellowed:

'Now, Jos!'

And still more distantly the grim warning shot forth from the crowd:

'Now, Jos! Now, Jos!'

The nearer of the white dolls, as the red one approached, sprang forward. I could see a leg. And the ball was flying back in a magnificent curve into the skies; it passed out of my sight, and then I heard a bump on the slates of the roof of the grand stand, and it fell among the crowd in the stand-enclosure. But almost before the flight of the ball had commenced, a terrific roar of relief had rolled formidably round the field, and out of that roar, like rockets out of thick smoke, burst acutely ecstatic cries of adoration:

'Bravo, Jos!'

'Good old Jos!'

The leg had evidently been Jos's leg. The nearer of these two white dolls must be Jos, darling of fifteen thousand frenzied people.

Stirling punched a neighbour in the side to attract his attention.

'What's the score?' he demanded of the neighbour, who scowled and then grinned.

'Twoone–agen uz!' The other growled. 'It'll take our b——s all their time to draw. They're playing a man short.'

'Accident?'

'No! Referee ordered him off for rough play.'

Several spectators began to explain, passionately, furiously, that the referee's action was utterly bereft of common sense and justice; and I gathered that a less gentlemanly crowd would undoubtedly have lynched the referee. The explanations died down, and everybody except me resumed his fierce watch on the field.

I was recalled from the exercise of a vague curiosity upon the set, anxious faces around me by a crashing, whooping cheer which in volume and sincerity of joy surpassed all noises in my experience. This massive cheer reverberated round the field like the echoes of a battleship's broadside in a fiord. But it was human, and therefore more terrible than guns. I instinctively thought: 'If such are the symptoms of pleasure, what must be the symptoms of pain or disappointment?' Simultaneously with the expulsion of the unique noise the expression of the faces changed. Eyes sparkled; teeth became prominent in enormous, uncontrolled smiles. Ferocious satisfaction had to find vent in ferocious gestures, wreaked either upon dead wood or upon the living tissues of fellow-creatures. The gentle, mannerly sound of hand-clapping was a kind of light froth on the surface of the billowy sea of heartfelt applause. The host of the fifteen thousand might have just had their lives saved, or their children snatched from destruction and their wives from dishonour; they might have been preserved from bankruptcy, starvation, prison, torture; they might have been rewarding with their impassioned worship a band of national heroes. But it was not so. All that had happened was that the ball had rolled into the net of the Manchester Rovers' goal. Knype had drawn level. The reputation of the Five Towns before the jury of expert opinion that could distinguish between first-class football and second-class was maintained intact. I could hear specialists around me proving that though Knype had yet five League matches to play, its situation was safe. They pointed excitedly to a huge hoarding at one end of the ground on which appeared names of other clubs with changing figures. These clubs included the clubs which Knype would have to meet before the end of the season, and the figures indicated their fortunes on various grounds similar to this ground all over the country. If a goal was scored in Newcastle, or in Southampton, the very Peru of first-class football, it was registered on that board and its possible effect on the destinies of Knype was instantly assessed. The calculations made were dizzying.

Then a little flock of pigeons flew up and separated, under the illusion that they were free agents and masters of the air, but really wafted away to fixed destinations on the stupendous atmospheric waves of still-continued cheering.

After a minute or two the ball was restarted, and the greater noise had diminished to the sensitive uneasy murmur which responded like a delicate instrument to the fluctuations of the game. Each feat and manœuvre of Knype drew generous applause in proportion to its intention or its success, and each sleight of the Manchester Rovers, successful or not, provoked a holy disgust. The attitude of the host had passed beyond morality into religion.

Then, again, while my attention had lapsed from the field, a devilish, a barbaric, and a deafening yell broke from those fifteen thousand passionate hearts. It thrilled me; it genuinely frightened me. I involuntarily made the motion of swallowing. After the thunderous crash of anger from the host came the thin sound of a whistle. The game stopped. I heard the same word repeated again and again, in divers tones of exasperated fury:

'Foul!'

I felt that I was hemmed in by potential homicides, whose arms were lifted in the desire of murder and whose features were changed from the likeness of man into the corporeal form of some pure and terrible instinct.

And I saw a long doll rise from the ground and approach a lesser doll with threatening hands.

'Foul! Foul!'

'Go it, Jos! Knock his neck out! Jos! He tripped thee up!'

There was a prolonged gesticulatory altercation between the three black dolls in leather leggings and several of the white and the red dolls. At last one of the mannikins in leggings shrugged his shoulders, made a definite gesture to the other two, and walked away towards the edge of the field nearest the stand. It was the unprincipled referee; he had disallowed the foul. In the protracted duel between the offending Manchester forward and the great, honest Jos Myatt he had given another point to the enemy. As soon as the host realized the infamy it yelled once more in heightened fury. It seemed to surge in masses against the thick iron railings that alone stood between the referee and death. The discreet referee was approaching the grand stand as the least unsafe place. In a second a handful of executioners had somehow got on to the grass. And in the next second several policemen were in front of them, not striking nor striving to intimidate, but heavily pushing them into bounds.

'Get back there!' cried a few abrupt, commanding voices from the stand.

The referee stood with his hands in his pockets and his whistle in his mouth. I think that in that moment of acutest suspense the whole of his earthly career must have flashed before him in a phantasmagoria. And then the crisis was past. The inherent gentlemanliness of the outraged host had triumphed and the referee was spared.

'Served him right if they'd man-handled him!' said a spectator.

'Ay!' said another, gloomily, 'ay! And th' Football Association 'ud ha' fined us maybe a hundred quid and disqualified th' ground for the rest o' th' season!'

'D—n th' Football Association!'

'Ay! But you canna'!'

'Now, lads! Play up, Knype! Now, lads! Give 'em hot hell!' Different voices heartily encouraged the home team as the ball was thrown into play.

The fouling Manchester forward immediately resumed possession of the ball. Experience could not teach him. He parted with the ball and got it again, twice. The devil was in him and in the ball. The devil was driving him towards Myatt. They met. And then came a sound quite new: a cracking sound, somewhat like the snapping of a bough, but sharper, more decisive.

'By Jove!' exclaimed Stirling. 'That's his bone!'

And instantly he was off down the staircase and I after him. But he was not the first doctor on the field. Nothing had been unforeseen in the wonderful organization of this enterprise. A pigeon sped away and an official doctor and an official stretcher appeared, miraculously, simultaneously. It was tremendous. It inspired awe in me.

'He asked for it!' I heard a man say as I hesitated on the shore of the ocean of mud.

Then I knew that it was Manchester and not Knype that had suffered. The confusion and hubbub were in a high degree disturbing and puzzling. But one emotion emerged clear: pleasure. I felt it myself. I was aware of joy in that the two sides were now levelled to ten men apiece. I was mystically identified with the Five Towns, absorbed into their life. I could discern on every face the conviction that a divine providence was in this affair, that God could not be mocked. I too had this conviction. I could discern also on every face the fear lest the referee might give a foul against the hero Myatt, or even order him off the field, though of course the fracture was a simple accident. I too had this fear. It was soon dispelled by the news which swept across the entire enclosure like a sweet smell, that the referee had adopted the theory of a simple accident. I saw vaguely policemen, a stretcher, streaming crowds, and my ears heard a monstrous universal babbling. And then the figure of Stirling detached itself from the moving disorder and came to me.

'Well, Myatt's calf was harder than the other chap's, that's all,' he said.

'Which *is* Myatt?' I asked, for the red and the white dolls had all vanished at close quarters, and were replaced by unrecognizably gigantic human animals, still clad, however, in dolls' vests and dolls' knickerbockers.

Stirling warningly jerked his head to indicate a man not ten feet away from me. This was Myatt, the hero of the host and the darling of populations. I gazed up at him. His mouth and his left knee were red with blood, and he was piebald with thick patches of mud from his tousled crown to his enormous boot. His blue eyes had a heavy, stupid, honest glance; and of the three qualities stupidity predominated. He seemed to be all feet, knees, hands and elbows. His head was very small – the sole remainder of the doll in him.

A little man approached him, conscious – somewhat too obviously conscious – of his right to approach. Myatt nodded.

'Ye'n settled *him*, seemingly, Jos!' said the little man.

'Well,' said Myatt, with slow bitterness. 'Hadn't he been blooming well begging and praying for it, aw afternoon? Hadn't he now?'

The little man nodded. Then he said in a lower tone:

'How's missis, like?'

'Her's altogether yet,' said Myatt. 'Or I'd none ha' played!'

'I've bet Watty half-a-dollar as it inna' a lad!' said the little man.

Myatt seemed angry.

'Wilt bet me half a *quid* as it inna' a lad?' he demanded, bending down and scowling and sticking out his muddy chin.

'Ay!' said the little man, not blenching.

'Evens?'

'Evens.'

'I'll take thee, Charlie,' said Myatt, resuming his calm.

The whistle sounded. And several orders were given to clear the field. Eight minutes had been lost over a broken leg, but Stirling said that the referee would surely deduct them from the official time, so that after all the game would not be shortened.

'I'll be up yon, to-morra morning,' said the little man.

Myatt nodded and departed. Charlie, the little man, turned on his heel and proudly rejoined the crowd. He had been seen of all in converse with supreme greatness.

Stirling and I also retired; and though Jos Myatt had not even done his doctor the honour of seeing him, neither of us, I think, was quite without a consciousness of glory: I cannot imagine why. The rest of the game was flat and tame. Nothing occurred. The match ended in a draw.

IV

We were swept from the football ground on a furious flood of humanity – carried forth and flung down a slope into a large waste space that separated the ground from the nearest streets of little reddish houses. At the bottom of the slope, on my suggestion, we halted for a few moments aside, while the current rushed forward and, spreading out, inundated the whole space in one marvellous minute. The impression of the multitude streaming from that gap in the wooden wall was like nothing more than the impression of a burst main which only the emptying of the reservoir will assuage. Anybody who wanted to commit suicide might have stood in front of that gap and had his wish. He would not have been noticed. The interminable and implacable infantry charge would have passed unheedingly over him. A silent, preoccupied host, bent on something else now, and perhaps teased by the inconvenient thought that after all a draw is not as good as a win! It hurried blindly, instinctively outwards, knees and chins protruding, hands deep in pockets, chilled feet stamping. Occasionally someone stopped or slackened to light a pipe, and on being curtly bunted onward by a blind force from behind, accepted the hint as an atom accepts the law of gravity. The fever and ecstasy were over. What fascinated the Southern in me was the grim taciturnity, the steady stare (vacant or dreaming), and the heavy, muffled, multitudinous tramp shaking the cindery earth. The flood continued to rage through the gap.

Our automobile had been left at the Haycock Hotel; we went to get it, braving the inundation. Nearly opposite the stableyard the electric trams started for Hanbridge, Bursley and Turnhill, and for Longshaw. Here the crowd was less dangerous, but still very formidable – to my eyes. Each tram as it came up was savagely assaulted, seized, crammed and possessed, with astounding rapidity. Its steps were the western bank of a Beresina. At a given moment the inured conductor, brandishing his leather-shielded arm with a pitiless gesture, thrust aspirants down into the mud and the tram rolled powerfully away. All this in silence.

After a few minutes a bicyclist swished along through the mud, taking the far side of the road, which was comparatively free. He wore grey trousers, heavy boots, and a dark cut-away coat, up the back of which a line of caked mud had deposited itself. On his head was a bowler hat.

'How do, Jos?' cried a couple of boys, cheekily. And then there were a few adult greetings of respect.

It was the hero, in haste.

'Out of it, there!' he warned impeders, between his teeth, and plugged on with bent head.

'He keeps the Foaming Quart up at Toft End,' said the doctor. 'It's the highest pub in the Five Towns. He used to be what they call a pot-hunter, a racing bicyclist, you know. But he's got past that and he'll soon be past football. He's thirty-four if he's a day. That's one reason why he's so independent – that and because he's almost the only genuine native in the team.'

'Why?' I asked. 'Where do they come from, then?'

'Oh!' said Stirling as he gently started the car. 'The club buys 'em, up and down the country. Four of 'em are Scots. A few years ago an Oldham club offered Knype £500 for Myatt, a big price – more than he's worth now! But he wouldn't go, though they guaranteed to put him into a first-class pub – a free house. He's never cost Knype anything except his wages and the goodwill of the Foaming Quart.'

'What are his wages?'

'Don't know exactly. Not much. The Football Association fix a maximum. I daresay about four pounds a week. *Hi there! Are you deaf?*'

'Thee mind what tha'rt about!' responded a stout loiterer in our path. 'Or I'll take thy ears home for my tea, mester.'

Stirling laughed.

In a few minutes we had arrived at Hanbridge, splashing all the way between two processions that crowded either footpath. And in the middle of the road was a third procession of trams, – tram following tram, each gorged with passengers, frothing at the step with passengers; not the lackadaisical trams that I had seen earlier in the afternoon in Crown Square; a different race of trams, eager and impetuous velocities. We reached the *Signal* offices. No crowd of urchins to salute us this time!

Under the earth was the machine-room of the *Signal*. It reminded me of the bowels of a ship, so full was it of machinery. One huge machine clattered slowly, and a folded green thing dropped strangely on to a little iron table in front of us. Buchanan opened it, and I saw that the broken leg was in it at length, together with a statement that in the *Signal*'s opinion the sympathy of every true sportsman would be with the disabled player. I began to say something to Buchanan, when suddenly I could not hear my own voice. The great machine, with another behind us, was working at a fabulous speed and with a fabulous clatter. All that my startled senses could clearly disentangle was that the blue arc-lights above us blinked occasionally, and that folded green papers were snowing down upon the iron table far faster than the eye could follow them. Tall lads in aprons elbowed me away and carried off the green papers in bundles, but not more quickly than the machine shed them. Buchanan put his lips to my ear. But I could hear nothing. I shook my head. He smiled, and led us out from the tumult.

'Come and see the boys take them,' he said at the foot of the stairs.

In a sort of hall on the ground floor was a long counter, and beyond the counter a system of steel railings in parallel lines, so arranged that a person entering at the public door could only reach the counter by passing up or down each alley in succession. These steel lanes, which absolutely ensured the triumph of right over might, were packed with boys – the ragged urchins whom we had seen playing in the street. But not urchins now; rather young tigers! Perhaps half a dozen had reached the counter; the rest were massed behind, shouting and quarrelling. Through a hole in the wall, at the level of the counter, bundles of papers shot continuously, and were snatched up by servers, who distributed them in smaller bundles to the hungry boys; who flung down metal discs in exchange and fled, fled madly as though fiends were after them, through a third door, out of the pandemonium into the darkling street. And unceasingly the green papers appeared at the hole in the wall and unceasingly they were plucked away and borne off by those maddened children, whose destination was apparently Aix or Ghent, and whose wings were their tatters.

'What are those discs?' I inquired.

'The lads have to come and buy them earlier in the day,' said Buchanan. 'We haven't time to sell this edition for cash, you see.'

'Well,' I said as we left, 'I'm very much obliged.'

'What on earth for?' Buchanan asked.

'Everything,' I said.

We returned through the squares of Hanbridge and by Trafalgar Road to Stirling's house at Bleakridge. And everywhere in the deepening twilight I could see the urchins, often hatless and sometimes scarcely shod, scudding over the lamp-reflecting mire with sheets of wavy green, and above the noises of traffic I could hear the shrill outcry: '*Signal.* Football Edition. Football Edition. *Signal.*' The world was being informed of the might of Jos Myatt, and of the averting of disaster from Knype, and of the results of over a hundred other matches – not counting Rugby.

V

During the course of the evening, when Stirling had thoroughly accustomed himself to the state of being in sole charge of an expert from the British Museum, London, and the high walls round his more private soul had yielded to my timid but constant attacks, we grew fairly intimate. And in particular the doctor proved to me that his reputation for persuasive raciness with patients was well founded. Yet up to the time of dessert I might have been justified in supposing that that much-praised 'manner' in a sick-room was nothing but a provincial legend. Such may be the influence of a quite inoffensive and shy Londoner in the country. At half-past ten, Titus being already asleep for the night in an arm-chair, we sat at ease over the fire in the study telling each other stories. We had dealt with the arts, and with medicine; now we were dealing with life, in those aspects of it which cause men to laugh and women uneasily to wonder. Once or twice we had mentioned the Brindleys. The hour for their arrival was come. But being deeply comfortable and content where I was, I felt no impatience. Then there was a tap on the window.

'That's Bobbie!' said Stirling, rising slowly from his chair. '*He* won't refuse whisky, even if you do. I'd better get another bottle.'

The tap was repeated peevishly.

'I'm coming, laddie!' Stirling protested.

He slippered out through the hall and through the surgery to the side door, I following, and Titus sneezing and snuffing in the rear.

'I say, mester,' said a heavy voice as the doctor opened the door. It was not Brindley, but Jos Myatt. Unable to locate the bell-push in the dark, he had characteristically attacked the sole illuminated window. He demanded, or he commanded, very curtly, that the doctor should go up instantly to the Foaming Quart at Toft End.

Stirling hesitated a moment.

'All right, my man,' said he, calmly.

'Now?' the heavy, suspicious voice on the door-step insisted.

'I'll be there before ye if ye don't sprint, man. I'll run up in the car.' Stirling shut the door. I heard footsteps on the gravel path outside.

'Ye heard?' said he to me. 'And what am I to do with ye?'

'I'll go with you, of course,' I answered.

'I may be kept up there a while.'

'I don't care,' I said roisterously. 'It's a pub and I'm a traveller.'

Stirling's household was in bed and his assistant gone home. While he and Titus got out the car I wrote a line for the Brindleys: 'Gone with doctor to see patient at Toft End. Don't wait up. – A. L.' This we pushed under Brindley's front door on our way forth. Very soon we were vibrating up a steep street on the first speed of the car, and the yellow reflections of distant furnaces began to shine over house roofs below us. It was exhilaratingly cold, a clear and frosty night, tonic, bracing after the enclosed warmth of the study. I was joyous, but silently. We had quitted the kingdom of the god Pan; we were in Lucina's realm, its consequence, where there is no laughter. We were on a mission.

'I didn't expect this,' said Stirling.

'No?' I said. 'But seeing that he fetched you this morning—'

'Oh! That was only in order to be sure, for himself. His sister was there, in charge. Seemed very capable. Knew all about everything. Until ye get to the high social status of a clerk or a draper's assistant people seem to manage to have their children without professional assistance.'

'Then do you think there's anything wrong?' I asked.

'I'd not be surprised.'

He changed to the second speed as the car topped the first bluff. We said no more. The night and the mission solemnized us. And gradually, as we rose towards the purple skies, the Five Towns wrote themselves out in fire on the irregular plain below.

'That's Hanbridge Town Hall,' said Stirling, pointing to the right. 'And that's Bursley Town Hall,' he said, pointing to the left. And there were many other beacons, dominating the jewelled street-lines that faded on the horizon into golden-tinted smoke.

The road was never quite free of houses. After occurring but sparsely for half a mile, they thickened into a village – the suburb of Bursley called Toft End. I saw a moving red light in front of us. It was the reverse of Myatt's bicycle lantern. The car stopped near the dark façade of the inn, of which two yellow windows gleamed. Stirling, under Myatt's shouted guidance, backed into an obscure yard under cover. The engine ceased to throb.

'Friend of mine,' he introduced me to Myatt. 'By the way, Loring, pass me my bag, will you? Mustn't forget that.' Then he extinguished the acetylene lamps, and there was no light in the yard except the ray of the bicycle lantern which Myatt held in his hand. We groped towards the house. Strange, every step that I take in the Five Towns seems to have the genuine quality of an adventure!

VI

In five minutes I was of no account in the scheme of things at Toft End, and I began to wonder why I had come. Stirling, my sole protector, had vanished up the dark stairs of the house, following a stout, youngish woman in a white apron, who bore a candle. Jos Myatt, behind, said to me: 'Happen you'd better go in there, mester,' pointing to a half-open door at the foot of the stairs. I went into a little room at the rear of the bar-parlour. A good fire burned in a small old-fashioned grate, but there was no other light. The inn was closed to customers, it being past eleven o'clock. On a bare table I perceived a candle, and ventured to put a match to it. I then saw almost exactly such a room as one would expect to find at the rear of the bar-parlour of an inn on the outskirts of an industrial town. It appeared to serve the double purpose of a living-room and of a retreat for favoured customers. The table was evidently one at which men drank. On a shelf was a row of bottles, more or less empty, bearing names famous in newspaper advertisements and in the House of Lords. The dozen chairs suggested an acute bodily discomfort such as would only be tolerated by a sitter all of whose sensory faculties were centred in his palate. On a broken chair in a corner was an insecure pile of books. A smaller table was covered with a chequered cloth on which were a few plates. Along one wall, under the window, ran a pitch-pine sofa upholstered with a stuff slightly dissimilar from that on the table. The mattress of the sofa was uneven and its surface wrinkled, and old newspapers and pieces of brown paper had been stowed away between it and the framework. The chief article of furniture was an effective walnut bookcase, the glass doors of which were curtained with red cloth. The window, wider than it was high, was also curtained with red cloth. The walls, papered in a saffron tint, bore framed advertisements and a few photographs of self-conscious persons. The ceiling was as obscure as heaven; the floor tiled, with a list rug in front of the steel fender.

I put my overcoat on the sofa, picked up the candle and glanced at the books in the corner: Lavater's indestructible work, a paper-covered *Whitaker*, the *Licensed Victuallers' Almanac*, *Johnny Ludlow*, the illustrated catalogue of the Exhibition of 1856, *Cruden's Concordance*, and seven or eight volumes of *Knight's Penny Encyclopædia*. While I was poring on these titles I heard movements overhead – previously there had been no sound whatever – and with guilty haste I restored the candle to the table and placed myself negligently in front of the fire.

'Now don't let me see ye up here any more till I fetch ye!' said a woman's distant voice – not crossly, but firmly. And then, crossly: 'Be off with ye now!'

Reluctant boots on the stairs! Jos Myatt entered to me. He did not speak at first; nor did I. He avoided my glance. He was still wearing the cut-away coat with the line of mud up the back. I took out my watch, not for the sake of information, but from mere nervousness, and the sight of the watch reminded me that it would be prudent to wind it up.

'Better not forget that,' I said, winding it.

'Ay!' said he, gloomily. 'It's a tip.' And he wound up his watch; a large, thick, golden one.

This watch-winding established a basis of intercourse between us.

'I hope everything is going on all right,' I murmured.

'What dun ye say?' he asked.

'I say I hope everything is going on all right,' I repeated louder, and jerked my head in the direction of the stairs, to indicate the place from which he had come.

'Oh!' he exclaimed, as if surprised. 'Now what'll ye have, mester?' He stood waiting. 'It's my call to-night.'

I explained to him that I never took alcohol. It was not quite true, but it was as true as most general propositions are.

'Neither me!' he said shortly, after a pause.

'You're a teetotaller too?' I showed a little involuntary astonishment.

He put forward his chin.

'What do *you* think?' he said confidentially and scornfully. It was precisely as if he had said: 'Do you think that anybody but a born ass would *not* be a teetotaller, in my position?'

I sat down on a chair.

'Take th' squab, mester,' he said, pointing to the sofa. I took it.

He picked up the candle; then dropped it, and lighted a lamp which was on the mantelpiece between his vases of blue glass. His movements were very slow, hesitating and clumsy. Blowing out the candle, which smoked for a long time, he went with the lamp to the bookcase. As the key of the bookcase was in his right pocket and the lamp in his right hand he had to change the lamp, cautiously, from hand to hand. When he opened the cupboard I saw a rich gleam of silver from every shelf of it except the lowest, and I could distinguish the forms of ceremonial cups with pedestals and immense handles.

'I suppose these are your pots?' I said.

'Ay!'

He displayed to me the fruits of his manifold victories. I could see him straining along endless cinder-paths and highroads under hot suns, his great knees going up and down like treadles amid the plaudits and howls of vast populations. And all that now remained of that glory was these debased and vicious shapes, magnificently useless, grossly ugly, with their inscriptions lost in a mess of flourishes.

'Ay!' he said again, when I had fingered the last of them.

'A very fine show indeed!' I said, resuming the sofa.

He took a penny bottle of ink and a pen out of the bookcase, and also, from the lowest shelf, a bag of money and a long narrow account book. Then he sat down at the table and commenced accountancy. It was clear that he regarded his task as formidable and complex. To see him reckoning the coins, manipulating the pen, splashing the ink, scratching the page; to hear him whispering consecutive numbers aloud, and muttering mysterious anathemas against the untamable naughtiness of figures – all this was painful, and with the painfulness of a simple exercise rendered difficult by inaptitude and incompetence. I wanted to jump up and cry to him: 'Get out of the way, man, and let me do it for you! I can do it while you are wiping hairs from your pen on your sleeve.' I was sorry for him because he was ridiculous – and even more grotesque than ridiculous. I felt, quite acutely, that it was a shame that he could not be for ever the central figure of a field of mud, kicking a ball into long and grandiose parabolas higher than gasometers, or breaking an occasional leg, surrounded by the violent affection of hearts whose melting-point was the exclamation, 'Good old Jos!' I felt that if he must repose his existence ought to have been so contrived that he could repose in impassive and senseless dignity, like a mountain watching the flight of time. The conception of him tracing symbols in a ledger, counting shillings and sixpences, descending to arithmetic, and suffering those humili ations which are the invariable preliminaries to legitimate fatherhood, was shocking to a nice taste for harmonious fitness . . . What, this precious and terrific organism, this slave with a specialty – whom distant towns had once been anxious to buy at the prodigious figure of five hundred pounds – obliged to sit in a mean chamber and wait silently while the woman of his choice encountered the supreme peril! And he would 'soon be past football!' He was 'thirty-four if a day!' It was the verge of senility! He was no longer worth five hundred pounds. Perhaps even now this jointed merchandise was only worth two hundred pounds! And 'they' – the shadowy directors, who could not kick a ball fifty feet and who would probably turn sick if they broke a leg – 'they' paid him four pounds a week for being the hero of a quarter of a million of people! He was the chief magnet to draw fifteen thousand sixpences and shillings of a Saturday afternoon into a company's cash box, and here he sat splitting his head over fewer sixpences and shillings than would fill a half-pint pot! Jos, you ought in justice to have been José, with a thin red necktie down your breast (instead of a line of mud up your back), and embroidered breeches on those miraculous legs, and an income of a quarter of a million pesetas, and the languishing acquiescence of innumerable mantillas. Every moment you were getting older and stiffer; every moment was bringing nearer the moment when young men would reply curtly to their doddering elders: 'Jos Myatt – who was 'e?'

The putting away of the ledger, the ink, the pen and the money was as exasperating as their taking out had been. Then Jos, always too large for the room, crossed the tiled floor and mended the fire. A poker was more suited to his capacity than a pen. He glanced about him, uncertain and anxious, and then crept to the door near the foot of the stairs and listened. There was no sound; and that was curious. The woman who was bringing into the world the hero's child made no cry that reached us below. Once or twice I had heard muffled movements not quite overhead – somewhere above – but naught else. The doctor and Jos's sister seemed to have retired into a sinister and dangerous mystery. I could not dispel from my mind pictures of what they were watching and what they were doing. The vast, cruel, fumbling clumsiness of Nature, her lack of majesty in crises that ought to be majestic, her incurable indignity, disgusted me, aroused my disdain. I wanted, as a philosopher of all the cultures, to feel that the present was indeed a majestic crisis, to be so esteemed by a superior man. I could not. Though the crisis possibly intimidated me somewhat, yet, on behalf of Jos Myatt, I was ashamed of it. This may be reprehensible, but it is true.

He sat down by the fire and looked at the fire. I could not attempt to carry on a conversation with him, and to avoid the necessity for any talk at all, I extended myself on the sofa and averted my face, wondering once again why I had accompanied the doctor to Toft End. The doctor was now in another, an inaccessible world. I dozed, and from my doze I was roused by Jos Myatt going to the door on the stairs.

'Jos,' said a voice. 'It's a girl.'

Then a silence.

I admit there was a flutter in my heart. Another soul, another formed and unchangeable temperament, tumbled into the world! Whence? Whither? . . . As for the quality of majesty – yes, if silver trumpets had announced the advent, instead of a stout, aproned woman, the moment could not have been more majestic in its sadness. I say 'sadness', which is the inevitable and sole effect of these eternal and banal questions, 'Whence? Whither?'

'Is her bad?' Jos whispered.

'Her's pretty bad,' said the voice, but cheerily. 'Bring me up another scuttle o' coal.'

When he returned to the parlour, after being again dismissed, I said to him:

'Well, I congratulate you.'

'I thank ye!' he said, and sat down. Presently I could hear him muttering to himself, mildly: 'Hell! Hell! Hell!'

I thought: 'Stirling will not be very long now, and we can depart home.'

I looked at my watch. It was a quarter to two. But Stirling did not appear, nor was there any message from him or sign. I had to submit to the predicament. As a faint chilliness from the window affected my back I drew my overcoat up to my shoulders as a counterpane. Through a gap between the red curtains of the window I could see a star blazing. It passed behind the curtain with disconcerting rapidity. The universe was swinging and whirling as usual.

VII

Sounds of knocking disturbed me. In the few seconds that elapsed before I could realize just where I was and why I was there, the summoning knocks were repeated. The early sun was shining through the red blind. I sat up and straightened my hair, involuntarily composing my attitude so that nobody who might enter the room should imagine that I had been other than patiently wide-awake all night. The second door of the parlour – that leading to the bar-room of the Foaming Quart – was open, and I could see the bar itself, with shelves rising behind it and the upright handles of a beer-engine at one end. Someone whom I could not see was evidently unbolting and unlocking the principal entrance to the inn. Then I heard the scraping of a creaky portal on the floor.

'Well, Jos lad!'

It was the voice of the little man, Charlie, who had spoken with Myatt on the football field.

'Come in quick, Charlie. It's cowd,' said the voice of Jos Myatt, gloomily.

'Ay! Cowd it is, lad! It's above three mile as I've walked, and thou knows it, Jos. Give us a quartern o' gin.'

The door grated again and a bolt was drawn.

The two men passed together behind the bar, and so within my vision. Charlie had a grey muffler round his neck; his hands were far in his pockets and seemed to be at strain, as though trying to prevent his upper and his lower garments from flying apart. Jos Myatt was extremely dishevelled. In the little man's demeanour towards the big one there was now none of the self-conscious pride in the mere fact of acquaintance that I had noticed on the field. Clearly the two were intimate friends, perhaps relatives. While Jos was dispensing the gin, Charlie said, in a low tone:

'Well, what luck, Jos?'

This was the first reference, by either of them, to the crisis.

Jos deliberately finished pouring out the gin. Then he said:

'There's two on 'em, Charlie.'

'Two on 'em? What mean'st tha', lad?'

'I mean as it's twins.'

Charlie and I were equally startled.

'Thou never says!' he murmured, incredulous.

'Ay! One o' both sorts,' said Jos.

'Thou never says!' Charlie repeated, holding his glass of gin steady in his hand.

'One come at summat after one o'clock, and th' other between five and six. I had for fetch old woman Eardley to help. It were more than a handful for Susannah and th' doctor.'

Astonishing, that I should have slept through these events!

'How is her?' asked Charlie, quietly, as it were casually. I think this appearance of casualness was caused by the stoic suppression of the symptoms of anxiety.

'Her's bad,' said Jos, briefly.

'And I am na' surprised,' said Charlie. And he lifted the glass. 'Well – here's luck.' He sipped the gin, savouring it on his tongue like a connoisseur, and gradually making up his mind about its quality. Then he took another sip.

'Hast seen her?'

'I seed her for a minute, but our Susannah wouldna' let me stop i' th' room. Her was raving like.'

'Missis?'

'Ay!'

'And th' babbies – hast seen *them?*'

'Ay! But I can make nowt out of 'em. Mrs Eardley says as her's never seen no finer.'

'Doctor gone?'

'That he has na'! He's bin up there all the blessed night, in his shirt-sleeves. I give him a stiff glass o' whisky at five o'clock and that's all as he's had.'

Charlie finished his gin. The pair stood silent.

'Well,' said Charlie, striking his leg. 'Swelp me bob! It fair beats me! Twins! Who'd ha' thought it? Jos, lad, thou mayst be thankful as it isna' triplets. Never did I think, as I was footing it up here this morning, as it was twins I was coming to!'

'Hast got that half quid in thy pocket?'

'What half quid?' said Charlie, defensively.

'Now then. Chuck us it over!' said Jos, suddenly harsh and overbearing.

'I laid thee half quid as it 'ud be a wench,' said Charlie, doggedly.

'Thou'rt a liar, Charlie!' said Jos. 'Thou laidst half a quid as it wasna' a boy.'

'Nay, nay!' Charlie shook his head.

'And a boy it is!' Jos persisted.

'It being a lad *and* a wench,' said Charlie, with a judicial air, 'and me 'aving laid as it 'ud be a wench, I wins.' In his accents and his gestures I could discern the mean soul, who on principle never paid until he was absolutely forced to pay. I could see also that Jos Myatt knew his man.

'Thou laidst me as it wasna' a lad,' Jos almost shouted. 'And a lad it is, I tell thee.'

'*And* a wench!' said Charlie; then shook his head.

The wrangle proceeded monotonously, each party repeating over and over again the phrases of his own argument. I was very glad that Jos did not know me to be a witness of the making of the bet; otherwise I should assuredly have been summoned to give judgment.

'Let's call it off, then,' Charlie suggested at length. 'That'll settle it. And it being twins—'

'Nay, thou old devil, I'll none call it off. Thou owes me half a quid, and I'll have it out of thee.'

'Look ye here,' Charlie said more softly. 'I'll tell thee what'll settle it. Which on 'em come first, th' lad or th' wench?'

'Th' wench come first,' Jos Myatt admitted, with resentful reluctance, dully aware that defeat was awaiting him.

'Well, then! Th' wench is thy eldest child. That's law, that is. And what was us betting about, Jos lad? Us was betting about thy eldest and no other. I'll admit as I laid it wasna' a lad, as thou sayst. And it *wasna'* a lad. First come is eldest, and us was betting about eldest.'

Charlie stared at the father in triumph.

Jos Myatt pushed roughly past him in the narrow space behind the bar, and came into the parlour. Nodding to me curtly, he unlocked the bookcase and took two crown pieces from a leathern purse which lay next to the bag. Then he returned to the bar and banged the coins on the counter with fury.

'Take thy brass!' he shouted angrily. 'Take thy brass! But thou'rt a damned shark, Charlie, and if anybody 'ud give me a plug o' bacca for doing it, I'd bash thy face in.'

The other sniggered contentedly as he picked up his money.

'A bet's a bet,' said Charlie.

He was clearly accustomed to an occasional violence of demeanour from Jos Myatt, and felt no fear. But he was wrong in feeling no fear. He had not allowed, in his estimate of the situation, for the exasperated condition of Jos Myatt's nerves under the unique experiences of the night.

Jos's face twisted into a hundred wrinkles and his hand seized Charlie by the arm whose hand held the coins.

'Drop 'em!' he cried loudly, repenting his naïve honesty. 'Drop 'em! Or I'll—'

The stout woman, her apron all soiled, now came swiftly and scarce heard into the parlour, and stood at the door leading to the bar-room.

'What's up, Susannah?' Jos demanded in a new voice.

'Well may ye ask what's up!' said the woman. 'Shouting and brangling there, ye sots!'

'What's up?' Jos demanded again, loosing Charlie's arm.

'Her's gone!' the woman feebly whimpered. 'Like that!' with a vague movement of the hand indicating suddenness. Then she burst into wild sobs and rushed madly back whence she had come, and the sound of her sobs diminished as she ascended the stairs, and expired altogether in the distant shutting of a door.

The men looked at each other.

Charlie restored the crown-pieces to the counter and pushed them towards Jos.

'Here!' he murmured faintly.

Jos flung them savagely to the ground. Another pause followed.

'As God is my witness,' he exclaimed solemnly, his voice saturated with feeling, 'as God is my witness,' he repeated, 'I'll ne'er touch a footba' again!'

Little Charlie gazed up at him sadly, plaintively, for what seemed a long while.

'It's good-bye to th' First League, then, for Knype!' he tragically muttered, at length.

VIII

Dr Stirling drove the car very slowly back to Bursley. We glided gently down into the populous valleys. All the stunted trees were coated with rime, which made the sharpest contrast with their black branches and the black mud under us. The high chimneys sent forth their black smoke calmly and tirelessly into the fresh blue sky. Sunday had descended on the vast landscape like a physical influence. We saw a snake of children winding out of a dark brown Sunday school into a dark brown chapel. And up from the valleys came all the bells of all the temples of all the different gods of the Five Towns, chiming, clanging, ringing, each insisting that it alone invited to the altar of the one God. And priests and acolytes of the various cults hurried occasionally along, in silk hats and bright neckties, and smooth coats with folded handkerchiefs sticking out of the pockets, busy, happy and self-important, the convinced heralds of eternal salvation: no doubt nor hesitation as to any fundamental truth had ever entered their minds. We passed through a long, straight street of new red houses with blue slate roofs, all gated and gardened. Here and there a girl with her hair in pins and a rough brown apron over a gaudy frock was stoning a front step. And half-way down the street a man in a scarlet jersey, supported by two women in blue bonnets, was beating a drum and crying aloud: 'My friends, you may die to-night. Where, I ask you, where—?' But he had no friends; not even a boy heeded him. The drum continued to bang in our rear.

I enjoyed all this. All this seemed to me to be fine, seemed to throw off the true, fine, romantic savour of life. I would have altered nothing in

it. Mean, harsh, ugly, squalid, crude, barbaric – yes, but what an intoxi-
cating sense in it of the organized vitality of a vast community unconscious
of itself! I would have altered nothing even in the events of the night. I
thought of the rooms at the top of the staircase of the Foaming Quart –
mysterious rooms which I had not seen and never should see, recondite
rooms from which a soul had slipped away and into which two had come,
scenes of anguish and of frustrated effort! Historical rooms, surely! And
yet not a house in the hundreds of houses past which we slid but possessed
rooms ennobled and made august by happenings exactly as impressive in
their tremendous inexplicableness.

The natural humanity of Jos Myatt and Charlie, their fashion of com-
porting themselves in a sudden stress, pleased me. How else should they
have behaved? I could understand Charlie's prophetic dirge over the ruin
of the Knype Football Club. It was not that he did not feel the tragedy
in the house. He had felt it, and because he had felt it he had uttered at
random, foolishly, the first clear thought that ran into his head.

Stirling was quiet. He appeared to be absorbed in steering, and
looked straight in front, yawning now and again. He was much more
fatigued than I was. Indeed, I had slept pretty well. He said, as we swerved
into Trafalgar Road and overtook the aristocracy on its way to chapel and
church:

'Well, ye let yeself in for a night, young man! No mistake!'

He smiled, and I smiled.

'What's going to occur up there?' I asked, indicating Toft End.

'What do you mean?'

'A man like that – left with two babies!'

'Oh!' he said. 'They'll manage that all right. His sister's a widow. She'll
go and live with him. She's as fond of those infants already as if they were
her own.'

We drew up at his double gates.

'Be sure ye explain to Brindley,' he said, as I left him, 'that it isn't my
fault ye've had a night out of bed. It was your own doing. I'm going to get
a bit of sleep now. See you this evening. Bob's asked me to supper.'

A servant was sweeping Bob Brindley's porch and the front door was
open. I went in. The sound of the piano guided me to the drawing-room.
Brindley, the morning cigarette between his lips, was playing Maurice

Ravel's 'L'heure espagnole'. He held his head back so as to keep the smoke out of his eyes. His children in their blue jerseys were building bricks on the carpet.

Without ceasing to play he addressed me calmly:

'You're a nice chap! Where the devil have you been?'

And one of the little boys, glancing up, said, with roguish, imitative innocence, in his high, shrill voice:

'Where the del you been?'

D. H. LAWRENCE

Daughters of the Vicar

I

Mr Lindley was first vicar of Aldecross. The cottages of this tiny hamlet had nestled in peace since their beginning, and the country folk had crossed the lanes and farm-lands, two or three miles, to the parish church at Greymeed, on the bright Sunday mornings.

But when the pits were sunk, blank rows of dwellings started up beside the high roads, and a new population, skimmed from the floating scum of workmen, was filled in, the cottages and the country people almost obliterated.

To suit the convenience of these new collier-inhabitants, a church must be built at Aldecross. There was not too much money. And so the little building crouched like a humped stone-and-mortar mouse, with two little turrets at the west corners for ears, in the fields near the cottages and the apple trees, as far as possible from the dwellings down the high road. It had an uncertain, timid look about it. And so they planted big-leaved ivy, to hide its shrinking newness. So that now the little church stands buried in its greenery, stranded and sleeping among the fields, while the brick houses elbow nearer and nearer, threatening to crush it down. It is already obsolete.

The Reverend Ernest Lindley, aged twenty-seven, and newly married, came from his curacy in Suffolk to take charge of his church. He was just an ordinary young man, who had been to Cambridge and taken orders. His wife was a self-assured young woman, daughter of a Cambridgeshire rector. Her father had spent the whole of his thousand a year, so that

Mrs Lindley had nothing of her own. Thus the young married people came to Aldecross to live on a stipend of about a hundred and twenty pounds, and to keep up a superior position.

They were not very well received by the new, raw, disaffected population of colliers. Being accustomed to farm labourers, Mr Lindley had considered himself as belonging indisputably to the upper or ordering classes. He had to be humble to the county families, but still, he was of their kind, whilst the common people were something different. He had no doubts of himself.

He found, however, that the collier population refused to accept this arrangement. They had no use for him in their lives, and they told him so, callously. The women merely said, 'they were throng,' or else, 'Oh, it's no good you coming here, we're Chapel.' The men were quite good-humoured so long as he did not touch them too nigh, they were cheerfully contemptuous of him, with a preconceived contempt he was powerless against.

At last, passing from indignation to silent resentment, even, if he dared have acknowledged it, to conscious hatred of the majority of his flock, and unconscious hatred of himself, he confined his activities to a narrow round of cottages, and he had to submit. He had no particular character, having always depended on his position in society to give him position among men. Now he was so poor, he had no social standing even among the common vulgar tradespeople of the district, and he had not the nature nor the wish to make his society agreeable to them, nor the strength to impose himself where he would have liked to be recognized. He dragged on, pale and miserable and neutral.

At first his wife raged with mortification. She took on airs and used a high hand. But her income was too small, the wrestling with tradesmen's bills was too pitiful, she only met with general, callous ridicule when she tried to be impressive.

Wounded to the quick of her pride, she found herself isolated in an indifferent, callous population. She raged indoors and out. But soon she learned that she must pay too heavily for her outdoor rages, and then she only raged within the walls of the rectory. There her feeling was so strong, that she frightened herself. She saw herself hating her husband, and she knew that, unless she were careful, she would smash her form of life and bring catastrophe upon him and upon herself. So in very fear, she went quiet. She hid, bitter and beaten by fear, behind the only shelter she had in the world, her gloomy, poor parsonage.

Children were born one every year; almost mechanically, she continued to perform her maternal duty, which was forced upon her. Gradually, broken by the suppressing of her violent anger and misery and disgust, she became an invalid and took to her couch.

The children grew up healthy, but unwarmed and rather rigid. Their father and mother educated them at home, made them very proud and very genteel, put them definitely and cruelly in the upper classes, apart from the vulgar around them. So they lived quite isolated. They were good-looking, and had that curiously clean, semi-transparent look of the genteel, isolated poor.

Gradually Mr and Mrs Lindley lost all hold on life, and spent their hours, weeks and years merely haggling to make ends meet, and bitterly repressing and pruning their children into gentility, urging them to ambition, weighting them with duty. On Sunday morning the whole family, except the mother, went down the lane to church, the long-legged girls in skimpy frocks, the boys in black coats and long, grey, unfitting trousers. They passed by their father's parishioners with mute, clear faces, childish mouths closed in pride that was like a doom to them, and childish eyes already unseeing. Miss Mary, the eldest, was the leader. She was a long, slim thing with a fine profile and a proud, pure look of submission to a high fate. Miss Louisa, the second, was short and plump and obstinate-looking. She had more enemies than ideals. She looked after the lesser children, Miss Mary after the elder. The collier children watched this pale, distinguished procession of the vicar's family pass mutely by, and they were impressed by the air of gentility and distance, they made mock of the trousers of the small sons, they felt inferior in themselves, and hate stirred their hearts.

In her time, Miss Mary received as governess a few little daughters of tradesmen; Miss Louisa managed the house and went among her father's church-goers, giving lessons on the piano to the colliers' daughters at thirteen shillings for twenty-six lessons.

II

One winter morning, when his daughter Mary was about twenty years old, Mr Lindley, a thin, unobtrusive figure in his black overcoat and his wideawake, went down into Aldecross with a packet of white papers under his arm. He was delivering the parish almanacs.

A rather pale, neutral man of middle age, he waited while the train thumped over the level-crossing, going up to the pit which rattled busily just along the line. A wooden-legged man hobbled to open the gate, Mr Lindley passed on. Just at his left hand, below the road and the railway, was the red roof of a cottage, showing through the bare twigs of apple trees. Mr Lindley passed round the low wall, and descended the worn steps that led from the highway down to the cottage which crouched darkly and quietly away below the rumble of passing trains and the clank of coal-carts in a quiet little under-world of its own. Snowdrops with tight-shut buds were hanging very still under the bare currant bushes.

The clergyman was just going to knock when he heard a clinking noise, and turning saw through the open door of a black shed just behind him an elderly woman in a black lace cap stooping among reddish big cans, pouring a very bright liquid into a tundish. There was a smell of paraffin. The woman put down her can, took the tundish and laid it on a shelf, then rose with a tin bottle. Her eyes met those of the clergyman.

'Oh, is it you, Mr Lin'ley!' she said, in a complaining tone. 'Go in.'

The minister entered the house. In the hot kitchen sat a big, elderly man with a great grey beard, taking snuff. He grunted in a deep, muttering voice, telling the minister to sit down, and then took no more notice of him, but stared vacantly into the fire. Mr Lindley waited.

The woman came in, the ribbons of her black lace cap, or bonnet, hanging on her shawl. She was of medium stature, everything about her was tidy. She went up a step out of the kitchen, carrying the paraffin tin. Feet were heard entering the room up the step. It was a little haberdashery shop, with parcels on the shelves of the walls, a big, old-fashioned sewing machine with tailor's work lying round it, in the open space. The woman went behind the counter, gave the child who had entered the paraffin bottle, and took from her a jug.

'My mother says shall yer put it down,' said the child, and she was gone. The woman wrote in a book, then came into the kitchen with her jug. The husband, a very large man, rose and brought more coal to the already hot fire. He moved slowly and sluggishly. Already he was going dead; being a tailor, his large form had become an encumbrance to him. In his youth he had been a great dancer and boxer. Now he was taciturn, and inert. The minister had nothing to say, so he sought for his phrases. But John Durant took no notice, existing silent and dull.

Mrs Durant spread the cloth. Her husband poured himself beer into a mug, and began to smoke and drink.

'Shall you have some?' he growled through his beard at the clergyman, looking slowly from the man to the jug, capable of this one idea.

'No, thank you,' replied Mr Lindley, though he would have liked some beer. He must set the example in a drinking parish.

'We need a drop to keep us going,' said Mrs Durant.

She had rather a complaining manner. The clergyman sat on uncomfortably while she laid the table for the half-past ten lunch. Her husband drew up to eat. She remained in her little round arm-chair by the fire.

She was a woman who would have liked to be easy in her life, but to whose lot had fallen a rough and turbulent family, and a slothful husband who did not care what became of himself or anybody. So, her rather good-looking square face was peevish, she had that air of having been compelled all her life to serve unwillingly, and to control where she did not want to control. There was about her, too, that masterful *aplomb* of a woman who has brought up and ruled her sons: but even them she had ruled unwillingly. She had enjoyed managing her little haberdashery-shop, riding in the carrier's cart to Nottingham, going through the big warehouses to buy her goods. But the fret of managing her sons she did not like. Only she loved her youngest boy, because he was her last, and she saw herself free.

This was one of the houses the clergyman visited occasionally. Mrs Durant, as part of her regulation, had brought up all her sons in the Church. Not that she had any religion. Only, it was what she was used to. Mr Durant was without religion. He read the fervently evangelical 'Life of John Wesley' with a curious pleasure, getting from it a satisfaction as from the warmth of the fire, or a glass of brandy. But he cared no more about John Wesley, in fact, than about John Milton, of whom he had never heard.

Mrs Durant took her chair to the table.

'I don't feel like eating,' she sighed.

'Why – aren't you well?' asked the clergyman, patronizing.

'It isn't that,' she sighed. She sat with shut, straight mouth. 'I don't know what's going to become of us.'

But the clergyman had ground himself down so long, that he could not easily sympathize.

'Have you any trouble?' he asked.

'Ay, have I any trouble!' cried the elderly woman. 'I shall end my days in the workhouse.'

The minister waited unmoved. What could she know of poverty, in her little house of plenty!

'I hope not,' he said.

'And the one lad as I wanted to keep by me—' she lamented.

The minister listened without sympathy, quite neutral.

'And the lad as would have been a support to my old age! What is going to become of us?' she said.

The clergyman, justly, did not believe in the cry of poverty, but wondered what had become of the son.

'Has anything happened to Alfred?' he asked.

'We've got word he's gone for a Queen's sailor,' she said sharply.

'He has joined the Navy!' exclaimed Mr Lindley. 'I think he could scarcely have done better – to serve his Queen and country on the sea . . .'

'He is wanted to serve *me*,' she cried. 'And I wanted my lad at home.'

Alfred was her baby, her last, whom she had allowed herself the luxury of spoiling.

'You will miss him,' said Mr Lindley, 'that is certain. But this is no regrettable step for him to have taken – on the contrary.'

'That's easy for you to say, Mr Lindley,' she replied tartly. 'Do you think I want my lad climbing ropes at another man's bidding, like a monkey—?'

'There is no *dishonour*, surely, in serving in the Navy?'

'Dishonour this dishonour that,' cried the angry old woman. 'He goes and makes a slave of himself, and he'll rue it.'

Her angry, scornful impatience nettled the clergyman and silenced him for some moments.

'I do not see,' he retorted at last, white at the gills and inadequate, 'that the Queen's service is any more to be called slavery than working in a mine.'

'At home he was at home, and his own master. *I* know he'll find a difference.'

'It may be the making of him,' said the clergyman. 'It will take him away from bad companionship and drink.'

Some of the Durants' sons were notorious drinkers, and Alfred was not quite steady.

'And why indeed shouldn't he have his glass?' cried the mother. 'He picks no man's pocket to pay for it!'

The clergyman stiffened at what he thought was an allusion to his own profession, and his unpaid bills.

'With all due consideration, I am glad to hear he has joined the Navy,' he said.

'Me with my old age coming on, and his father working very little! I'd thank you to be glad about something else besides that, Mr Lindley.'

The woman began to cry. Her husband, quite impassive, finished his lunch of meat-pie, and drank some beer. Then he turned to the fire, as if there were no one in the room but himself.

'I shall respect all men who serve God and their country on the sea, Mrs Durant,' said the clergyman stubbornly.

'That is very well, when they're not your sons who are doing the dirty work. – It makes a difference,' she replied tartly.

'I should be proud if one of my sons were to enter the Navy.'

'Ay – well – we're not all of us made alike—'

The minister rose. He put down a large folded paper.

'I've brought the almanac,' he said.

Mrs Durant unfolded it.

'I do like a bit of colour in things,' she said, petulantly.

The clergyman did not reply.

'There's that envelope for the organist's fund—' said the old woman, and rising, she took the thing from the mantelpiece, went into the shop, and returned sealing it up.

'Which is all I can afford,' she said.

Mr Lindley took his departure, in his pocket the envelope containing Mrs Durant's offering for Miss Louisa's services. He went from door to door delivering the almanacs, in dull routine. Jaded with the monotony of the business, and with the repeated effort of greeting half-known people, he felt barren and rather irritable. At last he returned home.

In the dining-room was a small fire. Mrs Lindley, growing very stout, lay on her couch. The vicar carved the cold mutton; Miss Louisa, short and plump and rather flushed, came in from the kitchen; Miss Mary, dark, with a beautiful white brow and grey eyes, served the vegetables; the children chattered a little, but not exuberantly. The very air seemed starved.

'I went to the Durants,' said the vicar, as he served out small portions of mutton; 'it appears Alfred has run away to join the Navy.'

'Do him good,' came the rough voice of the invalid.

Miss Louisa, attending to the youngest child, looked up in protest.

'Why has he done that?' asked Mary's low, musical voice.

'He wanted some excitement, I suppose,' said the vicar. 'Shall we say grace?'

The children were arranged, all bent their heads, grace was pronounced, at the last word every face was being raised to go on with the interesting subject.

'He's just done the right thing, for once,' came the rather deep voice of the mother; 'save him from becoming a drunken sot, like the rest of them.'

'They're not *all* drunken, mama,' said Miss Louisa, stubbornly.

'It's no fault of their upbringing if they're not. Walter Durant is a standing disgrace.'

'As I told Mrs Durant,' said the vicar, eating hungrily, 'it is the best thing he could have done. It will take him away from temptation during the most dangerous years of his life – how old is he – nineteen?'

'Twenty,' said Miss Louisa.

'Twenty!' repeated the vicar. 'It will give him wholesome discipline and set before him some sort of standard of duty and honour – nothing could have been better for him. But—'

'We shall miss him from the choir,' said Miss Louisa, as if taking opposite sides to her parents.

'That is as it may be,' said the vicar. 'I prefer to know he is safe in the Navy, than running the risk of getting into bad ways here.'

'Was he getting into bad ways?' asked the stubborn Miss Louisa.

'You know, Louisa, he wasn't quite what he used to be,' said Miss Mary gently and steadily. Miss Louisa shut her rather heavy jaw sulkily. She wanted to deny it, but she knew it was true.

For her he had been a laughing, warm lad, with something kindly and something rich about him. He had made her feel warm. It seemed the days would be colder since he had gone.

'Quite the best thing he could do,' said the mother with emphasis.

'I think so,' said the vicar. 'But his mother was almost abusive because I suggested it.'

He spoke in an injured tone.

'What does she care for her children's welfare?' said the invalid. 'Their wages is all her concern.'

'I suppose she wanted him at home with her,' said Miss Louisa.

'Yes, she did – at the expense of his learning to be a drunkard like the rest of them,' retorted her mother.

'George Durant doesn't drink,' defended her daughter.

'Because he got burned so badly when he was nineteen – in the pit – and that frightened him. The Navy is a better remedy than that, at least.'

'Certainly,' said the vicar. 'Certainly.'

And to this Miss Louisa agreed. Yet she could not but feel angry that he had gone away for so many years. She herself was only nineteen.

III

It happened when Miss Mary was twenty-three years old, that Mr Lindley was very ill. The family was exceedingly poor at the time, such a lot of money was needed, so little was forthcoming. Neither Miss Mary nor Miss Louisa had suitors. What chance had they? They met no eligible young men in Aldecross. And what they earned was a mere drop in a void. The girls' hearts were chilled and hardened with fear of this perpetual, cold penury, this narrow struggle, this horrible nothingness of their lives.

A clergyman had to be found for the church work. It so happened the son of an old friend of Mr Lindley's was waiting three months before taking up his duties. He would come and officiate, for nothing. The young clergyman was keenly expected. He was not more than twenty-seven, a Master of Arts of Oxford, had written his thesis on Roman Law. He came of an old Cambridgeshire family, had some private means, was going to take a church in Northamptonshire with a good stipend, and was not married. Mrs Lindley incurred new debts, and scarcely regretted her husband's illness.

But when Mr Massy came, there was a shock of disappointment in the house. They had expected a young man with a pipe and a deep voice, but with better manners than Sidney, the eldest of the Lindleys. There arrived instead a small, chétif man, scarcely larger than a boy of twelve, spectacled, timid in the extreme, without a word to utter at first; yet with a certain inhuman self-sureness.

'What a little abortion!' was Mrs Lindley's exclamation to herself on first seeing him, in his buttoned-up clerical coat. And for the first time for many days, she was profoundly thankful to God that all her children were decent specimens.

He had not normal powers of perception. They soon saw that he lacked the full range of human feelings, but had rather a strong, philosophical mind, from which he lived. His body was almost unthinkable, in intellect he was something definite. The conversation at once took a balanced, abstract tone when he participated. There was no spontaneous exclamation, no violent assertion or expression of personal conviction, but all cold, reasonable assertion. This was very hard on Mrs Lindley. The little man would look at her, after one of her pronouncements, and then give, in his thin voice, his own calculated version, so that she felt as if she were tumbling into thin air through a hole in the flimsy floor on which their conversation stood. It was she who felt a fool. Soon she was reduced to a hardy silence.

Still, at the back of her mind, she remembered that he was an unattached gentleman, who would shortly have an income altogether of six or seven hundred a year. What did the man matter, if there were pecuniary ease! The man was a trifle thrown in. After twenty-two years her sentimentality was ground away, and only the millstone of poverty mattered to her. So she supported the little man as a representative of a decent income.

His most irritating habit was that of a sneering little giggle, all on his own, which came when he perceived or related some illogical absurdity on the part of another person. It was the only form of humour he had. Stupidity in thinking seemed to him exquisitely funny. But any novel was unintelligibly meaningless and dull, and to an Irish sort of humour he listened curiously, examining it like mathematics, or else simply not hearing. In normal human relationship he was not there. Quite unable to take part in simple everyday talk, he padded silently round the house, or sat in the dining-room looking nervously from side to side, always apart in a cold, rarefied little world of his own. Sometimes he made an ironic remark, that did not seem humanly relevant, or he gave his little laugh, like a sneer. He had to defend himself and his own insufficiency. And he answered questions grudgingly, with a yes or no, because he did not see their import and was nervous. It seemed to Miss Louisa he scarcely distinguished one person from another, but that he liked to be near her, or to Miss Mary, for some sort of contact which stimulated him unknown.

Apart from all this, he was the most admirable workman. He was unremittingly shy, but perfect in his sense of duty: as far as he could conceive Christianity, he was a perfect Christian. Nothing that he realized he could do for anyone did he leave undone, although he was so incapable of coming into contact with another being, that he could not proffer help. Now he attended assiduously to the sick man, investigated all the affairs of the parish or the church which Mr Lindley had in control, straightened out accounts, made lists of the sick and needy, padded round with help and to see what he could do. He heard of Mrs Lindley's anxiety about her sons, and began to investigate means of sending them to Cambridge. His kindness almost frightened Miss Mary. She honoured it so, and yet she shrank from it. For, in it all Mr Massy seemed to have no sense of any person, any human being whom he was helping: he only realized a kind of mathematical working out, solving of given situations, a calculated well-doing. And it was as if he had accepted the Christian tenets as axioms. His religion consisted in what his scrupulous, abstract mind approved of.

Seeing his acts, Miss Mary must respect and honour him. In consequence she must serve him. To this she had to force herself, shuddering and yet desirous, but he did not perceive it. She accompanied him on his visiting in the parish, and whilst she was cold with admiration for him, often she was touched with pity for the little padding figure with bent shoulders, buttoned up to the chin in his overcoat. She was a handsome, calm girl, tall, with a beautiful repose. Her clothes were poor, and she wore a black silk scarf, having no furs. But she was a lady. As the people saw her walking down Aldecross beside Mr Massy, they said:

'My word, Miss Mary's got a catch. Did ever you see such a sickly little shrimp!'

She knew they were talking so, and it made her heart grow hot against them, and she drew herself as it were protectively towards the little man beside her. At any rate, she could see and give honour to his genuine goodness.

He could not walk fast, or far.

'You have not been well?' she asked, in her dignified way.

'I have an internal trouble.'

He was not aware of her slight shudder. There was silence, whilst she bowed to recover her composure, to resume her gentle manner towards him.

He was fond of Miss Mary. She had made it a rule of hospitality that he should always be escorted by herself or by her sister on his visits in the parish, which were not many. But some mornings she was engaged. Then Miss Louisa took her place. It was no good Miss Louisa's trying to adopt to Mr Massy an attitude of queenly service. She was unable to regard him save with aversion. When she saw him from behind, thin and bent-shouldered, looking like a sickly lad of thirteen, she disliked him exceedingly, and felt a desire to put him out of existence. And yet a deeper justice in Mary made Louisa humble before her sister.

They were going to see Mr Durant, who was paralysed and not expected to live. Miss Louisa was crudely ashamed at being admitted to the cottage in company with the little clergyman.

Mrs Durant was, however, much quieter in the face of her real trouble.

'How is Mr Durant?' asked Louisa.

'He is no different – and we don't expect him to be,' was the reply. The little clergyman stood looking on.

They went upstairs. The three stood for some time looking at the bed, at the grey head of the old man on the pillow, the grey beard over the sheet. Miss Louisa was shocked and afraid.

'It is so dreadful,' she said, with a shudder.

'It is how I always thought it would be,' replied Mrs Durant.

Then Miss Louisa was afraid of her. The two women were uneasy, waiting for Mr Massy to say something. He stood, small and bent, too nervous to speak.

'Has he any understanding?' he asked at length.

'Maybe,' said Mrs Durant. 'Can you hear, John?' she asked loudly. The dull blue eye of the inert man looked at her feebly.

'Yes, he understands,' said Mrs Durant to Mr Massy. Except for the dull look in his eyes, the sick man lay as if dead. The three stood in silence. Miss Louisa was obstinate but heavy-hearted under the load of unliving-ness. It was Mr Massy who kept her there in discipline. His non-human will dominated them all.

Then they heard a sound below, a man's footsteps, and a man's voice called subduedly:

'Are you upstairs, mother?'

Mrs Durant started and moved to the door. But already a quick, firm step was running up the stairs.

'I'm a bit early, mother,' a troubled voice said, and on the landing they saw the form of the sailor. His mother came and clung to him. She was suddenly aware that she needed something to hold on to. He put his arms round her, and bent over her, kissing her.

'He's not gone, mother?' he asked anxiously, struggling to control his voice.

Miss Louisa looked away from the mother and son who stood together in the gloom on the landing. She could not bear it that she and Mr Massy should be there. The latter stood nervously, as if ill at ease before the emotion that was running. He was a witness, nervous, unwilling, but dispassionate. To Miss Louisa's hot heart it seemed all, all wrong that they should be there.

Mrs Durant entered the bedroom, her face wet.

'There's Miss Louisa and the vicar,' she said, out of voice and quavering.

Her son, red-faced and slender, drew himself up to salute. But Miss Louisa held out her hand. Then she saw his hazel eyes recognize her for a moment, and his small white teeth showed in a glimpse of the greeting she used to love. She was covered with confusion. He went round to the bed; his boots clicked on the plaster floor, he bowed his head with dignity.

'How are you, dad?' he said, laying his hand on the sheet, faltering. But the old man stared fixedly and unseeing. The son stood perfectly still for a few minutes, then slowly recoiled. Miss Louisa saw the fine outline of his breast, under the sailor's blue blouse, as his chest began to heave.

'He doesn't know me,' he said, turning to his mother. He gradually went white.

'No, my boy!' cried the mother, pitiful, lifting her face. And suddenly she put her face against his shoulder, he was stooping down to her, holding her against him, and she cried aloud for a moment or two. Miss Louisa saw his sides heaving, and heard the sharp hiss of his breath. She turned away, tears streaming down her face. The father lay inert upon the white bed, Mr Massy looked queer and obliterated, so little now that the sailor with his sunburned skin was in the room. He stood waiting. Miss Louisa wanted to die, she wanted to have done. She dared not turn round again to look.

'Shall I offer a prayer?' came the frail voice of the clergyman, and all kneeled down.

Miss Louisa was frightened of the inert man upon the bed. Then she felt a flash of fear of Mr Massy, hearing his thin, detached voice. And then, calmed, she looked up. On the far side of the bed were the heads of the mother and son, the one in the black lace cap, with the small white nape of the neck beneath, the other, with brown, sun-scorched hair too close and wiry to allow of a parting, and neck tanned firm, bowed as if unwillingly. The great grey beard of the old man did not move, the prayer continued. Mr Massy prayed with a pure lucidity, that they all might conform to the higher Will. He was like something that dominated the bowed heads, something dispassionate that governed them inexorably. Miss Louisa was afraid of him. And she was bound, during the course of the prayer, to have a little reverence for him. It was like a foretaste of inexorable, cold death, a taste of pure justice.

That evening she talked to Mary of the visit. Her heart, her veins were possessed by the thought of Alfred Durant as he held his mother in his arms; then the break in his voice, as she remembered it again and again, was like a flame through her; and she wanted to see his face more distinctly in her mind, ruddy with the sun, and his golden-brown eyes, kind and careless, strained now with a natural fear, the fine nose tanned hard by the sun, the mouth that could not help smiling at her. And it went through her with pride, to think of his figure, a straight, fine jet of life.

'He is a handsome lad,' said she to Miss Mary, as if he had not been a year older than herself. Underneath was the deeper dread, almost hatred, of the inhuman being of Mr Massy. She felt she must protect herself and Alfred from him.

'When I felt Mr Massy there,' she said, 'I almost hated him. What right had he to be there!'

'Surely he has all right,' said Miss Mary after a pause. 'He is *really* a Christian.'

'He seems to me nearly an imbecile,' said Miss Louisa.

Miss Mary, quiet and beautiful, was silent for a moment:

'Oh, no,' she said. 'Not *imbecile*—'

'Well then – he reminds me of a six months' child – or a five months' child – as if he didn't have time to get developed enough before he was born.'

'Yes,' said Miss Mary, slowly. 'There is something lacking. But there is something wonderful in him: and he is really *good*—'

'Yes,' said Miss Louisa, 'it doesn't seem right that he should be. What right has *that* to be called goodness!'

'But it *is* goodness,' persisted Mary. Then she added, with a laugh: 'And come, you wouldn't deny that as well.'

There was a doggedness in her voice. She went about very quietly. In her soul, she knew what was going to happen. She knew that Mr Massy was stronger than she, and that she must submit to what he was. Her physical self was prouder, stronger than he, her physical self disliked and despised him. But she was in the grip of his moral, mental being. And she felt the days allotted out to her. And her family watched.

IV

A few days after, old Mr Durant died. Miss Louisa saw Alfred once more, but he was stiff before her now, treating her not like a person, but as if she were some sort of will in command and he a separate, distinct will waiting in front of her. She had never felt such utter steel-plate separation from anyone. It puzzled her and frightened her. What had become of him? And she hated the military discipline – she was antagonistic to it. Now he was not himself. He was the will which obeys set over against the will which commands. She hesitated over accepting this. He had put himself out of her range. He had ranked himself inferior, subordinate to her. And that was how he would get away from her, that was how he would avoid all connection with her: by fronting her impersonally from the opposite camp, by taking up the abstract position of an inferior.

She went brooding steadily and sullenly over this, brooding and brooding. Her fierce, obstinate heart could not give way. It clung to its own rights. Sometimes she dismissed him. Why should he, inferior, trouble her?

Then she relapsed to him, and almost hated him. It was his way of getting out of it. She felt the cowardice of it, his calmly placing her in a superior class, and placing himself inaccessibly apart, in an inferior, as if she, the sensient woman who was fond of him, did not count. But she was not going to submit. Dogged in her heart she held on to him.

V

In six months' time Miss Mary had married Mr Massy. There had been no love-making, nobody had made any remark. But everybody was tense and callous with expectation. When one day Mr Massy asked for Mary's hand, Mr Lindley started and trembled from the thin, abstract voice of the little man. Mr Massy was very nervous, but so curiously absolute.

'I shall be very glad,' said the vicar, 'but of course the decision lies with Mary herself.' And his still feeble hand shook as he moved a Bible on his desk.

The small man, keeping fixedly to his idea, padded out of the room to find Miss Mary. He sat a long time by her, while she made some conversation, before he had readiness to speak. She was afraid of what was coming, and sat stiff in apprehension. She felt as if her body would rise and fling him aside. But her spirit quivered and waited. Almost in expectation she waited, almost wanting him. And then she knew he would speak.

'I have already asked Mr Lindley,' said the clergyman, while suddenly she looked with aversion at his little knees, 'if he would consent to my proposal.' He was aware of his own disadvantage, but his will was set.

She went cold as she sat, and impervious, almost as if she had become stone. He waited a moment nervously. He would not persuade her. He himself never even heard persuasion, but pursued his own course. He looked at her, sure of himself, unsure of her, and said:

'Will you become my wife, Mary?'

Still her heart was hard and cold. She sat proudly.

'I should like to speak to mama first,' she said.

'Very well,' replied Mr Massy. And in a moment he padded away.

Mary went to her mother. She was cold and reserved.

'Mr Massy has asked me to marry him, mama,' she said. Mrs Lindley went on staring at her book. She was cramped in her feeling.

'Well, and what did you say?'

They were both keeping calm and cold.

'I said I would speak to you before answering him.'

This was equivalent to a question. Mrs Lindley did not want to reply to it. She shifted her heavy form irritably on the couch. Miss Mary sat calm and straight, with closed mouth.

'Your father thinks it would not be a bad match,' said the mother, as if casually.

Nothing more was said. Everybody remained cold and shut-off. Miss Mary did not speak to Miss Louisa, the Reverend Ernest Lindley kept out of sight.

At evening Miss Mary accepted Mr Massy.

'Yes, I will marry you,' she said, with even a little movement of tenderness towards him. He was embarrassed, but satisfied. She could see him making some movement towards her, could feel the male in him, something cold and triumphant, asserting itself. She sat rigid, and waited.

When Miss Louisa knew, she was silent with bitter anger against everybody, even against Mary. She felt her faith wounded. Did the real things to her not matter after all? She wanted to get away. She thought of Mr Massy. He had some curious power, some unanswerable right. He was a will that they could not controvert. – Suddenly a flush started in her. If he had come to her she would have flipped him out of the room.

He was never going to touch *her.* And she was glad. She was glad that her blood would rise and exterminate the little man, if he came too near to her, no matter how her judgment was paralysed by him, no matter how he moved in abstract goodness. She thought she was perverse to be glad, but glad she was. 'I would just flip him out of the room,' she said, and she derived great satisfaction from the open statement. Nevertheless, perhaps she ought still to feel that Mary, on her plane, was a higher being than herself. But then Mary was Mary, and she was Louisa, and that also was inalterable.

Mary, in marrying him, tried to become a pure reason such as he was, without feeling or impulse. She shut herself up, she shut herself rigid against the agonies of shame and the terror of violation which came at first. She *would* not feel, and she *would* not feel. She was a pure will acquiescing to him. She elected a certain kind of fate. She would be good and purely just, she would live in a higher freedom than she had ever known, she would be free of mundane care, she was a pure will towards right. She had sold herself, but she had a new freedom. She had got rid of her body. She had sold a lower thing, her body, for a higher thing, her freedom from material things. She considered that she paid for all she got from her husband. So, in a kind of independence, she moved proud and free. She had paid with her body: that was henceforward out of consideration. She was glad to be rid of it. She had bought her position in the world – that henceforth was taken for granted. There remained only the direction of her activity towards charity and high-minded living.

She could scarcely bear other people to be present with her and her husband. Her private life was her shame. But then, she could keep it hidden. She lived almost isolated in the rectory of the tiny village miles from the railway. She suffered as if it were an insult to her own flesh, seeing the repulsion which some people felt for her husband, or the special manner they had of treating him, as if he were a 'case'. But most people were uneasy before him, which restored her pride.

If she had let herself, she would have hated him, hated his padding round the house, his thin voice devoid of human understanding, his bent little shoulders and rather incomplete face that reminded her of an abortion. But rigorously she kept to her position. She took care of him and was just to him. There was also a deep craven fear of him, something slave-like.

There was not much fault to be found with his behaviour. He was scrupulously just and kind according to his lights. But the male in him was cold and self-complete, and utterly domineering. Weak, insufficient little thing as he was, she had not expected this of him. It was something in the bargain she had not understood. It made her hold her head, to keep still. She knew, vaguely, that she was murdering herself. After all, her body was not quite so easy to get rid of. And this manner of disposing of it – ah, sometimes she felt she must rise and bring about death, lift her hand for utter denial of everything, by a general destruction.

He was almost unaware of the conditions about him. He did not fuss in the domestic way, she did as she liked in the house. Indeed, she was a great deal free of him. He would sit obliterated for hours. He was kind, and almost anxiously considerate. But when he considered he was right, his will was just blindly male, like a cold machine. And on most points he was logically right, or he had with him the right of the creed they both accepted. It was so. There was nothing for her to go against.

Then she found herself with child, and felt for the first time horror, afraid before God and man. This also she had to go through – it was the right. When the child arrived, it was a bonny, healthy lad. Her heart hurt in her body, as she took the baby between her hands. The flesh that was trampled and silent in her must speak again in the boy. After all, she had to live – it was not so simple after all. Nothing was finished completely. She looked and looked at the baby, and almost hated it, and suffered an anguish of love for it. She hated it because it made her live again in the flesh, when she *could* not live in the flesh, she could not. She wanted to trample her flesh down, down, extinct, to live in the mind. And now there was this child. It was too cruel, too racking. For she must love the child. Her purpose was broken in two again. She had to become amorphous, purposeless, without real being. As a mother, she was a fragmentary, ignoble thing.

Mr Massy, blind to everything else in the way of human feeling, became obsessed by the idea of his child. When it arrived, suddenly it filled the whole world of feeling for him. It was his obsession, his terror was for its safety and well-being. It was something new, as if he himself had been born a naked infant, conscious of his own exposure, and full of apprehension. He who had never been aware of anyone else, all his life, now was aware of nothing but the child. Not that he ever played with it, or kissed it, or tended it. He did nothing for it. But it dominated him, it filled, and at the same time emptied his mind. The world was all baby for him.

This his wife must also bear, his question: 'What is the reason that he cries?' – his reminder, at the first sound: 'Mary, that is the child,' – his restlessness if the feeding-time were five minutes past. She had bargained for this – now she must stand by her bargain.

VI

Miss Louisa, at home in the dingy vicarage, had suffered a great deal over her sister's wedding. Having once begun to cry out against it, during the engagement, she had been silenced by Mary's quiet: 'I don't agree with you about him, Louisa, I *want* to marry him.' Then Miss Louisa had been angry deep in her heart, and therefore silent. This dangerous state started the change in her. Her own revulsion made her recoil from the hitherto undoubted Mary.

'I'd beg the streets barefoot first,' said Miss Louisa, thinking of Mr Massy.

But evidently Mary could perform a different heroism. So she, Louisa the practical, suddenly felt that Mary, her ideal, was questionable after all. How could she be pure – one cannot be dirty in act and spiritual in being. Louisa distrusted Mary's high spirituality. It was no longer genuine for her. And if Mary were spiritual and misguided, why did not her father protect her? Because of the money. He disliked the whole affair, but he backed away, because of the money. And the mother frankly did not care: her daughters could do as they liked. Her mother's pronouncement:

'Whatever happens to *him*, Mary is safe for life,' – so evidently and shallowly a calculation, incensed Louisa.

'I'd rather be safe in the workhouse,' she cried.

'Your father will see to that,' replied her mother brutally. This speech, in its indirectness, so injured Miss Louisa that she hated her mother deep, deep in her heart, and almost hated herself. It was a long time resolving itself out, this hate. But it worked and worked, and at last the young woman said:

'They are wrong – they are all wrong. They have ground out their souls for what isn't worth anything, and there isn't a grain of love in them anywhere. And I *will* have love. They want us to deny it. They've never found it, so they want to say it doesn't exist. But I *will* have it. I *will* love – it is my birthright. I will love the man I marry – that is all I care about.'

So Miss Louisa stood isolated from everybody. She and Mary had parted over Mr Massy. In Louisa's eyes, Mary was degraded, married to Mr Massy. She could not bear to think of her lofty, spiritual sister degraded in the body like this. Mary was wrong, wrong, wrong: she was not superior, she was flawed, incomplete. The two sisters stood apart. They still loved each other, they would love each other as long as they lived. But they had parted ways. A new solitariness came over the obstinate Louisa, and her heavy jaw set stubbornly. She was going on her own way. But which way? She was quite alone, with a blank world before her. How could she be said to have any way? Yet she had her fixed will to love, to have the man she loved.

VII

When her boy was three years old, Mary had another baby, a girl. The three years had gone by monotonously. They might have been an eternity, they might have been brief as a sleep. She did not know. Only, there was always a weight on top of her, something that pressed down her life. The only thing that had happened was that Mr Massy had had an operation. He was always exceedingly fragile. His wife had soon learned to attend to him mechanically, as part of her duty.

But this third year, after the baby girl had been born, Mary felt oppressed and depressed. Christmas drew near: the gloomy, unleavened Christmas of the rectory, where all the days were of the same dark fabric. And Mary was afraid. It was as if the darkness were coming upon her.

'Edward, I should like to go home for Christmas,' she said, and a certain terror filled her as she spoke.

'But you can't leave baby,' said her husband, blinking.

'We can all go.'

He thought, and stared in his collective fashion.

'Why do you wish to go?' he asked.

'Because I need a change. A change would do me good, and it would be good for the milk.'

He heard the will in his wife's voice, and was at a loss. Her language was unintelligible to him. And while she was breeding, either about to have a child, or nursing, he regarded her as a special sort of being.

'Wouldn't it hurt baby to take her by the train?' he said.

'No,' replied the mother, 'why should it?'

They went. When they were in the train, it began to snow. From the window of his first-class carriage the little clergyman watched the big flakes sweep by, like a blind drawn across the country. He was obsessed by thought of the baby, and afraid of the draughts of the carriage.

'Sit right in the corner,' he said to his wife, 'and hold baby close back.'

She moved at his bidding, and stared out of the window. His eternal presence was like an iron weight on her brain. But she was going partially to escape for a few days.

'Sit on the other side, Jack,' said the father. 'It is less draughty. Come to this window.'

He watched the boy in anxiety. But his children were the only beings in the world who took not the slightest notice of him.

'Look, mother, look!' cried the boy. 'They fly right in my face' – he meant the snowflakes.

'Come into this corner,' repeated his father, out of another world.

'He's jumped on this one's back, mother, an' they're riding to the bottom!' cried the boy, jumping with glee.

'Tell him to come on this side,' the little man bade his wife.

'Jack, kneel on this cushion,' said the mother, putting her white hand on the place.

The boy slid over in silence to the place she indicated, waited still for a moment, then almost deliberately, stridently cried:

'Look at all those in the corner, mother, making a heap,' and he pointed to the cluster of snowflakes with finger pressed dramatically on the pane, and he turned to his mother a bit ostentatiously.

'All in a heap!' she said.

He had seen her face, and had her response, and he was somewhat assured. Vaguely uneasy, he was reassured if he could win her attention.

They arrived at the vicarage at half-past two, not having had lunch.

'How are you, Edward?' said Mr Lindley, trying on his side to be fatherly. But he was always in a false position with his son-in-law, frustrated before him, therefore, as much as possible, he shut his eyes and ears to him. The vicar was looking thin and pale and ill-nourished. He had gone quite grey. He was, however, still haughty; but, since the growing-up of his children, it was a brittle haughtiness, that might break at any moment and leave the vicar only an impoverished, pitiable figure. Mrs Lindley took all the notice of her daughter, and of the children. She ignored her son-in-law. Miss Louisa was clucking and laughing and rejoicing over the baby. Mr Massy stood aside, a bent, persistent little figure.

'Oh a pretty! – a little pretty! oh a cold little pretty come in a railway-train!' Miss Louisa was cooing to the infant, crouching on the hearthrug opening the white woollen wraps and exposing the child to the fireglow.

'Mary,' said the little clergyman, 'I think it would be better to give baby a warm bath; she may take a cold.'

'I think it is not necessary,' said the mother, coming and closing her hand judiciously over the rosy feet and hands of the mite. 'She is not chilly.'

'Not a bit,' cried Miss Louisa. 'She's not caught cold.'

'I'll go and bring her flannels,' said Mr Massy, with one idea.

'I can bath her in the kitchen then,' said Mary, in an altered, cold tone.

'You can't, the girl is scrubbing there,' said Miss Louisa. 'Besides, she doesn't want a bath at this time of day.'

'She'd better have one,' said Mary, quietly, out of submission. Miss Louisa's gorge rose, and she was silent. When the little man padded down with the flannels on his arm, Mrs Lindley asked:

'Hadn't *you* better take a hot bath, Edward?'

But the sarcasm was lost on the little clergyman. He was absorbed in the preparations round the baby.

The room was dull and threadbare, and the snow outside seemed fairy-like by comparison, so white on the lawn and tufted on the bushes. Indoors the heavy pictures hung obscurely on the walls, everything was dingy with gloom.

Except in the fireglow, where they had laid the bath on the hearth.

Mrs Massy, her black hair always smoothly coiled and queenly, kneeled by the bath, wearing a rubber apron, and holding the kicking child. Her husband stood holding the towels and the flannels to warm. Louisa, too cross to share in the joy of the baby's bath, was laying the table. The boy was hanging on the door-knob, wrestling with it to get out. His father looked round.

'Come away from the door, Jack,' he said, ineffectually. Jack tugged harder at the knob as if he did not hear. Mr Massy blinked at him.

'He must come away from the door, Mary,' he said. 'There will be a draught if it is opened.'

'Jack, come away from the door, dear,' said the mother, dexterously turning the shiny wet baby on to her towelled knee, then glancing round: 'Go and tell Auntie Louisa about the train.'

Louisa, also afraid to open the door, was watching the scene on the hearth. Mr Massy stood holding the baby's flannel, as if assisting at some ceremonial. If everybody had not been subduedly angry, it would have been ridiculous.

'I want to see out of the window,' Jack said. His father turned hastily.

'Do *you* mind lifting him on to a chair, Louisa,' said Mary hastily. The father was too delicate.

When the baby was flannelled, Mr Massy went upstairs and returned with four pillows, which he set in the fender to warm. Then he stood watching the mother feed her child, obsessed by the idea of his infant.

Louisa went on with her preparations for the meal. She could not have told why she was so sullenly angry. Mrs Lindley, as usual, lay silently watching.

Mary carried her child upstairs, followed by her husband with the pillows. After a while he came down again.

'What is Mary doing? Why doesn't she come down to eat?' asked Mrs Lindley.

'She is staying with baby. The room is rather cold. I will ask the girl to put in a fire.' He was going absorbedly to the door.

'But Mary has had nothing to eat. It is *she* who will catch cold,' said the mother, exasperated.

Mr Massy seemed as if he did not hear. Yet he looked at his mother-in-law, and answered:

'I will take her something.'

He went out. Mrs Lindley shifted on her couch with anger. Miss Louisa glowered. But no one said anything, because of the money that came to the vicarage from Mr Massy.

Louisa went upstairs. Her sister was sitting by the bed, reading a scrap of paper.

'Won't you come down and eat?' the younger asked.

'In a moment or two,' Mary replied, in a quiet, reserved voice, that forbade anyone to approach her.

It was this that made Miss Louisa most furious. She went downstairs, and announced to her mother:

'I am going out. I may not be home to tea.'

VIII

No one remarked on her exit. She put on her fur hat, that the village people knew so well, and the old Norfolk jacket. Louisa was short and plump and plain. She had her mother's heavy jaw, her father's proud brow, and her own grey, brooding eyes that were very beautiful when she smiled. It was true, as the people said, that she looked sulky. Her chief attraction was her glistening, heavy, deep-blonde hair, which shone and gleamed with a richness that was not entirely foreign to her.

'Where am I going?' she said to herself, when she got outside in the snow. She did not hesitate, however, but by mechanical walking found herself descending the hill towards Old Aldecross. In the valley that was black with trees, the colliery breathed in stertorous pants, sending out high conical columns of steam that remained upright, whiter than the snow on the hills, yet shadowy, in the dead air. Louisa would not acknowledge to herself whither she was making her way, till she came to the railway crossing. Then the bunches of snow in the twigs of the apple tree that leaned towards the fence told her she must go and see Mrs Durant. The tree was in Mrs Durant's garden.

Alfred was now at home again, living with his mother in the cottage below the road. From the highway hedge, by the railway crossing, the snowy garden sheered down steeply, like the side of a hole, then dropped straight in a wall. In this depth the house was snug, its chimney just level with the road. Miss Louisa descended the stone stairs, and stood below in the little backyard, in the dimness and the semi-secrecy. A big tree leaned overhead, above the paraffin hut. Louisa felt secure from all the world down there. She knocked at the open door, then looked round. The tongue of garden narrowing in from the quarry bed was white with snow: she thought of the thick fringes of snowdrops it would show beneath the currant bushes in a month's time. The ragged fringe of pinks hanging over the garden brim behind her was whitened now with snow-flakes, that in summer held white blossom to Louisa's face. It was pleasant, she thought, to gather flowers that stooped to one's face from above.

She knocked again. Peeping in, she saw the scarlet glow of the kitchen, red firelight falling on the brick floor and on the bright chintz cushions. It was alive and bright as a peep-show. She crossed the scullery, where still an almanac hung. There was no one about. 'Mrs Durant,' called Louisa softly, 'Mrs Durant.'

She went up the brick step into the front room, that still had its little shop counter and its bundles of goods, and she called from the stair-foot. Then she knew Mrs Durant was out.

She went into the yard to follow the old woman's footsteps up the garden path.

She emerged from the bushes and raspberry canes. There was the whole quarry bed, a wide garden white and dimmed, brindled with dark bushes, lying half submerged. On the left, overhead, the little colliery train rumbled by. Right away at the back was a mass of trees.

Louisa followed the open path, looking from right to left, and then she gave a cry of concern. The old woman was sitting rocking slightly among the ragged snowy cabbages. Louisa ran to her, found her whimpering with little, involuntary cries.

'Whatever have you done?' cried Louisa, kneeling in the snow.

'I've – I've – I was pulling a brussel-sprout stalk – and – oh-h! – something tore inside me. I've had a pain,' the old woman wept from shock and suffering, gasping between her whimpers, – 'I've had a pain there – a long time – and now – oh – oh!' She panted, pressed her hand on her side, leaned as if she would faint, looking yellow against the snow. Louisa supported her.

'Do you think you could walk now?' she asked.

'Yes,' gasped the old woman.

Louisa helped her to her feet.

'Get the cabbage – I want it for Alfred's dinner,' panted Mrs Durant. Louisa picked up the stalk of brussel-sprouts, and with difficulty got the old woman indoors. She gave her brandy, laid her on the couch, saying:

'I'm going to send for a doctor – wait just a minute.'

The young woman ran up the steps to the public-house a few yards away. The landlady was astonished to see Miss Louisa.

'Will you send for a doctor at once to Mrs Durant,' she said, with some of her father in her commanding tone.

'Is something the matter?' fluttered the landlady in concern.

Louisa, glancing out up the road, saw the grocer's cart driving to East-wood. She ran and stopped the man, and told him.

Mrs Durant lay on the sofa, her face turned away, when the young woman came back.

'Let me put you to bed,' Louisa said. Mrs Durant did not resist.

Louisa knew the ways of the working people. In the bottom drawer of the dresser she found dusters and flannels. With the old pit-flannel she snatched out the oven shelves, wrapped them up, and put them in the bed. From the son's bed she took a blanket, and, running down, set it before the fire. Having undressed the little old woman, Louisa carried her upstairs.

'You'll drop me, you'll drop me!' cried Mrs Durant.

Louisa did not answer, but bore her burden quickly. She could not light a fire, because there was no fire-place in the bedroom. And the floor was plaster. So she fetched the lamp, and stood it lighted in one corner.

'It will air the room,' she said.

'Yes,' moaned the old woman.

Louisa ran with more hot flannels, replacing those from the oven shelves. Then she made a bran-bag and laid it on the woman's side. There was a big lump on the side of the abdomen.

'I've felt it coming a long time,' moaned the old lady, when the pain was easier, 'but I've not said anything; I didn't want to upset our Alfred.'

Louisa did not see why 'our Alfred' should be spared.

'What time is it?' came the plaintive voice.

'A quarter to four.'

'Oh!' wailed the old lady, 'he'll be here in half an hour, and no dinner ready for him.'

'Let me do it?' said Louisa, gently.

'There's that cabbage – and you'll find the meat in the pantry – and there's an apple pie you can hot up. But *don't you* do it—!'

'Who will, then?' asked Louisa.

'I don't know,' moaned the sick woman, unable to consider.

Louisa did it. The doctor came and gave serious examination. He looked very grave.

'What is it, doctor?' asked the old lady, looking up at him with old, pathetic eyes in which already hope was dead.

'I think you've torn the skin in which a tumour hangs,' he replied.

'Ay!' she murmured, and she turned away.

'You see, she may die any minute – and it *may* be swaled away,' said the old doctor to Louisa.

The young woman went upstairs again.

'He says the lump may be swaled away, and you may get quite well again,' she said.

'Ay!' murmured the old lady. It did not deceive her. Presently she asked:

'Is there a good fire?'

'I think so,' answered Louisa.

'He'll want a good fire,' the mother said. Louisa attended to it.

Since the death of Durant, the widow had come to church occasionally, and Louisa had been friendly to her. In the girl's heart the purpose was fixed. No man had affected her as Alfred Durant had done, and to that she kept. In her heart, she adhered to him. A natural sympathy existed between her and his rather hard, materialistic mother.

Alfred was the most lovable of the old woman's sons. He had grown up like the rest, however, headstrong and blind to everything but his own will. Like the other boys, he had insisted on going into the pit as soon as he left school, because that was the only way speedily to become a man, level with all the other men. This was a great chagrin to his mother, who would have liked to have this last of her sons a gentleman.

But still he remained constant to her. His feeling for her was deep and unexpressed. He noticed when she was tired, or when she had a new cap.

And he bought little things for her occasionally. She was not wise enough to see how much he lived by her.

At the bottom he did not satisfy her, he did not seem manly enough. He liked to read books occasionally, and better still he liked to play the piccolo. It amused her to see his head nod over the instrument as he made an effort to get the right note. It made her fond of him, with tenderness, almost pity, but not with respect. She wanted a man to be fixed, going his own way without knowledge of women. Whereas she knew Alfred depended on her. He sang in the choir because he liked singing. In the summer he worked in the garden, attended to the fowls and pigs. He kept pigeons. He played on Saturday in the cricket or football team. But to her he did not seem the man, the independent man her other boys had been. He was her baby – and whilst she loved him for it, she was a little bit contemptuous of him.

There grew up a little hostility between them. Then he began to drink, as the others had done; but not in their blind, oblivious way. He was a little self-conscious over it. She saw this, and she pitied it in him. She loved him most, but she was not satisfied with him because he was not free of her. He could not quite go his own way.

Then at twenty he ran away and served his time in the Navy. This made a man of him. He had hated it bitterly, the service, the subordination. For years he fought with himself under the military discipline, for his own self-respect, struggling through blind anger and shame and a cramping sense of inferiority. Out of humiliation and self-hatred, he rose into a sort of inner freedom. And his love for his mother, whom he idealised, remained the fact of hope and of belief.

He came home again, nearly thirty years old, but naïve and inexperienced as a boy, only with a silence about him that was new: a sort of dumb humility before life, a fear of living. He was almost quite chaste. A strong sensitiveness had kept him from women. Sexual talk was all very well among men, but somehow it had no application to living women. There were two things for him, the *idea* of women, with which he sometimes debauched himself, and real women, before whom he felt a deep uneasiness, and a need to draw away. He shrank and defended himself from the approach of any woman. And then he felt ashamed. In his innermost soul he felt he was not a man, he was less than the normal man. In Genoa he went with an under officer to a drinking house where the cheaper sort of girl came in to look for lovers. He sat there with his glass, the girls looked at him, but they never came to him. He knew that if they did come he could only pay for food and drink for them, because he felt a pity for them, and was anxious lest they lacked good necessities. He could not have gone with one of them: he knew it, and was ashamed, looking with curious envy at the swaggering, easy-passionate Italian whose body went to a woman by instinctive impersonal attraction. They were men, he was not a man. He sat feeling short, feeling like a leper. And he went away imagining sexual scenes between himself and a woman, walking wrapt in this indulgence. But when the ready woman presented herself, the very fact that she was a palpable woman made it impossible for him to touch her. And this incapacity was like a core of rottenness in him.

So several times he went, drunk, with his companions, to the licensed prostitute houses abroad. But the sordid insignificance of the experience appalled him. It had not been anything really: it meant nothing. He felt as if he were, not physically, but spiritually impotent: not actually impotent, but intrinsically so.

He came home with this secret, never changing burden of his unknown, unbestowed self torturing him. His navy training left him in perfect physical condition. He was sensible of, and proud of his body. He bathed and used dumb-bells, and kept himself fit. He played cricket and football. He read books and began to hold fixed ideas which he got from the Fabians. He played his piccolo, and was considered an expert. But at the bottom of his soul was always this canker of shame and incompleteness: he was miserable beneath all his healthy cheerfulness, he was uneasy and felt despicable among all his confidence and superiority of ideas. He would have changed with any mere brute, just to be free of himself, to be free of this shame of self-consciousness. He saw some collier lurching straight forward without misgiving, pursuing his own satisfactions, and he envied him. Anything, he would have given anything for this spontaneity and this blind stupidity which went to its own satisfaction direct.

IX

He was not unhappy in the pit. He was admired by the men, and well enough liked. It was only he himself who felt the difference between himself and the others. He seemed to hide his own stigma. But he was never sure that the others did not really despise him for a ninny, as being less a man than they were. Only he pretended to be more manly, and was surprised by the ease with which they were deceived. And, being naturally cheerful, he was happy at his work. He was sure of himself there. Naked to the waist, hot and grimy with labour, they squatted on their heels for a few minutes and talked, seeing each other dimly by the light of the safety lamps, while the black coal rose jutting round them, and the props of wood stood like little pillars in the low, black, very dark temple. Then the pony came and the gang-lad with a message from Number 7, or with a bottle of water from the horse-trough or some news of the world above. The day passed pleasantly enough. There was an ease, a go-as-you-please about the day underground, a delightful camaraderie of men shut off alone from the rest of the world, in a dangerous place, and a variety of labour, holing, loading, timbering, and a glamour of mystery and adventure in the atmosphere, that made the pit not unattractive to him when he had again got over his anguish of desire for the open air and the sea.

This day there was much to do and Durant was not in humour to talk. He went on working in silence through the afternoon.

'Loose-all' came, and they tramped to the bottom. The whitewashed underground office shone brightly. Men were putting out their lamps. They sat in dozens round the bottom of the shaft, down which black, heavy drops of water fell continuously into the sump. The electric lights shone away down the main underground road.

'Is it raining?' asked Durant.

'Snowing,' said an old man, and the younger was pleased. He liked to go up when it was snowing.

'It'll just come right for Christmas,' said the old man.

'Ay,' replied Durant.

'A green Christmas, a fat churchyard,' said the other sententiously.

Durant laughed, showing his small, rather pointed teeth.

The cage came down, a dozen men lined on. Durant noticed tufts of snow on the perforated, arched roof of the chain, and he was pleased. He wondered how it liked its excursion underground. But already it was getting soppy with black water.

He liked things about him. There was a little smile on his face. But underlying it was the curious consciousness he felt in himself.

The upper world came almost with a flash, because of the glimmer of snow. Hurrying along the bank, giving up his lamp at the office, he smiled to feel the open about him again, all glimmering round him with snow. The hills on either side were pale blue in the dusk, and the hedges looked savage and dark. The snow was trampled between the railway lines. But far ahead, beyond the black figures of miners moving home, it became smooth again, spreading right up to the dark wall of the coppice.

To the west there was a pinkness, and a big star hovered half revealed. Below, the lights of the pit came out crisp and yellow among the darkness of the buildings, and the lights of Old Aldecross twinkled in rows down the bluish twilight.

Durant walked glad with life among the miners, who were all talking animatedly because of the snow. He liked their company, he liked the white dusky world. It gave him a little thrill to stop at the garden gate and see the light of home down below, shining on the silent blue snow.

X

By the big gate of the railway, in the fence, was a little gate, that he kept locked. As he unfastened it, he watched the kitchen light that shone on to the bushes and the snow outside. It was a candle burning till night set in, he thought to himself. He slid down the steep path to the level below. He liked making the first marks in the smooth snow. Then he came through the bushes to the house. The two women heard his heavy boots ring outside on the scraper, and his voice as he opened the door:

'How much worth of oil do you reckon to save by that candle, mother?' He liked a good light from the lamp.

He had just put down his bottle and snap-bag and was hanging his coat behind the scullery door, when Miss Louisa came upon him. He was startled, but he smiled.

His eyes began to laugh – then his face went suddenly straight, and he was afraid.

'Your mother's had an accident,' she said.

'How?' he exclaimed.

'In the garden,' she answered. He hesitated with his coat in his hands. Then he hung it up and turned to the kitchen.

'Is she in bed?' he asked.

'Yes,' said Miss Louisa, who found it hard to deceive him. He was silent. He went into the kitchen, sat down heavily in his father's old chair, and began to pull off his boots. His head was small, rather finely shapen. His brown hair, close and crisp, would look jolly whatever happened. He wore heavy moleskin trousers that gave off the stale, exhausted scent of the pit. Having put on his slippers, he carried his boots into the scullery.

'What is it?' he asked, afraid.

'Something internal,' she replied.

He went upstairs. His mother kept herself calm for his coming. Louisa felt his tread shake the plaster floor of the bedroom above.

'What have you done?' he asked.

'It's nothing, my lad,' said the old woman, rather hard. 'It's nothing. You needn't fret, my boy, it's nothing more the matter with me than I had yesterday, or last week. The doctor said I'd done nothing serious.'

'What were you doing?' asked her son.

'I was pulling up a cabbage, and I suppose I pulled too hard; for, oh – there was such a pain—'

Her son looked at her quickly. She hardened herself.

'But who doesn't have a sudden pain sometimes, my boy. We all do.'

'And what's it done?'

'I don't know,' she said, 'but I don't suppose it's anything.'

The big lamp in the corner was screened with a dark green screen, so that he could scarcely see her face. He was strung tight with apprehension and many emotions. Then his brow knitted.

'What did you go pulling your inside out at cabbages for,' he asked, 'and the ground frozen? You'd go on dragging and dragging, if you killed yourself.'

'Somebody's got to get them,' she said.

'You needn't do yourself harm.'

But they had reached futility.

Miss Louisa could hear plainly downstairs. Her heart sank. It seemed so hopeless between them.

'Are you sure it's nothing much, mother?' he asked, appealing, after a little silence.

'Ay, it's nothing,' said the old woman, rather bitter.

'I don't want you to – to – to be badly – you know.'

'Go an' get your dinner,' she said. She knew she was going to die: moreover, the pain was torture just then. 'They're only cosseting me up a bit because I'm an old woman. Miss Louisa's *very* good – and she'll have got your dinner ready, so you'd better go and eat it.'

He felt stupid and ashamed. His mother put him off. He had to turn away. The pain burned in his bowels. He went downstairs. The mother was glad he was gone, so that she could moan with pain.

He had resumed the old habit of eating before he washed himself. Miss Louisa served his dinner. It was strange and exciting to her. She was strung up tense, trying to understand him and his mother. She watched him as he sat. He was turned away from his food, looking in the fire. Her soul watched him, trying to see what he was. His black face and arms were uncouth, he was foreign. His face was masked black with coal-dust. She could not see him, she could not even know him. The brown eyebrows, the steady eyes, the coarse, small moustache above the closed mouth – these were the only familiar indications. What was he, as he sat there in his pit-dirt? She could not see him, and it hurt her.

She ran upstairs, presently coming down with the flannels and the bran-bag, to heat them, because the pain was on again.

He was half-way through his dinner. He put down the fork, suddenly nauseated.

'They will soothe the wrench,' she said. He watched, useless and left out.

'Is she bad?' he asked.

'I think she is,' she answered.

It was useless for him to stir or comment. Louisa was busy. She went upstairs. The poor old woman was in a white, cold sweat of pain. Louisa's face was sullen with suffering as she went about to relieve her. Then she sat and waited. The pain passed gradually, the old woman sank into a state of coma. Louisa still sat silent by the bed. She heard the sound of water downstairs. Then came the voice of the old mother, faint but unrelaxing:

'Alfred's washing himself – he'll want his back washing—'

Louisa listened anxiously, wondering what the sick woman wanted.

'He can't bear if his back isn't washed—' the old woman persisted, in a cruel attention to his needs. Louisa rose and wiped the sweat from the yellowish brow.

'I will go down,' she said soothingly.

'If you would,' murmured the sick woman.

Louisa waited a moment. Mrs Durant closed her eyes, having discharged her duty. The young woman went downstairs. Herself, or the man, what did they matter? Only the suffering woman must be considered.

Alfred was kneeling on the hearthrug, stripped to the waist, washing himself in a large panchion of earthenware. He did so every evening, when he had eaten his dinner; his brothers had done so before him. But Miss Louisa was strange in the house.

He was mechanically rubbing the white lather on his head, with a repeated, unconscious movement, his hand every now and then passing over his neck. Louisa watched. She had to brace herself to this also. He bent his head into the water, washed it free of soap, and pressed the water out of his eyes.

'Your mother said you would want your back washing,' she said.

Curious how it hurt her to take part in their fixed routine of life! Louisa felt the almost repulsive intimacy being forced upon her. It was all so common, so like herding. She lost her own distinctness.

He ducked his face round, looking up at her in what was a very comical way. She had to harden herself.

'How funny he looks with his face upside down,' she thought. After all, there was a difference between her and the common people. The water in which his arms were plunged was quite black, the soap-froth was darkish. She could scarcely conceive him as human. Mechanically, under the influence of habit, he groped in the black water, fished out soap and flannel, and handed them backward to Louisa. Then he remained rigid and submissive, his two arms thrust straight in the panchion, supporting the weight of his shoulders. His skin was beautifully white and unblemished, of an opaque, solid whiteness. Gradually Louisa saw it: this also was what he was. It fascinated her. Her feeling of separateness passed away: she ceased to draw back from contact with him and his mother. There was this living centre. Her heart ran hot. She had reached some goal in this beautiful, clear, male body. She loved him in a white, impersonal heat. But the sun-burnt, reddish neck and ears: they were more personal, more curious. A tenderness rose in her, she loved even his queer ears. A person – an intimate being he was to her. She put down the towel and went upstairs again, troubled in her heart. She had only seen one human being in her life – and that was Mary. All the rest were strangers. Now her soul was going to open, she was going to see another. She felt strange and pregnant.

'He'll be more comfortable,' murmured the sick woman abstractedly, as Louisa entered the room. The latter did not answer. Her own heart was heavy with its own responsibility. Mrs Durant lay silent awhile, then she murmured plaintively:

'You mustn't mind, Miss Louisa.'

'Why should I?' replied Louisa, deeply moved.

'It's what we're used to,' said the old woman.

And Louisa felt herself excluded again from their life. She sat in pain, with the tears of disappointment distilling her heart. Was that all?

Alfred came upstairs. He was clean, and in his shirt-sleeves. He looked a workman now. Louisa felt that she and he were foreigners, moving in different lives. It dulled her again. Oh, if she could only find some fixed relations, something sure and abiding.

'How do you feel?' he said to his mother.

'It's a bit better,' she replied wearily, impersonally. This strange putting herself aside, this abstracting herself and answering him only what she thought good for him to hear, made the relations between mother and son poignant and cramping to Miss Louisa. It made the man so ineffectual, so nothing. Louisa groped as if she had lost him. The mother was real and positive – he was not very actual. It puzzled and chilled the young woman.

'I'd better fetch Mrs Harrison?' he said, waiting for his mother to decide.

'I suppose we shall have to have somebody,' she replied.

Miss Louisa stood by, afraid to interfere in their business. They did not include her in their lives, they felt she had nothing to do with them, except as a help from outside. She was quite external to them. She felt hurt and powerless against this unconscious difference. But something patient and unyielding in her made her say:

'I will stay and do the nursing: you can't be left.'

The other two were shy, and at a loss for an answer.

'Wes'll manage to get somebody,' said the old woman wearily. She did not care very much what happened, now.

'I will stay until tomorrow, in any case,' said Louisa. 'Then we can see.'

'I'm sure you've no right to trouble yourself,' moaned the old woman. But she must leave herself in any hands.

Miss Louisa felt glad that she was admitted, even in an official capacity. She wanted to share their lives. At home they would need her, now Mary had come. But they must manage without her.

'I must write a note to the vicarage,' she said.

Alfred Durant looked at her inquiringly, for her service. He had always that intelligent readiness to serve, since he had been in the Navy. But there was a simple independence in his willingness, which she loved. She felt nevertheless it was hard to get at him. He was so deferential, quick to take the slightest suggestion of an order from her, implicitly, that she could not get at the man in him.

He looked at her very keenly. She noticed his eyes were golden brown, with a very small pupil, the kind of eyes that can see a long way off. He stood alert, at military attention. His face was still rather weather-reddened.

'Do you want pen and paper?' he asked, with deferential suggestion to a superior, which was more difficult for her than reserve.

'Yes, please,' she said.

He turned and went downstairs. He seemed to her so self-contained, so utterly sure in his movement. How was she to approach him? For he would take not one step towards her. He would only put himself entirely and impersonally at her service, glad to serve her, but keeping himself quite removed from her. She could see he felt real joy in doing anything for her, but any recognition would confuse him and hurt him. Strange it was to her, to have a man going about the house in his shirt-sleeves, his waistcoat unbuttoned, his throat bare, waiting on her. He moved well, as if he had plenty of life to spare. She was attracted by his completeness. And yet, when all was ready, and there was nothing more for him to do, she quivered, meeting his questioning look.

As she sat writing, he placed another candle near her. The rather dense light fell in two places on the overfoldings of her hair till it glistened heavy and bright, like a dense golden plumage folded up. Then the nape of her neck was very white, with fine down and pointed wisps of gold. He watched it as it were a vision, losing himself. She was all that was beyond him, of revelation and exquisiteness. All that was ideal and beyond him, she was that – and he was lost to himself in looking at her. She had no connection with him. He did not approach her. She was there like a wonderful distance. But it was a treat, having her in the house. Even with this anguish for his mother tightening about him, he was sensible of the wonder of living this evening. The candles glistened on her hair, and seemed to fascinate him. He felt a little awe of her, and a sense of uplifting, that he and she and his mother should be together for a time, in the strange, unknown atmosphere. And, when he got out of the house, he was afraid. He saw the stars above ringing with fine brightness, the snow beneath just visible, and a new night was gathering round him. He was afraid almost with obliteration. What was this new night ringing about him, and what was he? He could not recognize himself nor any of his surroundings. He was afraid to think of his mother. And yet his chest was conscious of her, and of what was happening to her. He could not escape from her, she carried him with her into an unformed, unknown chaos.

XI

He went up the road in an agony, not knowing what it was all about, but feeling as if a red-hot iron were gripped round his chest. Without thinking, he shook two or three tears on to the snow. Yet in his mind he did not believe his mother would die. He was in the grip of some greater consciousness. As he sat in the hall of the vicarage, waiting whilst Mary put things for Louisa into a bag, he wondered why he had been so upset. He felt abashed and humbled by the big house, he felt again as if he were one of the rank and file. When Miss Mary spoke to him, he almost saluted.

'An honest man,' thought Mary. And the patronage was applied as salve to her own sickness. She had station, so she could patronize: it was almost all that was left to her. But she could not have lived without having a certain position. She could never have trusted herself outside a definite place, nor respected herself except as a woman of superior class.

As Alfred came to the latch-gate, he felt the grief at his heart again, and saw the new heavens. He stood a moment looking northward to the Plough climbing up the night, and at the far glimmer of snow in distant fields. Then his grief came on like physical pain. He held tight to the gate, biting his mouth, whispering 'Mother!' It was a fierce, cutting, physical pain of grief, that came on in bouts, as his mother's pain came on in bouts, and was so acute he could scarcely keep erect. He did not know where it came from, the pain, nor why. It had nothing to do with his thoughts. Almost it had nothing to do with him. Only it gripped him and he must submit. The whole tide of his soul, gathering in its unknown towards this expansion into death, carried him with it helplessly, all the fritter of his thought and consciousness caught up as nothing, the heave passing on towards its breaking, taking him further than he had ever been. When the young man had regained himself, he went indoors, and there he was almost gay. It seemed to excite him. He felt in high spirits: he made whimsical fun of things. He sat on one side of his mother's bed, Louisa on the other, and a certain gaiety seized them all. But the night and the dread was coming on.

Alfred kissed his mother and went to bed. When he was half undressed the knowledge of his mother came upon him, and the suffering seized him in its grip like two hands, in agony. He lay on the bed screwed up tight. It lasted so long, and exhausted him so much, that he fell asleep, without having the energy to get up and finish undressing. He awoke after midnight to find himself stone cold. He undressed and got into bed, and was soon asleep again.

At a quarter to six he woke, and instantly remembered. Having pulled on his trousers and lighted a candle, he went into his mother's room. He put his hand before the candle flame so that no light fell on the bed.

'Mother!' he whispered.

'Yes,' was the reply.

There was a hesitation.

'Should I go to work?'

He waited, his heart was beating heavily.

'I think I'd go, my lad.'

His heart went down in a kind of despair.

'You want me to?'

He let his hand down from the candle flame. The light fell on the bed. There he saw Louisa lying looking up at him. Her eyes were upon him. She quickly shut her eyes and half buried her face in the pillow, her back turned to him. He saw the rough hair like bright vapour about her round head, and the two plaits flung coiled among the bedclothes. It gave him a shock. He stood almost himself, determined. Louisa cowered down. He looked, and met his mother's eyes. Then he gave way again, and ceased to be sure, ceased to be himself.

'Yes, go to work, my boy,' said the mother.

'All right,' replied he, kissing her. His heart was down at despair, and bitter. He went away.

'Alfred!' cried his mother faintly.

He came back with beating heart.

'What, mother?'

'You'll always do what's right, Alfred?' the mother asked, beside herself in terror now he was leaving her. He was too terrified and bewildered to know what she meant.

'Yes,' he said.

She turned her cheek to him. He kissed her, then went away, in bitter despair. He went to work.

XII

By midday his mother was dead. The word met him at the pit-mouth. As he had known, inwardly, it was not a shock to him, and yet he trembled. He went home quite calmly, feeling only heavy in his breathing.

Miss Louisa was still at the house. She had seen to everything possible.

Very succinctly, she informed him of what he needed to know. But there was one point of anxiety for her.

'You *did* half expect it – it's not come as a blow to you?' she asked, looking up at him. Her eyes were dark and calm and searching. She too felt lost. He was so dark and inchoate.

'I suppose – yes,' he said stupidly. He looked aside, unable to endure her eyes on him.

'I could not bear to think you might not have guessed,' she said.

He did not answer.

He felt it a great strain to have her near him at this time. He wanted to be alone. As soon as the relatives began to arrive, Louisa departed and came no more. While everything was arranging, and a crowd was in the house, whilst he had business to settle, he went well enough, with only those uncontrollable paroxysms of grief. For the rest, he was superficial. By himself, he endured the fierce, almost insane bursts of grief which passed again and left him calm, almost clear, just wondering. He had not known before that everything could break down, that he himself could break down, and all be a great chaos, very vast and wonderful. It seemed as if life in him had burst its bounds, and he was lost in a great, bewildering flood, immense and unpeopled. He himself was broken and spilled out amid it all. He could only breathe panting in silence. Then the anguish came on again.

When all the people had gone from the Quarry Cottage, leaving the young man alone with an elderly housekeeper, then the long trial began. The snow had thawed and frozen, a fresh fall had whitened the grey, this then began to thaw. The world was a place of loose grey slosh. Alfred had nothing to do in the evenings. He was a man whose life had been filled up with small activities. Without knowing it, he had been centralized, polarized in his mother. It was she who had kept him. Even now, when the old housekeeper had left him, he might still have gone on in his old way. But the force and balance of his life was lacking. He sat pretending to read, all the time holding his fists clenched, and holding himself in, enduring he did not know what. He walked the black and sodden miles of field-paths, till he was tired out: but all this was only running away from whence he must return. At work he was all right. If it had been summer he might have escaped by working in the garden till bedtime. But now, there was no escape, no relief, no help. He, perhaps, was made for action rather than for understanding; for doing than for being. He was shocked out of his activities, like a swimmer who forgets to swim.

For a week, he had the force to endure this suffocation and struggle, then he began to get exhausted, and knew it must come out. The instinct of self-preservation became strongest. But there was the question: Where was he to go? The public-house really meant nothing to him, it was no good going there. He began to think of emigration. In another country he would be all right. He wrote to the emigration offices.

On the Sunday after the funeral, when all the Durant people had attended church, Alfred had seen Miss Louisa, impassive and reserved, sitting with Miss Mary, who was proud and very distant, and with the other Lindleys, who were people removed. Alfred saw them as people remote. He did not think about it. They had nothing to do with his life. After service Louisa had come to him and shaken hands.

'My sister would like you to come to supper one evening, if you would be so good.'

He looked at Miss Mary, who bowed. Out of kindness, Mary had proposed this to Louisa, disapproving of herself even as she did so. But she did not examine herself closely.

'Yes,' said Durant awkwardly, 'I'll come if you want me.' But he vaguely felt that it was misplaced.

'You'll come tomorrow evening, then, about half-past six.'

He went. Miss Louisa was very kind to him. There could be no music, because of the babies. He sat with his fists clenched on his thighs, very quiet and unmoved, lapsing, among all those people, into a kind of muse or daze. There was nothing between him and them. They knew it as well as he. But he remained very steady in himself, and the evening passed slowly. Mrs Lindley called him 'young man'.

'Will you sit here, young man?'

He sat there. One name was as good as another. What had they to do with him?

Mr Lindley kept a special tone for him, kind, indulgent, but patronizing. Durant took it all without criticism or offence, just submitting. But he did not want to eat – that troubled him, to have to eat in their presence.

He knew he was out of place. But it was his duty to stay yet awhile. He answered precisely, in monosyllables.

When he left he winced with confusion. He was glad it was finished. He got away as quickly as possible. And he wanted still more intensely to go right away, to Canada.

Miss Louisa suffered in her soul, indignant with all of them, with him too, but quite unable to say why she was indignant.

XIII

Two evenings after, Louisa tapped at the door of the Quarry Cottage, at half-past six. He had finished dinner, the woman had washed up and gone away, but still he sat in his pit dirt. He was going later to the New Inn. He had begun to go there because he must go somewhere. The mere contact with other men was necessary to him, the noise, the warmth, the forgetful flight of the hours. But still he did not move. He sat alone in the empty house till it began to grow on him like something unnatural.

He was in his pit dirt when he opened the door.

'I have been wanting to call – I thought I would,' she said, and she went to the sofa. He wondered why she wouldn't use his mother's round armchair. Yet something stirred in him, like anger, when the housekeeper placed herself in it.

'I ought to have been washed by now,' he said, glancing at the clock, which was adorned with butterflies and cherries, and the name of 'T. Brooks, Mansfield.' He laid his black hands along his mottled dirty arms. Louisa looked at him. There was the reserve, and the simple neutrality towards her, which she dreaded in him. It made it impossible for her to approach him.

'I am afraid,' she said, 'that I wasn't kind in asking you to supper.'

'I'm not used to it,' he said, smiling with his mouth, showing the interspaced white teeth. His eyes, however, were steady and unseeing.

'It's not *that*,' she said hastily. Her repose was exquisite and her dark grey eyes rich with understanding. He felt afraid of her as she sat there, as he began to grow conscious of her.

'How do you get on alone?' she asked.

He glanced away to the fire.

'Oh—' he answered, shifting uneasily, not finishing his answer.

Her face settled heavily.

'How close it is in this room. You have such immense fires. I will take off my coat,' she said.

He watched her take off her hat and coat. She wore a cream cashmir blouse embroidered with gold silk. It seemed to him a very fine garment, fitting her throat and wrists close. It gave him a feeling of pleasure and cleanness and relief from himself.

'What were you thinking about, that you didn't get washed?' she asked, half intimately. He laughed, turning aside his head. The whites of his eyes showed very distinct in his black face.

'Oh,' he said, 'I couldn't tell you.'

There was a pause.

'Are you going to keep this house on?' she asked.

He stirred in his chair, under the question.

'I hardly know,' he said. 'I'm very likely going to Canada.'

Her spirit became very quiet and attentive.

'What for?' she asked.

Again he shifted restlessly on his seat.

'Well' – he said slowly – 'to try the life.'

'But which life?'

'There's various things – farming or lumbering or mining. I don't mind much what it is.'

'And is that what you want?'

He did not think in these times, so he could not answer.

'I don't know,' he said, 'till I've tried.'

She saw him drawing away from her for ever.

'Aren't you sorry to leave this house and garden?' she asked.

'I don't know,' he answered reluctantly. 'I suppose our Fred would come in – that's what he's wanting.'

'You don't want to settle down?' she asked.

He was leaning forward on the arms of his chair. He turned to her. Her face was pale and set. It looked heavy and impassive, her hair shone richer as she grew white. She was to him something steady and immovable and eternal presented to him. His heart was hot in an anguish of suspense.

Sharp twitches of fear and pain were in his limbs. He turned his whole body away from her. The silence was unendurable. He could not bear her to sit there any more. It made his heart go hot and stifled in his breast.

'Were you going out to-night?' she asked.

'Only to the New Inn,' he said.

Again there was silence.

She reached for her hat. Nothing else was suggested to her. She *had* to go. He sat waiting for her to be gone, for relief. And she knew that if she went out of that house as she was, she went out a failure. Yet she continued to pin on her hat; in a moment she would have to go. Something was carrying her.

Then suddenly a sharp pang, like lightning, seared her from head to foot, and she was beyond herself.

'Do you want me to go?' she asked, controlled, yet speaking out of a fiery anguish, as if the words were spoken from her without her intervention.

He went white under his dirt.

'Why?' he asked, turning to her in fear, compelled.

'Do you want me to go?' she repeated.

'Why?' he asked again.

'Because I wanted to stay with you,' she said, suffocated, with her lungs full of fire.

His face worked, he hung forward a little, suspended, staring straight into her eyes, in torment, in an agony of chaos, unable to collect himself. And as if turned to stone, she looked back into his eyes. Their souls were exposed bare for a few moments. It was agony. They could not bear it. He dropped his head, whilst his body jerked with little sharp twitchings.

She turned away for her coat. Her soul had gone dead in her. Her hands trembled, but she could not feel any more. She drew on her coat. There was a cruel suspense in the room. The moment had come for her to go. He lifted his head. His eyes were like agate, expressionless, save for the black points of torture. They held her, she had no will, no life any more. She felt broken.

'Don't you want me?' she said helplessly.

A spasm of torture crossed his eyes, which held her fixed.

'I – I—' he began, but he could not speak. Something drew him from his chair to her. She stood motionless, spellbound, like a creature given up as prey. He put his hand tentatively, uncertainly, on her arm. The expression of his face was strange and inhuman. She stood utterly motionless. Then clumsily he put his arms round her, and took her, cruelly, blindly, straining her till she nearly lost consciousness, till he himself had almost fallen.

Then, gradually, as he held her gripped, and his brain reeled round, and he felt himself falling, falling from himself, and whilst she, yielded up, swooned to a kind of death of herself, a moment of utter darkness came over him, and they began to wake up again as if from a long sleep. He was himself.

After a while his arms slackened, she loosened herself a little, and put her arms round him, as he held her. So they held each other close, and hid each against the other for assurance, helpless in speech. And it was ever her hands that trembled more closely upon him, drawing him nearer into her, with love.

And at last she drew back her face and looked up at him, her eyes wet, and shining with light. His heart, which saw, was silent with fear. He was with her. She saw his face all sombre and inscrutable, and he seemed eternal to her. And all the echo of pain came back into the rarity of bliss, and all her tears came up.

'I love you,' she said, her lips drawn and sobbing. He put down his head against her, unable to hear her, unable to bear the sudden coming of the peace and passion that almost broke his heart. They stood together in silence whilst the thing moved away a little.

At last she wanted to see him. She looked up. His eyes were strange and glowing, with a tiny black pupil. Strange, they were, and powerful over her. And his mouth came to hers, and slowly her eyelids closed, as his mouth sought hers closer and closer, and took possession of her.

They were silent for a long time, too much mixed up with passion and grief and death to do anything but hold each other in pain and kiss with long, hurting kisses wherein fear was transfused into desire. At last she disengaged herself. He felt as if his heart were hurt, but glad, and he scarcely dared look at her.

'I'm glad,' she said also.

He held her hands in passionate gratitude and desire. He had not yet the presence of mind to say anything. He was dazed with relief.

'I ought to go,' she said.

He looked at her. He could not grasp the thought of her going, he knew he could never be separated from her any more. Yet he dared not assert himself. He held her hands tight.

'Your face is black,' she said.

He laughed.

'Yours is a bit smudged,' he said.

They were afraid of each other, afraid to talk. He could only keep her near to him. After a while she wanted to wash her face. He brought her some warm water, standing by and watching her. There was something he wanted to say, that he dared not. He watched her wiping her face, and making tidy her hair.

'They'll see your blouse is dirty,' he said.

She looked at her sleeves and laughed for joy.

He was sharp with pride.

'What shall you do?' he asked.

'How?' she said.

He was awkward at a reply.

'About me,' he said.

'What do you want me to do?' she laughed.

He put his hand out slowly to her. What did it matter!

'But make yourself clean,' she said.

XIV

As they went up the hill, the night seemed dense with the unknown. They kept close together, feeling as if the darkness were alive and full of knowledge, all around them. In silence they walked up the hill. At first the street lamps went their way. Several people passed them. He was more shy than she, and would have let her go had she loosened in the least. But she held firm.

Then they came into the true darkness, between the fields. They did not want to speak, feeling closer together in silence. So they arrived at the Vicarage gate. They stood under the naked horse-chestnut tree.

'I wish you didn't have to go,' he said.

She laughed a quick little laugh.

'Come tomorrow,' she said, in a low tone, 'and ask father.'

She felt his hand close on hers.

She gave the same sorrowful little laugh of sympathy. Then she kissed him, sending him home.

At home, the old grief came on in another paroxysm, obliterating Louisa, obliterating even his mother for whom the stress was raging like a burst of fever in a wound. But something was sound in his heart.

XV

The next evening he dressed to go to the vicarage, feeling it was to be done, not imagining what it would be like. He would not take this seriously. He was sure of Louisa, and this marriage was like fate to him. It filled him also with a blessed feeling of fatality. He was not responsible, neither had her people anything really to do with it.

They ushered him into the little study, which was fireless. By and by the vicar came in. His voice was cold and hostile as he said:

'What can I do for you, young man?'

He knew already, without asking.

Durant looked up at him, again like a sailor before a superior. He had the subordinate manner. Yet his spirit was clear.

'I wanted, Mr Lindley—' he began respectfully, then all the colour suddenly left his face. It seemed now a violation to say what he had to say. What was he doing there? But he stood on, because it had to be done. He held firmly to his own independence and self-respect. He must not be indecisive. He must put himself aside: the matter was bigger than just his personal self. He must not feel. This was his highest duty.

'You wanted—' said the vicar.

Durant's mouth was dry, but he answered with steadiness:

'Miss Louisa – Louisa – promised to marry me—'

'You asked Miss Louisa if she would marry you – yes—' corrected the vicar. Durant reflected he had not asked her this:

'If she would marry me, sir. I hope you – don't mind.'

He smiled. He was a good-looking man, and the vicar could not help seeing it.

'And my daughter was willing to marry you?' said Mr Lindley.

'Yes,' said Durant seriously. It was pain to him, nevertheless. He felt the natural hostility between himself and the elder man.

'Will you come this way?' said the vicar. He led into the dining-room, where were Mary, Louisa, and Mrs Lindley. Mr Massy sat in a corner with a lamp.

'This young man has come on your account, Louisa?' said Mr Lindley.

'Yes,' said Louisa, her eyes on Durant, who stood erect, in discipline. He dared not look at her, but he was aware of her.

'You don't want to marry a collier, you little fool,' cried Mrs Lindley harshly. She lay obese and helpless upon the couch, swathed in a loose, dove-grey gown.

'Oh, hush, mother,' cried Mary, with quiet intensity and pride.

'What means have you to support a wife?' demanded the vicar's wife roughly.

'I!' Durant replied, starting. 'I think I can earn enough.'

'Well, and how much?' came the rough voice.

'Seven and six a day,' replied the young man.

'And will it get to be any more?'

'I hope so.'

'And are you going to live in that poky little house?'

'I think so,' said Durant, 'if it's all right.'

He took small offence, only was upset, because they would not think him good enough. He knew that, in their sense, he was not.

'Then she's a fool, I tell you, if she marries you,' cried the mother roughly, casting her decision.

'After all, mama, it is Louisa's affair,' said Mary distinctly, 'and we must remember—'

'As she makes her bed, she must lie — but she'll repent it,' interrupted Mrs Lindley.

'And after all,' said Mr Lindley, 'Louisa cannot quite hold herself free to act entirely without consideration for her family.'

'What do you want, papa?' asked Louisa sharply.

'I mean that if you marry this man, it will make my position very difficult for me, particularly if you stay in this parish. If you were moving quite away, it would be simpler. But living here in a collier's cottage, under my nose, as it were – it would be almost unseemly. I have my position to maintain, and a position which may not be taken lightly.'

'Come over here, young man,' cried the mother, in her rough voice, 'and let us look at you.'

Durant, flushing, went over and stood – not quite at attention, so that he did not know what to do with his hands. Miss Louisa was angry to see him standing there, obedient and acquiescent. He ought to show himself a man.

'Can't you take her away and live out of sight?' said the mother. 'You'd both of you be better off.'

'Yes, we can go away,' he said.

'Do you want to?' asked Miss Mary clearly.

He faced round. Mary looked very stately and impressive. He flushed.

'I do if it's going to be a trouble to anybody,' he said.

'For yourself, you would rather stay?' said Mary.

'It's my home,' he said, 'and that's the house I was born in.'

'Then' – Mary turned clearly to her parents, 'I really don't see how you can make the conditions, papa. He has his own rights, and if Louisa wants to marry him—'

'Louisa, Louisa!' cried the father impatiently. 'I cannot understand why Louisa should not behave in the normal way. I cannot see why she should only think of herself, and leave her family out of count. The thing is enough in itself, and she ought to try to ameliorate it as much as possible. And if—'

'But I love the man, papa,' said Louisa.

'And I hope you love your parents, and I hope you want to spare them as much of the – the loss of prestige, as possible.'

'We *can* go away to live,' said Louisa, her face breaking to tears. At last she was really hurt.

'Oh, yes, easily,' Durant replied hastily, pale, distressed.

There was dead silence in the room.

'I think it would really be better,' murmured the vicar, mollified.

'Very likely it would,' said the rough-voiced invalid.

'Though I think we ought to apologize for asking such a thing,' said Mary haughtily.

'No,' said Durant. 'It will be best all round.' He was glad there was no more bother.

'And shall we put up the banns here or go to the registrar?' he asked clearly, like a challenge.

'We will go to the registrar,' replied Louisa decidedly.

Again there was a dead silence in the room.

'Well, if you will have your own way, you must go your own way,' said the mother emphatically.

All the time Mr Massy had sat obscure and unnoticed in a corner of the room. At this juncture he got up, saying:

'There is baby, Mary.'

Mary rose and went out of the room, stately; her little husband padded after her. Durant watched the fragile, small man go, wondering.

'And where,' asked the vicar, almost genial, 'do you think you will go when you are married?'

Durant started.

'I was thinking of emigrating,' he said.

'To Canada? or where?'

'I think to Canada.'

'Yes, that would be very good.'

Again there was a pause.

'We shan't see much of you then, as a son-in-law,' said the mother, roughly but amicably.

'Not much,' he said.

Then he took his leave. Louisa went with him to the gate. She stood before him in distress.

'You won't mind them, will you?' she said humbly.

'I don't mind them, if they don't mind me!' he said. Then he stooped and kissed her.

'Let us be married soon,' she murmured, in tears.

'All right,' he said. 'I'll go tomorrow to Barford.'

RUDYARD KIPLING

The Village that Voted the Earth was Flat

Our drive till then had been quite a success. The other men in the car were my friend Woodhouse, young Ollyett, a distant connection of his, and Pallant, the M.P. Woodhouse's business was the treatment and cure of sick journals. He knew by instinct the precise moment in a newspaper's life when the impetus of past good management is exhausted and it fetches up on the dead-centre between slow and expensive collapse and the new start which can be given by gold injections – and genius. He was wisely ignorant of journalism; but when he stooped on a carcase there was sure to be meat. He had that week added a half-dead, halfpenny evening paper to his collection, which consisted of a prosperous London daily, one provincial ditto, and a limp-bodied weekly of commercial leanings. He had also, that very hour, planted me with a large block of the evening paper's common shares, and was explaining the whole art of editorship to Ollyett, a young man three years from Oxford, with coir-matting-coloured hair and a face harshly modelled by harsh experiences, who, I understood, was assisting in the new venture. Pallant, the long, wrinkled M.P., whose voice is more like a crane's than a peacock's, took no shares, but gave us all advice.

'You'll find it rather a knacker's yard,' Woodhouse was saying. 'Yes, I know they call me The Knacker; but it will pay inside a year. All my papers do. I've only one motto: Back your luck and back your staff. It'll come out all right.'

Then the car stopped, and a policeman asked our names and addresses for exceeding the speed-limit. We pointed out that the road ran absolutely straight for half a mile ahead without even a side-lane. 'That's just what we depend on,' said the policeman unpleasantly.

'The usual swindle,' said Woodhouse under his breath. 'What's the name of this place?'

'Huckley,' said the policeman. 'H-u-c-k-l-e-y,' and wrote something in his note-book at which young Ollyett protested. A large red man on a grey horse who had been watching us from the other side of the hedge shouted an order we could not catch. The policeman laid his hand on the rim of the right driving-door (Woodhouse carries his spare tyres aft), and it closed on the button of the electric horn. The grey horse at once bolted, and we could hear the rider swearing all across the landscape.

'Damn it, man, you've got your silly fist on it! Take it off!' Woodhouse shouted.

'Ho!' said the constable, looking carefully at his fingers as though we had trapped them. 'That won't do you any good either,' and he wrote once more in his note-book before he allowed us to go.

This was Woodhouse's first brush with motor law, and since I expected no ill consequences to myself, I pointed out that it was very serious. I took the same view myself when in due time I found that I, too, was summonsed on charges ranging from the use of obscene language to endangering traffic.

Judgment was done in a little pale-yellow market-town with a small, Jubilee clock-tower and a large corn-exchange. Woodhouse drove us there in his car. Pallant, who had not been included in the summons, came with us as moral support. While we waited outside, the fat man on the grey horse rode up and entered into loud talk with his brother magistrates. He said to one of them – for I took the trouble to note it down – 'It falls away from my lodge-gates, dead straight, three-quarters of a mile. I'd defy any one to resist it. We rooked seventy pounds out of 'em last month. No car can resist the temptation. You ought to have one your side the county, Mike. They simply can't resist it.'

'Whew!' said Woodhouse. 'We're in for trouble. Don't you say a word – or Ollyett either! I'll pay the fines and we'll get it over as soon as possible. Where's Pallant?'

'At the back of the court somewhere,' said Ollyett. 'I saw him slip in just now.'

The fat man then took his seat on the Bench, of which he was chairman, and I gathered from a bystander that his name was Sir Thomas

Ingell, Bart., M.P., of Ingell Park, Huckley. He began with an allocution pitched in a tone that would have justified revolt throughout empires. Evidence, when the crowded little court did not drown it with applause, was given in the pauses of the address. They were all very proud of their Sir Thomas, and looked from him to us, wondering why we did not applaud too.

Taking its time from the chairman, the Bench rollicked with us for seventeen minutes. Sir Thomas explained that he was sick and tired of processions of cads of our type, who would be better employed breaking stones on the road than in frightening horses worth more than themselves or their ancestors. This was after it had been proved that Woodhouse's man had turned on the horn purposely to annoy Sir Thomas, who 'happened to be riding by'! There were other remarks too – primitive enough, – but it was the unspeakable brutality of the tone, even more than the quality of the justice, or the laughter of the audience that stung our souls out of all reason. When we were dismissed – to the tune of twenty-three pounds, twelve shillings and sixpence – we waited for Pallant to join us, while we listened to the next case – one of driving without a licence. Ollyett with an eye to his evening paper, had already taken very full notes of our own, but we did not wish to seem prejudiced.

'It's all right,' said the reporter of the local paper soothingly. 'We never report Sir Thomas *in extenso*. Only the fines and charges.'

'Oh, thank you,' Ollyett replied, and I heard him ask who every one in court might be. The local reporter was very communicative.

The new victim, a large, flaxen-haired man in somewhat striking clothes, to which Sir Thomas, now thoroughly warmed, drew public attention, said that he had left his licence at home. Sir Thomas asked him if he expected the police to go to his home address at Jerusalem to find it for him; and the court roared. Nor did Sir Thomas approve of the man's name, but insisted on calling him 'Mr Masquerader', and every time he did so, all his people shouted. Evidently this was their established *auto-da-fé*.

'He didn't summons me – because I'm in the House, I suppose. I think I shall have to ask a Question,' said Pallant, reappearing at the close of the case.

'I think *I* shall have to give it a little publicity too,' said Woodhouse.

'We can't have this kind of thing going on, you know.' His face was set and quite white. Pallant's, on the other hand, was black, and I know that my very stomach had turned with rage. Ollyett was dumb.

'Well, let's have lunch,' Woodhouse said at last. 'Then we can get away before the show breaks up.'

We drew Ollyett from the arms of the local reporter, crossed the Market Square to the Red Lion and found Sir Thomas's 'Mr Masquerader' just sitting down to beer, beef and pickles.

'Ah!' said he, in a large voice. 'Companions in misfortune. Won't you gentlemen join me?'

'Delighted,' said Woodhouse. 'What did you get?'

'I haven't decided. It might make a good turn, but – the public aren't educated up to it yet. It's beyond 'em. If it wasn't, that red dub on the Bench would be worth fifty a week.'

'Where?' said Woodhouse. The man looked at him with unaffected surprise.

'At any one of My places,' he replied. 'But perhaps you live here?'

'Good heavens!' cried young Ollyett suddenly. 'You *are* Masquerier, then? I thought you were!'

'Bat Masquerier.' He let the words fall with the weight of an international ultimatum. 'Yes, that's all I am. But you have the advantage of me, gentlemen.'

For the moment, while we were introducing ourselves, I was puzzled. Then I recalled prismatic music-hall posters – of enormous acreage – that had been the unnoticed background of my visits to London for years past. Posters of men and women, singers, jongleurs, impersonators and audacities of every draped and undraped brand, all moved on and off in London and the Provinces by Bat Masquerier – with the long wedge-tailed flourish following the final 'r'.

'*I* knew you at once,' said Pallant, the trained M.P., and I promptly backed the lie. Woodhouse mumbled excuses. Bat Masquerier was not moved for or against us any more than the frontage of one of his own palaces.

'I always tell My people there's a limit to the size of the lettering,' he said. 'Overdo that and the ret'na doesn't take it in. Advertisin' is the most delicate of all the sciences.'

'There's one man in the world who is going to get a little of it if I live for the next twenty-four hours,' said Woodhouse, and explained how this would come about.

Masquerier stared at him lengthily with gun-metal-blue eyes.

'You mean it?' he drawled; the voice was as magnetic as the look.

'*I* do,' said Ollyett. 'That business of the horn alone ought to have him off the Bench in three months.' Masquerier looked at him even longer than he had looked at Woodhouse.

'He told *me*,' he said suddenly, 'that my home-address was Jerusalem. You heard that?'

'But it was the tone – the tone,' Ollyett cried.

'You noticed that, too, did you?' said Masquerier. 'That's the artistic temperament. You can do a lot with it. And I'm Bat Masquerier,' he went on. He dropped his chin in his fists and scowled straight in front of him . . . 'I made the Silhouettes – I made the Trefoil and the Jocunda. I made 'Dal Benzaguen.' Here Ollyett sat straight up, for in common with the youth of that year he worshipped Miss Vidal Benzaguen of the Trefoil immensely and unreservedly. '"*Is* that a dressing-gown or an ulster you're supposed to be wearing?" You heard *that*? . . . "And I suppose you hadn't time to brush your hair either?" You heard *that*? . . . Now, you hear *me*!' His voice filled the coffee-room, then dropped to a whisper as dreadful as a surgeon's before an operation. He spoke for several minutes. Pallant muttered 'Hear! hear!' I saw Ollyett's eye flash – it was to Ollyett that Masquerier addressed himself chiefly, – and Woodhouse leaned forward with joined hands.

'Are you *with* me?' he went on, gathering us all up in one sweep of the arm. 'When I begin a thing I see it through, gentlemen. What Bat can't break, breaks him! But I haven't struck that thing yet. This is no one-turn turn-it-down show. This is business to the dead finish. Are you with me, gentlemen? Good! Now, we'll pool our assets. One London morning, and one provincial daily, didn't you say? One weekly commercial ditto and one M.P.'

'Not much use, I'm afraid,' Pallant smirked.

'But privileged. *But* privileged,' he returned. 'And we have also my little team – London, Blackburn, Liverpool, Leeds – I'll tell you about Manchester later – and Me! Bat Masquerier.' He breathed the name reverently into his tankard. 'Gentlemen, when our combination has finished with

Sir Thomas Ingell, Bart., M.P., and everything else that is his, Sodom and Gomorrah will be a winsome bit of Merrie England beside 'em. I must go back to town now, but I trust you gentlemen will give me the pleasure of your company at dinner to-night at the Chop Suey – the Red Amber Room – and we'll block out the scenario.' He laid his hand on young Ollyett's shoulder and added: 'It's your brains I want.' Then he left, in a good deal of astrakhan collar and nickel-plated limousine, and the place felt less crowded.

We ordered our car a few minutes later. As Woodhouse, Ollyett and I were getting in, Sir Thomas Ingell, Bart., M.P., came out of the Hall of Justice across the square and mounted his horse. I have sometimes thought that if he had gone in silence he might even then have been saved, but as he settled himself in the saddle he caught sight of us and must needs shout: 'Not off yet? You'd better get away and you'd better be careful.' At that moment Pallant, who had been buying picture-postcards, came out of the inn, took Sir Thomas's eye and very leisurely entered the car. It seemed to me that for one instant there was a shade of uneasiness on the baronet's grey-whiskered face.

'I hope,' said Woodhouse after several miles, 'I hope he's a widower.'

'Yes,' said Pallant. 'For his poor, dear wife's sake I hope that, very much indeed. I suppose he didn't see me in Court. Oh, here's the parish history of Huckley written by the Rector and here's your share of the picture-postcards. Are we all dining with this Mr Masquerier to-night?'

'Yes!' said we all.

If Woodhouse knew nothing of journalism, young Ollyett, who had graduated in a hard school, knew a good deal. Our halfpenny evening paper, which we will call *The Bun* to distinguish her from her prosperous morning sister, *The Cake*, was not only diseased but corrupt. We found this out when a man brought us the prospectus of a new oil-field and demanded sub-leaders on its prosperity. Ollyett talked pure Brasenose to him for three minutes. Otherwise he spoke and wrote trade-English – a toothsome amalgam of Americanisms and epigrams. But though the slang changes the game never alters, and Ollyett and I and, in the end, some others enjoyed it immensely. It was weeks ere we could see the wood for the trees, but so soon as the staff realised that they had proprietors who backed them right or wrong, and specially when they were wrong (which is the sole secret of journalism), and that their fate did not hang on any passing owner's passing mood, they did miracles.

But we did not neglect Huckley. As Ollyett said our first care was to create an 'arresting atmosphere' round it. He used to visit the village of week-ends, on a motor-bicycle with a side-car; for which reason I left the actual place alone and dealt with it in the abstract. Yet it was I who drew first blood. Two inhabitants of Huckley wrote to contradict a small, quite solid paragraph in *The Bun* that a hoopoe had been seen at Huckley and had, 'of course, been shot by the local sportsmen.' There was some heat in their letters, both of which we published. Our version of how the hoopoe got his crest from King Solomon was, I grieve to say, so inaccurate that the Rector himself – no sportsman as he pointed out, but a lover of accuracy – wrote to us to correct it. We gave his letter good space and thanked him.

'This priest is going to be useful,' said Ollyett. 'He has the impartial mind. I shall vitalise him.'

Forthwith he created M. L. Sigden, a recluse of refined tastes who in *The Bun* demanded to know whether this Huckley-of-the-Hoopoe was the Hugly of his boyhood and whether, by any chance, the fell change of name had been wrought by collusion between a local magnate and the railway, in the mistaken interests of spurious refinement. 'For I knew it and loved it with the maidens of my day – *eheu ab angulo!* – as Hugly,' wrote M. L. Sigden from Oxford.

Though other papers scoffed, *The Bun* was gravely sympathetic. Several people wrote to deny that Huckley had been changed at birth. Only the Rector – no philosopher as he pointed out, but a lover of accuracy – had his doubts, which he laid publicly before Mr M. L. Sigden, who suggested, through *The Bun*, that the little place might have begun life in Anglo-Saxon days as 'Hogslea' or among the Normans as 'Argilé,' on account of its much clay. The Rector had his own ideas too (he said it was mostly gravel), and M. L. Sigden had a fund of reminiscences. Oddly enough – which is seldom the case with free reading-matter – our subscribers rather relished the correspondence, and contemporaries quoted freely.

'The secret of power,' said Ollyett, 'is not the big stick. It's the liftable stick.' (This means the 'arresting' quotation of six or seven lines.) 'Did you see the *Spec.* had a middle on "Rural Tenacities" last week. That was all Huckley. I'm doing a "Mobiquity" on Huckley next week.'

Our 'Mobiquities' were Friday evening accounts of easy motor-bike-*cum*-side-car trips round London, illustrated (we could never get that machine to work properly) by smudgy maps. Ollyett wrote the stuff with a fervour and a delicacy which I always ascribed to the side-car. His account of Epping Forest, for instance, was simply young love with its soul at its lips. But his Huckley 'Mobiquity' would have sickened a soap-boiler. It chemically combined loathsome familiarity, leering suggestion, slimy piety and rancid 'social service' in one fuming compost that fairly lifted me off my feet.

'Yes,' said he, after compliments. 'It's the most vital, arresting and dynamic bit of tump I've done up to date. *Non nobis gloria!* I met Sir Thomas Ingell in his own park. He talked to me again. He inspired most of it.'

'Which? The "glutinous native drawl," or "the neglected adenoids of the village children"?' I demanded.

'Oh, no! That's only to bring in the panel doctor. It's the last flight we – I'm proudest of.'

This dealt with 'the crepuscular penumbra spreading her dim limbs over the boskage'; with 'jolly rabbits'; with a herd of 'gravid polled Angus'; and with the 'arresting, gipsy-like face of their swart, scholarly owner – as well known at the Royal Agricultural Shows as that of our late King-Emperor'.

'"Swart" is good and so's "gravid",' said I, 'but the panel doctor will be annoyed about the adenoids.'

'Not half as much as Sir Thomas will about his face,' said Ollyett. 'And if you only knew what I've left out!'

He was right. The panel doctor spent his week-end (this is the advantage of Friday articles) in overwhelming us with a professional counterblast of no interest whatever to our subscribers. We told him so, and he, then and there, battered his way with it into the *Lancet* where they are keen on glands, and forgot us altogether. But Sir Thomas Ingell was of sterner stuff. He must have spent a happy week-end too. The letter which we received from him on Monday proved him to be a kinless loon of upright life, for no woman, however remotely interested in a man, would have let it pass the home wastepaper-basket. He objected to our references to his own herd, to his own labours in his own village, which he said was a Model Village, and to our infernal insolence; but he objected most to our invoice of his features. We wrote him courteously to ask whether the letter was meant for publication. He, remembering, I presume, the Duke of Wellington, wrote back, 'publish and be damned.'

'Oh! This is too easy,' Ollyett said as he began heading the letter.

'Stop a minute,' I said. 'The game is getting a little beyond us. To-night's the Bat dinner.' (I may have forgotten to tell you that our dinner with Bat Masquerier in the Red Amber Room of the Chop Suey had come to be a weekly affair.) 'Hold it over till they've all seen it.'

'Perhaps you're right,' he said. 'You might waste it.'

At dinner, then, Sir Thomas's letter was handed round. Bat seemed to be thinking of other matters, but Pallant was very interested.

'I've got an idea,' he said presently. 'Could you put something into *The Bun* to-morrow about foot-and-mouth disease in that fellow's herd?'

'Oh, plague if you like,' Ollyett replied. 'They're only five measly Shorthorns. I saw one lying down in the park. She'll serve as a substratum of fact.'

'Then, do that; and hold the letter over meanwhile. I think *I* come in here,' said Pallant.

'Why?' said I.

'Because there's something coming up in the House about foot-and-mouth, and because he wrote me a letter after that little affair when he fined you. 'Took ten days to think it over. Here you are,' said Pallant. 'House of Commons paper, you see.'

We read:

DEAR PALLANT – Although in the past our paths have not lain much together, I am sure you will agree with me that on the floor of the House all members are on a footing of equality. I make bold, therefore, to approach you in a matter which I think capable of a very different interpretation from that which perhaps was put upon it by your friends. Will you let them know that that was the case and that I was in no way swayed by animus in the exercise of my magisterial duties, which as you, as a brother magistrate, can imagine are frequently very distasteful to – Yours very sincerely,

T. Ingell.

P.S. – I have seen to it that the motor vigilance to which your friends took exception has been considerably relaxed in my district.

'What did you answer?' said Ollyett, when all our opinions had been expressed.

'I told him I couldn't do anything in the matter. And I couldn't – then. But you'll remember to put in that foot-and-mouth paragraph. I want something to work upon.'

'It seems to me *The Bun* has done all the work up to date,' I suggested. 'When does *The Cake* come in?'

'*The Cake*,' said Woodhouse, and I remembered afterwards that he spoke like a Cabinet Minister on the eve of a Budget, 'reserves to itself the fullest right to deal with situations as they arise.'

'Ye-eh!' Bat Masquerier shook himself out of his thoughts. '"Situations as they arise." I ain't idle either. But there's no use fishing till the swim's baited. You' – he turned to Ollyett – 'manufacture very good ground-bait . . . I always tell My people— What the deuce is that?'

There was a burst of song from another private dining-room across the landing. 'It ees some ladies from the Trefoil,' the waiter began.

'Oh, I know that. What are they singing, though?'

He rose and went out, to be greeted by shouts of applause from that merry company. Then there was silence, such as one hears in the form-room after a master's entry. Then a voice that we loved began again: 'Here we go gathering nuts in May – nuts in May – nuts in May!'

'It's only 'Dal – and some nuts,' he explained when he returned. 'She says she's coming in to dessert.' He sat down, humming the old tune to himself, and till Miss Vidal Benzaguen entered, he held us speechless with tales of the artistic temperament.

We obeyed Pallant to the extent of slipping into *The Bun* a wary paragraph about cows lying down and dripping at the mouth, which might be read either as an unkind libel or, in the hands of a capable lawyer, as a piece of faithful nature-study.

'And besides,' said Ollyett, 'we allude to "gravid polled Angus". I am advised that no action can lie in respect of virgin Shorthorns. Pallant wants us to come to the House to-night. He's got us places for the Strangers' Gallery. I'm beginning to like Pallant.'

'Masquerier seems to like you,' I said.

'Yes, but I'm afraid of him,' Ollyett answered with perfect sincerity. 'I am. He's the Absolutely Amoral Soul. I've never met one yet.'

We went to the House together. It happened to be an Irish afternoon, and as soon as I had got the cries and the faces a little sorted out, I gathered there were grievances in the air, but how many of them was beyond me.

'It's all right,' said Ollyett of the trained ear. 'They've shut their ports against – oh yes – export of Irish cattle! Foot-and-mouth disease at Ballyhellion. *I* see Pallant's idea!'

The House was certainly all mouth for the moment, but, as I could feel, quite in earnest. A Minister with a piece of typewritten paper seemed to be fending off volleys of insults. He reminded me somehow of a nervous huntsman breaking up a fox in the face of rabid hounds.

'It's question-time. They're asking questions,' said Ollyett. 'Look! Pallant's up.'

There was no mistaking it. His voice, which his enemies said was his one parliamentary asset, silenced the hubbub as toothache silences mere singing in the ears. He said:

'Arising out of that, may I ask if any special consideration has recently been shown in regard to any suspected outbreak of this disease on *this* side of the Channel?'

He raised his hand; it held a noon edition of *The Bun*. We had thought it best to drop the paragraph out of the later ones. He would have continued, but something in a grey frock-coat roared and bounded on a bench opposite, and waved another *Bun*. It was Sir Thomas Ingell.

'As the owner of the herd so dastardly implicated—' His voice was drowned in shouts of 'Order!' – the Irish leading.

'What's wrong?' I asked Ollyett. 'He's got his hat on his head, hasn't he?'

'Yes, but his wrath should have been put as a question.'

'Arising out of that, Mr Speaker, Sirrr!' Sir Thomas bellowed through a lull, 'are you aware that – that all this is a conspiracy – part of a dastardly conspiracy to make Huckley ridiculous – to make *us* ridiculous? Part of a deep-laid plot to make *me* ridiculous, Mr Speaker, Sir!'

The man's face showed almost black against his white whiskers, and he struck out swimmingly with his arms. His vehemence puzzled and held the House for an instant, and the Speaker took advantage of it to lift his pack from Ireland to a new scent. He addressed Sir Thomas Ingell in tones of measured rebuke, meant also, I imagine, for the whole House, which lowered its hackles at the word. Then Pallant, shocked and pained: 'I can only express my profound surprise that in response to my simple question the honourable member should have thought fit to indulge in a personal attack. If I have in any way offended—'

Again the Speaker intervened, for it appeared that he regulated these matters.

He, too, expressed surprise, and Sir Thomas sat back in a hush of reprobation that seemed to have the chill of the centuries behind it. The Empire's work was resumed.

'Beautiful!' said I, and I felt hot and cold up my back.

'And now we'll publish his letter,' said Ollyett.

We did – on the heels of his carefully reported outburst. We made no comment. With that rare instinct for grasping the heart of a situation which is the mark of the Anglo-Saxon, all our contemporaries and, I should say, two-thirds of our correspondents demanded how such a person could be made more ridiculous than he had already proved himself to be. But beyond spelling his name 'Injle,' we alone refused to hit a man when he was down.

'There's no need,' said Ollyett. 'The whole press is on the huckle from end to end.'

Even Woodhouse was a little astonished at the ease with which it had come about, and said as much.

'Rot!' said Ollyett. 'We haven't really begun. Huckley isn't news yet.'

'What do you mean?' said Woodhouse, who had grown to have great respect for his young but by no means distant connection.

'Mean? By the grace of God, Master Ridley, I mean to have it so that when Huckley turns over in its sleep, Reuters and the Press Association jump out of bed to cable.' Then he went off at score about certain restorations in Huckley Church which, he said – and he seemed to spend his every week-end there – had been perpetrated by the Rector's predecessor, who had abolished a 'leper-window' or a 'squinch-hole' (whatever these may be) to institute a lavatory in the vestry. It did not strike me as stuff for which Reuters or the Press Association would lose much sleep, and I left him declaiming to Woodhouse about a fourteenth-century font which, he said, he had unearthed in the sexton's tool-shed.

My methods were more on the lines of peaceful penetration. An odd copy, in *The Bun*'s rag-and-bone library, of Hone's *Every-Day Book* had revealed to me the existence of a village dance founded, like all village dances, on Druidical mysteries connected with the Solar Solstice (which is always unchallengeable) and Midsummer Morning, which is dewy and refreshing to the London eye. For this I take no credit – Hone being a mine any one can work – but that I rechristened that dance, after I had revised it, 'The Gubby' is my title to immortal fame. It was still to be witnessed, I wrote, 'in all its poignant purity at Huckley, that last home of significant mediæval survivals'; and I fell so in love with my creation that I kept it back for days, enamelling and burnishing.

'You's better put it in,' said Ollyett at last. 'It's time we asserted ourselves again. The other fellows are beginning to poach. You saw that thing in the *Pinnacle* about Sir Thomas's Model Village? He must have got one of their chaps down to do it.'

'Nothing like the wounds of a friend,' I said. 'That account of the non-alcoholic pub alone was—'

'I liked the bit best about the white-tiled laundry and the Fallen Virgins who wash Sir Thomas's dress shirts. Our side couldn't come within a mile of that, you know. We haven't the proper flair for sexual slobber.'

'That's what I'm always saying,' I retorted. 'Leave 'em alone. The other fellows are doing our work for us now. Besides I want to touch up my "Gubby Dance" a little more.'

'No. You'll spoil it. Let's shove it in to-day. For one thing it's Literature. I don't go in for compliments as you know, but, etc. etc.'

I had a healthy suspicion of young Ollyett in every aspect, but though I knew that I should have to pay for it, I fell to his flattery, and my priceless article on the 'Gubby Dance' appeared. Next Saturday he asked me to bring out *The Bun* in his absence, which I naturally assumed would be connected with the little maroon side-car. I was wrong.

On the following Monday I glanced at *The Cake* at breakfast-time to make sure, as usual, of her inferiority to my beloved but unremunerative *Bun.* I opened on a heading: 'The Village that Voted the Earth was Flat.' I read . . . I read that the Geoplanarian Society – a society devoted to the proposition that the earth is flat – had held its Annual Banquet and Exercises at Huckley on Saturday, when after convincing addresses, amid scenes of the greatest enthusiasm, Huckley village had decided by an unanimous vote of 438 that the earth was flat. I do not remember that I breathed again till I had finished the two columns of description that followed. Only one man could have written them. They were flawless – crisp, nervous, austere yet human, poignant, vital, arresting – most distinctly arresting – dynamic enough to shift a city – and quotable by whole sticks at a time. And there was a leader, a grave and poised leader, which tore me in two with mirth, until I remembered that I had been left out – infamously and unjustifiably dropped. I went to Ollyett's rooms. He was breakfasting, and, to do him justice, looked conscience-stricken.

'It wasn't my fault,' he began. 'It was Bat Masquerier. I swear *I* would have asked you to come if—'

'Never mind that,' I said. 'It's the best bit of work you've ever done or will do. Did any of it happen?'

'Happen? Heavens! D'you think even *I* could have invented it?'

'Is it exclusive to *The Cake*?' I cried.

'It cost Bat Masquerier two thousand,' Ollyett replied. 'D'you think he'd let any one else in on that? But I give you my sacred word I knew nothing about it till he asked me to come down and cover it. He had Huckley posted in three colours, "The Geoplanarians' Annual Banquet and Exercises." Yes, he invented "Geoplanarians". He wanted Huckley to think it meant aeroplanes. Yes, I know that there is a real Society that thinks the world's flat – they ought to be grateful for the lift – but Bat made his own. He did! He created the whole show, I tell you. He swept out half his Halls for the job. Think of that – on a Saturday! They – we went down in motor char-à-bancs – three of 'em – one pink, one primrose, and one forget-me-not blue – twenty people in each one and "The Earth *is* Flat" on each side and across the back. I went with Teddy Rickets and Lafone from the Trefoil, and both the Silhouette Sisters, and – wait a minute! – the Crossleigh Trio. You know the Every-Day Dramas Trio at the Jocunda – Ada Crossleigh, "Bunt" Crossleigh, and little Victorine? Them. And there was Hoke Ramsden, the lightning-change chap in *Morgiana and Drexel* – and there was Billy Turpeen. Yes, you know him! The North London Star. "I'm the Referee that got himself disliked at Blackheath." *That* chap! And there was Mackaye – that one-eyed Scotch fellow that all Glasgow is crazy about. Talk of subordinating yourself for Art's sake! Mackaye was the earnest inquirer who got converted at the end of the meeting. And there was quite a lot of girls I didn't know, and – oh, yes – there was 'Dal! 'Dal Benzaguen herself! We sat together, going and coming. She's all the darling there ever was. She sent you her love, and she told me to tell you that she won't forget about Nellie Farren. She says you've given her an ideal to work for. She? Oh, she was the Lady Secretary to the Geoplanarians, of course. I forget who were in the other brakes – provincial stars mostly – but they played up gorgeously. The art of the music-hall's changed since your day. They didn't overdo it a bit. You see, people who believe the earth is flat don't dress quite like other people. You may have noticed that I hinted at that in my account. It's a rather flat-fronted Ionic style – neo-Victorian, except for the bustles, 'Dal told me, – but 'Dal looked heavenly in it! So did little Victorine. And there was a girl in the blue brake – she's a provincial – but she's coming to town this winter and she'll knock 'em – Winnie Deans. Remember that! She told Huckley how she had suffered for the Cause as a governess in a rich family where they believed that the world is round, and how she threw up her job sooner than teach immoral geography. That was at the overflow meeting outside the Baptist chapel. She knocked 'em to sawdust! We must look out for Winnie . . . But Lafone! Lafone was beyond everything. Impact, personality – conviction – the whole bag o' tricks! He sweated conviction. Gad, he convinced *me* while he was speaking! (Him? He was President of the Geoplanarians, of course. Haven't you read my account?) It *is* an infernally plausible theory. After all, no one has actually proved the earth is round, have they?'

'Never mind the earth. What about Huckley?'

'Oh, Huckley got tight. That's the worst of these model villages if you let 'em smell fire-water. There's one alcoholic pub in the place that Sir Thomas can't get rid of. Bat made it his base. He sent down the banquet in two motor lorries – dinner for five hundred and drinks for ten thousand.

Huckley voted all right. Don't you make any mistake about that. No vote, no dinner. A unanimous vote – exactly as I've said. At least, the Rector and the Doctor were the only dissentients. We didn't count them. Oh yes, Sir Thomas was there. He came and grinned at us through his park gates. He'll grin worse to-day. There's an aniline dye that you rub through a stencil-plate that eats about a foot into any stone and wears good to the last. Bat had both the lodge-gates stencilled "The Earth *is* flat!" and all the barns and walls they could get at . . . Oh Lord, but Huckley was drunk! We had to fill 'em up to make 'em forgive us for not being aeroplanes. Unthankful yokels! D'you realise that Emperors couldn't have commanded the talent Bat decanted on 'em? Why, 'Dal alone was . . . And by eight o'clock not even a bit of paper left! The whole show packed up and gone, and Huckley hoo-raying for the earth being flat.'

'Very good,' I began. 'I am, as you know, a one-third proprietor of *The Bun.*'

'I didn't forget that,' Ollyett interrupted. 'That was uppermost in my mind all the time. I've got a special account for *The Bun* to-day – it's an idyll – and just to show how I thought of you, I told 'Dal, coming home, about your Gubby Dance, and she told Winnie. Winnie came back in our char-à-banc. After a bit we had to get out and dance it in a field. It's quite a dance the way we did it – and Lafone invented a sort of gorilla lockstep procession at the end. Bat had sent down a film-chap on the chance of getting something. He was the son of a clergyman – a most dynamic personality. He said there isn't anything for the cinema in meetings *qua* meetings – they lack action. Films are a branch of art by themselves. But he went wild over the Gubby. He said it was like Peter's vision at Joppa. He took about a million feet of it. Then I photoed it exclusive for *The Bun*. I've sent 'em in already, only remember we must eliminate Winnie's left leg in the first figure. It's too arresting . . . And there you are! But I tell you I'm afraid of Bat. That man's the Personal Devil. He did it all. He didn't even come down himself. He said he'd distract his people.'

'Why didn't he ask me to come?' I persisted.

'Because he said you'd distract me. He said he wanted my brains on ice. He got 'em. I believe it's the best thing I've ever done.' He reached for *The Cake* and re-read it luxuriously. 'Yes, out and away the best – supremely quotable,' he concluded, and – after another survey – 'By God, what a genius I was yesterday!'

I would have been angry, but I had not the time. That morning, Press agencies grovelled to me in *The Bun* office for leave to use certain photos, which, they understood, I controlled, of a certain village dance. When I had sent the fifth man away on the edge of tears, my self-respect came back a little. Then there was *The Bun*'s poster to get out. Art being elimination, I fined it down to two words (one too many, as it proved) – 'The Gubby!' in red, at which our manager protested; but by five o'clock he told me that I was *the* Napoleon of Fleet Street. Ollyett's account in *The Bun* of the Geoplanarians' Exercises and Love Feast lacked the supreme shock of his version in *The Cake*, but it bruised more; while the photos of 'The Gubby' (which, with Winnie's left leg, was why I had set the doubtful press to work so early) were beyond praise and, next day, beyond price. But even then I did not understand.

A week later, I think it was, Bat Masquerier telephoned to me to come to the Trefoil.

'It's your turn now,' he said. 'I'm not asking Ollyett. Come to the stage-box.'

I went, and, as Bat's guest, was received as Royalty is not. We sat well back and looked out on the packed thousands. It was *Morgiana and Drexel*, that fluid and electric review which Bat – though he gave Lafone the credit – really created.

'Ye-es,' said Bat dreamily, after Morgiana had given 'the nasty jar' to the Forty Thieves in their forty oil 'combinations'. 'As you say, I've got 'em and I can hold 'em. What a man does doesn't matter much; and how he does it don't matter either. It's the *when* – the psychological moment. 'Press can't make up for it; money can't; brains can't. A lot's luck, but all the rest is genius. I'm not speaking about My people now. I'm talking of Myself.'

Then 'Dal – she was the only one who dared – knocked at the door and stood behind us all alive and panting as Morgiana. Lafone was carrying the police-court scene, and the house was ripped up crossways with laughter.

'Ah! Tell a fellow now,' she asked me for the twentieth time, 'did you love Nellie Farren when you were young?'

'Did we love her?' I answered. '"If the earth and the sky and the sea" – There were three million of us, 'Dal, and we worshipped her.'

'How did she get it across?' 'Dal went on.

'She was Nellie. The houses used to coo over her when she came on.'

'I've had a good deal, but I've never been cooed over yet,' said 'Dal wistfully.

'It isn't the how, it's the when,' Bat repeated. 'Ah!'

He leaned forward as the house began to rock and peal full-throatedly. 'Dal fled. A sinuous and silent procession was filing into the police-court to a scarcely audible accompaniment. It was dressed – but the world and all its picture-palaces know how it was dressed. It danced and it danced, and it danced the dance which bit all humanity in the leg for half a year, and it wound up with the lockstep finale that mowed the house down in swathes, sobbing and aching. Somebody in the gallery moaned, 'Oh Gord, the Gubby!' and we heard the word run like a shudder, for they had not a full breath left among them. Then 'Dal came on, an electric star in her dark hair, the diamonds flashing in her three-inch heels – a vision that made no sign for thirty counted seconds while the police-court scene dissolved behind her into Morgiana's Manicure Palace, and they recovered themselves. The star on her forehead went out, and a soft light bathed her as she took – slowly, slowly to the croon of adoring strings – the eighteen paces forward. We saw her first as a queen alone; next as a queen for the first time conscious of her subjects, and at the end, when her hands fluttered, as a woman delighted, awed not a little, but transfigured and illuminated with sheer, compelling affection and goodwill. I caught the broken mutter of welcome – the coo which is more than tornadoes of applause. It died and rose and died again lovingly.

'She's got it across,' Bat whispered. 'I've never seen her like this. I told her to light up the star, but I was wrong, and she knew it. She's an artist.'

''Dal, you darling!' some one spoke, not loudly but it carried through the house.

'Thank *you*!' 'Dal answered, and in that broken tone one heard the last fetter riveted. 'Good evening, boys! I've just come from – now – where the dooce was it I have come from?' She turned to the impassive files of the Gubby dancers, and went on: 'Ah, so good of you to remind me, you dear, bun-faced things. I've just come from the village – The Village that Voted the Earth was Flat.'

She swept into that song with the full orchestra. It devastated the habitable earth for the next six months. Imagine, then, what its rage and pulse must have been at the incandescent hour of its birth! She only gave the chorus once. At the end of the second verse, 'Are you *with* me, boys?' she cried, and the house tore it clean away from her – '*Earth* was flat – *Earth* was flat. Flat as my hat – Flatter than that' – drowning all but the bassoons and double-basses that marked the word.

'Wonderful,' I said to Bat. 'And it's only "Nuts in May" with variations.'

'Yes – but *I* did the variations,' he replied.

At the last verse she gestured to Carlini the conductor, who threw her up his baton. She caught it with a boy's ease. 'Are you *with* me?' she cried once more, and – the maddened house behind her – abolished all the instruments except the guttural belch of the double-basses on '*Earth*' – 'The Village that voted the *Earth* was flat – *Earth* was flat!' It was delirium. Then she picked up the Gubby dancers and led them in a clattering improvised lockstep thrice round the stage till her last kick sent her diamond-hilted shoe catherine-wheeling to the electrolier.

I saw the forest of hands raised to catch it, heard the roaring and stamping pass through hurricanes to full typhoon; heard the song, pinned down by the faithful double-basses as the bull-dog pins down the bellowing bull, overbear even those; till at last the curtain fell and Bat took me round to her dressing-room, where she lay spent after her seventh call. Still the song, through all those white-washed walls, shook the reinforced concrete of the Trefoil as steam pile-drivers shake the flanks of a dock.

'I'm all out – first time in my life. Ah! Tell a fellow now, did I get it across?' she whispered huskily.

'You know you did,' I replied as she dipped her nose deep in a beaker of barley-water. 'They cooed over you.'

Bat nodded. 'And poor Nellie's dead – in Africa, ain't it?'

'I hope I'll die before they stop cooing,' said 'Dal.

'"*Earth* was flat – *Earth* was flat!"' Now it was more like mine-pumps in flood.

'They'll have the house down if you don't take another,' some one called.

'Bless 'em!' said 'Dal, and went out for her eighth, when in the face of that cataract she said yawning, 'I don't know how *you* feel, children, but *I'm* dead. You be quiet.'

'Hold a minute,' said Bat to me. 'I've got to hear how it went in the provinces. Winnie Deans had it in Manchester, and Ramsden at Glasgow – and there are all the films too. I had rather a heavy week-end.'

The telephones presently reassured him.

'It'll do,' said he. 'And *he* said my home address was Jerusalem.' He left me humming the refrain of 'The Holy City.' Like Ollyett I found myself afraid of that man.

When I got out into the street and met the disgorging picture-palaces capering on the pavements and humming it (for he had put the gramophones on with the films), and when I saw far to the south the red electrics flash 'Gubby' across the Thames, I feared more than ever.

A few days passed which were like nothing except, perhaps, a suspense of fever in which the sick man perceives the searchlights of the world's assembled navies in act to converge on one minute fragment of wreckage – one only in all the black and agony-strewn sea. Then those beams focussed themselves. Earth as we knew it – the full circuit of our orb – laid the weight of its impersonal and searing curiosity on this Huckley which had voted that it was flat. It asked for news about Huckley – where and what it might be, and how it talked – it knew how it danced – and how it thought in its wonderful soul. And then, in all the zealous, merciless press, Huckley was laid out for it to look at, as a drop of pond water is exposed on the sheet of a magic-lantern show. But Huckley's sheet was only coterminous with the use of type among mankind. For the precise moment that was necessary, Fate ruled it that there should be nothing of first importance in the world's idle eye. One atrocious murder, a political crisis, an incautious or heady continental statesman, the mere catarrh of a king, would have wiped out the significance of our message, as a passing cloud annuls the urgent helio. But it was halcyon weather in every respect. Ollyett and I did not need to lift our little fingers any more than the Alpine climber whose last sentence has unkeyed the arch of the avalanche. The thing roared and pulverised and swept beyond eyesight all by itself – all by itself. And once well away, the fall of kingdoms could not have diverted it.

Ours is, after all, a kindly earth. While The Song ran and raped it with the cataleptic kick of 'Ta-ra-ra-boom-de-ay', multiplied by the West African significance of 'Everybody's doing it', plus twice the infernal elementality of a certain tune in *Dona et Gamma* when for all practical purposes, literary, dramatic, artistic, social, municipal, political, commercial, and administrative, the Earth *was* flat, the Rector of Huckley wrote to us – again as a lover of accuracy – to point out that the Huckley vote on 'the alleged flatness of this scene of our labours here below' was *not* unanimous; he and the doctor having voted against it. And the great Baron Reuter himself (I am sure it could have been none other) flashed that letter in full to the front, back, and both wings of this scene of our labours. For Huckley was News. *The Bun* also contributed a photograph which cost me some trouble to fake.

'We are a vital nation,' said Ollyett while we were discussing affairs at a Bat dinner. 'Only an Englishman could have written that letter at this present juncture.'

'It reminded me of a tourist in the Cave of the Winds under Niagara. Just one figure in a mackintosh. But perhaps you saw our photo?' I said proudly.

'Yes,' Bat replied. 'I've been to Niagara, too. And how's Huckley taking it?'

'They don't quite understand, of course,' said Ollyett. 'But it's bringing pots of money into the place. Ever since the motor-bus excursions were started—'

'I didn't know they had been,' said Pallant.

'Oh yes. Motor char-à-bancs – uniformed guides and key-bugles included. They're getting a bit fed up with the tune there nowadays,' Ollyett added.

'They play it under his windows, don't they?' Bat asked. 'He can't stop the right of way across his park.'

'He cannot,' Ollyett answered. 'By the way, Woodhouse, I've bought that font for you from the sexton. I paid fifteen pounds for it.'

'What am I supposed to do with it?' asked Woodhouse.

'You give it to the Victoria and Albert Museum. It is fourteenth-century work all right. You can trust me.'

'Is it worth it – now?' said Pallant. 'Not that I'm weakening, but merely as a matter of tactics?'

'But this is true,' said Ollyett. 'Besides, it is my hobby, I always wanted to be an architect. I'll attend to it myself. It's too serious for *The Bun* and miles too good for *The Cake*.'

He broke ground in a ponderous architectural weekly, which had never heard of Huckley. There was no passion in his statement, but mere fact backed by a wide range of authorities. He established beyond doubt that the old font at Huckley had been thrown out, on Sir Thomas's instigation, twenty years ago, to make room for a new one of Bath stone adorned with Limoges enamels; and that it had lain ever since in a corner of the sexton's shed. He proved, with learned men to support him, that there was only one other font in all England to compare with it. So Woodhouse bought it and presented it to a grateful South Kensington which said it would see the earth still flatter before it returned the treasure to purblind Huckley. Bishops by the benchful and most of the Royal Academy, not to mention 'Margaritas ante Porcos', wrote fervently to the papers. *Punch* based a political cartoon on it; the *Times* a third leader, 'The Lust of Newness'; and the *Spectator* a scholarly and delightful middle, 'Village Haussmania'. The vast amused outside world said in all its tongues and types: 'Of course! This is just what Huckley would do!' And neither Sir Thomas nor the Rector nor the sexton nor any one else wrote to deny it.

'You see,' said Ollyett, 'this is much more of a blow to Huckley than it looks – because every word of it's true. Your Gubby dance was inspiration, I admit, but it hadn't its roots in—'

'Two hemispheres and four continents so far,' I pointed out.

'Its roots in the hearts of Huckley was what I was going to say. Why don't you ever come down and look at the place? You've never seen it since we were stopped there.'

'I've only my week-ends free,' I said, 'and you seem to spend yours there pretty regularly – with the side-car. I was afraid—'

'Oh, *that's* all right,' he said cheerily. 'We're quite an old engaged couple now. As a matter of fact, it happened after "the gravid polled Angus" business. Come along this Saturday. Woodhouse says he'll run us down after lunch. He wants to see Huckley too.'

Pallant could not accompany us, but Bat took his place.

'It's odd,' said Bat, 'that none of us except Ollyett has ever set eyes on Huckley since that time. That's what I always tell My people. Local colour is all right after you've got your idea. Before that, it's a mere nuisance.' He regaled us on the way down with panoramic views of the success – geographical and financial – of 'The Gubby' and The Song.

'By the way,' said he, 'I've assigned 'Dal all the gramophone rights of "The Earth". She's a born artist. 'Hadn't sense enough to hit me for triple-dubs the morning after. She'd have taken it out in coos.'

'Bless her! And what'll she make out of the gramophone rights?' I asked.

'Lord knows!' he replied. 'I've made fifty-four thousand my little end of the business, and it's only just beginning. Hear *that*!'

A shell-pink motor-brake roared up behind us to the music on a key-bugle of 'The Village that Voted the Earth was Flat'. In a few minutes we overtook another, in natural wood, whose occupants were singing it through their noses.

'I don't know that agency. It must be Cook's,' said Ollyett. 'They *do* suffer.' We were never out of ear-shot of the tune the rest of the way to Huckley.

Though I knew it would be so, I was disappointed with the actual aspect of the spot we had – it is not too much to say – created in the face of the nations. The alcoholic pub; the village green; the Baptist chapel; the church; the sexton's shed; the Rectory whence the so-wonderful letters had come; Sir Thomas's park gate-pillars still violently declaring 'The Earth *is* flat', were as mean, as average, as ordinary as the photograph of a room where a murder has been committed. Ollyett, who, of course, knew the place specially well, made the most of it to us. Bat, who had employed it as a back-cloth to one of his own dramas, dismissed it as a thing used and emptied, but Woodhouse expressed my feelings when he said: 'Is that all – after all we've done?'

'*I* know,' said Ollyett soothingly. '"Like that strange song I heard Apollo sing: When Ilion like a mist rose into towers." I've felt the same sometimes, though it has been Paradise for me. But they *do* suffer.'

The fourth brake in thirty minutes had just turned into Sir Thomas's park to tell the Hall that 'The *Earth* was flat'; a knot of obviously American tourists were kodaking his lodge gates; while the tea-shop opposite the lych-gate was full of people buying postcards of the old font as it had lain twenty years in the sexton's shed. We went to the alcoholic pub and congratulated the proprietor.

'It's bringin' money to the place,' said he. 'But in a sense you can buy money too dear. It isn't doin' us any good. People are laughin' at us. That's what they're doin' . . . Now, with regard to that Vote of ours you may have heard talk about . . .'

'For Gorze sake, chuck that votin' business,' cried an elderly man at the door. 'Money-gettin' or no money-gettin', we're fed up with it.'

'Well, I do think,' said the publican, shifting his ground, 'I do think Sir Thomas might ha' managed better in some things.'

'He tole me,' – the elderly man shouldered his way to the bar – 'he tole me twenty years ago to take an' lay that font in my tool-shed. He *tole* me so himself. An' now, after twenty years, me own wife makin' me out little better than the common 'angman!'

'That's the sexton,' the publican explained. 'His good lady sells the postcards – if you 'aven't got some. But we feel Sir Thomas might ha' done better.'

'What's he got to do with it?' said Woodhouse.

'There's nothin' we can trace 'ome to 'im in so many words, but we think he might 'ave saved us the font business. Now, in regard to that votin' business—'

'Chuck it! Oh, chuck it!' the sexton roared, 'or you'll 'ave me cuttin' my throat at cock-crow. 'Ere's another parcel of fun-makers!'

A motor-brake had pulled up at the door and a multitude of men and women immediately descended. We went out to look. They bore rolled banners, a reading-desk in three pieces, and, I specially noticed, a collapsible harmonium, such as is used on ships at sea.

'Salvation Army?' I said, though I saw no uniforms.

Two of them unfurled a banner between poles which bore the legend: 'The Earth *is* flat.' Woodhouse and I turned to Bat. He shook his head. 'No, no! Not me . . . If I had only seen their costumes in advance!'

'Good Lord!' said Ollyett. 'It's the genuine Society!'

The company advanced on the green with the precision of people well broke to these movements. Scene-shifters could not have been quicker with the three-piece rostrum, nor stewards with the harmonium. Almost before its cross-legs had been kicked into their catches, certainly before

the tourists by the lodge-gates had begun to move over, a woman sat down
to it and struck up a hymn:

> Hear ther truth our tongues are telling,
>> Spread ther light from shore to shore,
> God hath given man a dwelling
>> Flat and flat for evermore.

> When ther Primal Dark retreated,
>> When ther deeps were undesigned,
> He with rule and level meted
>> Habitation for mankind!

I saw sick envy on Bat's face. 'Curse Nature,' he muttered. 'She gets ahead
of you every time. To think *I* forgot hymns and a harmonium!'

Then came the chorus:

> Hear ther truth our tongues are telling,
>> Spread ther light from shore to shore –
> Oh, be faithful! Oh, be truthful!
>> Earth is flat for evermore.

They sang several verses with the fervour of Christians awaiting their
lions. Then there were growlings in the air. The sexton, embraced by the
landlord, two-stepped out of the pub-door. Each was trying to outroar
the other. 'Apologising in advarnce for what he says,' the landlord shouted:
'You'd better go away' (here the sexton began to speak words). 'This isn't
the time nor yet the place for – for any more o' this chat.'

The crowd thickened. I saw the village police-sergeant come out of his
cottage buckling his belt.

'But surely,' said the woman at the harmonium, 'there must be some
mistake. We are not suffragettes.'

'Damn it! They'd be a change,' cried the sexton. 'You get out of this!
Don't talk! *I* can't stand it for one! Get right out, or we'll font you!'

The crowd which was being recruited from every house in sight echoed
the invitation. The sergeant pushed forward. A man beside the reading-desk

said: 'But surely we are among dear friends and sympathisers. Listen to me for a moment.'

It was the moment that a passing char-à-banc chose to strike into The Song. The effect was instantaneous. Bat, Ollyett, and I, who by divers roads have learned the psychology of crowds, retreated towards the tavern door. Woodhouse, the newspaper proprietor, anxious, I presume, to keep touch with the public, dived into the thick of it. Every one else told the Society to go away at once. When the lady at the harmonium (I began to understand why it is sometimes necessary to kill women) pointed at the stencilled park pillars and called them 'the cromlechs of our common faith', there was a snarl and a rush. The police-sergeant checked it, but advised the Society to keep on going. The Society withdrew into the brake fighting, as it were, a rearguard action of oratory up each step. The collapsed harmonium was hauled in last, and with the perfect unreason of crowds, they cheered it loudly, till the chauffeur slipped in his clutch and sped away. Then the crowd broke up, congratulating all concerned except the sexton, who was held to have disgraced his office by having sworn at ladies. We strolled across the green towards Woodhouse, who was talking to the police-sergeant near the park-gates. We were not twenty yards from him when we saw Sir Thomas Ingell emerge from the lodge and rush furiously at Woodhouse with an uplifted stick, at the same time shrieking: 'I'll teach you to laugh, you—' but Ollyett has the record of the language. By the time we reached them, Sir Thomas was on the ground; Woodhouse, very white, held the walking-stick and was saying to the sergeant:

'I give this person in charge for assault.'

'But, good Lord!' said the sergeant, whiter than Woodhouse. 'It's Sir Thomas.'

'Whoever it is, it isn't fit to be at large,' said Woodhouse. The crowd suspecting something wrong began to reassemble, and all the English horror of a row in public moved us, headed by the sergeant, inside the lodge. We shut both park-gates and lodge-door.

'You saw the assault, sergeant,' Woodhouse went on. 'You can testify I used no more force than was necessary to protect myself. You can testify that I have not even damaged this person's property. (Here! take your stick, you!) You heard the filthy language he used.'

'I – I can't say I did,' the sergeant stammered.

'Oh, but *we* did!' said Ollyett, and repeated it, to the apron-veiled horror of the lodge-keeper's wife.

Sir Thomas on a hard kitchen chair began to talk. He said he had 'stood enough of being photographed like a wild beast', and expressed loud regret that he had not killed 'that man', who was 'conspiring with the sergeant to laugh at him.'

"Ad you ever seen 'im before, Sir Thomas?' the sergeant asked.

'No! But it's time an example was made here. I've never seen the sweep in my life.'

I think it was Bat Masquerier's magnetic eye that recalled the past to him, for his face changed and his jaw dropped. 'But I have!' he groaned. 'I remember now.'

Here a writhing man entered by the back door. He was, he said, the village solicitor. I do not assert that he licked Woodhouse's boots, but we should have respected him more if he had and been done with it. His notion was that the matter could be accommodated, arranged and compromised for gold, and yet more gold. The sergeant thought so too. Woodhouse undeceived them both. To the sergeant he said, 'Will you or will you not enter the charge?' To the village solicitor he gave the name of his lawyers, at which the man wrung his hands and cried, 'Oh, Sir T., Sir T.!' in a miserable falsetto, for it was a Bat Masquerier of a firm. They conferred together in tragic whispers.

'I don't dive after Dickens,' said Ollyett to Bat and me by the window, 'but every time *I* get into a row I notice the police-court always fills up with his characters.'

'I've noticed that too,' said Bat. 'But the odd thing is you mustn't give the public straight Dickens – not in My business. I wonder why that is.'

Then Sir Thomas got his second wind and cursed the day that he, or it may have been we, were born. I feared that though he was a Radical he might apologise and, since he was an M.P., might lie his way out of the difficulty. But he was utterly and truthfully beside himself. He asked foolish questions – such as what we were doing in the village at all, and how much blackmail Woodhouse expected to make out of him. But neither Woodhouse nor the sergeant nor the writhing solicitor listened. The upshot of their talk, in the chimney-corner, was that Sir Thomas stood engaged to appear next Monday before his brother magistrates on charges of assault, disorderly conduct, and language calculated, etc. Ollyett was specially careful about the language.

Then we left. The village looked very pretty in the late light – pretty and tuneful as a nest of nightingales.

'You'll turn up on Monday, I hope,' said Woodhouse, when we reached town. That was his only allusion to the affair.

So we turned up – through a world still singing that the Earth was flat – at the little clay-coloured market-town with the large Corn Exchange and the small Jubilee memorial. We had some difficulty in getting seats in the court. Woodhouse's imported London lawyer was a man of commanding personality, with a voice trained to convey blasting imputations by tone. When the case was called, he rose and stated his client's intention not to proceed with the charge. His client, he went on to say, had not entertained, and, of course, in the circumstances could not have entertained, any suggestion of accepting on behalf of public charities any moneys that might have been offered to him on the part of Sir Thomas's estate. At the same time, no one acknowledged more sincerely than his client the spirit in which those offers had been made by those entitled to make them. But, as a matter of fact – here he became the man of the world colloguing with his equals – certain – er – details had come to his client's knowledge *since* the lamentable outburst, which . . . He shrugged his shoulders. Nothing was served by going into them, but he ventured to say that, had those painful circumstances only been known earlier, his client would – again 'of course' – never have dreamed— A gesture concluded the sentence, and the ensnared Bench looked at Sir Thomas with new and withdrawing eyes. Frankly, as they could see, it would be nothing less than cruelty to proceed further with this – er – unfortunate affair. He asked leave, therefore, to withdraw the charge *in toto*, and at the same time to express his client's deepest sympathy with all who had been in any way distressed, as his client had been, by the fact and the publicity of proceedings which he could, of course, again assure them that his client would never have dreamed of instituting if, as he hoped he had made plain, certain facts had been before his client at the time when . . . But he had said enough. For his fee it seemed to me that he had.

Heaven inspired Sir Thomas's lawyer – all of a sweat lest his client's language should come out – to rise up and thank him. Then, Sir Thomas – not yet aware what leprosy had been laid upon him, but grateful to escape on any terms – followed suit. He was heard in interested silence, and people drew back a pace as Gehazi passed forth.

'You hit hard,' said Bat to Woodhouse afterwards. 'His own people think he's mad.'

'You don't say so? I'll show you some of his letters to-night at dinner,' he replied.

He brought them to the Red Amber Room of the Chop Suey. We forgot to be amazed, as till then we had been amazed, over The Song or 'The Gubby,' or the full tide of Fate that seemed to run only for our sakes. It did not even interest Ollyett that the verb 'to huckle' had passed into the English leader-writers' language. We were studying the interior of a soul, flash-lighted to its grimiest corners by the dread of 'losing its position'.

'And then it thanked you, didn't it, for dropping the case?' said Pallant.

'Yes, and it sent me a telegram to confirm.' Woodhouse turned to Bat. 'Now d'you think I hit too hard?' he asked.

'No–o!' said Bat. 'After all – I'm talking of every one's business now – one can't ever do anything in Art that comes up to Nature in any game in life. Just think how this thing has—'

'Just let me run through that little case of yours again,' said Pallant, and picked up *The Bun* which had it set out in full.

'Any chance of 'Dal looking in on us to-night?' Ollyett began.

'She's occupied with her Art too,' Bat answered bitterly. 'What's the use of Art? Tell me, some one!' A barrel-organ outside promptly pointed out that the *Earth* was flat. 'The gramophone's killing street organs, but I let loose a hundred-and-seventy-four of those hurdygurdys twelve hours after The Song,' said Bat. 'Not counting the Provinces.' His face brightened a little.

'Look here!' said Pallant over the paper. 'I don't suppose you or those asinine J.P.'s knew it – but your lawyer ought to have known that you've all put your foot in it most confoundedly over this assault case.'

'What's the matter?' said Woodhouse.

'It's ludicrous. It's insane. There isn't two penn'orth of legality in the whole thing. Of course, you could have withdrawn the charge, but the way you went about it is childish – besides being illegal. What on earth was the Chief Constable thinking of?'

'Oh, he was a friend of Sir Thomas's. They all were for that matter,' I replied.

'He ought to be hanged. So ought the Chairman of the Bench. I'm talking as a lawyer now.'

'Why, what have we been guilty of? Misprision of treason or compounding a felony – or what?' said Ollyett.

'I'll tell you later.' Pallant went back to the paper with knitted brows, smiling unpleasantly from time to time. At last he laughed.

'Thank you!' he said to Woodhouse. 'It ought to be pretty useful – for us.'

'What d'you mean?' said Ollyett.

'For our side. They are all Rads who are mixed up in this – from the Chief Constable down. There must be a Question. There must be a Question.'

'Yes, but I wanted the charge withdrawn in my own way,' Woodhouse insisted.

'That's nothing to do with the case. It's the legality of your silly methods. You wouldn't understand if I talked till morning.' He began to pace the room, his hands behind him. 'I wonder if I can get it through our Whip's thick head that it's a chance . . . That comes of stuffing the Bench with radical tinkers,' he muttered.

'Oh, sit down!' said Woodhouse.

'Where's your lawyer to be found now?' he jerked out.

'At the Trefoil,' said Bat promptly. 'I gave him the stage-box for to-night. He's an artist too.'

'Then I'm going to see him,' said Pallant. 'Properly handled this ought to be a godsend for our side.' He withdrew without apology.

'Certainly, this thing keeps on opening up, and up,' I remarked inanely.

'It's beyond me!' said Bat. 'I don't think if I'd known I'd have ever . . . Yes, I would, though. He said my home address was—'

'It was his tone – his tone!' Ollyett almost shouted. Woodhouse said nothing, but his face whitened as he brooded.

'Well, any way,' Bat went on, 'I'm glad I always believed in God and Providence and all those things. Else I should lose my nerve. We've put it over the whole world – the full extent of the geographical globe. We couldn't stop it if we wanted to now. It's got to burn itself out. I'm not in charge any more. What d'you expect'll happen next. Angels?'

I expected nothing. Nothing that I expected approached what I got. Politics are not my concern, but, for the moment, since it seemed that they were going to 'huckle' with the rest, I took an interest in them. They impressed me as a dog's life without a dog's decencies, and I was confirmed in this when an unshaven and unwashen Pallant called on me at ten o'clock one morning, begging for a bath and a couch.

'Bail too?' I asked. He was in evening dress and his eyes were sunk feet in his head.

'No,' he said hoarsely. 'All night sitting. Fifteen divisions. 'Nother to-night. Your place was nearer than mine, so—' He began to undress in the hall.

When he awoke at one o'clock he gave me lurid accounts of what he said was history, but which was obviously collective hysteria. There had been a political crisis. He and his fellow M.P.'s had 'done things' – I never quite got at the things – for eighteen hours on end, and the pitiless Whips were even then at the telephones to herd 'em up to another dog-fight. So he snorted and grew hot all over again while he might have been resting.

'I'm going to pitch in my question about that miscarriage of justice at Huckley this afternoon, if you care to listen to it,' he said. 'It'll be absolutely thrown away – in our present state. I told 'em so; but it's my only chance for weeks. P'raps Woodhouse would like to come.'

'I'm sure he would. Anything to do with Huckley interests us,' I said.

'It'll miss fire, I'm afraid. Both sides are absolutely cooked. The present situation has been working up for some time. You see the row was bound to come, etc. etc.,' and he flew off the handle once more.

I telephoned to Woodhouse, and we went to the House together. It was a dull, sticky afternoon with thunder in the air. For some reason or other, each side was determined to prove its virtue and endurance to the utmost. I heard men snarling about it all round me. 'If they won't spare us, we'll show 'em no mercy.' 'Break the brutes up from the start. They can't stand late hours.' 'Come on! No shirking! I know *you*'ve had a Turkish bath,' were some of the sentences I caught on our way. The House was packed already, and one could feel the negative electricity of a jaded crowd wrenching at one's own nerves, and depressing the afternoon soul.

'This is bad!' Woodhouse whispered. 'There'll be a row before they've finished. Look at the Front Benches!' And he pointed out little personal signs by which I was to know that each man was on edge. He might have spared himself. The House was ready to snap before a bone had been thrown. A sullen minister rose to reply to a staccato question. His supporters cheered defiantly. 'None o' that! None o' that!' came from the Back Benches. I saw the Speaker's face stiffen like the face of a helmsman as he humours a hard-mouthed yacht after a sudden following sea. The trouble was barely met in time. There came a fresh, apparently causeless gust a few minutes later – savage, threatening, but futile. It died out – one could hear the sigh – in sudden wrathful realisation of the dreary hours ahead, and the ship of state drifted on.

Then Pallant – and the raw House winced at the torture of his voice – rose. It was a twenty-line question, studded with legal technicalities. The gist of it was that he wished to know whether the appropriate Minister was aware that there had been a grave miscarriage of justice on such and such a date, at such and such a place, before such and such justices of the peace, in regard to a case which arose—

I heard one desperate, weary 'damn!' float up from the pit of that torment. Pallant sawed on – 'out of certain events which occurred at the village of Huckley.'

The House came to attention with a parting of the lips like a hiccough, and it flashed through my mind . . . Pallant repeated, 'Huckley. The village—'

'That voted the *Earth* was flat.' A single voice from a back Bench sang it once like a lone frog in a far pool.

'*Earth* was flat,' croaked another voice opposite.

'*Earth* was flat.' There were several. Then several more.

It was, you understand, the collective, over-strained nerve of the House, snapping, strand by strand to various notes, as the hawser parts from its moorings.

'The Village that voted the *Earth* was flat.' The tune was beginning to shape itself. More voices were raised and feet began to beat time. Even so it did not occur to me that the thing would—

'The Village that voted the *Earth* was flat!' It was easier now to see who were not singing. There were still a few. Of a sudden (and this proves the fundamental instability of the cross-bench mind) a cross-bencher leaped on his seat and there played an imaginary double-bass with tremendous maestro-like wagglings of the elbow.

The last strand parted. The ship of state drifted out helpless on the rocking tide of melody.

> The Village that voted the *Earth* was flat!
> The Village that voted the *Earth* was flat!

The Irish first conceived the idea of using their order-papers as funnels wherewith to reach the correct '*vroom – vroom*' on '*Earth*'. Labour, always conservative and respectable at a crisis, stood out longer than any other section, but when it came in it was howling syndicalism. Then, without distinction of Party, fear of constituents, desire for office, or hope of emolument, the House sang at the tops and at the bottoms of their voices, swaying their stale bodies and epileptically beating with their swelled feet. They sang 'The Village that voted the *Earth* was flat': first, because they wanted to, and secondly – which is the terror of that song – because they could not stop. For no consideration could they stop.

Pallant was still standing up. Some one pointed at him and they laughed. Others began to point, lunging, as it were, in time with the tune. At this moment two persons came in practically abreast from behind the Speaker's chair, and halted appalled. One happened to be the Prime Minister and the other a messenger. The House, with tears running down their cheeks, transferred their attention to the paralysed couple. They pointed six hundred forefingers at them. They rocked, they waved, and they rolled while they pointed, but still they sang. When they weakened for an instant, Ireland would yell: 'Are ye *with* me, bhoys?' and they all renewed their strength like Antaeus. No man could say afterwards what happened in the Press or the Strangers' Gallery. It was the House, the hysterical and abandoned House of Commons that held all eyes, as it deafened all ears. I saw both Front Benches bend forward, some with their foreheads on their despatch-boxes, the rest with their faces in their hands; and their moving shoulders jolted the House out of its last rag of decency. Only the Speaker remained unmoved. The entire press of Great Britain bore witness next day that he had not even bowed his head. The Angel of the Constitution, for vain was the help of man, foretold him the exact moment at which the House would have broken into 'The Gubby.' He is reported to have said: 'I heard the Irish beginning to shuffle it. So I adjourned'. Pallant's version is that he added: 'And I was never so grateful to a private member in all my life as I was to Mr Pallant.'

He made no explanation. He did not refer to orders or disorders. He simply adjourned the House till six that evening. And the House adjourned – some of it nearly on all fours.

I was not correct when I said that the Speaker was the only man who did not laugh. Woodhouse was beside me all the time. His face was set and quite white – as white, they told me, as Sir Thomas Ingell's when he went, by request, to a private interview with his Chief Whip.

STACY AUMONIER

The Great Unimpressionable

Ned Picklekin was a stolid chunk of a young man, fair, blue-eyed, with his skin beaten to a uniform tint of warm red by the sun and wind. For he was the postman at the village at Ashalton. Except for two hours in the little sorting-office, he spent the whole day on his bicycle, invariably accompanied by his Irish terrier, Toffee. Toffee was as well-known on the countryside as Ned himself. He took the business of delivering letters as seriously as his master. He trotted behind the bicycle with his tongue out, and waited panting outside the gates of gardens while the important government business was transacted. He never barked, and had no time for fighting common, unofficial dogs. When the letters were delivered, his master would return to his bicycle, and say: 'Coom ahn, boy!' and Toffee would immediately jump up, and fall into line. They were great companions.

Ned lived with his mother, and also he walked out with a young lady. Her name was Ettie Skinner, and she was one of the three daughters of old Charlie Skinner, the corn-merchant. Charlie Skinner had a little establishment in the station-yard. He was a widower, and he and his three daughters lived in a cottage in Neap's Lane. It was very seldom necessary to deliver letters at the Skinners' cottage, but every morning Ned had to pass up Neap's Lane, and so, when he arrived at the cottage, he dismounted, and rang his bicycle bell. The signal was understood by Ettie, who immediately ran out to the gate, and a conversation somewhat on this pattern usually took place:

'Hulloa!'

'Hulloa!'

'All right?'

'Ay.'

'Busy?'

'Ay. Mendin' some old cla'es.'

'Oo-ay!'

'Looks like mebbe a shower.'

'Mebbe.'

'Comin' along to-night?'

'Ay, if it doan't rain.'

'Well, so long!'

'So long, Ned.'

In the evenings the conversation followed a very similar course. They waddled along the lanes side by side, and occasionally gave each other a punch. Ned smoked his pipe all the time, and Toffee was an unembarrassed cicerone. He was a little jealous of this unnecessary female, but he behaved with a resigned acquiescence. His master could do no wrong. His master was a god, a being apart from all others.

It cannot be said that Ned was a romantic lover. He was solemn, direct, imperturbable. He was a Saxon of Saxons, matter-of-fact, incorruptible, unimaginative, strong-willed, conscientious, not very ambitious, and suspicious of the unusual and the unknown. When the war broke out, he said:

'Ay, but this is a bad business!'

And then he thought about it for a month. At the end of that time he made up his mind to join. He rode up Neap's Lane one morning and rang his bell. When Ettie appeared the usual conversation underwent a slight variant:

'Hulloa!'

'Hulloa!'

'All right?'

'Ay.'

'Doin' much?'

'Oo – mendin' pa's night-gown.'

'Oh! I be goin' to jine up.'

'Oo-oh! Be 'ee?'

'Ay.'

'When be goin'?'

'Monday with Dick Thursby and Len Cotton. An' I think young Walters, and Binnie Short mebbe.'

'Oh, I say!'

'Ay. Comin' along to-night?'

'Ay, if it doan't rain.'

'Well, see you then.'

'So long, Ned.'

On the following Monday Ned said good-bye to his mother, and sweetheart, and to Toffee, and he and the other four boys walked over to the recruiting-office at Carchester. They were drafted into the same unit, and sent up to Yorkshire to train. (Yorkshire being one hundred and fifty miles away was presumably the most convenient and suitable spot).

They spent five months there, and then Len Cotton was transferred to the Machine Gun Corps, and the other four were placed in an infantry regiment and sent out to India. They did not get an opportunity of returning to Ashalton, but the night before they left Ned wrote to his mother:

Dear Mother, I think we are off to-morrow. They don't tell us where we are going but they seem to think it's India because of the Eastern kit served out and so on. Everything all right, the grub is fine. Young Walters has gone sick with a bile on his neck. Hope you are all right. See Toffee don't get into Mr Mears yard for this is about the time he puts down that poison for the rats. Everything all O.K. love from Ned.

He wrote a very similar letter to Ettie, only leaving out the instructions about Toffee, and adding, 'don't get overdoing it now the warm weathers on.'

They touched at Gibraltar, Malta, Alexandria, and Aden. At all these places he merely sent the cryptic post-card. He did not write a letter again until he had been three weeks up in the hills in India. As a matter of fact it had been a terribly rough passage nearly all the way, especially in the Mediterranean, and nearly all the boys had been sea-sick most of the time. Ned had been specially bad and in the Red Sea had developed a slight fever. In India he had been sent to a rest-camp up in the hills. He wrote:

Dear mother, everything all right. The grub is fine. I went a bit sick coming out but nothing. Quite all O.K. now. This is a funny place. The people would make you laugh to look at. We beat the 2nd Royal Scots by two goals to one. I wasn't playing but Binnie played a fine game at half-back. He stopped their centre forward an old league player. time and again. Hope you are keeping all right. Does Henry Thatcham take Toffee out regler. Everything serene. love from Ned.

In this letter the words '2nd Royal Scots' were deleted by the censor.

India at that time was apparently a kind of training-ground for young recruits. There were a few recalcitrant hill-tribes upon whom to practise the latest developments of military science, and Ned was mixed up in one or two of these little scraps. He proved himself a good soldier, doing precisely what he was told and being impervious to danger. They were five months in India, and then the regiment was suddenly drafted back to Egypt. Big things were afoot. No one knew what was going to happen. They spent ten days in a camp near Alexandria. They were then detailed for work in connection with the protection of the banks of the Canal, and Ned was stationed near the famous pyramid of Gizeh. He wrote to his mother:

Dear mother, 'everything all right. Pretty quiet so far. This is a funny place. Young Walters has gone sick again. We had the regimental sports Thursday. Me and Bert Carter won the three-legged race. The grub is fine and we get dates and figs for nuts. Hope your cold is all right by now. Thanks for the parcel which I got on the 27th. Everything all right. Glad to hear about Mrs Parsons having the twins and that. Glad to hear Toffee all right and so with love your loving son Ned.

They had not been at Gizeh for more than a week before they were sent back to Alexandria and placed on a transport. In fifteen days after touching at Imbros, Ned and his companions found themselves on Gallipoli peninsula. Heavy fighting was in progress. They were rushed up to the front line. For two days and nights they were in action and their numbers were reduced to one-third their original size. For thirty hours they were without water and were being shelled by gas, harried by flame-throwers, blasted by shrapnel and high-explosive. At the end of that time they crawled back to the beach at night through prickly brambles which poisoned them and set up septic wounds if they scratched them. They lay there dormant for two days, but still under shell-fire, and then were hurriedly re-formed into a new regiment, and sent to another part of the line. This went on continuously for three weeks, and then a terrible storm and flood occurred. Hundreds of men – some alive and some partly alive – were drowned in the ravines. Ned and his company lost all their kit, and slept in water for three nights running. At the end of four weeks he obtained five days' rest at the base. He wrote to Ettie:

Dear Ettie,

A long time since I had a letter from you. Hope all right. Everything all right so far. We had a bad storm but the weather now keeps fine. Had a fine bathe this morning. There was a man in our company could make you laugh. He is an Irish Canadian. He plays the penny whistle fine and sings a bit too. Sorry to say young Walters died. He got enteric and phewmonnia and so on. I expect his people will have heard all right. How is old Mrs Walters? Dick Thursby got a packet too and Mrs Quinby's boy I forget his name. How are them white rabbits of yours. I met a feller as used to take the milk round for Mr Brand up at Bodes farm. Funny wasn't it. Well nothing more now. I hope this finds you as it leaves me your affectionate Ned.

Ned was three months on Gallipoli peninsula, but he left before the evacuation. During the whole of that time he was never not under shell-fire. He took part in seven attacks. On one occasion he went over the top with twelve hundred others, of whom only one hundred and seven returned. Once he was knocked unconscious by a mine explosion which killed sixty-seven men. At the end of that period he was shot through the back by a sniper. He was put in a dressing-station, and a gentleman in a white overall came and stuck a needle into his chest and left him there in a state of nudity for twelve hours. Work at the field hospitals was very congested just then. He became a bit delirious and was eventually put on a hospital ship with a little tag tied to him. After some vague and restless period he found himself again at Imbros and in a very comfortable hospital. He stayed there six weeks and his wound proved to be slight. The bone was only grazed. He wrote to his mother:

Dear mother,
Everything all right. I had a scratch but nothing. I hope you enjoyed
the flower show. How funny meeting Mrs Perks. We have a fine time
here. The grub is fine. Sorry to say Binnie Short went under. He got
gassed one night when he hadn't his mask on. The weather is mild and
pleasant. Glad to hear Henry takes Toffee out all right. Have not heard
from Ettie for some time. We had a fine concert on Friday. A chap
played the flute lovely. Hope you are now all right again.

Your loving son, Ned.

In bed in the hospital at Imbros a bright idea occurred to Ned. He made his
will. Such an idea would never have occurred to him had it not been forced
upon him by the unusual experiences of the past year. He suddenly realised
that of all the boys who had left the village with him only Len Cotton, as
far as he knew, remained. So one night he took a blunt-pointed pencil,
and laboriously wrote on the space for the will at the end of his pay-book:

I leave everything Ive got to my mother Anne Picklekin including Toffee. I hope Henry Thatcham will continue to look after Toffee except
the silver bowl which I won at the rabbit show at Oppleford. This I leave
to Ettie Skinner as a memorial of me.

One day Ned enjoyed a great excitement. He was under discharge from
the hospital, and a rumour got round that he and some others were to be
sent back to England. They hung about the island for three days, and were
then packed into an Italian fruit-steamer – which had been converted into
a transport. It was very overcrowded and the weather was hot. They sailed
one night and reached another island before dawn. They spent three weeks
doing this. They only sailed at night, for the seas about there were reported
to be infested with submarines. Every morning they put in at some island
in the Greek archipelago, or at some port on the mainland. At one place
there was a terrible epidemic of illness, owing to some Greek gentleman
having sold the men some doped wine. Fifteen of them died. Ned escaped
from this, as he had not had any of the wine. He was practically a
teetotaller except for an occasional glass of beer. But he was far from
happy on that voyage. The seas were rough and the transport ought to

have been broken up years ago, and this didn't seem to be the right route for England.

At length they reached a large port called Salonika. They never went into the town, but were sent straight out to a camp in the hills ten miles away. The country was very wild and rugged, and there was great difficulty with water. Everything was polluted and malarial. There was very little fighting apparently, but plenty of sickness. He found himself in a Scottish regiment. At least, it was called Scottish, but the men came from all parts of the world, from Bow Street to Hong-Kong.

There was to be no Blighty after all, but still – there it was! He continued to drill, and march, and clean his rifle and play the mouth-organ and football. And then one morning he received a letter from his mother, which had followed him from Imbros. It ran as follows:

My Dear Ned, –

How are you, dear? I hope you keep all right. My corf is now pretty middlin otherwise nothin to complain of. Now dear I have to tell you something which greives me dear. Im afraid its no good keepin it from you ony longer dear. Ettie is walkin out with another feller. A feller from the air station called Alf Mullet. I taxed her with it and she says yes it is so dear. Now dear you mustnt take on about this. I told her off I says it was a disgraceful and you out there fightin for your country and that. And she says nothin excep yes there it was and she couldnt help it and her feelins had been changed you being away and that. Now dear you must put a good face on this and remember theres just as good fish in the sea as ever came out of it as they say dear. One of Mr Beans rabbits died Sunday they think it over-eating you never know with rabbits. Keep your feet warm dear I hope you got them socks I sent. Lizzie was at chapel Sunday she had on her green lawn looked very nice I thought but I wish she wouldnt get them spots on her face perhaps its only the time of year. Toffee is all right he had a fight with a hairdale Thursday Henry says got one of his eres bitten but nothin serous. So now dear I must close as Mrs Minchin wants me to go and take tea with her has Florrie has gone to the schooltreat at Furley. And so dear with love your lovin Mother.

When he had finished reading this letter he uttered an exclamation, and a cockney friend sitting on the ground by his side remarked:

'What's the matter, mate?'

Ned took a packet of cigarettes out of his pocket and lighted one. Then he said:

'My girl's jilted me.'

The cockney laughed and said:

'Gawd! is that all? I thought it was somethin' serious!'

He was cleaning his rifle with an oil rag, and he continued:

'Don't you worry, mate. Women are like those blinkin' little Greek islands, places to call at but not to stay. What was she like?'

'Oo – all right.'

'Pretty?'

'Ay – middlin'.'

''As she got another feller?'

'Ay.'

'Oh, well, it's all in the gime. If you *will* go gallivanting about these foreign parts enjoyin' yerself, what d'yer expect? What time's kick-off this afternoon?'

'Two o'clock.'

'Reckon we're goin' to win?'

'I doan't know. 'Pends upon whether McFarlane turns out.'

'Yus, 'e's a wonderful player. Keeps the team together like.'

'Ay.'

'Are you playin'?'

'Ay. I'm playin' right half.'

'Are yer? Well, you'll 'ave yer 'ands full. You'll 'ave to tackle Curly Snider.'

'Ay.'

Ned's team won the match that afternoon, and he wrote to his mother afterwards:

DEAR MOTHER, –

We just had a great game against 15/Royal South Hants. McFarlane played centre half and he was in great form. We lead 2–0 at half-time and they scored one at the beginnin of the second half but Davis got thro towards the end and we beat them by 3–1. I was playin quite a good game I think but McFarlane is a real first class. I got your letter all right, am glad your corf is getting all right. I was sorry about Ettie but of course she knows what she wants I spose. You dont say what Toffee did to the other dog. You might tell Henery to let me have a line about this. Fancy Liz being at chapel. I almos forget what shes like. Everything is all right. The grub is fine. This is a funny place all rocks and planes. The Greeks are a stinkin lot for the most part so must now close with love.

NED.

Having completed this letter, Ned got out his pay-book and revised his will. Ettie Skinner was now deleted, and the silver bowl won at the rabbit-show at Oppleford was bequeathed to Henry Thatcham in consideration of his services in taking Toffee out for runs.

They spent a long and tedious eight months on the plains of Macedonia, dodging malaria and bullets, cracking vermin in their shirts, playing football, ragging, quarrelling, drilling, manœuvring, and, most demoralising of all, hanging about. And then a joyous day dawned. This hybrid Scottish regiment were ordered home! They left Salonica in a French liner and ten days later arrived at Malta. But in the meantime the gods had been busy. The wireless operators had been flashing their mysterious signals all over the Mediterranean and the Atlantic. At Malta the order was countermanded. They remained there long enough to coal, but the men were not even given shore leave. The next day they turned Eastwards again and made for Alexandria.

The cockney was furious. He had the real genius of the grouser, with the added venom of the man who in the year of grace had lived by his wits and now found his wits enclosed in an iron cylinder. It was a disgusting anticlimax.

'When I left that filthy 'ole,' he exclaimed, 'I swore to God I'd try and never remember it again. And now I'm darned if we ain't goin' back there. As if once ain't enough in a man's lifetime! It's like the blooming cat with the blankety mouse!'

'Eh, well, mon,' interjected a Scotsman, 'there's ane thing. They canna keel ye no but once.'

'It ain't the killing I mind. It's the blooming mucking about. What d'yer say, Pickles?'

'Ah, well . . . there it is,' said Ned sententiously.

There was considerable 'mucking about' in Egypt, and then they started off on a long trek through the desert, marching on wire mesh that had been laid down by the engineers. There was occasional skirmishing, sniping, fleas, delay, and general discomfort. One day, in Southern Palestine, Ned was out with a patrol party just before sun-down. They were trekking across the sand between two oases when shots rang out. Five of the party fell. The rest were exposed in the open to foes firing from concealment on two sides. The position was hopeless. They threw up their hands. Two more shots rang out and the cockney next to Ned fell forward with a bullet through his throat. Then dark figures came across the sands towards them. There were only three left, Ned, a Scotsman, and a boy who had been a clerk in a drapery store at Lewisham before the war. He said:

'Well, are they going to kill us?'

'No,' said the Scotsman. 'Onyway, keep your hands weel up and pray to God.'

A tall man advanced, and to their relief beckoned them to follow. They fell into single file.

'These are no Tur-r-ks at all,' whispered the Scotsman. 'They're some nomadic Arab tribe.'

The Scotsman had attended evening continuation classes at Peebles, and was rather fond of the word 'nomadic'.

They were led to one of the oases, and instructed to sit down. The Arabs sat round them, armed with rifles. They remained there till late at night, when another party arrived, and a rope was produced. They were handcuffed and braced together, and then by gesticulation told to march. They trailed across the sand for three hours and a half. There was no moon, but the night was tolerably clear. At length they came to another oasis, and were bidden to halt. They sat on the sand for twenty minutes, and one of the Arabs gave them some water. Then a whistle blew, and they were kicked and told to follow. The party wended its way through a grove of cedar-trees. It was pitch-dark. At last they came to a halt by a large hut. There was much coming and going. When they entered the hut, in charge of their guard, they were blinded by a strong light. The hut was comfortably furnished and lighted by electric light. At a table sat a stout, pale-faced man, with a dark moustache – obviously a German. By his side stood a tall German orderly. The German official looked tired and bored. He glanced at the prisoners and drew some papers towards him.

'Come and stand here in front of my desk,' he said in English.

They advanced, and he looked at each one carefully. Then he yawned, dipped his pen in ink, tried it on a sheet of paper, swore, and inserted a fresh nib.

'Now, you,' he said, addressing the Scotchman, when he had completed these operations. 'Name, age, profession, regiment. Smartly.'

He obtained all these particulars from each man. Then he got up and came round the table, and looking right into the eyes of the clerk from Lewisham, he said:

'We know, of course, in which direction your brigade is advancing, but from which direction is the brigade commanded by Major-General Forbes Fittleworth advancing?'

The three of them all knew this, for it was common gossip of the march. But the clerk from Lewisham said:

'I don't know.'

The German turned from him to the Scotsman and repeated the question.

'I don't know,' answered the Scotsman.

'From which direction is the brigade commanded by Major-General Forbes Fittleworth advancing?' he said to Ned.

'Naw! I doan't know,' replied Ned.

And then a horrible episode occurred. The German suddenly whipped out a revolver and shot the clerk from Lewisham through the body twice. He gave a faint cry and crumbled forward. Without taking the slightest notice of this horror, the German turned deliberately and held the revolver pointed at Ned's face. In a perfectly unimpassioned, toneless voice he repeated:

'From which direction is the brigade commanded by Major-General Forbes Fittleworth advancing?'

In the silence which followed, the only sound seemed to be the drone of some machine, probably from the electric-light plant. The face of Ned was mildly surprised but quite impassive. He answered without a moment's hesitation:

'Naw! I doan't know.'

There was a terrible moment in which the click of the revolver could almost be heard. It seemed to hover in front of his face for an unconscionable time, then suddenly the German lowered it with a curse, and leaning forward, he struck Ned on the side of his face with the flat of his hand. He treated the Scotsman in the same way, causing his nose to bleed. Both of the men remained quite impassive. Then he walked back to his seat, and said calmly:

'Unless you can refresh your memories within the next two hours you will both share the fate of – that swine. You will now go out to the plantation at the back and dig your graves. Dig three graves.'

He spoke sharply in Arabic to the guards, and they were led out. They were handed a spade each, two Arabs held torches for them to work by, and four others hovered in a circle twelve paces away. The soil was light sand, and digging was fairly easy. Each man dug his own grave, making it about four feet deep. When it came to the third grave the Scotsman whispered:

'Dig deep, mon.'

'Deeper than others?'

'Ay, deep enough to make a wee trench.'

'I see.'

They made it very deep, working together and whispering. When it was practically completed, apparently a sudden quarrel arose between the men. They swore at each other, and the Scotsman sprang out of the trench and gripped Ned by the throat. A fearful struggle began to take place on the edge of the grave. The guard ran up and tried to separate them. And then, during the brief confusion there was a sudden dramatic development. Simultaneously they snatched their spades. Both the men with the torches were knocked senseless, and one of them fell into the third grave. The torches were stamped out and a rifle went off. It was fired by a guard near the hut, and the bullet struck another Arab who was trying to use his bayonet. Ned brought a fourth man down with his spade and seized his rifle, and the Scotsman snatched the rifle of the man who had been shot, and they both leapt back into their purposely prepared trench.

'We shallna be able to hold this long, but we'll give them a grand run for their money,' said the Scotsman.

The body of one Arab was lying on the brink of their trench and the other in the trench itself. Fortunately they both had bandoliers, which Ned and his companion instantly removed.

'You face east and I'll take west,' said the Scotsman, his eyes glittering in the dim light. 'I'm going to try and scare that Boche devil.'

He peppered away at the hut, putting bullets through every window and smashing the telephone connection, which was a fine target at the top of a post against the sky. Bullets pinged over their heads from all directions, but there was little chance of them being rushed while their ammunition held out. However, it became necessary to look ahead. It was the Scotsman's idea in digging the graves to plan them in zig-zag formation. The end of the furthest one was barely ten paces from a clump of aloes. He now got busy with his spade whilst Ned kept guard in both directions, occasionally firing at the hut and then in the opposite direction into the darkness. In half-an-hour the Scotsman had made a shallow connection between the three graves, leaving just enough room to crawl through. They then in turn donned the turbans of the two fallen Arabs, who were otherwise dressed in a kind of semi-European uniform.

They ended up with a tremendous fusillade against the hut, riddling it with bullets; then they crept to the end of the furthest grave, and leaving their rifles, they made a sudden dash across the open space to the group of aloes, bending low and limping like wounded Arabs. They reached them in safety, but there were many open spaces to cover yet. As they emerged from the trees Ned stumbled on a dark figure. He kicked it and ran. They both ran zig-zag fashion, and tore off their turbans as they raced along. They covered nearly a hundred yards, and then bullets began to search them out again. They must have gone nearly a mile before the Scotsman gave a sudden slight groan.

'I'm hit,' he said.

He stumbled on into a clump of bushes, and fell down.

'Is it bad?' asked Ned.

'Eh, laddie, I'm doon,' he said quietly. He put his hand to his side. He had been shot through the lungs. Ned stayed with him all night, and they were undisturbed. Just before dawn the Scotsman said:

'Eh, mon, but yon was a bonny fight,' and he turned on his back and died.

Ned made a rough grave with his hands, and buried his companion. He took his identification disc and his pocket-book and small valuables, with the idea of returning them to his kin if he should get through himself. He also took his water-flask, which still fortunately contained a little water. He lay concealed all day, and at night he boldly donned his turban, issued forth and struck a caravan-trail. He continued this for four days and nights, hiding in the day-time and walking at nights. He lived on figs and dates, and one night he raided a village and caught a fowl, which also nearly cost him his life.

On the fourth night his water gave out, and he was becoming light-headed. He stumbled on into the darkness. He was a desperate man. All the chances were against him, and he felt unmoved and fatalistic. He drew his clasp-knife and gripped it tightly in his right hand. He was hardly conscious of what he was doing, and where he was going. The moon was up, and after some hours he suddenly beheld a small oblong hut. He got it into his head that this was the hut where his German persecutor was. He crept stealthily towards it.

'I'll kill that swine,' he muttered.

He was within less than a hundred yards of the hut, when a voice called out:

''Alt! Who goes there?'

'It's me,' he said. 'Doan't thee get in my way. I want to kill him. I'm going to kill him. I'm going to stab him through his black heart.'

'What the hell—!'

The sentry was not called upon to use his rifle, for the turbaned figure fell forward in a swoon.

Three weeks later Ned wrote to his mother from Bethlehem (where Christ was born), and this is what he said:

Dear Mother, –

Everything going on all right. I got three parcels here altogether as I had been away copped by some black devils an unfriendly tribe. I got back all right though. The ointment you sent was fine and so was them rock cakes. What a funny thing about Belle getting lost at the picnick. We got an awful soaking from the Mid-Lancs Fusiliers on Saturday. They had two league cracks playing one a wonderful centreforward. He scored three goals. They beat us by 7–0. The weather is hot but quite plessant at night. We have an old sergeant who was born in America does wonderful tricks with string and knots and so on. He tells some very tall yarns. You have to take them with a pinch of salt. Were getting fine grub here pretty quiet so far. Hope Henry remembers to wash Toffee with that stuff every week or so. Sorry to hear Len Cotton killed. Is his sister still walking out with that feller at Aynham. I never think he was much class for her getting good money though. Hope you have not had any more trouble with the boiler. That was a good price to get for that old buck rabbit. Well there's nothing more just now and so with love your loving son.

Ned.

Ned went through the Palestine campaign and was slightly wounded in the thigh. After spending some time in hospital he was sent to the coast and put on duty looking after Turkish prisoners. He remained there six months and was then shipped to Italy. On the way the transport was torpedoed. He was one of a party of fifty-seven picked up by French destroyers. He had been for over an hour in the water in his life-belt. He was landed in Corsica and there he developed pneumonia. He only wrote his mother one short note about this:

Dear Mother, –

Have been a bit dicky owing to falling in the water and getting wet. But going on all right. Nurses very nice and one of the doctors rowed for Cambridge against Oxford. I forget the year but Cambridge won by two and a half lengths. We have very nice flowers in the ward. Well not much to write about and so with love your loving son,

Ned.

Ned was fit again in a few weeks and he was sent up to the Italian front. He took part in several engagements and was transferred to the French front during the last months of the war. He was in the great retreat in March, 1918, and in the advance in July. After the armistice he was with the army of occupation on the banks of the Rhine. His mother wrote to him there:

My Dear Ned, –

Am glad that the fightin us now all over dear. How relieved you must be. Mr Filter was in Sunday. He thinks there will be no difficulty about you gettin your job back when you come back dear. Miss Siffkins as been deliverin but as Mr Filter says its not likely a girl is going to be able to deliver letters not like a man can and that dear. So now you will be comin home soon dear. That will be nice. We had a pleesant afternoon at the Church needlewomens gild. Miss Barbary Banstock sang very pleesantly abide with me and the vicar told a very amusing story about a little girl and a prince she didn't know he was a prince and talked to him just as though he was a man it was very amusin dear. I hear Ettie is goin to get married next month they wont get me to the weddin was it ever so I call it disgraceful and I have said so. Maud Bean is expectin in April that makes her forth in three years. Mr Bean as lost three more rabbits they say its rats this time. The potaters are a poor lot this time but the runners and cabbidge promiss well. So now dear I will close. Hoppin to have your back dear soon.

     Your loving mother.

It was, however, the autumn before Ned was demobilised. One day in early October he came swinging up the village street carrying a white kit-bag slung across his left shoulder. He looked more bronzed and perhaps a little thinner, but otherwise little altered by his five years of war experiences. The village of Ashalton was quite unaltered, but he observed several strange faces; he only met two acquaintances on the way to his mother's cottage, and they both said:

'Hullo, Ned! Ye're home agen then!'

In each case he replied:

'Ay,' and grinned, and walked on.

He entered his mother's cottage, and she was expecting him. The lamp was lighted and a grand tea was spread. There was fresh boiled beetroot, tinned salmon, salad, cake, and a large treacle tart. She embraced him and said:

'Well, Ned! Ye're back then.'

He replied: 'Ay.'

'Ye're lookin' fine,' she said. 'What a fine suit they've given ye!'

'Ay,' he replied.

'I expect you want yer tea?'

'Ay.'

He had dropped his kit-bag, and he moved luxuriously round the little parlour, looking at all the familiar objects. Then he sat down, and his mother brought the large brown tea-pot from the hob and they had a cosy tea. She told him all the very latest news of the village, and all the gossip of the countryside, and Ned grinned and listened. He said nothing at all. The tea had progressed to the point when Ned's mouth was full of treacle tart, when his mother suddenly stopped, and said:

'Oh, dear, I'm afraid I have somethin' distressin' to tell ye, dear.'

'O-oh? what's that?'

'Poor Toffee was killed.'

'What!'

Ned stopped suddenly in the mastication of the treacle tart. His eyes bulged and his cheeks became very red. He stared at his mother wildly, and repeated:

'What's that? What's that ye say, Mother?'

'Poor Toffee, my dear. It happened right at the cross-roads. Henry was takin' him out. It seems he ran round in front of a steam-roller, and a motor came round the corner sudden. Henry called out, but too late. Went right over his back. Poor Henry was quite upset. He brought him home. What's the matter, dear?'

Ned had pushed his chair back, and he stood up. He stared at his mother like a man who has seen horror for the first time.

'Where is – where was—' he stammered.

'We buried 'im, dear, under the little mound beyond the rabbit hutches.'

Ned staggered across the room like a drunken man, and repeated dismally:

'The little mound beyond the rabbit hutches!'

He lifted the latch, and groped his way into the garden. His mother followed him. He went along the mud path, past the untenanted hutches covered with tarpaulin. Some tall sunflowers stared at him insolently. A fine rain was beginning to fall. In the dim light he could just see the little mound – signifying the spot where Toffee was buried. He stood there bare-headed, gazing at the spot. His mother did not like to speak. She tiptoed back to the door. But after a time she called out:

'Ned! . . . Ned!'

He did not seem to hear, and she waited patiently. At the end of several minutes she called again:

'Ned! . . . Ned dear, come and finish your tea.'

He replied quite quietly:

'All right, Mother.'

But he kept his face averted, for he did not want his mother to see the tears which were streaming down his cheeks.

VIOLA MEYNELL

The Letter

There came a day when it was realized at the farm that Jessie was no longer working. It was this that brought the truth of her condition suddenly forward, as nothing else had done, into the full glare of recognition and disapproval. Until now it had been lurking in the background, half ignored, or at least postponed in the perpetually behind-hand pressure of farm life. For some time she had been slackening off; she gave no helping hand at the anxious time of harvest, and at last she stopped milking, with inconceivable inconvenience. In that work-ridden household the matter had at last become prominent and disastrous. George Troubridge evidently thought that by setting her to tasks different from those to which she was accustomed he could still draw service out of his daughter. His wife in similar circumstances always worked right up to the end. But all the same, it was his wife who now defended the girl from the necessity to perform these tasks, telling him sharply that he could see for himself that she wasn't fit for work. Never, however, was a defence more coldly put forward, purely on its merits, and without a touch of personal bias in Jessie's favour. This protection of her by her mother was like the cold intervention of the law against some popular act of mob justice.

Once made a conspicuous question, therefore, the whole matter emerged out of its silence. 'Something'll have to be done,' said George Troubridge. Repeating this several times, the necessity took a more definite form in his mind. 'She'll have to write to him and tell him,' he said doggedly. 'I don't care who he is, he's got to be told. You'll have to make her sit down and write to him,' he said to his wife in the presence of the girl; and Jessie's sudden flood of tears at that pronouncement only made him more certain that he was right.

At first it was just a blow dealt her by her father, but presently it became something gradually closing her in on every side – that she must write. No matter how often her father or mother repeated it, the effect on Jessie was the same – one stiff, frightened look and she was dissolved in tears which made her eyes swollen for hours. So that even when the subject might have been laid aside for a time – as everything but death gets laid aside for the immediate task in farm life – people were constantly being reminded of it by the sight of the girl's tear-stained face.

As she was no longer driven here and there by her work, and had strange free-time to dispose of, she began to spend hours in the fields and woods, and there at any rate she could feel a little removed from the necessity to write her letter. But how odd an inhabitant she felt of the familiar places! She was nearly eighteen, and had never lived anywhere else, and yet she felt a stranger now. Everything was new to her. There was one thing that she had never considered in the past about the roads and paths her feet used to cover so swiftly and lightly, and that was whether they were up or downhill. The country had been all flat beneath her swift, untiring feet. Now it rose and fell in so marked a way that this seemed to be the most noticeable thing about it. The slightest gradient shortened her breath and reminded her of her distress and weakness. As for all the village girls who could move quickly and lightly, she still might be their contemporary, but she was no longer of their kind; she was of an age and kind all to herself. She was more like an old man she met creeping up the lane than like those who used to be her playmates.

One day when she came down pale in the early morning her father, pressed by the excess of things to do, just found time, amidst all his preparations for market, to be fretted intolerably by the sight of her uselessness.

'Have you written that letter?' he asked.

'No.'

'Then you'll write it today! You've got plenty of time on your hands, by the look of it.' He slammed the door – all his useful work on one side of it, all her useless tears on the other.

She did what she could to help her mother through her tears; but Mrs Troubridge, busy giving the younger children their breakfast, and nursing in her arms the youngest of all, seemed to Jessie silently to repeat her father's command, if only because she had been present when it was made and had heard it and had not contradicted it. The very children by their mere complacence were of the same mind as their father. The servant-girl, because she had run so quickly to fetch his leggings when he asked for them, was obviously of his mind.

She felt alone with the impossibility that confronted her. With dismay she watched her mother. Mrs Troubridge reached down from a shelf a box that for years had contained a few pieces of best note-paper, and laid one of the sheets, almost as thick as blotting-paper, and with fretted edges, on the table for Jessie. The girl gave one helpless look at it and went out.

It had not rained, and yet when her arm touched a low branch heavy drops hung on her sleeve. No surface was exempt from the drenching wet. Even the tiny scarlet field-poppy, with petals so flimsy that they seemed to be made of nothing but light and redness, had to support a layer of moisture. The sun, wherever it was, could do nothing; it was one of those autumn days of dew and mist too heavy to lift, when midday is no lighter than dawn.

Jessie walked slowly, breathing hard. Her thin face, in which the youth and beauty should have been so full of flitting subtle things to say, had now the simplest and singlest look in the world, the look of suffering. It was not mental strain that marked her; she had not lived long enough to be marked by the kind of trouble that writes slowly on young faces. But her body's woes, with their much quicker signals, had reduced all the sparkle to languor, and she was a pale, haggard beauty instead of a fresh rosy one.

She had not walked far through the first field before each of her ankles was bound round and round with threads of moist cobweb, spun between one stalk and another. If those threads had been cords, she would have been a close prisoner, neatly caught and fastened up. But as it was she went idly through the stubble, unconscious that with each step she was bursting bonds, dragging chains, and escaping a thousand prisons. From the bonds and prisons she was conscious of there was no escape. She knew that the letter must be written, for her father was determined.

The knowledge that she must write overwhelmed her with simple, mystified dismay. What could she say to him? She had said so little to him at any time – never anything that was not timid and shy, and breathed out wildly and gently on the secret pulses of love. When her father said angrily, 'You'll write to him and tell him!' she seemed to have a hard harangue of threats and disgrace and retribution thrust upon her with which to speak to him, instead of those soft broken flowers of speech which were all that she could remember or imagine with him; and her mind and heart were powerless and refused.

She was out as long as possible that day, until clinging round each of her ankles was such a mass of the threads of cobweb that they seemed woven into soft grey fabric. The day faded away early from the light it had never really seemed to attain. When evening came she was at home getting the younger children to bed, while downstairs the evening that awaited her held nothing but her father's homecoming, and the sheet of note-paper lying on the table.

After supper her father asked the dreaded question, which her mother answered for her.

'No, she hasn't written yet.'

'She's got to do as she's told, do you hear?'

'Yes, the girl knows that.'

'Then why hasn't she done it?'

Mrs Troubridge explained.

'She says she doesn't know what to say.'

George Troubridge took this in slowly. His silence continued to listen to the words after they were spoken; it also allowed the difficulty, though without acknowledging that he was himself beaten by it. He was sitting at his ease in the cosy lamp-lit room, but his hard limbs seemed to be so stiff-shaped as to be beyond the comfortable ministrations of the arm-chair. Two of the elder children were playing cards at the table. Their Aunt Isabel, whose status in the house as Mrs Troubridge's sister gave her the privilege of doing twice as much work as any maid, came and sat down with her mending. But because the younger children were in bed, and the indoor man gone to his quarters, and the hour come when it was unlikely that George Troubridge would be interrupted again that night, a suitable degree of privacy seemed to have been achieved.

'She doesn't know what to say, doesn't she?' began Mr Troubridge. 'Oh, so she doesn't know what to say,' he repeated, gaining time. Sudden inspiration came to him. 'Well, then, let her tell him he's got her into trouble and he'll have to do something about it. Let her tell him that.'

'Yes, and she must tell him a man might be the highest in the land, but it doesn't excuse him,' said his wife, catching the inspiration herself. 'And she must say he'll never have any rest to his mind nor enjoy any of his blessings unless he does something for her and the child,' she proclaimed doubtfully.

Each time they stopped speaking Jessie made a faint movement, not a reply, but something more dutiful than absolute stillness would have been. Her downcast eyes and helpless mouth just stirred – a faint, dumb, despairing signal of obedience.

'So you don't know what to say, don't you?' said George Troubridge once more. 'Well, then tell him that what with dear labour and cheap corn, and what with the taxes, and the market flooded with imports, you might say I'm a ruined man. You tell him that. And the harder I work, the more money I lose, by the look of it,' he grumbled. 'And so it's going on, by what I can see. And it isn't likely I'm going to pay for his wrong-doing. That's what you've got to tell him.'

'And tell him,' said Mrs Troubridge, 'that you've had a bad time with it so far, shocking bad; and that you've been as good as useless in the house for some time past.'

'And you must say,' came from Mrs Troubridge's hard-worked sister, startling them all with unexpectedness, 'that a man should do everything in his power to atone for such wickedness – yes, everything, and then he could never do enough.' Her face was flushed and her eyes bright with indignation.

This outburst closed the subject; anything added at that moment would have been an anticlimax, and no further material for Jessie's letter was supplied to her that night.

But when she woke up the next morning she knew that the letter had come closer, and she did not see how she could avoid writing it that day.

That night her father asked:

'Has she written to him?'

'No, she hasn't exactly written yet,' replied her mother.

'Then why hasn't she?'

'Well, she didn't really know if that's all she has to say.'

He reflected.

'She can tell him I've always been a fair man myself, and I look for fair treatment from others. But there's no fairness in how this is! None at all! And she's got to let him know it.'

Another day went by and when evening came the sight of her immediately reminded her father.

'Has she done what she's told?' he asked.

'Not yet,' said her mother, 'but now that she knows what she's got to say, she'll be writing. I was just wondering whether that's all, or whether there's anything else she ought to add.'

They meditated, with the slightly pleasant consciousness that the execution of this disagreeable duty did at any rate provide the opportunity to distinguish oneself by the value of the ideas one contributed to the letter. It was to Mrs Troubridge that the honours fell this evening.

'I was thinking,' she said, 'that she might also put that a girl's fair name is her all, and that once she's lost that she's lost everything.'

'Yes,' said Mr Troubridge, 'she can put a piece about that if she likes.'

Jessie went out the next day to wander in her father's big fields. Today only the early morning was misty, and the dark-gold sun of autumn shone powerfully, scattering the vapours. The fields were of an unusual size; it would seem at first as if this were a wide undivided sweep of tilled land, until far away could be seen the hedges that squared-in the vast spaces and made them, after all, into fields – but such fields as required a mammoth sowing, and made large ricks and filled great barns. Passing into one of these fields with her tired distressed walk, Jessie could hardly see its limits. For one of those great fields was large enough to contain rises and falls, to hold not only the deeply coloured sunshine close around her, but also the mists of autumn in its distant parts. When afternoon came she and the red setting sun stood in the same field, at either end of it.

In the grandeur and spaciousness of the day her thoughts passed beyond her immediate preoccupation, and opened her mind to memories and to faint thrills of the future. Earlier in the day she had thought she would have done best to stay at home in the arm-chair. But as she wandered her weariness passed away for once. She entered a field that from the gate was nothing but monotonous stubble from end to end; she came out of the same field with her hands full of bright yellow and white and purple wild-flowers gathered from the profusion lurking in that colourless stubble. She passed into a little wood, and came out of it with her face bright, leaving it lingeringly as if she had never wished to leave it again. And then when she could delay no longer she turned her footsteps toward home.

Going indoors she saw the sheet of letter-paper lying where it had waited so long for her. With a leap of her heart she knew she was to write to him, and she sat at the table and took up the pen.

Do not be angry at getting these few lines from one you have perhaps forgotten now you are so far away. It is because I had such a happy day, and it seems as if I am speaking to you now. Excuse me for telling you what a joyful thing happened today. I passed through Hayter's copse where I lost the bracelet you gave me and where we searched so long. I've spent many an hour looking for it since then, but after all these months I found it today at my feet in some moss.

I went also by the lane where you sprained your ankle, and how I wish with all my heart you had never had that pain to bear and need never know what it is to suffer pain. If these few lines could bring you a hundredth part of what I wish you would be happy for always.

JESSIE

That evening her father, when he came indoors and settled himself in his arm-chair, said:

'Has the girl written that letter yet?'

'Yes,' said her mother, 'she's written.'

'She has written? Oh well, never mind. Only I was going to tell her another bit to put in if she hadn't written yet. Here I've been to market today with the pigs and the chicken and had a terrible bad trade; they didn't make much above what they cost me to rear. How's that going to pay for extra expenses? And what's the good of me going out to earn sixpence if she stops at home and spends a shilling! Just let her tell him that!'

'Yes, but the letter's written,' his wife reminded him.

'So it is. Well, then, let Tom slip along to the cross-roads and catch the postman with it.'

A. E. COPPARD

Olive and Camilla

They had lived and travelled together for twenty years, and this is a part of their history: not much, but all that matters. Ever since reaching marriageable age they had been together, and so neither had married, though Olive had had her two or three occasions of perilous inducement. Being women, they were critical of each other, inseparably critical; being spinsters, they were huffy, tender, sullen, and demure and had quarrelled with each other ten thousand times in a hundred different places during their 'wanderings up and down Europe'. That was the phrase Camilla used in relating their maidenly Odyssey, which had comprised a multitude of sojourns in the pensions of Belgium, Switzerland, Italy, and France. They quarrelled in Naples and repented in Rome; exploded in anger at Arles, were embittered at Interlaken, parted for ever at Lake Garda, Taormina, and Bruges; but running water never fouls, they had never really been apart, not anywhere. Olive was like that, and so was her friend; such natures could nowise be changed. Camilla Hobbs, slight and prim, had a tiny tinkling mind that tinkled all day long; she was all things to little nothings. The other, Olive Sharples, the portly one, had a mind like a cuckoo-clock; something came out and cried 'Cuckoo' now and again, quite sharply, and was done with it. They were moulded thus, one supposes, by the hand of Providence; it could be neither evaded nor altered, it could not even be mitigated, for in Camilla's prim mind and manner there was a prim deprecation of Olive's boorish nature, and for her part Olive resented Camilla's assumption of a superior disposition. Saving a precious month or two in Olive's favour they were both now of a sad age, an age when the path of years slopes downwards to a yawning inexplicable gulf.

'Just fancy!' Camilla said on her forty-fifth birthday – they were at Chamonix then – 'we are ninety between us!'

Olive glowered at her friend, though a couple of months really is nothing. 'When I am fifty,' she declared, 'I shall kill myself.'

'But why?' Camilla was so interested.

'God, I don't know!' returned Olive.

Camilla brightly brooded for a few moments. 'You'll find it very hard to commit suicide; it's not easy, you know, not at all. I've heard time and time again that it's most difficult . . .'

'Pooh!' snorted Olive.

'But I tell you! I tell you I knew a cook at Leamington who swallowed ground glass in her porridge, pounds and pounds, and nothing came of it.'

'Pooh!' Olive was contemptuous. 'Never say die.'

'Well, that's just what people say who can't do it!'

The stream of their companionship was far from being a rill of peaceful water, but it flowed, more and more like a cataract it flowed, and was like to flow on as it had for those twenty years. Otherwise they were friendless! Olive had had enough money to do as she modestly liked, for though she was impulsive her desires were frugal, but Camilla had had nothing except a grandmother. In the beginning of their friendship Olive had carried the penurious Camilla off to Paris, where they mildly studied art and ardently pursued the practice of water-colour painting. Olive, it might be said, transacted doorways and alleys, very shadowy and grim, but otherwise quite nice; and Camilla did streams with bending willow and cow on bank, really sweet. In a year or two Camilla's grandmother died of dropsy and left her a fortune, much larger than Olive's, in bank stock, insurance stock, distillery, coal – oh, a mass of money! And when something tragical happened to half of Olive's property – it was in salt shares or jute shares, such unstable friable material – it became the little fluttering Camilla's joy to play the fairy godmother in her turn. So there they were in a bondage less sentimental than appeared, but more sentimental than was known.

They returned to England for George V's coronation. In the train from Chamonix a siphon of soda-water that Camilla imported into the carriage – it was an inexplicable thing, that bottle of soda-water, as Olive said after the catastrophe: God alone knew why she had bought it – Camilla's siphon, what with the jolting of the train and its own gasobility, burst on the rack. Just burst! A handsome young Frenchwoman travelling in their compartment was almost convulsed with mirth, but Olive, sitting just below the bottle, was drenched, she declared, to the midriff. Camilla lightly deprecated the coarseness of the expression. How could *she* help it if a bottle took it into its head to burst like that! In abrupt savage tones Olive merely repeated that she was soaked to the midriff, and to Camilla's horror she began to divest herself of some of her clothing. Camilla rushed to the windows, pulled down the blinds, and locked the corridor door. The young Frenchwoman sat smiling while Olive removed her corsets and her wetted linen; Camilla rummaged so feverishly in Olive's suitcase that the compartment began to look as if arranged for a jumble sale; there were garments and furbelows strewn everywhere. But at last Olive completed her toilet, the train stopped at a station, the young Frenchwoman got out. Later in the day, when they were nearing Paris, Olive's corsets could not be found.

'What did you do with them?' Olive asked Camilla.

'But I don't think I touched them, Olive. After you took them off I did not see them again. Where do you think you put them? Can't you remember?'

She helped Olive unpack the suitcase, but the stays were not there. And she helped Olive to repack.

'What am I to do?' asked Olive.

Camilla firmly declared that the young Frenchwoman who had travelled with them in the morning must have stolen them.

'What for?' asked Olive.

'Well, what do people steal things for?' There was an air of pellucid reason in Camilla's question, but Olive was scornful.

'Corsets!' she exclaimed.

'I knew a cripple once,' declared Olive, 'who stole an ear-trumpet.'

'That French girl wasn't a cripple.'

'No,' said Camilla, 'but she was married – at least, she wore a wedding ring. She looked as deep as the sea. I am positive she was up to no good.'

'Bosh!' said Olive. 'What the devil are you talking about?'

'Well, you should not throw your things about as you do.'

'Soda-water,' snapped Olive, with ferocious dignity, 'is no place for a railway carriage.'

'You mean—?' asked Camilla with the darling sweetness of a maid of twenty.

'I mean just what I say.'

'Oh no, you don't,' purred the triumphant one; and she repeated Olive's topsy-turvy phrase. 'Ha, ha, that's what you said.'

'I did not! Camilla, why are you such a liar? You know it annoys me.'

'But I tell you, Olive—'

'I did not! It's absurd. You're a fool.'

Well, they got to England and in a few days it began to appear to them as the most lovely country they had ever seen. It was not only that, it was their homeland. Why have we stayed away so long? Why did we not come back before? It was so marvellously much better than anything else in the world, they were sure of that. So much better, too, than their youthful recollection of it, so much improved; and the cleanness! Why did we never come back? Why have we stayed away so long? They did not know; it was astonishing to find your homeland so lovely. Both felt that they could not bear to leave England again; they would settle down and build a house, it was time; their joint age was ninety! But, alas, it was difficult, it was impossible, to dovetail their idea of a house into one agreeable abode.

'I want,' said Olive Sharples, 'just an English country cottage with a few conveniences. That's all I can afford and all I want.'

So she bought an acre of land at the foot of a green hill in the Chilterns and gave orders for the erection of the house of her dreams. Truly it was a charming spot, pasture and park and glebe and spinney and stream, *deliciously* remote, quite half a mile from *any* village, and only to be reached by a *mere* lane. No sooner had her friend made this decision than Camilla too bought land there, half a dozen acres adjoining Olive's, and began to build the house of *her* dreams, a roomy house with a loggia and a balcony, planting her land with fruit trees. The two houses were built close together, by the same men, and Camilla could call out greetings to Olive from her bedroom window before Olive was up in the morning, and Olive could hear her – though she did not always reply. Had Olive suffered herself to peer steadily into her secret thoughts in order to discover her present feeling about Camilla, she would have been perplexed; she might even have been ashamed, but for the comfort of old acquaintance such telescopic introspection was denied her. The new cottage brought her felicity, halcyon days; even her bedroom contented her, so small and clean and bare it was. Beyond bed, washing-stand, mirror, and rug there was almost nothing, and yet she felt that if she were not exceedingly careful she would break something. The ceiling was virgin white, the walls the colour of butter, the floor the colour of chocolate. The grate had never had a fire in it; not a shovelful of ashes had ever been taken from it, and, please God – so it seemed to indicate – never would be. But the bed was soft and reposeful. Oh, heavenly sleep!

The two friends dwelt thus in isolation; there they were, perhaps this was happiness. The isolation was tempered by the usual rural society, a squire who drank, a magistrate who was mad, and a lime-burner whose daughters had been to college and swore like seamen. There was the agreeable Mr Kippax, a retired fellmonger, in whom Camilla divined a desire to wed somebody – Olive perhaps. He was sixty and played on the violoncello. Often Olive accompanied him on Camilla's grand piano. Crump, crump, he would go; and primp, primp, Olive would reply. He was a serious man, and once when they were alone he asked Olive why she was always so sad.

'I don't know. Am I?'

'Surely,' he said, grinning, running his fingers through his long grey hair. 'Why are you?'

And Olive thought and thought. 'I suppose I want impossible things.'

'Such as—?' he interrogated.

'I do not know. I only know that I shall never find them.'

Then there were the vicarage people, a young vicar with a passionate complexion who had once been an actor and was now something of an invalid, having had a number of his ribs removed for some unpleasant purpose; charming Mrs Vicar and a tiny baby. Oh, and Mrs Lassiter, the wife of a sea captain far away on the seas; yet she was content, and so by inference was the sea captain, for he never came home. There was a dearth of colour in her cheeks, it had crowded into her lips, her hair, her eyes. So young, so beautiful, so trite, there was a fragrant imbecility about her.

Olive and Camilla seldom went out together: the possession of a house is often as much of a judgment as a joy, and as full of ardours as of raptures. Gardens, servants, and tradespeople were not automata that behaved like eight-day clocks, by no means. Olive had an eight-day clock, a small competent little thing; it had to be small to suit her room, but Camilla had three – three eight-day clocks. And on the top of the one in the drawing-room – and really Camilla's house seemed a positive little mansion, all crystal and mirror and white pillars and soft carpets, but it wasn't a mansion any more than Olive's was a cottage – well, on the mantelpiece of the drawing-room, on top of Camilla's largest eight-day clock, there stood the bronze image of a dear belligerent little lion copied in miniature from a Roman antique. The most adorable creature it was, looking as if it were about to mew, for it was no bigger than a kitten although a grown-up lion with a mane and an expression of annoyance as if it had been insulted by an ox – a toy ox. The sweep of its tail was august; the pads of its feet were beautiful crumpled cushions, with claws (like the hooks of a tiny ship) laid on the cushions. Simply ecstatic with anger, most adorable, and Olive loved it as it raged there on Camilla's eight-day clock. But clocks are not like servants. No servant would stay there for long, the place was so lonely, they said, dreadful! And in wet weather the surroundings and approach – there was only a green lane, and half a mile of that – were so muddy, dreadful mud; and when the moon was gone everything was steeped in darkness, and that was dreadful too! As neither Camilla nor Olive could mitigate these natural but unpleasing features – they were, of course, the gifts of Providence – the two ladies, Camilla at any rate, suffered from an ever recurrent domestic Hail and Farewell. What, Camilla would inquire, *did* the servants want? There was the village, barely a mile away; if you climbed the hill you could see it spendidly, a fine meek little village; the woods, the hills, the fields, positively thrust their greenness upon it, bathed it as if in a prism – so that the brown chimney-pots looked red and the yellow ones blue. And the church was new, or so nearly new that you might call it a good second-hand; it was made of brown bricks. Although it had no tower, or even what you might call a belfry, it had got a little square fat chimney over the front gable with a cross of yellow bricks worked into the face of the chimney, while just below that was a bell cupboard stuffed with sparrows' nests. And there were unusual advantages in the village – watercress, for instance. But Camilla's servants came and went, only Olive's Quincy Pugh remained. She was a dark young woman with a white amiable face, amiable curves to her body, the elixir of amiability in her blood, and it was clear to Camilla that *she* only remained because of Luke Feedy. He was the gardener, chiefly employed by Camilla, but he also undertook the work of Olive's plot. Unfortunately Olive's portion was situated immediately under the hill and, fence it how they would, the rabbits always burrowed in and stole Olive's vegetables. They never seemed to attack Camilla's more abundant acreage.

Close beside their houses there was a public footway, but seldom used, leading up into the hills. Solemn steep hills they were, covered with long fawn-hued grass that was never cropped or grazed, and dotted with thousands of pert little juniper bushes, very dark, and a few whitebeam trees whose foliage when tossed by the wind shook on the hillside like bushes of entangled stars. Half-way up the hill path was a bulging bank that tempted climbers to rest, and here, all unknown to Camilla, Olive caused an iron bench to be fixed so that tired persons could recline in comfort and view the grand country that rolled away before them. Even at midsummer it was cool on that height, just as in winter it took the sunbeams warmly. The air roving through the long fawn-hued grass had a soft caressing movement. Darkly green at the foot of the hill began the trees and hedges that diminished in the pastoral infinity of the vale, farther and farther yet, so very far and wide. At times Olive would sit on her iron bench in clear sunlight and watch a shower swilling over half a dozen towns while beyond them, seen through the inundating curtain, very remote indeed lay the last hills of all, brightly glowing and contented. Often Olive would climb to her high seat and bask in the delight, but soon Camilla discovered that the bench was the public gift of Olive. Thereupon lower down the hill Camilla caused a splendid ornate bench of teak with a foot-rest to be installed in a jolly nook surrounded by tall juniper bushes like cypresses, and she planted three or four trailing roses thereby. Whenever Camilla had visitors she would take them up the hill to sit on her splendid bench; even Olive's visitors preferred Camilla's bench and remarked upon its superior charm. So much more handsome it was, and yet Olive could not bear to sit there at all, never alone. And soon she gave up going even to the iron one.

Thus they lived in their rather solitary houses, supporting the infirmities of the domestic spirit by mutual commiseration, and coming to date occasions by the names of those servants – Georgina, Rose, Elizabeth, Sue – whoever happened to be with them when such and such an event occurred. These were not remarkable in any way. The name of Emma Tooting, for instance, only recalled a catastrophe to the parrot. One day she had actually shut the cockatoo – it was a stupid bird, always like a parson nosing about in places where it was not wanted – she had accidentally shut the cockatoo in the oven. The fire had not long been lit, the oven was not hot, Emma Tooting was brushing it out, the cockatoo was watching. Emma Tooting was called away for a few moments by the baker in the yard, came back, saw the door open, slammed it to with her foot, pulled out blower, went upstairs to make bed, came down later to make fire, heard most horrible noises in kitchen, couldn't tell where, didn't know they came from the oven, thought it was the devil, swooned straight away – and the cockatoo was baked. The whole thing completely unnerved Emma Tooting and she gave notice. Such a good cook, too. Mrs Lassiter and the lime-burner – that was a mysterious business – were thought to have been imprudent in Minnie Hopplecock's time; at any rate, suspicion was giddily engendered then.

'I shouldn't be surprised,' Camilla had declared, 'if they were all the way, myself. Of course, I don't know, but it would not surprise me one bit. You see, we've only instinct to go upon, suspicion, but what else has anyone ever to go upon in such matters? She is so deep, she's deep as the sea; and as for men—! No, I've only my intuitions, but they are sufficient, otherwise what is the use of an intuition? And what *is* the good of shutting your eyes to the plain facts of life?'

'But why him?' inquired Olive brusquely.

'I suspect him, Olive.' Camilla, calmly adjusting a hair-slide, peered at her yellow carpet, which had a design in it, a hundred times repeated, of a spool of cord in red and a shuttlecock in blue. 'I suspect him, just as I suspect the man who quotes Plato to me.'

Mr Kippax that is – thought Olive. 'But isn't that what Plato's for?' she asked.

'I really don't know what Plato is for, Olive; I have never read Plato; in fact I don't read him at all; I can't read him with enjoyment. Poetry, now, is a thing I can enjoy – like a bath – but I can't talk about it. Can you? I never talk about the things that are precious to me; it's natural to be reserved and secretive. I don't blame Maude Lassiter for that; I don't blame her at all, but she'll be lucky if she gets out of this with a whole skin: it will only be by the skin of her teeth.'

'I'd always be content,' Olive said, 'if I could have the skin of my teeth for a means of escape.'

'Quite so,' agreed Camilla, 'I'm entirely with you. Oh, yes.'

Among gardeners Luke Feedy was certainly the pearl. He had come from far away, a man of thirty or thirty-five, without a wife or a home in the world, and now he lodged in the village at Mrs Thrupcott's cottage; the thatch of her roof was the colour of shag tobacco; her husband cut your hair in his vegetable garden for twopence a time. Luke was tall and powerful, fair and red. All the gardening was done by him, both Olive's and Camilla's, and all the odd and difficult jobs from firewood down to the dynamo for electric light that coughed in Camilla's shed. Bluff but comely, a pleasant man, a very conversational man, and a very attractable man; the maids were always uncommon friendly to him. And so even was Olive, Camilla observed, for she had actually bought him a gun to keep the rabbits out of the garden. Of course a gun was no use for that – Luke said so – yet, morning or evening, Olive would perambulate with the gun, inside or outside the gardens, while Luke Feedy taught her the use of it, until one October day, when it was drawing on to evening – bang! – Olive had killed a rabbit. Camilla had rushed to her balcony. 'What is it?' she cried in alarm, for the gun had not often been fired before and the explosion was terrifying. Fifty yards away, with her back towards her, Olive in short black fur jacket, red skirt, and the Cossack boots she wore, was standing quite still holding the gun across her breast. The gardener stalked towards a bush at the foot of the hill, picked up a limp contorted bundle by its long ears, and brought it back to Olive. She had no hat on, her hair was ruffled, her face had gone white. The gardener held up the rabbit, a small soft thing, dead, but its eyes still stared, and its forefeet drooped in a gesture that seemed to beseech pity. Olive swayed away, the hills began to twirl, the house turned upside down, the gun fell from her hands. 'Hullo!' cried Luke Feedy, catching the swooning woman against his shoulder. Camilla saw it all and flew to their aid, but by the time she had got down to the garden Feedy was there too, carrying Olive to her own door. Quincy ran for a glass of water, Camilla petted her, and soon all was well. The gardener stood in the room holding his hat against his chest with both hands. A huge fellow he looked in Olive's small apartment. He wore breeches and leggings and a grey shirt with the sleeves uprolled, a pleasant comely man, very powerful, his voice seemed to excite a quiver in the air.

'What a fool I am!' said Olive disgustedly.

'Oh, no,' commented the gardener. 'Oh no, ma'am; it stands to reason—' He turned to go about his business, but said: 'I should have a sip o' brandy now, ma'am, if you'll excuse me mentioning it.'

'Cognac!' urged Camilla.

'Don't go, Luke,' Olive cried.

'I'll fetch that gun in, ma'am, I fancy it's going to rain.' He stalked away, found his coat and put it on (for it was time to go home), and then he fetched in the gun. Camilla had gone.

'Take it away, please,' cried Olive. 'I never want to see it again. Keep it. Do what you like, it's yours.'

'Thank you, ma'am,' said the imperturbable Feedy. Two small glasses of cognac and a long slim bottle stood upon a table in the alcove. Olive, still a little wan, pushed one towards him.

'Your very good health, ma'am.' Feedy tipped the thimbleful of brandy into his mouth, closed his lips, pursed them, gazed at the ceiling, and sighed. Olive now switched on the light, for the room was growing dimmer every moment. Then she sat down on the settee that faced the fire. An elegant little settee in black satin with crimson piping. The big man stood by the shut door and stared at the walls; he could not tell whether they were blue or green or grey, but the skirting was white and the fireplace was tiled with white tiles. Old and dark the furniture was, though, and the mirror over the mantel was egg-shaped in a black frame. In the alcove made by the bow window stood the round table on crinkled legs, and the alcove itself was lined with a bench of tawny velvet cushions. Feedy put his empty glass upon the table.

'Do have some more; help yourself,' said Olive, and Luke refilled the glass and drank again amid silence. Olive did not face him – she was staring into the fire – but she could feel his immense presence. There was an aroma, something of earth, something of man, about him, strange and exciting. A shower of rain dashed at the windows.

'You had better sit down until the rain stops.' Olive poked a tall hassock to the fireplace with her foot, and Luke, squatting upon it, his huge boots covering quite a large piece of the rug there, twirled the half-empty glass between his finger and thumb.

'Last time I drunk brandy,' he mused, 'was with a lady in her room, just this way.'

Olive could stare at him now.

'She was mad,' he explained.

'Oh,' said Olive, as if disappointed.

'She's dead now,' continued Luke, sipping.

Olive, without uttering a word, seemed to encourage his reminiscence.

'A Yorkshire lady she was, used to live in the manor house, near where I was then; a lonely place. Her brother had bought it because it was lonely, and sent her there to keep her quiet because she had been crossed in love, as they say, and took to drink for the sorrow of it; rich family, bankers, Croxton the name, if you ever heard of them?'

Olive, lolling back and sipping brandy, shook her head.

'A middling-size lady, about forty-five she was, but very nice to look at – you'd never think she was daft – and used to live at the big house with only a lot of servants and a butler in charge of her, name of Scrivens. None of her family ever came near her, nobody ever came to visit her. There was a big motor-car and they kept some horses, but she always liked to be tramping about alone; everybody knew her, poor daft thing, and called her Miss Mary, 'stead of by her surname, Croxton, a rich family; bankers they were. Quite daft. One morning I was going to my work – I was faggoting then in Hanging Copse – and I'd got my bill-hook, my axe, and my saw in a bag on my back, when I see Miss Mary coming down the road towards me. 'Twas a bright spring morning and cold 'cause 'twas rather early; a rare wind on, and blew sharp enough to shave you; it blew the very pigeons out the trees, but she'd got neither jacket or hat and her hair was wild. "Good morning, miss," I said, and she said: "Good morning," and stopped. So I stopped, too; I didn't quite know what to be at, so I said: "Do you know where you are going?"'

'Look here,' interrupted Olive, glancing vacantly around the room. 'It's still raining; light your pipe.'

'Thank you, ma'am.' Luke began to prepare his pipe. '"Do you know where you're going?" I asked her, "No," she says. "I've lost my way; where am I?" and she put' – Luke paused to strike a match and ignite the tobacco – 'put her arm in my arm and said: "Take me home." "You're walking away from home," I said, so she turned back with me and we started off to her home. Two miles away or more it was. "It is kind of you," she says, and she kept on chattering as if we were two cousins, you might say. "You ought to be more careful and have your jacket on," I said to her. "I didn't think, I can't help it," she says; "it's the time 'o love; as soon as the elder leaf is as big as a mouse's ear I want to be blown about the world," she says. Of course she was thinking to find someone as she'd lost. She dropped a few tears. "You must take care of yourself these rough mornings," I said, "or you'll be catching the inflammation." Then we come to a public-house, The Bank of England's the name of it, and Miss Mary asks me if we could get some refreshment there. "That you can't," I said ('cause I knew about her drinking), "it's shut," so on we went as far as Bernard's Bridge. She had to stop a few minutes there to look over in the river, all very blue and crimped with the wind; and there was a boat-house there, and a new boat cocked upside down on some trestles on the landing, and a chap laying on his back blowing in the boat with a pair of bellows. Well, on we goes, and presently she pulls out her purse. "I'm putting you to a lot of trouble," she says. "Not at all, miss," I said, but she give me a sovereign, then and there, she give me a sovereign.'

Olive was staring at the man's hands; the garden soil was chalky, and his hands were covered with fine milky dust that left the skin smooth and the markings very plain.

'I didn't want to take the money, ma'am, but I had to, of course; her being such a grand lady it wasn't my place to refuse.'

Olive had heard of such munificence before; the invariable outcome, the denouement of Feedy's stories, the crown, the peak, the apex of them all was that somebody, at some point or other, gave him a sovereign. Neither more nor less. Never anything else. Olive thought it unusual for so *many* people . . .

'– and I says: "I'm very pleased, miss, to be a help to anyone in trouble." "That's most good of you," she said to me. "That's most good of you; it's the time of year I must go about the world, or I'd die," she says. By and by we come to the manor house and we marched arm in arm right up to the front door and I rong the bell. I was just turning away to leave her there, but she laid hold of my arm again. "I want you to stop," she says, "you've been so kind to me." It was a bright fresh morning, and I rong the bell. "I want you to stop," she says. Then the butler opened the door. "Scrivens," she says, "this man has been very kind to me; give him a

sovereign, will you." Scrivens looked very straight at me, but I gave him
as good as he sent, and the lady stepped into the hall. I had to follow her.
"Come in," she says, and there was I in the dining-room, while Scrivens
nipped off somewhere to get the money. Well, I had to set down on a
chair while she popped out at another door. I hadn't hardly set down when
in she come again with a lighted candle in one hand and a silver teapot
in the other. She held the teapot up and says: "Have some?" and then she
got two little cups and saucers out of a chiffonier and set them on the
table and filled them out of the silver teapot. "There you are," she says,
and she up with her cup and dronk it right off. I couldn't see no milk and
no sugar and I was a bit flabbergasted, but I takes a swig – and what do
you think? It was brandy, just raw brandy; nearly made the tears come out
of my eyes, 'specially that first cup. All of a sudden she dropped on a sofy
and went straight off to sleep, and there was I left with that candle burning on the table in broad daylight. Course I blew it out, and the butler
came in and gave me the other sovereign, and I went off to my work. Rare
good-hearted lady, ma'am. Pity,' sighed the gardener. He sat hunched on
the hassock, staring into the fire, and puffing smoke. There was attraction
in the lines of his figure squatting beside her hearth, a sort of huge power.
Olive wondered if she might sketch him some time, but she had not
sketched for years now. He said that the rain had stopped, and got up to
go. Glancing at the window Olive saw it was quite dark; the panes were
crowded on the outside with moths trying to get in to the light.

'What a lot of mawths there be!' said Luke.

Olive went to the window to watch them. Swarms of fat brown furry
moths with large heads pattered and fluttered silently about the shut
panes, forming themselves into a kind of curtain on the black window.
Now and then one of their eyes would catch a reflection from the light
and it would burn with a fiery crimson glow.

'Good night, ma'am,' the gardener said, taking the gun away with him.
Outside, he picked up the dead rabbit and put it in his pocket. Olive drew
the curtains; she did not like the moths' eyes, they were demons' eyes,
and they filled her with melancholy. She took the tall brandy bottle from
the table and went to replace it in a cabinet. In the cabinet she saw her
little silver teapot, a silver teapot on a silver tray with a bowl and a jug.
Something impelled her to fill the teapot from the long slim bottle. She

poured out a cup and drank it quickly. Another. Then she switched out the light, stumbled to the couch, and fell upon it, laughing stupidly and kicking her heels with playful fury.

That was the beginning of Olive's graceless decline, her pitiable lapse into intemperance. Camilla one May evening had trotted across to Olive's cottage; afterwards she could recall every detail of that tiniest of journeys; rain had fallen and left a sort of crisp humidity in the gloomy air; on the pathway to Olive's door she nearly stepped on a large hairy caterpillar solemnly confronting a sleek nude slug. That lovely tree by Olive's door was desolated, she remembered; the blossoms had fallen from the flowering cherry tree so wonderfully bloomed; its virginal bridal had left only a litter and a breath of despair. And then inside Olive's hall was the absurd old blunderbuss hanging on a strap, its barrel so large that you could slip an egg into it. Camilla fluttered into her friend's drawing-room. 'Olive could you lend me your gridiron?' And there was Olive lounging on the settee simply incredibly drunk! In daylight! It was about six o'clock of a May day. And Olive was so indecently jovial that Camilla, smitten with grief, burst into tears and rushed away home again.

She came back of course; she never ceased coming back, hour by hour, day after day; never would she leave Olive alone to her wretched debauches. Camilla was drenched with compunction, filled with divine energy; until she had dragged Olive from her trough, had taken her to live with her again under her own cherishing wings, she would have no rest. But Olive was not always tipsy, and though moved by Camilla's solicitude, she refused to budge, or 'make an effort', or do any of the troublesome things so dear to the heart of a friend. Fond as she was of Camilla, she had a disinclination – of course she was fond of her, there was nothing she would not do for Camilla Hobbs – a disinclination to reside with her again. What if they had lived together for twenty years? It is a great nuisance that one's loves are determined not by judgment but by the feelings. There are two simple tests of any friendly relationship: can you happily share your bed with your friend, and can you, without unease, watch him or her partake of food? If you can do either of these things with amiability, to say nothing of joy, it is well between you; if you can do both it is a sign that your affection is rooted in immortal soil. Now, Olive was forthright about food; she just ate it, that was what it was for. But she knew that even at breakfast Camilla would cut her bread into little cubes or little diamonds; if she had been able to she would surely have cut it into little lozenges or little marbles; in fact, the butter was patted into balls the same as you had in restaurants. Every shred of fat would be laboriously shaved from the rasher and discarded. The cube or the diamond would be rolled in what Camilla called the 'jewse' – for her to swallow the grease but not the fat was a horrible mortification to Olive – rolled and rolled and then impaled by the fork. Snip off a wafer of bacon, impale it; a triangle of white egg, impale that; plunge the whole into the yolk. Then, so carefully, with such desperate care, a granule of salt, the merest breath of pepper. Now the knife must pursue with infinite patience one or two minuscular crumbs idling in the plate and at last wipe them gloatingly upon the mass. With her fork lavishly furnished and elegantly poised, Camilla would then bend to peer at sentences in her correspondence and perhaps briskly inquire:

'Why are you so glum this morning, Olive?'

Of course Olive would not answer.

'Aren't you feeling well, dear?' Camilla would exasperatingly persist, still toying with her letters.

'What?' Olive would say.

Camilla would pop the loaded fork into her mouth, her lips would close tightly upon it, and when she drew the fork slowly from her encompassing lips it would be empty, quite empty and quite clean. Repulsive!

'Why are you so glum?'

'I'm not!'

'Sure? Aren't you?' Camilla would impound another little cube or diamond and glance smilingly at her letters. On that count alone Olive could not possibly resume life with her.

As for sleeping with Camilla – not that it was suggested that she should, but it was the test – Olive's distaste for sharing a bed was ineradicable. In the whole of her life Olive had never known a woman with whom it would have been anything but an intensely unpleasant experience, neither decent nor comfortable. Olive was deeply virginal. And yet there had been two or three men who, perhaps, if it had not been for Camilla – such a prude, such a killjoy – she might – well, goodness only knew. But Camilla had been a jealous harpy, always fond, Olive was certain, of the very men who had been fond of Olive. Even Edgar Salter, who had dallied with them one whole spring in Venice. Why, there was one day in a hayfield on the Lido when the grass was mown in May – it was, oh, fifteen years ago. And before that, in Paris, Hector Dubonnel, and Willie Macmaster! Camilla had been such a lynx, such a collar-round-the-neck, that Olive had found the implications, the necessities of romance quite beyond her grasp. Or, perhaps, the men themselves – they were not at all like the bold men you read about, they were only like the oafs you meet and meet and meet. Years later, in fact not ten years ago, there was the little Italian count in Rouen. They were all dead now, yes, perhaps they were dead. Or married. What was the use? What did it all matter?

Olive would lie abed till midday in torpor and vacancy, and in the afternoon she would mope and mourn in dissolute melancholy. The soul loves to rehearse painful occasions. At evening the shadows cast by the down-going sun would begin to lie aslant the hills and then she would look out of her window, and seeing the bold curves bathed in the last light, she would exclaim upon her folly. 'I have not been out in the sunlight all day; it would be nice to go and stand on the hill now and feel the warmth just once.' No, she was too weary to climb the hill, but she would certainly go tomorrow, early, and catch the light coming from the opposite heaven. Now it was too late, or too damp, and she was very dull. The weeks idled by until August came with the rattle of the harvest reapers, and then September with the boom of the sportsman's gun in the hollow coombs. Camilla one evening was sitting with her, Camilla who had become a most tender friend, who had realized her extremity, her inexplicable grief; Camilla who was a nuisance, a bore, who knew she was not to be trusted alone with her monstrous weakness for liquor, who constantly urged her to cross the garden and live in peace with her. No, no, she would not. 'I should get up in the night and creep away,' she thought to herself, 'and leave her to hell and the judgment,' but all she would reply to Camilla was: 'Enjoy your own life, and I'll do mine. Don't want to burden yourself with a drunken old fool like me.'

'Olive! Olive! What are you saying?'

'Drunken fool,' repeated Olive sourly. 'Don't badger me any

more, let me alone, leave me as I am. I – I'll – I dunno – perhaps I'll marry Feedy.'

'Nonsense,' cried Camilla shrilly. She turned on the light and drew the blinds over the alcove window. 'Nonsense,' she cried again over her shoulder. 'Nonsense.'

'You let me alone, I ask you,' commanded her friend. 'Do as I like.'

'But you can't – you can't think – why, don't be stupid!'

'I might. Why shouldn't I? He's a proper man; teach me a lot of things.'

Camilla shuddered. 'But you can't. You can't, he is going to marry somebody else.'

'What's that?' sighed Olive. 'Who? Oh God, you're not thinking to marry him yourself, are you? You're not going—'

'Stuff! He's going to marry Quincy. He told me so himself. I'd noticed them for some time, and then, once, I came upon them suddenly, and really—! Honest love-making is all very well, but, of course, one has a responsibility to one's servants. I spoke to him most severely, and he told me.'

'Told you what?'

'That they were engaged to be married, so what—'

'Quincy?'

'Yes, so what can one do?'

'Do? God above!' cried Olive. She touched a bell and Quincy came in answer. 'Is this true?'

Quincy looked blankly at Miss Sharples.

'Are you going to marry Mr Feedy?'

'Yes'm.'

'When are you going to marry Mr Feedy?' Olive had risen on unsteady legs.

'As soon as we can get a house, ma'am.'

'When will that be?'

The girl smiled. She did not know; there were no houses to be had.

'I won't have it!' shouted Olive suddenly, swaying. 'But no, I won't, I won't! You wretched devil! Go away, go off. I won't have you whoring about with that man, I tell you. Go off, off with you; pack your box!'

The flushing girl turned savagely and went out, slamming the door.

'Oh, I'm drunk,' moaned Olive, falling to the couch again. 'I'm sodden. Camilla, what shall I do?'

'Olive, listen! Olive! Now you *must* come to live with me; you won't be able to replace her. What's the good? Shut up the house and let me take care of you.'

'No, stupid wretch I am. Don't want to burden yourself with a stupid wretch.' With her knuckle Olive brushed a tear from her haggard eyes.

'Nonsense, darling!' cried her friend. 'I want you immensely. Just as we once were, when we were so fond of each other. Aren't you fond of me still, Olive? You'll come, and we'll be so happy again. Shall we go abroad?'

Olive fondled her friend's hand with bemused caresses. 'You're too good, Camilla, and I ought to adore you. I do, I do, and I'm a beast.'

'No, no, listen.'

'Yes, I am. I'm a beast. I tell you I have wicked envious feelings about you, and sneer at you, and despise you in a low secret way. And yet you are, oh, Camilla, yes, you are true and honest and kind, and I know it, I know it.' She broke off and stared tragically at her friend. 'Camilla, were you ever in love?'

The question startled Camilla.

'Were you?' repeated Olive. 'I've never known you to be. Were you ever in love?'

'Oh – sometimes – yes – sometimes.'

Olive stared for a moment with a look of silent contempt, then almost guffawed.

'Bah! Sometimes! Good Lord, Camilla. Oh no, no, you've never been in love. Oh no, no.'

'But yes, of course,' Camilla persisted, with a faint giggle.

'Who? Who with?'

'Why, yes, of course, twenty times at least,' admitted the astonishing Camilla.

'But listen, tell me,' cried Olive, sitting up eagerly as her friend sat down beside her on the couch. 'Tell me – it's you and I – tell me. Really in love?'

'Everybody is in love,' said Camilla slowly, 'some time or another, and I was very solemnly in love – well – four times. Olive, you mustn't reproach yourself for – for all this. I've been – I've been bad, too.'

'Four times! Four times! Perhaps you will understand me, Camilla, now. I've been in love all my life. Any man could have had me, but none did, not one.'

'Never mind, dear. I was more foolish than you, that's all, Olive.'

'Foolish! But how? It never went very far?'

'As far as I could go.'

Olive eyed her friend, the mournful, repentant, drooping Camilla. 'What do you mean? How far?'

Camilla shrugged her shoulders. 'As far as love takes you,' she said.

'Yes, but –' pursued Olive, 'do you mean—?'

'I could go no further,' Camilla explained quickly.

'But how – what – were you ever really and truly a lover?'

'If you must know – that is what I mean.'

'Four times!'

Camilla nodded.

'But I mean, Camilla, were you really, really, a mistress?'

'Olive, only for a very little while. Oh, my dear,' she declined on Olive's breast, 'you see, you see, I've been worse, much worse than you. And it's all over. And you'll come back and be good too?'

But her friend's eagerness would suffer no caresses; Olive was sobered and alert. 'But – this, I can't understand – while we were together – inseparable we were. Who – did I know them? Who were they?'

Camilla, unexpectedly, again fairly giggled. 'Well, then, I wonder if you can remember the young man we knew at Venice—?'

'Edgar Salter, was it?' Olive snapped at the name.

'Yes.'

'And the others? Willie Macmaster and Hercules and Count Filippo!' Olive was now fairly raging. Camilla sat with folded hands. 'Camilla Hobbs, you're a fiend,' screamed Olive, 'a fiend, a fiend, an impertinent immoral fool. Oh, how I loathe you!'

'Miss Sharples,' said Camilla, rising primly, 'I can only say I despise you.'

'A fool!' shrieked Olive, burying her face in the couch; 'an extraordinary person with a horrible temper and intolerant as a – yes, you are. Oh, intolerable beast!'

'I can hardly expect you to realize, in your present state,' returned

Camilla, walking to the door, 'how disgusting you are to me. You are like a dog that barks at every passer.'

'There are people whose minds are as brutal as their words. Will you cease annoying me, Camilla!'

'You imagine' – Camilla wrenched open the door – 'you imagine that I'm trying to annoy you. How strange!'

'Oh, you've a poisonous tongue and a poisonous manner; I'm dreadfully ashamed of you.'

'Indeed.' Camilla stopped and faced her friend challengingly.

'Yes.' Olive sat up, nodding wrathfully. 'I'm ashamed and deceived and disappointed. You've a coarse soul. Oh,' she groaned, 'I want kindness, friendship, pity, pity, pity, pity, most of all, pity. I cannot bear it.' She flung herself again to the couch and sobbed forlornly.

'Very well, Olive, I will leave you. Good night.'

Olive did not reply and Camilla passed out of the room to the front door and opened that. Then: 'Oh,' she said, 'how beautiful, Olive!' She came back into Olive's room and stood with one hand grasping the edge of the door, looking timidly at her friend. 'There's a new moon and a big star and a thin fog over the barley field. Come and see.'

She went out again to the porch and Olive rose and followed her. 'See,' cried Camilla, 'the barley is goosenecked now, it is ripe for cutting.'

Olive stood staring out long and silently. It was exquisite as an Eden evening, with a sleek young moon curled in the fondling clouds; it floated into her melancholy heart. Sweet light, shadows, the moon, the seat, the long hills, the barley field, they twirled in her heart with disastrous memories of Willie Macmaster, Edgar Salter, Hercules, and Count Filippo. All lost, all gone now, and Quincy Pugh was going to marry the gardener.

'Shall I come with you, Camilla? Yes, I can't bear it any longer; I'll come with you now, Camilla, if you'll have me.'

Camilla's response was tender and solicitous.

'I'll tell Quincy,' said Olive. 'She and Luke can have this cottage, just as it is. I shan't want it ever again! They can get married at once.' Camilla was ecstatic. 'And then will you tell me, Camilla,' said Olive, taking her friend's arm, 'all about – all about – those men!'

'I will, darling; yes, yes, I will,' cried Camilla. 'Oh, come along.'

E. M. DELAFIELD

Holiday Group

I

The Reverend Herbert Cliff-Hay's legacy had been paid at last. It seemed almost incredible, they had waited for it so long, talked about it so much, and alas! borrowed money upon it twice already. It reached them, indeed, in a terribly diminished form, what with death duties, and mysterious stamps, and fees of which they had had no previous cognisance.

The Reverend Herbert paid back all the borrowed money, and paid the premium on little Martin's Educational Annuity Policy a whole month before it was actually due, and took out a brand new Educational Annuity Policy for little Theodore, who had reached the age of nineteen months without his parents' having been able to afford this so necessary outlay on his behalf.

Their second child, Constance, being a girl, Herbert had not thought it necessary to do more than open a Post-Office Savings Account for her. Constance, as a matter of fact, would have been his favourite child, if he had considered it right to have a favourite child – which he didn't – but with boys, one had to think about education. The legacy paid their debts, enabled him to put a tiny nest-egg into the bank, and caused Herbert to make an announcement to his wife.

'We are going to have a holiday,' he said. 'A real holiday, Julia.'

Julia looked startled.

'A second honeymoon!' he cried.

'Except for the children . . .' hinted Julia, rather tactlessly, and almost indelicately.

'Naturally,' said the Reverend Herbert, frowning. He told her his plan.

He had kept twenty pounds out of the legacy, in cash – in his desk. It was there at this very moment. And it was all to be spent on a holiday, at the sea.

Herbert's living was a country one, and so they hadn't felt justified in going away every summer. It was, in fact, three years since they had been away – before Theodore was born, said Julia reminiscently.

Constance, aged four, had never even seen the sea.

'When did you think of going, darling? It's the end of June now – shall we be able to get in anywhere?'

'Oh yes, I think so,' said the Reverend Herbert brightly and firmly, meaning really that he hoped so. 'Of course, we shouldn't care for one of the fashionable, expensive, crowded places, should we, dear?'

'No. But even—'

'Cornwall, now, or North Devon – and that wouldn't be too long a journey, which would mean less expense. We needn't feel bound to any one date. Smith will take duty for me any Sunday I like, and we can get away on a Monday, and stay till the following Saturday week.'

'What about Ethel?'

Ethel was their general servant. It was very difficult for Mrs Cliff-Hay to find a servant, and still more difficult for her to keep one. Ethel had been with them six months, and Julia's great preoccupation in life, after the welfare of Herbert and the children, was how to make certain that Ethel would never leave.

'Ethel will look after the house, of course.'

'Dear, she won't sleep here alone, I'm perfectly certain. You know what girls are.'

'Well, well, we can settle about Ethel later, surely,' said the Reverend Herbert rather peevishly. 'Here am I, full of a surprise plan which I hope will be a joy and a pleasure to you, and all you can talk about is the wretched Ethel!'

It did indeed seem ungrateful, looked at in that way.

'I didn't really mean it like that,' said Julia – although she had really meant it exactly like that. 'Of course it's a glorious idea, Herbert, and so kind of you to think of it all. I'd love it, naturally.'

'It would do you good, dear,' said Herbert, mollified at once. 'We'll cast off all responsibilities, for once, and simply enjoy ourselves. After all, we're still young,' he added wistfully. And Julia, in quick response to the wistfulness, answered at once: 'Of course we are!'

She, as a matter of fact, was thirty-five, and Herbert eight years older. But she had a suspicion that they both looked more – Herbert because he was getting fat, and she because her hair was turning grey so very quickly. (It wouldn't have shown, though, if her hair had only been fair instead of dark brown.)

Julia wrote to various places about rooms, and found, as she had expected, that everything was full up already, until the middle of October.

'If one was on the spot . . .' said Herbert thoughtfully. 'I think, dearest, the only thing would be, if you didn't very much mind, for you to go yourself to one of these places – say Bewlaigh, which is the shortest journey – and go round the town, and find a lodging or one of the less expensive hotels or boarding-houses. It'll really save you time and trouble in endless writing, in the long run, and you're sure to find something.'

Julia was rather astonished. He had never suggested that she should go away anywhere by herself, before, but it just showed how much his mind was set upon this plan of a holiday.

Julia went to Bewlaigh, a journey of about two-and-a-half hours by train. It was a nice hot day, and the sea looked very blue, and there were people bathing, and children playing on the sands and climbing over the rocks, and Julia thought of Martin and Constance and Theodore, and made up her mind then and there that she *wouldn't* go home until she'd found rooms for them.

The place was small – only one cinema, no Pierrots, no bathing-machines, and only a very tiny pier. It couldn't really be full up.

The station was in the middle of the little town, and she walked slowly up the parade, not looking much at the white, shining, square houses with green shutters, and striped sun-blinds, and gardens, that lined the roads, because she knew that these would be the most expensive of all the lodgings.

Anything not directly overlooking the blue, sparkling sea would be cheaper.

She turned up a little side road, called Prospect Road. The Prospect, if taken literally, referred to a number of small, grey stone villas, all exactly alike, duplicated in two long rows. Almost every window had a card in it, bearing the word: *Apartments.*

Julia tried the first one.

'Full up till the end of September,' said the woman pleasantly.

The next one was full up till October. So were the third and the fourth and the fifth. The fifth doubted very much if there was anything to be had anywhere in Bewlaigh so late in the day. Rooms were generally booked in the winter, or the early spring – sometimes the year before, if people wanted to return to the same house.

But Julia could *try* Mrs Parker, in York Terrace – the last house but one on the left as you went down.

Julia said that she was much obliged, and went to York Terrace. She had expected to have great difficulty in finding what she wanted, and was neither surprised, nor very much discouraged.

With three children and not much money, it was never easy to get in anywhere.

She passed a pink house, with 'Board-Residence' placarded on the balcony, on her way to York Terrace, and went in, just in case, and asked for the manageress.

The manageress thought she *might* have rooms, when would it be for?

'Any date in July or August,' said Julia. 'Two rooms, and a double bed and a single one in each, or else three single beds in one room, for the children—'

'Oh,' said the manageress, differently. 'Oh, I'm sorry, but we don't really care about taking children. How old would they be?'

'Five and four and nearly two,' said Julia, conscious that these were, of all ages, the most damning.

'I'm sorry,' said the manageress firmly.

They wished one another a good morning, and separated.

York Terrace was on the top of a hill. It would be a terrific climb up from the sands, but it needn't take more than fifteen minutes even with the pram.

'The last house but one on the left, as you went down . . .'

It was called, poetically, 'Eventide'. It reminded Julia vaguely of some hymn, which seemed suitable. Perhaps a good omen, or was that being superstitious?

'Mrs Parker?'

'Yes.'

'I was wondering if you had any rooms vacant any time in July or August—' glibly began Julia, in the formula that she had now used seven times within an hour.

'Any time in July or August,' said Mrs Parker. *'Any* time.'

'I've the middle of July practically vacant, owing to a party having failed. How long would you be wanting the rooms, and for how many?'

Julia gave particulars, not slurring the ages of the children.

Her heart leapt when Mrs Parker asked if she would care to see the rooms.

One front bedroom – one back one on the same floor, the requisite number of beds, and a small sitting-room downstairs.

'What are your terms for these rooms?'

'Six guineas a week, after the first week in July. I have to try and make up, in the season, for all the rest of the year, when I may get no let at all,' said Mrs Parker mournfully.

Six guineas wasn't too bad. But Julia knew about landladies.

'Does that include cooking and attendance?'

'Yes.'

'Lighting – if any?'

'Lighting is an extra. It varies so much.'

'Baths?'

'Baths is naturally an extra. Sixpence, a hot bath is.'

'And what about early-morning tea?' said Mrs Cliff-Hay, having learnt all the moves in the game by painful experience three and a half years ago at Ilfracombe.

She could see that Mrs Parker, while resenting this catechism, at the same time respected her for it. She replied curtly, but not unkindly, that early-morning tea would be sixpence – without bread and butter.

'Just the two cups,' said Mrs Parker.

Julia engaged the rooms.

'In time for tea on the 15th,' said Mrs Parker. 'Shall I order in some bread, and milk, and butter, and what quantity of milk shall you be requiring, and will you want cake, or jam, for tea?'

Julia gave the required information.

'Plain or fancy?' Mrs Parker further demanded, referring to the cakes for tea.

It was evident that she had been keeping lodgings for years, Julia thought, and said, 'Plain, please. Buns. Six penny ones would do. We shall be bringing the baby's pram.'

'That'll be all right. At the back.'

All being thus made clear between them, Julia Cliff-Hay promised to send a postcard confirming the time of their arrival, and walked back to the station again.

As there wasn't a train for an hour and a half, she had time to go slowly, and to have a cup of tea on the way.

Herbert, hearing of her success, was delighted, and said twice in the course of the evening that it would be a second honeymoon, and although Julia – who had been young, ignorant, and frightened, at the time – had not enjoyed her honeymoon at all, she had long ago succeeded in forgetting this with her conscious mind, and now agreed with him quite happily, and looked forward eagerly to the holiday.

The question of Ethel was settled about a week later, after a good deal of difficulty. She was to go home to her mother and take the Cliff-Hays' cat with her, and the Rectory was to be shut up, and the gardener would keep an eye on it.

'But Ethel's mother always puts some nonsense into her head, and goodness knows if we shall ever get her back,' thought Julia. 'And if Ethel isn't here, and the house is empty, we can't very well have in the sweep, as I should have liked. It'll have to wait till we get back.'

When twelve o'clock on the 15th of July came, the packing was done, the suit-case and portmanteau belonging to Herbert, and a small tin trunk containing the effects of Julia and the three children, were locked and labelled, the basket, with sandwiches and bananas in it, stood ready. Ethel, with the protesting cat in a little hamper, waited at the back door, the village Ford that was to take them to the station was due in twenty minutes – and Herbert, Julia and their two elder children waited anxiously for the infant Theodore to wake from his morning sleep, so that the pram could be put into its sacking and get its label tied to the handle.

'You know how it'll upset him if we do wake him. I'd wake him in a minute, if it didn't mean that he'll be so cross all the way down,' said Julia for about the seventh time.

'That's all very well, dear, but I can't tie the covering on to the pram all in a minute, and we do *not* want to miss the train.'

'Miss the train!' echoed Martin, aged five, in great dismay.

'Shall I have a spade, Daddy?' said little Constance.

'If you're good, dear.'

'I can't think why he's sleeping so late this morning – it's always the way when one doesn't want them to—'

Julia made a hasty trip to the front door, outside which stood the pram. Theodore, inside it, still slept peacefully.

'Daddy, shall I have a spade?' Constance said, earnestly.

'Yes, darling.'

'A real spade, Daddy?'

'Yes, yes, certainly, when we get there. I say, Julia, you must really wake the child. This is nonsense.'

'I'd wake him in a minute, if it didn't mean that he'll be so cross all the way down. I can't think why he's sleeping like this – he never does as a rule, but it's always the way—'

Ethel appeared in the hall.

'The car is just coming up the lane, 'm. Didn't we ought to wake Baby?'

'He'll be so cross – there! isn't he moving?'

'Mummie,' said Constance in a voice of passionate and uncontrollable anxiety, '*can't* I have a spade?'

'Certainly, my pet, you shall have a spade. I promise you. Well, if that's the car, Ethel . . .'

Ethel darted towards the pram.

Theodore was awakened, and cried pitifully, and Julia hurried him into the house, and changed all the clothes he had on for other, similar clothes, that were clean instead of dirty, and Herbert tied up the pram and helped the driver to put the luggage on the car.

'Martin dear, run and tell Mother that we shall miss the train,' said Herbert, who had all his life suffered from train-fever.

Martin rushed in, shrieking: 'We shall miss the train, we shall miss the train!' And Julia said, 'Oh no, darling', soothingly, and finished off Baby as quickly as she could, and ran out with him to the car.

'Can I sit in front?' said Martin.

'No, me,' said Constance.

'Daddy will sit in front.'

'With me on his lap—'

'No, me!'

'It's Martin's turn,' said Julia, who had to remember these things. 'Constance darling, come and sit with Mother and Theodore in the back.'

'Tell me a story, Mother!' cried Constance.

Julia immediately said, 'Once upon a time there was a little pig who lived in a wood and – wave good-bye to Ethel, darling – Baby wave his little hand – ta-ta, Ethel! Are you all right. Herbert?'

'Quite, thank you, dear. Have you any room for your feet?'

'Yes, thank you . . . Lived in a wood and went out every day to look for acorns . . .'

The story lasted until they reached the station, when Julia said: 'Get out carefully, my pet, and wait for Mother.'

'Am I going to have a spade for the sands?'

'Yes, you shall all have spades.'

On these lines, the journey proceeded. Herbert was very kind, and took his turn in amusing the fractious Theodore, and Julia told stories, and reassured Constance about her spade, and from time to time smiled her pleasure at the holiday having really begun, and received Herbert's equally pleased and sympathetic smile in return. And it was a fine day, even if not a very warm one.

Everything was ready for them at 'Eventide,' down to the six plain buns upon the tea-table; and the moment tea was finished, they went out.

'To the shops, please, dear,' Julia said. 'I've got to order the things for our meals to-morrow. It's Sunday, you know, and she's got nothing in for us, except just the milk and the bread.'

'And shall we get my spade now, Mother?' said Constance in a trustful, uncomplaining voice.

'Yes, of course. Poor little thing, you have been patient!' cried Julia, really believing this, owing to the fabulous number of times that she had heard her daughter's request.

'Will you let me have some money, Herbert?'

'I'll come with you,' said the Reverend Herbert, and he took Martin's hand.

'Is the pram undone, darling? Because of Baby. It's too early to put him to bed, and besides, I couldn't leave him alone, in a strange room, anyway – but we ought to hurry, because the shops shut at six.'

They unwrapped the pram, and set out. Julia had a list, and they went – as fast as the pram, the narrow streets, the people, their unfamiliarity with the locality, and the short legs of Martin and Constance – would permit from the butcher to the grocer, and the grocer to the greengrocer, and the greengrocer to the baker. Everything seemed to be a little more expensive than the same things would have been at home, but one expected that, on a holiday.

When the shopping was done – and it included spades, buckets and sand-shoes for all the children – it was time for Julia to go back and put Theodore to bed.

Herbert took the other two down to the sands. He was so good about the children, Julia reflected thankfully. Even at home, where he was busy, he often helped her with them on Ethel's afternoon out. Theodore was good, and went to sleep quickly, and Julia had done nearly all the unpacking before Herbert and the elder children came back, and she had to put Martin and Constance to bed.

At half-past seven Mr and Mrs Cliff-Hay had supper. Mrs Parker had made it perfectly clear that when she said 'No cooking' in the evenings, she included things like potatoes, or even cocoa. But Julia had brought a spirit lamp, and boiled water herself, which made them independent.

After supper Herbert wanted to go for a walk, and Julia, who didn't like leaving the children, and was very tired besides, reluctantly went with him. She was but an abstracted companion, and Herbert, disappointed, was quite ready to come in again by nine o'clock. By ten, Julia, who could scarcely keep her eyes open, having seen that Martin and Constance and Theodore were all sleeping, went to bed herself.

'You won't be quite so tired, I hope, at nights, after a few days' holiday,' said the Reverend Herbert, when he in his turn got into the double bed.

He tried to make his voice sound only kind, and not resentful, but the effort was wasted upon Julia, who was sleeping like the dead.

II

The days sped by, only too quickly.

The order of them was always the same.

Between six and half-past six, Theodore woke, and was taken into his parents' bed so that he might not disturb the other two children, who seldom opened their eyes till seven o'clock. At half-past seven Mrs Parker brought the early-morning tea – without bread and butter – and Julia got up, and washed and dressed and brushed the three children.

At half-past eight they had breakfast.

Then the sands – Julia doing the necessary shopping on the way. There was always something to be ordered, or bought, for the children.

The weather wasn't too bad, for an English July. Julia thought it rather chilly, but then she had to adjust her pace to that of the baby, who could only toddle about, or sit on the sands scooping holes with his fingers.

While Theodore had his sleep in the pram, the others bathed.

Julia, years ago, had liked swimming, and Herbert was 'very good at it'. It brought home to her the fact that she was no longer very young, when she found herself secretly rather dreading the daily treat of the bathe. Perhaps it was the difference between being able to swim with Herbert, and having to remain close to the edge of the water, encouraging Martin, who was inclined to be nervous, and calling out 'Yes, I see, darling,' to Constance, who was under the impression that she was swimming if she stuck her fat arms straight out in front of her, and kicked the water with her feet.

Herbert, as usual, was goodness itself.

He tried, although not successfully, to teach the two elder children to swim, and he squeezed out their wet bathing-dresses while Julia hurriedly dried and dressed them in the bathing-machine, and then he generally struck out to sea again, so as to give her time to dress herself before he sought the bathing machine. Still feeling damp and mottled, Julia would hasten out into the rather fitful sunshine, and distribute buns to the children, and try to warm her slightly discoloured hands by rubbing them in the sand. At least she kept her hair dry, for it was no longer the sort of hair that one rather enjoyed wetting, for the sake of letting it dry in the open air afterwards . . .

Her thoughts went back to other holiday-times, which, strangely enough, seemed not at all remote, when she hadn't been 'Mother,' but only Julia, and Mamma had been 'Mother' – the omniscient, all-powerful and ever-present universal provider.

Was it possible that Mamma, who had been dead ten years, had then felt exactly as Julia felt now?

She could certainly remember a reluctance, at the time incomprehensible, on the part of Mamma to join in delightful hill-climbing expeditions, or early-morning swims, at Weymouth.

Every year they had gone to Weymouth, Papa and Mamma and Julia.

One hadn't realised, in those days, that one was lucky to be taken to a nice hotel, where nobody bothered about 'extras', and there was a real meal at the end of the day as a matter of course – not just a slice of cold ham, and bread and cheese, and cocoa made over a spirit lamp.

('Oh, what a pig I am, to think about the food like that!' thought Julia. 'Though really it's on Herbert's account – except the cocoa, which is such a comfort when one's cold or tired . . .')

Had Papa and Mamma really been well off? Julia, who had inherited their small savings, knew that they hadn't, although, of course, the value of money had altered altogether since the War. It had just been that, in the past, she hadn't had the responsibility of any of it – hadn't known or cared how the holiday was paid for, how the plans were made, how the meals were ordered, or anything else.

She had gone on being blissfully irresponsible until she was quite grown-up. She could remember the last Weymouth holiday before Papa's death, when she had just left school, and she had wanted to go every night to the concert on the pier, with the school friend who was staying with her. Papa had taken them, and Mamma, to their incredulous astonishment, evening after evening, had declared that she preferred to go to bed.

'But she was much older then, than I am now,' reflected Julia.

'Mother, look at me!' screamed Constance.

'I see, darling. Wonderful!'

'But did I turn head-over-heels?'

'Well – very nearly. Next time it'll be quite.'

'Mother, may I have the last bun?'

'No, Martin dear. It's really too near dinner-time.'

'Then will you help me to build a castle exactly like the one we made yesterday?'

Julia got up, feeling stiff.

'Did I nearly turn head-over-heels?'

'Very nearly.'

Herbert emerged from the bathing-machine.

'Daddy, I turned head-over-heels.'

'Nearly,' Julia inserted automatically.

'I nearly turned head-over-heels.'

'Did you, dear? Well, Julia, did you enjoy the water? You look cold, my dear. If you didn't stay in the shallow water so much, but went right out of your depth at once, you wouldn't feel cold.'

'The walk up the hill will warm me.'

The steep ascent to York Terrace was not much liked by Martin and Constance with their short legs, and Julia always told them a story while they climbed.

Herbert pushed the pram.

After dinner, the two elder children were sent to rest for an hour on their beds, and Julia amused the baby downstairs, and Herbert read the paper.

Then they all went on the sands again, or once or twice for an excursion by charabanc, but the children were too young to enjoy these, and rendered the whole family unpopular with their fellow-passengers, except, indeed, with those who had with them children of the same age.

But Julia, unreasonably, didn't like being told that 'the little ones were all alike,' and never let this opening lead to anything further.

Tea – the day fell naturally into the categorical division of time that separated one meal from another – was generally taken at their lodgings. The café in the High Street, where there was a small string band, was amusing, but it cost money, and little Theodore was really too young for that sort of place, and Constance, who was easily made bilious, was sure to eat something that would disagree with her later.

Very soon after tea Theodore was put to bed, and the other two children played in the sitting-room, since it would be too much for them to walk down to the sea and back once more.

Julia came downstairs, read about 'Little Black Sambo' or 'The Story of Peter Rabbit', and then took Constance and Martin upstairs. When she came down again it was usually nearly seven o'clock, and there was only time to do the mending that always seemed to be required on one garment or another.

At half-past seven, supper – that cold and skimpy meal that was disposed of in rather less than twenty minutes.

'How the time flies, doesn't it? I can't believe we've been here so long already. What about a little walk this evening?'

'Yes – only I don't much like leaving the children – if Baby did happen to wake—'

'Surely, with two women in the house—'

'Dear, I can't possibly ask Mrs Parker to go to him, and it wouldn't be any good if she did, either—'

'I suppose not. Well. You're not tired, are you, Julia?'

'Did I yawn? It must be the air. It's much stronger than the air at home.'

'It'll do us all good. The children look quite different.'

'Yes, don't they?' she said eagerly, and then immediately yawned again.

'Julia!' exclaimed the Reverent Herbert. The truth was, as they both knew too well, that Julia was intolerably sleepy. She was often sleepy at home, too, since she had never been without a baby in her room after the first year of her marriage, and was always awakened early in the mornings – but at home she sat at her desk in the evenings, or sometimes played the piano, and kept herself awake that way.

At home, also, Herbert was busy, and took it for granted that she should go to bed before he did, but on a holiday – a second honeymoon – things should have been different.

He was kind, as ever – but he evidently didn't understand it.

Julia tried going to bed very early indeed, and getting some sleep before Herbert came up, on the understanding that he should wake her, when she would then be fresh and lively and ready for conversation.

But she wasn't fresh or lively, and indeed it proved to be almost impossible to wake her without the employment of real physical violence.

'And yet,' said the Reverend Herbert, rather reproachfully, 'if one of the children so much as turns over in the night, you're awake directly.'

Julia wondered, but did not like to ask, if that was perhaps the reason she was so sleepy now. She said feebly that she thought there was an

Instinct which woke mothers on behalf of their children. 'When we get home,' she said hopefully, 'and I know that Martin and Constance are in their own nursery with Ethel next door, I shan't wake so early in the mornings, and then I shan't be so tired at night. Besides, it's this wonderful sea-air. It's – doing – wonders.'

Julia's eyes grew fixed and watery, the muscles of her jaw became strangely set, and she tightly compressed her lips, in the suppression of an enormous yawn.

'Go to bed, my dear,' said her husband forbearingly. And she looked so miserable that he added, entirely to try and comfort her for her inadequacy. 'It's the sea-air.'

Right up to the very last day of their fortnight at 'Eventide' the sea-air continued to demonstrate its effects upon Julia.

The final evening was marred by the usual discrepancy between the visitors' attitude towards their bill, and that of the landlady.

'Of course, I knew she'd stick it on at the end, as they always do,' said Julia, 'but really! When it comes to cruet, sixpence – and neither of us touches mustard or pepper, and I'm sure the poor children haven't eaten six-pennyworth of salt, the whole time they've been here.'

'Absurd! But still, if that's the only extra—'

'The only extra!' cried Julia. 'Why, the whole thing is extras. And she's put down that hideous glass vase that Baby smashed in our room as valued at three-and-eightpence.'

'Shall I have her in?' said the Reverend Herbert wearily. 'It's no use letting that sort of person think that one doesn't know one's being robbed.'

'No, of course it isn't.'

They both of them dreaded the interview with Mrs Parker, and knew that they had no possible chance of getting the better of her, but they felt, confusedly and miserably, that in some mysterious way they owed it to their caste to show Mrs Parker that her extortions were resented by them.

Julia, in a deprecating, apologetic voice, called Mrs Parker.

An interview on lines exceedingly familiar to Mrs Parker ensued.

At the end of thirty-seven minutes, the sum at the foot of Mrs Parker's bill, reduced by half-a-crown, had been paid by the Reverend Herbert, and the bill duly receipted by the landlady.

'Thank you, sir,' said Mrs Parker, her voice suddenly pitched in a more natural key. 'I'm sure I hope you've all enjoyed your stay?'

'Very much indeed, thank you. It's done us all so much good.'

'A thorough rest,' said Herbert, not without a glance at Julia.

'Perhaps we shall come again another year.'

'I hope so, sir, I'm sure. Good night, sir, good night, 'm.'

'Good night, Mrs Parker,' they replied together with amiable smiles.

The door shut behind Mrs Parker.

'I suppose they're all alike,' said Julia tolerantly. 'After all, they've their living to get.'

'It must be a dog's life. And extortionate though she's been, she's let us down pretty lightly over the damage the children did. I saw that ink-stain on the counterpane myself.'

'And naughty little Constance's hole in the wall, over the bed—'

'It isn't everywhere where they'll take children at all.'

'No, that's true. One might do a great deal worse than come here another year. I mean, supposing we're able to afford another holiday one year.'

'Now that we've got this legacy, Julia dearest, and that our debts are all paid, I want to afford a holiday every year,' said the Reverend Herbert, adding, with unwonted effusiveness, for he was a reserved man, 'You and I, and little Martin and Constance and the baby – and perhaps other little ones, if we should be blessed with them. To get right away from home cares and worries and responsibilities, and have a thorough rest and change. I value it on your account even more than on my own.'

Julia laid her thin hand upon his plump one, and her eyes – her tired eyes – filled with the easy tears of utter contentment. She thought, as she had often thought before, that she was a very fortunate woman. Her heart swelled with gratitude at the thought of her kind husband, her splendid children, and the wonderful holiday that they had all had together.

DOROTHY EDWARDS

A Country House

From the day when I first met my wife she has been my first consideration always. It is only fair that I should treat her so, because she is young. When I met her she was a mere child, with black ringlets down her back and big blue eyes. She put her hair up to get married. Not that I danced attendance on her. That is nonsense. But from the very first moment I saw her I allowed all those barriers and screens that one puts up against people's curiosity to melt away. Nobody can do more than that. It takes many years to close up all the doors to your soul. And then a woman comes along, and at the first sight of her you push them all open, and you become a child again. Nobody can do more than that.

And then at the first sight of a stranger she begins talking about 'community of interests' and all that sort of thing. I must tell you we live in the country, a long way from a town, so we have no electric light. It is a disadvantage, but you must pay something for living in the country. It is a big house, too, and carrying lamps and candles from one end of it to another is hard. Not that it worries me. I have lived here since I was born. I can find my way about in the dark. But it is natural that a woman would not like it.

I had thought about it for a long time. I do not know anything about electrical engineering, but there is a stream running right down the garden; not a very small stream either. Now why not use the water for a little power-station of our own and make our own electricity?

I went up to town and called at the electricians. They would send someone down to look at it. But they could not send anyone until September. Their man was going for his holidays the next day. He would be away until September. Now I suddenly felt that there was a great hurry. I wanted it done before September. They had no one else they could send, and it would take some time if I decided to have it done. I asked them to send for the electrician. I would pay him anything he liked if he would put off his holiday. They sent for him, and he came in and listened to my proposal.

At this point I ought to describe his appearance. He was tall, about forty years old. He had blue eyes, and grey hair brushed straight up. His hair might have been simply fair, not grey. I cannot remember that now. He had almost a military appearance, only he was shy, reserved, and rather prim. His voice was at least an octave deeper than is natural in a speaking voice. He smiled as though he was amused at everyone else's amusement, only this was not contemptuous. Do not think for a moment that I regard this as a melodrama. I do not. I saw at once that he was a nice fellow, something out of the ordinary, not a villain at all.

He smiled when I asked him to put off his vacation. Nothing could be done until he had had a look at the place, and he was perfectly willing to come down that evening to see it. If it were possible to start work at once, something could perhaps be arranged. I was pleased with this, and I invited him to stay the night with us.

At five o'clock he was standing on the office steps with a very small bag, which he carried as if it were too light for him. He climbed into the car, and sat in silence during the whole long drive. When we reached the avenue of trees just before we turn in at my gate (although it was still twilight, under the trees it was quite dark, because they are so thick), he said, 'I should imagine this was very dark at night?'

'Yes, as black as pitch,' I said.

'It would be a good thing to have a light here. It looks dangerous.'

'No, I don't want one here,' I said. 'Nobody uses this road at night but I, and I know it in the dark. Light in the house will be enough.'

I wonder if he thought that unreasonable or not. He was silent again. We turned in at the gate. My wife came across the lawn to meet us. I do not know how to describe her. That day she had a large white panama hat and a dress with flowers on it. I said before that she had black hair and blue eyes. She is tall, too, and she still looks very young. The electrician – his name was Richardson – stood with his feet close together and bowed from the waist. I told her that I had brought him here to see if it was possible to put in electric light.

'In the house?' she said. 'That would be lovely. Is it possible at all?'

'I hope so,' said Richardson in his deep voice. I could see that she was surprised at it.

'We don't know yet,' I said; 'we must take him to see the stream.'

She came with us. The stream runs down by the side of the house, curving a little with the slope of the garden, until it joins the larger stream which flows between the garden wall and the fields. We followed it down, not going round by the paths, but jumping over flower-beds and lawns. Richardson looked all the time at the water, except once when he helped my wife across a border.

'There is enough water,' he said, 'and I suppose it is fuller than this sometimes?'

'Yes, when it rains,' said my wife. 'Sometimes it is impossible to cross the stepping-stones without getting one's shoes wet.'

Now I will tell you where the stepping-stones are. Where the stream curves most a wide gravelled path crosses it, and some high stones have been put in the water. When we came down as far as that Richardson said, 'This is the place where we could have it. We could put a small engine-house here, and the water could afterwards be carried through pipes to join the stream down below, forming a sort of triangle with the hypotenuse underground.'

I asked him if he was certain that it could be done.

'I think so,' he said seriously.

My wife smiled at him. 'I hope the building will not be ugly; it would spoil the garden.'

Richardson smiled in the amused way and answered, 'It will, but it will not be high. We must have it at least half underground, with steps to go down to it. Would it be possible to plant some thick trees round it? Yews, so long as they do not interfere with the wires.'

'Oh yes, thank you,' she said. 'I believe we could have that.'

Richardson looked about him a bit more, and he took some measurements with a tape-measure from his pocket. Then we went back to the house. At dinner I asked him where he meant to spend his holiday.

'I am not sure,' he said seriously. 'I thought perhaps the Yorkshire moors would be a good place.'

'You won't find anything better than this,' I said. 'Put off your holiday until September.'

My wife moved to the door. 'Would you have to stay here during the work?' she asked.

'Or somewhere near here, madam,' he said.

'Yes, of course, here,' she said, and walked out of the room. Richardson bowed from the waist again.

We arranged it easily. He would not put it off, but he would make this his holiday. He would bring his motor bike here and explore the country around. He could be here always when there was anything for him to do, and he considered our invitation to him to stay here more than enough compensation for the change of his plans.

Afterwards in the drawing-room he asked my wife if she was fond of music.

'That is what she *is* fond of,' I said. 'She plays the piano.'

What can anyone do with a strange man in the drawing-room but play the piano to him? She played a Chopin nocturne. Now I could watch girls dancing to Chopin's music all day, but to play Chopin to a stranger that you meet for the first time! What must he think of you? I can understand her playing even the nocturnes when she is alone. When one is alone one is in the mood for anything. But to choose to play them when she is meeting someone for the first time! That is simply wrong. Chopin's nights are like days. There is no difference, except that they are rounded off. That is nonsense. Night does not round things off. Night is a distorter. These nocturnes come of never having spent his nights alone, of spending them either in an inn or in someone else's bedroom. No! How do I know what Chopin did? But I tell you they are the result of thinking of darkness as the absence of the sun's light. It is better to think of it as a vapour rising from the depths of the earth and perhaps bringing many things with it.

But he liked it. That is, Richardson liked the nocturne. He asked her to play another. While she turned over the pages I said aloud, 'Night isn't like that. Night is a distorter.'

My wife looked into the darkness outside the window.

Richardson looked at her, then he looked at me in uncertainty. She began to play, and he, for a moment pretending to be apologetic, studied her music with concentration.

Why didn't they ask me what I meant? I could have proved it to them. In any case it was an interesting point.

She played a lot of Chopin. Then as she came from the piano she said, 'You are fond of music too. Do you play?'

'No,' he said. 'It was my great ambition to be a 'cellist, but I never learnt to play it well, and I haven't one now. It is my favourite instrument.'

'It is only the heavy father of a violin,' I said. But I said it only because all that Chopin had annoyed me. I like the 'cello very much.

'I have never liked anything better than the piano,' said my wife. 'I am sorry you do not play.'

'He sings,' I said.

He smiled with amusement.

'Do you?' she asked eagerly.

'Yes,' he said, half bowing from where he sat.

'I knew by your speaking voice,' I said. 'Please let us hear you.'

'I will bring some songs with me if you wish it,' he said. 'That is very kind of you,' and he leaned back in his chair and cut off all communication with us.

We sat in silence until my wife left us. Then we talked a little about the electric light and then went to bed.

The next day the work began. Until the small building was up and the pipes laid from it back to the stream, Richardson could do nothing more than see that the measurements were right. He carried a small black notebook, and kept looking at it and then looking up at us and saying, 'This is no work at all, you know; it is simply like a holiday.'

He brought his motor bike down, but he went for few rides. Most of the time he spent looking at the first few bricks of the building, or crossing and recrossing the stream over the stepping-stones, with no hat on, and his black notebook open in one hand, as though he were making some very serious calculations. I do not suppose he was for a moment.

As I said before, I do not regard this as a melodrama. I do not consider him a villain, but, on the contrary, a nice enough fellow, but it was irritating to me the way he wandered round in a circle looking for something to do.

In the daytime he could look after himself, but in the evening we treated him as a guest.

The second day he was here, after tea I suggested taking him for a walk. He bowed with one hand behind his back, and he kept it there afterwards. I noticed it particularly. My wife came too. We walked down the garden. Richardson, still with his hand behind his back, walking just behind her, talked to her about the work, and he said the same things over twice.

When we got to the bottom of the garden and through the door which opens on the bank of the stream she gave a cry of horror. And I will tell you why. It was because I had had the grass and weeds on the banks cut.

She turned to Richardson. 'I am so sorry,' she said. 'You should have seen this before it was cut. It was very pretty. What were those white flowers growing on the other side?'

'Hemlock,' I said. 'It had to be cut.'

'I don't see why,' she said. 'It is a pity to spoil such a beautiful place for the sake of tidiness.' She turned to him petulantly.

Now that is all nonsense. A place must be tidy. There were bulrushes and water-lilies as it was. What more must she have? A lot of weeds dripping down into the water! There is a difference between garden flowers and weeds. If you want weeds, then do not have gardens. And I suppose I am insensible to beauty because I keep the place cut and trimmed. Nonsense! Suppose my wife took off her clothes and ran about the garden like a bacchante! Perhaps I should like it very much, but I should shut her up in her room all the same.

We walked along in silence over the newly cut grass. It was yellow already with having been left uncut too long. I went first across the bridge, and my two friends who admire Chopin so much came after. We were in the cornfield now, and I will tell you what it is like. There is a little hill just opposite the bridge, and the corn grows on top of it and on its slopes. It is a very small hill, but the country around is flat, and from the top of it you can see over the trees a long distance. We began to walk up the path to the top. The corn was cut and stood up in sheaves. That is what I like.

When we reached the top Richardson took his hand from behind his back and looked around him. There is a lake a few miles away, and on either side of it the land rises and there are trees. Beyond that again is the sea. And from the hill the sea looks nearer than it is and the lake like a bay. Richardson thought it was a bay. I thought so too when I was a child.

'I did not know the sea was so near,' he said.

'It isn't near,' I answered. 'That is a lake. There are even houses in between it and the sea, only you cannot see them.'

He took a deep breath. 'You know, it is very kind of you to let me stay here. It is very beautiful. I have not seen a place I like better. I am most grateful. And the work is simply nothing. It is a real holiday.' At this point he fingered the black notebook which stuck out of his pocket.

If things had not happened as they did he might have come down often; he might have spent his week-ends here. He was not a bad sort of fellow.

He did not want to leave the hill, but my wife did not like walking about on the stubble in her thin shoes. We walked back by the path which leads between a low wall and some small fir-trees to the back of the house. I had the path made for her, because she prefers that walk.

After dinner Richardson sang. His voice was all right, deep like his speaking voice, only not so steady. She played for him, and he stood up at attention, except that, with his right arm bent stiffly at the elbow and pressed to his side, he clutched the lapel of his coat. He sang some Brahms. It was quite nice.

I went to write some letters, and afterwards I walked about in the garden. When I returned they had left the piano and were talking. He was very fond of Strauss. She had not heard the *Alpine* symphony. We were so far from everywhere here.

The time went on. Richardson grew more restless every day. And yet he was lethargic too. He hardly left the house and garden, and he still wandered back and forth by the work. He did not interfere with the men by giving unnecessary orders, but he still studied his notebook as though there were important calculations there. I know all this, because I watched him as if he were my brother.

My wife used to go down there to sit sometimes in the mornings. But he hardly spoke to her then. It is natural that a man would not care to talk about music and all that when the men were working in the sun. It was curious how much interest we all took in the little building and the pipes and the water, and yet when we thought of the electric light in the house, which was to be the result, all the romance was gone out of it. This is not simply my experience. It was so with my wife and Richardson too. I know by my own observation of them. The minute the building was finished we went down to see it. Nothing but a yellow brick hut with steps to go down, and an opening like the mouth of a letter-box in the wall nearest the stream.

'The water is shut off now,' said Richardson. 'We have to put a grating in it before the water comes through.'

There was a hole in the concrete floor too, and from that the pipes would lead back to the stream. The first pipe was there with a big curve in it. It was nice to see it getting on. After that they dug a ditch and put the pipes down. He helped them to dig.

Every night he sang and my wife played, but I did not always stay in the drawing-room. One night, though, I remember particularly, he sang a song by Hugo Wolf about a girl whose lover had gone, and while the men and women were binding the corn she went to the top of a hill, and the wind played with the ribbon that he had put in her hat. It was something like that; I have forgotten it. I asked him to sing it again. I suppose they were pleased that I liked something. He sang it.

> An dem Hut mein Rosenband, von seiner Hand
> Spielet in dem Winde.

Now I should think that the hill that she climbed in that song was like the hill in our cornfield, and the girl sat there for hours 'like one lost in a dream.'

The days passed, and everything remained the same except the work, and that went on quickly. We walked about together sometimes. One evening we went again through the door to the little river where the grass had been cut. We were going along the bank talking when we heard a splash, and there was a boy swimming in the water. I shouted to him, and told him to come out and not swim there again. His white back flashed through the water to a bush on the other side, and he began to dress behind it. When I turned back she said, 'Why did you send him away? It looked so nice.'

'He can go somewhere else to swim,' I said.

Richardson said nothing.

'He does no harm here, surely?' she said.

Bulrushes and water-lilies are not enough for her. She must have weeds and naked boys too. And do you think *she* ever bathed in a river when she was a child, and hid behind a bush when someone was coming? No, of course not. And does she think the boy wants to be seen bathing? And if he is not to be seen when he is here, he might as well go somewhere else.

We never talked about anything except the work, and he talked about music with my wife. They never said anything illuminating on the subject, though. It is a funny thing that you can spend days and weeks with a man and never mention anything but water-pipes and electricity. But, after all, you can't talk about God and Immortality to a man you hardly know. Anyhow, it is nice to see someone so much interested in his work. No. That is nonsense. He was not interested in his work. When the engine came we were enthusiastic, and he was as miserable as sin. What business has an electrician to get excited over yellow bricks and water-pipes? He was restless. He could not settle to anything. If he read a book, half the time it would be open on his knee and he looking away from it. I noticed him very particularly.

The day before everything was finished and he was to go – he was not waiting to see the light actually put in the rooms – I was chalking out a garden-bed just at the bottom of the garden by the door. It is a shady place, and I meant to plant violets there, especially white violets – not in August, of course, but it was better to get it prepared while I thought of it. I heard them coming along on the other side of the wall.

She was saying, 'Before I was married I stayed with my music master in London. He had two sons but no daughters. His wife was very fond of me. That was the happiest time of my life. One of the sons is a first violin now. I went to a symphony concert when we were in London once and saw him play. I don't know what happened to the other one.'

'Let us sit down here,' said Richardson.

I knew there was something wrong with him by his voice. I detected that at once.

I suppose they sat down on the large tree-stump outside. They were silent for a moment. I suppose she was looking at the water and he was looking at her.

Then he said, beginning as though he were talking to himself, and yet apologising too, 'Please forgive me, I ought not to say it. I have never been to a place which has given me such pleasure as this. I have never noticed scenery or nature much before. When one likes a place, it is because one went to it in childhood or something of that sort. But this has been so very beautiful while I have been here. I suppose from the beginning I knew I could not come here again. It is impossible. Forgive me saying so.' His voice became deeper as he went on, I noticed that.

'Oh, but you must come here again,' she said anxiously. 'There is no one here at all, and we have so many tastes in common.'

'No,' he said; 'you think I don't mean it. I walked up and down in the garden just now and I came to a decision. At first I thought I would not speak a word to you, but afterwards I decided it would not make any great difference if I did. People do not change their lives suddenly. That is, they don't except in literature. And now I feel at peace about it. No harm at all – none. I do not mean that literature is artificial, you know, only that it is concerned with different people.'

Now what word had he spoken that a husband could not listen to? And yet we would have looked very interesting from an aeroplane or from a window in heaven.

And do you suppose she wanted to know what he was talking about?

All she said was, 'Oh, but my husband has asked you to come here himself. You must come often, and bring your songs. There is no one here to talk about music to. And I cannot go to any concerts, we are so far from everywhere.'

He was silent. They stood up, and I waited for them to come through the door. I suppose nobody could expect me to hide behind a tree so as to cause them no embarrassment. 'Excuse me, I was just passing at this moment. Please go on with your pleasant conversation.' However, they chose to go back by the other way along the bank of the stream.

We spent dinner very pleasantly. Nobody spoke a word. Richardson was not fully aware that we were in the room. He looked at the tablecloth. I did not go away to write letters after dinner. I never left the drawing-room. I suppose no one could expect me to do that. After the music we sat round the empty grate and said nothing, and we went very late to bed.

The next morning, after breakfast, I went up to the flagstaff. If you climb up the steep bank at the left of the house and walk along until you come to a narrow path with trees growing there, you come to a ledge, and the flagstaff has been put there, because it can be seen above the trees. I was standing there disentangling the rope to pull the flag up when he came up to me.

'What time are you going?' I asked, and pulled out my watch.

'At eleven,' he said.

'I suppose you think it funny that I should be putting the flag up on the day that you go?'

'I did not know you had a flagstaff,' he said. 'I suppose it can be seen even from the sea?'

'Yes.'

He was silent, and he looked across at the house.

'Where is my wife?' I asked.

'In the drawing-room, practising.'

'I hope you will send in your bill as soon as possible.'

'Oh yes,' he said. 'It will come from the firm, you know. They pay me. I wanted to walk round the cornfield before I go.'

I pulled up the flag and fastened the cord. 'I'll come with you,' I said.

We walked in silence to the top of the hill, and he stood and looked all round, at the house and at the sea. Taking leave of it, of course.

'In the village down there,' I said, 'there is a very nice girl called Agnes. She isn't pretty, but she is very nice.'

Now Agnes was the name of the girl in the song by Hugo Wolf, but I knew he would not see that. He looked at me in surprise. Then he took out his watch and said he must go. There was no need for that. If you go away on a motor bike why go exactly at eleven? He had to keep himself to a time, that is what it was. We turned to go down the hill.

'I put up the flag because it is my birthday,' I said, though that was not true.

He looked at me without listening to what I said.

When we got back to the house his motor bike was standing outside the gate ready. He went into the house to fetch his cap, and my wife came out with him. Half-way to the gate he turned to her and thanked her. He had never experienced such pleasure in a holiday before. Then he shook hands with me and said nothing.

'Come down to see us often,' I said. 'Come whenever you like, for week-ends.'

'Oh yes,' said my wife, 'please come, and bring your music.'

He looked embarrassed. I was watching him. I knew he would be. He looked at the ground and mumbled, 'Thank you very much. Goodbye.' Then he turned and went out through the gate, and in a few minutes he drove away under the trees.

She went into the house. She thinks he will come again, call, and listen to her playing Chopin.

I went to sit down by the engine-house. The engine was working, and it throbbed noisily, while there was hardly any water in the curve of the stream. It has made a great difference to the garden. Up above the flag waved senselessly in the wind.

JOHN BUCHAN

The King of Ypres

Private Peter Galbraith, of the 3rd Lennox Highlanders, awoke with a splitting headache and the consciousness of an intolerable din. At first he thought it was the whistle from the forge, which a year ago had pulled him from his bed when he was a puddler in Motherwell. He scrambled to his feet, and nearly cracked his skull against a low roof. That, and a sound which suggested that the heavens were made of canvas which a giant hand was rending, cleared his wits and recalled him to the disagreeable present. He lit the dottle in his pipe, and began to piece out his whereabouts.

Late the night before, the remnants of his battalion had been brought in from the Gheluvelt trenches to billets in Ypres. That last week he had gone clean off his sleep. He had not been dry for a fortnight, his puttees had rotted away, his greatcoat had disappeared in a mud-hole, and he had had no stomach for what food could be got. He had seen half his battalion die before his eyes, and day and night the shells had burst round him till the place looked like the ironworks at Motherwell on a foggy night. The worst of it was that he had never come to grips with the Boches, which he had long decided was the one pleasure left to him in life. He had got far beyond cursing, though he had once had a talent that way. His mind was as sodden as his body, and his thoughts had been focussed on the penetrating power of a bayonet when directed against a plump Teutonic chest. There had been a German barber in Motherwell called Schultz, and he imagined the enemy as a million Schultzes – large, round men who talked with the back of their throat.

In billets he had scraped off the worst part of the mud, and drunk half a bottle of wine which a woman had given him. It tasted like red ink, but anything liquid was better than food. Sleep was what he longed for, but he could not get it. The Boches were shelling the town, and the room he shared with six others seemed as noisy as the Gallowgate on a Saturday night. He wanted to get deep down into the earth where there was no sound; so, while the others snored, he started out to look for a cellar. In the black darkness, while the house rocked to the shell reverberations, he had groped his way down the stairs, found a door which led to another flight, and, slipping and stumbling, had come to a narrow, stuffy chamber which smelt of potatoes. There he had lain down on some sacks and fallen into a frowsty slumber.

His head was spinning, but the hours of sleep had done him good. He felt a slight appetite for breakfast, as well as an intolerable thirst. He groped his way up the stairs, and came out in a dilapidated hall lit by a dim November morning.

There was no sign of the packs which had been stacked there the night before. He looked for a Boche's helmet which he had brought in as a souvenir, but that was gone. Then he found the room where he had been billeted. It was empty, and only the stale smell of tobacco told of its occupants.

Lonely, disconsolate, and oppressed with thoughts of future punishment, he moved towards the street door. Suddenly the door of a side room opened and a man came out, a furtive figure with a large, pasty face. His pockets bulged, and in one hand was a silver candlestick. At the sight of Galbraith he jumped back and held up a pistol.

'Pit it down, man, and tell's what's come ower this place?' said the soldier. For answer, a bullet sang past his ear and shivered a plaster Venus.

Galbraith gave his enemy the butt of his rifle and laid him out. From his pockets he shook out a mixed collection of loot. He took possession of his pistol, and kicked him with some vehemence into a cupboard.

'That yin's a thief,' was his spoken reflection. 'There's something michty wrong wi' Wipers the day.'

His head was clearing, and he was getting very wroth. His battalion had gone off and left him in a cellar, and miscreants were abroad. It was time for a respectable man to be up and doing. Besides, he wanted his breakfast. He fixed his bayonet, put the pistol in his pocket, and emerged into the November drizzle.

The streets suddenly were curiously still. The occasional shell-fire came to his ears as if through layers of cotton-wool. He put this down to dizziness from lack of food, and made his way to what looked like an *estaminet*. The place was full of riotous people who were helping themselves to drinks, while a distracted landlord wrung his hands. He flew to Galbraith, the tears running down his cheeks, and implored him in broken words.

'Vere ze Engleesh?' he cried. 'Ze méchants rob me. Zere is une émeute. Vere ze officers?'

'That's what I'm wantin' to ken mysel',' said Galbraith.

'Zey are gone,' wailed the innkeeper. 'Zere is no gendarme or anyzing, and I am rob.'

'Where's the polis? Get the Provost, man. D'ye tell me there's no polis left?'

'I am rob,' the wail continued. 'Ze méchants rob ze magasins and ve vill be assassinés.'

Light was dawning upon Private Galbraith. The British troops had left Ypres for some reason which he could not fathom, and there was no law or order in the little city. At other times he had hated the law as much as any man, and his relations with the police had often been strained. Now he realised that he had done them an injustice. Disorder suddenly seemed to him the one thing intolerable. Here had he been undergoing a stiff discipline for weeks, and if that was his fate no civilian should be allowed on the loose. He was a British soldier – marooned here by no fault of his own – and it was his business to keep up the end of the British Army and impose the King's peace upon the unruly. His temper was getting hot, but he was curiously happy. He marched into the *estaminet*. 'Oot o' here, ye scum!' he bellowed. 'Sortez, ye cochons!'

The revellers were silent before the apparition. Then one, drunker than the rest, flung a bottle which grazed his right ear. That put the finishing touch to his temper. Roaring like a bull, he was among them, prodding their hinder parts with his bayonet, and now and then reversing his rifle to crack a head. He had not played centre-forward in the old days at Celtic Park for nothing. The place emptied in a twinkling – all but one man whose legs could not support him. Him Private Galbraith seized by the scruff and the slack of his trousers, and tossed into the street.

'Now I'll hae my breakfast,' he said to the trembling landlord.

Private Galbraith, much the better for his exercise, made a hearty meal of bread and cold ham, and quenched his thirst with two bottles of Hazebrouck beer. He had also a little brandy and pocketed the flask, for which the landlord refused all payment. Then, feeling a giant refreshed, he sallied into the street.

'I'm off to look for your Provost,' he said. 'If ye have ony mair trouble, ye'll find me at the Toun Hall.'

A shell had plumped into the middle of the causeway, and the place was empty. Private Galbraith, despising shells, swaggered up the open, his disreputable kilt swinging about his putteeless legs, the remnant of a bonnet set well on the side of his shaggy red head, and the light of battle in his eyes. For once he was arrayed on the side of the angels, and the thought encouraged him mightily. The brandy had fired his imagination.

Adventure faced him at the next corner. A woman was struggling with two men – a slim pale girl with dark hair. No sound came from her lips, but her eyes were bright with terror. Galbraith started to run, shouting sound British oaths. The men let the woman go, and turned to face him. One had a pistol, and for the second time that day a bullet just missed its mark. An instant later a clean bayonet thrust had ended the mortal career of the marksman, and the other had taken to his heels.

'I'll learn thae lads to be sae free wi' their popguns,' said the irate soldier. 'Haud up, Mem. It's a' by wi' noo. Losh! The wumman's fentit.'

Private Galbraith was as shy of women as of his Commanding Officer, and he had not bargained for this duty. She was clearly a lady from her dress and appearance, and this did not make it easier. He supported her manfully, addressing to her the kind of encouragements which a groom gives to a horse. 'Canny now, Mem. Haud up! Ye've no cause to be feared.'

Then he remembered the brandy in his pocket, and with much awkwardness managed to force some drops between her lips. To his vast relief she began to come to. Her eyes opened and stared uncomprehendingly at her preserver. Then she found her voice.

'Thank God, the British have come back!' she said in excellent English.

'No, Mem; not yet. It's just me, Private Galbraith, "C" Company, 3rd Battalion, Lennox Highlanders. Ye keep some bad lots in this toun.'

'Alas! what can we do? The place is full of spies, and they will stir up the dregs of the people and make Ypres a hell. Oh, why did the British go? Our good men are all with the army, and there are only old folk and wastrels left.'

'Rely upon me, Mem,' said Galbraith stoutly. 'I was just settin' off to find your Provost.'

She puzzled at the word, and then understood.

'He has gone!' she cried. 'The Maire went to Dunkirk a week ago, and there is no authority in Ypres.'

'Then we'll make yin. Here's the minister. We'll speir at him.'

An old priest, with a lean, grave face, had come up.

'Ah, Mam'selle Omèrine,' he cried, 'the devil in our city is unchained. Who is this soldier?'

The two talked in French, while Galbraith whistled and looked at the sky. A shrapnel shell was bursting behind the cathedral, making a splash of colour in the November fog. Then the priest spoke in careful and constrained English.

'There is yet a chance for a strong man. But he must be very strong. Mam'selle will summon her father, Monsieur le Procureur, and we will meet at the Mairie. I will guide you there, *mon brave*.'

The Grande Place was deserted, and in the middle there was a new gaping shell-hole. At the door of a great building, which Galbraith assumed to be the Town Hall, a feeble old porter was struggling with a man. Galbraith scragged the latter and pitched him into the shell-hole. There was a riot going on in a café on the far side which he itched to have a hand in, but he postponed that pleasure to a more convenient season.

Twenty minutes later, in a noble room with frescoed and tapestried walls, there was a strange conference. The priest was there, and Galbraith, and Mam'selle Omèrine, and her father, M. St Marais. There was a doctor too, and three elderly citizens, and an old warrior who had left an arm on the Yser. Galbraith took charge, with Mam'selle as his interpreter, and in half an hour had constituted a Committee of Public Safety. He had nervous folk to deal with.

'The Germans may enter at any moment, and then we will all be hanged,' said one.

'Nae doot,' said Galbraith; 'but ye needna get your throats cut afore they come.'

'The city is full of the ill-disposed,' said another. 'The Boches have their spies in every alley. We who are so few cannot control them.'

'If it's spies,' said Galbraith firmly, 'I'll take on the job my lone. D'ye think a terrier dowg's feared of a wheen rottens?'

In the end he had his way, with Mam'selle's help, and had put some confidence into civic breasts. It took him the best part of the afternoon to collect his posse. He got every wounded Belgian that had the use of his legs, some well-grown boys, one or two ancients, and several dozen robust women. There was no lack of weapons, and he armed the lot with a strange collection of French and English rifles, giving pistols to the section leaders. With the help of the Procureur, he divided the city into beats and gave his followers instructions. They were drastic orders, for the situation craved for violence.

He spent the evening of his life. So far as he remembered afterwards, he was in seventeen different scraps. Strayed revellers were leniently dealt with – the canal was a cooling experience. Looters were rounded up, and, if they showed fight, summarily disposed of. One band of bullies made a stout resistance, killed two of his guards, and lost half a dozen dead. He got a black eye, a pistol-bullet through his sleeve, a wipe on the cheek from a carving-knife, and he lost the remnants of his bonnet. Fifty-two prisoners spent the night in the cellars of the Mairie.

About midnight he found himself in the tapestried chamber. 'We'll hae to get a Proclamation,' he had announced; 'a gude strong yin, for we maun conduct this job according to the rules.' So the Procureur had a document drawn up bidding all inhabitants of Ypres keep indoors except between the hours of 10 a. m. and noon, and 3 and 5 p. m.; forbidding the sale of alcohol in all forms; and making theft and violence and the carrying of arms punishable by death. There was a host of other provisions which Galbraith imperfectly understood, but when the thing was translated to him he approved its spirit. He signed the document in his large sprawling hand – 'Peter Galbraith, 1473, Pte., 3rd Lennox Highlanders, Acting Provost of Wipers.'

'Get that prentit,' he said, 'and pit up copies at every street corner and on a' the public-hooses. And see that the doors o' the publics are boardit up. That'll do for the day. I'm feelin' verra like my bed.'

Mam'selle Omèrine watched him with a smile. She caught his eye and dropped him a curtsey.

'Monsieur le Roi d'Ypres,' she said.

He blushed hotly.

*

For the next few days Private Galbraith worked harder than ever before in his existence. For the first time he knew responsibility, and that toil which brings honour with it. He tasted the sweets of office; and he, whose aim in life had been to scrape through with the minimum of exertion, now found himself the inspirer of the maximum in others.

At first he scorned advice, being shy and nervous. Gradually, as he felt his feet, he became glad of other people's wisdom. Especially he leaned on two, Mam'selle Omèrine and her father. Likewise the priest, whom he called the minister.

By the second day the order in Ypres was remarkable. By the third day it was phenomenal; and by the fourth a tyranny. The little city for the first time for seven hundred years fell under the sway of a despot. A citizen had to be on his best behaviour, for the Acting Provost's eye was on him. Never was seen so sober a place. Three permits for alcohol and no more were issued, and then only on the plea of medical necessity. Peter handed over to the doctor the flask of brandy he had carried off from the *estaminet* – Provosts must set an example.

The Draconian code promulgated the first night was not adhered to. Looters and violent fellows went to gaol instead of the gallows. But three spies were taken and shot after a full trial. That trial was the master effort of Private Galbraith – based on his own regimental experience and memories of a Sheriff Court in Lanarkshire, where he had twice appeared for poaching. He was extraordinarily punctilious about forms, and the three criminals – their guilt was clear, and they were the scum of creation – had something more than justice. The Acting Provost pronounced sentence, which the priest translated, and a file of *mutilés* in the yard did the rest.

'If the Boches get in here we'll pay for this day's work,' said the judge cheerfully; 'but I'll gang easier to the grave for havin' got rid o' thae swine.'

On the fourth day he had a sudden sense of dignity. He examined his apparel, and found it very bad. He needed a new bonnet, a new kilt, and puttees, and he would be the better of a new shirt. Being aware that commandeering for personal use ill suited with his office, he put the case before the Procureur, and a *Commission de Ravitaillement* was appointed. Shirts and puttees were easily got, but the kilt and bonnet were difficulties. But next morning Mam'selle Omèrine brought a gift. It was a bonnet with such a dicing round the rim as no Jock ever wore, and a skirt – it is the truest word – of that pattern which graces the persons of small girls in France. It was not the Lennox tartan, it was not any kind of tartan, but Private Galbraith did not laugh. He accepted the garments with a stammer of thanks – 'They're awfu' braw, and I'm much obliged, Mem' – and, what is more, he put them on. The Ypriotes saw his splendour with approval. It was a proof of his new frame of mind that he did not even trouble to reflect what his comrades would think of his costume, and that he kissed the bonnet affectionately before he went to bed.

That night he had evil dreams. He suddenly saw the upshot of it all – himself degraded and shot as a deserter, and his brief glory pricked like a bubble. Grim forebodings of court-martials assailed him. What would Mam'selle think of him when he was led away in disgrace – he who for a little had been a king? He walked about the floor in a frenzy of disquiet, and stood long at the window peering over the Place, lit by a sudden blink of moonlight. It could never be, he decided. Something desperate would happen first. The crash of a shell a quarter of a mile off reminded him that he was in the midst of war – war with all its chances of cutting knots.

Next morning no Procureur appeared. Then came the priest with a sad face and a sadder tale. Mam'selle had been out late the night before on an errand of mercy, and a shell, crashing through a gable, had sent an avalanche of masonry into the street. She was dead, without pain, said the priest, and in the sure hope of Heaven.

The others wept, but Private Galbraith strode from the room, and in a very little time was at the house of the Procureur. He saw his little colleague laid out for death after the fashion of her Church, and his head suddenly grew very clear and his heart hotter than fire.

'I maun resign this job,' he told the Committee of Public Safety. 'I've been forgettin' that I'm a sodger and no a Provost. It's my duty to get a nick at thae Boches.'

They tried to dissuade him, but he was adamant. His rule was over, and he was going back to serve.

But he was not allowed to resign. For that afternoon, after a week's absence, the British troops came again into Ypres.

They found a decorous little city, and many people who spoke of 'le Roi' – which they assumed to signify the good King Albert. Also, in a corner of the cathedral yard, sitting disconsolately on the edge of a fallen monument, Company Sergeant-Major Macvittie of the 3rd Lennox Highlanders found Private Peter Galbraith.

'Ma God, Galbraith, ye've done it this time! *You'll* catch it in the neck! Absent for a week wi'out leave, and gettin' yoursel' up to look like Harry Lauder! You come along wi' me!'

'I'll come quiet,' said Galbraith with strange meekness. He was wondering how to spell Omèrine St Marais in case he wanted to write it in his Bible.

The events of the next week were confusing to a plain man. Galbraith was very silent, and made no reply to the chaff with which at first he was greeted. Soon his fellows forbore to chaff him, regarding him as a doomed man who had come well within the pale of the ultimate penalties.

He was examined by his Commanding Officer, and interviewed by still more exalted personages. The story he told was so bare as to be unintelligible. He asked for no mercy, and gave no explanations. But there were other witnesses besides him – the priest, for example, and Monsieur St Marais, in a sober suit of black and very dark under the eyes.

By-and-by the court gave its verdict. Private Peter Galbraith was found guilty of riding roughshod over the King's Regulations; he had absented himself from his battalion without permission; he had neglected his own duties and usurped without authority a number of superior functions; he had been the cause of the death or maltreatment of various persons who, whatever their moral deficiencies, must be regarded for the purposes of the case as civilian Allies. The Court, however, taking into consideration the exceptional circumstances in which Private Galbraith had been placed, inflicted no penalty and summarily discharged the prisoner.

Privately, his Commanding Officer and the still more exalted personages shook hands with him, and told him that he was a devilish good fellow and a credit to the British Army.

But Peter Galbraith cared for none of these things. As he sat again in the trenches at St Eloi in six inches of water and a foot of mud, he asked his neighbour how many Germans were opposite them.

'I was hearin' that there was maybe fifty thoosand,' was the answer.

Private Galbraith was content. He thought that the whole fifty thousand would scarcely atone for the death of one slim, dark-eyed girl.

Author Biographies

DANIEL DEFOE (*c.* 1660–1731) was born Daniel Foe in Cripplegate, London. An early career as a merchant ended in failure and debt, and at the turn of the eighteenth century Defoe turned to polemical and other writings. The extent of his writings is hotly debated, and many anonymous pamphlets of Whiggish tendency are ascribed to his name. Certainly his are a group of novels published between 1719 and 1724, including *Robinson Crusoe*, *Moll Flanders* and *Roxana*. He died while in hiding from his many creditors.

JONATHAN SWIFT (1667–1745) was born and died in Dublin. He was a clergyman, and only started publishing the fantastical satires for which he became famous in the first years of the eighteenth century. A member of the inner circle of the Tory government under Queen Anne, he spent the last thirty years of his life in a sort of internal exile, writing hilarious, excoriating satires on the new Whig establishment, including *Gulliver's Travels*, *A Modest Proposal* and a disconcerting body of poetry. He invented the name 'Vanessa'. He was a pillar of the Tory Augustan group of writers, with John Gay and Alexander Pope.

HENRY FIELDING (1707–54), one of the greatest of European novelists, began his writing career by writing fifteen plays. His career in prose fiction started almost accidentally, with parodies of Richardson's wildly popular *Pamela*. *Joseph Andrews*, *Jonathan Wild* and, supremely, *Tom Jones* stand at the summit of eighteenth-century fiction. He also established, with his brother, the first London police force, and represented humanitarian causes to his age. His health was destroyed at a relatively young age, and he died in Lisbon.

HANNAH MORE (1745–1833) was a poet, religious writer and philanthropist. Born in Bristol, she was first educated and subsequently taught at a boarding school established by her father. After suffering the consequences of a breach of promise suit, she established herself in the London circles of David Garrick and Samuel Johnson. She achieved great success and prominence both as the author of moral tracts and, subsequently, as a generous philanthropist, setting up schools for all classes of person against considerable opposition.

MARY LAMB (1764–1847) was the daughter of a London legal family, and her siblings included the writer Charles Lamb. By the 1790s, her parents were incapacitated and needed constant care by Mary. In a moment of mental collapse, she murdered her mother and was promptly committed to a mental institution. Her brother Charles extracted her, and committed to live with her in a state of celibacy. For the next decades, Mary lived a secure life, with only occasional short periods of insanity. Her career as a writer developed in partnership with her brother, and led to success and financial security.

JAMES HOGG (1770–1835) was born into a very humble family near Ettrick, Scotland. He taught himself to read while working as a shepherd, and was given encouragement by enlightened employers. Discovering the work of Burns, he published a volume of Scottish pastorals in 1801, attracting the attention of Scott, Galt and other literary figures. He was regarded as an uncouth and somewhat problematic figure by his society. His major work, *The Private Memoirs and Confessions of a Justified Sinner*, only ascended into the status of classic on its being discovered by the French novelist André Gide in the mid-twentieth century.

JOHN GALT (1779–1839) was born in Ayrshire, the son of a sea captain. Moving to London in 1804 and travelling in Europe, he befriended Lord Byron. His writing was carried out between business ventures worldwide. In 1824, Galt was appointed secretary to the Canada Company. His employers complained of his lack of basic business skills, and he was dismissed from his post. Back in Britain, he was imprisoned for his debts. A city in Ontario, no longer extant, was named after him.

FREDERICK MARRYAT (1792–1848) went to sea at the age of thirteen, subsequently seeing action against Napoleon, designing a lifeboat, carrying out important scientific endeavour, and behaving with admirable bravery throughout. He resigned his commission in 1830 and wrote a series of splendidly outgoing novels, of which *Mr Midshipman Easy* was the most successful and remains highly readable.

WILLIAM THACKERAY (1811–63) was born in Calcutta. He turned to writing after he had squandered his inheritance on gambling and other pastimes. After his marriage to Isabella Shawe and the birth of three daughters, Thackeray wrote very prolifically to support them. His wife plunged into a serious depression after the birth of their third child. His biggest success, *Vanity Fair* (1847–8) transformed his fortunes. He was the first editor of the *Cornhill Magazine* and died of a stroke at fifty-two.

ELIZABETH GASKELL (1810–65) was born in Cheyne Walk, London, but was sent as a tiny child to live in Cheshire. In 1832, she married a Unitarian minister, and her thinking and work thereafter expressed the human aspects of social idealism. Subsequently, her husband was appointed professor of history, literature and logic at Manchester New College, introducing her to intense theological and philosophical debate. Her first novel, *Mary Barton*, was initially attacked by local and national press on the grounds of its hostility to employers and ignorance of economics. Her new fame introduced her to a wider circle; her considerable network of acquaintances of all classes created a world in her novels unusual even among Victorian novelists for its solidity and breadth. She was much admired by her contemporaries, and wrote the first biography of her friend Charlotte Brontë.

ANTHONY TROLLOPE (1815–82) was the son of a failed barrister, and had it impressed upon him that, despite any lack of means, he was a gentleman. In 1834 he took a job at the Post Office, subsequently transferring to Ireland to avoid trouble with his employer. He started publishing novels in 1847, reaching great success with the first of the 'Barchester' novels, *The Warden*, in 1855. Thereafter, he became a novelist of celebrated efficiency, publishing nearly four dozen novels in thirty-five years. He wrote one of the best of authors' autobiographies, and was one of the first users of the term 'short story'.

WILKIE COLLINS (1824–89) was one of the first, and is still among the most outstanding, writers of sensational fiction. He was a friend of Dickens, who encouraged him with commissions and joint endeavours, and his novels of the 1860s are some of the most enduring and compelling of the century. In later years, after Dickens's death, his fiction took on an increasing interest in physical grotesquerie and writing to a set topic. By Victorian standards, Collins's private life was extremely unconventional: he divided his time between two mistresses, taking on a false name for life with one of them.

CHARLES DICKENS (1812–70) is one of the greatest of all writers in the English language. A traumatic childhood at the hands of chaotic parents, including a stint in a blacking factory, fed his imagination and his fierce sense of injustice. Working as a journalist, he published his first sketches in 1834, and in 1836 *The Pickwick Papers* introduced him to a colossal audience which never left him. Even the irregularity of his private life, in which he was much condemned for leaving his wife, did not dent his immense popularity. He was the busy editor of a series of journals, a keen performer, as well as the author of his incomparable novels. He died, worn out by touring and his workload, at fifty-eight.

THOMAS HARDY (1840–1928) trained as an architect, but his principal work is his spectacularly horrible house in Dorset, Max Gate. From 1871 to 1895, he published novels, the last two of which, *Tess of the d'Urbervilles* and *Jude the Obscure*, attracted fierce criticism on moral grounds. Thereafter, he wrote nothing but poetry. His first marriage ended with a long estrangement and the sudden death of his wife, much commemorated in a sequence of remorseful poetry; his second, to his secretary, putting up with the remorseful poetry, lasted the rest of his life. She published his autobiography under her own name, as a biography, according to his wishes. His coffin was carried by the Prime Minister, the Leader of the Opposition and the greatest writers of the day, including Kipling and Housman. His heart was buried with his first wife; the rest of him in Westminster Abbey.

MARGARET OLIPHANT (1828–97) was a keen writer in childhood, publishing her first novel in her very early twenties. She married her cousin, a stained-glass artist of delicate health, who died in 1859, leaving her with three children and no income. For the rest of her life, she wrote prolifically to support her family, including, after the late 1860s, her ruined brother and his family. She lived for most of her life in Windsor. Of her nearly 100 novels, the best-regarded are the 'Chronicles of Carlingford', including the classic *Miss Marjoribanks*.

ROBERT LOUIS STEVENSON (1850–94) was born the son of an Edinburgh lighthouse engineer. A sickly child, he was a compulsive teller of stories before he could read or write. He abandoned the family trade of engineer, first for law and then for life in the London literary world. Required to travel for the sake of his health, he met an American woman, Fanny Osbourne, in the South of France. He followed her to California, bringing himself near death with the strains of the journey. After marrying her in 1880, Stevenson travelled in search of an ideal climate for his health, writing his most successful works on the way. In 1888, he sailed into the Pacific, settling in 1890 in Samoa, where he took the native title of a teller of tales. He sank from critical esteem after his death until quite recently, but his popularity among readers never declined.

ARTHUR CONAN DOYLE (1859–1930) was, like many great writers, originally a doctor. Born in Edinburgh, he took his medical career very seriously, undertaking research and serving as the medical officer on whalers and African ships. During an unsuccessful period as a GP and an ophthalmologist, he took to writing fiction. In 1886 he published his first Sherlock Holmes adventure, *A Study in Scarlet*. The Holmes and Watson stories were colossally popular, as were many of Doyle's other works, including historical novels and fantasy adventures. He was an accomplished sportsman, who once took W. G. Grace's wicket, an advocate of justice and, after the Great War, a committed spiritualist.

ARTHUR MORRISON (1863–1945) was the son of an engine fitter at the London docks, a detail he later sought to conceal. His entry into publishing was as the author of comic verse for a magazine covering bicycling. In the 1890s, he turned away from genre fiction towards highly authentic stories of working-class London life, collected as *Tales of Mean Streets* (1894). This and the novel *A Child of the Jago* (1896) attained a classic status which comes and goes in public awareness. After 1909 he retired from writing and devoted himself to the collection and study of Chinese and Japanese works of art. Very little is known of the last twenty-five years of Morrison's life, which were spent very quietly in Buckinghamshire.

'MRS ERNEST LEVERSON' (ADA LEVERSON) (1862–1933) came from a mercantile family with racy offspring. One sibling refused to marry Sir Arthur Sullivan and was one of the first translators of Proust; another had an affair with Puccini. Leverson ran off with her husband at nineteen, immortalizing the bizarre atmosphere of her marriage in a trilogy of novels, *The Little Ottleys*. She was a famous wit and friend to many of the great, including Beerbohm, the Sitwells and, most famously, Oscar Wilde, whom she loyally stood by and who called her 'Sphinx'.

EVELYN SHARP (1869–1955) is best known as a militant suffragette. Her career as a novelist preceded that, however, including novels such as *All the Way to Fairyland*. She boldly took a flat in London on her own at the age of twenty-four, encouraging Whistler to ask her, 'Not understood at home, I suppose?' An interest in the 1890s topic of the New Woman led to a career as a journalist and campaigner for women's rights, an effective speechmaker and fighter for the rights of working-class women. A promise made to her mother never to go to prison in support of the suffrage was lifted in 1911, and she subsequently was imprisoned for smashing Government windows. She was one of the few suffragettes to continue the militant campaign during the Great War.

T. BARON RUSSELL (1865–1931) was primarily an advertising consultant, son of the librarian of a circulating library. Russell wrote memorable advertisements for liver pills and other patent medicines, and restructured the way in which agents for advertising were paid. As advertising manager of *The Times*, he inaugurated the newspaper's book club, and became the first advertising consultant in the UK. Aside from his single contribution to the *Yellow Book*, he published two novels of life in drapers' shops. His second novel was rather remarkably reviewed for the *Daily Express* by James Joyce, who observed that it had 'unsentimental vigour' but that the book's binding was 'as ugly as one could reasonably expect'. After the publication of this review, the editor of the *Daily Express* threatened to kick Joyce down the stairs, and Russell's career turned to advertising.

JOSEPH CONRAD (1857–1924) was born ethnically Polish in what is now Ukraine, but a Russian subject, and grew up in an atmosphere of political activism. Orphaned at eleven, at thirteen he decided to become a sailor. He went to sea at sixteen, serving for almost twenty years. In 1886, he became a British subject, and from 1894 started publishing fiction in English, his third language. His critiques of imperialism specify Belgian and French endeavours, not the British. His novels were critically acclaimed for many years before he achieved any serious success in the marketplace. His first bestseller was the intricate *Chance* (1913). A writer of melancholy elegance, he continues to be vividly controversial among readers.

H. G. WELLS (1866–1946) was born in Kent of lower-middle-class stock. He benefited from the spread of libraries and, after an apprenticeship as a draper, became first a pupil-teacher in a school and later a scholar of biology at the Normal School of Science, subsequently Imperial College, under T. H. Huxley. He took up teaching and began to write. A marriage to a cousin was succeeded by one to a student, and subsequently a large number of affairs, including one with Rebecca West that resulted in a child. His works include major early inventions in science fiction as well as penetrating studies of society, especially the superb *Tono-Bungay*, and non-fiction drawing on Fabian principles; in *The Shape of Things to Come* (1933) he predicted, accurately enough, that the next world war would break out in January 1940. He lived long enough, and remained argumentative enough, to call George Orwell 'you shit'.

M. R. JAMES (1862–1936) was director of the Fitzwilliam Museum, Cambridge, provost of King's College, Cambridge and Eton College successively between 1893 and 1936. He was a mediaevalist and antiquarian by trade. His ghost stories remain peerless, and he codified the important rules of the genre, including 'Reticence conduces to effect, blatancy ruins it.' The outbreaks of terror in his stories often unwittingly reveal the fastidiousness of a bachelor don who could, clearly, imagine nothing worse than being intimately touched by another.

'SAKI' (HECTOR HUGH MONRO) (1870–1916) was born in Burma but was brought up in England by a puritanical grandmother and aunts, whose presence is made clear in his malevolent short stories. He was a journalist and foreign correspondent in the Balkans and Russia. The often macabre and decidedly camp qualities of his stories descend from Wilde and, especially, Ada Leverson, and were published to an appreciative Tory-anarchist readership. His pen-name may come from a boy in the *Rubaiyat of Omar Khayyam*. He volunteered at forty-three as an ordinary trooper for the Great War, and was shot by a sniper during the Battle of the Ancre in 1916. His last words are reliably reported as 'Put that bloody cigarette out.'

G. K. CHESTERTON (1874–1936) was an all-round man of letters, writing poetry, novels, journalism, essays, criticism and dramas.

Initially an Anglican, he turned increasingly to an energetic and noisy Roman Catholicism. He became very popular in the radio age. His writing has been seen as tawdry as well as ingenious; his brilliantly paradoxical fiction includes *The Man Who Was Thursday*, in which God turns out to be an anarchist bowling bombs at the populace, his disciples policemen in heavy disguise. He was a colossal man of 6'4" and, in his prime, weighing 20 stone. He was preserved by P. G. Wodehouse in a celebrated simile, when a shattering noise is described as sounding 'like G. K. Chesterton falling on a sheet of tin'.

MAX BEERBOHM (1872–1956) was a wit, essayist, novelist and caricaturist and the most brilliant parodist in the English language. His parodies of Henry James have never been equalled, and astonished even their subject with their virtuosity. The son of a rich Lithuanian grain merchant, he met Wilde, Beardsley and William Rothenstein while he was still at Oxford. The elegant refinement of his prose style early led to him being dismissed from a job writing letters for a theatrical company, as it took him far too long. He married in 1910, moving to Rapallo in Italy, where he never, in the following forty-six years, learned to speak Italian.

ARNOLD BENNETT (1867–1931) was born in what would later be called Stoke-on-Trent. After moving to London to work as a solicitor's clerk, he found success as a journalist, and subsequently writing fiction. He never, in a very profitable career, gave up journalism. In 1903, he moved to Paris to be closer to the sources of French realism, such as Zola and Maupassant; the first major result of this endeavour, *The Old Wives' Tale*, has always been regarded as a masterpiece. His other great novels are the *Clayhanger* trilogy, *The Card* and *Riceyman Steps*, which combine a specificity of detail with a verve all but unique in English fiction. As he was dying, of typhoid, in 1931, he was one of the last to receive the honour of having the street outside his house muffled with a thick layer of straw. His novels have never stopped commanding the respect and love of practising novelists and ordinary readers.

D. H. LAWRENCE (1885–1930) was born the son of a Nottinghamshire miner. He won scholarships to Nottingham High School, leaving at sixteen to become a clerk, then a teacher. His first successes as a writer came in 1908 with a short story for Ford Madox Hueffer (later Ford). In 1912, he met Frieda Weekley, née von Richthofen, who left her husband for him; they eloped together to Germany. *Sons and Lovers* was published in 1913. During the Great War Lawrence and Frieda lived in poverty in Cornwall, where they were regarded as German spies, Lawrence working on *Women in Love*, unpublishable until 1920. After being required to leave Cornwall under the Defence of the Realm Act, Lawrence and Frieda took the first opportunity to leave England. They travelled to Italy, Ceylon (now Sri Lanka) and New Mexico. Lawrence went on being harried by the British authorities, and his last novel, *Lady Chatterley's Lover*, was not published until 1960, after a celebrated obscenity trial.

RUDYARD KIPLING (1865–1936) was born in Bombay. His family was immensely well connected: his uncle was Edward Burne-Jones and his cousin Stanley Baldwin. As a tiny child, he was boarded in Southsea with a couple given to abominable cruelty, and later, at a school of military inclination. At sixteen, he returned to India. Visits to Simla resulted in the stories collected as *Plain Tales from the Hills*. In 1889, he came back to England the long way, via America; his American wife Carrie drew him back in the 1890s. First success came with writing about India, poems, short stories, fiction for children and novels, written in America. After his return to England in 1896, Kipling became a controversial but passionately loved poet of Empire, and was awarded the Nobel Prize in 1907. The death of his son in the Great War led to a detachment from the official version. He went on living an active public life, writing with the unforgettable energy that has sometimes been mischaracterized as vulgarity.

STACY AUMONIER (1877–1928) was a writer of short stories immensely highly regarded in his lifetime. He was a London child of a family of artists, a gifted writer and a much admired stage performer. In his obituary, the *Observer* claimed that 'no man had more friends'.

Galsworthy described him as 'one of the best short story writers of all time' and thought that he would 'outlive all the writers of his day'. The stories have a frequent structural ingenuity, occasionally verging on the very odd.

VIOLA MEYNELL (1885–1956) was the daughter of a well-known publisher and niece of the great battle painter Lady Butler. Her parents were pillars of late-Victorian literary society. She married a Sussex farmer, and maintained friendships and correspondence with a number of important writers, not all of whom were well known at the time – she was an early supporter of D. H. Lawrence.

A. E. COPPARD (1878–1957) was the child of deprived circumstances, leaving school at nine. He did not publish until the 1920s, when he was living in Oxford. He was well regarded by his contemporaries, and was one of the first authors to be seriously collected by connoisseurs of small presses – some of his later stories were written to be produced in small numbers in luxury editions for the benefit of collectors.

E. M. DELAFIELD (EDMÉE ELIZABETH MONICA DASHWOOD) (1890–1943) was the daughter of a Count de la Pasture. At twenty-one, she entered a convent of an enclosed order in Belgium, only leaving when she learned that her sister was planning to join another enclosed order, meaning that they would never meet. During the war, she worked as a nurse, publishing her first novel in 1917. She was a professional and accomplished author during the 1920s and 1930s, attaining popular success with *Diary of a Provincial Lady* in 1930.

DOROTHY EDWARDS (1903–34) had a short and tragic life. She came from a political family in Wales, the daughter of a socialist and vegetarian schoolmaster, and had an early ambition to become an opera singer. Her political activism and elegant writing brought her to the attention of Bloomsbury in the person of David Garnett, who first adopted her as a protégée and lodger, then asked her to make other arrangements when he tired of her. Without any income, and struggling with serious depression, she returned home to Wales, and committed suicide by throwing herself in front of a train. She published a novel, *Winter Sonata*, and a collection of short stories, *Rhapsody*. Both are remarkable.

JOHN BUCHAN (1875–1940) was, in worldly terms, the most important of great British novelists after Disraeli. He was the son of a Free Church of Scotland minister. After university in Glasgow and Oxford, he became a diplomat's secretary and was called to the Bar. With the outbreak of the Great War, Buchan took on official duties, including Director of Information in the Intelligence Corps. Some papers relating to his wartime activities are still classified. His famous *The Thirty-Nine Steps* and his masterpiece, *Greenmantle*, were published during this busy time. After the war, he continued his busy public life, in 1927 being elected MP for the Combined Scottish Universities. In 1935 he was made Baron Tweedsmuir, and shortly afterwards appointed Governor General of Canada. He was given a state funeral in his adoptive country.

Acknowledgements

'The Great Unimpressionable', Stacy Aumonier.

First published in *Pictorial Review* (November 1919) and then in Stacy Aumonier, *The Golden Windmill and Other Stories* (New York: The Macmillan Company, 1921).

'Enoch Soames', Max Beerbohm.

First published in *The Century Illustrated Monthly Magazine* (May 1916) and then in Max Beerbohm, *Seven Men* (London: William Heinemann, 1919). Reprinted by permission of Berlin Associates Ltd.

'The Matador of the Five Towns', Arnold Bennett.

First published in *The English Review* (April 1909) and then in Arnold Bennett, *The Matador of the Five Towns and Other Stories* (London: Methuen and Co., 1912).

'The King of Ypres', John Buchan.

First published in *The Illustrated London News* (December 1915) and then in John Buchan, *The Watcher by the Threshold* (New York: George H. Doran Co., 1918).

'The Honour of Israel Gow', G. K. Chesterton.

First published (as 'The Strange Justice') in *The Saturday Evening Post* (25 March 1911) and then in G. K. Chesterton, *The Innocence of Father Brown* (London: Cassell & Company, 1911).

'Mrs Badgery', Wilkie Collins.

First published in *Household Words* (26 September 1857) and then in *Novels and Tales reprinted from Household Words, conducted by Charles Dickens*, vol. 6 (Leipzig: Bernhard Tauchnitz, 1857).

'Amy Foster', Joseph Conrad.

First published in *The Illustrated London News* (14–28 December 1901) and then in Joseph Conrad, *Typhoon and Other Stories* (London: William Heinemann, 1903).

'Olive and Camilla', A. E. Coppard.

First published in A. E. Coppard, *The Field of Mustard* (London: Jonathan Cape, 1926). Reprinted by permission of David Higham Associates. Copyright © A. E. Coppard, 1926.

'A True Relation of the Apparition of One Mrs Veal', Daniel Defoe.

First published as Anon., *A True Relation of the Apparition of one Mrs. Veal, The next Day after Her Death: to one Mrs. Bargrave At Canterbury. The 8th September, 1705* (London: Printed for B. Bragg, at the Black Raven in Pater-Noster-Row, 1706).

'Holiday Group', E. M. Delafield.

First published in [Alec Waugh (ed.)], *Georgian Stories 1926* (London: Chapman and Hall, 1926).

'Mrs Lirriper's Lodgings', Charles Dickens.

First published in *All the Year Round*, The Extra Christmas Number (December 1863), and then in Charles Dickens, *The Uncommercial Traveller and Additional Christmas Stories* (Boston: Ticknor and Fields, 1867).

'Silver Blaze', Arthur Conan Doyle.

First published (as 'The Adventure of Silver Blaze') in *The Strand Magazine* (December 1892) and then in *The Memoirs of Sherlock Holmes* (London: George Newnes, 1894).

'A Country House', Dorothy Edwards.

First published in *The Calendar of Modern Letters* (August 1925) and then in Edward J. O'Brien (ed.), *The Best Short Stories of 1926: English (With an Irish Supplement)* (London: Jonathan Cape, 1927) and Dorothy Edwards, *Rhapsody* (London: Wishart and Co., 1927).

'The Female Husband', Henry Fielding.

First published as Anon., *The Female Husband: or, The Surprising History of Mrs. Mary, alias Mr. George Hamilton, Who was convicted of having married a Young Woman of Wells and lived with her as her Husband. Taken from Her own Mouth since her Confinement* (London: Printed for M. Cooper, at the Globe in Pater-noster-Row, 1746).

'The Howdie', John Galt. [Unfinished.]

First published (Parts 1 and 2) in *Tait's Edinburgh Magazine* (September–October 1832) and then (Part 1) in John Galt, *The Howdie and Other Tales*, ed. William Roughead (Edinburgh and London: T. N. Foulis Ltd, 1923).

'Six Weeks at Heppenheim', Elizabeth Gaskell.

First published in *The Cornhill Magazine* (May 1862) and then in Mrs [Elizabeth] Gaskell, *The Grey Woman and Other Tales* (London: Smith, Elder and Co., 1865).

'The Three Strangers', Thomas Hardy.

First published in *Longman's Magazine* (March 1883) and then in Thomas Hardy, *Wessex Tales: Strange, Lively and Commonplace*, 2 vols. (London: Macmillan and Co., 1888), vol. 1.

Acknowledgements

'John Gray o'Middleholm', James Hogg.

 First published in James Hogg, *Winter Evening Tales, collected among the Cottagers in the South of Scotland*, 2 vols. (Edinburgh: Oliver & Boyd; and London: G. & W. B. Whittaker, 1820), vol. 1.

'The Stalls of Barchester Cathedral', M. R. James.

 First published (as 'The Stalls of Barchester Cathedral: Materials for a Ghost Story') in *Contemporary Review* (April 1910) and then in Montague Rhodes James, *More Ghost Stories of an Antiquary* (London: Edward Arnold, 1911).

'The Village that Voted the Earth Was Flat', Rudyard Kipling.

 First published in Rudyard Kipling, *A Diversity of Creatures* (London: Macmillan and Co., 1917).

'The Farm House', Mary Lamb.

 First published in [Charles and Mary Lamb], *Mrs. Leicester's School: or, The History of Several Young Ladies, related by Themselves* (London: M. J. Godwin, 1809).

'Daughters of the Vicar', D. H. Lawrence.

 First published in D. H. Lawrence, *The Prussian Officer and Other Stories* (London: Duckworth & Co., 1914).

'Suggestion', Mrs Ernest Leverson.

 First published in *The Yellow Book* (April 1895).

'South West and by West three-quarters West', Frederick Marryat.

 First published in The Author of 'Peter Simple', etc. etc. [Frederick Marryat], *Olla Podrida*, 3 vols. (London: Longman, Orme, Brown, Green and Longmans, 1840), vol. 3.

'The Letter', Viola Meynell.

 First published in Viola Meynell, *Young Mrs. Cruse* (London: Edward Arnold & Co., 1924). Reprinted by permission of Paul Dallyn. Copyright © Viola Meynell, 1924.

'Betty Brown, the St Giles's Orange Girl: with Some Account of Mrs Sponge, the Money Lender', Hannah More.

 First published as a chapbook (and in the series 'Cheap Repository of Moral and Religious Tracts'), Signed 'Z' [Hannah More] (London: Sold by J. Marshall and R. White, and by J. Hatchard; and Bath: by S. Hazard, [between 1795 and 1806]), and then in Hannah More, *Stories for the Middle Ranks of Society, and Tales for the Common People*, 2 vols. (London: T. Cadell and W. Davies, 1818), vol. 2.

'Behind the Shade', Arthur Morrison.

 First published in *Tales of Mean Streets* (London: Methuen & Co., 1894). Reprinted by permission of Methuen Publishing Ltd.

Acknowledgements

'The Library Window', Margaret Oliphant.

First published in *Blackwood's Edinburgh Magazine* (January 1896) and then in Mrs [Margaret] Oliphant, *Stories of the Seen and the Unseen* (Edinburgh and London: William Blackwood and Sons, 1902).

'A Guardian of the Poor', T. Baron Russell.

First published in *The Yellow Book* (April 1896).

'The Unrest-Cure', Saki.

First published in *The Westminster Gazette* (1 April 1910) and then in H. H. Munro ('Saki'), *The Chronicles of Clovis* (London: John Lane, The Bodley Head, 1911).

'In Dull Brown', Evelyn Sharp.

First published in *The Yellow Book* (January 1896).

'The Body Snatcher', Robert Louis Stevenson. First published in [*The*] *Pall Mall* [*Gazette*] *Christmas 'Extra'* (December 1884).

'Directions to the Footman', Jonathan Swift.

First published in Revd. Dr Swift, *Directions to Servants in General; And in particular to The Butler, Cook, Footman, Coachman, Groom, House-Steward, and Land-Steward, Porter, Dairy-Maid, Chamber-Maid, Nurse, Laundress, House-Keeper, Tutoress, or Governess* (Dublin: Printed by George Faulkner, 1745).

'A Little Dinner at Timmins's', William Thackeray.

First published in *Punch* (27 May–29 July 1848) and then in W. M. Thackeray, *Miscellanies: Prose and Verse*, vol. 3 (London: Bradbury and Evans, 1856).

'An Unprotected Female at the Pyramids', Anthony Trollope.

First published in *Cassell's Illustrated Family Paper* (6–13 October 1860) and then in Anthony Trollope, *Tales of All Countries* (London: Chapman and Hall, 1861).

'The Magic Shop', H. G. Wells.

First published in *The Strand Magazine* (June 1903) and then in H. G. Wells, *Twelve Stories and a Dream* (London: Macmillan and Co., 1903). Reprinted by permission of United Agents LLP on behalf of The Literary Executors of the Estate of H. G. Wells.

Every effort has been made to trace the copyright-holders of the copyright material in this book and credit the sources of the stories. Penguin regrets any oversight and upon written notification will rectify any omission in future reprints or editions. The editor and publisher gratefully acknowledge the above for permission to reprint stories.